Miss Marple Meets Murder

MISS MARPLE MEETS MURDER

including
The Mirror Crack'd
A Pocket Full of Rye
At Bertram's Hotel
The Moving Finger

By AGATHA CHRISTIE

NELSON DOUBLEDAY, INC.
Garden City, New York

Contents

The Mirror Crack'd

Chapter One

Miss Jane Marple was sitting by her window. The window looked over her garden, once a source of pride to her. That was no longer so. Nowadays she looked out of the window and winced. Active gardening had been forbidden her for some time now. No stooping, no digging, no planting—at most a little light pruning. Old Laycock, who came three times a week, did his best, no doubt. But his best, such as it was (which was not much), was only the best according to his lights, and not according to those of his employer. Miss Marple knew exactly what she wanted done, and when she wanted it done, and instructed him duly. Old Laycock then displayed his particular genius which was that of enthusiastic agreement and subsequent lack of performance.

"That's right, missus. We'll have them mecosoapies there and the Canterburys along the wall and as you say, it ought to be got on with first thing next week."

Laycock's excuses were always reasonable, and strongly resembled those of Captain George's in *Three Men in a Boat* for avoiding going to sea. In the captain's case the wind was always wrong, either blowing offshore or inshore, or coming from the unreliable west, or the even more treacherous east. Laycock's was the weather. Too dry—too wet—waterlogged—a nip of frost in the air. Or else something of great importance had to come first (usually to do with cabbages or Brussels sprouts, of which he liked to grow inordinate quantities). Laycock's own principles of gardening were simple, and no employer, however knowledgeable, could wean him from them.

They consisted of a great many cups of tea, sweet and strong, as an encouragement to effort, a good deal of sweeping up of leaves in the autumn, and a certain amount of bedding out of his own favourite plants, mainly asters and salvias—to "make a nice show," as he put it, in summer. He was all in favour of syringing roses for green-fly, but was slow to get around to it, and a demand for deep trenching for sweet peas was usually countered by the remark that you ought to see his own sweet peas! A proper treat last year, and no fancy stuff done beforehand.

To be fair, he was attached to his employers, humoured their fancies in horticulture (so far as no actual hard work was involved) but vegetables he knew to be the real stuff of life; a nice Savoy, or a bit of curly kale; flowers were fancy stuff such as ladies liked to go in for, having nothing better to do with their time. He showed his affection by producing presents of the aforementioned asters, salvias, lobelia edging, and summer chrysanthemums.

"Been doing some work at them new houses over at the Development. Want their gardens laid out nice, they do. More plants than they needed so I brought along a few, and I've put 'em in where them old-fashioned roses ain't looking so well."

Thinking of these things, Miss Marple averted her eyes from the garden, and picked up her knitting.

One had to face the fact: St. Mary Mead was not the place it had been. In a sense, of course, nothing was what it had been. You could blame the war (both the wars), or the younger generation, or women going out to work, or the atom bomb, or just the Government—but what one really meant was the simple fact that one was growing old. Miss Marple, who was a very sensible old lady, knew that quite well. It was just that, in a queer way, she felt it more in St. Mary Mead, because it had been her home for so long.

St. Mary Mead, the old-world core of it, was still there. The Blue Boar was there, and the church and the vicarage and the little nest of Queen Anne and Georgian houses, of which hers was one. Miss Hartnell's house was still there, and also Miss Hartnell, fighting progress to the last gasp. Miss Wetherby had passed on and her house was now inhabited by the bank manager and his family, having been given a face-lift by the painting of doors and windows a bright royal blue. There were new people in most of the other old houses, but the houses themselves were little changed in appearance since the people who had bought them had done so because they liked what the house agent called "old-world charm." They just added another bathroom, and spent a good deal of money on plumbing, electric cookers, and dishwashers.

But though the houses looked much as before, the same could hardly be said of the village street. When shops changed hands there, it was with a view to immediate and intemperate modernization. The fishmonger was unrecognizable with new super windows behind which the refrigerated fish gleamed. The butcher had remained conservative—good meat is good meat, if you have the money to pay for it. If not, you take the cheaper cuts and the tough joints and like it! Barnes, the grocer, was still there, unchanged, for which Miss Hartnell and Miss Marple and others daily thanked heaven. So obliging, comfortable chairs to sit in by the counter, and cozy discussions as to cuts of bacon, and varieties of cheese. At the end of the street, however, where Mr. Toms had once had his basket shop stood a glittering new supermarket—anathema to the elderly ladies of St. Mary Mead.

"Packets of things one's never even heard of," exclaimed Miss Hartnell. "All these great packets of breakfast cereal instead of cooking a child a proper breakfast of bacon and eggs. And you're expected to take a basket yourself and go round looking for things—it takes a quarter of an hour sometimes to find all one wants—and usually made up in inconvenient sizes, too much or too little. And then a long queue waiting to pay as you go out. Most tiring. Of course it's all very well for the people from the Development—"

At this point she stopped.

Because, as was now usual, the sentence came to an end there. The Development, Period, as they would say in modern terms. It had an entity of its own, and a capital letter.

II

Miss Marple uttered a sharp exclamation of annoyance. She'd dropped a stitch again. Not only that, she must have dropped it some time ago. Not until now, when she had to decrease for the neck and count the stitches, had she realized the fact. She took up a spare pin, held the knitting sideways to the light and peered anxiously. Even her new spectacles didn't seem to do any good. And that, she reflected, was because obviously there came a time when oculists, in spite of their luxurious waiting-rooms, their up-to-date instruments, the bright lights they flashed into your eyes, and the very high fees they charged, couldn't do anything much more for you. Miss Marple reflected with some nostalgia on how good her eyesight had been a few (well, not perhaps a *few*) years ago. From the vantage-point of her garden, so admirably placed to see all that was going on in St. Mary Mead, how little had escaped her noticing eye! And with the help of her bird glasses—(an interest in birds was *so* useful)—she had been able to see— She broke off there and let her thoughts run back over the past. Ann Protheroe in her summer frock going along to the Vicarage garden. And Colonel Protheroe—poor man—a very tiresome and unpleasant man, to be sure—but to be murdered like that— She shook her head and went on to thoughts of Griselda, the vicar's pretty young wife. Dear Griselda—such a faithful friend—a Christmas card every year. That attractive baby of hers was a strapping young man now, and with a very good job. Engineering, was it? He always had enjoyed taking his mechanical trains to pieces. Beyond the Vicarage, there had been the stile and the field path with Farmer Giles's cattle beyond in the meadows where now—now . . .

The Development.

And why not? Miss Marple asked herself sternly. These things had to be. The houses were necessary, and they were very well built, or so she had been told. "Planning," or whatever they called it. Though why everything had to be called a Close, she couldn't imagine. Aubrey Close and Longwood Close, and Grandison Close and all the rest of them. Not really Closes at all. Miss Marple knew what a Close was perfectly. Her uncle had been a Canon of Chichester Cathedral. As a child she had gone to stay with him in the Close.

It was like Cherry Baker who always called Miss Marple's old-world overcrowded drawing-room the "lounge." Miss Marple corrected her gently, "It's the drawing-room, Cherry." And Cherry, because she was young and kind, endeavoured to remember, though it was obvious that to her "drawing-room" was a very funny word to use—and "lounge" came slipping out. She had of late, however, compromised on "living-room." Miss Marple liked Cherry very much. Her name was Mrs. Baker and she came from the Development. She was one of the detachment of young wives who shopped at the supermarket and wheeled prams about the quiet streets of St. Mary Mead. They were all smart and well turned out. Their hair was crisp and curled. They laughed and talked and called to one another. They were like a happy flock of birds. Owing to the insidious snares of installment buying, they were always in need of ready money, though their husbands all earned good wages; and so they came and did housework or cooking. Cherry was a quick and efficient cook, she was an intelligent girl, took telephone calls correctly and was quick to spot inaccuracies in the tradesmen's books. She was not much given to turning mattresses, and as far as washing up went, Miss Marple always now passed the pantry door with her head turned away so as not to observe Cherry's method, which was that of thrusting everything into the sink together and letting loose a snowstorm of detergent on it. Miss Marple had quietly removed her old Worcester tea set from daily circulation and put it in the corner cabinet whence it only emerged on special occasions. Instead she had purchased a modern service with a pattern of pale grey on white and no gilt on it whatsoever to be washed away in the sink.

How different it had been in the past. . . . Faithful Florence, for instance, that grenadier of a parlourmaid—and there had been Amy and Clara and Alice, those "nice little maids"—arriving from St. Faith's Orphanage to be "trained," and then going on to better-paid jobs elsewhere. Rather simple, some of them had been, and frequently adenoidal, and Amy distinctly moronic. They had gossiped and chattered with the other maids in the village and walked out with the fishmonger's assistant, or the under-gardener at the Hall, or one of Mr. Barnes, the grocer's, numerous assistants. Miss Marple's mind went back over them affectionately, thinking of all the little woolly coats she had knitted for their subsequent offspring. They had not been very good with the telephone, and no good at all at arithmetic. On the other hand, they knew how to wash up, and how to make a bed. They had had skills, rather than education. It was odd that nowadays it should be the educated girls who went in for all the domestic chores. Students from abroad, girls *au pair*, university students in the vacation, young married women like Cherry Baker, who lived in spurious Closes on new building developments.

There were still, of course, people like Miss Knight. This last thought came suddenly as Miss Knight's tread overhead made the lustres on the mantelpiece tinkle warningly. Miss Knight had obviously had her afternoon rest and would now go out for her afternoon walk. In a moment she would come to ask Miss Marple if she could get her anything in the town. The thought of Miss Knight brought the usual reaction to Miss Marple's mind. Of course, it was very generous of dear Raymond (her nephew) and nobody could be kinder than Miss Knight, and of course that attack of bronchitis had left her very weak, and Dr. Haydock had said very firmly that she must not go on sleeping alone in the house with only someone coming in daily, but— She stopped there. Because it was no use going on with the thought which was "If only it could have been someone other than Miss Knight." But there wasn't much choice for elderly ladies nowadays. Devoted maidservants had gone out of fashion. In real illness you could have a proper hospital nurse, at vast expense and procured with difficulty, or you could go to hospital. But after that critical phase of illness had passed, you were down to the Miss Knights.

There wasn't, Miss Marple reflected, anything wrong about the Miss Knights other than the fact that they were madly irritating. They were full of kindness, ready to feel affection towards their charges, to humour them, to be bright and cheerful with them and in general to treat them as slightly mentally afflicted children.

"But I," said Miss Marple to herself, "although I may be old, am *not* a mentally afflicted child."

At this moment, breathing rather heavily, as was her custom, Miss Knight bounced brightly into the room. She was a big, rather flabby woman of fifty-six with yellowing grey hair very elaborately arranged, glasses, a long thin nose, and below it a good-natured mouth and a weak chin.

"Here we are!" she exclaimed with a kind of beaming boisterousness, meant to cheer and enliven the sad twilight of the aged. "I hope *we*'ve had our little snooze?"

"I have been knitting," Miss Marple replied, putting some emphasis on the pronoun, "and," she went on, confessing her weakness with distaste and shame, "I've dropped a stitch."

"Oh dear, dear," said Miss Knight. "Well, we'll soon put that right, won't we?"

"*You* will," said Miss Marple. "*I*, alas, am unable to do so."

The slight acerbity of her tone passed quite unnoticed. Miss Knight, as always, was eager to help.

"There," she said after a few moments. "There you are, dear. Quite all right now."

Though Miss Marple was perfectly agreeable to be called "dear" (and even "ducks") by the woman at the greengrocer or the girl at the paper shop, it annoyed her intensely to be called "dear" by Miss Knight. Another of those things that elderly ladies have to bear. She thanked Miss Knight politely.

"And now I'm just going out for my wee toddle," said Miss Knight humorously. "Shan't be long."

"Please don't dream of hurrying back," said Miss Marple politely and sincerely.

"Well, I don't like to leave you too long on your own, dear, in case you get moped."

"I assure you I am quite happy," said Miss Marple. "I probably shall have"—she closed her eyes—"a little nap."

"That's right, dear. Anything I can get you?"

Miss Marple opened her eyes and considered.

"You might go into Longdon's and see if the curtains are ready. And perhaps another skein of the blue wool from Mrs. Wisley. And a box of black currant lozenges at the chemist's. And change my book at the library —but don't let them give you anything that isn't on my list. This last one was too terrible. I couldn't read it." She held out *The Spring Awakens*.

"Oh, dear, dear! Didn't you like it? I thought you'd love it. Such a pretty story."

"And if it isn't too far for you, perhaps you wouldn't mind going as far as Halletts and see if they have one of those up-and-down egg whisks—*not* the turn-the-handle kind."

(She knew very well they had nothing of the kind, but Halletts was the farthest shop possible.)

"If all this isn't too much—" she murmured.

But Miss Knight replied with obvious sincerity.

"Not at all. I shall be delighted."

Miss Knight loved shopping. It was the breath of life to her. One met acquaintances, and had the chance of a chat, one gossiped with the assistants, and had the opportunity of examining various articles in the various shops. And one could spend quite a long time engaged in these pleasant occupations without any guilty feeling that it was one's duty to hurry back.

So Miss Knight started off happily, after a last glance at the frail old lady resting so peacefully by the window.

After waiting a few minutes in case Miss Knight should return for a shopping bag, or her purse, or a handkerchief (she was a great forgetter and returner), and also to recover from the slight mental fatigue induced by thinking of so many unwanted things to ask Miss Knight to get, Miss Marple rose briskly to her feet, cast aside her knitting and strode purposefully across the room and into the hall. She took down her summer coat from its peg, a stick from the hall stand, and exchanged her bedroom slippers for a pair of stout walking shoes. Then she left the house by the side door.

"It will take her at least an hour and a half," Miss Marple estimated to herself. "Quite that—with all the people from the Development doing their shopping."

Miss Marple visualized Miss Knight at Longdon's making abortive inquiries *re* curtains. Her surmises were remarkably accurate. At this moment Miss Knight was exclaiming, "Of course, I felt quite sure in my own mind they wouldn't be ready yet. But of course I said I'd come along and see when the old lady spoke about it. Poor old dears, they've got so little to look forward to. One must humour them. And she's a sweet old lady. Failing a little now, it's only to be expected—their faculties get dimmed. Now that's a pretty material you've got there. Do you have it in any other colours?"

A pleasant twenty minutes passed. When Miss Knight had finally departed, the senior assistant remarked with a sniff, "Failing, is she? I'll believe that when I see it for myself. Old Miss Marple has always been as sharp as a needle, and I'd say she still is." She then gave her attention to a young woman in tight trousers and a sailcloth jersey who wanted plastic material with crabs on it for bathroom curtains.

"Emily Waters, that's who she reminds me of," Miss Marple was saying to herself, with the satisfaction it always gave her to match up a human personality with one known in the past. "Just the same bird brain. Let me see, what happened to Emily?"

Nothing much, was her conclusion. She had once nearly got engaged to a curate, but after an understanding of several years the affair had fizzled out. Miss Marple dismissed her nurse attendant from her mind and gave her attention to her surroundings. She had traversed the garden rapidly, only observing as it were from the corner of her eye that Laycock had cut down the old-fashioned roses in a way more suitable to hybrid teas, but she did not allow this to distress her, or distract her from the delicious pleasure of having escaped for an outing entirely on her own. She had a happy feeling of adventure. She turned to the right, entered the Vicarage gate, took the path through the Vicarage garden and came out on the right of way. Where the stile had been there was now an iron swing gate giving on to a tarred asphalt path. This led to a neat little bridge over the stream and on the other side of the stream, where once there had been meadows with cows, there was the Development.

Chapter Two

WITH THE FEELING of Columbus setting out to discover a new world, Miss Marple passed over the bridge, continued on to the path and within four minutes was actually in Aubrey Close.

Of course Miss Marple had seen the Development from the Market Basing Road, that is, had seen from afar its Closes and rows of neat well-built houses, with their television masts and their blue and pink and yellow and green painted doors and windows. But until now it had only had the reality of a map, as it were. She had not been in it and of it. But now she was here, observing the brave new world that was springing up, the world that by all accounts was foreign to all she had known. It was like a neat model built with child's bricks. It hardly seemed real to Miss Marple.

The people, too, looked unreal. The trousered young women, the rather sinister-looking young men and boys, the exuberant bosoms of the fifteen-year-old girls. Miss Marple couldn't help thinking that it all looked terribly depraved. Nobody noticed her much as she trudged along. She turned out of Aubrey Close and was presently in Darlington Close. She went slowly and as she went she listened avidly to the snippets of conversation between mothers wheeling prams, to the girls addressing young men, to the sinister-looking Teds (she supposed they were Teds) exchanging dark remarks with each other. Mothers came out on doorsteps calling to their children who, as usual, were busy doing all the things they had been told not to do. Children, Miss Marple reflected gratefully, never changed. And presently she began to smile, and noted down in her mind her usual series of recognitions.

That woman is just like Carry Edwards—and the dark one is just like that Hooper girl—she'll make a mess of her marriage just as Mary Hooper did. Those boys—the dark one is just like Edward Leeke, a lot of wild talk but no harm in him—a nice boy, really—the fair one is Mrs. Bedwell's Josh all over again. Nice boys, both of them. The one like Gregory Binns won't do very well, I'm afraid. I expect he's got the same sort of mother. . . .

She turned a corner into Walsingham Close and her spirits rose every moment.

The new world was the same as the old. The houses were different, the streets were called Closes, the clothes were different, the voices were different, but the human beings were the same as they always had been. And though using slightly different phraseology, the subjects of conversation were the same.

By dint of turning corners in her exploration, Miss Marple had rather lost her sense of direction and had arrived at the edge of the housing estate again. She was now in Carrisbrook Close, half of which was still "under construction." At the first-floor window of a nearly finished house a young couple were standing. Their voices floated down as they discussed the amenities.

"You must admit it's a nice position, Harry."

"Other one was just as good."

"This one's got two more rooms."

"And you've got to pay for 'em."

"Well, I *like* this one."

"You would!"

"Ow, don't be such a spoil-sport. You know what Mum said."

"Your Mum never stops saying."

"Don't you say nothing against Mum. Where'd I have been without her? And she might have cut up nastier than she did, I can tell you that. She could have taken you to court."

"Oh, come off it, Lily."

"It's a good view of the hills. You can almost see—" She leaned far out, twisting her body to the left "You can almost see the reservoir—"

She leant farther still, not realizing that she was resting her weight on loose boards that had been laid across the sill. They slipped under the pressure of her body, sliding outwards, carrying her with them. She screamed, trying to regain her balance.

"Harry—!"

The young man stood motionless—a foot or two behind her. He took one step backwards—

Desperately, clawing at the wall, the girl righted herself.

"Oo!" She let out a frightened breath. "I near as nothing fell out. Why didn't you get hold of me?"

"It was all so quick. Anyway, you're all right."

"That's all you know about it. I nearly went, I tell you. And look at the front of my jumper, it's all mussed."

Miss Marple went on a little way, then on impulse, she turned back.

Lily was outside in the road waiting for the young man to lock up the house.

Miss Marple went up to her and spoke rapidly in a low voice.

"If I were you, my dear, I shouldn't marry that young man. You want someone whom you can rely upon if you're in danger. You must excuse me for saying this to you—but I feel you ought to be warned."

She turned away and Lily stared after her.

"Well, of all the—"

Her young man approached.

"What was she saying to you, Lil?"

Lily opened her mouth—then shut it again.

"Giving me the gipsy's warning, if you want to know."

She eyed him in a thoughtful manner.

Miss Marple, in her anxiety to get away quickly, turned a corner, stumbled over some loose stones and fell.

A woman came running out of one of the houses.

"Oh, dear, what a nasty spill! I hope you haven't hurt yourself?"

With almost excessive goodwill she put her arms round Miss Marple and tugged her to her feet.

"No bones broken, I hope? There we are. I expect you feel rather shaken."

Her voice was loud and friendly. She was a plump, squarely built woman of about forty, brown hair just turning grey, blue eyes, and a big generous mouth that seemed to Miss Marple's rather shaken gaze to be far too full of white shining teeth.

"You'd better come inside and sit down and rest a bit. I'll make you a cup of tea."

Miss Marple thanked her. She allowed herself to be led through the blue-painted door and into a small room full of bright cretonne-covered chairs and sofas.

"There you are," said her rescuer, establishing her on a cushioned armchair. "You sit quiet and I'll put the kettle on."

She hurried out of the room which seemed rather restfully quiet after her departure. Miss Marple took a deep breath. She was not really hurt, but the fall had shaken her. Falls at her age were not to be encouraged. With luck, however, she thought guiltily, Miss Knight need never know. She moved her arms and legs gingerly. Nothing broken. If she could only get home all right. Perhaps, after a cup of tea—

The cup of tea arrived almost as the thought came to her. Brought on a tray with four sweet biscuits on a little plate.

"There you are." It was placed on a small table in front of her. "Shall I pour it out for you? Better have plenty of sugar."

"No sugar, thank you."

"You must have sugar. Shock, you know. I was abroad with ambulances during the war. Sugar's wonderful for shock." She put four lumps in the cup and stirred vigorously. "Now you get that down, and you'll feel as right as rain."

Miss Marple accepted the dictum.

"A kind woman," she thought. "She reminds me of someone—now who is it?"

"You've been very kind to me," she said, smiling.

"Oh, that's nothing. The little ministering angel, that's me. I love helping people." She looked out of the window as the latch of the outer gate clicked. "Here's my husband home. Arthur—we've got a visitor."

She went out into the hall and returned with Arthur who looked rather bewildered. He was a thin pale man, rather slow in speech.

"This lady fell down—right outside our gate, so of course I brought her in."

"Your wife is very kind, Mr.—?"

"Badcock's the name."

"Mr. Badcock. I'm afraid I've given her a lot of trouble."

"Oh, no trouble to Heather. Heather enjoys doing things for people." He looked at her curiously. "Were you on your way anywhere in particular?"

"No, I was just taking a walk. I live in St. Mary Mead, the house beyond the Vicarage. My name is Marple."

"Well, I never!" exclaimed Heather. "So *you're* Miss Marple. I've heard about you. You're the one who does all the murders."

"Heather! What *do* you—"

"Oh, you know what I mean. Not actually do murders—find out about them. That's right, isn't it?"

Miss Marple murmured modestly that she had been mixed up in murders once or twice.

"I heard there have been murders here, in this village. They were talking about it the other night at the Bingo Club. There was one at Gossington Hall. I wouldn't buy a place where there'd been a murder. I'd be sure it was haunted."

"The murder wasn't committed in Gossington Hall. A dead body was brought there."

"Found in the library on the hearthrug, that's what they said?"

Miss Marple nodded.

"Did you ever? Perhaps they're going to make a film of it. Perhaps that's why Marina Gregg has bought Gossington Hall."

"Marina Gregg?"

"Yes. She and her husband. I forget his name—he's a producer, I think, or a director—Jason something. But Marina Gregg, she's lovely, isn't she? Of course she hasn't been in so many pictures of late years—she was ill for a long time. But I still think there's never anybody like her. Did you see her in *Carmanella*? And *The Price of Love,* and *Mary of Scotland*? She's not so young any more, but she'll always be a wonderful actress. I've always been a terrific fan of hers. When I was a teen-ager I used to dream about her. The big thrill of my life was when there was a big show in aid of the St. John's Ambulance in Bermuda, and Marina Gregg came to open it. I was mad with excitement, and then on the very day I came down with a temperature and the doctor said I couldn't go. But I wasn't going to be beaten. I didn't actually feel too bad. So I got up and put a lot of make-up on my face and went along. I was introduced to her and she talked to me for quite three minutes and gave me her autograph. It was wonderful. I've never forgotten that day."

Miss Marple stared at her.

"I hope there were no—unfortunate aftereffects?" she said anxiously.

Heather Badcock laughed.

"None at all. Never felt better. What I say is, if you want a thing, you've got to take risks. I always do."

She laughed again, a happy strident laugh.

Arthur Badcock said admiringly, "There's never any holding Heather. She always gets away with things."

"Alison Wilde," murmured Miss Marple, with a nod of satisfaction.

"Pardon?" said Mr. Badcock.

"Nothing. Just someone I used to know."

Heather looked at her inquiringly.

"You reminded me of her, that is all."

"Did I? I hope she was nice."

"She was very nice indeed," said Miss Marple slowly. "Kind, healthy, full of life."

"But she had her faults, I suppose?" laughed Heather. "I have."

"Well, Alison always saw her own point of view so clearly that she didn't always see how things might appear to, or affect, other people."

"Like the time you took in that evacuated family from a condemned cottage and they went off with all our teaspoons," Arthur said.

"But, Arthur!—I couldn't have turned them away. It wouldn't have been kind."

"They were family spoons," said Mr. Badcock sadly. "Georgian. Belonged to my mother's grandmother."

"Oh, do forget those old spoons, Arthur. You do harp so."

"I'm not very good at forgetting, I'm afraid."

Miss Marple looked at him thoughtfully.

"What's your friend doing now?" asked Heather of Miss Marple with kindly interest.

Miss Marple paused a moment before answering.

"Alison Wilde? Oh—she died."

Chapter Three

"I'm GLAD to be back," said Mrs. Bantry. "Although, of course, I've had a wonderful time."

Miss Marple nodded appreciatively, and accepted a cup of tea from her friend's hand.

When her husband, Colonel Bantry, had died some years ago, Mrs. Bantry had sold Gossington Hall and the considerable amount of land attached to it, retaining for herself what had been the East Lodge, a charming porticoed little building replete with inconvenience, where even a gardener had refused to live. Mrs. Bantry had added to it the essentials of modern life, a built-on kitchen of the latest type, a new water supply from the main, electricity, and a bathroom. This had all cost her a great deal, but not nearly so much as an attempt to live at Gossington Hall would have done. She had also retained the essentials of privacy, about three quarters of an acre of garden nicely ringed with trees, so that, as she explained, "Whatever they do with Gossington, I shan't really see it or worry."

For the last few years she had spent a good deal of the year travelling about, visiting children and grandchildren in various parts of the globe, and coming back from time to time to enjoy the privacies of her own home. Gossington Hall itself had changed hands once or twice. It had been run as a guest house, failed, and been bought by four people who had shared it as four roughly divided flats and subsequently quarrelled. Finally the Ministry of Health had bought it for some obscure purpose for which they eventually did not want it. The Ministry had now resold it—and it was this sale which the two friends were discussing.

"I have heard rumours, of course," said Miss Marple.

"Naturally," said Mrs. Bantry. "It was even said that Charlie Chaplin and all his children were coming to live here. That would have been wonderful fun; unfortunately there isn't a word of truth in it. No, it's definitely Marina Gregg."

"How very lovely she was," said Miss Marple with a sigh. "I always remember those early films of hers. *Bird of Passage* with that handsome

Joel Roberts. And the Mary, Queen of Scots film. And of course it was very sentimental, but I did enjoy *Comin' Thru the Rye*. Oh, dear, that was a long time ago."

"Yes," said Mrs. Bantry. "She must be—what do you think? Forty-five? Fifty?"

Miss Marple thought nearer fifty.

"Has she been in anything lately? Of course I don't go very often to the cinema nowadays."

"Only small parts, I think," said Mrs. Bantry. "She hasn't been a star for quite a long time. She had that bad nervous breakdown. After one of her divorces."

"Such a lot of husbands they all have," said Miss Marple. "It must really be very tiring."

"It wouldn't suit me," said Mrs. Bantry. "After you've fallen in love with a man and married him and got used to his ways and settled down comfortably—to go and throw it all up and start again! It seems to me madness."

"I can't presume to speak," said Miss Marple with a little spinsterish cough, "never having married. But it seems, you know, a pity."

"I suppose they can't help it really," said Mrs. Bantry vaguely. "With the kind of lives they have to live. So public, you know. I met her," she added. "Marina Gregg, I mean, when I was in California."

"What was she like?" Miss Marple asked with interest.

"Charming," said Mrs. Bantry. "So natural and unspoiled." She added thoughtfully, "It's like a kind of livery really."

"What is?"

"Being unspoiled and natural. You learn how to do it, and then you have to go on being it all the time. Just think of the hell of it—never to be able to chuck something and say, 'Oh, for the Lord's sake stop bothering me.' I dare say that in sheer self-defence you have to have drunken parties, or orgies."

"She's had five husbands, hasn't she?" Miss Marple asked.

"At least. An early one that didn't count, and then a foreign prince or count, and then another film star, Robert Truscott, wasn't it? That was built up as a great romance. But it only lasted four years. And then Isidore Wright, the playwright. That was rather serious and quiet, and she had a baby—apparently she'd always longed to have a child—she's even half-adopted a few strays—anyway this was the real thing. Very much built up. Motherhood with a capital M. And then, I believe, it was an imbecile, or queer or something—and it was after that that she had this breakdown and started to take drugs and all that, and threw up her parts."

"You seem to know a lot about her," said Miss Marple.

"Well, naturally," said Mrs. Bantry. "When she bought Gossington I was interested. She married the present man about two years ago, and they say she's quite all right again now. He's a producer—or do I mean a director? I always get mixed. He was in love with her when they were quite young, but he didn't amount to very much in those days. But now, I believe, he's got quite famous. What's his name now? Jason—Jason something—Jason Hudd, no, Rudd, that's it. They've bought Gossington because it's handy for"—she hesitated—"Elstree?" she hazarded.

Miss Marple shook her head.

"I don't think so," she said. "Elstree's in North London."

"It's the fairly new studios. Hellingforth—that's it. Sounds so Finnish, I always think. About six miles from Market Basing. She's going to do a film on Elizabeth of Austria, I believe."

"What a lot you know," said Miss Marple, "about the private lives of film stars. Did you learn it all in California?"

"Not really," said Mrs. Bantry. "Actually I get it from the extraordinary magazines I read at my hairdresser's. Most of the stars I don't even know by name, but as I said because Marina Gregg and her husband have bought Gossington, I was interested. Really the things those magazines say! I don't suppose half of it is true—probably not a quarter. I don't believe Marina Gregg is a nymphomaniac, I don't think she drinks, probably she doesn't even take drugs, and quite likely she just went away to have a nice rest and didn't have a nervous breakdown at all!—but it's true that she is coming here to live."

"Next week, I heard," said Miss Marple.

"As soon as that? I know she's lending Gossington for a big fête on the twenty-third in aid of St. John's Ambulance Corps. I suppose they've done a lot to the house?"

"Practically everything," said Miss Marple. "Really, it would have been much simpler, and probably cheaper, to have pulled it down and built a new house."

"Bathrooms, I suppose?"

"Six new ones, I hear. And a palm court. And a pool. And what I believe they call picture windows, and they've knocked your husband's study and the library into one to make a music room."

"Arthur will turn in his grave. You know how he hated music. Tone-deaf, poor dear. His face, when some kind friend took us to the opera!

He'll probably come back and haunt them." She stopped and then said abruptly, "Does anyone ever hint that Gossington might be haunted?"

Miss Marple shook her head.

"It isn't," she said with certainty.

"That wouldn't prevent people saying it was," Mrs. Bantry pointed out.

"Nobody ever has said so." Miss Marple paused and then said, "People aren't really foolish, you know. Not in villages."

Mrs. Bantry shot her a quick look. "You've always stuck to that, Jane. And I won't say that you're not right."

She suddenly smiled.

"Marina Gregg asked me, very sweetly and delicately, if I wouldn't find it very painful to see my old home occupied by strangers. I assured her that it wouldn't hurt me at all. I don't think she quite believed me. But after all, as you know, Jane, Gossington wasn't our home. We weren't brought up there as children—that's what really counts. It was just a house with a nice bit of shooting and fishing attached that we bought when Arthur retired. We thought of it, I remember, as a house that would be nice and easy to run! How we can ever have thought that, I can't imagine! All those staircases and passages. Only four servants! *Only!* Those were the days, ha ha!" She added suddenly: "What's all this about your falling down! That Knight woman ought not to let you go out by yourself."

"It wasn't poor Miss Knight's fault. I gave her a lot of shopping to do and then I—"

"Deliberately gave her the slip? I see. Well, you shouldn't do it, Jane. Not at your age."

"How did you hear about it?"

Mrs. Bantry grinned.

"You can't keep any secrets in St. Mary Mead. You've often told me so. Mrs. Meavy told me."

"Mrs. Meavy?" Miss Marple looked at sea.

"She comes in daily. She's from the Development."

"Oh, the Development." The usual pause happened.

"What were you doing in the Development?" asked Mrs. Bantry curiously.

"I just wanted to see it. To see what the people were like."

"And what did you think they were like?"

"Just the same as everyone else. I don't quite know if that was disappointing or reassuring."

"Disappointing, I should think."

"No. I think it's reassuring. It makes you—well—recognize certain types

—so that when anything occurs—one will understand quite well why and for what reason."

"Murder, do you mean?"

Miss Marple looked shocked.

"I don't know why you should assume that I think of murder all the time."

"Nonsense, Jane. Why don't you come out boldly, and call yourself a criminologist and have done with it?"

"Because I am nothing of the sort," said Miss Marple with spirit. "It is simply that I have a certain knowledge of human nature—that is only natural after having lived in a small village all my life."

"You probably have something there," said Mrs. Bantry thoughtfully, "though most people wouldn't agree, of course. Your nephew Raymond always used to say this place was a complete backwater."

"Dear Raymond," said Miss Marple indulgently. She added: "He's always been so kind. He's paying for Miss Knight, you know."

The thought of Miss Knight induced a new train of thought and she rose and said: "I'd better be going back now, I suppose."

"You didn't walk all the way here, did you?"

"Of course not. I came in Inch."

This somewhat enigmatic pronouncement was received with complete understanding. In days very long past, Mr. Inch had been the proprietor of two cabs which met trains at the local station and which were also hired by the local ladies to take them "calling," out to tea parties, and occasionally, with their daughters, to such frivolous entertainments as dances. In the fullness of time, Inch, a cheery red-faced man of seventy-odd, gave place to his son—known as "young Inch" (he was then aged forty-five)—though old Inch still continued to drive such elderly ladies as considered his son too young and irresponsible. To keep up with the times, young Inch abandoned horse vehicles for motorcars. He was not very good with machinery and in due course a certain Mr. Bardwell took over from him. The name Inch persisted. Mr. Bardwell in due course sold out to Mr. Roberts, but in the telephone book *Inch's Taxi Service* was still the official name, and the old ladies of the community continued to refer to their journeys as going somewhere "in Inch," as though they were Jonah and Inch was a whale.

II

"Dr. Haydock called," said Miss Knight reproachfully. "I told him you'd gone to tea with Mrs. Bantry. He said he'd call in again tomorrow."

She helped Miss Marple off with her wraps.

"And now, I expect, we're tired out," she said accusingly.

"*You* may be," said Miss Marple. "*I* am not."

"You come and sit cozy by the fire," said Miss Knight, as usual paying no attention. ("You don't need to take much notice of what the old dears say. I just humour them.") "And how would we fancy a nice cup of Ovaltine? Or Horlicks for a change?"

Miss Marple thanked her and said she would like a small glass of dry sherry. Miss Knight looked disapproving.

"I don't know what the doctor would say to that, I'm sure," she said, when she returned with the glass.

"We will make a point of asking him tomorrow morning," said Miss Marple.

On the following morning Miss Knight met Dr. Haydock in the hall, and did some agitated whispering.

The elderly doctor came into the room rubbing his hands, for it was a chilly morning.

"Here's our doctor to see us," said Miss Knight gaily. "Can I take your gloves, Doctor?"

"They'll be all right here," said Haydock, casting them carelessly on a table. "Quite a nippy morning."

"A little glass of sherry perhaps?" suggested Miss Marple.

"I heard you were taking to drink. Well, you should never drink alone."

The decanter and glasses were already on a small table by Miss Marple. Miss Knight left the room.

Dr. Haydock was a very old friend. He had semi-retired, but came to attend certain of his old patients.

"I hear you've been falling about," he said as he finished his glass. "It won't do, you know, not at your age. I'm warning you. And I hear you didn't want to send for Sandford."

Sandford was Haydock's partner.

"That Miss Knight of yours sent for him anyway—and she was quite right."

"I was only bruised and shaken a little. Dr. Sandford said so. I could have waited quite well until you were back."

"Now look here, my dear. I can't go on forever. And Sandford, let me tell you, has better qualifications than I have. He's a first-class man."

"The younger doctors are all the same," said Miss Marple. "They take your blood pressure, and whatever's the matter with you, you get some kind of mass-produced variety of new pills. Pink ones, yellow ones, brown ones. Medicine nowadays is just like a supermarket—all packaged up."

"Serve you right if I prescribed leeches, and black draught, and rubbed your chest with camphorated oil."

"I do that myself when I've got a cough," said Miss Marple with spirit, "and very comforting it is."

"We don't like getting old, that's what it is," said Haydock gently. "I hate it."

"You're quite a young man compared to me," said Miss Marple. "And I don't really mind getting old—not that in itself. It's the lesser indignities."

"I think I know what you mean."

"Never being alone! The difficulty of getting out for a few minutes by oneself. And even my knitting—such a comfort that has always been, and I really am a good knitter. Now I drop stitches all the time—and quite often I don't even know I've dropped them."

Haydock looked at her thoughtfully.

Then his eyes twinkled.

"There's always the opposite."

"Now what do you mean by that?"

"If you can't knit, what about unravelling for a change? Penelope did."

"I'm hardly in her position."

"But unravelling's rather in your line, isn't it?"

He rose to his feet.

"I must be getting along. What I'd prescribe for you is a nice juicy murder."

"That's an outrageous thing to say!"

"Isn't it? However, you can always make do with the depth the parsley sank into the butter on a summer's day. I always wondered about that. Good old Holmes. A period piece, nowadays, I suppose. But he'll never be forgotten."

Miss Knight bustled in after the doctor had gone.

"There," she said, "we look *much* more cheerful. Did the doctor recommend a tonic?"

"He recommended me to take an interest in murder."

"A nice detective story?"

"No," said Miss Marple. "Real life."

"Goodness," exclaimed Miss Knight. "But there's not likely to be a murder in this quiet spot."

"Murders," said Miss Marple, "can happen anywhere. And do."

"At the Development, perhaps?" mused Miss Knight. "A lot of those Teddy-looking boys carry knives."

But the murder, when it came, was not at the Development.

Chapter Four

MRS. BANTRY stepped back a foot or two, surveyed herself in the glass, made a slight adjustment to her hat (she was not used to wearing hats), drew on a pair of good quality leather gloves and left the lodge, closing the door carefully behind her. She had the most pleasurable anticipations of what lay in front of her. Some three weeks had passed since her talk with Miss Marple. Marina Gregg and her husband had arrived at Gossington Hall and were now more or less installed there.

There was to be a meeting there this afternoon of the main persons involved in the arrangements for the fête in aid of the St. John's Ambulance. Mrs. Bantry was not among those on the committee, but she had received a note from Marina Gregg asking her to come and have tea beforehand. It had recalled their meeting in California and had been signed, "Cordially, Marina Gregg." It had been handwritten, not typewritten. There is no denying that Mrs. Bantry was both pleased and flattered. After all, a celebrated film star is a celebrated film star, and elderly ladies, though they may be of local importance, are aware of their complete unimportance in the world of celebrities. So Mrs. Bantry had the pleased feeling of a child for whom a special treat had been arranged.

As she walked up the drive Mrs. Bantry's keen eyes went from side to side registering her impressions. The place had been smartened up since the days when it had passed from hand to hand. "No expense spared," said Mrs. Bantry to herself, nodding in satisfaction. The drive afforded no view of the flower garden and for that Mrs. Bantry was just as pleased. The flower garden and its special herbaceous border had been her own particular delight in the far-off days when she had lived at Gossington Hall. She permitted regretful and nostalgic memories of her irises. The best iris garden of any in the county, she told herself with a fierce pride.

Faced by a new front door in a blaze of new paint, she pressed the bell. The door was opened with gratifying promptness by what was undeniably an Italian butler. She was ushered by him straight to the room which had been Colonel Bantry's library. This, as she had already heard, had been thrown into one with the study. The result was impressive. The walls were panelled, the floor was parquet. At one end was a grand piano and halfway along the wall was a superb record player. At the other end of the room was a small island, as it were, which comprised Persian rugs, a tea table and some chairs. By the tea table sat Marina Gregg, and leaning against the mantelpiece was what Mrs. Bantry at first thought to be the ugliest man she had ever seen.

Just a few moments previously when Mrs. Bantry's hand had been advanced to press the bell, Marina Gregg had been saying in a soft, enthusiastic voice to her husband:

"This place is right for me, Jinks, just right. It's what I've always wanted. *Quiet*. English quiet and the English countryside. I can see myself living here, living here all my life if need be. And we'll adopt the English way of life. We'll have afternoon tea every afternoon with China tea and my lovely Georgian tea service. And we'll look out of the window on those lawns and that English herbaceous border. I've come home at last, that's what I feel. I feel that I can settle down here, that I can be quiet and happy. It's going to be home, this place. That's what I feel. *Home.*"

And Jason Rudd (known to his wife as Jinks) had smiled at her. It was an acquiescent smile, indulgent, but it held its reserve because, after all, he had heard it very often before. Perhaps this time it would be true. Perhaps this was the place that Marina Gregg might feel at home. But he knew her early enthusiasms so well. She was always so sure that at last she had found exactly what she wanted. He said in his deep voice:

"That's grand, honey. That's just grand. I'm glad you like it."

"Like it? I adore it. Don't you adore it, too?"

"Sure," said Jason Rudd. "Sure."

It wasn't too bad, he reflected to himself. Good, solidly built, rather ugly

Victorian. It had, he admitted, a feeling of solidity and security. Now that the worst of its fantastic inconveniences had been ironed out, it would be quite reasonably comfortable to live in. Not a bad place to come back to from time to time. With luck, he thought, Marina wouldn't start taking a dislike to it for perhaps two years to two years and a half. It all depended.

Marina said, sighing softly:

"It's so wonderful to feel well again. Well and strong. Able to cope with things."

And he said again: "Sure, honey, sure."

And it was at that moment that the door opened and the Italian butler had ushered in Mrs. Bantry.

Marina Gregg's welcome was all that was charming. She came forward, hands outstretched, saying how delightful it was to meet Mrs. Bantry again. And what a coincidence that they should have met that time in San Francisco and that two years later she and Jinks should actually buy the house that had once belonged to Mrs. Bantry. And she did hope, she really did hope that Mrs. Bantry wouldn't mind terribly the way they'd pulled the house about and done things to it and she hoped she wouldn't feel that they were terrible intruders living here.

"Your coming to live here is one of the most exciting things that has ever happened in this place," said Mrs. Bantry cheerfully, and she looked towards the mantelpiece. Whereupon, almost as an afterthought, Marina Gregg said:

"You don't know my husband, do you? Jason, this is Mrs. Bantry."

Mrs. Bantry looked at Jason Rudd with some interest. Her first impression that this was one of the ugliest men she had ever seen became qualified. He had interesting eyes. They were, she thought, more deeply sunk in his head than any eyes she had seen. Deep quiet pools, said Mrs. Bantry to herself, and felt like a romantic lady novelist. The rest of his face was distinctly craggy, almost ludicrously out of proportion. His nose jutted upwards and a little red paint would have transformed it into the nose of a clown very easily. He had, too, a clown's big sad mouth. Whether he was at this moment in a furious temper or whether he always looked as though he were in a furious temper she did not quite know. His voice when he spoke was unexpectedly pleasant. Deep and slow.

"A husband," he said, "is always an afterthought. But let me say with my wife that we're very glad to welcome you here. I hope you don't feel that it ought to be the other way about."

"You must get it out of your head," said Mrs. Bantry, "that I've been driven forth from my old home. It never was my old home. I've been congratulating myself ever since I sold it. It was a most inconvenient house to run. I liked the garden, but the house became more and more of a worry. I've had a perfectly splendid time ever since, travelling abroad and going and seeing my married daughters and my grandchildren and my friends in all the different parts of the world."

"Daughters," said Marina Gregg, "you have daughters and sons?"

"Two sons and two daughters," said Mrs. Bantry, "and pretty widely spaced. One in Kenya, one in South Africa. One near Texas and the other, thank goodness, in London."

"Four," said Marina Gregg. "Four—and grandchildren?"

"Nine up to date," said Mrs. Bantry. "It's great fun being a grandmother. You don't have any of the worry of parental responsibility. You can spoil them in the most unbridled way—"

Jason Rudd interrupted her. "I'm afraid the sun catches your eyes," he said, and went to a window to adjust the blind. "You must tell us all about this delightful village," he said as he came back.

He handed her a cup of tea.

"Will you have a hot scone or a sandwich, or this cake? We have an Italian cook and she makes quite good pastry and cakes. You see we have quite taken to your English afternoon tea."

"Delicious tea, too," said Mrs. Bantry, sipping the fragrant beverage.

Marina Gregg smiled and looked pleased. The sudden nervous movement of her fingers which Jason Rudd's eye had noticed a minute or two previously, was stilled again. Mrs. Bantry looked at her hostess with great admiration. Marina Gregg's heyday had been before the rise to supreme importance of vital statistics. She could not have been described as Sex Incarnate, or "The Bust" or "The Torso." She had been long and slim and willowy. The bones of her face and head had had some of the beauty associated with those of Garbo. She had brought personality to her pictures rather than mere sex. The sudden turn of her head, the opening of the deep lovely eyes, the faint quiver of her mouth, all these were what brought to one suddenly that feeling of breathtaking loveliness that comes not from regularity of feature but from some sudden magic of the flesh that catches the onlooker unawares. She still had this quality though it was not now so easily apparent. Like many film and stage actresses, she had what seemed to be a habit of turning off personality at will. She could retire into herself, be quiet, gentle, aloof, disappointing to an eager fan. And then suddenly the turn of the head, the movement of the hands, the sudden smile and the magic was there.

One of her greatest pictures had been *Mary, Queen of Scots*, and it was of her performance in that picture that Mrs. Bantry was reminded now as she watched her. Mrs. Bantry's eye switched to the husband. He too was watching Marina. Off guard for a moment, his face expressed clearly his feelings. "Good Lord," said Mrs. Bantry to herself, "the man adores her."

She didn't know why she should feel so surprised. Perhaps because film stars and their love affairs and their devotion were so written up in the press, that one never expected to see the real thing with one's own eyes. On an impulse she said:

"I do hope you'll enjoy it here and that you'll be able to stay here some time. Do you expect to have the house for long?"

Marina opened wide surprised eyes as she turned her head. "I want to stay here always," she said. "Oh, I don't mean that I shan't have to go away a lot. I shall, of course. There's a possibility of my making a film in North Africa next year although nothing's settled yet. No, but this will be my home. I shall come back here. I shall always be able to come back here." She sighed. "That's what's so wonderful. That's what's so very wonderful. To have found a home at last."

"I see," said Mrs. Bantry, but at the same time she thought to herself, "All the same I don't believe for a moment that it will be like that. I don't believe you're the kind that can ever settle down."

Again she shot a quick surreptitious glance at Jason Rudd. He was not scowling now. Instead he was smiling, a sudden very sweet and unexpected smile, but it was a sad smile. "He knows it, too," thought Mrs. Bantry.

The door opened and a woman came in. "Bartletts want you on the telephone, Jason," she said.

"Tell them to call back."

"They said it was urgent."

He sighed and rose. "Let me introduce you to Mrs. Bantry," he said. "Ella Zielinsky, my secretary."

"Have a cup of tea, Ella," said Marina as Ella Zielinsky acknowledged the introduction with a smiling "pleased to meet you."

"I'll have a sandwich," said Ella. "I don't go for China tea."

Ella Zielinsky was, at a guess, thirty-five. She wore a well-cut suit, a ruffled blouse and appeared to breathe self-confidence. She had short-cut black hair and a wide forehead.

"You used to live here, so they tell me," she said to Mrs. Bantry.

"It's a good many years ago now," said Mrs. Bantry. "After my husband's death I sold it, and it's passed through several hands since then."

"Mrs. Bantry really says she doesn't hate the things we've done to it," said Marina.

"I should be frightfully disappointed if you hadn't," said Mrs. Bantry. "I came up here all agog. I can tell you the most splendid rumours have been going around the village."

"Never knew how difficult it was to get hold of plumbers in this country," said Miss Zielinsky, chomping a sandwich in a businesslike way. "Not that that's been really my job," she went on.

"Everything is your job," said Marina, "and you know it is, Ella. The domestic staff and the plumbing and arguing with the builders."

"They don't seem ever to have heard of a picture window in this country."

Ella looked towards the window. "It's a nice view, I must admit."

"A lovely old-fashioned rural English scene," said Marina. "This house has got atmosphere."

"It wouldn't look so rural if it wasn't for the trees," said Ella Zielinsky. "That housing estate down there grows while you look at it."

"That's new since my time," said Mrs. Bantry.

"You mean there was nothing but the village when you lived here?" Mrs. Bantry nodded.

"It must have been hard to do your shopping."

"I don't think so," said Mrs. Bantry. "I think it was frightfully easy."

"I understand having a flower garden," said Ella Zielinsky, "but you folks over here seem to grow all your vegetables as well. Wouldn't it be much easier to buy them—there's a supermarket?"

"It's probably coming to that," said Mrs. Bantry, with a sigh. "They don't taste the same, though."

"Don't spoil the atmosphere, Ella," said Marina.

The door opened and Jason looked in. "Darling," he said to Marina, "I hate to bother you, but would you mind? They just want your private view about this."

Marina sighed and rose. She trailed languidly towards the door. "Always something," she murmured. "I'm so sorry, Mrs. Bantry. I don't really think that this will take longer than a minute or two."

"Atmosphere," said Ella Zielinsky, as Marina went out and closed the door. "Do you think the house has got atmosphere?"

"I can't say I ever thought of it that way," said Mrs. Bantry. "It was just a house. Rather inconvenient in some ways and very nice and cozy in other ways."

"That's what I should have thought," said Ella Zielinsky. She cast a quick direct look at Mrs. Bantry. "Talking of atmosphere, when did the murder take place here?"

"No murder ever took place here," said Mrs. Bantry.

"Oh, come now. The stories I've heard. There are always stories, Mrs. Bantry. On the hearthrug, right there, wasn't it?" said Miss Zielinsky, nodding towards the fireplace.

"Yes," said Mrs. Bantry. "That was the place."

"So there was a murder?"

Mrs. Bantry shook her head. "The murder didn't take place here. The girl who had been killed was brought here and planted in this room. She'd nothing to do with us."

Miss Zielinsky looked interested.

"Possibly you had a bit of difficulty making people believe that?" she remarked.

"You're quite right there," said Mrs. Bantry.

"When did you find it?"

"The housemaid came in in the morning," said Mrs. Bantry, "with early morning tea. We had housemaids then, you know."

"I know," said Miss Zielinsky, "wearing print dresses that rustled."

"I'm not sure about the print dress," said Mrs. Bantry, "it may have been overalls by then. At any rate, she burst in and said there was a body in the library. I said 'nonsense,' then I woke up my husband and we came down to see."

"And there it was," said Miss Zielinsky. "My, the way things happen." She turned her head sharply towards the door and then back again. "Don't talk about it to Miss Gregg, if you don't mind," she said. "It's not good for her, that sort of thing."

"Of course. I won't say a word," said Mrs. Bantry. "I never do talk about it, as a matter of fact. It all happened so long ago. But won't she—Miss Gregg, I mean—won't she hear it anyway?"

"She doesn't come very much in contact with reality," said Ella Zielinsky. "Film stars can lead a fairly insulated life, you know. In fact very often one has to take care that they do. Things upset them. Things upset her. She's been seriously ill the last year or two, you know. She only started making a comeback a year ago."

"She seems to like the house," said Mrs. Bantry, "and to feel she will be happy here."

"I expect it'll last a year or two," said Ella Zielinsky.

"Not longer than that?"

"Well, I rather doubt it. Marina is one of those people, you know, who are always thinking they've found their heart's desire. But life isn't as easy as that, is it?"

"No," said Mrs. Bantry forcefully, "it isn't."

"It'll mean a lot to him if she's happy here," said Miss Zielinsky. She ate two more sandwiches in an absorbed, rather gobbling fashion in the manner of those who cram food into themselves as though they have an important train to catch. "He's a genius, you know," she went on. "Have you seen any of the pictures he's directed?"

Mrs. Bantry felt slightly embarrassed. She was of the type of woman who when she went to the cinema went entirely for the picture. The long lists of casts, directors, producers, photography and the rest of it passed her by. Very frequently, indeed, she did not even notice the names of the stars. She was not, however, anxious to call attention to this failing on her part.

"I get so mixed up," she said.

"Of course, he's got a lot to contend with," said Ella Zielinsky. "He's got her as well as everything else, and she's not easy. You've got to keep her happy, you see; and it's not really easy, I suppose, to keep people happy. Unless—that is—they—they are—" She hesitated.

"Unless they're the happy kind," suggested Mrs. Bantry. "Some people," she added thoughtfully, "enjoy being miserable."

"Oh, Marina isn't like that," said Ella Zielinsky, shaking her head. "It's more that her ups and downs are so violent. You know—far too happy one moment, far too pleased with everything and delighted with everything and how wonderful she feels. Then, of course, some little thing happens and down she goes to the opposite extreme."

"I suppose that's temperament," said Mrs. Bantry vaguely.

"That's right," said Ella Zielinsky. "Temperament. They've all got it, more or less, but Marina Gregg has got it more than most people. Don't we know it! The stories I could tell you!" She ate the last sandwich. "Thank God I'm only the social secretary."

Chapter Five

THE THROWING OPEN of the grounds of Gossington Hall for the benefit of the St. John's Ambulance Association was attended by a quite unprecedented number of people. Shilling admission fees mounted up in a highly satisfactory fashion. For one thing, the weather was good, a clear sunny day. But the preponderant attraction was undoubtedly the enormous local curiosity to know exactly what these "film people" had done to Gossington Hall. The most extravagant assumptions were entertained. The swimming pool in particular caused immense satisfaction. Most people's ideas of Hollywood stars were of sun-bathing by a pool in exotic surroundings and in exotic company. That the climate of Hollywood might be more suited to swimming pools than that of St. Mary Mead failed to be considered. After all, England always has one fine hot week in the summer and there is always one day that the Sunday papers publish articles on How to Keep Cool, How to Have Cool Suppers and How to Make Cool Drinks. The pool was almost exactly what everyone had imagined it might be. It was large, its waters were blue, it had a kind of exotic pavilion for changing and was surrounded with a highly artificial plantation of hedges and shrubs. The reactions of the multitude were exactly as might have been expected and hovered over a wide range of remarks.

"O-oh, isn't it lovely!"

"Two penn'orth of splash here, all right!"

"Reminds me of that holiday camp I went to."

"Wicked luxury *I* call it. It oughtn't to be allowed."

"Look at all that fancy marble. It must have cost the earth!"

"Don't see why these people think they can come over here and spend all the money they like."

"Perhaps this'll be on the telly sometime. That'll be fun."

Even Mr. Sampson, the oldest man in St. Mary Mead, boasting proudly of being ninety-six though his relations insisted firmly that he was only eighty-eight, had staggered along supporting his rheumatic legs with a stick, to see the excitement. He gave it his highest praise: "Wicked, this!" He smacked his lips hopefully. "Ah, there'll be a lot of wickedness here, I don't doubt. Naked men and women drinking and smoking what they call in the papers them reefers. There'll be all that, I expect. Ah yes," said Mr. Sampson with enormous pleasure, "there'll be a lot of wickedness."

It was felt that the final seal of approval had been set on the afternoon's entertainment. For an extra shilling people were allowed to go into the house, and study the new music room, the drawing-room, the completely unrecognizable dining-room, now done in dark oak and Spanish leather, and a few other joys.

"Never think this was Gossington Hall, would you, now?" said Mr. Sampson's daughter-in-law.

Mrs. Bantry strolled up fairly late and observed with pleasure that the money was coming in well and that the attendance was phenomenal.

The large marquee in which tea was being served was jammed with people. Mrs. Bantry hoped the buns were going to go round. There seemed some very competent women, however, in charge. She herself made a beeline for the herbaceous border and regarded it with a jealous eye. No expense had been spared on the herbaceous border, she was glad to note, and it was a proper herbaceous border, well planned and arranged and expensively stocked. No personal labours had gone into it, she was sure of that. Some good gardening firm had been given the contract, no doubt. But aided by carte blanche and the weather, they had turned out a very good job.

Looking round her, she felt there was a faint flavour of a Buckingham Palace garden party about the scene. Everybody was craning to see all they could see, and from time to time a chosen few were led into one of the more secret recesses of the house. She herself was presently approached by a willowy young man with long wavy hair.

"Mrs. Bantry? You *are* Mrs. Bantry?"

"I'm Mrs. Bantry, yes."

"Hailey Preston." He shook hands with her. "I work for Mr. Rudd. Will you come up to the second floor? Mr. and Mrs. Rudd are asking a few special friends up there."

Duly honoured, Mrs. Bantry followed him. They went in through what had been called in her time the garden door. A red cord cordoned off the bottom of the main stairs. Hailey Preston unhooked it and she passed through. Just in front of her Mrs. Bantry observed Councillor and Mrs. Allcock. The latter who was stout was breathing heavily.

"Wonderful what they've done, isn't it, Mrs. Bantry?" panted Mrs. Allcock. "I'd like to have a look at the bathrooms, I must say, but I suppose I shan't get the chance." Her voice was wistful.

At the top of the stairs Marina Gregg and Jason Rudd were receiving this specially chosen élite. What had once been a spare bedroom had been thrown into the landing so as to make a wide lounge-like effect. Giuseppe the butler was officiating with drinks.

A stout man in livery was announcing guests.

"Councillor and Mrs. Allcock," he boomed.

Marina Gregg was being, as Mrs. Bantry had described her to Miss Marple, completely natural and charming. She could already hear Mrs. Allcock saying later, "—and so unspoiled, you know, in spite of being so famous."

How very nice of Mrs. Allcock to come, *and* the Councillor, and she did hope that they'd enjoy their afternoon. "Jason, please look after Mrs. Allcock."

Councillor and Mrs. Allcock were passed on to Jason and drinks.

"Oh, Mrs. Bantry, it *is* nice of you to come."

"I wouldn't have missed it for the world," said Mrs. Bantry and moved on purposefully towards the martinis.

The young man called Hailey Preston ministered to her in a tender manner and then made off, consulting a little list in his hand, to fetch, no doubt, more of the Chosen to the Presence. It was all being managed very well, Mrs. Bantry thought, turning, martini in hand, to watch the next arrivals. The vicar, a lean, ascetic man, was looking vague and slightly bewildered. He said earnestly to Marina Gregg:

"Very nice of you to ask me. I'm afraid, you know, I haven't got a television set myself, but of course I—er—I—well, of course my young people keep me up to the mark."

Nobody knew what he meant. Miss Zielinsky, who was also on duty, administered a lemonade to him with a kindly smile. Mr. and Mrs. Badcock were next up the stairs. Heather Badcock, flushed and triumphant, came a little ahead of her husband.

"Mr. and Mrs. Badcock," boomed the man in livery.

"Mrs. Badcock," said the vicar, turning back, lemonade in hand, "the indefatigable secretary of the association. She's one of our hardest workers. In fact I don't know what St. John's would do without her."

"I'm sure you've been wonderful," said Marina.

"You don't remember me?" said Heather, in an arch manner. "How should you, with all the hundreds of people you meet. And anyway, it was years ago. In Bermuda, of all places in the world. I was there with one of our ambulance units. Oh, it's a long time ago now."

"Of course," said Marina Gregg, once more all charm and smiles.

"I remember it all so well," said Mrs. Badcock. "I was thrilled, you know, absolutely thrilled. I was only a girl at the time. To think there was a chance of seeing Marina Gregg in the flesh—oh! I was a mad fan of yours always."

"It's too kind of you, really too kind of you," said Marina sweetly, her eyes beginning to hover faintly over Heather's shoulder towards the next arrivals.

"I'm not going to detain you," said Heather, "but I must—"

"Poor Marina Gregg," said Mrs. Bantry to herself. "I suppose this kind of thing is always happening to her! The patience they need!"

Heather was continuing in a determined manner with her story.

Mrs. Allcock breathed heavily at Mrs. Bantry's shoulder.

"The changes they've made here! You wouldn't believe till you saw for yourself. What it must have cost . . ."

"—I didn't feel really ill—and I thought I just must—"

"This is vodka." Mrs. Allcock regarded her glass suspiciously. "Mr. Rudd asked if I'd like to try it. Sounds very Russian. I don't think I like it very much . . ."

"—I said to myself; I won't be beaten! I put a lot of make-up on my face—"

"I suppose it would be rude if I just put it down somewhere." Mrs. Allcock sounded desperate.

Mrs. Bantry reassured her kindly.

"Not at all. Vodka ought really to be thrown straight down the throat" —Mrs. Allcock looked startled—"but that needs practice. Put it down on the table and get yourself a martini from that tray the butler's carrying."

She turned back to hear Heather Badcock's triumphant peroration.

"I've never forgotten how wonderful you were that day. It was a hundred times worth it."

Marina's response was this time not so automatic. Her eyes, which had wavered over Heather Badcock's shoulder, now seemed to be fixed on the wall midway up the stairs. She was staring and there was something so ghastly in her expression that Mrs. Bantry half took a step forward. Was the woman going to faint? What on earth could she be seeing that gave her that basilisk look? But before she could reach Marina's side, the latter had recovered herself. Her eyes, vague and unfocused, returned to Heather and the charm of manner was turned on once more, albeit a shade mechanically.

"What a nice little story. Now, what will you have to drink? Jason! A cocktail?"

"Well, really I usually have lemonade or orange juice."

"You must have something better than that," said Marina. "This is a feast day, remember."

"Let me persuade you to an American daiquiri," said Jason, appearing with a couple in his hand. "They're Marina's favourites, too."

He handed one to his wife.

"I shouldn't drink any more," said Marina. "I've had three already." But she accepted the glass.

Heather took her drink from Jason. Marina turned away to meet the next person who was arriving.

Mrs. Bantry said to Mrs. Allcock, "Let's go and see the bathrooms."

"Oh, do you think we can? Wouldn't it look rather rude?"

"I'm sure it wouldn't," said Mrs. Bantry. She spoke to Jason Rudd. "We want to explore your wonderful new bathrooms, Mr. Rudd. May we satisfy this purely domestic curiosity?"

"Sure," said Jason, grinning. "Go and enjoy yourselves, girls. Draw yourselves baths if you like."

Mrs. Allcock followed Mrs. Bantry along the passage.

"That was ever so kind of you, Mrs. Bantry. I must say I wouldn't have dared myself."

"One has to dare if one wants to get anywhere," said Mrs. Bantry.

They went along the passage, opening various doors. Presently "Ahs" and "Ohs" began to escape Mrs. Allcock and two other women who had joined the party.

"I do like the pink one," said Mrs. Allcock. "Oh, I like the pink one a lot."

"I like the one with the dolphin tiles," said one of the other women.

Mrs. Bantry acted the part of hostess with complete enjoyment. For a moment she had really forgotten that the house no longer belonged to her.

"All those showers!" said Mrs. Allcock with awe. "Not that I really like showers. I never know how you keep your head dry."

"It'd be nice to have a peep into the bedrooms," said one of the other women wistfully, "but I suppose it'd be a bit too nosy. What do you think?"

"Oh, I don't think we could do that," said Mrs. Allcock. They both looked hopefully at Mrs. Bantry.

"Well," said Mrs. Bantry, "no, I suppose we oughtn't to—" Then she took pity on them. "But—I don't think anyone would know if we have one peep." She put her hand on a door handle.

But that had been attended to. The bedrooms were locked. Everyone was very disappointed.

"I suppose they've got to have some privacy," said Mrs. Bantry kindly.

They retraced their steps along the corridor. Mrs. Bantry looked out of one of the landing windows. She noted below her Mrs. Meavy (from the Development) looking incredibly smart in a ruffled organdie dress. With Mrs. Meavy, she noticed, was Miss Marple's Cherry, whose last name for the moment Mrs. Bantry could not remember. They seemed to be enjoying themselves and were laughing and talking.

Suddenly the house felt to Mrs. Bantry old, worn-out and highly artificial. In spite of its new gleaming paint, its alterations, it was in essence a tired old Victorian mansion. "I was wise to go," thought Mrs. Bantry. "Houses are like everything else. There comes a time when they've just had their day. This has had its day. It's been given a face lift, but I don't really think it's done it any good."

Suddenly a slight rise in the hum of voices reached her. The two women with her started forward.

"What's happening?" said one. "It sounds as though something's happening."

They stepped back along the corridor towards the stairs. Ella Zielinsky came rapidly along and passed them. She tried a bedroom door and said quickly, "Oh, damn. Of course they've locked them all."

"Is anything the matter?" asked Mrs. Bantry.

"Someone's taken ill," said Miss Zielinsky shortly.

"Oh dear, I'm sorry. Can I do anything?"

"I suppose there's a doctor here somewhere?"

"I haven't seen any of our local doctors," said Mrs. Bantry, "but there's almost sure to be one here."

"Jason's telephoning," said Ella Zielinsky, "but she seems pretty bad."

"Who is it?" asked Mrs. Bantry.

"A Mrs. Badcock, I think."

"Heather Badcock? But she looked so well just now."

Ella Zielinsky said impatiently, "She's had a seizure, or a fit, or something. Do you know if there's anything wrong with her heart or anything like that?"

"I don't really know anything about her," said Mrs. Bantry. "She's new since my day. She comes from the Development."

"The Development? Oh, you mean that housing estate. I don't even know where her husband is or what he looks like."

"Middle-aged, fair, unobtrusive," said Mrs. Bantry. "He came with her so he must be about somewhere."

Ella Zielinsky went into a bathroom. "I don't know really what to give her," she said. "Sal volatile, do you think, something like that?"

"Is she faint?" said Mrs. Bantry.

"It's more than that," said Ella Zielinsky.

"I'll see if there's anything I can do," said Mrs. Bantry. She turned away and walked rapidly back towards the head of the stairs. Turning a corner, she cannoned into Jason Rudd.

"Have you seen Ella?" he said. "Ella Zielinsky?"

"She went along there into one of the bathrooms. She was looking for something. Sal volatile—something like that."

"She needn't bother," said Jason Rudd.

Something in his tone struck Mrs. Bantry. She looked up sharply. "Is it bad?" she said. "Really bad?"

"You could call it that," said Jason Rudd. "The poor woman's dead."

"Dead!" Mrs. Bantry was really shocked. She said, as she had said before, "But she looked so well just now."

"I know. I know," said Jason. He stood there, scowling. "What a thing to happen!"

Chapter Six

"HERE WE ARE," said Miss Knight, settling a breakfast tray on the bed table beside Miss Marple. "And how are we this morning? I see we've got our curtains pulled back," she added with a slight note of disapproval in her voice.

"I wake early," said Miss Marple. "You probably will when you're my age," she added.

"Mrs. Bantry rang up," said Miss Knight, "about half an hour ago. She wanted to talk to you but I said she'd better ring up again after you'd had your breakfast. I wasn't going to disturb you at that hour, before you'd even had a cup of tea or anything to eat."

"When my friends ring up," said Miss Marple, "I prefer to be told."

"I'm sorry, I'm sure," said Miss Knight, "but it seemed to me very inconsiderate. When you've had your nice tea and your boiled egg and your toast and butter, we'll see."

"Half an hour ago," said Miss Marple thoughtfully, "that would have been—let me see—eight o'clock."

"Much too early," reiterated Miss Knight.

"I don't believe Mrs. Bantry would have rung me up then unless it was for some particular reason," said Miss Marple. "She doesn't usually ring up in the early morning."

"Oh well, dear, don't fuss your head about it," said Miss Knight soothingly. "I expect she'll be ringing up again very shortly. Or would you like me to get her for you?"

"No, thank you," said Miss Marple. "I prefer to eat my breakfast while it's hot."

"Hope I haven't forgotten anything," said Miss Knight cheerfully.

But nothing had been forgotten. The tea had been properly made with boiling water, the egg had been boiled exactly three and three-quarter minutes, the toast was evenly browned, the butter was arranged in a nice little pat and the small jar of honey stood beside it. In many ways undeniably Miss Knight was a treasure. Miss Marple ate her breakfast and enjoyed it. Presently the whirr of a vacuum cleaner began below. Cherry had arrived.

Competing with the whirr of the vacuum cleaner was a fresh tuneful voice singing one of the latest popular tunes of the day. Miss Knight, coming in for the breakfast tray, shook her head.

"I really wish that young woman wouldn't go singing all over the house," she said. "It's not what I call respectful."

Miss Marple smiled a little. "It would never enter Cherry's head that she would have to be respectful," she remarked. "Why should she?"

Miss Knight sniffed and said, "Very different to what things used to be."

"Naturally," said Miss Marple. "Times change. That is a thing which has to be accepted." She added, "Perhaps you'll ring up Mrs. Bantry now and find out what it was she wanted."

Miss Knight bustled away. A minute or two later there was a rap on the door and Cherry entered. She was looking bright and excited and extremely pretty. A plastic overall rakishly patterned with sailors and naval emblems was tied round her dark blue dress.

"Your hair looks nice," said Miss Marple.

"Went for a perm yesterday," said Cherry. "A bit stiff still, but it's going to be all right. I came up to see if you'd heard the news."

"What news?" said Miss Marple.

"About what happened at Gossington Hall yesterday. You know there was a big do there for the St. John's Ambulance?"

Miss Marple nodded. "What happened?" she asked.

"Somebody died in the middle of it. A Mrs. Badcock. Lives round the corner from us. I don't suppose you'd know her."

"Mrs. Badcock?" Miss Marple sounded alert. "But I do know her. I think—yes, that was the name—she came out and picked me up when I fell down the other day. She was very kind."

"Oh, Heather Badcock's kind all right," said Cherry. "Overkind, some people say. They call it interfering. Well, anyway, she up and died. Just like that."

"Died! But what of?"

"Search me," said Cherry. "She'd been taken into the house because of her being the secretary of the St. John's Ambulance, I suppose. She and the mayor and a lot of others. As far as I heard, she had a glass of something and about five minutes later she was took bad and died before you could snap your fingers."

"What a shocking occurrence," said Miss Marple. "Did she suffer from heart trouble?"

"Sound as a bell, so they say," Cherry said. "Of course, you never know, do you? I suppose you can have something wrong with your heart and nobody knowing about it. Anyway, I can tell you this. They've not sent her home."

Miss Marple looked puzzled. "What do you mean, not sent her home?"

"The body," said Cherry, her cheerfulness unimpaired. "The doctor said there'd have to be an autopsy. Post-mortem—whatever you call it. He said he hadn't attended her for anything and there was nothing to show the cause of death. Looks funny to me," she added.

"Now what do you mean by funny?" said Miss Marple.

"Well." Cherry considered. "Funny. As though there was something behind it."

"Is her husband terribly upset?"

"Looks as white as a sheet. Never saw a man as badly hit, to look at—that is to say."

Miss Marple's ears, long attuned to delicate nuances, led her to cock her head slightly on one side like an inquisitive bird.

"Was he so very devoted to her?"

"He did what she told him and gave her her own way," said Cherry, "but that doesn't always mean you're devoted, does it? It may mean you haven't got the courage to stick up for yourself."

"You didn't like her?" asked Miss Marple.

"I hardly know her really," said Cherry. "Knew her, I mean. I don't—didn't—dislike her. But she's just not my type. Too interfering."

"You mean inquisitive, nosy?"

"No, I don't," said Cherry. "I don't mean that at all. She was a very kind woman and she was always doing things for people. And she was always quite sure she knew the best thing to do. What they thought about it wouldn't have mattered. I had an aunt like that. Very fond of seedcake herself and she used to bake seedcakes for people and take them to them, and she never troubled to find out whether they liked seedcake or not. There are people can't bear it, just can't stand the flavour of caraway. Well, Heather Badcock was a bit like that."

"Yes," said Miss Marple thoughtfully, "yes, she would have been. I knew someone a little like that. Such people," she added, "live dangerously—though they don't know it themselves."

Cherry stared at her. "That's a funny thing to say. I don't quite get what you mean."

Miss Knight bustled in. "Mrs. Bantry seems to have gone out," she said. "She didn't say where she was going."

"I can guess where she's going," said Miss Marple. "She's coming here. I shall get up now," she added.

II

Miss Marple had just ensconced herself in her favourite chair by the window when Mrs. Bantry arrived. She was slightly out of breath.

"I've got plenty to tell you, Jane," she said.

"About the fête?" asked Miss Knight. "You went to the fête yesterday, didn't you? I was there myself for a short time early in the afternoon. The tea tent was very crowded. An astonishing lot of people seemed to be there. I didn't catch a glimpse of Marina Gregg, though, which was rather disappointing."

She picked a little dust off a table and said brightly, "Now I'm sure you two want to have a nice little chat together," and went out of the room.

"She doesn't seem to know anything about it," said Mrs. Bantry. She fixed her friend with a keen glance. "Jane, I believe you *do* know."

"You mean about the death yesterday?"

"You always know everything," said Mrs. Bantry. "I cannot think how."

"Well, really, dear," said Miss Marple, "in the same way one always has known everything. My daily helper, Cherry Baker, brought the news. I expect the butcher will be telling Miss Knight presently."

"And what do you think of it?" said Mrs. Bantry.

"What do I think of what?" said Miss Marple.

"Now don't be aggravating, Jane, you know perfectly what I mean. There's this woman—whatever her name is—"

"Heather Badcock," said Miss Marple.

"She arrives full of life and spirit. I was there when she came. And about a quarter of an hour later she sits down in a chair, says she doesn't feel well, gasps a bit and dies. What do you think of *that?*"

"One mustn't jump to conclusions," said Miss Marple. "The point is, of course, what did a medical man think of it?"

Mrs. Bantry nodded. "There's to be an inquest and a post-mortem," she said. "That shows what they think of it, doesn't it?"

"Not necessarily," said Miss Marple. "Anyone may be taken ill and die suddenly and they have to have a post-mortem to find out the cause."

"It's more than that," said Mrs. Bantry.

"How do you know?" said Miss Marple.

"Dr. Sandford went home and rang up the police."

"Who told you that?" said Miss Marple, with great interest.

"Old Briggs," said Mrs. Bantry. "At least, he didn't tell me. You know he goes down after hours in the evening to see Dr. Sandford's garden, and he was clipping something quite close to the study and he heard the doctor ringing up the police station in Much Benham. Briggs told his daughter and his daughter mentioned it to the postwoman and she told me," said Mrs. Bantry.

Miss Marple smiled. "I see," she said, "that St. Mary Mead has not changed very much from what it used to be."

"The grapevine is much the same," agreed Mrs. Bantry. "Well, now, Jane, tell me what you think?"

"One thinks, of course, of the husband," said Miss Marple reflectively. "Was he there?"

"Yes, he was there. You don't think it would be suicide," said Mrs. Bantry.

"Certainly not suicide," said Miss Marple decisively. "She wasn't the type."

"How did you come across her, Jane?"

"It was the day I went for a walk to the Development, and fell down near her house. She was kindness itself. She was a very kind woman."

"Did you see the husband? Did he look as though he'd like to poison her?"

"You know what I mean," Mrs. Bantry went on as Miss Marple showed some slight signs of protesting. "Did he remind you of Major Smith or Bertie Jones or someone you've known years ago who did poison a wife, or tried to?"

"No," said Miss Marple, "he didn't remind me of anyone I know." She added, "But she did."

"Who—Mrs. Badcock?"

"Yes," said Miss Marple, "she reminded me of someone called Alison Wilde."

"And what was Alison Wilde like?"

"She didn't know at all," said Miss Marple slowly, "what the world was like. She didn't know what people were like. She'd never thought about them. And so, you see, she couldn't guard against things happening to her."

"I don't really think I understand a word of what you're saying," said Mrs. Bantry.

"It's very difficult to explain exactly," said Miss Marple apologetically. "It comes really from being self-centred and I don't mean selfish by that," she added. "You can be kind and unselfish and even thoughtful. But if you're like Alison Wilde, you never really know what you may be doing. And so you never know what may happen to you."

"Can't you make that a little clearer?" said Mrs. Bantry.

"Well, I suppose I could give you a sort of figurative example. This isn't anything that actually happened, it's just something I am inventing."

"Go on," said Mrs. Bantry.

"Well, supposing you went into a shop, say, and you knew the proprietress had a son who was the spivvy young juvenile delinquent type. He was there listening while you told his mother about some money you had in the house, or some silver or a piece of jewellery. It was something you were excited and pleased about and you wanted to talk about it. And you also perhaps mention an evening that you were going out. You even say you never lock the house. You're interested in what you're saying, what you're telling her, because it's so very much in your mind. And then, say, on that particular evening you come home because you've forgotten something and there's this bad lot of a boy in the house, caught in the act, and he turns round and coshes you."

"That might happen to almost anybody nowadays," said Mrs. Bantry.

"Not quite," said Miss Marple; "most people have a sense of protection. They realize when it's unwise to say or do something because of the person or persons who are taking in what you say, and because of the kind of character that those people have. But as I say, Alison Wilde never thought of anybody else but herself— She was the sort of person who tells you what they've done and what they've seen and what they've felt and what they've heard. They never mention what any other people said or did. Life is a kind of one-way track—just their own progress through it. Other people seem to them just like—like wallpaper in a room." She paused and then said, "I think Heather Badcock was that kind of person."

Mrs. Bantry said, "You think she was the sort of person who might have butted into something without knowing what she was doing?"

"And without realizing that it was a dangerous thing to do," said Miss Marple. She added, "It's the only reason I can possibly think of why she should have been killed. If, of course," added Miss Marple, "we are right in assuming that murder *has* been committed."

"You don't think she was blackmailing someone?" Mrs. Bantry suggested.

"Oh, no," Miss Marple assured her. "She was a kind, good woman. She'd never have done anything of *that* kind." She added vexedly, "The whole thing seems to me very unlikely. I suppose it can't have been—"

"Well?" Mrs. Bantry urged her.

"I just wondered if it might have been the wrong murder," said Miss Marple thoughtfully.

The door opened and Dr. Haydock breezed in, Miss Knight twittering behind him.

"Ah, at it already, I see," said Dr. Haydock, looked at the two ladies. "I came in to see how your health was," he said to Miss Marple, "but I needn't ask. I see you've begun to adopt the treatment that I suggested."

"Treatment, Doctor?"

Dr. Haydock pointed a finger at the knitting that lay on the table beside her. "Unravelling," he said. "I'm right, aren't I?"

Miss Marple twinkled very slightly in a discreet, old-ladyish kind of way.

"You will have your joke, Dr. Haydock," she said.

"You can't pull the wool over my eyes, my dear lady. I've known you too many years. Sudden death at Gossington Hall and all the tongues of St. Mary Mead are wagging. Isn't that so? Murder suggested long before anybody even knows the result of the inquest."

"When is the inquest to be held?" asked Miss Marple.

"The day after tomorrow," said Dr. Haydock, "and by that time," he said, "you ladies will have reviewed the whole story, decided on the verdict and decided on a good many other points too, I expect. Well," he added, "I shan't waste my time here. It's no good wasting time on a patient that doesn't need my ministrations. Your cheeks are pink, your eyes are bright, you've begun to enjoy yourself. Nothing like having an interest in life. I'll be on my way." He stomped out again.

"I'd rather have him than Sandford any day," said Mrs. Bantry.

"So would I," said Miss Marple. "He's a good friend, too," she added thoughtfully. "He came, I think, to give me the go-ahead sign."

"Then it *was* murder," said Mrs. Bantry. They looked at each other. "At any rate, the doctors think so."

Miss Knight brought in cups of coffee. For once in their lives, both ladies were too impatient to welcome this interruption. When Miss Knight had gone, Miss Marple started immediately.

"Now then, Dolly, you were there—"

"I practically saw it happen," said Mrs. Bantry, with modest pride.

"Splendid," said Miss Marple. "I mean—well, you know what I mean. So you can tell just exactly what happened from the moment she arrived."

"I'd been taken into the house," said Mrs. Bantry. "Snob status."

"Who took you in?"

"Oh, a willowy-looking young man. I think he's Marina Gregg's secretary or something like that. He took me in, up the staircase. They were having a kind of reunion reception committee at the top of the stairs."

"On the landing?" said Miss Marple, surprised.

"Oh, they've altered all that. They've knocked the dressing-room and bedroom down so that you've got a big sort of alcove, practically a room. It's very attractive-looking."

"I see. And who was there?"

"Marina Gregg, being natural and charming, looking lovely in a sort of willowy grey-green dress. And the husband, of course, and that woman Ella Zielinsky I told you about. She's their social secretary. And there were about—oh, eight or ten people, I should think. Some of them I knew, some of them I didn't. Some I think were from the studios—the ones I didn't know. There was the vicar and Dr. Sandford's wife. He wasn't there himself until later, and Colonel and Mrs. Clittering and the High

Sheriff. And I think there was someone from the press there. And a young woman with a big camera taking photographs."

Miss Marple nodded.

"Go on."

"Heather Badcock and her husband arrived just after me. Marina Gregg said nice things to me, then to somebody else, oh, yes—the vicar— and then Heather Badcock and her husband came. She's the secretary, you know, of the St. John's Ambulance. Somebody said something about that and how hard she worked and how valuable she was. And Marina Gregg said some pretty things. Then Mrs. Badcock, who struck me, I must say, Jane, as rather a tiresome sort of woman, began some long rigmarole of how years before she'd met Marina Gregg somewhere. She wasn't awful tactful about it since she urged exactly how long ago and the year it was and everything like that. I'm sure that actresses and film stars and people don't really like being reminded of the exact age they are. Still, she wouldn't think of that, I suppose."

"No," said Miss Marple, "she wasn't the kind of woman who would have thought of that. Well?"

"Well, there was nothing particular in that except for the fact that Marina Gregg didn't do her usual stuff."

"You mean she was annoyed?"

"No, no, I don't mean that. As a matter of fact I'm not at all sure that she heard a word of it. She was staring, you know, over Mrs. Badcock's shoulder, and when Mrs. Badcock had finished her rather silly story of how she got out of a bed of sickness and sneaked out of the house to go and meet Marina and get her autograph, there was a sort of odd silence. Then I saw her face."

"Whose face? Mrs. Badcock's?"

"No. Marina Gregg's. It was as though she hadn't heard a word the Badcock woman was saying. She was staring over her shoulder right at the wall opposite. Staring with—I can't explain it to you—"

"But do try, Dolly," siad Miss Marple, "because I think perhaps that this might be important."

"She had a kind of frozen look," said Mrs. Bantry, struggling with words, "as though she'd seen something that—oh, dear me, how hard it is to describe things. Do you remember the Lady of Shalott? *The mirror crack'd from side to side; 'The doom has come upon me,' cried the Lady of Shalott.* Well, that's what she looked like. People laugh at Tennyson nowadays, but the Lady of Shalott always thrilled me when I was young and it still does."

"She had a frozen look," repeated Miss Marple thoughtfully. "And she was looking *over* Mrs. Badcock's shoulder at the wall. What was on that wall?"

"Oh! A picture of some kind, I think," said Mrs. Bantry. "You know, Italian. I think it was a copy of a Bellini Madonna, but I'm not sure. A picture where the Virgin is holding up a laughing child."

Miss Marple frowned. "I can't see that a *picture* could give her that expression."

"Especially as she must see it every day," agreed Mrs. Bantry.

"There were people coming up the stairs still, I suppose?"

"Oh, yes, there were."

"Who were they, do you remember?"

"You mean she might have been looking at one of the people coming up the stairs?"

"Well, it's possible, isn't it?" said Miss Marple.

"Yes—of course— Now let me see. There was the mayor, all dressed up too with his chains and all, and his wife, and there was a man with long hair and one of those funny beards they wear nowadays. Quite a young man. And there was the girl with the camera. She'd taken her position on the stairs so as to get photos of people coming up and having their hands shaken by Marina, and—let me see, two people I didn't know. Studio people, I think, and the Grices from Lower Farm. There may have been others, but that's all I can remember now."

"Doesn't sound very promising," said Miss Marple. "What happened next?"

"I think Jason Rudd nudged her or something because all of a sudden she seemed to pull herself together and she smiled at Mrs. Badcock, and she began to say all the usual things. You know, sweet, unspoilt, natural, charming, the usual bag of tricks."

"And then?"

"And then Jason Rudd gave them drinks."

"What kind of drinks?"

"Daiquiris, I think. He said they were his wife's favourites. He gave one to her and one to the Badcock woman."

"That's very interesting," said Miss Marple. "Very interesting indeed. And what happened after that?"

"I don't know, because I took a gaggle of women to look at the bathrooms. The next thing I knew was when the secretary woman came rushing along and said someone had been taken ill."

Chapter Seven

THE INQUEST, when it was held, was short and disappointing. Evidence of identification was given by the husband, and the only other evidence was medical. Heather Badcock had died as a result of four grains of hy-ethyl-dexyl-barbo-quindelorytate, or, let us be frank, some such name! There was no evidence to show how the drug was administered.

The inquest was adjourned for a fortnight.

After it was concluded, Detective-Inspector Frank Cornish joined Arthur Badcock.

"Could I have a word with you, Mr. Badcock?"

"Of course, of course."

Arthur Badcock looked more like a chewed-out bit of string than ever. "I can't understand it," he muttered. "I simply can't understand it."

"I've got a car here," said Cornish. "We'll drive back to your house, shall we? Nicer and more private there."

"Thank you, sir. Yes, yes, I'm sure that would be much better."

They drew up at the neat little blue-painted gate of No. 3 Arlington Close. Arthur Badcock led the way and the inspector followed him. He drew out his latchkey but before he had inserted it into the door, it was opened from inside. The woman who opened it stood back looking slightly embarrassed. Arthur Badcock looked startled.

"Mary," he said.

"I was just getting you ready some tea, Arthur. I thought you'd need it when you came back from the inquest."

"That's very kind of you, I'm sure," said Arthur Badcock gratefully. "Er—" he hesitated. "This is Inspector Cornish, Mrs. Bain. She's a neighbour of mine."

"I see," said Inspector Cornish.

"I'll get another cup," said Mrs. Bain.

She disappeared and rather doubtfully Arthur Badcock showed the inspector into the bright cretonne-covered sitting-room to the right of the hall.

"She's very kind," said Arthur Badcock. "Very kind always."

"You've known her a long time?"

"Oh, no. Only since we came here."

"You've been here two years, I believe, or is it three?"

"Just about three now," said Arthur. "Mrs. Bain only got here about six months ago," he explained. "Her son works near here and so, after her husband's death, she came down to live here and he boards with her."

Mrs. Bain appeared at this point bringing the tray from the kitchen. She was a dark, rather intense-looking woman of about forty years of age. She had gipsy colouring that went with her dark hair and eyes. There was something a little odd about her eyes. They had a watchful look. She put down the tray on the table and Inspector Cornish said something pleasant and noncommittal. Something in him, some professional instinct, was on the alert. The watchful look in the woman's eyes, the slight start she had given when Arthur introduced him had not passed unnoticed. He was familiar with that slight uneasiness in the presence of the police. There were two kinds of uneasiness. One was the kind of natural alarm and distrust as of those who might have offended unwittingly against the majesty of the law, but there was a second kind. And it was the second kind that he felt sure was present here. Mrs. Bain, he thought, had had at some time some connection with the police, something that had left her wary and ill at ease. He made a mental note to find out a little more about Mary Bain. Having set down the tea tray, and refused to partake herself, saying she had to get home, she departed.

"Seems a nice woman," said Inspector Cornish.

"Yes, indeed. She's very kind, a very good neighbour, a very sympathetic woman," said Arthur Badcock.

"Was she a great friend of your wife?"

"No. No, I wouldn't say that. They were neighbourly and on pleasant terms. Nothing special about it though."

"I see. Now, Mr. Badcock, we want as much information as we can from you. The findings of the inquest have been a shock to you, I expect?"

"Oh, they have, Inspector. Of course I realized that you must think something was wrong, and I almost thought so myself because Heather has always been such a healthy woman. Practically never a day's illness. I said to myself, 'There *must* be something wrong.' But it seems so incredible, if you understand what I mean, Inspector. Really quite incredible. What is this stuff—this hy-ethyl-hex—" he came to a stop.

"There is an easier name for it," said the inspector. "It's sold under a trade name, the trade name of Calmo. Ever come across it?"

Arthur Badcock shook his head, perplexed.

"It's more used in America than here," said the inspector. "They prescribe it very freely over there, I understand."

"What's it for?"

"It induces, or so I understand, a happy and tranquil state of mind," said Cornish. "It's prescribed for those under strain; suffering anxiety, depression, melancholy, sleeplessness and a good many other things. The properly prescribed dose is not dangerous, but overdoses are not to be advised. It would seem that your wife took something like six times the ordinary dose."

Badcock stared. "Heather never took anything like that in her life," he said. "I'm sure of it. She wasn't one for taking medicines anyway. She was never depressed or worried. She was one of the most cheerful women you could possibly imagine."

The inspector nodded. "I see. And no doctor had prescribed anything of this kind for her?"

"No. Certainly not. I'm sure of that."

"Who was her doctor?"

"She's on Dr. Sim's panel, but I don't think she's been to him once since we've been here."

Inspector Cornish said thoughtfully, "So she doesn't seem the kind of woman to have been likely to need such a thing, or to have taken it?"

"She didn't, Inspector, I'm sure she didn't. She must have taken it by a mistake of some kind."

"It's a very difficult mistake to imagine," said Inspector Cornish. "What did she have to eat and drink that afternoon?"

"Well, let me see. For lunch—"

"You needn't go back as far as lunch," said Cornish. "Given in such quantity, the drug would act quickly and suddenly. Tea. Go back to tea."

"Well, we went into the marquee in the grounds. It was a terrible scrum in there, but we managed in the end to get a bun each and a cup of tea. We finished it as quickly as possible because it was very hot in the marquee and we came out again."

"And that's all she had, a bun and a cup of tea there?"

"That's right, sir."

"And after that you went into the house. Is that right?"

"Yes. The young lady came and said that Miss Marina Gregg would be very pleased to see my wife if she would like to come into the house. Of course my wife was delighted. She had been talking about Marina Gregg for days. Everybody was excited. Oh, well, you know that, Inspector, as well as anyone does."

"Yes, indeed," said Cornish. "My wife was excited, too. Why, from all around people were paying their shilling to go in and see Gossington Hall and what had been done there, and hoping to catch a glimpse of Marina Gregg herself."

"The young lady took us into the house," said Arthur Badcock, "and up the stairs. That's where the party was. On the landing up there. But it looked quite different from what it used to look like, so I understand. It was more like a room, a sort of big hollowed-out place with chairs and tables with drinks on them. There were about ten or twelve people there, I suppose."

Inspector Cornish nodded. "And you were received there—by whom?"

"By Miss Marina Gregg herself. Her husband was with her. I've forgotten his name now."

"Jason Rudd," said Inspector Cornish.

"Oh, yes, not that I noticed him at first. Well, anyway, Miss Gregg greeted Heather very nicely and seemed very pleased to see her, and Heather was talking and telling a story of how she'd once met Miss Gregg years ago in the West Indies and everything seemed as right as rain."

"Everything seemed right as rain," echoed the inspector. "And then?"

"And then Miss Gregg said what would we have? And Miss Gregg's husband, Mr. Rudd, got Heather a kind of cocktail. A dickery or something like that."

"A daiquiri."

"That's right, sir. He brought two. One for her and one for Miss Gregg."

"And you, what did you have?"

"I had a sherry."

"I see. And you three stood there drinking your drinks together?"

"Well, not quite like that. You see there were more people coming up the stairs. There was the mayor, for one, and some other people—an American gentleman and lady, I think—so we moved off a bit."

"And your wife drank her daiquiri then?"

"Well, no, not then, she didn't."

"Well, if she didn't drink it then, when did she drink it?"

Arthur Badcock stood frowning in remembrance. "I think—she set it down on one of the tables. She saw some friends there. I think it was someone to do with St. John's Ambulance who'd driven over from Much Benham or somewhere like that. Anyway, they got to talking together."

"And when did she drink her drink?"

Arthur Badcock again frowned. "It was a little after that," he said. "It was getting rather more crowded by then. Somebody jogged Heather's elbow and her glass got spilt."

"What's that?" Inspector Cornish looked up sharply. "Her drink was spilt?"

"Yes, that's how I remember it. . . . She'd picked it up and I think she took a little sip and made rather a face. She didn't really like cocktails, you know, but all the same she wasn't going to be downed by that. Anyway, as she stood there, somebody jogged her elbow and the glass spilled over. It went down her dress and I think it went on Miss Gregg's dress, too. Miss Gregg couldn't have been nicer. She said it didn't matter at all and it would make no stain and she gave Heather her handkerchief to wipe up Heather's dress, and then she passed over the drink she was holding and said, 'Have this, I haven't touched it yet.'"

"She handed over her own drink, did she?" said the inspector. "You're sure of that?"

Arthur Badcock paused a moment while he thought. "Yes, I'm quite sure of that," he said.

"And your wife took the drink?"

"Well, she didn't want to at first, sir. She said, 'Oh, no, I couldn't do that,' and Miss Gregg laughed and said, 'I've had far too much to drink already.'"

"And so your wife took that glass and did what with it?"

"She turned away a little and drank it, rather quick, I think. And then we walked a little way along the corridor, looking at some of the pictures and the curtains. Lovely curtain stuff it was, like nothing we'd seen before. Then I met a pal of mine, Councillor Allcock, and I was just passing the time of day with him when I looked round and saw Heather was sitting in a chair looking rather odd, so I came to her and said, 'What's the matter?' She said she felt a little queer."

"What kind of queerness?"

"I don't know, sir. I didn't have time. Her voice sounded very queer and thick and her head was rolling a little. All of a sudden she made a great half gasp and her head fell forward. She was dead, sir, dead."

Chapter Eight

"St. Mary Mead, you say?" Chief-Inspector Craddock looked up sharply. The assistant commissioner was a little surprised.

"Yes," he said, "St. Mary Mead. Why? Does it—"

"Nothing really," said Dermot Craddock.

"It's quite a small place, I understand," went on the other. "Though of course there's a great deal of building development going on there now. Practically all the way from St. Mary Mead to Much Benham, I understand. Hellingforth Studios," he added, "are on the other side of St. Mary Mead, towards Market Basing." He was still looking slightly inquiring. Dermot Craddock felt that he should perhaps explain.

"I know someone living there," he said. "At St. Mary Mead. An old lady. A very old lady by now. Perhaps she's dead, I don't know. But if not—"

The assistant commissioner took his subordinate's point, or at any rate thought he did.

"Yes," he said, "it would give you an 'in' in a way. One needs a bit of local gossip. The whole thing is a curious business."

"The County have called us in?" Dermot asked.

"Yes. I've got the chief constable's letter here. They don't seem to feel that it's necessarily a local affair. The largest house in the neighbourhood, Gossington Hall, was recently sold as a residence for Marina Gregg, the film star, and her husband. They're shooting a film at their new studios, at Hellingforth, in which she is starring. A fête was held in the grounds in aid of St. John's Ambulance. The dead woman—her name is Mrs. Heather Badcock—was the local secretary of this and had done most of the administrative work for the fête. She seems to have been a competent, sensible person, well liked locally."

"One of those bossy women?" suggested Craddock.

"Very possibly," said the assistant commissioner. "Still, in my experience, bossy women seldom get themselves murdered. I can't think why not. When you come to think of it, it's rather a pity. There was a record attendance at the fête, it seems, good weather, everything running to plan. Marina Gregg and her husband held a kind of small private reception in

Gossington Hall. About thirty or forty people attended this. The local notables, various people connected with the St. John's Ambulance Association, several friends of Marina Gregg herself, and a few people connected with the studios. All very peaceful, nice and happy. But, fantastically and improbably, Heather Badcock was poisoned there."

Dermot Craddock said thoughtfully, "An odd place to choose."

"That's the chief constable's point of view. If anyone wanted to poison Heather Badcock, why choose that particular afternoon and circumstances? Hundreds of much simpler ways of doing it. A risky business anyway, you know, to slip a dose of deadly poison into a cocktail in the middle of twenty or thirty people milling about. Somebody ought to have seen something."

"It definitely was in the drink?"

"Yes, it was definitely in the drink. We have the particulars here. One of those long inexplicable names that doctors delight in, but actually a fairly common prescription in America."

"In America. I see."

"Oh, this country, too. But these things are handed out much more freely on the other side of the Atlantic. Taken in small doses, beneficial."

"Supplied on prescription or can it be bought freely?"

"No. You have to have a prescription."

"Yes, it's odd," said Dermot. "Heather Badcock have any connection with these film people?"

"None whatever."

"Any member of her own family at this do?"

"Her husband."

"Her husband," said Dermot thoughtfully.

"Yes, one always thinks that way," agreed his superior officer, "but the local man—Cornish, I think his name is—doesn't seem to think there's anything in that, although he does report that Badcock seemed ill at ease and nervous, but he agrees that respectable people often are like that when interviewed by the police. They appear to have been quite a devoted couple."

"In other words, the police there don't think it's their pigeon. Well, it ought to be interesting. I take it I'm going down there, sir?"

"Yes. Better get there as soon as possible, Dermot. Who do you want with you?"

Dermot considered for a moment or two.

"Tiddler, I think," he said thoughtfully. "He's a good man and, what's more, he's a film fan. That might come in useful."

The assistant commissioner nodded. "Good luck to you," he said.

II

"Well!" exclaimed Miss Marple, going pink with pleasure and surprise. "This *is* a surprise. How are you, my dear boy—though you're hardly a boy now. What are you—a Chief-Inspector or this new thing they call a Commander?"

Dermot explained his present rank.

"I suppose I need hardly ask what you are doing down here," said Miss Marple. "Our local murder is considered worthy of the attention of Scotland Yard."

"They handed it over to us," said Dermot, "and so, naturally, as soon as I got down here I came to headquarters."

"Do you mean—" Miss Marple fluttered a little.

"Yes, Aunty," said Dermot disrespectfully, "I mean you."

"I'm afraid," said Miss Marple regretfully, "I'm very much out of things nowadays. I don't get out much."

"You get out enough to fall down and be picked up by a woman who's going to be murdered ten days later," said Dermot Craddock.

Miss Marple made the kind of noise that would once have been written down as "tut-tut."

"I don't know where you hear these things," she said.

"You should know," said Dermot Craddock. "You told me yourself that in a village everybody knows everything."

"And just off the record," he added, "did you think she was going to be murdered as soon as you looked at her?"

"Of course not, of course not," exclaimed Miss Marple. "What an idea!"

"You didn't see that look in her husband's eye that reminded you of Harry Simpson or David Jones or somebody you've known years ago, and who subsequently pushed his wife off a precipice?"

"No, I did not!" said Miss Marple. "I'm sure Mr. Badcock would never do a wicked thing of that kind. At least," she added thoughtfully, "I'm nearly sure."

"But human nature being what it is—" murmured Craddock wickedly.

"Exactly," said Miss Marple. She added, "I dare say, after the first natural grief, he won't miss her very much. . . ."

"Why? Did she bully him?"

"Oh, no," said Miss Marple, "but I don't think that she—well, she wasn't a considerate woman. Kind, yes. Considerate—no. She would be fond of him and look after him when he was ill and see to his meals and be a good housekeeper, but I don't think she would ever—well, that she would ever even know what he might be feeling or thinking. That makes rather a lonely life for a man."

"Ah," said Dermot, "and is his life less likely to be lonely in future?"

"I expect he'll marry again," said Miss Marple. "Perhaps quite soon. And probably, which is such a pity, a woman of much the same type. I mean he'll marry someone with a stronger personality than his own."

"Anyone in view?" asked Dermot.

"Not that I know of," said Miss Marple. She added regretfully, "But I know so little."

"Well, what do you *think*?" urged Dermot Craddock. "You've never been backward in thinking things."

"I think," said Miss Marple unexpectedly, "that you ought to go and see Mrs. Bantry."

"Mrs. Bantry? Who is she? One of the film lot?"

"No," said Miss Marple, "she lives in the East Lodge at Gossington. She was at the party that day. She used to own Gossington at one time. She and her husband, Colonel Bantry."

"She was at the party. And she saw something?"

"I think she must tell you herself what it was she saw. You mayn't think it has any bearing on the matter, but I think it might be—just might be—suggestive. Tell her I sent you to her and—ah, yes, perhaps you'd better just mention the Lady of Shalott."

Dermot Craddock looked at her with his head just slightly on one side.

"The Lady of Shalott," he said. "Those are the code words, are they?"

"I don't know that I should put it that way," said Miss Marple, "but it will remind her of what I mean."

Dermot Craddock got up. "I shall be back," he warned her.

"That is very nice of you," said Miss Marple. "Perhaps if you have time, you would come and have tea with me one day. If you still drink tea," she added, rather wistfully. "I know that so many young people nowadays only go out to drinks and things. They think that afternoon tea is a very out-moded affair."

"I'm not as young as all that," said Dermot Craddock. "Yes, I'll come and have tea with you one day. We'll have tea and gossip, and talk about the village. Do you know any of the film stars, by the way, or any of the studio lot?"

"Not a thing," said Miss Marple, "except what I hear," she added.

"Well, you usually hear a good deal," said Dermot Craddock. "Good-bye. It's been very nice to see you."

III

"Oh, how do you do?" said Mrs. Bantry, looking slightly taken aback when Dermot Craddock had introduced himself and explained who he was. "How very exciting to see you. Don't you always have sergeants with you?"

"I've got a sergeant down here, yes," said Craddock. "But he's busy."

"On routine inquiries?" asked Mrs. Bantry hopefully.

"Something of the kind," said Dermot gravely.

"And Jane Marple sent you to me," said Mrs. Bantry, as she ushered him into her small sitting-room. "I was just arranging some flowers," she explained. "It's one of those days when flowers won't do anything you want them to. They fall out, or stick up where they shouldn't stick up or won't lie down where you want them to lie down. So I'm thankful to have a distraction, and especially such an exciting one. So it really was murder, was it?"

"Did you think it was murder?"

"Well, it could have been an accident, I suppose," said Mrs. Bantry. "Nobody's said anything definite, officially, that is. Just that rather silly piece about no evidence to show by whom or in what way the poison was administered. But, of course, we all talk about it as murder."

"And about who did it?"

"That's the odd part of it," said Mrs. Bantry. "We don't. Because I really don't see who *can* have done it."

"You mean as a matter of definite physical fact you don't see who could have done it?"

"Well, no, not that. I suppose it would have been difficult but not impossible. No, I mean I don't see who could have *wanted* to do it."

"Nobody, you think, could have wanted to kill Heather Badcock?"

"Well, frankly," said Mrs. Bantry, "I can't imagine anybody wanting to kill Heather Badcock. I've seen her quite a few times, on local things, you know. Girl Guides and St. John's Ambulance, and various parish things. I found her a rather trying sort of woman. Very enthusiastic about every-thing and a bit given to overstatement, and just a little bit of a gusher. But you don't want to murder people for that. She was the kind of woman who in the old days if you'd seen her approaching the front door, you'd have hurried out to say to your parlourmaid—which was an institution we had in those days and very useful, too—and told her to say 'Not at home' or 'Not at home to visitors,' if she had conscientious scruples about the truth."

"You mean that one might take pains to avoid Mrs. Badcock, but one would have no urge to remove her permanently."

"Very well put," said Mrs. Bantry, nodding approval.

"She had no money to speak of," mused Dermot, "so nobody stood to gain by her death. Nobody seems to have disliked her to the point of hatred. I don't suppose she was blackmailing anybody?"

"She wouldn't have dreamed of doing such a thing, I'm sure," said Mrs. Bantry. "She was the conscientious and high-principled kind."

"And her husband wasn't having an affair with someone else?"

"I shouldn't think so," said Mrs. Bantry. "I only saw him at the party. He looked like a bit of chewed string. Nice but wet."

"Doesn't leave much, does it?" said Dermot Craddock. "One falls back on the assumption that she knew something."

"Knew something?"

"To the detriment of somebody else."

Mrs. Bantry shook her head again. "I doubt it," she said. "I doubt it very much. She struck me as the kind of woman who if she had known anything about anyone, couldn't have helped talking about it."

"Well, that washes that out," said Dermot Craddock, "so we'll come, if we may, to my reasons for coming to see you. Miss Marple, for whom I have the greatest admiration and respect, told me that I was to say to you the Lady of Shalott."

"Oh, *that!*" said Mrs. Bantry.

"Yes," said Craddock. "*That!* Whatever it is."

"People don't read much Tennyson nowadays," said Mrs. Bantry.

"A few echoes come back to me," said Dermot Craddock. "She looked out to Camelot, didn't she?

> "Out flew the web and floated wide;
> The mirror crack'd from side to side;
> 'The curse has come upon me,' cried
> The Lady of Shalott."

"Exactly. She did," said Mrs. Bantry.

"I beg your pardon. Who did? Did what?"

"Looked like that," said Mrs. Bantry.

"Who looked like what?"

"Marina Gregg."

"Ah. Marina Gregg. When was this?"

"Didn't Jane Marple tell you?"

"She didn't tell me anything. She sent me to you."

"That's tiresome of her," said Mrs. Bantry, "because she can always tell things better than I can. My husband always used to say that I was so abrupt that he didn't know what I was talking about. Anyway, it may have been only my fancy. But when you see anyone looking like that you can't help remembering it."

"Please tell me," said Dermot Craddock.

"Well, it was at the party. I call it a party because what can one call things? But it was just a sort of reception up at the top of the stairs where they've made a kind of recess. Marina Gregg was there and her husband. They fetched some of us in. They fetched me, I suppose, because I once owned the house, and they fetched Heather Badcock and her husband because she'd done all the running of the fête, and the arrangements. And we happened to go up the stairs at about the same time, so I was standing there, you see, when I noticed it."

"Quite. When you noticed what?"

"Well, Mrs. Badcock went into a long spiel as people do when they meet celebrities. You know, how wonderful it was, and what a thrill and they'd always hoped to see them. And she went into a long story of how she'd once met her years ago and how exciting it had been. And I thought, in my own mind, you know, what a bore it must be for these poor celebrities to have to say all the right things. And then I noticed that Marina Gregg wasn't saying the right things. She was just staring."

"Staring—at Mrs. Badcock?"

"No—no, it looked as though she'd forgotten Mrs. Badcock altogether. I mean, I don't believe she'd even heard what Mrs. Badcock was saying. She was just staring with what I call this Lady of Shalott look, as though she'd seen something awful. Something frightening, something that she could hardly believe she saw and couldn't bear to see."

" 'The curse has come upon me?' " suggested Dermot Craddock helpfully.

"Yes, just that. That's why I called it the Lady of Shalott look."

"But what was she looking *at*, Mrs. Bantry?"

"Well, I wish I knew," said Mrs. Bantry.

"She was at the top of the stairs, you say?"

"She was looking over Mrs. Badcock's head—no, more over one shoulder, I think."

"Straight at the middle of the staircase?"

"It might have been a little to one side."

"And there were people coming up the staircase?"

"Oh, yes, I should think about five or six people."

"Was she looking at one of these people in particular?"

"I can't possibly tell," said Mrs. Bantry. "You see, I wasn't facing that way. I was looking at *her*. My back was to the stairs. I thought perhaps she was looking at one of the pictures."

"But she must know the pictures quite well if she's living in the house."

"Yes, yes, of course. No, I suppose she must have been looking at one of the people. I wonder which."

"We have to try and find out," said Dermot Craddock. "Can you remember at all who the people were?"

"Well, I know the mayor was one of them, and his wife. There was someone who I think was a reporter, with red hair, because I was introduced to him later, but I can't remember his name. I never hear names. Galbraith—something like that. Then there was a big black man. I don't mean a Negro—I just mean very dark, forceful-looking. And an actress with him. A bit overblonde and the minky kind. And old General Barnstaple from Much Benham. He's practically ga-ga now, poor boy. I don't think *he* could have been anybody's doom. Oh, and the Grices from the farm."

"Those are all the people you can remember?"

"Well, there may have been others. But you see I wasn't—well, I mean I wasn't noticing particularly. I know that the mayor and General Barnstaple and the Americans did arrive about that time. And there were people taking photographs. One I think was a local man, and there was a girl from London, an arty-looking girl with long hair and a rather large camera."

"And you think it was one of those people who brought that look to Marina Gregg's face?"

"I didn't really think anything," said Mrs. Bantry with complete frankness. "I just wondered what on earth made her look like that, and then I didn't think of it any more. But afterwards one remembers about these things. But of course," added Mrs. Bantry with honesty, "I may have imagined it. After all, she may have had a sudden toothache or a safety pin run into her or a sudden violent colic. The sort of thing where you try to go on as usual and not to show anything, but your face can't help looking awful."

Dermot Craddock laughed. "I'm glad to see you're a realist, Mrs. Bantry," he said. "As you say, it may have been something of that kind. But it's certainly just one interesting little fact that might be a pointer."

He shook hands and departed to present his official credentials in Much Benham.

Chapter Nine

"So LOCALLY you've drawn a blank?" said Craddock, offering his cigarette case to Frank Cornish.

"Completely," said Cornish. "No enemies, no quarrels, on good terms with her husband."

"No question of another woman or another man?"

The other shook his head. "Nothing of that kind. No hint of scandal anywhere. She wasn't what you'd call the sexy kind. She was on a lot of committees and things like that and there were some small local rivalries, but nothing beyond that."

"There wasn't anyone else the husband wanted to marry? No one in the office where he worked?"

"He's in Biddle and Russell, the estate agents and valuers. There's Florrie West with adenoids, and Miss Grundle, who is at least fifty and as plain as a haystack—nothing much there to excite a man. Though for all that I shouldn't be surprised if he did marry again soon."

Craddock looked interested.

"A neighbour," explained Cornish. "A widow. When I went back with him from the inquest, she'd gone in and was making him tea and looking after him generally. He seemed surprised and grateful. If you ask me, she's made up her mind to marry him, but he doesn't know it yet, poor chap."

"What sort of a woman is she?"

"Good-looking," admitted the other. "Not young, but handsome in a gipsyish sort of way. High colour. Dark eyes."

"What's her name?"

"Bain. Mrs. Bain. Mary Bain. She's a widow."

"What'd her husband do?"

"No idea. She's got a son working near here who lives with her. She seems a quiet, respectable woman. All the same, I've a feeling I've seen her before." He looked at his watch. "Ten to twelve. I've made an appointment for you at Gossington Hall at twelve o'clock. We'd best be going."

II

Dermot Craddock's eyes, which always looked gently inattentive, were in actuality making a close mental note of the features of Gossington Hall. Inspector Cornish had taken him there, had delivered him over to a young man called Hailey Preston, and had then taken a tactful leave. Since then, Dermot Craddock had been gently nodding at intervals as he listened to the flood of talk emanating from Mr. Preston. Hailey Preston, he gathered, was a kind of public relations or personal assistant, or private secretary, or more likely, a mixture of all three, to Jason Rudd. He talked. He talked freely and at length without much modulation and managing miraculously not to repeat himself too often. He was a pleasant young man, anxious that his own views, reminiscent of those of Dr. Pangloss that all was for the best in the best of all possible worlds, should be shared by anyone in whose company he happened to be. He said several times and in different ways what a terrible shame this had been, how worried everyone had been, how Marina was absolutely prostrated, how Mr. Rudd was more upset than he could possibly say, how it absolutely beat anything that a thing like that should happen, didn't it? Possibly there might have been some kind of allergy to some particular kind of substance? He just put that forward as an idea—allergies were extraordinary things. Chief-Inspector Craddock was to count on every possible cooperation that Hellingforth Studios or any of their staff could give. He was to ask any questions he wanted, go anywhere he liked. If they could help in any way, they would do so. They all had the greatest respect for Mrs. Badcock and appreciated her strong social sense and the valuable work she had done for the St. John's Ambulance Association.

He then started again, not in the same words but using the same motifs. No one could have been more eagerly cooperative. At the same time he endeavoured to convey how very far this was from the cellophane world of studios; and Mr. Jason Rudd and Miss Marina Gregg, or any of the people in the house who surely were going to do their utmost to help in any way they possibly could. Then he nodded gently some forty-four times. Dermot Craddock took advantage of the pause to say:

"Thank you very much."

It was said quietly but with a kind of finality that brought Mr. Hailey Preston up with a jerk. He said:

"Well—" and paused inquiringly.

"You said I might ask questions?"

"Sure. Sure. Fire ahead."

"Is this where she died?"

"Mrs. Badcock?"

"Mrs. Badcock. Is this the place?"

"Yes, sure. Right here. At least, well, actually I can show you the chair."

They were standing on the landing recess. Hailey Preston walked a short way along the corridor and pointed out a rather phony-looking oak armchair.

"She was sitting right there," he said. "She said she didn't feel well. Someone went to get her something, and then she just died, right there."

"I see."

"I don't know if she'd seen a physician lately. If she'd been warned that she had anything wrong with her heart—"

"She had nothing wrong with her heart," said Dermot Craddock. "She was a healthy woman. She died of six times the maximum dose of a substance whose official name I will not try to pronounce but which I understand is generally known as Calmo."

"I know, I know," said Hailey Preston. "I take it myself sometimes."

"Indeed? That's very interesting. You find it has a good effect?"

"Marvellous. Marvellous. It bucks you up and it soothes you down, if you understand what I mean. Naturally," he added, "you have to take it in the proper dosage."

"Would there be supplies of this substance in the house?"

He knew the answer to the question, but he put it as though he did not. Hailey Preston's answer was frankness itself.

"Loads of it, I should say. There'll be a bottle of it in most of the bathroom cupboards here."

"Which doesn't make our task easier."

"Of course," said Hailey Preston, "she might have used the stuff herself and taken a dose, and as I say, had an allergy."

Craddock looked unconvinced—Hailey Preston sighed and said:

"You're quite definite about the dosage?"

"Oh, yes. It was a lethal dose and Mrs. Badcock did not take any such things herself. As far as we can make out the only things she ever took were bicarbonate of soda or aspirin."

Hailey Preston shook his head and said, "That sure gives us a problem. Yes, it sure does."

"Where did Mr. Rudd and Miss Gregg receive their guests?"

"Right here." Hailey Preston went to the spot at the top of the stairs.

Chief-Inspector Craddock stood beside him. He looked at the wall opposite him. In the centre was an Italian Madonna and child. A good copy, he presumed, of some well-known picture. The blue-robed Madonna held aloft the infant Jesus and both child and mother were laughing. Little groups of people stood on either side, their eyes upraised to the child. One of the more pleasing Madonnas, Dermot Craddock thought. To the right and left of this picture were two narrow windows. The whole effect was very charming, but it seemed to him that there was emphatically nothing there that could cause a woman to look like the Lady of Shalott whose doom had come upon her.

"People, of course, were coming up the stairs?" he asked.

"Yes. They came in driblets, you know. Not too many at once. I shepherded up some, Ella Zielinsky, that's Mr. Rudd's secretary, brought some of the others. We wanted to make it all pleasant and informal."

"Were you here yourself at the time Mrs. Badcock came up?"

"I'm ashamed to tell you, Chief-Inspector Craddock, that I just can't remember. I had a list of names, I went out and I shepherded people in. I introduced them, saw to drinks, then I'd go out and come up with the next batch. At the time I didn't know this Mrs. Badcock by sight, and she wasn't one of the ones on my list to bring up."

"What about a Mrs. Bantry?"

"Ah, yes, she's the former owner of this place, isn't she? I believe she, and Mrs. Badcock and her husband, did come up about the same time." He paused. "And the mayor came just about then. He had a big chain on and a wife with yellow hair, wearing royal blue with frills. I remember all of them. I didn't pour drinks for any of them because I had to go down and bring up the next lot."

"Who did pour drinks for them?"

"Why, I can't exactly say. There were three or four of us on duty. I know I went down the stairs just as the mayor was coming up."

"Who else was on the stairs as you went down, if you can remember?"

"Jim Galbraith, one of the newspaper boys who was covering this, and three or four others whom I didn't know. There were a couple of photographers, one of the locals, I don't remember his name, and an arty girl from London, who rather specializes in queer angle shots. Her camera was set right up in that corner so that she could get a view of Miss Gregg receiving. Ah, now let me think, I rather fancy that that was when Ardwyck Fenn arrived."

"And who is Ardwyck Fenn?"

Hailey Preston looked shocked. "He's a big shot, Chief-Inspector. A very big shot in the television and moving picture world. We didn't even know he was in this country."

"His turning up was a surprise?"

"I'll say it was," said Preston. "Nice of him to come and quite unexpected."

"Was he an old friend of Miss Gregg's and Mr. Rudd's?"

"He was a close friend of Marina's a good many years ago when she was married to her second husband. I don't know how well Jason knew him."

"Anyway, it was a pleasant surprise when he arrived?"

"Sure it was. We were all delighted."

Craddock nodded and passed from that to other subjects. He made meticulous inquiries about the drinks, their ingredients, how they were served, who served them, what servants and hired servants were on duty. The answer seemed to be, as Inspector Cornish had already hinted was the case, that although any one of thirty people *could* have poisoned Heather Badcock with the utmost ease, yet at the same time any one of the thirty might have been seen doing so! It was, Craddock reflected, a big chance to take.

"Thank you," he said at last, "now I would like, if I may, to speak to Miss Marina Gregg."

Hailey Preston shook his head.

"I'm sorry," he said, "I really am sorry, but that's right out of the question."

Craddock's eyebrows rose.

"Surely!"

"She's prostrated. She's absolutely prostrated. She's got her own physician here looking after her. He wrote out a certificate. I've got it here. I'll show it to you."

Craddock took it and read it.

"I see," he said. He asked, "Does Marina Gregg always have a physician in attendance?"

"They're very high-strung, all these actors and actresses. It's a big strain, this life. It's usually considered desirable in the case of the big shots that they should have a physician who understands their constitution and their nerves. Maurice Gilchrist has a very big reputation. He's looked after Miss Gregg for many years now. She's had a great deal of illness, as you may have read, in the last few years. She was hospitalized for a very long time. It's only about a year ago that she got her strength and health back."

"I see."

Hailey Preston seemed relieved that Craddock was not making any more protest.

"You'll want to see Mr. Rudd?" he suggested. "He'll be—" he looked at his watch—"he'll be back from the studios in about ten minutes if that's all right for you."

"That'll do admirably," said Craddock. "In the meantime, is Dr. Gilchrist actually here in the house?"

"He is."

"Then I'd like to talk to him."

"Why, certainly. I'll fetch him right away."

The young man bustled away. Dermot Craddock stood thoughtfully at the top of the stairs. Of course this frozen look that Mrs. Bantry had described might have been entirely Mrs. Bantry's imagination. She was, he thought, a woman who would jump to conclusions. At the same time he thought it quite likely that the conclusion to which she had jumped was a just one. Without going so far as to look like the Lady of Shalott seeing doom coming upon her, Marina Gregg might have seen something that vexed or annoyed her. Something that had caused her to have been negligent to a guest to whom she was talking. Somebody had come up those stairs, perhaps, who could be described as an unexpected guest—an unwelcome guest?

He turned at the sound of footsteps. Hailey Preston was back, and with him was Dr. Maurice Gilchrist. Dr. Gilchrist was not at all as Dermot Craddock had imagined him. He had no suave bedside manner, neither was he theatrical in appearance. He seemed, on the face of it, a blunt, hearty, matter-of-fact man. He was dressed in tweeds, slightly florid tweeds to the English idea. He had a thatch of brown hair and observant, keen dark eyes.

"Dr. Gilchrist? I am Chief-Inspector Dermot Craddock. May I have a word or two with you in private?"

The doctor nodded. He turned along the corridor and went along it almost to the end, then he pushed the door open and invited Craddock to enter.

"No one will disturb us here," he said.

It was obviously the doctor's own bedroom, a very comfortably appointed one. Dr. Gilchrist indicated a chair and then sat down himself.

"I understand," said Craddock, "that Miss Marina Gregg, according to you, is unable to be interviewed. What's the matter with her, Doctor?"

Gilchrist shrugged his shoulders very slightly.

"Nerves," he said. "If you were to ask her questions now she'd be in a state bordering on hysteria within ten minutes. I can't permit that. If you'd like to send your police doctor to see me, I'd be willing to give him my views. She was unable to be present at the inquest for the same reason."

"How long," asked Craddock, "is such a state of things likely to continue?"

Dr. Gilchrist looked at him and smiled. It was a likeable smile.

"If you want my opinion," he said, "a human opinion, that is, not a medical one, any time within the next forty-eight hours, she'll be not only willing, but asking to see you! She'll be wanting to ask questions. She'll be wanting to answer your questions. They're like that!" He leaned forward. "I'd like to try and make you understand if I can, Chief-Inspector, a little bit what makes these people act the way they do. The motion picture life is a life of continuous strain, and the more successful you are, the greater the strain. You live always, all day, in the public eye. When you're on location, when you're working, it's hard monotonous work with long hours. You're there in the morning, you sit and you wait. You do your small bit, the bit that's being shot over and over again. If you're rehearsing on the stage, you'd be rehearsing as likely as not a whole act, or at any rate, a part of an act. The thing would be in sequence, it would be more or less human and credible. But when you're shooting a picture, everything's taken out of sequence. It's a monotonous, grinding business. It's exhausting. You live in luxury, of course; you have soothing drugs, you have baths and creams and powders and medical attention, you have relaxations and parties and people, but you're always in the public eye. You can't enjoy yourself quietly. You can't really—ever relax."

"I can understand that," said Dermot. "Yes, I can understand."

"And there's another thing," went on Gilchrist. "If you adopt this career, and especially if you're any good at it, you are a certain kind of person. You're a person—or so I've found in my experience—with a skin too few—a person who is plagued the whole time with diffidence. A terrible feeling of inadequacy, of apprehension that you can't do what's required of you. People say that actors and actresses are vain. That isn't true. They're not conceited about themselves; they're obsessed with themselves, yes, but they need reassurance the whole time. They must be continually reassured. Ask Jason Rudd. He'll tell you the same. You have to make them feel they can do it, to assure them they can do it, take them over and over again over the same thing, encouraging them the whole time until you get the effect you want. But they are always doubtful of themselves. And that makes them, in an ordinary, human, unprofessional word: nervy. Damned nervy! A mass of nerves. And the worse their nerves are, the better they are at the job."

"That's interesting," said Craddock. "Very interesting." He paused, adding: "Though I don't see quite why you—"

"I'm trying to make you understand Marina Gregg," said Maurice Gilchrist. "You've seen her pictures, no doubt."

"She's a wonderful actress," said Dermot, "wonderful. She has a personality, a beauty, a sympathy."

"Yes," said Gilchrist, "she has all those, and she's had to work like the devil to produce the effects that she has produced. In the process her nerves get shot to pieces, and she's not actually a strong woman physically. Not as strong as you need to be. She's got one of those temperaments that swing to and fro between despair and rapture. She can't help it. She's made that way. She's suffered a great deal in her life. A large part of the suffering has been her own fault, but some of it hasn't. None of her marriages has been happy, except, I'd say, this last one. She's married to a man now who loves her dearly and who's loved her for years. She's sheltering in that love and she's happy in it. At least, at the moment she's happy in it. One can't say how long all that will last. The trouble with her is that either she thinks that at last she's got to that spot or place or that moment in her life where everything's like a fairy tale come true, that nothing can go wrong, that she'll never be unhappy again; or else she's down in the dumps, a woman whose life is ruined, who's never known love and happiness and who never will again." He added dryly, "If she could only stop halfway between the two, it'd be wonderful for her; and the world would lose a fine actress."

He paused, but Dermot Craddock did not speak. He was wondering why Maurice Gilchrist was saying what he did. Why this close detailed analysis of Marina Gregg? Gilchrist was looking at him. It was as though he was urging Dermot to ask one particular question. Dermot wondered very much what the question was that he ought to ask. He said at last slowly, with the air of one feeling his way:

"She's been very much upset by this tragedy happening here?"

"Yes," said Gilchrist, "she has."

"Almost unnaturally so?"

"That depends," said Dr. Gilchrist.

"On what does it depend?"

"On her reason for being so upset."

"I suppose," said Dermot, feeling his way, "that it was a shock, a sudden death happening like that in the midst of a party."

He saw very little response in the face opposite him. "Or might it," he said, "be something more than that?"

"You can't tell, of course," said Dr. Gilchrist, "how people are going to react. You can't tell, however well you know them. They can always surprise you. Marina might have taken this in her stride. She's a soft-hearted creature. She might say, 'Oh, poor, poor woman, how tragic. I wonder how it could have happened.' She could have been sympathetic without really caring. After all, deaths do occasionally occur at studio parties. Or she might, if there wasn't anything very interesting going on, choose—choose unconsciously, mind you—to dramatize herself over it. She might decide to throw a scene. Or there might be some quite different reason."

Dermot decided to take the bull by the horns. "I wish," he said, "you would tell me what you really think?"

"I don't know," said Dr. Gilchrist, "I can't be sure." He paused and then said, "There's professional etiquette, you know. There's the relationship between doctor and patient."

"She has told you something?"

"I don't think I could go as far as that."

"Did Marina Gregg know this woman, Heather Badcock? Had she met her before?"

"I don't think she knew her from Adam," said Dr. Gilchrist. "No. That's not the trouble. If you ask me, it's nothing to do with Heather Badcock."

Dermot said, "This stuff, this Calmo. Does Marina Gregg ever use it herself?"

"Lives on it, pretty well," said Dr. Gilchrist. "So does everyone else around here," he added. "Ella Zielinsky takes it, Hailey Preston takes it, half the boiling takes it—it's the fashion at this moment. They're all much the same, these things. People get tired of one and they try a new one that comes out, and they think it's wonderful, and that it makes all the difference."

"And does it make all the difference?"

"Well," said Gilchrist, "it makes *a* difference. It does its work. It calms you or it peps you up, makes you feel you could do things which otherwise you might fancy that you couldn't. I don't prescribe them more than I can help, but they're not dangerous taken properly. They help people who can't help themselves."

"I wish I knew," said Dermot Craddock, "what it is that you are trying to tell me."

"I'm trying to decide," said Gilchrist, "what is my duty. There are two duties. There's the duty of a doctor to his patient. What his patient says to him is confidential and must be kept so. But there's another point of view. You can fancy that there is danger to a patient. You have to take steps to avoid the danger."

He stopped. Craddock looked at him and waited.

"Yes," said Dr. Gilchrist. "I think I know what I must do. I must ask you, Chief-Inspector Craddock, to keep what I am telling you confidential. Not from your colleagues, of course. But as far as regards the outer world, particularly people in the house here. Do you agree?"

"I can't bind myself," said Craddock. "I don't know what will arise. In general terms, yes, I agree. That is to say, I imagine that any piece of information you gave me I should prefer to keep to myself and to my colleagues."

"Now listen," said Gilchrist, "this mayn't mean anything at all. Women say anything when they're in the state of nerves Marina Gregg is in now. I'm telling you something which she said to me. There may be nothing in it at all."

"What did she say?" asked Craddock.

"She broke down after this thing happened. She sent for me. I gave her a sedative. I stayed there beside her, holding her hand, telling her to calm down, telling her things were going to be all right. Then, just before she went off into unconsciousness, she said, 'It was meant for *me*, Doctor.'"

Craddock stared. "She said that, did she? And afterwards—the next day?"

"She never alluded to it again. I raised the point once. She evaded it. She said, 'Oh, you must have made a mistake. I'm sure I never said anything like that. I expect I was half doped at the time.'"

"But you think she meant it?"

"She meant it all right," said Gilchrist. "That's not to say that it is so," he added warningly. "Whether someone meant to poison her or meant to poison Heather Badcock, I don't know. You'd probably know better than I would. All I do say is that Marina Gregg definitely thought and believed that that dose was meant for her."

Craddock was silent for some moments. Then he said, "Thank you, Dr. Gilchrist. I appreciate what you have told me and I realize your motive. If what Marina Gregg said to you was founded on fact, it may mean, may it not, that there is still danger to her?"

"That's the point," said Gilchrist. "That's the whole point."

"Have you any reason to believe that that might be so?"

"No, I haven't."

"No idea what her reason for thinking so was?"

"No."

"Thank you."

Craddock got up. "Just one thing more, Doctor. Do you know if she said the same thing to her husband?"

Slowly Gilchrist shook his head. "No," he said, "I'm quite sure of that. She didn't tell her husband."

His eyes met Dermot's for a few moments, then he gave a brief nod of his head and said, "You don't want me any more? All right. I'll go back and have a look at the patient. You shall talk to her as soon as it's possible."

He left the room and Craddock remained, pursing his lips up and whistling very softly beneath his breath.

Chapter Ten

"JASON'S BACK NOW," said Hailey Preston. "Will you come with me, Chief-Inspector? I'll take you to his room."

The room which Jason Rudd used partly for office and partly for a sitting-room was on the first floor. It was comfortably but not luxuriously furnished. It was a room which had little personality and no indication of the private tastes or predilection of its user. Jason Rudd rose from the desk at which he was sitting and came forward to meet Dermot. It was wholly unnecessary, Dermot thought, for the room to have a personality; the user of it had so much. Hailey Preston had been an efficient and voluble gas-bag. Gilchrist had force and magnetism. But here was a man whom, as Dermot immediately admitted to himself, it would not be easy to read. In the course of his career, Craddock had met and summed up many people. By now he was fully adept in realizing the potentialities and very often reading the thoughts of most of the people with whom he came in contact. But he felt at once that one would be able to gauge only so much of Jason Rudd's thoughts as Jason Rudd himself permitted. The eyes, deep-set and thoughtful, perceived but would not easily reveal. The ugly, rugged head spoke of an excellent intellect. The clown's face could repel you or attract you. Here, thought Dermot Craddock to himself, is where I sit and listen and take very careful notes.

"Sorry, Chief-Inspector, if you've had to wait for me. I was held up by some small complication over at the studios. Can I offer you a drink?"

"Not just now, thank you, Mr. Rudd."

The clown's face suddenly crinkled into a kind of ironic amusement.

"Not the house to take a drink in, is that what you're thinking?"

"As a matter of fact it wasn't what I was thinking."

"No, no, I suppose not. Well, Chief-Inspector, what do you want to know? What can I tell you?"

"Mr. Preston has answered very adequately all the questions I have put to him."

"And that has been helpful to you?"

"Not as helpful as I could wish."

Jason Rudd looked inquiring.

"I've also seen Dr. Gilchrist. He informs me that your wife is not yet strong enough to be asked questions."

"Marina," said Jason Rudd, "is very sensitive. She's subject, frankly, to nerve storms. And murder at such close quarters, is, as you will admit, likely to produce a nerve storm."

"It is not a pleasant experience," Dermot Craddock agreed dryly.

"In any case I doubt if there is anything my wife could tell you that you could not learn equally well from me. I was standing beside her when the thing happened, and frankly I would say that I am a better observer than my wife."

"The first question I would like to ask," said Dermot, "(and it is a question that you have probably answered already but for all that, I would like to ask it again) had you or your wife any previous acquaintance with Heather Badcock?"

Jason Rudd shook his head.

"None whatever. I certainly have never seen the woman before in my life. I had had two letters from her on behalf of the St. John's Ambulance Association, but I had not met her personally until about five minutes before her death."

"But she claimed to have met your wife?"

Jason Rudd nodded.

"Yes, some twelve or thirteen years ago, I gather. In Bermuda. Some big garden party in aid of ambulances, which Marina opened for them, I think, and Mrs. Badcock, as soon as she was introduced, burst into some long rigmarole of how although she was in bed with 'flu, she had got up and had managed to come to this affair and had asked for and got my wife's autograph."

Again the ironical smile crinkled his face.

"That, I may say, is a very common occurrence, Chief-Inspector. Large mobs of people are usually lined up to obtain my wife's autograph, and it is a moment that they treasure and remember. Quite understandably, it is an event in their lives. Equally naturally it is not likely that my wife would remember one out of a thousand or so autograph hunters. She had, quite frankly, no recollection of ever having seen Mrs. Badcock before."

"That I can well understand," said Craddock. "Now I have been told, Mr. Rudd, by an onlooker that your wife was slightly distrait during the few moments that Heather Badcock was speaking to her. Would you agree that such was the case?"

"Very possibly," said Jason Rudd. "Marina is not particularly strong.

She was, of course, used to what I may describe as her public social work, and could carry out her duties in that line almost automatically. But towards the end of a long day she was inclined occasionally to flag. This may have been such a moment. I did not, I may say, observe anything of the kind myself. No, wait a minute, that is not quite true. I do remember that she was a little slow in making her reply to Mrs. Badcock. In fact I think I nudged her very gently in the ribs."

"Something had perhaps distracted her attention?" said Dermot.

"Possibly, but it may have been just a momentary lapse through fatigue."

Dermot Craddock was silent for a few minutes. He looked out of the window where the view was the somewhat sombre one over the woods surrounding Gossington Hall. He looked at the pictures on the walls, and finally he looked at Jason Rudd. Jason Rudd's face was attentive but nothing more. There was no guide to his feelings. He appeared courteous and completely at ease, but he might, Craddock thought, be actually nothing of the kind. This was a man of very high mental calibre. One would not, Dermot thought, get anything out of him that he was not prepared to say unless one put one's cards on the table. Dermot took his decision. He would do just that.

"Has it occurred to you, Mr. Rudd, that the poisoning of Heather Badcock may have been entirely accidental? That the real intended victim was your wife?"

There was a silence. Jason Rudd's face did not change its expression. Dermot waited. Finally Jason Rudd gave a deep sigh and appeared to relax.

"Yes," he said quietly, "you're quite right, Chief-Inspector. I have been sure of it all along."

"But you have said nothing to that effect, not to Inspector Cornish, not at the inquest?"

"No."

"Why not, Mr. Rudd?"

"I could answer you very adequately by saying that it was merely a belief on my part unsupported by any kind of evidence. The facts that led me to deduce it were facts equally accessible to the law, which was probably better qualified to decide than I was. I know nothing about Mrs. Badcock personally. She might have enemies, someone might have decided to administer a fatal dose to her on this particular occasion, though it would seem a very curious and farfetched decision. But it might have been chosen conceivably for the reason that at a public occasion of this kind the issues would be more confused, the number of strangers present would be considerable, and just for that reason it would be more difficult to bring home to the person in question the commission of such a crime. All that is true, but I am going to be frank with you, Chief-Inspector. That was *not* my reason for keeping silent. I will tell you what that reason was. I didn't want my wife to suspect for one moment that it was she who had narrowly escaped dying by poison."

"Thank you for your frankness," said Dermot. "Not that I quite understand your motive in keeping silent."

"No? Perhaps it is a little difficult to explain. You would have to know Marina to understand. She is a person who badly needs happiness and security. Her life has been highly successful in the material sense. She has won renown artistically, but her personal life has been one of deep unhappiness. Again and again she has thought that she has found happiness and was wildly and unduly elated thereby, and has had her hopes dashed to the ground. She is incapable, Mr. Craddock, of taking a rational, prudent view of life. In her previous marriages she was expected, like a child reading a fairy story, to live happy ever afterwards."

Again the ironic smile changed the ugliness of the clown's face into a strange, sudden sweetness.

"But marriage is not like that, Chief-Inspector. There can be no rapture continued indefinitely. We are fortunate indeed if we can achieve a life of quiet content, affection, and serene and sober happiness." He added, "Perhaps you are married, Chief-Inspector?"

"I have not so far that good, or bad, fortune," he murmured.

"In our world, the moving picture world, marriage is a fully occupational hazard. Film stars marry often. Sometimes happily, sometimes disastrously, but seldom permanently. In that respect I should not say that Marina has had any undue cause to complain, but to one of her temperament things of that kind matter very deeply. She imbued herself with the idea that she was unlucky, that nothing would ever go right for her. She has always been looking desperately for the same things: love, happiness, affection, security. She was wildly anxious to have children. According to some medical opinion, the very strength of that anxiety frustrated its object. One very celebrated physician advised the adoption of a child. He said it is often the case that when an intense desire for maternity is assuaged by having adopted a baby, a child is born naturally shortly afterwards. Marina adopted no less than three children. For a time she got a certain amount of happiness and serenity, but it was not the real thing. You can imagine her delight when eleven years ago she found she was going to have a child. Her pleasure and delight were quite indescribable. She was in good health and the doctors assured her that there was every reason to believe that everything would go well. As you may or may not know, the result was tragedy. The child, a boy, was born mentally deficient, imbecile. The result was disastrous. Marina had a complete breakdown and was severely ill for years, confined to a sanatorium. Though her recovery was slow, she did recover. Shortly after that we married and she began once more to take an interest in life and to feel that perhaps she could be happy. It was difficult at first for her to get a worthwhile contract for a picture. Everyone was inclined to doubt whether her health would stand the strain. I had to battle for that." Jason Rudd's lips set firmly together. "Well, the battle was successful. We have started shooting the picture. In the meantime we bought this house and set about altering it. Only about a fortnight ago Marina was saying to me how happy she was, and how she felt at last she was going to be able to settle down to a happy home life, her troubles behind her. I was a little nervous because, as usual, her expectations were too optimistic. But there was no doubt that she was happy. Her nervous symptoms disappeared, there was a calmness and a quietness about her that I had never seen before. Everything was going well until—" he paused. His voice became suddenly bitter. "Until this happened! That women had to die—*here!* That in itself was shock enough. I couldn't risk—I was determined not to risk—Marina's knowing that an attempt had been made on *her* life. That would have been a second, perhaps fatal, shock. It might have precipitated another mental collapse."

He looked directly at Dermot.

"Do you understand—now?"

"I see your point of view," said Craddock, "but forgive me, isn't there one aspect that you are neglecting? You give me your conviction that an attempt was made to poison your wife. Doesn't that danger still remain? If a poisoner does not succeed, isn't it likely that the attempt may be repeated?"

"Naturally I've considered that," said Jason Rudd, "but I am confident that, being forewarned, so to speak, I can take all reasonable precautions for my wife's safety. I shall watch over her and arrange that others shall watch over her. The great thing, I feel, is that she herself should not know that any danger threatened her."

"And you think," said Dermot cautiously, "that she does not know?"

"Of course not. She has no idea."

"You're sure of that?"

"Certain. Such an idea would never occur to her."

"But it occurred to you," Dermot pointed out.

"That's very different," said Jason Rudd. "Logically, it was the only solution. But my wife isn't logical, and to begin with she could not possibly imagine that anyone would want to do away with her. Such a possibility would simply not occur to her mind."

"You may be right," said Dermot slowly, "but that leaves us now with several other questions. Again, let me put this bluntly. Whom do you suspect?"

"I can't tell you."

"Excuse me, Mr. Rudd, do you mean by that you can't or that you won't?"

Jason Rudd spoke quickly. "Can't. Can't every time. It seems to me just as impossible as it would seem to her that anyone would dislike her enough—should have a sufficient grudge against her—to do such a thing. On the other hand, on the sheer, downright evidence of the facts, that is exactly what must have occurred."

"Will you outline the facts to me as you see them?"

"If you like. The circumstances are quite clear. I poured out two daiquiri cocktails from an already prepared jug. I took them to Marina and to Mrs. Badcock. What Mrs. Badcock did I do not know. She moved on, I presume, to speak to someone she knew. My wife had her drink in her hand. At that moment the mayor and his wife were approaching. She put down her glass, as yet untouched, and greeted them. Then there were more greetings. An old friend we'd not seen for years, some other locals and one or two people from the studios. During that time the glass containing the cocktail stood on the table which was situated at that time behind us since we had both moved forward a little to the top of the stairs. One or two photographs were taken of my wife talking to the mayor, which we hoped would please the local population, at the special request of the representatives of the local newspaper. While this was being done I brought some fresh drinks to a few of the last arrivals. During that time my wife's glass must have been poisoned. Don't ask me how it was done, it cannot have been easy to do. On the other hand, it is startling, if anyone has the nerve to do an action openly and unconcernedly, how little people are likely to notice it! You ask me if I have suspicions; all I can say is that at least one of about twenty people might have done it. People, you see, were moving about in little groups, talking, occasionally going off to have a look at the alterations which had been done to the house. There was movement, continual movement. I've thought and I've thought, I've racked my brains but there is nothing, absolutely *nothing* to direct my suspicions to any particular person."

He paused and gave an exasperated sigh.

"I dare say you've heard the next part before."

"I should like to hear it again from you."

"Well, I had come back towards the head of the stairs. My wife had turned towards the table and was just picking up her glass. There was a slight exclamation from Mrs. Badcock. Somebody must have jogged her arm and the glass slipped out of her fingers and was broken on the floor. Marina did the natural hostess's act. Her own skirt had been slightly touched with the liquid. She insisted no harm was done, used her own handkerchief to wipe Mrs. Badcock's skirt and insisted on her having her own drink. If I remember, she said, 'I've had far too much already.' So that was that. But I can assure you of this. The fatal dose could not have been added *after* that, for Mrs. Badcock immediately began to drink from the glass. As you know, four or five minutes later she was dead. I wonder —how I wonder—what the poisoner must have felt when he realized how badly his scheme had failed. . . ."

"All this occurred to you at the time?"

"Of course not. At the time I concluded, naturally enough, that this woman had had some kind of a seizure. Perhaps heart, coronary thrombosis, something of that sort. It never occurred to me that *poisoning* was involved. Would it occur to you—would it occur to anybody?"

"Probably not," said Dermot. "Well, your account is clear enough and you seem sure of your facts. You say you have no suspicion of any particular person. I can't quite accept that, you know."

"I assure you it's the truth."

"Let us approach it from another angle. Who is there who could wish to harm your wife? It all sounds melodramatic if you put it this way, but what enemies has she got?"

Jason Rudd made an expressive gesture.

"Enemies? Enemies? It's so hard to define what one means by an enemy. There's plenty of envy and jealousy in the world my wife and I occupy. There are always people who say malicious things, who'll start a whispering campaign, who will do someone they are jealous of a bad turn if the opportunity occurs. But that doesn't mean that any of those people is a murderer, or indeed even a likely murderer. Don't you agree?"

"Yes, I agree. There must be something beyond petty dislikes or envies. Is there anyone whom your wife has injured, say, in the past?"

Jason Rudd did not rebut this easily. Instead he frowned.

"Honestly, I don't think so," he said at last, "and I may say I've given a lot of thought to that point."

"Anything in the nature of a love affair, an association with some man?"

"There have of course been affairs of that kind. It may be considered, I suppose, that Marina has occasionally treated some man badly. But there is nothing to cause any lasting ill-will. I'm sure of it."

"What about women? Any woman who has had a lasting grudge against Miss Gregg?"

"Well," said Jason Rudd, "you can never tell with women. I can't think of any particular one offhand."

"Who'd benefit financially by your wife's death?"

"Her will benefits various people, but not to any large extent. I suppose the people who'd benefit, as you put it, financially, would be myself as her husband and from another angle, possibly the star who might replace her in this film. Though, of course, the film might be abandoned altogether. These things are very uncertain."

"Well, we need not go into all that now," said Dermot.

"And I have your assurance that Marina will not be told that she is in possible danger?"

"We shall have to go into that matter," said Dermot. "I want to impress upon you that you are taking quite a considerable risk there. However, the matter will not arise for some days since your wife is still under medical care. Now there is one more thing I would like you to do. I would like you to write down for me as accurately as you can every single person who was in that recess at the top of the stairs, or whom you saw coming up the stairs at the time of the murder."

"I'll do my best, but I'm rather doubtful. You'd do far better to consult my secretary, Ella Zielinsky. She has a most accurate memory and also lists of the local people who were there. If you'd like to see her now—"

"I would like to talk to Miss Ella Zielinsky very much," said Dermot.

Chapter Eleven

SURVEYING Dermot Craddock unemotionally through her large horn-rimmed spectacles, Ella Zielinsky seemed to him almost too good to be true. With quiet businesslike alacrity she whipped out of a drawer a typewritten sheet and passed it across to him.

"I think I can be fairly sure that there are no omissions," she said. "But it is just possible that I may have included one or two names—local names they will be—who were not actually there. That is to say who may have left earlier or who may not have been found and brought up. Actually, I'm pretty sure that it is correct."

"A very efficient piece of work if I may say so," said Dermot.

"Thank you."

"I suppose—I am quite an ignoramus in such things—that you have to attain a high standard of efficiency in your job?"

"One has to have things pretty well taped, yes."

"What exactly does your job comprise? Are you a kind of liaison officer, so to speak, between the studios and Gossington Hall?"

"No. I've nothing to do with the studios, actually, though of course I naturally take messages from there on the telephone or send them. My job is to look after Miss Gregg's social life, her public and private engagements, and to supervise in some degree the running of the house."

"You like the job?"

"It's extremely well paid and I find it reasonably interesting. I didn't, however, bargain for murder," she added dryly.

"Did it seem very incredible to you?"

"So much so that I am going to ask you if you are really sure it *is* murder?"

"Six times the dose of hy-ethyl-mexine, et cetera, could hardly be anything else."

"It might have been an accident of some kind."

"And how would you suggest such an accident could have occurred?"

"More easily than you'd imagine, since you don't know the set-up. This house is simply full of drugs of all kinds. I don't mean dope when I say drugs. I mean properly prescribed remedies, but, like most of these things, what they call, I understand, the lethal dose is not very far removed from the therapeutic dose."

Dermot nodded.

"These theatrical and picture people have the most curious lapses in their intelligence. Sometimes it seems to me that the more of an artistic genius you are, the less common sense you have in everyday life."

"That may well be."

"What with all the bottles, cachets, powders, capsules, and little boxes that they carry about with them; what with popping in a tranquillizer here and a tonic there and a pep pill somewhere else, don't you think it would be easy enough that the whole thing might get mixed up?"

"I don't see how it could apply in this case."

"Well, I think it could. Somebody, one of the guests, may have wanted a sedative, or a reviver, and whipped out his or her little container which they carry around and possibly because they were talking to someone or possibly because they hadn't remembered the dose because they hadn't had one for some time, might have put too much in a glass. Then their mind was distracted and they went off somewhere, and let's say this Mrs. What's-her-name comes along, thinks it's her glass, picks it up and drinks it. That's surely a more feasible idea than anything else?"

"You don't think that all those possibilities haven't been gone into, do you?"

"No, I suppose not. But there were a lot of people there and a lot of glasses standing about with drinks in them. It happens often enough, you know, that you pick up the wrong glass and drink out of it."

"Then you don't think that Heather Badcock was deliberately poisoned? You think that she drank out of somebody else's glass?"

"I can't imagine anything more likely to happen."

"In that case," said Dermot, speaking carefully, "it would have had to be Marina Gregg's glass. You realize that? Marina handed her her own glass."

"Or what she thought was her own glass," Ella Zielinsky corrected him. "You haven't talked to Marina yet, have you? She's extremely vague. She'd pick up any glass that looked as though it were hers, and drink it. I've seen her do it again and again."

"She takes Calmo?"

"Oh, yes, we all do."

"You too, Miss Zielinsky?"

"I'm driven to it sometimes," said Ella Zielinsky. "These things are rather imitative, you know."

"I shall be glad," said Dermot, "when I am able to talk to Miss Gregg. She—er—seems to be prostrated for a very long time."

"That's just throwing a temperament," said Ella Zielinsky. "She dramatizes herself a good deal, you know. She'd never take murder in her stride."

"As you manage to do, Miss Zielinsky?"

"When everybody about you is in a continual state of agitation," said Ella dryly, "it develops in you a desire to go to the opposite extreme."

"You learn to take a pride in not turning a hair when some shocking tragedy occurs?"

She considered. "It's not a really nice trait, perhaps. But I think if you didn't develop that sense, you'd probably go round the bend yourself."

"Was Miss Gregg—is Miss Gregg a difficult person to work for?"

It was something of a personal question, but Dermot Craddock regarded it as a kind of test. If Ella Zielinsky raised her eyebrows and tacitly demanded what this had to do with the murder of Mrs. Badcock, he would be forced to admit that it had nothing to do with it. But he wondered if Ella Zielinsky might perhaps enjoy telling him what she thought of Marina Gregg.

"She's a great artist. She's got a personal magnetism that comes over on the screen in the most extraordinary way. Because of that, one feels it's rather a privilege to work with her. Taken purely personally, of course, she's hell!"

"Ah," said Dermot.

"She has no kind of moderation, you see. She's up in the air or down in the dumps and everything is always terrifically exaggerated, and she changes her mind and there are an enormous lot of things that one must never mention or allude to because they upset her."

"Such as?"

"Well, naturally mental breakdown, or sanatoriums for mental cases. I think it is quite to be understood that she should be sensitive about that. And anything to do with children."

"Children? In what way?"

"Well, it upsets her to see children, or to hear of people being happy with children. If she hears someone is going to have a baby or has just had a baby, it throws her into a state of misery at once. She can never have another child herself, you see, and the only one she did have is batty. I don't know if you knew that?"

"I had heard it, yes. It's all very sad and unfortunate. But after a good many years you'd think she'd forget about it a little."

"She doesn't. It's an obsession with her. She broods on it."

"What does Mr. Rudd feel about it?"

"Oh, it wasn't his child. It was her last husband's, Isidore Wright's."

"Ah yes, her last husband. Where is he now?"

"He married again and lives in Florida," said Ella Zielinsky promptly.

"Would you say that Marina Gregg had made many enemies in her life?"

"Not unduly so. Not more than most, that is to say. There are always rows over other women or other men or over contracts or jealousy—all those things."

"She wasn't as far as you know afraid of anyone?"

"Marina? *Afraid* of anyone? I don't think so. Why? Why should she be?"

"I don't know," said Dermot. He picked up the list of names. "Thank you very much, Miss Zielinsky. If there's anything else I want to know, I'll come back. May I?"

"Certainly. I'm only too anxious—we're all only too anxious—to do anything we can to help."

II

"Well, Tom, what have you got for me?"

Detective-Sergeant Tiddler grinned appreciatively. His name was not Tom, it was William, but the combination of Tom Tiddler had always been too much for his colleagues.

"What gold and silver have you picked up for me?" continued Dermot Craddock.

The two were staying at the Blue Boar, and Tiddler had just come back from a day spent at the studios.

"The proportion of gold is very small," said Tiddler. "Not much gossip. No startling rumours. One or two suggestions of suicide."

"Why suicide?"

"They thought she might have had a row with her husband and be trying to make him sorry. That line of country. But that she didn't really mean to go so far as doing herself in."

"I can't see that that's a very hopeful line," said Dermot.

"No, of course it isn't. They know nothing about it, you see. They don't know anything except what they're busy on. It's all highly technical and there's an atmosphere of 'the show must go on,' or as I suppose one ought to say, the picture must go on, or the shooting must go on. I don't know any of the right terms. All they're concerned about is when Marina Gregg will get back to the set. She's mucked up a picture once or twice before by staging a nervous breakdown."

"Do they like her on the whole?"

"I should say they consider her the devil of a nuisance but for all that, they can't help being fascinated by her when she's in the mood to fascinate them. Her husband's besotted about her, by the way."

"What do they think of him?"

"They think he's the finest director or producer or whatever it is that there's ever been."

"No rumours of his being mixed up with some other star or some woman of some kind?"

Tom Tiddler stared. "No," he said, "no. Not a hint of such a thing. Why, do you think there might be?"

"I wondered," said Dermot. "Marina Gregg is convinced that that lethal dose was meant for her."

"Is she now? Is she right?"

"Almost certainly, I should say," Dermot replied. "But that's not the point. The point is that she hasn't told her husband so, only her doctor."

"Do you think she would have told him if—"

"I just wondered," said Craddock, "whether she might have had at the back of her mind an idea that her husband had been responsible. The doctor's manner was a little peculiar. I may have imagined it, but I don't think I did."

"Well, there were no such rumours going about at the studios," said Tom. "You hear that sort of thing soon enough."

"She herself is not embroiled with any other man?"

"No, she seems to be devoted to Rudd."

"No interesting snippets about her past?"

Tiddler grinned. "Nothing to what you can read in a film magazine any day of the week."

"I think I'll have to read a few," said Dermot, "to get the atmosphere."

"The things they say and hint!" said Tiddler.

"I wonder," said Dermot thoughtfully, "if my Miss Marple reads film magazines."

"Is that the old lady who lives in the house by the church?"

"That's right."

"They say she's sharp," said Tiddler. "They say there's nothing goes on here that Miss Marple doesn't hear about. She may not know much about the film people, but she ought to be able to give you the low-down on the Badcocks all right."

"It's not as simple as it used to be," said Dermot. "There's a new social life springing up here. A housing estate, big building development. The Badcocks are fairly new and come from there."

"I didn't hear much about the locals of course," said Tiddler. "I concentrated on the sex life of film stars and such things."

"You haven't brought back very much," grumbled Dermot. "What about Marina Gregg's past, anything about that?"

"Done a bit of marrying in her time, but not more than most. Her first husband didn't like getting the chuck, so they said, but he was a very ordinary sort of bloke. He was a realtor or something like that. What is a realtor, by the way?"

"I think it means in the real estate business."

"Oh well, anyway, he didn't line up as very glamorous so she got rid of him and married a foreign count or prince. That lasted hardly any time at all, but there don't seem to be any bones broken. She just shook him off and teamed up with number three. Film star Robert Truscott. That was said to be a passionate love match. His wife didn't much like letting go of him, but she had to take it in the end. Big alimony. As far as I can make out, everybody's hard up because they've got to pay so much alimony to all their ex-wives."

"But it went wrong?"

"Yes. She was the brokenhearted one, I gather. But another big romance came along a year or two later. Isidore Somebody—a playwright."

"It's an exotic life," said Dermot. "Well, we'll call it a day now. Tomorrow we've got to get down to a bit of hard work."

"Such as?"

"Such as checking a list I've got here. Out of twenty-odd names we ought to be able to do some elimination, and out of what's left we'll have to look for X."

"Any idea who X is?"

"Not in the least. If it isn't Jason Rudd, that is." He added with a wry and ironic smile, "I shall have to go to Miss Marple and get briefed on local matters."

Chapter Twelve

MISS MARPLE was pursuing her own method of research.

"It's very kind of you, Mrs. Jameson, very kind of you indeed. I can't tell you how grateful I am."

"Oh, don't mention it, Miss Marple. I'm sure I'm glad to oblige you. I suppose you'll want the latest ones?"

"No, no, not particularly," said Miss Marple. "In fact I think I'd rather have some of the older numbers."

"Well, here you are then," said Mrs. Jameson, "there's a nice armful and I can assure you we shan't miss them. Keep them as long as you like. Now it's too heavy for you to carry. Jenny, how's your perm doing?"

"She's all right, Mrs. Jameson. She's had her rinse and now she's having a good dry-out."

"In that case, dear, you might just run along with Miss Marple here, and carry these magazines for her. No, really, Miss Marple, it's no trouble at all. Always pleased to do anything we can for you."

How kind people were, Miss Marple thought, especially when they'd known you practically all their lives. Mrs. Jameson, after long years of running a hairdressing parlour, had steeled herself to going as far in the cause of progress as to repaint her sign and call herself: "DIANE. Hair Stylist." Otherwise the shop remained much as before and catered in much the same way to the needs of its clients. It turned you out with a nice firm perm: it accepted the task of shaping and cutting for the younger generation and the resultant mess was accepted without too much recrimination. But the bulk of Mrs. Jameson's clientele was a bunch of solid, stick-in-the-mud middle-aged ladies who found it extremely hard to get their hair done the way they wanted it anywhere else.

"Well, I never," said Cherry the next morning, as she prepared to run a virulent Hoover round the lounge as she still called it in her mind. "What's all this?"

"I am trying," said Miss Marple, "to instruct myself a little in the moving picture world."

She laid aside *Movie News* and picked up *Amongst the Stars*.

"It's really very interesting. It reminds one so much of so many things."

"Fantastic lives they must lead," said Cherry.

"Specialized lives," said Miss Marple. "Highly specialized. It reminds me very much of the things a friend of mine used to tell me. She was a hospital nurse. The same simplicity of outlook and all the gossip and the rumours. And good-looking doctors causing any amount of havoc."

"Rather sudden, isn't it, this interest of yours?" said Cherry.

"I'm finding it difficult to knit nowadays," said Miss Marple. "Of course the print of these is rather small, but I can always use a magnifying glass."

Cherry looked at her curiously.

"You're always surprising me," she said. "The things you take an interest in."

"I take an interest in everything," said Miss Marple.

"I mean taking up new subjects at your age."

Miss Marple shook her head.

"They aren't really new subjects. It's human nature I'm interested in, you know, and human nature is much the same whether it's film stars or hospital nurses or people in St. Mary Mead or," she added thoughtfully, "people who live in the Development."

"Can't see much likeness between me and a film star," said Cherry laughing, "more's the pity. I suppose it's Marina Gregg and her husband coming to live at Gossington Hall that set you off on this."

"That and the very sad event that occurred there," said Miss Marple.

"Mrs. Badcock, you mean? It was bad luck, that."

"What do you think of it in the—" Miss Marple paused with the "D" hovering on her lips. "What do you and your friends think about it?" she amended her question.

"It's a queer do," said Cherry. "Looks as though it were murder, doesn't it, though of course the police are too cagey to say so outright. Still, that's what it looks like."

"I don't see what else it could be," said Miss Marple.

"It couldn't be suicide," agreed Cherry, "not with Heather Badcock."

"Did you know her well?"

"No, not really. Hardly at all. She was a bit of a nosy parker you know. Always wanting you to join this, join that, turn up for meetings at so-and-so. Too much energy. Her husband got a bit sick of it sometimes, I think."

"She doesn't seem to have had any real enemies."

"People used to get a bit fed up with her sometimes. The point is, I don't see who could have murdered her unless it was her husband. And he's a very meek type. Still, the worm will turn, or so they say. I've always heard that Crippen was ever so nice a man and that man Haigh, who pickled them all in acid—they said he couldn't have been more charming! So one never knows, does one?"

"Poor Mr. Badcock," said Miss Marple.

"And people say he was upset and nervy at the fête that day—before it happened, I mean—but people always say that kind of thing afterwards. If you ask me, he's looking better now than he's looked for years. Seems to have got a bit more spirit and go in him."

"Indeed?" said Miss Marple.

"Nobody *really* thinks he did it," said Cherry. "Only, if he didn't, who did? I can't help thinking myself it must have been an accident of some kind. Accidents do happen. You think you know all about mushrooms and go out and pick some. One fungus gets in among them and there you are, rolling about in agony and lucky if the doctor gets to you in time."

"Cocktails and glasses of sherry don't seem to lend themselves to accident," said Miss Marple.

"Oh, I don't know," said Cherry. "A bottle of something or other could have got in by mistake. Somebody I knew took a dose of concentrated D.D.T. once. Horribly ill they were."

"Accident," said Miss Marple thoughtfully. "Yes, it certainly seems the best solution. I must say I can't believe that in the case of Heather Badcock it could have been deliberate murder. I won't say it's impossible. Nothing is impossible, but it doesn't seem like it. No, I think the truth lies somewhere here." She rustled her magazines and picked up another one.

"You mean you're looking for some special story about someone?"

"No," said Miss Marple. "I'm just looking for odd mentions of people and a way of life and something—some little something that might help." She returned to her perusal of the magazines and Cherry removed her vacuum cleaner to the upper floor. Miss Marple's face was pink and interested, and being slightly deaf now, she did not hear the footsteps that came along the garden path towards the drawing-room window. It was only when a slight shadow fell on the page that she looked up. Dermot Craddock was standing smiling at her.

"Doing your homework, I see," he remarked.

"Inspector Craddock, how very nice to see you. And how kind to spare time to come and see me. Would you like a cup of coffee, or possibly a glass of sherry?"

"A glass of sherry would be splendid," said Dermot. "Don't you move," he added. "I'll ask for it as I come in."

He went round by the side door and presently joined Miss Marple.

"Well," he said, "is all that bumph giving you ideas?"

"Rather too many ideas," said Miss Marple. "I'm not often shocked, you know, but this does shock me a little."

"What, the private lives of film stars?"

"Oh, no," said Miss Marple, "not *that!* That all seems to be most natural, given the circumstances and the money involved and the opportunities for propinquity. Oh, no, that's natural enough. I mean the way they're written about. I'm rather old-fashioned, you know, and I feel that that really shouldn't be allowed."

"It's news," said Dermot Craddock, "and some pretty nasty things can be said in the way of fair comment."

"I know," said Miss Marple. "It makes me sometimes very angry. I expect you think it's silly of me reading all these. But one does so badly want to be *in* things, and of course sitting here in the house I can't really know as much about things as I would like to."

"That's just what I thought," said Dermot Craddock, "and that's why I've come to tell you about them."

"But, my dear boy, excuse me, would your superiors really approve of that?"

"I don't see why not," said Dermot. "Here," he added, "I have a list. A list of people who were there on that landing during the short time of Heather Badcock's arrival until her death. "We've eliminated a lot of people, perhaps precipitately, but I don't think so. We've eliminated the mayor and his wife and Alderman somebody and his wife and a great many of the locals, though we've kept in the husband. If I remember rightly, you were always very suspicious of husbands."

"They are often the obvious suspects," said Miss Marple apologetically, "and the obvious is so often right."

"I couldn't agree with you more," said Craddock.

"But which husband, my dear boy, are you referring to?"

"Which one do you think?" asked Dermot. He eyed her sharply.

Miss Marple looked at him.

"Jason Rudd?" she asked.

"Ah!" said Craddock. "Your mind works just as mine does. I don't think it was Arthur Badcock, because you see, I don't think that Heather Badcock was meant to be killed. I think the intended victim was Marina Gregg."

"That would seem almost certain, wouldn't it?" said Miss Marple.

"And so," said Craddock, "as we both agree on that, the field widens. To tell you who was there on that day, what they saw or said they saw, and where they were or said they were, is only a thing you could have observed for yourself if you'd been there. So my superiors, as you call them, couldn't possibly object to my discussing that with you, could they?"

"That's very nicely put, my dear boy," said Miss Marple.

"I'll give you a little précis of what I was told and then we'll come to the list."

He gave a brief résumé of what he had heard, and then he produced his list.

"It must be one of these," he said. "My godfather Sir Henry Clithering told me that you once had a club here. You called it the Tuesday Night Club. You all dined with each other in turn and then someone would tell a story—a story of some real-life happening which had ended in mystery. A mystery of which only the teller of the tale knew the answer. And every time, so my grandfather told me, you guessed right. So I thought I'd come along and see if you'd do a bit of guessing for me this morning."

"I think that is a rather frivolous way of putting it," said Miss Marple reprovingly, "but there is one question I should like to ask."

"Yes?"

"What about the children?"

"The children? There's only one. An imbecile child in a sanatorium in America. Is that what you mean?"

"No," said Miss Marple, "that's not what I mean. It's very sad of course. One of those tragedies that seem to happen and there's no one to blame for it. No, I meant the children that I've seen mentioned in some article here." She tapped the papers in front of her. "Children that Marina Gregg adopted. Two boys, I think, and a girl. In one case a mother with a lot of children and very little money to bring them up in this country, wrote to her, and asked if she couldn't take a child. There was a lot of very silly false sentiment written about that. About the mother's unselfishness and the wonderful home and education and future the child was going to have. I can't find out much about the other two. One I think was a foreign refugee and the other was some American child. Marina Gregg adopted them at different times. I'd like to know what's happened to them."

Dermot Craddock looked at her curiously. "It's odd that you should think of that," he said. "I did just vaguely wonder about those children myself. But how do you connect them up?"

"Well," said Miss Marple, "as far as I can hear or find out, they're not living with her now, are they?"

"I expect they were provided for," said Craddock. "In fact, I think that the adoption laws would insist on that. There was probably money settled on them in trust."

"So when she got—tired of them," said Miss Marple with a very faint pause before the word "tired," "they were dismissed! After being brought up in luxury with every advantage. Is that it?"

"Probably," said Craddock. "I don't know exactly." He continued to look at her curiously.

"Children feel things, you know," said Miss Marple, nodding her head. "They feel things more than the people around them ever imagine. The sense of hurt, of being rejected, of not belonging. It's a thing that you don't get over just because of advantages. Education is no substitute for it, or comfortable living, or an assured income, or a start in a profession. It's the sort of thing that might rankle."

"Yes. But all the same, isn't it rather farfetched to think that— Well, what exactly do you think?"

"I haven't got as far as that," said Miss Marple. "I just wondered where they were and how old they would be now? Grown up, I should imagine, from what I've read here."

"I could find out, I suppose," said Dermot Craddock slowly.

"Oh, I don't want to bother you in any way, or even to suggest that my little idea's worth while at all."

"There's no harm," said Dermot Craddock, "in having that checked up on." He made a note in his little book. "Now do you want to look at my list?"

"I don't really think I should be able to do anything useful about that. You see, I wouldn't know who the people were."

"Oh, I could give you a running commentary," said Craddock. "Here we are. *Jason Rudd, husband* (husbands always highly suspicious). Everyone says that Jason Rudd adored her. That is suspicious in itself, don't you think?"

"Not necessarily," said Miss Marple with dignity.

"He's been very active in trying to conceal the fact that his wife was the object of attack. He hadn't hinted any suspicion of such a thing to the police. I don't know why he thinks we're such asses as not to think of it for ourselves. We've considered it from the first. But anyway, that's his story. He was afraid that knowledge of that fact might get to his wife's ears and that she'd go into a panic about it."

"Is she the sort of woman who goes into panics?"

"Yes, she's neurasthenic, throws temperaments, has nervous breakdowns, gets in states."

"That might not mean any lack of courage," Miss Marple objected.

"On the other hand," said Craddock, "if she knows quite well that she was the object of the attack, it's also possible that she may know who did it."

"You mean she knows who did it—but does not want to disclose the fact?"

"I just say it's a possibility, and if so, one rather wonders why not? It looks as though the motive, the root of the matter, was something she didn't want to come to her husband's ear."

"That is certainly an interesting thought," said Miss Marple.

"Here are a few more names. The secretary, Ella Zielinsky. An extremely competent and efficient young woman."

"In love with the husband, do you think?" asked Miss Marple.

"I should think definitely," answered Craddock, "but why should you think so?"

"Well, it so often happens," said Miss Marple. "And therefore not very fond of poor Marina Gregg, I expect?"

"Therefore possible motive for murder," said Craddock.

"A lot of secretaries and employees are in love with their employers' husbands," said Miss Marple, "but very, very few of them try to poison them."

"Well, we must allow for exceptions," said Craddock. "Then there were two local and one London photographer, and two members of the press. None of them seem likely but we will follow them up. There was the woman who was formerly married to Marina Gregg's second or third husband. She didn't like it when Marina Gregg took her husband away. Still, that's about eleven or twelve years ago. It seems unlikely that she'd make a visit here at this juncture on purpose to poison Marina because of that. Then there's a man called Ardwyck Fenn. He was once a very close friend of Marina Gregg's. He hasn't seen her for years. He was not known to be in this part of the world, and it was a great surprise when he turned up on this occasion."

"She would be startled then when she saw him?"

"Presumably yes."

"Startled—and possibly frightened."

"'*The doom has come upon me,*'" said Craddock. "That's the idea. Then there was young Hailey Preston dodging about that day, doing his stuff. Talks a good deal but definitely heard nothing, saw nothing and knew nothing. Almost too anxious to say so. Does anything there ring a bell?"

"Not exactly," said Miss Marple. "Plenty of interesting possibilities. But I'd still like to know a little more about the children."

He looked at her curiously. "You've got quite a bee in your bonnet about that, haven't you?" he said. "All right, I'll find out."

Chapter Thirteen

"I suppose it couldn't possibly have been the mayor?" said Inspector Cornish wistfully.

He tapped the paper with the list of names on it with his pencil. Dermot Craddock grinned.

"Wishful thinking?" he asked.

"You could certainly call it that," said Cornish. "Pompous, canting old hypocrite!" he went on. "Everybody's got it in for him. Throws his weight about, ultrasanctimonious, and neck-deep in graft for years past!"

"Can't you ever bring it home to him?"

"No," said Cornish. "He's too slick for that. He's always just on the right side of the law."

"It's tempting, I agree," said Dermot Craddock, "but I think you'll have to banish that rosy picture from your mind, Frank."

"I know, I know," said Cornish. "He's a possible, but a wildly improbable. Who else have we got?"

Both men studied the list again. There were still eight names on it.

"We're pretty well agreed," said Craddock, "that there's nobody missed out from here?" There was a faint question in his voice. Cornish answered it.

"I think you can be pretty sure that's the lot. After Mrs. Bantry came the vicar, and after that the Badcocks. There were then eight people on the stairs. The mayor and his wife, Joshua Grice and wife from Lower Farm. Donald McNeil of the Much Benham *Herald and Argus*. Ardwyck Fenn, U.S.A. Miss Lola Brewster, U.S.A., moving picture star. There you are. In addition there was an arty photographer from London with a camera set up on the angle of the stairs. If, as you suggest, this Mrs. Bantry's story of Marina Gregg having a 'frozen look' was occasioned by someone she saw on the stairs, you've got to take your pick among that lot. Mayor regretfully out. Grices out—never been away from St. Mary Mead, I should say. That leaves four. Local journalist unlikely, photographer girl had been there for half an hour already, so why should Marina react so late in the day? What does that leave?"

"Sinister strangers from America," said Craddock with a faint smile.

"You've said it."

"They're our best suspects by far, I agree," said Craddock. "They turned up unexpectedly. Ardwyck Fenn was an old flame of Marina's whom she had not seen for years. Lola Brewster was once married to Marina Gregg's third husband, who got a divorce from her in order to marry Marina. It was not, I gather, a very amicable divorce."

"I'd put her down as Suspect Number One," said Cornish.

"Would you, Frank? After a lapse of about fifteen years or so, and having remarried twice herself since then?"

Cornish said that you never knew with women. Dermot accepted that as a general dictum, but remarked that it seemed odd to him to say the least of it.

"But you agree that it lies between them?"

"Possibly. But I don't like it very much. What about the hired help who were serving the drinks?"

"Discounting the 'frozen look' we've heard so much about? Well, we've checked up in a general way. Local catering firm from Market Basing had the job—for the fête, I mean. Actually in the house, there was the butler, Giuseppe, in charge; and two local girls from the studios' canteen. I know both of them. Not overbright, but harmless."

"Pushing it back at me, are you? I'll go and have a word with the reporter chap. He might have seen something helpful. Then to London. Ardwyck Fenn, Lola Brewster—and the photographer girl—what's her name?—Margot Bence. She also might have seen something."

Cornish nodded. "Lola Brewster is my best bet," he said. He looked curiously at Craddock. "You don't seem as sold on her as I am."

"I'm thinking of the difficulties," said Dermot slowly.

"Of putting poison into Marina's glass without anybody seeing her."

"Well, that's the same for everybody, isn't it? It was a mad thing to do."

"Agreed it was a mad thing to do, but it would be a madder thing for someone like Lola Brewster than for anybody else."

"Why?" asked Cornish.

"Because she was a guest of some importance. She's a somebody, a big name. Everyone would be looking at her."

"True enough," Cornish admitted.

"The locals would nudge each other and whisper and stare, and after Marina Gregg and Jason Rudd had greeted her, she'd have been passed on for the secretaries to look after. It wouldn't be easy, Frank. However adroit you were, you couldn't be sure *someone* wouldn't see you. That's the snag there, and it's a big snag."

"As I say, isn't that snag the same for everybody?"

"No," said Craddock. "Oh, no. Far from it. Take the butler now, Giuseppe. He's busy with the drinks and glasses, and pouring things out, with handing them. He could put a pinch or a tablet or two of Calmo in a glass easily enough."

"Giuseppe?" Frank Cornish reflected. "Do you think he did?"

"No reason to believe so," said Craddock, "but we might find a reason. A nice solid bit of motive, that is to say. Yes, he could have done it. Or one of the catering staff could have done it. Unfortunately they weren't on the spot—a pity."

"Someone might have managed to get himself or herself deliberately planted in the firm for the purpose."

"You mean it might have been as premeditated as all that?"

"We don't know anything about it yet," said Craddock vexedly. "We absolutely don't know the first thing about it. Not until we prise what we want to know out of Marina Gregg, or out of her husband. They *must* know or suspect—but they're not telling. And we don't know yet *why* they're not telling. We've a long way to go."

He paused and then resumed: "Discounting the 'frozen look' which may have been pure coincidence, there are other people who could have done it fairly easily. The secretary woman, Ella Zielinsky. She was also busy with glasses, with handing things to people. Nobody would be watching *her* with any particular interest. The same applies to that willow wand of a young man—I've forgotten his name. Hailey—Hailey Preston? That's right. There would be a good opportunity for either of them. In fact if either of them *had* wanted to do away with Marina Gregg, it would have been far safer to do so on a public occasion."

"Anyone else?"

"Well, there's always the husband," said Craddock.

"Back to husbands again," said Cornish, with a faint smile. "We thought it was that poor devil, Badcock, before we realized that Marina was the intended victim. Now we've transferred our suspicions to Jason Rudd. He seems devoted enough though, I must say."

"He has the reputation of being so," said Craddock, "but one never knows."

"If he wanted to get rid of her, wouldn't divorce be much easier?"

"It would be far more usual," agreed Dermot, "but there may be a lot of ins and outs to this business that we don't know yet."

The telephone rang. Cornish took up the receiver.

"What? Yes? Put them through. Yes, he's here." He listened for a moment, then put his hand over the receiver and looked at Dermot. "Miss Marina Gregg," he said, "is feeling very much better. She is quite ready to be interviewed."

"I'd better hurry along," said Dermot Craddock, "before she changes her mind."

II

At Gossington Hall, Dermot Craddock was received by Ella Zielinsky. She was, as usual, brisk and efficient.

"Miss Gregg is waiting for you, Mr. Craddock," she said.

Dermot looked at her with some interest. From the beginning he had found Ella Zielinsky an intriguing personality. He had said to himself, "A poker face if I ever saw one." She had answered any questions he had asked with the utmost readiness. She had shown no signs of keeping anything back, but what she really thought or felt or even knew about the business, he still had no idea. There seemed to be no chink in the armour of her bright efficiency. She might know no more than she said she did; she might know a good deal. The only thing he was sure of—and he had to admit to himself that he had no reasons to adduce for that surety—was that she was in love with Jason Rudd. It was, as he said, an occupational disease of secretaries. It probably meant nothing. But the fact did at least suggest a motive and he was sure, quite sure, that she was concealing something. It might be love, it might be hate. It might, quite simply, be guilt. She might have taken her opportunity that afternoon, or she might have deliberately planned what she was going to do. He could see her in the part quite easily, as far as the execution of it went. Her swift but unhurried movements, moving here and there looking after guests, handing glasses to one or another, taking glasses away, her eyes marking the spot where Marina had put her glass down on the table. And then, perhaps at the very moment when Marina had been greeting the arrivals from the States, with surprise and joyous cries and everybody's eyes turned towards their meeting, she could have quietly and unobtrusively dropped the fatal dose into that glass. It would require audacity, nerve, swiftness. She would have had all those. Whatever she had done, she would not have looked guilty while she was doing it. It would have been a simple, brilliant crime, a crime that could hardly fail to be successful. But chance had ruled otherwise. In the rather crowded floor space someone had joggled Heather Badcock's arm. Her drink had been spilt, and Marina, with her natural impulsive grace, had quickly proffered her own glass, standing there untouched. And so the wrong woman had died.

A lot of pure theory, and probably hooey at that, said Dermot Craddock to himself at the same time as he was making polite remarks to Ella Zielinsky.

"One thing I wanted to ask you, Miss Zielinsky. The catering was done by a Market Basing firm, I understand?"

"Yes."

"Why was that particular firm chosen?"

"I really don't know," said Ella. "That doesn't lie among my duties. I know Mr. Rudd thought it would be more tactful to employ somebody local rather than to employ a firm from London. The whole thing was really quite a small affair from our point of view."

"Quite." He watched her as she stood frowning a little and looking down. A good forehead, a determined chin, a figure which could look quite voluptuous if it was allowed to do so, a hard mouth, an acquisitive mouth. The eyes? He looked at them in faint surprise. The lids were reddened. He wondered. Had she been crying? It looked like it. And yet he could have sworn she was not the type of young woman to cry. She looked up at him, and as though she read his thoughts, she took out her handkerchief and blew her nose heartily.

"You've got a cold," he said.

"Not a cold. Hay fever. It's an allergy of some kind, really. I always get it at this time of year."

There was a low buzz. There were two phones in the room, one on the table and one on another table in the corner. It was the latter one that was beginning to buzz. Ella Zielinsky went over to it and picked up the receiver.

"Yes," she said, "he's here. I'll bring him up at once." She put the receiver down again. "Marina's ready for you," she said.

III

Marina Gregg received Craddock in a room on the first floor, which was obviously her own private sitting-room opening out of her bedroom. After the accounts of her prostration and her nervous state, Dermot Craddock had expected to find a fluttering invalid. But although Marina was half re-clining on a sofa, her voice was vigorous and her eyes were bright. She had very little make-up on, but in spite of this she did not look her age, and he was struck very forcibly by the subdued radiance of her beauty. It was the exquisite line of cheek and jawbone, the way the hair fell loosely and naturally to frame her face. The long sea-green eyes, the pencilled eyebrows, owing something to art but more to nature, and the warmth and sweetness of her smile, all had a subtle magic. She said:

"Chief-Inspector Craddock? I've been behaving disgracefully. I do apol-ogize. I just let myself go to pieces after this awful thing. I could have snapped out of it, but I didn't. I'm ashamed of myself." The smile came, rueful, sweet, turning up the corners of the mouth. She extended a hand and he took it.

"It was only natural," he said, "that you should feel upset."

"Well, everyone was upset," said Marina. "I'd no business to make out it was worse for me than anyone else."

"Hadn't you?"

She looked at him for a minute and then nodded. "Yes," she said, "you're very perceptive. Yes, I had." She looked down and with one long forefinger gently stroked the arm of the sofa. It was a gesture he had no-ticed in one of her films. It was a meaningless gesture, yet it seemed fraught with significance. It had a kind of musing gentleness.

"I'm a coward," she said, her eyes still cast down. "Somebody wanted to kill me, and I didn't want to die."

"Why do you think someone wanted to kill you?"

Her eyes opened wide. "Because it was my glass—*my* drink—that had been tampered with. It was just a mistake that that poor stupid woman got it. That's what's so horrible and so tragic. Besides—"

"Yes, Miss Gregg?"

She seemed a little uncertain about saying more.

"You had other reasons perhaps for believing that you were the intended victim?"

She nodded.

"What reasons, Miss Gregg?"

She paused a minute longer before saying, "Jason says I must tell you all about it."

"You've confided in him then?"

"Yes . . . I didn't want to at first—but Dr. Gilchrist put it to me that I must. And then I found that he thought so too. He'd thought it all along but—it's rather funny really"—a rueful smile curled her lips again—"he didn't want to alarm me by telling me. Really!" Marina sat up with a sudden vigorous movement. "Darling Jinks! Does he think I'm a complete fool?"

"You haven't told me yet, Miss Gregg, why you should think anyone wanted to kill you."

She was silent for a moment and then with a sudden, brusque gesture, she stretched out for her handbag, opened it, took out a piece of paper and thrust it into his hand. He read it. Typed on it was one line of writing: *Don't think you'll escape next time.*

Craddock said sharply, "When did you get this?"

"It was on my dressing-table when I came back from the bath."

"So someone in the house—"

"Not necessarily. Someone could have climbed up the balcony outside my window and pushed it through there. I think they meant it to frighten me still more, but actually it didn't. I just felt furiously angry and sent word to you to come and see me."

Dermot Craddock smiled. "Possibly a rather unexpected result for whoever sent it. Is this the first kind of message like that you've had?"

Again Marina hesitated. Then she said, "No, it isn't."

"Will you tell me about any others?"

"It was three weeks ago, when we first came here. It came to the studio, not here. It was quite ridiculous. It was just a message. Not typewritten that time. In capital letters. It said, 'Prepare to die.'" She laughed. There was perhaps a very faint tinge of hysteria in the laugh. The mirth was genuine enough. "It was so silly," she said. "Of course one often gets crank messages, threats, things like that. I thought it was probably religious, you know. Someone who didn't approve of film actresses. I just tore it up and threw it into the wastepaper basket."

"Did you tell anyone about it, Miss Gregg?"

Marina shook her head. "No, I never said a word to anyone. As a matter of fact, we were having a bit of worry at the moment about the scene we were shooting. I just couldn't have thought of anything but that at the moment. Anyway, as I say, I thought it was either a silly joke or one of those religious cranks who write and disapprove of play-acting and things like that."

"And after that, was there another?"

"Yes. On the day of the fête. One of the gardeners brought it to me, I think. He said someone had left a note for me and was there any answer? I thought perhaps it had to do with the arrangements. I just tore it open. It said, 'Today will be your last day on earth.' I just crumpled it up and said, 'No answer.' Then I called the man back and asked him who gave it to him. He said it was a man with spectacles on a bicycle. Well, I mean, what could you do about that? I thought it was more silliness. I didn't think—I didn't think for a moment it was a real genuine threat."

"Where's that note now, Miss Gregg?"

"I've no idea. I was wearing one of those coloured Italian silk coats and I think, as far as I can remember, that I crumpled it up and shoved it into the pocket of it. But it's not there now. It probably fell out."

"And you've no idea who wrote those notes, Miss Gregg? Who inspired them. Not even now?"

Her eyes opened widely. There was a kind of innocent wonder in them that he took note of. He admired it, but he did not believe in it.

"How can I tell? How can I possibly tell?"

"I think you might have quite a good idea, Miss Gregg."

"I haven't. I assure you I haven't."

"You're a very famous person," said Dermot. "You've had great successes. Successes in your profession, and personal successes, too. Men have fallen in love with you, wanted to marry you, have married you. Women have been jealous and envied you. Men have been in love with you and rebuffed by you. It's a pretty wide field, I agree, but I should think you must have some idea who could have written those notes."

"It could have been anybody."

"No, Miss Gregg, it couldn't have been *anybody*. It could possibly have been one of quite a lot of people. It could be someone quite humble, a dresser, an electrician, a servant; or it could be someone among the ranks of your friends, or so-called friends. But you must have some idea. Some name, more than one name, perhaps, to suggest."

The door opened and Jason Rudd came in. Marina turned to him. She swept out an arm appealingly.

"Jinks, darling, Mr. Craddock is insisting that I must know who wrote those horrid notes. And I don't. You know I don't. Neither of us know. We haven't got the least idea."

"Very urgent about that," thought Craddock. "Very urgent. Is Marina Gregg afraid of what her husband might say?"

Jason Rudd, his eyes dark with fatigue and the scowl on his face deeper than usual, came over to join them. He took Marina's hand in his.

"I know it sounds unbelievable to you, Inspector," he said, "but honestly neither Marina nor I has any idea about this business."

"So you're in the happy position of having no enemies, is that it?" The irony was manifest in Dermot's voice.

Jason Rudd flushed a little. "Enemies? That's a very biblical word, Inspector. In that sense, I can assure you I can think of no enemies. People who dislike one, would like to get the better of one, would do a mean turn to one if they could, in malice and uncharitableness, yes. But it's a long step from that to putting an overdose of poison in a drink."

"Just now, in speaking to your wife, I asked her who could have written or inspired those letters. She said she didn't know. But when we come to the actual action, it narrows it down. *Somebody actually put the poison in that glass.* And that's a fairly limited field, you know."

"I saw nothing," said Jason Rudd.

"I certainly didn't," said Marina. "Well, I mean—if I had seen anyone putting anything in my glass, I wouldn't have drunk the stuff, would I?"

"I can't help believing, you know," said Dermot Craddock gently, "that you do know a little more than you're telling me."

"It's not *true*," said Marina. "Tell him that that isn't true, Jason!"

"I assure you," said Jason Rudd, "that I am completely and absolutely at a loss. The whole thing's fantastic. I might believe it was a joke—a joke that had somehow gone wrong—that had proved dangerous, done by a person who never dreamt that it would be dangerous. . . ."

There was a slight question in his voice, then he shook his head. "No. I see that idea doesn't appeal to you."

"There's one more thing I should like to ask you," said Dermot Craddock. "You remember Mr. and Mrs. Badcock's arrival, of course. They came immediately after the vicar. You greeted them, I understand, Miss Gregg, in the same charming way as you had received all your guests. But I am told by an eyewitness that immediately after greeting them you looked over Mrs. Badcock's shoulder and that you saw something which seemed to alarm you. Is that true, and if so, what was it?"

Marina said quickly, "Of course it isn't true. Alarm me—what should have alarmed me?"

"That's what we want to know," said Dermot Craddock patiently. "My witness is very insistent on the point, you know."

"Who was your witness? What did he or she say they saw?"

"You were looking at the staircase," said Dermot Craddock. "There were people coming up that staircase. There was a journalist, there was Mr. Grice and his wife, elderly residents in this place, there was Mr. Ardwyck Fenn who had just arrived from the States, and there was Miss Lola Brewster. Was it the sight of one of those people that upset you, Miss Gregg?"

"I tell you I wasn't upset." She almost barked the words.

"And yet your attention wavered from greeting Mrs. Badcock. She had said something to you which you left unanswered because you were staring past her at something else."

Marina Gregg took hold on herself. She spoke quickly and convincingly.

"I can explain that, I really can. If you knew anything about acting, you'd be able to understand quite easily. There comes a moment, even when you know a part well—in fact, it usually happens when you *do* know a part well—when you go on with it mechanically. Smiling, making the proper movements and gestures, saying the words with the usual inflections. But your mind isn't on it. And quite suddenly there's a horrible blank moment when you don't know where you are, where you've got to in the play, what your next lines are! Drying up, that's what we call it. Well, that's what happened to me. I'm not terribly strong, as my husband will tell you. I've had rather a strenuous time, and a good deal of nervous apprehension about this film. I wanted to make a success of this fête and to be nice and pleasant and welcoming to everybody. But one does say the same things over and over again, mechanically, to the people who are always saying the same things to you. You know, how they've always wanted to meet you. How they once saw you outside a theatre in San Francisco—or travelled in a plane with you. Something silly, really, but one has to be nice about it and say things. Well, as I'm telling you, one does that automatically. One doesn't need to think what to say because one's said it so often before. Suddenly, I think, a wave of tiredness came over me. My brain went blank. Then I realized that Mrs. Badcock had been telling me a long story which I hadn't really heard at all, and was now looking at me in an eager sort of way and that I hadn't answered her or said any of the proper things. It was just tiredness."

"Just tiredness," said Dermot Craddock slowly. "You insist on that, Miss Gregg?"

"Yes, I do. I can't see why you don't believe me."

Dermot Craddock turned towards Jason Rudd. "Mr. Rudd," he said, "I think you're more likely to understand my meaning than your wife is. I am concerned, very much concerned, for your wife's safety. There has been an attempt on her life, there have been threatening letters. That means, doesn't it, that there is someone who was here on the day of the fête and possibly is still here, someone in very close touch with this house and what goes on in it. That person, whoever it is, may be slightly insane. It's not just a question of threats. Threatened men live long, as they say. The same goes for women. But whoever it was didn't stop at threats. A deliberate attempt was made to poison Miss Gregg. Don't you see, in the whole nature of things, that attempt is bound to be repeated? There's only one way to achieve safety. That is to give me all the clues you can. I don't say that you *know* who that person is, but I think that you must be able to give a guess or to have a vague idea. Won't you tell me the truth? Or if, which is possible, you yourself do not know the truth, won't you urge your wife to do so? It's in the interests of her own safety that I'm asking you."

Jason Rudd turned his head slowly. "You hear what Inspector Craddock says, Marina," he said. "It's possible, as he says, that you may know something that I do not. If so, for God's sake, don't be foolish about it. If you've the least suspicion of *anyone,* tell it to us now."

"But I haven't." Her voice rose in a wail. "You must believe me."

"Who were you afraid of that day?" asked Dermot.

"I wasn't afraid of anyone."

"Listen, Miss Gregg, of the people on the stairs or coming up it, there were two friends whom you were surprised to see, whom you had not seen for a long time and whom you did not expect to see that day. Mr. Ardwyck Fenn and Miss Brewster. Had you any special emotions when you suddenly saw them coming up the stairs? You didn't know they were coming, did you?"

"No, we'd no idea they were even in England," said Jason Rudd.

"I was delighted," said Marina, "absolutely delighted!"

"Delighted to see Miss Brewster?"

"Well—" she shot him a quick, faintly suspicious glance.

Craddock said, "Lola Brewster was, I believe, originally married to your third husband, Robert Truscott?"

"Yes, that's so."

"He divorced her in order to marry you."

"Oh, everyone knows about that," said Marina Gregg impatiently. "You needn't think it's anything you've found out. There was a bit of a rumpus at the time, but there wasn't any bad feeling about it in the end."

"Did she make threats against you?"

"Well—in a way, yes. But, oh dear, I wish I could explain. No one takes those sort of threats seriously. It was at a party, she'd had a lot of drink. She might have taken a pot shot at me with a pistol if she'd had one. But luckily she didn't. All that was *years* ago! None of these things last, these emotions! They don't, really they don't. That's true, isn't it, Jason?"

"I'd say it was true enough," said Jason Rudd, "and I can assure you, Mr. Craddock, that Lola Brewster had no opportunity on the day of the fête of poisoning my wife's drink. I was close beside her most of the time. The idea that Lola would suddenly, after a long period of friendliness, come to England, and arrive at our house all prepared to poison my wife's drink—why, the whole idea's absurd!"

"I appreciate your point of view," said Craddock.

"It's not only that, it's a matter of *fact* as well. She was nowhere near Marina's glass."

"And your other visitor—Ardwyck Fenn?"

There was, he thought, a very slight pause before Jason Rudd spoke.

"He's a very old friend of ours," he said. "We haven't seen him for a good many years now, though we occasionally correspond. He's quite a big figure in American television."

"Was he an old friend of yours, too?" Dermot Craddock asked Marina.

Her breath came rather quickly as she replied. "Yes, oh yes. He—he was quite a friend of mine always, but I've rather lost sight of him of late years." Then with a sudden quick rush of words, she went on, "If you think that I looked up and saw Ardwyck and was frightened of him, it's nonsense. It's absolute *nonsense*. Why should I be frightened of him, what reason would I have to be frightened of him? We were great friends. I was just very, very pleased when I suddenly saw him. It was a delightful surprise, as I told you. Yes, a delightful surprise." She raised her head, looking at him, her face vivid and defiant.

"Thank you, Miss Gregg," said Craddock quietly. "If you should feel inclined at any moment to take me a little further into your confidence, I should strongly advise you to do so."

Chapter Fourteen

Mrs. Bantry was on her knees. A good day for hoeing. Nice dry soil. But hoeing wouldn't do everything. Thistles now, and dandelions. She dealt vigorously with these pests.

She rose to her feet, breathless but triumphant, and looked out over the hedge on to the road. She was faintly surprised to see the dark-haired secretary whose name she couldn't remember coming out of the public call box that was situated near the bus stop on the other side of the road.

What was her name now? It began with a B—or was it an R? No, *Zielinsky*, that was it. Mrs. Bantry remembered just in time, as Ella crossed the road and came into the drive past the Lodge.

"Good morning, Miss Zielinsky," she called in a friendly tone.

Ella Zielinsky jumped. It was not so much a jump, as a shy—the shy of a frightened horse. It surprised Mrs. Bantry.

"Good morning," said Ella, and added quickly: "I came down to telephone. There's something wrong with our line today."

Mrs. Bantry felt more surprise. She wondered why Ella Zielinsky bothered to explain her action. She responded civilly.

"How annoying for you. Do come in and telephone any time you want to."

"Oh—thank you very much . . ." Ella was interrupted by a fit of sneezing.

"You've got hay fever," said Mrs. Bantry with immediate diagnosis. "Try weak bicarbonate of soda and water."

"Oh, that's all right. I have some very good patent stuff in an atomizer. Thank you all the same."

She sneezed again as she moved away, walking briskly up the drive.

Mrs. Bantry looked after her. Then her eyes returned to her garden. She looked at it in a dissatisfied fashion. Not a weed to be seen anywhere.

"Othello's occupation's gone," Mrs. Bantry murmured to herself confusedly. "I dare say I'm a nosy old woman but I would like to know if—"

A moment of irresolution and then Mrs. Bantry yielded to temptation. She was going to be a nosy old woman and the hell with it! She strode indoors to the telephone, lifted the receiver and dialled. A brisk transatlantic voice spoke.

"Gossington Hall."

"This is Mrs. Bantry, at the East Lodge."

"Oh, good morning, Mrs. Bantry. This is Hailey Preston. I met you on the day of the fête. What can I do for you?"

"I thought perhaps I could do something for you. If your telephone's out of order—"

His astonished voice interrupted her.

"Our telephone out of order? There's been nothing wrong with it. Why did you think so?"

"I must have made a mistake," said Mrs. Bantry. "I don't always hear very well," she explained unblushingly.

She put the receiver back, waited a minute, then dialled once more.

"Jane? Dolly here."

"Yes, Dolly. What is it?"

"Well, it seems rather odd. That secretary woman was dialling from the public call box in the road. She took the trouble to explain to me quite unnecessarily that she was doing so because the line at Gossington Hall was out of order. But I've rung up there, and it isn't. . . ."

She paused, and waited for intelligence to pronounce.

"In-deed," said Miss Marple thoughtfully. "Interesting."

"For what reason, do you think?"

"Well, clearly, she didn't want to be overheard—"

"Exactly."

"And there might be quite a number of reasons for that."

"Yes."

"Interesting," said Miss Marple again.

II

Nobody could have been more ready to talk than Donald McNeil. He was an amiable red-headed young man. He greeted Dermot Craddock with pleasure and curiosity.

"How are you getting along," he asked cheerfully, "got any little special tidbit for me?"

"Not as yet. Later perhaps."

"Stalling as usual. You're all the same. Affable oysters! Haven't you come to the stage yet of inviting someone to come and 'assist you in your inquiries'?"

"I've come to you," said Dermot Craddock with a grin.

"Is there a nasty *double-entendre* in that remark? Are you really suspicious that I murdered Heather Badcock and do you think I did it in mistake for Marina Gregg or that I meant to murder Heather Badcock all the time?"

"I haven't suggested anything," said Craddock.

"No, no, you wouldn't do that, would you? You'd be very correct. All right. Let's go into it. I was there. I had opportunity but had I any motive? Ah, that's what you'd like to know. What was my motive?"

"I haven't been able to find one so far," said Craddock.

"That's very gratifying. I feel safer."

"I'm just interested in what you may have seen that day."

"You've had that already. The local police had that straight away. It's humiliating. There I was on the scene of a murder. I practically *saw* the murder committed. I must have and yet I've no idea who did it. I'm ashamed to confess that the first I knew about it was seeing the poor, dear woman sitting on a chair gasping for breath and then pegging out. Of course it made a very good eyewitness account. It was a good scoop for me —and all that. But I'll confess to you that I feel humiliated that I don't know more. I ought to know more. And you can't kid me that the dose was meant for Heather Badcock. She was a nice woman who talked too much, but nobody gets murdered for that—unless of course they give away secrets. But I don't think anybody would ever have told Heather Badcock a secret. She wasn't the kind of woman who'd have been interested in other people's secrets. My view of her is of a woman who invariably talked about *herself*."

"That seems to be the generally accepted view," agreed Craddock.

"So we come to the famous Marina Gregg. I'm sure there are lots of wonderful motives for murdering Marina. Envy and jealousy and love tangles—all the stuff of drama. But who did it? Someone with a screw loose, I presume. There! You've had my valuable opinion. Is that what you wanted?"

"Not that alone. I understand that you arrived and came up the stairs about the same time as the vicar and the mayor."

"Quite correct. But that wasn't the first time I'd arrived. I'd been there earlier."

"I didn't know that."

"Yes. I was on a kind of roving commission, you know, going here and there. I had a photographer with me. I'd gone down to take a few local shots of the mayor arriving and throwing a hoopla and putting in a peg for buried treasure, and that kind of thing. Then I went back up again, not so much on the job, as to get a drink or two. The drink was good."

"I see. Now can you remember who else was on the staircase when you went up?"

"Margot Bence from London was there with her camera."

"You know her well?"

"Oh, I run against her quite often. She's a clever girl, who makes a success of her stuff. She takes all the fashionable things—first nights, gala performances—specializes in photographs from unusual angles. Arty! She was in a corner of the half landing, very well placed for taking anyone who came up and for taking the greetings going on at the top. Lola Brewster was just ahead of me on the stairs. Didn't know her at first. She's got a new rust-red hair-do. The very latest Fiji Islander type. Last time I saw her it was lank waves falling round her face and chin in a nice shade of auburn. There was a big dark man with her, American. I don't know who he was, but he looked important."

"Did you look at Marina Gregg herself at all as you were coming up?"

"Yes, of course I did."

"She didn't look upset at all or as though she'd had a shock or was frightened?"

"It's odd you should say that. I *did* think for a moment or two she was going to faint."

"I see," said Craddock thoughtfully. "Thanks. There's nothing else you'd like to tell me?"

McNeil gave him a wide innocent stare.

"What could there be?"

"I don't trust you," said Craddock.

"But you seem quite sure I didn't do it. Disappointing. Suppose I turn out to be her first husband. Nobody knows who he was except that he was so insignificant that even his name's been forgotten."

Dermot grinned.

"Married from your prep school?" he asked. "Or possibly in rompers! I must hurry. I've got a train to catch."

III

There was a neatly docketed pile of papers on Craddock's desk at New Scotland Yard. He gave a perfunctory glance through them, then threw a question over his shoulder.

"Where's Lola Brewster staying?"

"At the Savoy, sir. Suite eighteen hundred. She's expecting you."

"And Ardwyck Fenn?"

"He's at the Dorchester. First floor, one ninety."

"Good."

He picked up some cablegrams and read them through again before shoving them into his pocket. He smiled a moment to himself over the last one. "Don't say I don't do my stuff, Aunt Jane," he murmured under his breath.

He went out and made his way to the Savoy.

In Lola Brewster's suite Lola went out of her way to welcome him effusively. With the report he had just read in his mind, he studied her carefully. Quite a beauty still, he thought, in a lush kind of way, what you might call a trifle overblown, perhaps, but they still liked them that way. A completely different type, of course, from Marina Gregg. The amenities over, Lola pushed back her Fiji Islander hair, drew her generous lipsticked mouth into a provocative pout, and flickering blue eyelids over wide brown eyes, said:

"Have you come to ask me a lot more horrible questions? Like that local inspector did."

"I hope they won't be too horrible, Miss Brewster."

"Oh, but I'm sure they will be, and I'm sure the whole thing must have been some terrible mistake."

"Do you really think so?"

"Yes. It's all such nonsense. Do you really mean that someone tried to poison Marina? Who on earth would poison Marina? She's an absolute sweetie, you know. Everybody loves her."

"Including you?"

"I've always been devoted to Marina."

"Oh, come now, Miss Brewster, wasn't there a little trouble about eleven or twelve years ago?"

"Oh, that." Lola waved it away. "I was terribly nervy and distraught, and Rob and I had been having the most frightful quarrels. We were neither of us normal at the moment. Marina just fell wildly in love with him and rushed him off his feet, the poor pet."

"And you minded very much?"

"Well, I thought I did, Inspector. Of course I see now it was one of the best things that ever happened for me. I was really worried about the children, you know. Breaking up our home. I'm afraid I'd already realized that Rob and I were incompatible. I expect you know I got married to Eddie Groves as soon as the divorce went through? I think really I'd been in love with him for a long time, but of course I didn't want to break up my marriage, because of the children. It's so important, isn't it, that children should have a *home?*"

"Yet people say that actually you were terribly upset."

"Oh, people always say things," said Lola vaguely.

"You said quite a lot, didn't you, Miss Brewster? You went about threatening to shoot Marina Gregg, or so I understand."

"I've told you one *says* things. One's *supposed* to say things like that. Of course I wouldn't really shoot *anyone.*"

"In spite of taking a pot shot at Eddie Groves some few years later?"

"Oh, that was because we'd had an argument," said Lola. "I lost my temper."

"I have it on very good authority, Miss Brewster, that you said—and these are your exact words, or so I'm told" (he read from a notebook)— "'That bitch needn't think she'll get away with it. If I don't shoot her now I'll wait and get her in some other way. I don't care how long I wait, years if need be, but I'll get even with her in the end.'"

"Oh, I'm sure I never said anything of the kind." Lola laughed.

"I'm sure, Miss Brewster, that you did."

"People exaggerate so." A charming smile broke over her face. "I was just mad at the moment, you know," she murmured confidentially. "One says all sorts of things when one's mad with people. But you don't really think I'd wait fourteen years and come across to England and look up Marina and drop some deadly poison into her cocktail glass within three minutes of seeing her again?"

Dermot Craddock didn't really think so. It seemed to him wildly improbable. He merely said:

"I'm only pointing out to you, Miss Brewster, that there had been threats in the past and that Marina Gregg was certainly startled and frightened to see someone who came up the stairs that day. Naturally one feels that that someone must have been you."

"But darling Marina was delighted to see me! She kissed me and exclaimed how wonderful it was. Oh, really, Inspector, I do think that you're being very, very silly."

"In fact, you were all one big happy family?"

"Well, that's really much more true than all the things you've been thinking."

"And you've no ideas that could help us in any way? No ideas who might have killed her?"

"I tell you nobody would have wanted to kill Marina. She's a very silly woman anyway. Always making terrible fusses about her health, and changing her mind and wanting this, that and the other, and when she's got it being dissatisfied with it! I can't think why people are as fond of her as they are. Jason's always been absolutely mad about her. What that man has to put up with! But there it is. Everybody puts up with Marina, puts themselves out for her. Then she gives them a sad, sweet smile and thanks them! And apparently that makes them feel that the trouble is worth while. I really don't know how she does it. You'd better put the idea that somebody wanted to kill her right out of your head."

"I should like to," said Dermot Craddock. "Unfortunately I can't put it out of my head because, you see, it happened."

"What do you mean, *it happened?* Nobody has killed Marina, have they?"

"No. But the attempt was made."

"I don't believe it for a moment! I expect whoever it was meant to kill the other woman all the time—the one who *was* killed. I expect someone comes into money when she dies."

"She hadn't any money, Miss Brewster."

"Oh, well, there was some other reason. Anyway, I shouldn't worry about Marina if I were you. Marina is *always* all right!"

"Is she? She doesn't look a very happy woman to me."

"Oh, that's because she makes such a song and dance about everything. Unhappy love affairs. Not being able to have any children."

"She adopted some children, didn't she?" said Dermot with a lively remembrance of Miss Marple's urgent voice.

"I believe she did once. It wasn't a great success, I believe. She does these impulsive things and then wishes she hadn't."

"What happened to the children she adopted?"

"I've no idea. They just sort of vanished after a bit. She got tired of them, I suppose, like everything else."

"I see," said Dermot Craddock.

IV

Next—the Dorchester. Suite 190.

"Well, Chief-Inspector—" Ardwyck Fenn looked down at the card in his hand.

"Craddock."

"What can I do for you?"

"I hope you won't mind if I ask you a few questions."

"Not at all. It's this business at Much Benham. No—what's the actual name, St. Mary Mead?"

"Yes. That's right. Gossington Hall."

"Can't think what Jason Rudd wanted to buy a place like that for. Plenty of good Georgian houses in England—or even Queen Anne. Gossington Hall is a purely Victorian mansion. What's the attraction in that, I wonder?"

"Oh, there's some attraction—for some people, that is, in Victorian stability."

"Stability? Well, perhaps you've got something there. Marina, I suppose, had a feeling for stability. It's a thing she never had herself, poor girl, so I suppose that's why she always covets it. Perhaps this place will satisfy her for a bit."

"You know her well, Mr. Fenn?"

Ardwyck Fenn shrugged his shoulders.

"Well? I don't know that I'd say that. I've known her over a long period of years. Known her off and on, that is to say."

Craddock looked at him appraisingly. A dark man, heavily built, shrewd eyes behind thick glasses, heavy jowl and chin. Ardwyck Fenn went on:

"The idea is, I gather, from what I read in the newspapers, that this Mrs. Whatever-her-name-was was poisoned by mistake. That the dose was intended for Marina. Is that right?"

"Yes. That's it. The dose was in Marina Gregg's cocktail. Mrs. Badcock spilt hers and Marina handed over her drink to her."

"Well, that seems pretty conclusive. I really can't think, though, who would want to poison Marina. Especially as Lynette Brown wasn't there."

"Lynette Brown?" Craddock looked slightly at sea.

Ardwyck Fenn smiled. "If Marina breaks this contract, throws up this part—Lynette will get it and it would mean a good deal to Lynette to get it. But for all that, I don't imagine she'd send some emissary along with poison. Much too melodramatic an idea."

"It seems a little farfetched," said Dermot dryly.

"Ah, you'd be surprised what women will do when they're ambitious," said Ardwyck Fenn. "Mind you, death mayn't have been intended. It may have been just meant to give her a fright— Enough to knock her out but not to finish her."

Craddock shook his head. "It wasn't a borderline dose," he said.

"People make mistakes in doses, quite big ones."

"Is this really your theory?"

"Oh, no, it isn't. It was only a suggestion. I've no theory. I was only an innocent bystander."

"Was Marina Gregg very surprised to see you?"

"Yes, it was a complete surprise to her." He laughed amusedly. "Just couldn't believe her eyes when she saw me coming up the stairs. She gave me a very nice welcome, I must say."

"You hadn't seen her for a long time?"

"Not for four or five years, I should say."

"And some years before that there was a time when you and she were very close friends, I believe?"

"Are you insinuating anything in particular by that remark, Inspector Craddock?"

There was very little change in the voice, but there was something there that had not been there before. A hint of steel, of menace. Dermot felt suddenly that this man would be a very ruthless opponent.

"It would be as well, I think," said Ardwyck Fenn, "that you said exactly what you do mean."

"I'm quite prepared to do so, Mr. Fenn. I have to inquire into the past relations of everyone who was there on that day with Marina Gregg. It seems to have been a matter of common gossip that at the time I have just referred to, you were wildly in love with Marina Gregg."

Ardwyck Fenn shrugged his shoulders.

"One has these infatuations, Inspector. Fortunately, they pass."

"It is said that she encouraged you and that later she turned you down and that you resented the fact."

"It is said—it is said! I suppose you read all that in *Confidential?*"

"It has been told me by quite well-informed and sensible people."

Ardwyck Fenn threw back his head, showing the bull-like line of his neck.

"I had a yen for her at one time, yes," he admitted. "She was a beautiful and attractive woman and still is. To say that I ever threatened her is going a little far. I'm never pleased to be thwarted, Chief-Inspector, and most people who thwart me tend to be sorry that they have done so. But that principle applies mainly in my business life."

"You did, I believe, use your influence to have her dropped from a picture that she was making?"

Fenn shrugged his shoulders.

"She was unsuitable for the role. There was conflict between her and the director. I had money in that picture and I had no intention of jeopardizing it. It was, I assure you, purely a business transaction."

"But perhaps Marina Gregg did not think so?"

"Oh, naturally she did not think so. She would always think that anything like that was personal."

"She actually told certain friends of hers that she was afraid of you, I believe?"

"Did she? How childish. I expect she enjoyed the sensation."

"You think there was no need for her to be afraid of you?"

"Of course not. Whatever personal disappointment I might have had, I soon put it behind me. I've always gone on the principle that where women are concerned there are as good fish in the sea as ever came out of it."

"A very satisfactory way to go through life, Mr. Fenn."

"Yes, I think it is."

"You have a wide knowledge of the moving picture world?"

"I have financial interests in it."

"And therefore you are bound to know a lot about it?"

"Perhaps."

"You are a man whose judgment would be worth listening to. Can you suggest to me any person who is likely to have such a deep grudge against Marina Gregg that they would be willing to do away with her?"

"Probably a dozen," said Ardwyck Fenn, "that is to say, if they didn't have to do anything about it personally. If it was a mere matter of pressing a button in a wall, I dare say there'd be a lot of willing fingers."

"You were there that day. You saw her and talked to her. Do you think that among any of the people who were around you in the brief space of

time—from when you arrived to the moment when Heather Badcock died
—do you think that among them you can suggest—only suggest, mind you,
I'm asking you for nothing more than a guess—anyone who might poison
Marina Gregg?"

"I wouldn't like to say," said Ardwyck Fenn.

"That means that you have some idea?"

"It means that I have nothing to say on that subject. And that, Chief-
Inspector Craddock, is all you'll get out of me."

Chapter Fifteen

DERMOT CRADDOCK looked down at the last name and address he had
written in his notebook. The telephone number had been rung twice for
him, but there had been no response. He tried it now once more. He
shrugged his shoulders, got up and decided to go and see for himself.

Margot Bence's studio was in a cul-de-sac off the Tottenham Court
Road. Beyond the name on a plate on the side of a door, there was little to
identify it and certainly no form of advertising. Craddock groped his way
to the first floor. There was a large notice here painted in black on a white
board. "Margot Bence, Personality Photographer. Please enter."

Craddock entered. There was a small waiting-room but nobody in
charge of it. He stood there hesitating, then cleared his throat in a loud
and theatrical manner. Since that drew no attention, he raised his voice.

"Anybody here?"

He heard a flap of slippers behind a velvet curtain, the curtain was
pushed aside and a young man with exuberant hair and a pink and white
face peered round it.

"Terribly sorry, my dear," he said. "I didn't hear you. I had an absolutely new idea and I was just trying it out."

He pushed the velvet curtain farther aside and Craddock followed him
into an inner room. This proved to be unexpectedly large. It was clearly
the working studio. There were cameras, lights, arc lights, piles of drapery,
screens on wheels.

"Such a mess," said the young man, who was almost as willowy as

Hailey Preston. "But one finds it very hard to work, I think, unless one *does* get into a mess. Now what were you wanting to see us about?"

"I wanted to see Miss Margot Bence."

"Ah, Margot. Now what a pity. If you'd been half an hour earlier you'd have found her here. She's gone off to produce some photographs of models for *Fashion Dream*. You should have rung up, you know, to make an appointment. Margot's terribly busy these days."

"I did ring up. There was no reply."

"Of course," said the young man. "We took the receiver off. I remember now. It disturbed us." He smoothed down a kind of lilac smock that he was wearing. "Can I do anything for you? Make an appointment? I do a lot of Margot's business arrangements for her. You wanted to arrange for some photography somewhere? Private or business?"

"From that point of view, neither," said Dermot Craddock. He handed his card to the young man.

"How perfectly rapturous," said the young man. "C.I.D.! I believe, you know, I've seen pictures of you. Are you one of the Big Four or the Big Five, or is it perhaps the Big Six nowadays? There's so much crime about, they'd have to increase the numbers, wouldn't they? Oh dear, is that disrespectful? I'm afraid it is. I didn't mean to be disrespectful at all. Now, what do you want Margot for—not to arrest her, I hope."

"I just wanted to ask her one or two questions."

"She doesn't do indecent photographs or anything like that," said the young man anxiously. "I hope nobody's been telling you any stories of that kind, because it isn't true. Margot's very artistic. She does a lot of stage work and studio work. But her studies are terribly, terribly pure—almost prudish, I'd say."

"I can tell you quite simply why I want to speak to Miss Bence," said Dermot. "She was recently an eyewitness of a crime that took place near Much Benham, at a village called St. Mary Mead."

"Oh, my dear, of *course!* I know about *that*. Margot came back and told me about it. Hemlock in the cocktails, wasn't it? Something of that kind. So *bleak* it sounded! But all mixed up with St. John's Ambulance, which doesn't seem so bleak, does it? But haven't you already asked Margot questions about that—or was it somebody else?"

"One always finds there are more questions as the case goes on," said Dermot.

"You mean it develops. Yes, I can quite see that. Murder develops. Yes, like a photograph, isn't it?"

"It's very much like a photograph, really," said Dermot. "Quite a good comparison of yours."

"Well, it's very nice of you to say so, I'm sure. Now about Margot. Would you like to get hold of her right away?"

"If you can help me to do so, yes."

"Well, at the moment," said the young man, consulting his watch, "at the moment she'll be outside Keats' house at Hampstead Heath. My car's outside. Shall I run you up there?"

"That would be very kind of you, Mr.—?"

"Jethroe," said the young man, "Johnny Jethroe."

As they went down the stairs Dermot asked:

"Why Keats' house?"

"Well, you know we don't pose fashion photographs in the studio any more. We like them to seem natural, blown about by the wind. And if possible, some rather unlikely background. You know an Ascot frock against Wandsworth Prison, or a frivolous little suit outside a poet's house."

Mr. Jethroe drove rapidly but skilfully up Tottenham Court Road, through Camden Town and finally to the neighbourhood of Hampstead Heath. On the pavement near Keats' house a pretty little scene was being enacted. A slim girl wearing diaphanous organdie was standing clutching an immense black hat. On her knees, a little way behind her, a second girl was holding the first girl's skirt well pulled back so that it clung around her knees and legs. In a deep hoarse voice a girl with a camera was directing operations.

"For goodness' sake, Jane, get your behind down. It's showing behind her right knee. Get down flatter. That's it. No, more to the left. That's right. Now you're masked by the bush. That'll do. Hold it. We'll have one more. Both hands on the back of the hat this time. Head up. Good—now turn round, Elsie. Bend over. More. Bend! *Bend*, you've got to pick up that cigarette case. That's right. That's *heaven!* Got it! Now move over to the left. Same pose, only just turn your head over your shoulder. So."

"I can't see what you want to go taking photographs of my behind for," said the girl called Elsie rather sulkily.

"It's a lovely behind, dear. It looks smashing," said the photographer. "And when you turn your head, your chin comes up like the rising moon over a mountain. I don't think we need bother with any more."

"Hi—Margot," said Mr. Jethroe.

She turned her head. "Oh, it's you. What are you doing here?"

"I brought someone along to see you. Chief Detective-Inspector Crad-dock, C.I.D."

The girl's eyes turned swiftly on to Dermot. He thought they had a wary, searching look, but that, as he well knew, was nothing extraor-dinary. It was a fairly common reaction to detective-inspectors. She was a thin girl, all elbows and angles, but was an interesting shape for all that. A heavy curtain of black hair fell down on either side of her face. She looked dirty as well as sallow and not particularly prepossessing to his eyes. But he acknowledged that there was character there. She raised her eyebrows which were slightly raised by art already and remarked:

"And what can I do for you, Detective-Inspector Craddock?"

"How do you do, Miss Bence. I wanted to ask you if you would be so kind as to answer a few questions about that very unfortunate business at Gossington Hall, near Much Benham. You went there, if I remember, to take some photographs."

The girl nodded. "Of course. I remember quite well." She shot him a quick searching look. "I didn't see you there. Surely it was somebody else. Inspector—Inspector—"

"Inspector Cornish?" said Dermot.

"That's right."

"We were called in later."

"You're from Scotland Yard?"

"Yes."

"You butted in and took over from the local people. Is that it?"

"Well, it isn't quite a question of butting in, you know. It's up to the chief constable of the county to decide whether he thinks it'll be better handled by us."

"What makes him decide?"

"It very often turns on whether the case has a local background or whether it's a more—universal one. Sometimes, perhaps, an international one."

"And he decided, did he, that this was an international one?"

"Transatlantic, perhaps, would be a better word."

"They've been hinting that in the papers, haven't they? Hinting that the killer, whoever he was, was out to get Marina Gregg and got some wretched local woman by mistake. Is that true or is it a bit of publicity for their film?"

"I'm afraid there isn't much doubt about it, Miss Bence."

"What do you want to ask me? Have I got to come to Scotland Yard?"

He shook his head. "Not unless you like. We'll go back to your studio if you prefer."

"All right, let's do that. My car's just up the street."

She walked rapidly along the footpath. Dermot went with her. Jethroe called after them.

"So long, darling, I won't butt in. I'm sure you and the inspector are going to talk big secrets." He joined the two models on the pavement and began an animated discussion with them.

Margot got into the car, unlocked the door on the other side, and Dermot Craddock got in beside her. She said nothing at all during the drive back to Tottenham Court Road. She turned down the cul-de-sac and at the bottom of it drove through an open doorway.

"Got my own parking place here," she remarked. "It's a furniture depository place really, but they rent me a bit of space. Parking a car is one of the big headaches in London, as you probably know only too well, though I don't suppose you deal with traffic, do you?"

"No, that's not one of my troubles."

"I should think murder would be infinitely preferable," said Margot Bence.

She led the way back to the studio, motioned him to a chair, offered him a cigarette and sank down on the large ottoman opposite him. From behind the curtain of dark hair she looked at him in a sombre questioning way.

"Shoot, stranger," she said.

"You were taking photographs on the occasion of this death, I understand."

"Yes."

"You'd been engaged professionally?"

"Yes. They wanted someone to do a few specialized shots. I do quite a lot of that stuff. I do some work for film studios sometimes, but this time I was just taking photographs of the fête, and afterwards a few shots of special people being greeted by Marina Gregg and Jason Rudd. Local notabilities or other personalities. That sort of thing."

"Yes. I understand that. You had your camera on the stairs, I understand?"

"A part of the time, yes. I got a very good angle from there. You get people coming up the stairs below you and you could swivel round and get Marina shaking hands with them. You could get a lot of different angles without having to move much."

"I know, of course, that you answered some questions at the time as to whether you'd seen anything unusual, anything that might be helpful. They were general questions."

"Have you got more specialized ones?"

"A little more specialized, I think. You had a good view of Marina Gregg from where you were standing?"

She nodded. "Excellent."

"And of Jason Rudd?"

"Occasionally. But he was moving about more. Drinks and things and introducing people to one another. The locals to the celebrities. That kind of thing, I should imagine. I didn't see this Mrs. Baddeley—"

"Badcock."

"Sorry, Badcock. I didn't see her drink the fatal draught or anything like that. In fact, I don't think I really know which she was."

"Do you remember the arrival of the mayor?"

"Oh, yes. I remember the mayor all right. He had on his chain and his robes of office. I got one of him coming up the stairs—a close-up—rather a cruel profile, and then I got him shaking hands with Marina."

"Then you can fix that time at least in your mind. Mrs. Badcock and her husband came up the stairs to Marina Gregg immediately in front of him."

She shook her head. "Sorry. I still don't remember her."

"That doesn't matter so much. I presume that you had a pretty good view of Marina Gregg and that you had your eyes on her and were pointing the camera at her fairly often."

"Quite right. Most of the time. I'd wait till I got just the right moment."

"Do you know a man called Ardwyck Fenn by sight?"

"Oh, yes. I know him well enough. Television network—films, too."

"Did you take a photograph of him?"

"Yes, I got him coming up with Lola Brewster."

"That would be just after the mayor?"

She thought a minute then agreed. "Yes, about then."

"Did you notice that about that time Marina Gregg seemed to feel suddenly ill? Did you notice any unusual expression on her face?"

Margot Bence leant forward, opened a cigarette box and took out a cigarette. She lit it. Although she had not answered, Dermot did not press her. He waited, wondering what it was she was turning over in her mind. She said at last, abruptly:

"Why do you ask me that?"

"Because it's a question to which I am very anxious to have an answer—a reliable answer."

"Do you think my answer's likely to be reliable?"

"Yes I do, as a matter of fact. You must have the habit of watching people's faces very closely, waiting for certain expressions, certain propitious moments."

She nodded her head.

"Did you see anything of that kind?"

"Somebody else saw it too, did they?"

"Yes. More than one person, but it's been described rather differently."

"How did the other people describe it?"

"One person has told me that she was taken faint."

Margot Bence shook her head slowly.

"Someone else said that she was startled." He paused a moment then went on, "And somebody else describes her as having a frozen look on her face."

"Frozen," said Margot Bence thoughtfully.

"Do you agree to that last statement?"

"I don't know. Perhaps."

"It was put rather more fancifully still," said Dermot. "In the words of the late poet, Tennyson. *The mirror crack'd from side to side; 'The doom has come upon me,' cried the Lady of Shalott.*"

"There wasn't any mirror," said Margot Bence, "but if there had been, it might have cracked." She got up abruptly. "Wait," she said. "I'll do something better than describe it to you. I'll show you."

She pushed aside the curtain at the far end and disappeared for some moments. He could hear her uttering impatient mutterings under her breath.

"What hell it is," she said as she emerged again, "one never can find things when one wants them. I've got it now though."

She came across to him and put a glossy print into his hand. He looked down at it. It was a very good photograph of Marina Gregg. Her hand was clasped in the hand of a woman standing in front of her, and therefore with her back to the camera. But Marina Gregg was not looking at the woman. Her eyes stared not quite into the camera but slightly obliquely to the left. The interesting thing to Dermot Craddock was that the face expressed nothing whatever. There was no fear on it, no pain. The woman portrayed there was staring at something, something she saw, and the emotion it aroused in her was so great that she was physically unable to express it by any kind of facial expression. Dermot Craddock had seen such a look once on a man's face, a man who a second later had been shot dead. . . .

"Satisfied?" asked Margot Bence.

Craddock gave a deep sigh. "Yes, thank you. It's hard, you know, to make up one's mind if witnesses are exaggerating, if they are imagining they see things. But that's not so in this case. There *was* something to see and she saw it." He asked, "Can I keep this picture?"

"Oh, yes, you can have the print. I've got the negative."

"You didn't send it to the press?"

Margot Bence shook her head.

"I rather wonder why you didn't. After all, it's rather a dramatic photograph. Some paper might have paid a good price for it."

"I wouldn't care to do that," said Margot Bence. "If you look into somebody's soul by accident, you feel a bit embarrassed about cashing in."

"Did you know Marina Gregg at all?"

"No."

"You come from the States, don't you?"

"I was born in England. I was trained in America, though. I came over here, oh, about three years ago."

Dermot Craddock nodded. He had known the answers to his questions. They had been waiting for him among the other lists of information on his office table. The girl seemed straightforward enough. He asked:

"Where did you train?"

"Reingarden Studios. I was with Andrew Quilp for a time. He taught me a lot."

"Reingarden Studios and Andrew Quilp." Dermot Craddock was suddenly alert. The names struck a chord of remembrance.

"You lived in Seven Springs, didn't you?"

She looked amused.

"You seem to know a lot about me. Have you been checking up?"

"You're a well-known photographer, Miss Bence. There have been articles written about you, you know. Why did you come to England?"

She shrugged her shoulders.

"Oh, I like a change. Besides, as I told you, I was born in England although I went to the States as a child."

"Quite a young child, I think."

"Five years old, if you're interested."

"I am interested. I think, Miss Bence, you could tell me a little more than you have done."

Her face hardened. She stared at him.

"What do you mean by that?"

Dermot Craddock looked at her and risked it. It wasn't much to go on. Reingarden Studios and Andrew Quilp and the name of one town. But he felt rather as if old Miss Marple were at his shoulder egging him on.

"I think you knew Marina Gregg better than you say."

She laughed. "Prove it. You're imagining things."

"Am I? I don't think I am. And it *could* be proved, you know, with a little time and care. Come now, Miss Bence, hadn't you better admit the truth? Admit that Marina Gregg adopted you as a child and that you lived with her for four years."

She drew her breath in sharply with a hiss.

"You nosy bastard!" she said.

It startled him a little, it was such a contrast to her former manner. She got up, shaking her black head of hair.

"All right, all right, it's true enough! Yes. Marina Gregg took me over to America with her. My mother had eight kids. She lived in a slum somewhere. She was one of hundreds of people, I suppose, who write to any film actress they happen to see or hear about, spilling a hard-luck story, begging her to adopt the child a mother couldn't give advantages to. Oh, it's such a sickening business, all of it."

"There were three of you," said Dermot. "Three children adopted at different times from different places."

"That's right. Me and Rod and Angus. Angus was older than I was, Rod was practically a baby. We had a wonderful life. Oh, a wonderful life! All the advantages!" Her voice rose mockingly. "Clothes and cars and a wonderful house to live in and people to look after us, good schooling and teaching, and delicious food. Everything piled on! And she herself, our 'Mom.' 'Mom' in inverted commas, playing her part, crooning over us, being photographed with us! Ah, such a pretty sentimental picture."

"But she really wanted children," said Dermot Craddock. "That was real enough, wasn't it? It wasn't just a publicity stunt."

"Oh, perhaps. Yes, I think that was true. She wanted children. But she didn't want *us!* Not really. It was just a glorious bit of play-acting. 'My family' 'So lovely to have a family of my own.' And Izzy let her do it. He ought to have known better."

"Izzy was Isidore Wright?"

"Yes, her third husband or her fourth, I forget which. He was a wonderful man really. He understood her, I think, and he was worried sometimes about us. He was kind to us, but he didn't pretend to be a father. He didn't feel like a father. He only cared really about his own writing.

I've read some of his things since. They're sordid and rather cruel, but they're powerful. I think people will call him a great writer one day."

"And this went on until when?"

Margot Bence's smile curved suddenly. "Until she got sick of that particular bit of play-acting. No, that's not quite true. . . . She found she was going to have a child of her own."

"And then?"

She laughed with sudden bitterness "Then we'd had it! We weren't wanted any more. We'd done very well as little stop-gaps, but she didn't care a damn about us really, not a damn. Oh, she pensioned us off very prettily. With a home and a foster-mother and money for our education and a nice little sum to start us off in the world. Nobody can say that she didn't behave correctly and handsomely. But she'd never wanted us—all she wanted was a child of her own."

"You can't blame her for that," said Dermot gently.

"I don't blame her for wanting a child of her own, no! But what about us? She took us away from our own parents, from the places where we belonged. My mother sold me for a mess of pottage, if you like, but she didn't sell me for advantage to herself. She sold me because she was a damn silly woman who thought I'd get 'advantages' and 'education' and have a wonderful life. She thought she was doing the best for me. Best for me? If she only knew."

"You're still very bitter, I see."

"No, I'm not bitter now. I've got over that. I'm bitter because I'm remembering, because I've gone back to those days. We were all pretty bitter."

"All of you?"

"Well, not Rod. Rod never cared about anything. Besides, he was rather small. But Angus felt like I did, only I think he was more revengeful. He said that when he was grown up he would go and kill that baby she was going to have."

"You knew about the baby?"

"Oh, of course I knew. And everyone knows what happened. She went crazy with rapture about having it, and then when it was born it was an idiot! Served her right. Idiot or no idiot, she didn't want us back again."

"You hate her very much?"

"Why shouldn't I hate her? She did the worst thing to me that anyone can do to anyone else. Let them believe that they're loved and wanted and then show them that it's all a sham."

"What happened to your two—I'll call them brothers, for the sake of convenience."

"Oh, we all drifted apart later. Rod's farming somewhere in the Middle West. He's got a happy nature, and always had. Angus? I don't know. I lost sight of him."

"Did he continue to feel revengeful?"

"I shouldn't think so," said Margot. "It's not the sort of thing you can go on feeling. The last time I saw him, he said he was going on the stage. I don't know whether he did."

"You've remembered, though," said Dermot.

"Yes. I've remembered," said Margot Bence.

"Was Marina Gregg surprised to see you on that day or did she make the arrangements for your photography on purpose to please you?"

"She?" The girl smiled scornfully. "She knew nothing about the arrangements. I was curious to see her, so I did a bit of lobbying to get the job. As I say, I've got some influence with studio people. I wanted to see what she looked like nowadays." She stroked the surface of the table. "She didn't even recognize me. What do you think of that? I was with her for four years. From five years old to nine, and she didn't recognize me."

"Children change," said Dermot Craddock; "they change so much that you'd hardly know them. I have a niece I met the other day and I assure you I'd have passed her in the street."

"Are you saying that to make me feel better? I don't care really. Oh, what the hell, let's be honest. I do care. I did. She had a magic, you know. Marina! A wonderful calamitous magic that took hold of you. You can hate a person and still mind."

"You didn't tell her who you were?"

She shook her head. "No, I didn't tell her. That's the last thing I'd do."

"Did you try and poison her, Miss Bence?"

Her mood changed. She got up and laughed.

"What ridiculous questions you do ask! But I suppose you have to. It's part of your job. No, I can assure you I didn't kill her."

"That isn't what I asked you, Miss Bence."

She looked at him, frowning, puzzled.

"Marina Gregg," he said, "is still alive."

"For how long?"

"What do you mean by that?"

"Don't you think it's likely, Inspector, that someone will try again, and this time—this time, perhaps—they'll succeed?"

"Precautions will be taken."

"Oh, I'm sure they will. The adoring husband will look after her, won't he, and make sure that no harm comes to her?"

He was listening carefully to the mockery in her voice.

"What did you mean when you said you didn't ask me that?" she said, harking back suddenly.

"I asked you if you tried to kill her. You replied that you didn't kill her. That's true enough, but someone died, someone was killed."

"You mean I tried to kill Marina and instead I killed Mrs. What's-her-name. If you'd like me to make it quite clear, I didn't try to poison Marina and I didn't poison Mrs. Badcock."

"But you know perhaps who did?"

"I don't know anything, Inspector, I assure you."

"But you have some idea?"

"Oh, one always has ideas." She smiled at him, a mocking smile. "Among so many people it might be, mightn't it, the black-haired robot of a secretary, the elegant Hailey Preston, servants, maids, a masseur, the hairdresser, someone at the studios, so many people—*and one of them mightn't be what he or she pretended to be?*"

Then as he took an unconscious step towards her, she shook her head vehemently.

"Relax, Inspector," she said. "I'm only teasing you. Somebody's out for Marina's blood, but who it is I've no idea. Really. I've no idea at all."

Chapter Sixteen

AT No. 16 Aubrey Close, young Mrs. Baker was talking to her husband. Jim Baker, a big good-looking blond giant of a man, was intent on assembling a model construction unit.

"Neighbours!" said Cherry. She gave a toss of her black curly head. "Neighbours!" she said again with venom.

She carefully lifted the frying pan from the stove, then neatly shot its contents on to two plates, one rather fuller than the other. She placed the fuller one before her husband.

"Mixed grill," she announced.

Jim looked up and sniffed appreciatively.

"That's something like," he said. "What is today? My birthday?"

"You have to be well nourished," said Cherry.

She was looking very pretty in a cerise and white striped apron with little frills on it. Jim Baker shifted the component parts of a stratocruiser to make room for his meal. He grinned at his wife and asked:

"Who says so?"

"My Miss Marple for one!" said Cherry. "And if it comes to that," she added, sitting down opposite Jim and pulling her plate towards her, "I should say she could do with a bit more solid nourishment herself. That old cat of a White Knight of hers, gives her nothing but carbohydrates. It's all she can think of! A 'nice custard,' a 'nice bread and butter pudding,' a 'nice macaroni cheese.' Squashy puddings with pink sauce. And gas, gas, gas, all day. Talks her head off, she does."

"Oh, well," said Jim vaguely, "it's invalid diet, I suppose."

"Invalid diet!" said Cherry and snorted. "Miss Marple isn't an invalid—she's just old. Always interfering, too."

"Who, Miss Marple?"

"No. That Miss Knight. Telling me how to do things! She even tries to tell me how to cook! I know a lot more about cooking than she does."

"You're tops for cooking, Cherry," said Jim appreciatively.

"There's something to cooking," said Cherry, "something you can get your teeth into."

Jim laughed. "I'm getting my teeth into this all right. Why did your Miss Marple say that I needed nourishing? Did she think I looked run-down, the other day when I came in to fix that bathroom shelf?"

Cherry laughed. "I'll tell you what she said to me. She said 'You've got a handsome husband, my dear. A very handsome husband.' Sounds like one of those period books they read aloud on the telly."

"I hope you agreed with her?" said Jim with a grin.

"I said you were all right."

"All right, indeed! That's a nice lukewarm way of talking."

"And then she said, 'You must take care of your husband, my dear. Be sure you feed him properly. Men need plenty of good meat meals, well cooked.'"

"Hear, hear!"

"And she told me to be sure and prepare fresh food for you and not buy ready-made pies and things and slip them in the oven to warm up. Not that I do that often," added Cherry virtuously.

"You can't do it too seldom for me," said Jim. "They don't taste a bit the same."

"So long as you notice what you eat," said Cherry, "and aren't so taken up with those stratocruisers and things you're always building. And don't tell me you bought that set as a Christmas present for your nephew Michael. You bought it so that you could play with it yourself."

"He's not quite old enough for it yet," said Jim apologetically.

"And I suppose you're going on dithering about with it all the evening. What about some music? Did you get that new record you were talking about?"

"Yes, I did. Tchaikovski 1812."

"That's the loud one with the battle, isn't it?" said Cherry. She made a face. "Our Mrs. Hartwell won't half like that! Neighbours! I'm fed up with neighbours. Always grousing and complaining. I don't know which is the worst. The Hartwells or the Barnabys. The Hartwells start rapping on the wall as early as twenty to eleven sometimes. It's a bit thick! After all, even the telly and the B.B.C. go on later than that. Why shouldn't we have a bit of music if we like? And always asking us to turn it down low."

"You can't turn these things down low," said Jim with authority. "You don't get the tone unless you've got the volume. Everyone knows that. It's absolutely recognized in musical circles. And what about their cat—always coming over into our garden, digging up the beds, just when I've got it nice."

"I tell you what, Jim. I'm fed up with this place."

"You didn't mind your neighbours up in Huddersfield," remarked Jim.

"It wasn't the same there," said Cherry. "I mean, you're all independent there. If you're in trouble, somebody'd give you a hand and you'd give a hand to them. But you don't interfere. There's something about a new estate like this that makes people look sideways at their neighbours. Because we're all new, I suppose. The amount of backbiting and tale-telling and writing to the council and one thing and another round here beats me! People in real towns are too busy for it."

"You may have something there, my girl."

"D'you like it here, Jim?"

"The job's all right. And after all, this is a brand-new house. I wish there was a bit more room in it so that I could spread myself a bit more. It would be fine if I could have a workshop."

"I thought it was lovely at first," said Cherry, "but now I'm not so sure. The house is all right and I love the blue paint and the bathroom's nice, but I don't like the people and the *feeling* round here. Some of the people are nice enough. Did I tell you that Lily Price and that Harry of hers have broken off? It was a funny business that day in that house they went to look over. You know when she more or less fell out of the window. She said Harry just stood there like a stuck pig."

"I'm glad she's broken off with him. He's a no-good if I ever saw one," said Jim.

"No good marrying a chap just because a baby's on the way," said Cherry. "He didn't want to marry her, you know. He's not a very nice fellow. Miss Marple said he wasn't," she added thoughtfully. "She spoke to Lily about him. Lily thought she was crackers."

"Miss Marple? I didn't know she'd ever seen him?"

"Oh, yes, she was round here walking the day she fell down and Mrs. Badcock picked her up and took her into her house. Do you think Arthur and Mrs. Bain will make a match of it?"

Jim frowned as he picked up a bit of stratocruiser and consulted the instructional diagram.

"I do wish you'd listen when I'm talking," said Cherry.

"What did you say?"

"Arthur Badcock and Mary Bain."

"For the Lord's sake, Cherry, his wife's only just dead! You women! I've heard he's in a terrible state of nerves still—jumps if you speak to him."

"I wonder why. . . . I shouldn't have thought he'd take it that way, would you?"

"Can you clear off this end of the table a bit?" said Jim, relinquishing even a passing interest in the affairs of his neighbours. "Just so that I can spread some of these pieces out a bit."

Cherry heaved an exasperated sigh.

"To get any attention round here, you have to be a super jet, or a turbo prop," she said bitterly. "You and your constructional models!"

She piled the tray with the remains of supper and carried it over to the sink. She decided not to wash up, a necessity of daily life she always put off as long as possible. Instead, she piled everything into the sink, haphazard, slipped on a corduroy jacket and went out of the house, pausing to call over her shoulder:

"I'm just going to slip along to see Gladys Dixon. I want to borrow one of her *Vogue* patterns."

"All right, old girl." Jim bent over his model.

Casting a venomous look at her next-door neighbour's front door as she passed, Cherry went round the corner into Blenheim Close and stopped at

No. 16. The door was open and Cherry tapped on it and went into the hall calling out:

"Is Gladdy about?"

"Is that you, Cherry?" Mrs. Dixon looked out of the kitchen. "She's upstairs in her room, dressmaking."

"Right, I'll go up."

Cherry went upstairs to a small bedroom in which Gladys, a plump girl with a plain face, was kneeling on the floor, her cheeks flushed, and several pins in her mouth, tacking up a paper pattern.

"Hello, Cherry. Look, I got a lovely bit of stuff at Harper's sale in Much Benham. I'm going to do that crossover pattern with frills again, the one I did in Terylene before."

"That'll be nice," said Cherry.

Gladys rose to her feet, panting a little.

"Got indigestion now," she said.

"You oughtn't to do dressmaking right after supper," said Cherry, "bending over like that."

"I suppose I ought to slim a bit," said Gladys. She sat down on the bed.

"Any news from the studios?" asked Cherry, always avid for film news.

"Nothing much. There's a lot of talk still. Marina Gregg came back on the set yesterday—and she created something frightful."

"What about?"

"She didn't like the taste of her coffee. You know, they have coffee in the middle of the morning. She took one sip and said there was something wrong with it. Which was nonsense, of course. There couldn't have been. It comes in a jug straight from the canteen. Of course I always put hers in a special china cup, rather posh—different from the others—but it's the same coffee. So there couldn't have been anything wrong with it, could there?"

"Nerves, I suppose," said Cherry. "What happened?"

"Oh, nothing. Mr. Rudd just calmed everyone down. He's wonderful that way. He took the coffee from her and poured it down the sink."

"That seems to be rather stupid," said Cherry slowly.

"Why—what do you mean?"

"Well, if there was anything wrong with it—now nobody will ever know."

"Do you think there really might have been?" asked Gladys, looking alarmed.

"Well"—Cherry shrugged her shoulders—"there was something wrong with her cocktail the day of the fête wasn't there, so why not the coffee? If at first you don't succeed, try, try, try again."

Gladys shivered.

"I don't half like it, Cherry," she said. "Somebody's got it in for her all right. She's had more letters, you know, threatening her—and there was that bust business the other day."

"What bust business?"

"A marble bust. On the set. It's a corner of a room in some Austrian palace or other. Funny name like Shotbrown. Pictures and china and marble busts. This one was up on a bracket—suppose it hadn't been pushed back enough. Anyway, a heavy lorry went past out in the road and jarred it off—right on to the chair where Marina sits for her big scene with Count Somebody-or-other. Smashed it to smithereens! Lucky they weren't shooting at the time. Mr. Rudd, he said not to say a word about it to her, and he put another chair there, and when she came yesterday and asked why the chair had been changed, he said the other chair was the wrong period, and this gave a better angle for the camera. But he didn't half like it—I can tell you that."

The two girls looked at each other.

"It's exciting in a way," said Cherry slowly. "And yet—it isn't. . . ."

"I think I'm going to give up working in the canteen at the studios," said Gladys.

"Why? Nobody wants to poison you or drop marble busts on your head!"

"No. But it's not always the person who's meant to get done in who gets done in. It may be someone else. Like Heather Badcock that day."

"True enough," said Cherry.

"You know," said Gladys, "I've been thinking. I was up at the Hall that day, helping. I was quite close to them at the time."

"When Heather died?"

"No, when she spilt the cocktail. All down her dress. A lovely dress it was, too, royal blue nylon taffeta. She'd got it quite new for the occasion. And it was funny."

"What was funny?"

"I didn't think anything of it at the time. But it does seem funny when I think it over."

Cherry looked at her expectantly. She accepted the adjective "funny" in the sense that it was meant. It was not intended humorously.

"For goodness' sake, what was funny?" she demanded.

"I'm almost sure she did it on purpose."

"Spilt the cocktail on purpose?"

"Yes. And I do think that was funny, don't you?"

"On a brand-new dress? I don't believe it."

"I wonder now," said Gladys, "what Arthur Badcock will do with all Heather's clothes. That dress would clean all right. Or I could take out half a breadth, it's a lovely full skirt. Do you think Arthur Badcock would think it very awful of me if I wanted to buy it off him? It would need hardly any alteration—and it's lovely stuff."

"You wouldn't"—Cherry hesitated—"mind?"

"Mind what?"

"Well—having a dress that a woman had died in—I mean died that way. . . ."

Gladys stared at her.

"I hadn't thought of that," she admitted. She considered for a moment or two. Then she cheered up.

"I can't see that it really matters," she said. "After all, every time you buy something secondhand, somebody's usually worn it who has died, haven't they?"

"Yes. But it's not quite the same."

"I think you're being fanciful," said Gladys. "It's a lovely bright shade of blue, and really expensive stuff. About that funny business," she continued thoughtfully, "I think I'll go up to the hall tomorrow morning on my way to work and have a word with Mr. Giuseppe about it."

"Is he the Italian butler?"

"Yes. He's awfully handsome. Flashing eyes. He's got a terrible temper. When we go and help there, he chivvies us girls something terrible." She giggled. "But none of us really mind. He can be awfully nice sometimes. . . . Anyway, I might just tell him about it, and ask him what I ought to do."

"I don't see that you've got anything to tell," said Cherry.

"Well—it was funny," said Gladys, defiantly clinging to her favourite adjective.

"I think," said Cherry, "that you just want an excuse to go and talk to Mr. Giuseppe—and you'd better be careful, my girl. You know what these Italians are like! Affiliation orders all over the place. Hot-blooded and passionate, that's what they are."

Gladys sighed ecstatically.

Cherry looked at her friend's fat, slightly spotty face and decided that her warnings were unnecessary. Mr. Giuseppe, she thought, would have better fish to fry elsewhere.

II

"Aha!" said Dr. Haydock, "unravelling, I see."

He looked from Miss Marple to a pile of fluffy, white, fleecy wool.

"You advised me to try unravelling if I couldn't knit," said Miss Marple.

"You seem to have been very thorough about it."

"I made a mistake in the pattern right at the beginning. That made the whole thing go out of proportion, so I've had to unravel it all. It's a very elaborate pattern, you see."

"What are elaborate patterns to you? Nothing at all."

"I ought really, I suppose, with my bad eyesight, to stick to plain knitting."

"You'd find that very boring. Well, I'm flattered that you took my advice."

"Don't I always take your advice, Dr. Haydock?"

"You do when it suits you," said Dr. Haydock.

"Tell me, Doctor, was it really knitting you had in mind when you gave me that advice?"

"How are you getting on with unravelling the murder?" he asked.

He met the twinkle in her eyes and twinkled back at her.

"I'm afraid my faculties aren't quite what they were," said Miss Marple, shaking her head with a sigh.

"Nonsense," said Dr. Haydock. "Don't tell me you haven't formed some conclusions."

"Of course I have formed conclusions. Very definite ones."

"Such as?" asked Haydock inquiringly.

"If the cocktail glass was tampered with that day—and I don't see quite how that could have been done—"

"Might have had the stuff ready in an eyedropper," suggested Haydock.

"You are so professional," said Miss Marple admiringly. "But even then it seems to me so very peculiar that nobody saw it happen."

"Murder should not only be done, but be seen to be done! Is that it?"

"You know exactly what I mean," said Miss Marple.

"That was a chance the murderer had to take," said Haydock.

"Oh, quite so. I'm not disputing that for a moment. But there were, I have found by inquiry and adding up the persons, at least eighteen to

THE MIRROR CRACK'D 133

twenty people on the spot. It seems to me that among twenty people somebody must have seen that action occur."

Haydock nodded. "One would think so, certainly. But obviously no one
did."

"I wonder," said Miss Marple thoughtfully.

"What have you got in mind exactly?"

"Well, there are three possibilities. I'm assuming that at least one person would have seen something. One out of twenty. I think it's only reasonable to assume that."

"I think you're begging the question," said Haydock, "and I can see
looming ahead one of those terrible exercises in probability where six men
have white hats and six men have black and you have to work it out by
mathematics how likely it is that the hats will get mixed up and in what
proportion. If you start thinking about things like that, you would go
round the bend. Let me assure you of that!"

"I wasn't thinking of anything like that," said Miss Marple. "I was just
thinking of what is likely—"

"Yes," said Haydock thoughtfully, "you're very good at that. You always have been."

"It is likely, you know," said Miss Marple, "that out of twenty people
one at least should be an observant one."

"I give in," said Haydock. "Let's have the three possibilities."

"I'm afraid I'll have to put them rather sketchily," said Miss Marple. "I
haven't quite thought it out. Inspector Craddock, and probably Frank
Cornish before him, will have questioned everybody who was there, so the
natural thing would be that whoever saw anything of the kind would
have said so at once."

"Is that one of the possibilities?"

"No, of course it isn't," said Miss Marple, "because it hasn't happened.
What you have to account for is if one person did see something, why
didn't that person say so?"

"I'm listening."

"Possibility One," said Miss Marple, her cheeks going pink with animation. "The person who saw it didn't realize what they had seen. That
would mean, of course, that it would have to be rather a stupid person.
Someone, let us say, who can use their eyes but not their brains. The sort
of person who, if you asked them 'Did you see anyone put anything in
Marina Gregg's glass?' would answer, 'Oh, no,' but if you said 'Did you
see anyone put their hand over the top of Marina Gregg's glass?' would
say 'Oh, yes, of course I did!'"

Haydock laughed. "I admit," he said, "that one never quite allows for the moron in our midst. All right. I grant you Possibility One. The moron saw it, the moron didn't grasp what the action meant. And the second possibility?"

"This one's very farfetched, but I do think it is just a possibility. It might have been a person whose action in putting something in a glass was natural."

"Wait, wait, explain that a little more clearly."

"It seems to me nowadays," said Miss Marple, "that people are always adding things to what they eat and drink. In my young day it was considered to be very bad manners to take medicines with one's meals. It was on a par with blowing your nose at the dinner table. It just wasn't done. If you had to take pills or capsules, or a spoonful of something, you went out of the room to do so. That's not the case now. When staying with my nephew Raymond, I observed some of his guests seemed to arrive with quite a quantity of little bottles of pills and tablets. They take them with food, or before food, or after food. They keep aspirins and such things in their handbags and take them the whole time—with cups of tea or with their after-dinner coffee. You understand what I mean?"

"Oh, yes," said Dr. Haydock, "I've got your meaning now and it's interesting. You mean that someone—" he stopped. "Let me have it in your own words."

"I meant," said Miss Marple, "that it would be quite possible, audacious but possible, for someone to pick up that glass which as soon as it was in his hand or her hand, of course, would be assumed to be his or her own drink and to add whatever was added quite openly. In that case, you see, people wouldn't think twice of it."

"He—or she—couldn't be sure of that, though," Haydock pointed out.

"No," agreed Miss Marple, "it would be a gamble, a risk—but it could happen. And then," she went on, "there's the third possibility."

"Possibility One, a moron," said the doctor. "Possibility Two, a gambler —what's Possibility Three?"

"Somebody saw what happened and has held their tongue deliberately."

Haydock frowned. "For what reason?" he asked. "Are you suggesting blackmail? If so—"

"If so," said Miss Marple, "it's a very dangerous thing to do."

"Yes, indeed." He looked sharply at the placid old lady with the white fleecy wool on her lap. "Is the third possibility the one you consider the most probable one?"

"No," said Miss Marple, "I wouldn't go so far as that. I have, at the moment, insufficient grounds. Unless," she added carefully, "someone else gets killed."

"Do you think someone else is going to get killed?"

"I hope not," said Miss Marple, "I trust and pray not. But it so often happens, Dr. Haydock. That's the sad and frightening thing. It so often happens."

Chapter Seventeen

ELLA PUT DOWN the telephone receiver, smiled to herself and came out of the public telephone box. She was pleased with herself.

"Chief-Inspector God Almighty Craddock!" she said to herself. "I'm twice as good as he is at the job. Variations on the theme of: 'Fly, all is discovered!'"

She pictured to herself with a good deal of pleasure the reactions recently suffered by the person at the other end of the line. That faint menacing whisper coming through the receiver. *"I saw you . . ."*

She laughed silently, the corners of her mouth curving up in a feline cruel line. A student of psychology might have watched her with some interest. Never until the last few days had she had this feeling of power. She was hardly aware herself of how much the heady intoxication of it affected her. . . .

She passed the East Lodge and Mrs. Bantry, busy as usual in the garden, waved a hand to her.

"Damn that old woman," thought Ella. She could feel Mrs. Bantry's eyes following her as she walked up the drive.

A phrase came into her head for no particular reason.

The pitcher goes to the well once too often . . .

Nonsense. Nobody could suspect that it was she who had whispered those menacing words. . . .

She sneezed.

"Damn this hay fever," said Ella Zielinsky.

When she came into her office, Jason Rudd was standing by the window.

He wheeled round.

"I couldn't think where you were."

"I had to go and speak to the gardener. There were—" she broke off as she caught sight of his face.

She asked sharply: "What is it?"

His eyes seemed set deeper in his face than ever. All the gaiety of the clown was gone. This was a man under strain. She had seen him under strain before but never looking like this.

She said again, "What is it?"

He held a sheet of paper out to her. "It's the analysis of that coffee. The coffee that Marina complained about and wouldn't drink."

"You sent it to be analyzed?" She was startled. "But you poured it away down the sink. I saw you."

His wide mouth curled up in a smile. "I'm pretty good at sleight of hand, Ella," he said. "You didn't know that, did you? Yes, I poured most of it away, but I kept a little and I took it along to be analyzed."

She looked down at the paper in her hand.

"*Arsenic.*" She sounded incredulous.

"Yes, arsenic."

"So Marina was right about it tasting bitter?"

"She wasn't right about that. Arsenic has no taste. But her instinct was quite right."

"And we thought she was just being hysterical!"

"She is hysterical! Who wouldn't be? She has a woman drop dead at her feet practically. She gets threatening notes—one after another—there's not been anything today, has there?"

Ella shook her head.

"Who plants the damned things? Oh, well, I suppose it's easy enough—all these open windows. Anyone could slip in."

"You must mean we ought to keep the house barred and locked? But it's such hot weather. There's a man posted in the grounds, after all."

"Yes, and I don't want to frighten her more than she's frightened already. Threatening notes don't matter two hoots. But arsenic, Ella, arsenic's different. . . ."

"Nobody could tamper with food here in the house."

"Couldn't they, Ella? Couldn't they?"

"Not without being seen. No unauthorized person—"

He interrupted.

"People will do things for money, Ella."

"Hardly murder!"

"Even that. And they mightn't realize it *was* murder . . . The servants . . ."

"I'm sure the servants are all right."

"Giuseppe now. I doubt if I'd trust Giuseppe very far if it came to the question of money . . . He's been with us some time, of course, but—"

"Must you torture yourself like this, Jason?"

He flung himself down in the chair. He leaned forward, his long arms hanging down between his knees.

"What to do?" he said slowly and softly. "My God, what to do?"

Ella did not speak. She sat there watching him.

"She was happy here," said Jason. He was speaking more to himself than to Ella. He stared down between his knees at the carpet. If he had looked up, the expression on her face might perhaps have surprised him.

"She was happy," he said again. "She hoped to be happy and she *was* happy. She was saying so that day, the day Mrs. What's-her-name—"

"Bantry?"

"Yes. The day Mrs. Bantry came to tea. She said it was 'so peaceful.' She said that at last she'd found a place where she could settle down and be happy and feel secure. My goodness, secure!"

"Happy ever after?" Ella's voice held a slight tone of irony. "Yes, put like that, it sounds just like a fairy story."

"At any rate, she believed it."

"But you didn't," said Ella. "You never thought it would be like that?"

Jason Rudd smiled. "No. I didn't go the whole hog. But I did think that for a while, a year—two years—there might be a period of calm and content. It might have made a new woman of her. It might have given her confidence in herself. She can be happy, you know. When she is happy she's like a child. Just like a child. And now—*this* had to happen to her."

Ella moved restlessly. "Things have to happen to all of us," she said brusquely. "That's the way life is. You just have to take it. Some of us can, some of us can't. She's the kind that can't."

She sneezed.

"Your hay fever bad again?"

"Yes. By the way, Giuseppe's gone to London."

Jason looked faintly surprised.

"To London? Why?"

"Some kind of family trouble. He's got relations in Soho, and one of them's desperately ill. He went to Marina about it and she said it was all right, so I gave him the day off. He'll be back sometime tonight. You don't mind, do you?"

"No," said Jason, "I don't mind. . . ."

He got up and walked up and down.

"If I could take her away . . . now . . . at once."

"Scrap the picture? But just think—"

His voice rose.

"I can't think of anything but Marina. Don't you understand? She's in danger. That's all I can think about."

She opened her mouth impulsively, then closed it.

She gave another muffled sneeze and rose.

"I'd better get my atomizer."

She left the room and went to her bedroom, a word echoing in her mind.

Marina . . . Marina . . . Marina . . . Always Marina . . .

Fury rose up in her. She stilled it. She went into the bathroom and picked up the spray she used.

She inserted the nozzle into one nostril and squeezed.

The warning came a second too late. . . . Her brain recognized the unfamiliar odour of bitter almonds . . . but not in time to paralyze the squeezing fingers. . . .

Chapter Eighteen

FRANK CORNISH replaced the receiver.

"Miss Brewster is out of London for the day," he announced.

"Is she now?" said Craddock.

"Do you think she—"

"I don't know. I shouldn't think so, but I don't know. Ardwyck Fenn?"

"Out. I left word for him to ring you. And Margot Bence, Personality Photographer, has got an assignment somewhere in the country. Her pansy partner didn't know where—or said he didn't. And the butler's hooked it to London."

"I wonder," said Craddock thoughtfully, "if the butler has hooked it for good. I always suspect dying relatives. Why was he suddenly anxious to go to London today?"

"He could have put the cyanide in the atomizer easily enough before he left."

"Anybody could."

"But I think he's indicated. It could hardly be someone from outside."

"Oh, yes, it could. You'd have to judge your moment. You could leave a car in one of the side drives, wait until everyone is in the dining-room, say, and slip in through a window and upstairs. The shrubberies come close up to the house."

"Damn risky."

"This murderer doesn't mind taking risks, you know. That's been apparent all along."

"We've had a man on duty in the grounds."

"I know. One man wasn't enough. So long as it was a question of these anonymous letters, I didn't feel so much urgency. Marina Gregg herself is being well guarded. It never occurred to me that anyone else was in danger. I—"

The telephone rang. Cornish took the call.

"It's the Dorchester. Mr. Ardwyck Fenn is on the line."

He proffered the receiver to Craddock who took it.

"Mr. Fenn? This is Craddock here."

"Ah, yes. I heard you had rung me. I have been out all day."

"I am sorry to tell you, Mr. Fenn, that Miss Zielinsky died this morning —of cyanide poisoning."

"Indeed? I am shocked to hear it. An accident? Or not an accident?"

"Not an accident. Prussic acid had been put in an atomizer she was in the habit of using."

"I see. Yes, I see . . ." There was a short pause. "And why, may I ask, should you ring me about this distressing occurrence?"

"You knew Miss Zielinsky, Mr. Fenn."

"Certainly I knew her. I have known her for some years. But she was not an intimate friend."

"We hoped that you could, perhaps, assist us?"

"In what way?"

"We wondered if you could suggest any motive for her death. She is a stranger in this country. We know very little about her friends and associates and the circumstances of her life."

"I would suggest that Jason Rudd is the person to question about that."

"Naturally. We have done so. But there might be an off-chance that you might know something about her that he does not."

"I'm afraid that is not so. I know next to nothing about Ella Zielinsky except that she was a most capable young woman, and first-class at her job. About her private life I know nothing at all."

"So you have no suggestions to make?"

Craddock was ready for the decisive negative, but to his surprise it did not come. Instead there was a pause. He could hear Ardwyck Fenn breathing rather heavily at the other end.

"Are you still there, Chief-Inspector?"

"Yes, Mr. Fenn. I'm here."

"I have decided to tell you something that may be of assistance to you. When you hear what it is, you will realize that I have every reason to keep it to myself. But I judge that in the end that might be unwise. The facts are these. A couple of days ago I received a telephone call. A voice spoke to me in a whisper. It said—I am quoting now—*I saw you . . . I saw you put the tablets in the glass . . . You didn't know there had been an eyewitness, did you? That's all for now—very soon you will be told what you have to do.*"

Craddock uttered an ejaculation of astonishment.

"Surprising, was it not, Mr. Craddock? I will assure you categorically that the accusation was entirely unfounded. I did *not* put tablets in anybody's glass. I defy anyone to prove that I did. The suggestion is utterly absurd. But it would seem, would it not, that Miss Zielinsky was embarking on blackmail."

"You recognized her voice?"

"You cannot recognize a whisper. But it was Ella Zielinsky all right."

"How do you know?"

"The whisperer sneezed heavily before ringing off. I knew that Miss Zielinsky suffered from hay fever."

"And you think—what?"

"I think that Miss Zielinsky got hold of the wrong person at her first attempt. It seems to me possible that she was more successful later. Blackmail can be a dangerous game."

Craddock pulled himself together.

"I must thank you very much for your statement, Mr. Fenn. As a matter of form, I shall have to check upon your movements today."

"Naturally. My chauffeur will be able to give you precise information."

Craddock rang off and repeated what Fenn had said. Cornish whistled.

"Either that lets him out completely. Or else—"

"Or else it's a magnificent piece of bluff. It could be. He's the kind of man who has the nerve for it. If there's the least chance that Ella Zielinsky left a record of her suspicions, then this taking of the bull by the horns is a magnificent bluff."

"And his alibi?"

"We've come across some very good faked alibis in our time," said Craddock. "He could afford to pay a good sum for one."

II

It was past midnight when Giuseppe returned to Gossington. He took a taxi from Much Benham, as the last train on the branch line to St. Mary Mead had gone.

He was in very good spirits. He paid off the taxi at the gate, and took a short cut through the shrubbery. He opened the back door with his key. The house was dark and silent. Giuseppe shut and bolted the door. As he turned to the stair which led up to his own comfortable suite of bed and bath, he noticed that there was a draught. A window open somewhere, perhaps. He decided not to bother. He went upstairs smiling and fitted a key into his door. He always kept his suite locked. As he turned the key and pushed the door open he felt the pressure of a hard round ring in his back. A voice said, "Put your hands up and don't scream."

Giuseppe threw his hands up quickly. He was taking no chances. Actually there was no chance to take.

The trigger was pressed—once—twice.

Giuseppe fell forward. . . .

Bianca lifted her head from her pillow.

Was that a shot? . . . She was almost sure she had heard a shot. . . . She waited some minutes. Then she decided she had been mistaken and lay down again.

Chapter Nineteen

"IT'S TOO DREADFUL," said Miss Knight. She put down her parcels and gasped for breath.

"Something has happened?" asked Miss Marple.

"I really don't like to tell you about it, dear, I really don't. It might be a shock to you."

"If you don't tell me," said Miss Marple, "somebody else will."

"Dear, dear, that's true enough," said Miss Knight. "Yes, that's terribly true. Everybody talks too much, they say. And I'm sure there's a lot in that. I never repeat anything myself. Very careful I am."

"You were saying," said Miss Marple, "that something rather terrible had happened?"

"It really quite bowled me over," said Miss Knight. "Are you sure you don't feel the draught from that window, dear?"

"I like a little fresh air," said Miss Marple.

"Ah, but we mustn't catch cold, must we?" said Miss Knight archly. "I'll tell you what. I'll just pop out and make you a nice eggnog. We'd like that, wouldn't we?"

"I don't know whether *you* would like it," said Miss Marple. "*I* should be delighted for you to have it if you would like it."

"Now, now," said Miss Knight, shaking her finger, "so fond of our joke, aren't we?"

"But you were going to tell me something," said Miss Marple.

"Well, you mustn't worry about it," said Miss Knight, "and you mustn't let it make you nervous in any way, because I'm sure it's nothing to do with *us*. But with all these American gangsters and things like that, well, I suppose it's nothing to be surprised about."

"Somebody else has been killed," said Miss Marple, "is that it?"

"Oh, that's very sharp of you, dear. I don't know what should put such a thing into your head."

"As a matter of fact," said Miss Marple thoughtfully, "I've been expecting it."

"Oh, really!" exclaimed Miss Knight.

"Somebody always sees something," said Miss Marple, "only sometimes it takes a little while for them to realize what it is they have seen. Who is it who's dead?"

"The Italian butler. He was shot last night."

"I see," said Miss Marple thoughtfully. "Yes, very likely, of course, but I should have thought that he'd have realized before now the importance of what he saw—"

"Really!" exclaimed Miss Knight. "You talk as though you knew all about it. Why should he have been killed?"

"I expect," said Miss Marple thoughtfully, "that he tried to blackmail somebody."

"He went to London yesterday, they say."

"Did he now," said Miss Marple, "that's very interesting, and suggestive too, I think."

Miss Knight departed to the kitchen intent on the concoction of nourishing beverages. Miss Marple remained sitting thoughtfully till disturbed by the loud aggressive humming of the vacuum cleaner, assisted by Cherry's voice singing the latest favourite ditty of the moment, "I Said to You and You Said to Me."

Miss Knight popped her head round the kitchen door.

"Not quite so much noise, please, Cherry," she said. "You don't want to disturb dear Miss Marple, do you? You mustn't be thoughtless, you know."

She shut the kitchen door again as Cherry remarked, either to herself or the world at large, "And who said you could call me Cherry, you old jellybag?" The vacuum continued to whine while Cherry sang in a more subdued voice. Miss Marple called in a high clear voice:

"Cherry, come here a minute."

Cherry switched off the vacuum and opened the drawing-room door.

"I didn't mean to disturb you by singing, Miss Marple."

"Your singing is much pleasanter than the horrid noise that vacuum makes," said Miss Marple, "but I know one has to go with the times. It would be no use on earth asking any of you young people to use the dustpan and brush in the old-fashioned way."

"What, get down on my knees with a dustpan and brush?" Cherry registered alarm and surprise.

"Quite unheard of, I know," said Miss Marple. "Come in and shut the door. I called you because I wanted to talk to you."

Cherry obeyed and came towards Miss Marple looking inquiringly at her.

"We've not much time," said Miss Marple. "That old—Miss Knight, I mean—will come in any moment with an egg drink of some kind."

"Good for you, I expect. It'll pep you up," said Cherry encouragingly.

"Had you heard," asked Miss Marple, "that the butler at Gossington Hall was shot last night?"

"What, the Italian?" demanded Cherry.

"Yes. His name is Giuseppe, I understand."

"No," said Cherry, "I hadn't heard *that*. I heard that Mr. Rudd's secretary had a heart attack yesterday, and somebody said she was actually dead —but I suspect that was just a rumour. Who told you about the butler?"

"Miss Knight came back and told me."

"Of course I haven't seen anyone to speak to this morning," said Cherry, "not before coming along here. I expect the news has only just got round. Was he bumped off?" she demanded.

"That seems to be assumed," said Miss Marple, "whether rightly or wrongly, I don't quite know."

"This is a wonderful place for talk," said Cherry. "I wonder if Gladys got to see him or not," she added thoughtfully.

"Gladys?"

"Oh, a sort of friend of mine. She lives a few doors away. Works in the canteen at the studios."

"And she talked to you about Giuseppe?"

"Well, there was something that struck her as a bit funny, and she was going to ask him what he thought about it. But if you ask me, it was just an excuse—she's a bit sweet on him. Of course he's quite handsome and Italians do have a way with them—I told her to be careful about him, though. You know what Italians are."

"He went to London yesterday," said Miss Marple, "and only returned in the evening, I understand."

"I wonder if she managed to get to see him before he went?"

"Why did she want to see him, Cherry?"

"It was just something which she felt was a bit funny," said Cherry.

Miss Marple looked at her inquiringly. She was able to take the word "funny" at the valuation it usually had for the Gladyses of the neighbourhood.

"She was one of the girls who helped at the party there," explained Cherry. "The day of the fête. You know, when Mrs. Badcock got hers."

"Yes?" Miss Marple was looking more alert than ever, much as a fox terrier might look at a waiting rathole.

"And there was something that she saw that struck her as a bit funny."

"Why didn't she go to the police about it?"

"Well, she didn't really think it meant anything, you see," explained Cherry. "Anyway, she thought she'd better ask Mr. Giuseppe first."

"What was it that she saw that day?"

"Frankly," said Cherry, "what she told me seemed nonsense! I've wondered, perhaps, if she was just putting me off—and what she was going to see Mr. Giuseppe about was something quite different."

"What *did* she say?" Miss Marple was patient and pursuing.

Cherry frowned. "She was talking about Mrs. Badcock and the cocktail and she said she was quite near her at the time. And she said she did it herself."

"Did what herself?"

"Spilt her cocktail all down her dress, and ruined it."

"You mean it was clumsiness?"

"No, not clumsiness. Gladys said she did it on *purpose*—that she *meant* to do it. Well, I mean, that doesn't make sense, does it, however you look at it?"

Miss Marple shook her head, perplexed. "No," she said. "Certainly not —no, I can't see any sense in that."

"She'd got on a new dress, too," said Cherry. "That's how the subject came up. Gladys wondered whether she'd be able to buy it. Said it ought to clean all right but she didn't like to go and ask Mr. Badcock himself. She's very good at dressmaking, Gladys is, and she said it was lovely stuff. Royal blue artificial taffeta; and she said even if the stuff *was* ruined where the cocktail stained it, she could take out a seam—half a breadth say —because it was one of those full skirts."

Miss Marple considered this dressmaking problem for a moment and then set it aside.

"But you think your friend Gladys might have been keeping something back?"

"Well, I just wondered because I don't see if that's all she saw— Heather Badcock deliberately spilling her cocktail over herself—I don't see that there'd be anything to ask Mr. Giuseppe about, do you?"

"No, I don't," said Miss Marple. "But it's always interesting when one doesn't see," she added. "If you don't see what a thing means, you must be looking at it wrong way round, unless of course you haven't got full information. Which is probably the case here." She sighed. "It's a pity she didn't go straight to the police."

The door opened and Miss Knight bustled in holding a tall tumbler with a delicious pale yellow froth on top.

"Now here you are, dear," she said, "a nice little treat. We're going to enjoy this."

She pulled forward a little table and placed it beside her employer. Then she turned a glance on Cherry. "The vacuum cleaner," she said coldly, "is left in a most difficult position in the hall. I nearly fell over it. *Anyone* might have an accident."

"Righty-ho," said Cherry. "I'd better get on with things."

She left the room.

"Really," said Miss Knight, "that Mrs. Baker! I'm continually having to speak to her about something or other. Leaving vacuum cleaners all over the place and coming in here chattering to you when you want to be quiet."

"I called her in," said Miss Marple. "I wanted to speak to her."

"Well, I hope you mentioned the way the beds are made," said Miss Knight. "I was quite shocked when I came to turn down your bed last night. I had to make it all over again."

"That was very kind of you," said Miss Marple.

"Oh, I never grudge being helpful," said Miss Knight. "That's why I'm here, isn't it? To make a certain person we know as comfortable and happy as possible. Oh, dear, dear," she added, "you've pulled out a lot of your knitting again."

Miss Marple leaned back and closed her eyes. "I'm going to have a little rest," she said. "Put the glass here—thank you. And please don't come in and disturb me for at least three-quarters of an hour."

"Indeed I won't, dear," said Miss Knight. "And I'll tell that Mrs. Baker to be very quiet."

She bustled out purposefully.

II

The good-looking young American glanced round him in a puzzled way.

The ramifications of the housing estate perplexed him.

He addressed himself politely to an old lady with white hair and pink cheeks who seemed to be the only human being in sight.

"Excuse me, ma'am, but could you tell me where to find Blenheim Close?"

The old lady considered him for a moment. He had just begun to wonder if she was deaf, and had prepared himself to repeat his demand in a louder voice, when she spoke.

"Along here to the right, then turn left, second to the right again, and straight on. What number do you want?"

"Number sixteen." He consulted a small piece of paper. "Gladys Dixon."

"That's right," said the old lady. "But I believe she works at the Hellingforth Studios. In the canteen. You'll find her there if you want her."

"She didn't turn up this morning," explained the young man. "I want to get hold of her to come up to Gossington Hall. We're very shorthanded there today."

"Of course," said the old lady. "The butler was shot last night, wasn't he?"

The young man was slightly staggered by this reply.

"I guess news gets round pretty quickly in these parts," he said.

"It does indeed," said the old lady. "Mr. Rudd's secretary died of some kind of seizure yesterday, too, I understand."

She shook her head. "Terrible. Quite terrible. What are we coming to?"

Chapter Twenty

A LITTLE LATER in the day yet another visitor found his way to 16 Blenheim Close. Detective-Sergeant William (Tom) Tiddler.

In reply to his sharp knock on the smart yellow-painted door, it was opened to him by a girl of about fifteen. She had long straggly fair hair and was wearing tight black pants and an orange sweater.

"Miss Gladys Dixon live here?"

"You want Gladys? You're unlucky. She isn't here."

"Where is she? Out for the evening?"

"No. She's gone away. Bit of a holiday like."

"Where's she gone to?"

"That's telling," said the girl.

Tom Tiddler smiled at her in his most ingratiating manner. "May I come in? Is your mother at home?"

"Mum's out at work. She won't be in until half-past seven. But she can't tell you any more than I can. Gladys has gone off for a holiday."

"Oh, I see. When did she go?"

"This morning. All of a sudden like. Said she'd got the chance of a free trip."

"Perhaps you wouldn't mind giving me her address."

The fair-haired girl shook her head. "Haven't got an address," she said. "Gladys said she'd send us her address as soon as she knew where she was going to stay. As like as not she won't, though," she added. "Last summer she went to Newquay and never sent us as much as a postcard. She's slack that way and besides, she says, why do mothers have to bother all the time?"

"Did somebody stand her this holiday?"

"Must have," said the girl. "She's pretty hard up at the moment. Went to the sales last week."

"And you've no idea at all who gave her this trip or—er—paid for her going there?"

The fair girl bristled suddenly.

"Now don't you get any wrong ideas. Our Gladys isn't that sort. She and her boy friend may like to go to the same place for holidays in August, but there's nothing wrong about it. She pays for herself. So don't you get ideas, mister."

Tiddler said meekly that he wouldn't get ideas but he would like the address if Gladys Dixon should send a postcard.

He returned to the station with the result of his various inquiries. From the studios, he had learnt that Gladys Dixon had rung up that day and said she wouldn't be able to come to work for about a week. He had also learned some other things.

"No end of a shemozzle there's been there lately," he said. "Marina Gregg's been having hysterics most days. Said some coffee she was given was poisoned. Said it tasted bitter. Awful state of nerves she was in. Her husband took it and threw it down the sink and told her not to make so much fuss."

"Yes?" said Craddock. It seemed plain there was more to come.

"But word went round as Mr. Rudd didn't throw it all away. He kept some and had it analyzed and it was poison."

"It sounds to me," said Craddock, "very unlikely. I'll have to ask him about that."

II

Jason Rudd was nervous, irritable.

"Surely, Inspector Craddock," he said, "I was only doing what I had a perfect right to do."

"If you suspected anything was wrong with that coffee, Mr. Rudd, it would have been much better if you'd turned it over to us."

"The truth of it is that I didn't suspect for a moment that anything was wrong with it."

"In spite of your wife saying that it tasted odd?"

"Oh, that!" A faintly rueful smile came to Rudd's face. "Ever since the day of the fête everything that my wife has eaten or drunk has tasted odd. What with that and the threatening notes that have been coming—"

"There have been more of them?"

"Two more. One through the window down there. The other one was slipped in the letter box. Here they are if you would like to see them."

Craddock looked. They were printed, as the first one had been. One ran: *It won't be long now. Prepare yourself.*

The other one had a rough drawing of a skull and crossbones and below it was written: *This means you, Marina.*

Craddock's eyebrows rose.

"Very childish," he said.

"Meaning you discount them as dangerous?"

"Not at all," said Craddock. "A murderer's mind usually is childish. You've really no idea at all, Mr. Rudd, who sent these?"

"Not the least," said Jason. "I can't help feeling it's more like a macabre joke than anything else. It seemed to me perhaps—" he hesitated.

"Yes, Mr. Rudd?"

"It could be somebody local, perhaps, who—who had been excited by the poisoning on the day of the fête. Someone, perhaps, who has a grudge against the acting profession. There are rural pockets where acting is considered to be one of the devil's weapons."

"Meaning that you think Miss Gregg is not actually threatened? But what about this business of the coffee?"

"I don't even know how you got to hear about that," said Rudd with some annoyance.

Craddock shook his head.

"Everything's talked about. It always comes to one's ears sooner or later. But you should have come to us. Even when you got the result of the analysis you didn't let us know, did you?"

"No," said Jason. "No, I didn't. But I had other things to think about. Poor Ella's death, for one thing. And now this business of Giuseppe. Inspector Craddock, when can I get my wife away from here? She's half frantic."

"I can understand that. But there will be the inquests to attend."

"You do realize that her life is still in danger?"

"I hope not. Every precaution will be taken—"

"Every precaution! I've heard that before, I think . . . I must get her away from here, Craddock. I *must*."

III

Marina was lying on the chaise longue in her bedroom, her eyes closed. She looked grey with strain and fatigue.

Her husband stood there for a moment looking at her. Her eyes opened.

"Was that that Craddock man?"

"Yes."

"What did he come about? Ella?"

"Ella—and Giuseppe."

Marina frowned.

"Giuseppe? Have they found out who shot him?"

"Not yet."

"It's all like a nightmare. . . . Did he say we could go away?"

"He said—not yet."

"Why not? We must. Didn't you make him see that I can't go on waiting day after day for someone to kill me? It's fantastic."

"Every precaution will be taken."

"They said that before. Did it stop Ella being killed? Or Giuseppe? Don't you see, they'll get me in the end. . . . There was something in my coffee that day at the studio. I'm sure there was. . . . If only you hadn't poured it away! If we'd kept it, we could have had it analyzed or whatever you call it. We'd have known for sure. . . ."

"Would it have made you happier to know for sure?"

She stared at him, the pupils of her eyes widely dilated.

"I don't see what you mean. If they'd known for sure that someone was trying to poison me, they'd have let us leave here, they'd have let us get away."

"Not necessarily."

"But I can't go on like this! I can't . . . I can't . . . You must help me, Jason. You must do *something*. I'm frightened. I'm so terribly frightened . . . There's an enemy here. And I don't know who it is . . . It might be anyone—anyone. At the studios—or here in the house. Someone who hates me—but why? . . . why? . . . Someone who wants me dead . . . But who is it? Who is it? I thought—I was almost sure—it was Ella. But now—"

"You thought it was Ella?" Jason sounded astonished. "But why?"

"Because she hated me—oh, yes, she did. Don't men ever see these things? She was madly in love with you. I don't believe you had the least idea of it. But it can't be Ella, because Ella's dead. Oh, Jinks, Jinks—do help me—get me away from here—let me go somewhere safe . . . safe . . ."

She sprang up and walked rapidly up and down, turning and twisting her hands.

The director in Jason was full of admiration for those passionate, tortured movements. I must remember them, he thought. For Hedda Gabler, perhaps? Then, with a shock, he remembered that it was his wife he was watching.

He went to her and put his arms round her.

"It's all right, Marina—all right. I'll look after you."

"We must go away from this hateful house—at once. I hate this house—hate it."

"Listen, we can't go away immediately."

"Why not? Why *not?*"

"Because," said Rudd, "deaths cause complications . . . and there's something else to consider. Will running away do any good?"

"Of course it will. We'll get away from this person who hates me."

"If there's anyone who hates you that much, they could follow you easily enough."

"You mean—you mean— I shall never get away? I shall never be safe again?"

"Darling—it will be all right. I'll look after you. I'll keep you safe."

She clung to him.

"Will you, Jinks? Will you see that nothing happens to me?"

She sagged against him, and he laid her down gently on the chaise longue.

"Oh, I'm a coward," she murmured, "a coward . . . If I knew who it was—and why? . . . Get me my pills—the yellow ones—not the brown. I must have something to calm me."

"Don't take too many, for God's sake, Marina."

"All right—all right . . . Sometimes they don't have any effect any more. . . ." She looked up in his face.

She smiled, a tender exquisite smile.

"You'll take care of me, Jinks? Swear you'll take care of me . . ."

"Always," said Jason Rudd. "To the bitter end."

"You looked so—so odd when you said that."

Her eyes opened wide.

"Did I? How did I look?"

"I can't explain. Like—like a clown laughing at something terribly sad, that no one else has seen. . . ."

Chapter Twenty-one

It was a tired and depressed Inspector Craddock who came to see Miss Marple the following day.

"Sit down and be comfortable," she said. "I can see you've had a very hard time."

"I don't like to be defeated," said Inspector Craddock. "Two murders within twenty-four hours. Ah, well, I'm poorer at my job than I thought I was. Give me a nice cup of tea, Aunt Jane, with some thin bread and butter and soothe me with your earliest remembrances of St. Mary Mead."

Miss Marple clicked with her tongue in a sympathetic manner.

"Now it's no good talking like that, my dear boy, and I don't think tea and bread and butter is at all what you want. Gentlemen, when they've had a disappointment, want something stronger than tea."

As usual, Miss Marple said the word "gentlemen" in the way of someone describing a foreign species.

"I should advise a good stiff whisky and soda," she said.

"Would you really, Aunt Jane? Well, I won't say no."

"And I shall get it for you myself," said Miss Marple, rising to her feet.

"Oh, no, don't do that. Let me. Or what about Miss What's-her-name?"

"We don't want Miss Knight fussing about here," said Miss Marple. "She won't be bringing my tea for another twenty minutes, so that gives us a little peace and quiet. Clever of you to come to the window and not through the front door. Now we can have a nice quiet little time by ourselves."

She went to a corner cupboard, opened it and produced a bottle, a syphon of soda water and a glass.

"You are full of surprises," said Dermot Craddock. "I'd no idea that's what you kept in your corner cupboard. Are you quite sure you're not a secret drinker, Aunt Jane?"

"Now, now," Miss Marple admonished him. "I have never been an advocate of teetotalism. A little strong drink is always advisable on the premises in case there is a shock or an accident. Invaluable at such times. Or, of course, if a gentleman should arrive suddenly. There!" said Miss Marple, handing him her remedy with an air of quiet triumph. "And you don't need to joke any more. Just sit quietly there and relax."

"Wonderful wives there must have been in your young days," said Dermot Craddock.

"I'm sure, my dear boy, you would find the young lady of the type you refer to as a very inadequate helpmeet nowadays. Young ladies were not encouraged to be intellectual, and very few of them had university degrees or any kind of academic distinction."

"There are things that are preferable to academic distinctions," said Dermot. "One of them is knowing when a man wants a whisky and soda and giving it to him."

Miss Marple smiled at him affectionately.

"Come," she said. "Tell me all about it. Or as much as you are allowed to tell me."

"I think you probably know as much as I do. And very likely you have something up your sleeve. How about your dog's-body, your dear Miss Knight? What about her having committed the crime?"

"Now why should Miss Knight have done such a thing?" demanded Miss Marple, surprised.

"Because she's the most unlikely person," said Dermot. "It so often seems to hold good when you produce your answer."

"Not at all," said Miss Marple with spirit. "I have said over and over again, not only to you, my dear Dermot—if I may call you so—that it is always the *obvious* person who has done the crime. One thinks so often of the wife or the husband and so very often it *is* the wife or the husband."

"Meaning Jason Rudd?" He shook his head. "That man adores Marina Gregg."

"I was speaking generally," said Miss Marple, with dignity. "First we had Mrs. Badcock apparently murdered. One asked oneself who could have done such a thing and the first answer would naturally be the husband. So one had to examine that possibility. Then we decide that the real object of the crime was Marina Gregg and there again we have to look for the person most intimately connected with Marina Gregg, starting, as I say, with the husband. Because there is no doubt about it that husbands do, very frequently, want to make away with their wives, though sometimes, of course, they only *wish* to make away with their wives and do not actually do so. But I agree with you, my dear boy, that Jason Rudd really cares with all his heart for Marina Gregg. It *might* be very clever acting, though I can hardly believe that. And one certainly cannot see a motive of any kind for his doing away with her. If he wanted to marry somebody else there could, I should say, be nothing more simple. Divorce, if I may say so, seems second nature to film stars. A practical advantage does not seem to arise either. He is not a poor man by any means. He has his own career, and is, I understand, most successful in it. So we must go farther afield. But it certainly is difficult. Yes, very difficult."

"Yes," said Craddock, "it must hold particular difficulties for you because of course this film world is entirely new to you. You don't know the local scandals and animosities and all the rest of it."

"I know a little more than you may think," said Miss Marple. "I have studied very closely various numbers of *Confidential, Film Life, Film Talk* and *Film Topics.*"

Dermot Craddock laughed. He couldn't help it.

"I must say," he said, "it tickles me to see you sitting there and telling me what your course of literature has been."

"I found it very interesting," said Miss Marple. "They're not particularly well written, if I may say so. But it really is disappointing in a way that it is all so much the same as it used to be in my young days. *Modern Society* and *Tit Bits* and all the rest of them. A lot of gossip. A lot of scandal. A great preoccupation with who is in love with who, and all the rest of it. Really, you know, practically exactly the same sort of thing that goes on in St. Mary Mead. And in the Development, too. Human nature, I mean, is just the same everywhere. One comes back, I think, to the question of who could have been likely to want to kill Marina Gregg, to want to so much that having failed once they sent threatening letters and made repeated attempts to do so. Someone perhaps a little—" very gently she tapped her forehead.

"Yes," said Craddock, "that certainly seems indicated. And of course it doesn't always show."

"Oh, I know," agreed Miss Marple fervently. "Old Mrs. Pike's second boy, Alfred, *seemed* perfectly rational and normal. Almost painfully prosaic, if you know what I mean, but actually, it seems, he had the most abnormal psychology, or so I understand. Really positively dangerous. He seems quite happy and contented, so Mrs. Pike told me, now that he is in Fairways Mental Home. They understand him there, and the doctors think him a most interesting case. That of course pleases him very much. Yes, it all ended quite happily, but she had one or two very near escapes."

Craddock revolved in his mind the possibility of a parallel between someone in Marina Gregg's entourage and Mrs. Pike's second son.

"The Italian butler," continued Miss Marple, "the one who was killed. He went to London, I understand, on the day of his death. Does anyone know what he did there—if you are allowed to tell me, that is," she added conscientiously.

"He arrived in London at eleven-thirty in the morning," said Craddock, "and what he did in London nobody knows until at a quarter to two he visited his bank and made a deposit of five hundred pounds in cash. I may say that there was no confirmation of his story that he went to London to visit an ill relative or a relative who had got into trouble. None of his relatives there had seen him."

Miss Marple nodded her head appreciatively.

"Five hundred pounds," she said. "Yes, that's quite an interesting sum, isn't it? I should imagine it would be the first installment of a good many other sums, wouldn't you?"

"It looks that way," said Craddock.

"It was probably all the ready money the person he was threatening could raise. He may have pretended to be satisfied with that, or he may have accepted it as a down payment and the victim may have promised to raise further sums in the immediate future. It seems to knock out the idea that Marina Gregg's killer could have been someone in humble circumstances who had a private vendetta against her. It would also knock out, I should say, the idea of someone who'd obtained work as a studio helper or attendant or a servant or a gardener. Unless"—Miss Marple pointed out—"such a person may have been the active agent whereas the employing agent may not have been in the neighbourhood. Hence the visit to London."

"Exactly. We have in London Ardwyck Fenn, Lola Brewster and Margot Bence. All three were present at the party. All three of them could have met Giuseppe at an arranged meeting-place somewhere in London between the hours of eleven and a quarter to two. Ardwyck Fenn was out of his office during those hours, Lola Brewster had left her suite to go shopping, Margot Bence was not in her studio. By the way—"

"Yes?" said Miss Marple. "Have you something to tell me?"

"You asked me," said Dermot, "about the children. The children that Marina Gregg adopted before she knew she could have a child of her own."

"Yes, I did."

Craddock told her what he had learned.

"Margot Bence," said Miss Marple softly. "I had a feeling, you know, that it had something to do with children. . . ."

"I can't believe that after all these years—"

"I know, I know. One never can. But do you really, my dear Dermot, know very much about children? Think back to your own childhood. Can't you remember some incident, some happening that caused you grief, or a passion quite incommensurate with its real importance? Some sorrow or passionate resentment that has really never been equalled since? There was such a clever book, you know, written by that brilliant writer, Mr. Richard Hughes. I forget the name of it but it was about some children who had been through a hurricane. Oh, yes—the hurricane in Jamaica. What made a vivid impression on them was their cat rushing madly through the house. It was the only thing they remembered. But the whole of the horror and excitement and fear that they had experienced was bound up in that one incident."

"It's odd you should say that," said Craddock thoughtfully.

"Why, has it made you remember something?"

"I was thinking of when my mother died. I was five I think. Five or six. I was having dinner in the nursery, jam roll pudding. I was very fond of jam roll pudding. One of the servants came in and said to my nursery governess, 'Isn't it awful? There's been an accident and Mrs. Craddock has been killed.' . . . Whenever I think of my mother's death, d'you know what I see?"

"What?"

"A plate with jam roll pudding on it, and I'm staring at it. Staring at it and I can see as well now as then, how the jam oozed out of it at one side.

I didn't cry or say anything. I remember just sitting there as though I'd
been frozen stiff, staring at the pudding. And d'you know, even now if I
see in a shop or a restaurant or in anyone's house a portion of jam roll
pudding, a whole wave of horror and misery and despair comes over me.
Sometimes for a moment I don't remember *why*. Does that seem very
crazy to you?"

"No," said Miss Marple, "it seems entirely natural. It's very interesting,
that. It's given me a sort of idea. . . ."

The door opened and Miss Knight appeared bearing the tea tray.

"Dear, dear," she exclaimed, "and so we've got a visitor, have we? How
very nice. How do you do, Inspector Craddock. I'll just fetch another
cup."

"Don't bother," Dermot called after her, "I've had a drink instead."

Miss Knight popped her head back round the door.

"I wonder—could you just come here a minute, Mr. Craddock?"

Dermot joined her in the hall. She went to the dining-room and shut
the door.

"You will be careful, won't you," she said.

"Careful? In what way, Miss Knight?"

"Our old dear in there. You know, she's so interested in everything, but
it's not very good for her to get excited over murders and nasty things like
that. We don't want her to brood and have bad dreams. She's very old and
frail, and she really must lead a very sheltered life. She always has, you
know. I'm sure all this talk of murders and gangsters and things like that
is very, very bad for her."

Dermot looked at her with faint amusement.

"I don't think," he said gently, "that anything that you or I could say
about murders is likely unduly to excite or shock Miss Marple. I can assure you, my dear Miss Knight, that Miss Marple can contemplate murder
and sudden death and indeed crime of all kinds with the utmost equa-
nimity."

He went back to the drawing-room, and Miss Knight, clucking a little
in an indignant manner, followed him. She talked briskly during tea with
an emphasis on political news in the paper and the most cheerful subjects
she could think of. When she finally removed the tea tray and shut the
door behind her, Miss Marple drew a deep breath.

"At last we've got some peace," she said. "I hope I shan't murder that
woman someday. Now listen, Dermot, there are some things I want to
know."

"Yes? What are they?"

"I want to go over very carefully exactly what happened on the day of the fête. Mrs. Bantry has arrived, and the vicar shortly after her. Then come Mr. and Mrs. Badcock, and on the stairs at that time were the mayor and his wife, this man Ardwyck Fenn, Lola Brewster, a reporter from the *Herald and Argus* of Much Benham, and this photographer girl, Margot Bence. Margot Bence, you said, had her camera at an angle on the stairs and was taking photographs of the proceedings. Have you seen any of those photographs?"

"Actually I brought one to show you."

He took from his pocket an unmounted print. Miss Marple looked at it steadfastly. It showed Marina Gregg with Jason Rudd a little behind her to one side. Arthur Badcock, his hand to his face, looking slightly embarrassed, was standing back, while his wife had Marina Gregg's hand in hers and was looking up at her and talking. Marina was not looking at Mrs. Badcock. She was staring over her head looking, it seemed, full into the camera, or possibly just slightly to the left of it.

"*Very* interesting," said Miss Marple. "I've had descriptions, you know, of what this look was on her face. A frozen look. Yes, that describes it quite well. A look of doom. I'm not really so sure about that. It's more a kind of paralysis of feeling rather than apprehension of doom. Don't you think so? I wouldn't say it was actually fear, would you, although fear of course might take you that way. It might paralyze you. But I don't think it was fear. I think rather that it was *shock*. Dermot, my dear boy, I want you to tell me if you've got notes of it, what exactly Heather Badcock said to Marina Gregg on that occasion. I know roughly the gist of it, of course, but how near can you get to the actual words? I suppose you had accounts of it from different people."

Dermot nodded.

"Yes. Let me see. Your friend Mrs. Bantry, then Jason Rudd and I think Arthur Badcock. As you say, they varied a little in wording, but the gist of them was the same."

"I know. It's the variations that I want. I think it might help us."

"I don't see how," said Dermot, "though perhaps you do. Your friend Mrs. Bantry was probably the most definite on the point. As far as I remember—wait—I carry a good many of my jottings around with me."

He took out a small notebook from his pocket, looked through it to refresh his memory.

"I haven't got the exact words here," he said, "but I made a rough note. Apparently Mrs. Badcock was very cheerful, rather arch, and delighted with herself. She said something like 'I can't tell you how wonderful this is for me. You won't remember, but years ago in Bermuda—I got up from bed when I had chicken pox and came along to see you and you gave me an autograph and it's one of the proudest days of my life which I have never forgotten.'"

"I see," said Miss Marple, "she mentioned the place but not the date, did she?"

"Yes."

"And what did Rudd say?"

"Jason Rudd? He said that Mrs. Badcock told his wife that she'd got up from bed when she had the 'flu and had come to meet Marina and that she still had her autograph. It was a shorter account than your friend's, but the gist of it was the same."

"Did he mention the time and place?"

"No. I don't think he did. I think he said roughly that it was some ten or twelve years ago."

"I see. And what about Mr. Badcock?"

"Mr. Badcock said that Heather was extremely excited and anxious to meet Miss Gregg, that she was a great fan of Marina Gregg's and that she'd told him that once when she was ill as a girl she managed to get up and meet Miss Gregg and get her autograph. He didn't go into any close particulars, as it was evidently in the days before he was married to his wife. He impressed me as not thinking the incident of much importance."

"I see," said Miss Marple. "Yes, I see . . ."

"And what do you see?" asked Craddock.

"Not quite as much as I'd like to yet," said Miss Marple honestly, "but I have a sort of feeling if I only knew why she'd ruined her new dress—"

"Who—Mrs. Badcock?"

"Yes. It seems to me such a very odd thing—such an inexplicable one unless—of course— Dear me, I think I must be *very* stupid!"

Miss Knight opened the door and entered, switching the light on as she did so.

"I think we want a little light in here," she said brightly.

"Yes," said Miss Marple, "you are so right, Miss Knight. That is exactly what we did want. A little light. I think, you know, that at last we've got it."

The tête-à-tête seemed ended and Craddock rose to his feet.

"There only remains one thing," he said, "and that is for you to tell me just what particular memory from your own past is agitating your mind now."

"Everyone always teases me about that," said Miss Marple, "but I must say that I was reminded just for a moment of the Lauristons' parlourmaid."

"The Lauristons' parlourmaid?" Craddock looked completely mystified.

"She had, of course, to take messages on the telephone," said Miss Marple, "and she wasn't very good at it. She used to get the general *sense* right, if you know what I mean, but the way she wrote it down used to make quite nonsense of it sometimes. I suppose, really, because her grammar was so bad. The result was that some very unfortunate incidents occurred. I remember one in particular. A Mr. Burroughs, I think it was, rang up and said he had been to see Mr. Elvaston about the fence being broken down but he said that the fence wasn't his business at all to repair. It was on the other side of the property and he said he would like to know if that was really the case before proceeding further as it would depend on whether he was liable or not and it was important for him to know the proper lie of the land before instructing solicitors. A very obscure message, as you see. It confused rather than enlightened."

"If you're talking about parlourmaids," said Miss Knight with a little laugh, "that must have been a *very* long time ago. I haven't even heard of a parlourmaid for many years now."

"It was a good many years ago," said Miss Marple, "but nevertheless human nature was very much the same then as it is now. Mistakes were made for very much the same reasons. Oh dear," she added, "I *am* thankful that that girl is safely in Bournemouth."

"The girl? What girl?" asked Dermot.

"That girl who did dressmaking and went up to see Giuseppe that day. What was her name—Gladys something."

"Gladys Dixon?"

"Yes, that's the name."

"She's in *Bournemouth*, do you say? How on earth do you know that?"

"I know," said Miss Marple, "because I sent her there."

"What?" Dermot stared at her. "You? Why?"

"I went out to see her," said Miss Marple, "and I gave her some money and told her to take a holiday and not to write home."

"Why on earth did you do that?"

"Because I didn't want her to be killed, of course," said Miss Marple, and blinked at him placidly.

Chapter Twenty-two

"SUCH A SWEET LETTER from Lady Conway," Miss Knight said two days later as she deposited Miss Marple's breakfast tray. "You remember my telling you about her? Just a little, you know—" she tapped her forehead— "wanders sometimes. And her memory's bad. Can't recognize her relations always and tells them to go away."

"That might be shrewdness really," said Miss Marple, "rather than a loss of memory."

"Now, now," said Miss Knight, "aren't we being naughty to make suggestions like that? She's spending the winter at the Belgrave Hotel at Llandudno. *Such* a nice residential hotel. Splendid grounds and a very nice glassed-in terrace. She's most anxious for me to come and join her there." She sighed.

Miss Marple sat herself upright in bed.

"But please," she said, "if you are wanted—if you are needed there and would like to go—"

"No, no, I couldn't hear of it," cried Miss Knight. "Oh, no, I never meant anything like that. Why, what would Mr. Raymond West say? He explained to me that being here might turn out to be a permanency. I should never dream of not fulfilling my obligations. I was only just mentioning the fact in passing, so don't worry, dear," she added, patting Miss Marple on the shoulder. "We're not going to be deserted! No, no, indeed we're not! We're going to be looked after and cosseted and made very happy and comfortable always."

She went out of the room. Miss Marple sat with an air of determination, staring at her tray and failing to eat anything. Finally she picked up the receiver of the telephone and dialled with vigour.

"Dr. Haydock?"

"Yes?"

"Jane Marple here."

"And what's the matter with you? In need of my professional services?"

"No," said Miss Marple. "But I want to see you as soon as possible."

When Dr. Haydock came, he found Miss Marple still in bed waiting for him.

"You look the picture of health," he complained.

"That is why I wanted to see you," said Miss Marple. "To tell you that I am perfectly well."

"An unusual reason for sending for the doctor."

"I'm quite strong, I'm quite fit, and it's absurd to have anybody living in the house. So long as someone comes every day and does the cleaning and all that I don't see any need at all for having someone living here permanently."

"I dare say you don't, but I do," said Dr. Haydock.

"It seems to me you're turning into a regular old fuss-budget," said Miss Marple unkindly.

"And don't call me names!" said Dr. Haydock. "You're a very healthy woman for your age; you were pulled down a bit by bronchitis, which isn't good for the elderly. But to stay alone in a house at your age is a risk. Supposing you fall down the stairs one evening or fall out of bed or slip in the bath. There you'd lie and nobody know about it."

"One can imagine anything," said Miss Marple. "Miss Knight might fall down the stairs and I'd fall over her rushing out to see what had happened."

"It's no good your bullying me," said Dr. Haydock. "You're an old lady and you've got to be looked after in a proper manner. If you don't like this woman you've got, change her and get somebody else."

"That's not always so easy," said Miss Marple.

"Find some old servant of yours, someone that you like, and who's lived with you before. I can see this old hen irritates you. She'd irritate me. There must be some old servant somewhere. That nephew of yours is one of the best-selling authors of the day. He'd make it worth her while if you found the right person."

"Of course dear Raymond would do anything of that kind. He is most generous," said Miss Marple. "But it's not so easy to find the right person. Young people have their own lives to live, and so many of my faithful old servants, I am sorry to say, are dead."

"Well, you're not dead," said Dr. Haydock, "and you'll live a good deal longer if you take proper care of yourself."

He rose to his feet.

"Well," he said. "No good my stopping here. You look as fit as a fiddle. I shan't waste time taking your blood pressure or feeling your pulse or asking you questions. You're thriving on all this local excitement, even if you can't get about to poke your nose in as much as you'd like to do. Good-bye, I've got to go now and do some real doctoring. Eight to ten cases of German measles, half a dozen whooping coughs, and a suspected scarlet fever as well as my regulars!"

Dr. Haydock went out breezily— But Miss Marple was frowning . . . Something that he had said . . . what was it? Patients to see . . . the usual village ailments . . . village ailments? Miss Marple pushed her breakfast tray farther away with a purposeful gesture. Then she rang up Mrs. Bantry.

"Dolly? Jane here. I want to ask you something. Now pay attention. Is it true that you told Inspector Craddock that Heather Badcock told Marina Gregg a long pointless story about how she had chicken pox and got up in spite of it to go and meet Marina and get her autograph?"

"That was it more or less."

"*Chicken pox?*"

"Well, something like that. Mrs. Allcock was talking to me about vodka at the time, so I wasn't really listening closely."

"You're sure"—Miss Marple took a breath—"that she didn't say whooping cough?"

"Whooping cough?" Mrs. Bantry sounded astounded. "Of course not. She wouldn't have had to powder her face and do it up for whooping cough."

"I see—that's what you went by—her special mention of make-up?"

"Well, she laid stress on it—she wasn't the making-up kind. But I think you're right, it wasn't chicken pox . . . nettlerash, perhaps."

"You only say that," said Miss Marple coldly, "because you once had nettlerash yourself and couldn't go to a wedding. You're hopeless, Dolly, quite hopeless."

She put the receiver down with a bang, cutting off Mrs. Bantry's astonished protest of "Really, Jane."

Miss Marple made a ladylike noise of vexation like a cat sneezing to indicate profound disgust. Her mind reverted to the problem of her own domestic comfort. Faithful Florence? Could Faithful Florence, that grenadier of a former parlourmaid, be persuaded to leave her comfortable small house and come back to St. Mary Mead to look after her erstwhile mistress? Faithful Florence had always been very devoted to her. But Faithful Florence was very attached to her own little house. Miss Marple shook her head vexedly. A gay rat-tat-tat sounded at the door. On Miss Marple's calling, "Come in," Cherry entered.

"Come for your tray," she said. "Has anything happened? You're looking rather upset, aren't you?"

"I feel so helpless," said Miss Marple. "Old and helpless."

"Don't worry," said Cherry, picking up the tray. "You're very far from helpless. You don't know the things I hear about you in this place! Why, practically everybody in the Development knows about you now. All sorts of extraordinary things you've done. *They* don't think of you as the old and helpless kind. It's she puts it into your head."

"She?"

Cherry gave a vigorous nod of her head backwards towards the door behind her.

"Pussy, pussy," she said. "Your Miss Knight. Don't you let her get you down."

"She's very kind," said Miss Marple. "Really very kind," she added, in the tone of one who convinces herself.

"Care killed the cat, they say," said Cherry. "You don't want kindness rubbed into your skin, so to speak, do you?"

"Oh, well," said Miss Marple, sighing, "I suppose we all have our troubles."

"I should say we do," said Cherry. "I oughtn't to complain but I feel sometimes that if I live next door to Mrs. Hartwell any longer there's going to be a regrettable incident. Sour-faced old cat, always gossiping and complaining. Jim's pretty fed up, too. He had a first-class row with her last night. Just because we had the *Messiah* on a bit loud! You can't object to the *Messiah*, can you? I mean, it's religious."

"Did she object?"

"She created something terrible," said Cherry. "Banged on the wall and shouted and one thing and another."

"Do you have to have your music tuned in so loud?" asked Miss Marple.

"Jim likes it that way," said Cherry. "He says you don't get the tone unless you have full volume."

"It might," suggested Miss Marple, "be a little trying for anyone if they weren't musical."

"It's these houses being semi-detached," said Cherry. "Thin as anything, the walls. I'm not so keen really on all this new building, when you come to think of it. It looks all very prissy and nice but you can't express your personality without somebody being down on you like a ton of bricks."

Miss Marple smiled at her.

"You've got a lot of personality to express, Cherry," she said.

"D'you think so?" Cherry was pleased and she laughed. "I wonder," she began. Suddenly she looked embarrassed. She put down the tray and came back to the bed.

"I wonder if you'd think it cheek if I asked you something? I mean—you've only got to say 'out of the question' and that's that."

"Something you want me to do?"

"Not quite. It's those rooms over the kitchen. They're never used nowadays, are they?"

"No."

"Used to be a gardener and wife there once, so I heard. But that's old stuff. What I wondered—what Jim and I wondered—is if we could have them. Come and live here, I mean."

Miss Marple stared at her in astonishment.

"But your beautiful new house in the Development?"

"We're both fed up with it. We like gadgets, but you can have gadgets anywhere—and there would be a nice lot of room here, especially if Jim could have the room over the stables. He'd fix it up like new, and he could have all his construction models there, and wouldn't have to clear them away all the time. And if we had our stereogram there too, you'd hardly hear it."

"Are you really serious about this, Cherry?"

"Yes, I am. Jim and I, we've talked about it a lot. Jim could fix things for you any time—you know, plumbing or a bit of carpentry. And I'd look after you every bit as well as your Miss Knight does. I know you think I'm a bit slap-dash—but I'd try and take trouble with the beds and the washing-up—and I'm getting quite a dab at cooking. Did Beef Stroganoff last night, it's quite easy, really."

Miss Marple contemplated her.

Cherry was looking like an eager kitten—vitality and joy of life radiated from her. Miss Marple thought once more of Faithful Florence. Faithful Florence would, of course, keep the house far better. (Miss Marple put no faith in Cherry's promise.) But she was at least sixty-five—perhaps more. And would she really want to be uprooted? She might accept that out of her very real devotion for Miss Marple. But did Miss Marple really want sacrifices made for her? Wasn't she already suffering from Miss Knight's conscientious devotion to duty?

Cherry, however inadequate her housework, wanted to come. And she had qualities that to Miss Marple at this moment seemed of supreme importance.

Warm-heartedness, vitality, and a deep interest in everything that was going on.

"I don't want, of course," said Cherry, "to go behind Miss Knight's back in any way."

"Never mind about Miss Knight," said Miss Marple, coming to a decision. "She'll go off to someone called Lady Conway at a hotel in Llandudno—and enjoy herself thoroughly. We'll have to settle a lot of details, Cherry, and I shall want to talk to your husband—but if you really think you'd be happy. . . ."

"It'll suit us down to the ground," said Cherry. "And you really can rely on me doing things properly. I'll even use the dustpan and brush if you like."

Miss Marple laughed at this supreme offer.

Cherry picked up the breakfast tray again.

"I must get cracking. I got here late this morning—hearing about poor Arthur Badcock."

"Arthur Badcock? What happened to him?"

"Haven't you heard? He's up at the police station now," said Cherry. "They asked him if he'd come and 'assist them with their inquiries,' and you know what that always means."

"When did this happen?" demanded Miss Marple.

"This morning," said Cherry. "I suppose," she added, "that it got out about his once having been married to Marina Gregg."

"What!" Miss Marple sat up again. "Arthur Badcock was once married to Marina Gregg?"

"That's the story," said Cherry. "Nobody had any idea of it. It was Mr. Upshaw put it about. He's been to the States once or twice on business for his firm and so he knows a lot of gossip from over there. It was a long time ago, you know. Really before she'd begun her career. They were only married a year or two and then she won a film award and of course he wasn't good enough for her then, so they had one of those easy American divorces and he just faded out, as you might say. He's the fading-out kind, Arthur Badcock. He wouldn't make a fuss. He changed his name and came back to England. It's all ever so long ago. You wouldn't think anything like that mattered nowadays, would you? Still, there it is. It's enough for the police to go on, I suppose."

"Oh no," said Miss Marple. "Oh no. This mustn't happen. If I could only think what to do— Now, let me see." She made a gesture to Cherry. "Take the tray away, Cherry, and send Miss Knight up to me. I'm going to get up."

Cherry obeyed. Miss Marple dressed herself with fingers that fumbled slightly. It irritated her when she found excitement of any kind affected her. She was just hooking up her dress when Miss Knight entered.

"Did you want me? Cherry said—"

Miss Marple broke in incisively.

"Get Inch," she said.

"I beg your pardon," said Miss Knight, startled.

"Inch," said Miss Marple, "get Inch. Telephone for him to come at once."

"Oh, oh, I see. You mean the taxi people. But his name's Roberts, isn't it?"

"To me," said Miss Marple, "he is Inch and always will be. But anyway get him. He's to come here at once."

"You want to go for a little drive?"

"Just get him, can you?" said Miss Marple, "and hurry, please."

Miss Knight looked at her doubtfully and proceeded to do as she was told.

"We are feeling all right, dear, aren't we?" she said anxiously.

"We are both feeling very well," said Miss Marple, "and I am feeling particularly well. Inertia does not suit me, and never has. A practical course of action, that is what I have been wanting for a long time."

"Has that Mrs. Baker been saying something that has upset you?"

"Nothing has upset me," said Miss Marple. "I feel particularly well. I am annoyed with myself for being stupid. But really, until I got a hint from Dr. Haydock this morning—now I wonder if I remember rightly. Where is that medical book of mine?" She gestured Miss Knight aside and walked firmly down the stairs. She found the book she wanted on a shelf in the drawing-room. Taking it out she looked up the index, murmured "Page two hundred ten," turned to the page in question, read for a few moments, then nodded her head, satisfied.

"Most remarkable," she said, "most curious. I don't suppose anybody would ever have thought of it. I didn't myself, until the two things came together, so to speak."

Then she shook her head, and a little line appeared between her eyes. "If only there was someone . . ."

She went over in her mind the various accounts she had been given on that particular scene . . .

Her eyes widened in thought. There was someone—but would he, she wondered, be any good? One never knew with the vicar. He was quite unpredictable.

Nevertheless she went to the telephone and dialled.

"Good morning, Vicar, this is Miss Marple."

"Oh, yes, Miss Marple—anything I can do for you?"

"I wonder if you could help me on a small point. It concerns the day of the fête when poor Mrs. Badcock died. I believe you were standing quite near Miss Gregg when Mr. and Mrs. Badcock arrived."

"Yes—yes—I was just before them, I think. Such a tragic day."

"Yes, indeed. And I believe that Mrs. Badcock was recalling to Miss Gregg that they had met before in Bermuda. She had been ill in bed and had got up specially."

"Yes, yes, I do remember."

"And do you remember if Mrs. Badcock mentioned the illness she was suffering from?"

"I think now—let me see—yes, it was measles—at least not real measles—German measles—a much less serious disease. Some people hardly feel ill at all with it. I remember my cousin Caroline . . ."

Miss Marple cut off reminiscences of Cousin Caroline by saying firmly: "Thank you so much, Vicar," and replacing the receiver.

There was an awed expression on her face. One of the great mysteries of St. Mary Mead was what made the vicar remember certain things—only outstripped by the greater mystery of what the vicar could manage to forget!

"The taxi's here, dear," said Miss Knight, bustling in. "It's a very old one, and not too clean, I should say. I don't really like you driving in a thing like that. You might pick up some germ or other."

"Nonsense," said Miss Marple. Setting her hat firmly on her head and buttoning up her summer coat, she went out to the waiting taxi.

"Good morning, Roberts," she said.

"Good morning, Miss Marple. You're early this morning. Where do you want to go?"

"Gossington Hall, please," said Miss Marple.

"I'd better come with you, hadn't I, dear," said Miss Knight. "It won't take me a minute just to slip on outdoor shoes."

"No, thank you," said Miss Marple firmly. "I'm going by myself. Drive on, Inch. I mean Roberts."

Mr. Roberts drove on, merely remarking:

"Ah, Gossington Hall. Great changes there and everywhere nowadays. All that development. Never thought anything like that'd come to St. Mary Mead."

Upon arrival at Gossington Hall, Miss Marple rang the bell and asked to see Mr. Jason Rudd.

Giuseppe's successor, a rather shaky-looking elderly man, conveyed doubt.

"Mr. Rudd," he said, "does not see anybody without an appointment, madam. And today especially—"

"I have no appointment," said Miss Marple, "but I will wait," she added.

She stepped briskly past him into the hall and sat down on a hall chair.

"I'm afraid it will be quite impossible this morning, madam."

"In that case," said Miss Marple, "I shall wait until this afternoon."

Baffled, the new butler retired. Presently a young man came to Miss Marple. He had a pleasant manner and a cheerful, slightly American voice.

"I've seen you before," said Miss Marple. "In the Development. You asked me the way to Blenheim Close."

Hailey Preston smiled good-naturedly. "I guess you did your best, but you misdirected me badly."

"Dear me, did I?" said Miss Marple. "So many Closes, aren't there? Can I see Mr. Rudd?"

"Why, now, that's too bad," said Hailey Preston. "Mr. Rudd's a very busy man and he's—er—fully occupied this morning and really can't be disturbed."

"I'm sure he's very busy," said Miss Marple. "I came here quite prepared to wait."

"Why, I'd suggest now," said Hailey Preston, "that you should tell me what it is you want. I deal with all these things for Mr. Rudd, you see. Everyone has to see me first."

"I'm afraid," said Miss Marple, "that I want to see Mr. Rudd himself. And," she added, "I shall wait here until I do."

She settled herself more firmly in the large oak chair.

Hailey Preston hesitated, started to speak, finally turned away and went upstairs.

He returned with a large man in tweeds.

"This is Dr. Gilchrist, Miss—er—"

"Miss Marple."

"So you're Miss Marple," said Dr. Gilchrist. He looked at her with a good deal of interest.

Hailey Preston slipped away with celerity.

"I've heard about you," said Dr. Gilchrist. "From Dr. Haydock."

"Dr. Haydock is a very old friend of mine."

"He certainly is. Now you want to see Mr. Jason Rudd? Why?"

"It is necessary that I should," said Miss Marple.

Dr. Gilchrist's eyes appraised her.

"And you're camping here until you do?" he asked.

"Exactly."

"You would, too," said Dr. Gilchrist. "In that case I will give you a perfectly good reason why you cannot see Mr. Rudd. His wife died last night in her sleep."

"Dead!" exclaimed Miss Marple. "How?"

"An overdose of sleeping stuff. We don't want the news to leak out to the press for a few hours. So I'll ask you to keep this knowledge to yourself for the moment."

"Of course. Was it an accident?"

"That is definitely my view," said Gilchrist.

"But it could be suicide."

"It could—but most unlikely."

"Or someone could have given it to her?"

Gilchrist shrugged his shoulders.

"A most remote contingency. And a thing," he added firmly, "that would be quite impossible to prove."

"I see," said Miss Marple. She took a deep breath. "I'm sorry, but it's more necessary than ever that I should see Mr. Rudd."

Gilchrist looked at her.

"Wait here," he said.

Chapter Twenty-three

JASON RUDD looked up as Gilchrist entered.

"There's an old dame downstairs," said the doctor; "looks about a hundred. Wants to see you. Won't take no and says she'll wait. She'll wait till this afternoon, I gather, or she'll wait till this evening and she's quite capable, I should say, of spending the night here. She's got something she badly wants to say to you. I'd see her if I were you."

Jason Rudd looked up from his desk. His face was white and strained. "Is she mad?"

"No. Not in the least."

"I don't see why I— Oh, all right—send her up. What does it matter." Gilchrist nodded, went out of the room and called to Hailey Preston.

"Mr. Rudd can spare you a few minutes now, Miss Marple," said Hailey Preston, appearing again by her side.

"Thank you. That's very kind of him," said Miss Marple as she rose to her feet. "Have you been with Mr. Rudd long?" she asked.

"Why, I've worked with Mr. Rudd for the last two and a half years. My job is public relations generally."

"I see." Miss Marple looked at him thoughtfully. "You remind me very much," she said, "of someone I knew called Gerald French."

"Indeed? What did Gerald French do?"

"Not very much," said Miss Marple, "but he was a very good talker." She sighed. "He had had an unfortunate past."

"You don't say," said Hailey Preston, slightly ill at ease. "What kind of a past?"

"I won't repeat it," said Miss Marple. "He didn't like it talked about."

Jason Rudd rose from his desk and looked with some surprise at the slender elderly lady who was advancing towards him.

"You wanted to see me?" he said. "What can I do for you?"

"I am very sorry about your wife's death," said Miss Marple. "I can see it has been a great grief to you, and I want you to believe that I should not intrude upon you now or offer you sympathy unless it was absolutely necessary. But there are things that need badly to be cleared up unless an innocent man is going to suffer."

"An innocent man? I don't understand you."

"Arthur Badcock," said Miss Marple. "He is with the police now, being questioned."

"Questioned in connection with my wife's death? But that's absurd, absolutely absurd. He's never been near the place. He didn't even know her."

"I think he knew her," said Miss Marple. "He was married to her once."

"Arthur Badcock? But—he was—he was Heather Badcock's husband. Aren't you perhaps"—he spoke kindly and apologetically—"making a little mistake?"

"He was married to both of them," said Miss Marple. "He was married to your wife when she was very young, before she went into pictures."

Jason Rudd shook his head.

"My wife was first married to a man called Alfred Beadle. He was in real estate. They were not suited and they parted almost immediately."

"Then Alfred Beadle changed his name to Badcock," said Miss Marple. "He's in a real estate firm here. It's odd how some people never seem to like to change their job and want to go on doing the same thing. I expect really that's why Marina Gregg felt that he was no use to her. He couldn't have kept up with her."

"What you've told me is most surprising."

"I can assure you that I am not romancing or imagining things. What I'm telling you is sober fact. These things get round very quickly in a village, you know, though they take a little longer," she added, "in reaching the Hall."

"Well," Jason Rudd stalled, uncertain what to say, then he accepted the position, "and what do you want me to do for you, Miss Marple?" he asked.

"I want, if I may, to stand on the stairs at the spot where you and your wife received guests on the day of the fête."

He shot a quick doubtful glance at her. Was this, after all, just another sensation-seeker? But Miss Marple's face was grave and composed.

"Why certainly," he said, "if you want to do so. Come with me."

He led her to the staircase head and paused in the hollowed-out bay at the top of it.

"You've made a good many changes in the house since the Bantrys were here," said Miss Marple. "I like this. Now, let me see. The tables would be about here, I suppose, and you and your wife would be standing—"

"My wife stood here." Jason Rudd showed her the place. "People came up the stairs, she shook hands with them and passed them on to me."

"She stood here," said Miss Marple.

She moved over and took her place where Marina Gregg had stood. She remained there quite quietly without moving. Jason Rudd watched her. He was perplexed but interested. She raised her right hand slightly as though shaking hands, looked down the stairs as though to see people coming up it. Then she looked straight ahead of her. On the wall halfway up the stairs was a large picture, a copy of an Italian Old Master. On either side of it were narrow windows, one giving out on the garden and the other giving on to the end of the stables and the weathercock. But Miss Marple looked at neither of these. Her eyes were fixed on the picture itself.

"Of course you always hear a thing right the first time," she said. "Mrs.

Bantry told me that your wife stared at the picture and her face 'froze,' as she put it." She looked at the rich red and blue robes of the Madonna, a Madonna with her head slightly back, laughing up at the Holy Child that she was holding up in her arms. "Bellini's 'Laughing Madonna,'" she said. "A religious picture, but also a painting of a happy mother with her child. Isn't that so, Mr. Rudd?"

"I would say so, yes."

"I understand now," said Miss Marple. "I understand quite well. The whole thing is really very simple, isn't it?" She looked at Jason Rudd.

"Simple?"

"I think you know how simple it is," said Miss Marple.

There was a peal on the bell below.

"I don't think," said Jason Rudd, "I quite understand." He looked down the stairway. There was a sound of voices.

"I know that voice," said Miss Marple. "It's Inspector Craddock's voice, isn't it?"

"Yes, it seems to be Inspector Craddock."

"He wants to see you, too. Would you mind very much if he joined us?"

"Not at all as far as I am concerned. Whether he will agree—"

"I think he will agree," said Miss Marple. "There's really not much time now to be lost, is there? We've got to the moment when we've got to understand just how everything happened."

"I thought you said it was simple," said Jason Rudd.

"It was so simple," said Miss Marple, "that one just couldn't see it."

The decayed butler arrived at this moment up the stairs.

"Inspector Craddock is here, sir," he said.

"Ask him to join us here, please," said Jason Rudd.

The butler disappeared again and a moment or two later Dermot Craddock came up the stairs.

"You!" he said to Miss Marple. "How did you get here?"

"I came in Inch," said Miss Marple, producing the usual confused effect that that remark always caused.

From slightly behind her, Jason Rudd rapped his forehead interrogatively. Dermot Craddock shook his head.

"I was saying to Mr. Rudd," said Miss Marple, "—has that butler gone away—"

Dermot Craddock cast a look down the stairs.

"Oh, yes," he said, "he's not listening. Sergeant Tiddler will see to that."

"Then that is all right," said Miss Marple. "We could, of course, have gone into a room to talk, but I prefer it like this. Here we are on the spot where the thing happened, which makes it so much easier to understand."

"You are talking," said Jason Rudd, "of the day of the fête here, the day when Heather Badcock was poisoned."

"Yes," said Miss Marple, "and I'm saying that it is all very simple if one only looks at it in the proper way. It all began, you see, with Heather Badcock being the kind of person she was. It was inevitable, really, that something of that kind should happen someday to Heather."

"I don't understand what you mean," said Jason Rudd, "I don't understand at all."

"No, it has to be explained a little. You see, when my friend Mrs. Bantry, who was here, described the scene to me, she quoted a poem that was a great favourite in my youth, a poem of dear Lord Tennyson's, 'The Lady of Shalott.'" She raised her voice a little.

> "The mirror crack'd from side to side;
> 'The curse is come upon me,' cried
> The Lady of Shalott.

"That's what Mrs. Bantry saw, or thought she saw, though actually she misquoted and said doom instead of curse—perhaps a better word in the circumstances. She saw your wife speaking to Heather Badcock and heard Heather Badcock speaking to your wife and she saw this look of doom on your wife's face."

"Haven't we been over that a great many times?" said Jason Rudd.

"Yes, but we shall have to go over it once more," said Miss Marple. "There was that expression on your wife's face and she was looking not at Heather Badcock but at that picture. At a picture of a laughing, happy mother holding up a happy child. The mistake was that though there was doom foreshadowed in Marina Gregg's face, it was not on her the doom would come. The doom was to come upon Heather. Heather was doomed from the first moment that she began talking and boasting of an incident in the past."

"Could you make yourself a little clearer?" said Dermot Craddock.

Miss Marple turned to him.

"Of course I will. This is something that you know nothing about. You couldn't know about it, because nobody has told you what it was Heather Badcock actually said."

"But they have," protested Dermot. "They've told me over and over again. Several people have told me."

"Yes," said Miss Marple, "but you don't know because, you see, Heather Badcock didn't tell it to you."

"She hardly could tell it to me seeing she was dead when I arrived here," said Dermot.

"Quite so," said Miss Marple. "All you know is that she was ill but she got up from bed and came along to a celebration of some kind where she met Marina Gregg and spoke to her and asked for an autograph and was given one."

"I know," said Craddock with slight impatience. "I've heard all that."

"But you didn't hear the one operative phrase, because no one thought it was important," said Miss Marple. "Heather Badcock was ill in bed—with *German measles.*"

"German measles? What on earth has that got to do with it?"

"It's a very slight illness, really," said Miss Marple. "It hardly makes you feel ill at all. You have a rash which is easy to cover up with powder, and you have a little fever, but not very much. You feel quite well enough to go out and see people if you want to. And of course in repeating all this the fact that it was German measles didn't strike people particularly. Mrs. Bantry, for instance, just said that Heather had been ill in bed and mentioned chicken pox and nettlerash. Mr. Rudd here said that it was 'flu, but of course he did that on purpose. But I think myself that what Heather Badcock said to Marina Gregg was that she had had German measles and got up from bed and went off to meet Marina. And that's really the answer to the whole thing, because, you see, German measles is extremely infectious. People catch it very easily. And there's one thing about it which you've got to remember. If a woman contracts it in the first four months of—" Miss Marple spoke the next word with a slight Victorian modesty—"of—er—pregnancy, it may have a terribly serious effect. It may cause an unborn child to be born blind or to be born mentally affected."

She turned to Jason Rudd.

"I think I am correct in saying, Mr. Rudd, that your wife had a child who was born mentally afflicted and that she had never really recovered from the shock. She had always wanted a child, and when at last the child came, this was the tragedy that happened. A tragedy she had never forgotten, that she had not allowed herself to forget, and which ate into her as a kind of deep sore, an obsession."

"It's quite true," said Jason Rudd. "Marina developed German measles early on in her pregnancy and was told by the doctor that the mental affliction of her child was due to that cause. It was not a case of inherited insanity or anything of that kind. He was trying to be helpful, but I don't think it helped her much. She never knew how or when or from whom she had contracted the disease."

"Quite so," said Miss Marple, "she never knew until one afternoon here when a perfectly strange woman came up those stairs and told her the fact—told her, what was more—with a great deal of pleasure! With an air of being proud of what she'd done! *She* thought she'd been resourceful and brave and shown a lot of spirit in getting up from her bed, covering her face with make-up, and going along to meet the actress on whom she had such a crush and obtaining her autograph. It was a thing she had boasted of all through her life. Heather Badcock meant no harm. She never did mean harm, but there is no doubt that people like Heather Badcock (and like my old friend Alison Wilde), are capable of doing a lot of harm because they lack—not kindness, they have kindness—but any real consideration for the way their actions may affect other people. She thought always of what an action meant to *her*, never sparing a thought to what it might mean to somebody else."

Miss Marple nodded her head gently.

"So she died, you see, for a simple reason out of her own past. You must imagine what that moment meant to Marina Gregg. I think Mr. Rudd understands it very well. I think she had nursed all those years a kind of hatred for the unknown person who had been the cause of her tragedy. And here suddenly she meets that person face to face. And a person who is gay, jolly and pleased with herself. It was too much for her. If she had had time to think, to calm down, to be persuaded to relax—but she gave herself no time. Here was this woman who had destroyed her happiness and destroyed the sanity and health of her child. She wanted to punish her. She wanted to kill her. And unfortunately the means were to hand. She carried with her that well-known specific, Calmo. A somewhat dangerous drug because you had to be careful of the exact dosage. It was very easy to do. She put the stuff into her own glass. If by any chance anyone noticed what she was doing, they were probably so used to her pepping herself up or soothing herself down in any handy liquid that they'd hardly noticed it. It's possible that one person did see her, but I rather doubt it. I think that Miss Zielinsky did no more than guess. Marina Gregg put her glass down on the table and presently she managed to jog Heather Badcock's arm so that Heather Badcock spilt her own drink all down her new dress. And that's where the element of puzzle has come into the matter, owing to the fact that people cannot remember to use their pronouns properly.

"It reminds me so much of that parlourmaid I was telling you about," she added to Dermot. "I only had the account, you see, of what Gladys Dixon said to Cherry which simply was that she was worried about the ruin of Heather Badcock's dress with the cocktail spilt down it. What seemed so funny, she said, was that she did it on purpose. But the 'she' that Gladys referred to was not Heather Badcock, it was Marina Gregg. As Gladys said: 'She did it on purpose!' She jogged Heather's arm. Not by accident but because she *meant* to do so. We do know that she must have been standing very close to Heather because we have heard that she mopped up both Heather's dress and her own before pressing her cocktail on Heather. It was really," said Miss Marple meditatively, "a very perfect murder; because, you see, it was committed on the spur of the moment without pausing to think or reflect. She wanted Heather Badcock dead and a few minutes later Heather Badcock *was* dead. She didn't realize, perhaps, the seriousness of what she'd done and certainly not the danger of it until afterwards. But she realized it then. She was afraid, horribly afraid. Afraid that someone had seen her dope her own glass, that someone had seen her deliberately jog Heather's elbow, afraid that someone would accuse her of having poisoned Heather. She could see only one way out. To insist that the murder had been aimed at *her,* that *she* was the prospective victim. She tried that idea first on her doctor. She refused to let him tell her husband because I think she knew that her husband would not be deceived. She did fantastic things. She wrote notes to herself and arranged to find them in extraordinary places and at extraordinary moments. She doctored her own coffee at the studios one day. She did things that could really have been seen through fairly easily if one had happened to be thinking that way. They were seen through by one person."

"This is only a theory of yours," said Jason Rudd.

She looked at Jason Rudd.

"You can put it that way, if you like," said Miss Marple, "but you know quite well, don't you, Mr. Rudd, that I'm speaking the truth. You know, because you knew from the first. You knew because you heard that mention of German measles. You knew and you were frantic to protect her. But you didn't realize how much you would have to protect her from. You didn't realize that it was not only a question of hushing up one death, the death of a woman whom you might say quite fairly had brought her death on herself. But there were other deaths—the death of Giuseppe, a blackmailer, it is true, but a human being. And the death of Ella Zielinsky of whom I expect you were fond. You were frantic to protect Marina and also to prevent her from doing harm. All you wanted was to get her safely away somewhere. You tried to watch her all the time, to make sure that nothing more should happen."

She paused, and then coming nearer to Jason Rudd, she laid a gentle hand on his arm.

"I am very sorry for you," she said, "very sorry. I do realize the agony you've been through. You cared for her so much, didn't you?"

Jason Rudd turned slightly away.

"That," he said, "is, I believe, common knowledge."

"She was such a beautiful creature," said Miss Marple gently. "She had such a wonderful gift. She had a great power of love and hate, but no stability. That's what's so sad for anyone, to be born with no stability. She couldn't let the past go and she could never see the future as it really was, only as she imagined it to be. She was a great actress and a beautiful and very unhappy woman. What a wonderful Mary, Queen of Scots she was! I shall never forget her."

Sergeant Tiddler appeared suddenly on the stairs.

"Sir," he said, "can I speak to you a moment?"

Craddock turned.

"I'll be back," he said to Jason Rudd, then he went towards the stairs.

"Remember," Miss Marple called after him, "poor Arthur Badcock had nothing to do with this. He came to the fête because he wanted to have a glimpse of the girl he had married long ago. I should say she didn't even recognize him. Did she?" she asked Jason Rudd.

"I don't think so. She certainly never said anything to me. I don't think," he added thoughtfully, "she would recognize him."

"Probably not," said Miss Marple. "Anyway," she added, "he's quite innocent of wanting to kill her or anything of that kind. Remember that," she added to Dermot Craddock as he went down the stairs.

"He's not been in any real danger, I can assure you," said Craddock, "but of course when we found out that he had actually been Miss Marina Gregg's first husband we naturally had to question him on the point. Don't worry about him, Aunt Jane," he added in a low murmur, then he hurried down the stairs.

Miss Marple turned to Jason Rudd. He was standing there like a man in a daze, his eyes far away.

"Would you allow me to see her?" said Miss Marple.

He considered her for a moment or two, then he nodded.

"Yes, you can see her. You seem to—understand her very well."

He turned and Miss Marple followed him. He preceded her into the big bedroom and drew the curtains slightly aside.

Marina Gregg lay in the great white shell of the bed—her eyes closed, her hands folded.

So, Miss Marple thought, might the Lady of Shalott have lain in the boat that carried her down to Camelot. And there, standing musing, was a man with a rugged, ugly face, who might pass as a Lancelot of a later day.

Miss Marple said gently, "It's very fortunate for her that she—took an overdose. Death was really the only way of escape left to her. Yes—very fortunate she took that overdose—or—*was given it?*"

His eyes met hers, but he did not speak.

He said brokenly, "She was—so lovely—and she had suffered so much."

Miss Marple looked back again at the still figure.

She quoted softly the last lines of the poem:

> *"He said: 'She has a lovely face;*
> *God in His mercy lend her grace,*
> *The Lady of Shalott.'"*

A Pocket Full of Rye

Chapter One

IT WAS MISS SOMERS' turn to make the tea. Miss Somers was the newest and the most inefficient of the typists. She was no longer young and had a mild worried face like a sheep. The kettle was not quite boiling when Miss Somers poured the water onto the tea, but poor Miss Somers was never quite sure when a kettle was boiling. It was one of the many worries that afflicted her in life.

She poured out the tea and took the cups round with a couple of limp sweet biscuits in each saucer.

Miss Griffith, the efficient head typist, a gray-haired martinet who had been with Consolidated Investments Trust for sixteen years, said sharply: "Water not boiling again, Miss Somers!" and Miss Somers' worried meek face went pink and she said, "Oh dear, I did think it was boiling this time."

Miss Griffith thought to herself: "She'll last for another month, perhaps, just while we're so busy. . . . But really! The mess the silly idiot made of that letter to Eastern Developments—a perfectly straightforward job, and always so stupid over the tea. If it weren't so difficult to get hold of any intelligent typists—and the biscuit tin lid wasn't shut tightly last time, either. Really—"

Like so many of Miss Griffith's indignant inner communings, the sentence went unfinished.

At that moment Miss Grosvenor sailed in to make Mr. Fortescue's sacred tea. Mr. Fortescue had different tea, and different china and special biscuits. Only the kettle and the water from the cloakroom tap were the same. But on this occasion, being Mr. Fortescue's tea, the water boiled. Miss Grosvenor saw to that.

Miss Grosvenor was an incredibly glamorous blonde. She wore an expensively cut little black suit and her shapely legs were encased in the very best and most expensive black-market nylons.

She sailed back through the typists' room without deigning to give anyone a word or a glance. The typists might have been so many black beetles. Miss Grosvenor was Mr. Fortescue's own special personal secretary; unkind rumor always hinted that she was something more, but actually this was not true. Mr. Fortescue had recently married a second wife, both glamorous and expensive, and fully capable of absorbing all his attention. Miss Grosvenor was to Mr. Fortescue just a necessary part of the office décor, which was all very luxurious and very expensive.

Miss Grosvenor sailed back with the tray held out in front of her like a ritual offering. Through the inner office and through the waiting room, where the more important clients were allowed to sit, and through her own anteroom and finally with a light tap on the door she entered that holy of holies, Mr. Fortescue's office.

It was a large room with a gleaming expanse of parquet floor on which were dotted expensive oriental rugs. It was delicately paneled in pale wood and there were some enormous stuffed chairs upholstered in pale buff leather. Behind a colossal sycamore desk, the center and focus of the room, sat Mr. Fortescue himself.

Mr. Fortescue was less impressive than he should have been to match the room, but he did his best. He was a large flabby man with a gleaming bald head. It was his affectation to wear loosely-cut country tweed in his city office. He was frowning down at some papers on his desk when Miss Grosvenor glided up to him in her swanlike manner. Placing the tray on the desk at his elbow, she murmured in a low impersonal voice, "Your tea, Mr. Fortescue," and withdrew.

Mr. Fortescue's contribution to the ritual was a grunt.

Seated at her own desk again, Miss Grosvenor proceeded with the business in hand. She made two telephone calls, corrected some letters that were lying there typed ready for Mr. Fortescue to sign, and took one incoming call.

"Ay'm afraid it's impossible just now," she said in haughty accents. "Mr. Fortescue is in conference."

As she laid down the receiver she glanced at the clock. It was ten minutes past eleven.

It was just then that an unusual sound penetrated through the almost soundproof door of Mr. Fortescue's office. Muffled, it was yet fully recognizable, a strangled, agonized cry. At the same moment the buzzer on Miss Grosvenor's desk sounded in a long-drawn, frenzied summons. Miss

Grosvenor, startled for a moment into complete immobility, rose uncertainly to her feet. Confronted by the unexpected, her poise was shaken. However, she moved toward Mr. Fortescue's door in her usual statuesque fashion, tapped and entered.

What she saw upset her poise still further. Her employer behind his desk seemed contorted with agony. His convulsive movements were alarming to watch.

Miss Grosvenor said, "Oh dear, Mr. Fortescue, are you ill?" and was immediately conscious of the idiocy of the question. There was no doubt that Mr. Fortescue was very seriously ill. Even as she came up to him, his body was convulsed in a painful, spasmodic movement.

Words came out in jerky gasps.

"Tea—what the hell—you put in the tea—get help—quick, get a doctor—"

Miss Grosvenor fled from the room. She was no longer the supercilious blonde secretary. She was a thoroughly frightened woman who had lost her head.

She came running into the typists' office crying out, "Mr. Fortescue's having a fit—he's dying—we must get a doctor—he looks awful—I'm sure he's dying."

Reactions were immediate, and varied a good deal.

Miss Bell, the youngest typist, said, "If it's epilepsy we ought to put a cork in his mouth. Who's got a cork?"

Nobody had a cork.

Miss Somers said, "At his age it's probably apoplexy."

Miss Griffith said, "We must get a doctor—at once."

But she was hampered in her usual efficiency because in all her sixteen years of service it had never been necessary to call a doctor to the city office. There was her own doctor but that was at Streatham Hill. Where was there a doctor near here?

Nobody knew. Miss Bell seized a telephone directory and began looking up Doctors under D. But it was not a classified directory, and doctors were not automatically listed like taxis. Someone suggested a hospital, but which hospital? "It has to be the right hospital," Miss Somers insisted, "or else they won't come. Because of the National Health, I mean. It's got to be in the area."

Someone suggested that she dial Emergency at 999 but Miss Griffith was shocked at that and said it would mean the police and that would never do. For citizens of a country which enjoyed the benefits of Medical Service for all, a group of quite reasonably intelligent women showed incredible ignorance of correct procedure. Miss Bell started looking up Ambulances under A. Miss Griffith said, "There's his own doctor—he must have a doctor." Someone rushed for the private address book. Miss Griffith instructed the office boy to go out and find a doctor—somehow, anywhere. In the private address book, Miss Griffith found Sir Edwin Sandeman with an address in Harley Street. Miss Grosvenor, collapsed in a chair, wailed in a voice whose accent was noticeably less Mayfair than usual, "I made the tea just as usual—reely I did—there couldn't have been anything wrong in it. . . ."

"Wrong in it?" Miss Griffith paused, her hand on the dial of the telephone. "Why do you say that?"

"He said it—Mr. Fortescue—he said it was the tea—"

Miss Griffith's hand hovered irresolutely between Welbeck and 999. Miss Bell, young and hopeful, said: "We ought to give him some mustard and water—now. Isn't there any mustard in the office?"

There was no mustard in the office.

Some short while later Dr. Isaacs of Bethnal Green and Sir Edwin Sandeman met in the elevator just as two different ambulances drew up in front of the building. The telephone and the office boy had done their work.

Chapter Two

INSPECTOR NEELE sat in Mr. Fortescue's sanctum behind Mr. Fortescue's vast sycamore desk. One of his underlings with a notebook sat unobtrusively against the wall near the door.

Inspector Neele had a smart, soldierly appearance with crisp brown hair growing back from a rather low forehead. When he uttered the phrase "just a matter of routine" those addressed were wont to think spitefully: "And routine is about all you're capable of!" They would have been quite wrong. Behind his unimaginative appearance, Inspector Neele was a highly imaginative thinker, and one of his methods of investigation was to propound to himself fantastic theories of guilt which he applied to such persons as he was interrogating at the time.

Miss Griffith, whom he had at once picked out with an unerring eye as being the most suitable person to give him a succinct account of the events which had led to his being seated where he was, had just left the room, having given him an admirable résumé of the morning's happenings. Inspector Neele propounded to himself three separate, highly colored reasons why the faithful *doyenne* of the typists' room should have poisoned her employer's mid-morning cup of tea, and rejected them as unlikely.

He classified Miss Griffith as (a) not the type of a poisoner; (b) not in love with her employer; (c) no pronounced mental instability; (d) not a woman who cherished grudges. That really seemed to dispose of Miss Griffith except as a source of accurate information.

Inspector Neele glanced at the telephone. He was expecting a call from St. Jude's Hospital at any moment now.

It was possible, of course, that Mr. Fortescue's sudden illness was due to natural causes, but Dr. Isaacs of Bethnal Green had not thought so and Sir Edwin Sandeman of Harley Street had not thought so.

Inspector Neele pressed a buzzer conveniently situated at his left hand and demanded that Mr. Fortescue's personal secretary should be sent in to him.

Miss Grosvenor had recovered a little of her poise, but not much. She came in apprehensively, with nothing of the swanlike glide about her motions, and said at once defensively:

"I didn't do it!"

Inspector Neele murmured conversationally: "No?"

He indicated the chair where Miss Grosvenor was wont to place herself, pad in hand, when summoned to take down Mr. Fortescue's letters. She sat down now with reluctance and eyed Inspector Neele in alarm. Inspector Neele, his mind playing imaginatively on the themes—Seduction? Blackmail? Platinum Blonde in Court?, etc.—looked reassuring and just a little stupid.

"There wasn't anything wrong with the tea," said Miss Grosvenor. "There couldn't have been."

"*I* see," said Inspector Neele. "Your name and address, please?"

"Grosvenor. Irene Grosvenor."

"How do you spell it?"

"Oh. Like the Square."

"And your address?"

"14 Rushmoor Road, Muswell Hill."

Inspector Neele nodded in satisfied fashion.

"No seduction," he said to himself "No Love Nest. Respectable home with parents. No blackmail."

Another good set of speculative theories washed out.

"And so it was you who made the tea?" he said pleasantly.

"Well, I had to. I always do, I mean."

Unhurried, Inspector Neele took her closely through the morning ritual of Mr. Fortescue's Tea. The cup and saucer and teapot had already been packed up and dispatched to the appropriate quarter for analysis. Now Inspector Neele learned that Irene Grosvenor and only Irene Grosvenor had handled that cup and saucer and teapot. The kettle had been used for making the office tea and had been refilled from the cloakroom tap by Miss Grosvenor.

"And the tea itself?"

"It was Mr. Fortescue's own tea, special China tea. It's kept on the shelf in my room next door."

Inspector Neele nodded. He inquired about sugar and heard that Mr. Fortescue didn't take sugar.

The telephone rang. Inspector Neele picked up the receiver. His face changed a little.

"St. Jude's?"

He nodded to Miss Grosvenor in dismissal.

"That's all for now, thank you, Miss Grosvenor."

Miss Grosvenor sped out of the room hurriedly.

Inspector Neele listened carefully to the thin, unemotional tones speaking from St. Jude's Hospital. As the voice spoke he made a few cryptic signs with a pencil on the corner of the blotter in front of him.

"Died five minutes ago, you say?" he asked. His eye went to the watch on his wrist. Twelve forty-three, he wrote on the blotter.

The unemotional voice said that Doctor Bernsdorff himself would like to speak to Inspector Neele.

Inspector Neele said, "Right. Put him through," which rather scandalized the owner of the voice who had allowed a certain amount of reverence to seep into the official accents.

There were then various clicks, buzzes, and far-off ghostly murmurs. Inspector Neele sat patiently waiting.

Then without warning a deep bass roar caused him to shift the receiver an inch or two away from his ear.

"Hullo, Neele, you old vulture. At it again with your corpses?"

Inspector Neele and Professor Bernsdorff of St. Jude's had been brought together over a case of poisoning just over a year ago and had remained on friendly terms.

"Our man's dead, I hear, Doc."

"Yes. We couldn't do anything by the time he got here."

"And the cause of death?"

"There will have to be an autopsy, naturally. Very interesting case. Very interesting indeed. Glad I was able to be in on it."

The professional gusto in Bernsdorff's rich tones told Inspector Neele one thing, at least.

"I gather you don't think it was natural death," he said dryly.

"Not a dog's chance of it," said Dr. Bernsdorff robustly. "I'm speaking unofficially, of course," he added with belated caution.

"Of course. Of course. That's understood. He was poisoned?"

"Definitely. And what's more—this is quite unofficial, you understand—just between you and me—I'd be prepared to make a bet on what the poison was."

"In-deed?"

"Taxine, my boy. Taxine."

"Taxine? Never heard of it."

"I know. Most unusual. Really delightfully unusual! I don't say I'd have spotted it myself if I hadn't had a case only three or four weeks ago. Couple of kids playing dolls' tea-parties—pulled berries off a yew tree and used them for tea."

"Is that what it is? Yew berries?"

"Berries or leaves. Highly poisonous. Taxine, of course, is the alkaloid. Don't think I've heard of a case where it was used deliberately. Really most interesting and unusual. . . . You've no idea, Neele, how tired one gets of the inevitable weedkiller. Taxine is a real treat. Of course, I may be wrong—don't quote me, for Heaven's sake—but I don't think so. Interesting for you, too, I should think. Varies the routine!"

"A good time is to be had by all, is that the idea? With the exception of the victim."

"Yes, yes, poor fellow." Dr. Bernsdorff's tone was perfunctory. "Very bad luck on him."

"Did he say anything before he died?"

"Well, one of your fellows was sitting by him with a notebook. He'll have the exact details. He muttered something once about tea—that he'd been given something in his tea at the office—but that's nonsense, of course."

"Why is it nonsense?" Inspector Neele, who had been reviewing speculatively the picture of the glamorous Miss Grosvenor adding yew berries to a brew of tea, and finding it incongruous, spoke sharply.

"Because the stuff couldn't possibly have worked so soon. I understand the symptoms came on immediately after he had drunk the tea?"

"That's what they say."

"Well, there are very few poisons that act as quickly as that, apart from the cyanides, of course—and possibly pure nicotine—"

"And it definitely wasn't cyanide or nicotine?"

"My dear fellow. He'd have been dead before the ambulance arrived. Oh no, there's no question of anything of that kind. I did suspect strychnine, but the convulsions were not at all typical. Still unofficial, of course, but I'll stake my reputation it's taxine."

"How long would that take to work?"

"Depends. An hour. Two hours, three hours. Deceased looked like a hearty eater. If he had a big breakfast, that would slow things up."

"Breakfast," said Inspector Neele thoughtfully. "Yes, it looks like breakfast."

"Breakfast with the Borgias." Dr. Bernsdorff laughed cheerfully. "Well, good hunting, my lad."

"Thanks, doctor. I'd like to speak to my sergeant before you ring off."

Again there were clicks and buzzes and far-off ghostly voices. And then the sound of heavy breathing came through, an inevitable prelude to Sergeant Hay's conversation.

"Sir," he said urgently. "Sir."

"Neele here. Did the deceased say anything I ought to know?"

"Said it was the tea. The tea he had at the office. But the Medical Officer says not . . ."

"Yes, I know about that. Nothing else?"

"No, sir. But there's one thing that's odd. The suit he was wearing—I checked the contents of the pockets. The usual stuff—handkerchief, keys, change, wallet—but there was one thing that's downright peculiar. The right-hand pocket of his jacket. It had cereal in it."

"Cereal?"

"Yes, sir."

"What do you mean by cereal? Do you mean a breakfast food? Farmer's Glory or Wheatifax? Or do you mean corn or barley—"

"That's right, sir. Grain it was. Looked like rye to me. Quite a lot of it."

"I see. . . . Odd. . . . But it might have been a sample—something to do with a business deal."

"Quite so, sir—but I thought I'd better mention it."

"Quite right, Hay."

Inspector Neele sat staring ahead of him for a few moments after he had replaced the telephone receiver. His orderly mind was moving from Phase I to Phase II of the inquiry—from suspicion of poisoning to certainty of poisoning. Professor Bernsdorff's words may have been unofficial, but Professor Bernsdorff was not a man to be mistaken in his beliefs. Rex Fortescue had been poisoned and the poison had probably been administered one to three hours before the onset of the first symptoms. It seemed probable, therefore, that the office staff could be given a clean bill of health.

Neele got up and went into the outer office. A little desultory work was being done but the typewriters were not going at full speed.

"Miss Griffith? Can I have another word with you?"

"Certainly, Mr. Neele. Could some of the girls go out to lunch? It's long past their regular time. Or would you prefer that we get something sent in?"

"No. They can go to lunch. But they must return afterwards."

"Of course."

Miss Griffith followed Neele back into the private office. She sat down in her composed efficient way.

Without preamble, Inspector Neele said, "I have heard from St. Jude's Hospital. Mr. Fortescue died at 12:43."

Miss Griffith received the news without surprise, merely shook her head.

"I was afraid he was very ill," she said.

She was not, Neele noted, at all distressed.

"Will you please give me particulars of his home and family?"

"Certainly. I have already tried to get into communication with Mrs. Fortescue, but it seems she is out playing golf. She was not expected home to lunch. There is some uncertainty as to which course she is playing on." She added in an explanatory manner, "They live at Baydon Heath, you know, which is a center for three well-known golf courses."

Inspector Neele nodded. Baydon Heath was almost entirely inhabited by rich city men. It had an excellent train service, was only twenty miles from London and was comparatively easy to reach by car even in the rush of morning and evening traffic.

"The exact address, please, and the telephone number?"

"Baydon Heath 3400. The name of the house is Yewtree Lodge."

"What?" The sharp query slipped out before Inspector Neele could control it. "Did you say Yewtree Lodge?"

"Yes."

Miss Griffith looked faintly curious, but Inspector Neele had himself in hand again.

"Can you give me particulars of his family?"

"Mrs. Fortescue is his second wife. She is much younger than he is. They were married about two years ago. The first Mrs. Fortescue has been dead a long time. There are two sons and a daughter of the first marriage. The daughter lives at home and so does the elder son who is a partner in the firm. Unfortunately he is away in the North of England today on business. He is expected to return tomorrow."

"When did he go away?"

"The day before yesterday."

"Have you tried to get in touch with him?"

"Yes. After Mr. Fortescue was removed to the hospital I rang up the Midland Hotel in Manchester where I thought he might be staying, but he had left early this morning. I believe he was also going to Sheffield and Leicester, but I am not sure about that. I can give you the names of certain firms in those cities which he might be visiting."

Certainly an efficient woman, thought the Inspector, and if she murdered a man she would probably murder him very efficiently, too. But he forced himself to abandon these speculations and concentrate once more on Mr. Fortescue's home front.

"There is a second son, you said?"

"Yes. But owing to a disagreement with his father he lives abroad."

"Are both sons married?"

"Yes. Mr. Percival has been married for three years. He and his wife occupy a self-contained flat in Yewtree Lodge, though they are moving into their own house at Baydon Heath very shortly."

"You were not able to get in touch with Mrs. Percival Fortescue when you rang up this morning?"

"She had gone to London for the day." Miss Griffith went on, "Mr. Lancelot got married less than a year ago. To the widow of Lord Frederick Anstice. I expect you've seen pictures of her. In the *Tatler*—with horses, you know. And at point to points."

Miss Griffith sounded a little breathless and her cheeks were faintly flushed. Neele, who was quick to catch the moods of human beings, realized that this marriage had thrilled the snob and the romantic in Miss Griffith. The aristocracy was the aristocracy to Miss Griffith, and the fact that the late Lord Frederick Anstice had had a somewhat unsavory reputation in sporting circles was almost certainly not known to her. Freddie Anstice had blown his brains out just before an inquiry by the Stewards into the running of one of his horses. Neele remembered something vaguely about his wife. She had been the daughter of an Irish peer and had been married before to an airman who had been killed in the Battle of Britain.

And now, it seemed, she was married to the black sheep of the Fortescue family, for Neele assumed that the disagreement with his father, referred to primly by Miss Griffith, stood for some disgraceful incident in young Lancelot Fortescue's career.

Lancelot Fortescue! What a name! And what was the other son—Percival? He wondered what the first Mrs. Fortescue had been like? She'd had a curious taste in Christian names . . .

He drew the phone towards him and dialed TOL. He asked for Baydon Heath 3400.

Presently a man's voice said, "Baydon Heath 3400."

"I want to speak to Mrs. Fortescue or Miss Fortescue."

"Sorry. They aren't in, either of 'em."

The voice struck Inspector Neele as slightly alcoholic.

"Are you the butler?"

"That's right."

"Mr. Fortescue has been taken seriously ill."

"I know. They rung up and said so. But there's nothing I can do about it. Mr. Val's away up North and Mrs. Fortescue's out playing golf. Mrs. Val's gone to London but she'll be back for dinner and Miss Elaine's out with her Brownies."

"Is there no one in the house I can speak to about Mr. Fortescue's illness? It's important."

"Well—I don't know." The man sounded doubtful. "There's Miss Ramsbottom—but she don't ever speak over the phone. Or there's Miss Dove—she's what you might call the 'ousekeeper."

"I'll speak to Miss Dove, please."

"I'll try and get hold of her."

His retreating footsteps were audible through the phone. Inspector Neele heard no approaching footsteps but a minute or two later a woman's voice spoke.

"This is Miss Dove speaking."

The voice was low and well poised, with clear-cut enunciation. Inspector Neele formed a favorable picture of Miss Dove.

"I am sorry to have to tell you, Miss Dove, that Mr. Fortescue died in St. Jude's Hospital a short time ago. He was taken suddenly ill in his office. I am anxious to get in touch with his relatives—"

"Of course. I had no idea—" She broke off. Her voice had held no agitation, but it was shocked. She went on: "It is all most unfortunate. The person you really want to get in touch with is Mr. Percival Fortescue. He would be the one to see to all the necessary arrangements. You might be able to get in touch with him at the Midland in Manchester or possibly at the Grand in Leicester. Or you might try Shearer and Bonds of Leicester. I don't know their telephone number, I'm afraid, but I know they are a firm on whom he was going to call and they might be able to inform you where he would be likely to be today. Mrs. Fortescue will certainly be in to dinner and she may be in to tea. It will be a great shock to her. It must have been very sudden? Mr. Fortescue was quite well when he left here this morning."

"You saw him before he left?"

"Oh yes. What was it? Heart?"

"Did he suffer from heart trouble?"

"No—no—I don't think so—but I thought as it was so sudden—" She broke off. "Are you speaking from St. Jude's Hospital? Are you a doctor?"

"No, Miss Dove, I'm not a doctor. I'm speaking from Mr. Fortescue's office in the city. I am Detective Inspector Neele of the C.I.D. and I shall be coming down to see you as soon as I can get there."

"Detective Inspector? Do you mean—what do you mean?"

"It was a case of sudden death, Miss Dove, and when there is a sudden death we get called to the scene, especially when the deceased man hasn't seen a doctor lately, which I gather was the case?"

It was only the faintest suspicion of a question mark, but the young woman responded.

"I know. Percival made an appointment twice for him, but he wouldn't keep it. He was quite unreasonable—they've all been worried—"

She broke off and then resumed in her former assured manner.

"If Mrs. Fortescue returns to the house before you arrive, what do you want me to tell her?"

Practical as they make 'em, thought Inspector Neele.

Aloud he said, "Just tell her that in a case of sudden death we have to make a few inquiries. Routine inquiries."

He hung up.

Chapter Three

NEELE PUSHED the telephone away and looked sharply at Miss Griffith.

"So they've been worried about him lately," he said. "Wanted him to see a doctor. You didn't tell me that."

"I didn't think of it," said Miss Griffith, and added, "He never seemed to me really ill—"

"Not ill—but what?"

"Well, just odd. Unlike himself. Peculiar in his manner."

"Worried about something?"

"Oh no, not worried. It's we who were worried."

Inspector Neele waited patiently.

"It's difficult to say, really," said Miss Griffith. "He had moods, you know. Sometimes he was quite boisterous. Once or twice, frankly, I thought he had been drinking. . . . He boasted and told the most extraordinary stories which I'm sure couldn't possibly have been true. For most of the time I've been here he was always very close about his affairs—not giving anything away, you know. But lately he's been quite different, expansive, and positively—well, flinging money about. Most unlike his usual manner. Why, when the office boy had to go to his grandmother's funeral, Mr. Fortescue called him in and gave him a five-pound note and told him to put it on the second favorite and then roared with laughter. He wasn't —well, he just wasn't like himself. That's all I can say."

"As though, perhaps, he had something on his mind?"

"Not in the usual meaning of the term. It was as though he were looking forward to something pleasurable—exciting."

"Possibly a big deal that he was going to pull off?"

Miss Griffith agreed with more conviction. "Yes—yes, that's much more what I mean. As though everyday things didn't matter any more. He was excited. And some very odd-looking people came to see him on business. People who'd never been here before. It worried Mr. Percival dreadfully."

"Oh, it worried him, did it?"

"Yes. Mr. Percival's always been very much in his father's confidence, you see. His father relied on him. But lately—"

"Lately they weren't getting along so well?"

"Well, Mr. Fortescue was doing a lot of things that Mr. Percival thought unwise. Mr. Percival is always very careful and prudent. But suddenly his father didn't listen to him any more, and Mr. Percival was very upset."

"And they had a real row about it all?"

Inspector Neele was still probing.

"I don't know about a row. . . . Of course, I realize now Mr. Fortescue can't have been himself—shouting like that."

"Shouted, did he? What did he say?"

"He came right out in the typists' room—"

"So that you all heard?"

"Well—yes."

"And he called Percival names—abused him—swore at him . . . ? What did he say Percival had done?"

"It was more that he hadn't done anything . . . he called him a miserable, pettifogging little clerk. He said he had no large outlook, no conception of doing business in a big way. He said, 'I shall get Lance home again. He's worth ten of you—and he's married well. Lance has got guts even if he did risk a criminal prosecution once—' Oh dear, I oughtn't to have said that!" Miss Griffith, carried away as others before her had been under Inspector Neele's expert handling, was suddenly overcome with confusion.

"Don't worry," said Inspector Neele comfortingly. "What's past is past."

"Oh yes, it was a long time ago. Mr. Lance was just young and high-spirited and didn't really realize what he was doing."

Inspector Neele had heard that view before and didn't agree with it. But he passed on to fresh questions.

"Tell me a little more about the staff here."

Miss Griffith, hurrying to get away from her indiscretion, poured out information about the various personalities in the firm. Inspector Neele thanked her and then said he would like to see Miss Grosvenor again.

Detective Constable Waite sharpened his pencil. He remarked wistfully that this was a Ritzy joint. His glance wandered appreciatively over the huge chairs, the big desk and the indirect lighting.

"All these people have got Ritzy names, too," he said. "Grosvenor—that's something to do with a duke. And Fortescue—that's a classy name, too."

Inspector Neele smiled.

"His father's name wasn't Fortescue. Fontescu—and he came from somewhere in central Europe. I suppose this man thought Fortescue sounded better."

Detective Constable Waite looked at his superior officer with awe.

"So you know all about him?"

"I just looked up a few things before coming along on the call."

"Not got a record, had he?"

"Oh no. Mr. Fortescue was much too clever for that. He's had certain connections with the Black Market and put through one or two deals that are questionable, to say the least of it, but they've always been just within the law."

"I see," said Waite. "Not a nice man."

"A twister," said Neele. "But we've got nothing on him. The Inland Revenue have been after him for a long time, but he's been too clever for them. Quite a financial genius, the late Mr. Fortescue."

"The sort of man," said Constable Waite, "who might have enemies?" He spoke hopefully.

"Oh yes, certainly enemies. But he was poisoned at home, remember. Or so it would seem. You know, Waite, I see a kind of pattern emerging. An old-fashioned, familiar kind of pattern. The good boy, Percival. The bad boy, Lance—attractive to women. The wife who's younger than her husband and who's vague about which course she's going to play golf on. It's all very, very familiar. But there's one thing that sticks out in a most incongruous way."

Constable Waite asked "What's that?" just as the door opened and Miss Grosvenor, her poise restored, and once more her glamorous self, inquired haughtily,

"You wished to see me?"

"I wanted to ask you a few questions about your employer—your late employer, perhaps I should say."

"Poor soul," said Miss Grosvenor unconvincingly.

"I want to know if you have noticed any difference in him lately."

"Well, yes. I did, as a matter of fact."

"In what way?"

"I couldn't really say. . . . He seemed to talk a lot of nonsense. I couldn't really believe half of what he said. And then he lost his temper very easily, especially with Mr. Percival. Not with me, because of course I never argue. I just say, 'Yes, Mr. Fortescue,' whatever peculiar thing he says—said, I mean."

"Did he ever—well, make any passes at you?"

Miss Grosvenor replied rather regretfully, "Well, no, I couldn't exactly say that."

"There's just one other thing, Miss Grosvenor. Was Mr. Fortescue in the habit of carrying grain about in his pocket?"

Miss Grosvenor displayed a lively surprise.

"Grain? In his pocket? Do you mean, to feed pigeons or something?"

"It could have been for that purpose."

"Oh, I'm sure he didn't. Mr. Fortescue? Feed pigeons? Oh no."

"Could he have had barley—or rye—in his pocket today for any special reason? A sample, perhaps? Some deal in grain?"

"Oh no. He was expecting the Asiatic Oil people this afternoon. And the President of the Atticus Building Society. . . . No one else."

"Oh well—" Neele dismissed the subject and Miss Grosvenor with a wave of the hand.

"Lovely legs she's got," said Constable Waite with a sigh. "And super nylons—"

"Legs are no help to me," said Inspector Neele. "I'm left with what I had before. A pocket full of rye—and no explanation of it."

Chapter Four

MARY DOVE paused on her way downstairs and looked out through the big window on the stairs. A car had just driven up from which two men were alighting. The taller of the two stood for a moment with his back to the house surveying his surroundings. Mary Dove appraised the two men thoughtfully. Inspector Neele and presumably a subordinate.

She turned from the window and looked at herself in the full-length mirror that hung on the wall where the staircase turned. . . . She saw a small, demure figure with immaculate white collar and cuffs on a beige gray dress. Her dark hair was parted in the middle and drawn back in two shining waves to a knot in the back of her neck. . . . The lipstick she used was a pale rose color.

On the whole, Mary Dove was satisfied with her appearance. A very faint smile on her lips, she went on down the stairs.

Inspector Neele, surveying the house, was saying to himself:

Call it a lodge, indeed! Yewtree Lodge! The affectation of these rich people! The house was what he, Inspector Neele, would call a mansion. He knew what a lodge was. He'd been brought up in one. The lodge at the gates of Hartington Park, that vast, unwieldy Palladian house with its twenty-nine bedrooms which had now been taken over by the National Trust. The lodge had been small and attractive from the outside, and had been damp, uncomfortable and devoid of anything but the most primitive form of sanitation within. Fortunately these facts had been accepted as quite proper and fitting by Inspector Neele's parents. They had no rent to pay and nothing whatever to do except open and shut the gates when required, and there were always plenty of rabbits and an occasional pheasant or so for the pot. Mrs. Neele had never discovered the pleasures of electric irons, slow combustion stoves, airing cupboards, hot and cold water from taps, and the switching on of light by a mere flick of a finger. In winter the Neeles had an oil lamp, and in summer they went to bed when it got dark. They were a healthy family and a happy one, all thoroughly behind the times.

So when Inspector Neele heard the word Lodge, it was his childhood memories that stirred. But this place, this pretentiously named Yewtree Lodge was just the kind of mansion that rich people built themselves and then called it their "little place in the country." It wasn't in the country either, according to Inspector Neele's idea of the country. The house was a large, solid, red brick structure, sprawling lengthwise rather than upward, with rather too many gables, and a vast number of leaded paned windows. The gardens were highly artificial—all laid out in rose beds and pergolas and pools, and living up to the name of the house with large numbers of clipped yew hedges.

Plenty of yew here for anybody with a desire to obtain the raw material of taxine. Over on the right, behind the rose pergola, there was a bit of actual Nature left—a vast yew tree of the kind one associates with churchyards, its branches held up by stakes, like a kind of Moses of the forest world. That tree, the Inspector thought, had been there long before the rash of newly-built red brick houses had begun to spread over the countryside. It had been there before the golf courses had been laid out and the fashionable architects had walked round with their rich clients pointing out the advantages of the various sites. And since it was a valuable antique, the tree had been kept and incorporated in the new setup and had, perhaps, given its name to the new, desirable residence. Yewtree Lodge. And possibly the berries from that very tree—

Inspector Neele cut off these unprofitable speculations. Must get on with the job. He rang the bell.

It was opened promptly by a middle-aged man who fitted in quite accurately with the mental image Inspector Neele had formed of him over the phone. A man with a rather spurious air of smartness, a shifty eye and a rather unsteady hand.

Inspector Neele announced himself and his subordinate and had the pleasure of seeing an instant look of alarm come into the butler's eye. Neele did not attach too much importance to that. It might easily have nothing to do with the death of Rex Fortescue. It was quite possibly a purely automatic reaction.

"Has Mrs. Fortescue returned yet?"

"No, sir."

"Nor Mr. Percival Fortescue? Nor Miss Fortescue?"

"No, sir."

"Then I would like to see Miss Dove, please."

The man turned his head slightly. "Here's Miss Dove now—coming downstairs."

Inspector Neele took in Miss Dove as she came composedly down the wide staircase. This time the mental picture did not correspond with the reality. Unconsciously the word housekeeper had conjured up a vague impression of someone large and authoritative, dressed in black, with somewhere concealed about her a jingle of keys.

The Inspector was quite unprepared for the small, trim figure descending towards him. The soft dove-colored tones of her dress, the white collar and cuffs, the neat waves of hair, the faint Mona Lisa smile. It all seemed, somehow, just a little unreal, as though this young woman of under thirty was playing a part: not, he thought, the part of a housekeeper, but the part of Mary Dove. Her appearance was directed towards living up to her name.

She greeted him composedly. "Inspector Neele?"

"Yes. This is Sergeant Hay. Mr. Fortescue, as I told you through the phone, died in St. Jude's Hospital at 12:43. It seems likely that his death was the result of something he ate at breakfast this morning. I should be glad therefore if Sergeant Hay could be taken to the kitchen where he can make inquiries as to the food served."

Her eyes met his for a moment, thoughtfully; then she nodded.

"Of course," she said. She turned to the uneasily hovering butler.

"Crump, will you take Sergeant Hay out and show him whatever he wants to see."

The two men departed together. Mary Dove said to Neele, "Will you come in here?"

She opened the door of a room and preceded him into it. It was a characteristic apartment, clearly labeled "Smoking Room," with paneling, rich upholstery, large stuffed chairs, and a suitable set of sporting prints on the walls.

"Please sit down."

He sat and Mary Dove sat opposite him. She chose, he noticed, to face the light. An unusual preference for a woman. Still more unusual if a woman had anything to hide. But perhaps Mary Dove had nothing to hide.

"It is very unfortunate," she said, "that none of the family is available. Mrs. Fortescue may return at any minute. And so may Mrs. Val. I have sent wires to Mr. Percival Fortescue at various places."

"Thank you, Miss Dove."

"You say that Mr. Fortescue's death was caused by something he may have eaten for breakfast? Food poisoning, you mean?"

"Possibly." He watched her.

She said composedly, "It seems unlikely. For breakfast this morning there were bacon and scrambled eggs, coffee, toast and marmalade. There was also a cold ham on the sideboard, but that had been cut yesterday, and no one felt any ill effects. No fish of any kind was served, no sausages —nothing like that."

"I see you know exactly what was served."

"Naturally. I order the meals. For dinner last night—"

"No." Inspector Neele interrupted her. "It would not be a question of dinner last night."

"I thought the onset of food poisoning could sometimes be delayed as much as twenty-four hours."

"Not in this case. . . . Will you tell me exactly what Mr. Fortescue ate and drank before leaving the house this morning?"

"He had early tea brought to his room at eight o'clock. Breakfast was at a quarter past nine. Mr. Fortescue, as I have told you, had scrambled eggs, bacon, coffee, toast and marmalade."

"Any cereal?"

"No, he doesn't like cereals."

"The sugar for the coffee—is it lump sugar or granulated?"

"Lump. But Mr. Fortescue does not take sugar in his coffee."

"Is he in the habit of taking any medicines in the morning? Salts? A tonic? Some digestive remedy?"

"No, nothing of that kind."

"Did you have breakfast with him also?"

"No. I do not take meals with the family."

"Who was at breakfast?"

"Mrs. Fortescue. Miss Fortescue. Mrs. Val Fortescue. Mr. Percival Fortescue, of course, was away."

"And Mrs. and Miss Fortescue ate the same things for breakfast?"

"Mrs. Fortescue has only coffee, orange juice and toast. Mrs. Val and Miss Fortescue always eat a hearty breakfast. Besides eating scrambled eggs and cold ham, they would probably have a cereal as well. Mrs. Val drinks tea, not coffee."

Inspector Neele reflected for a moment. The opportunities seemed at least to be narrowing down. Three people, and three people only, had had breakfast with the deceased: his wife, his daughter and his daughter-in-law. Either of them might have seized an opportunity to add taxine to his cup of coffee. The bitterness of the coffee would have masked the bitter taste of the taxine. There was the early morning tea, of course, but Bernsdorff had intimated that the taste would be noticeable in tea. But perhaps, first thing in the morning, before the senses were alert. . . . He looked up to find Mary Dove watching him.

"Your questions about tonic and medicines seem to me rather odd, Inspector," she said. "It seems to imply that either there was something wrong with a medicine, or that something had been added to it. Surely neither of those processes could be described as food poisoning."

Neele eyed her steadily.

"I did not say, definitely, that Mr. Fortescue died of food poisoning. But—some kind of poisoning. In fact, just poisoning."

She repeated softly, "Poisoning. . . ."

She appeared neither startled nor dismayed, merely interested. Her attitude was of one sampling a new experience.

In fact, she said as much, remarking after a moment's reflection: "I have never had anything to do with a poisoning case before."

"It's not very pleasant," Neele informed her dryly.

"No, I suppose not. . . ."

She thought about it for a moment and then looked up at him with a sudden smile.

"I didn't do it," she said. "But I suppose everybody will tell you that!"

"Have you any idea who did do it, Miss Dove?"

She shrugged her shoulders. "Frankly, he was an odious man. Anybody might have done it."

"But people aren't poisoned just for being 'odious,' Miss Dove. There usually has to be a pretty solid motive."

"Yes, of course."

She was thoughtful.

"Do you care to tell me something about the household here?"

She looked up at him. He was a little startled to find her eyes cool and amused.

"This isn't exactly a statement you're asking me to make, is it? No, it couldn't be, because your Sergeant is busy upsetting the domestic staff. I shouldn't like to have what I say read out in court, but all the same I should rather like to say it—unofficially. Off the record, so to speak?"

"Go ahead then, Miss Dove. I've no witness, as you've already observed."

She leaned back, swinging one slim foot and narrowing her eyes.

"Let me start by saying that I've no feeling of loyalty to my employers. I work for them because it's a job that pays well and I insist that it should pay well."

"I was a little surprised to find you doing this type of job. It struck me that with your brains and education—"

"I ought to be confined in an office? Or compiling files in a Ministry? My dear Inspector Neele, this is the perfect racket. People will pay anything—anything—to be spared domestic worries. To find and engage a staff is a thoroughly tedious job. Writing to agencies, putting in advertisements, interviewing people, making arrangements for interviews, and finally keeping the whole thing running smoothly—it takes a certain capacity which most of these people haven't got."

"And suppose your staff, when you've assembled it, runs out on you? I've heard of such things."

Mary smiled. "If necessary, I can make the beds, dust the rooms, cook a meal and serve it without anyone noticing the difference. Of course, I don't advertise that fact. It might give rise to ideas. But I can always be sure of tiding over any little gap. But there aren't often gaps. I work only for the extremely rich who will pay anything to be comfortable. I pay top prices and so I get the best of what's going."

"Such as the butler?"

She threw him an amused, appreciative glance.

"There's always that trouble with a couple. Crump stays because of Mrs. Crump, who is one of the best cooks I've ever come across. She's a jewel, and one would put up with a good deal to keep her. Our Mr. Fortescue likes his food—liked, I should say. In this household nobody has any scruples and they have plenty of money. Butter, eggs, cream, Mrs. Crump can command what she likes. As for Crump, he just makes the grade. His silver's all right, and his waiting at table is not too bad. I keep the key of the wine cellar and a sharp eye on the whiskey and gin, and supervise his valeting."

Inspector Neele raised his eyebrows.

"The admirable Miss Crichton."

"I find one must know how to do everything oneself. Then—one need never do it. But you wanted to know my impression of the family."

"If you don't mind."

"They are really all quite odious. The late Mr. Fortescue was the kind of crook who is always careful to play safe. He boasted a great deal of his various smart dealings. He was rude and over-bearing in manner and was a definite bully. Mrs. Fortescue—Adele—is his second wife and about thirty years younger than he is. He came across her at Brighton. She was a manicurist on the lookout for big money. She is very good-looking—a real sexy piece, if you know what I mean."

Inspector Neele was shocked but managed not to show it. A girl like Mary Dove ought not to say such things, he felt.

The young lady was continuing composedly:

"Adele married him for his money, of course, and his son, Percival, and his daughter, Elaine, were simply livid about it. They're as nasty as they can be to her, but very wisely she doesn't care or even notice. She knows she's got the old man where she wants him. Oh dear, the wrong tense again. I haven't really grasped yet that he's dead. . . ."

"Let's hear about the son."

"Dear Percival? Val, as his wife calls him. Percival is a mealy-mouthed hypocrite. He's prim and sly and cunning. He's terrified of his father and has always let himself be bullied, but he's quite clever at getting his own way. Unlike his father, he's mean about money. Economy is one of his passions. That's why he's been so long about finding a house of his own. Having a suite of rooms here saved his pocket."

"And his wife?"

"Jennifer's meek and seems very stupid. But I'm not so sure. She was a hospital nurse before her marriage—nursed Percival through pneumonia to a romantic conclusion. The old man was disappointed by the marriage. He's a snob and wanted Percival to make what he called a 'good marriage.' He despises poor Mrs. Val and snubs her. She dislikes—disliked him a good deal, I think. Her principal interests are shopping and the cinema; her principal grievance is that her husband keeps her short of money."

"What about the daughter?"

"Elaine? I'm rather sorry for Elaine. She's not a bad sort. One of those great schoolgirls who never grow up. She plays games quite well, and runs Girl Guides and Brownies and all that sort of thing. There was some sort of affair not long ago with a disgruntled young schoolmaster, but Father discovered the young man had communistic ideas and came down on the romance like a ton of bricks."

"She hadn't got the spirit to stand up to him?"

"*She* had. It was the young man who ratted. A question of money yet again, I fancy. Elaine is not particularly attractive, poor dear."

"And the other son?"

"I've never seen him. He's attractive, by all accounts, and a thoroughly bad lot. Some little matter of a forged check in the past. He lives in East Africa."

"And is estranged from his father."

"Yes, Mr. Fortescue couldn't cut him off with a shilling because he'd already made him a junior partner in the firm, but he's held no communication with him for years, and in fact if Lance was ever mentioned, he used to say, 'Don't talk to me of that rascal. He's no son of mine.' All the same—"

"Yes, Miss Dove?"

Mary said slowly, "All the same, I shouldn't be surprised if old Fortescue hadn't been planning to get him back here."

"What makes you think that?"

"Because, about a month ago, old Fortescue had a terrific row with Percival—he found out something that Percival had been doing behind his back—I don't know what it was—and he was absolutely furious. Percival suddenly stopped being the white-headed boy. He's been quite different lately, too."

"Mr. Fortescue was quite different?"

"No. I meant Percival. He's gone about looking worried to death."

"Now, what about servants? You've already described the Crumps. Who else is there?"

"Gladys Martin is the parlourmaid or waitress, as they like to call themselves nowadays. She does the downstairs rooms, lays the tables, clears away and helps Crump wait at table. Quite a decent sort of girl, but very nearly half-witted. The adenoidal type."

Neele nodded.

"The housemaid is Ellen Curtis. Elderly, very crabbed, and very cross, but has been in good service and is a first-class housemaid. The rest is outside help—odd women who come in."

"And those are the only people living here?"

"There's old Miss Ramsbottom."

"Who is she?"

"Mr. Fortescue's sister-in-law—his first wife's sister. His wife was a good deal older than he was and her sister again is a good deal older than she—which makes her well over seventy. She has a room of her own on the second floor—does her own cooking and all that, with just a woman coming in to clean. She's rather eccentric and she never liked her brother-in-law, but she came here while her sister was alive and stayed on when she died. Mr. Fortescue never bothered about her much. She's quite a character, though, is Aunt Effie."

"And that is all."

"That's all."

"So we come to you, Miss Dove."

"You want particulars? I'm an orphan. I took a secretarial course at the St. Alfred's Secretarial College. I took a job as shorthand typist, left it and took another, decided I was in the wrong racket, and started on my present career. I have been with three different employers. After about a year or eighteen months, I get tired of a particular place and move on. I have been at Yewtree Lodge just over a year. I will type out the names and addresses of my various employers and give them, with a copy of my references, to Sergeant—Hay, is it? Will that be satisfactory?"

"Perfectly, Miss Dove." Neele was silent for a moment, enjoying a mental image of Miss Dove tampering with Mr. Fortescue's breakfast. His mind went back further, and he saw her methodically gathering yew berries in a little basket. With a sigh he returned to the present and reality. "Now, I would like to see the girl—er, Gladys—and then the housemaid, Ellen." He added as he rose, "By the way, Miss Dove, can you give me any idea why Mr. Fortescue would be carrying loose grain in his pocket?"

"Grain?" She stared at him with what appeared to be genuine surprise.

"Yes, grain. Does that suggest something to you, Miss Dove?"

"Nothing at all."

"Who looked after his clothes?"

"Crump."

"I see. Did Mr. Fortescue and Mrs. Fortescue occupy the same bedroom?"

"Yes. He had a dressing room and bath, of course, and so did she. . . ."

Mary glanced down at her wrist watch. "I really think that she ought to be back very soon now."

The Inspector had risen. He said in a pleasant voice:

"Do you know one thing, Miss Dove? It strikes me as very odd that even though there are three golf courses in the immediate neighborhood, it has yet not been possible to find Mrs. Fortescue on one of them before now?"

"It would not be so odd, Inspector, if she did not actually happen to be playing golf at all."

Mary's voice was dry. The Inspector said sharply:

"I was distinctly informed that she was playing golf."

"She took her golf clubs and announced her intention of doing so. She was driving her own car, of course."

He looked at her steadily, perceiving the inference.

"Whom was she playing with? Do you know?"

"I think it possible that it might be Mr. Vivian Dubois."

Neele contented himself by saying, "I see."

"I'll send Gladys in to you. She'll probably be scared to death." Mary paused for a moment by the door, then she said:

"I should hardly advise you to go too much by all I've told you. I'm a malicious creature."

She went out. Inspector Neele looked at the closed door and wondered. Whether actuated by malice or not, what she had told him could not fail to be suggestive. If Rex Fortescue had been deliberately poisoned, and it seemed almost certain that was the case, then the setup at Yewtree Lodge seemed highly promising. Motives appeared to be lying thick on the ground.

Chapter Five

THE GIRL who entered the room with obvious unwillingness was an unattractive, frightened-looking girl, who managed to look sluttish in spite of being tall and smartly dressed in a claret-colored uniform.

She said at once, fixing imploring eyes upon him:

"I didn't do anything. I didn't really. I don't know anything about it."

"That's all right," said Neele heartily. His voice had changed slightly. It sounded more cheerful and a good deal commoner in intonation. He wanted to put the frightened rabbit, Gladys, at her ease.

"Sit down here," he went on. "I just want to know about breakfast this morning."

"I didn't do anything at all."

"Well, you laid the breakfast, didn't you?"

"Yes, I did that." Even that admission came unwillingly. She looked both guilty and terrified, but Inspector Neele was used to witnesses who looked like that. He went on cheerfully, trying to put her at ease, asking questions: Who had come down first? And who next?

Elaine Fortescue had been the first down to breakfast. She'd come in just as Crump was bringing in the coffeepot. Mrs. Fortescue was down next, and then Mrs. Val, and the master last. They waited on themselves. The tea and coffee and the hot dishes were all on hot plates on the sideboard.

He learnt little of importance from her that he did not know already. The food and drink were as Mary Dove had described them. The master and Mrs. Fortescue and Miss Elaine took coffee and Mrs. Val took tea. Everything had been quite as usual.

Neele questioned her about herself and here she answered more readily. She'd been in the NAAFI, a sort of USO called Navy, Army, and Air Forces Institute, and after that in a café at Eastbourne. Then she thought she'd like to try private service and had come to Yewtree Lodge last September. She'd been there two months.

"And you like it?"

"Well, it's all right, I suppose." She added, "It's not so hard on your feet, but you don't get so much freedom. . . ."

"Tell me about Mr. Fortescue's clothes—his suits. Who looked after them? Brushed them and all that?"

Gladys looked faintly resentful. "Mr. Crump's supposed to. But half the time he makes me do it."

"Who brushed and pressed the suit Mr. Fortescue had on today?"

"I don't remember which one he wore. He's got ever so many."

"Have you ever found grain in the pocket of one of his suits?"

"Grain?" She looked puzzled.

"Rye, to be exact."

"Rye? That's bread, isn't it? A sort of black bread—got a nasty taste, I always think."

"That's bread made from rye. Rye is the grain itself. There was some found in the pocket of your master's coat."

"In his coat pocket?"

"Yes. Do you know how it got there?"

"Couldn't say, I'm sure. I never saw any."

He could get no more from her. For a moment or two he wondered if she knew more about the matter than she was willing to admit. She certainly seemed embarrassed and on the defensive, but on the whole he put it down to a natural fear of the police.

When he finally dismissed her, she asked:

"It's really true, is it? He's dead?"

"Yes, he's dead."

"Very sudden, wasn't it? They said when they rang up from the office that he'd had a kind of fit."

"Yes—it was a kind of fit."

Gladys said, "A girl I used to know had fits. Come on any time, they did. Used to scare me."

For the moment this reminiscence seemed to overcome her suspicions.

Inspector Neele made his way to the kitchen.

His reception was immediate and alarming. A woman of vast proportions, with a red face and armed with a rolling pin, stepped towards him in a menacing fashion.

"Police, indeed," she said. "Coming here and saying my cooking's poisoned the master. Nothing of the kind, I'd have you know. Anything I've sent in to the dining-room has been just what it should be. Coming here and saying I poisoned the master. I'll have the law on you, police or no police. No bad food's ever been served in this house."

It was some time before Inspector Neele could appease the irate artist. Sergeant Hay looked in grinning from the pantry, and Inspector Neele gathered that he had already run the gantlet of Mrs. Crump's wrath.

The scene was terminated by the ringing of the telephone.

Neele went out into the hall to find Mary Dove taking the call. She was writing down a message on a pad. Turning her head over her shoulder, she said, "It's a telegram."

The call concluded, she replaced the receiver and handed the pad on which she had been writing to the Inspector. The place of origin was Paris and the message ran as follows:

Fortescue Yewtree Lodge Baydon Heath Surrey. Sorry your letter delayed. Will be with you tomorrow about teatime. Shall expect roast veal for dinner. Lance.

Inspector Neele raised his eyebrows.

"So the Prodigal Son had been summoned home," he said.

Chapter Six

AT THE MOMENT when Rex Fortescue had been drinking his last cup of tea, Lance Fortescue and his wife had been sitting under the trees on the Champs Elysées watching the people walking past.

"It's all very well to say 'describe him,' Pat. I'm a rotten hand at descriptions. What do you want to know? The Guvnor's a bit of an old crook, you know. But you won't mind that? You must be used to that more or less."

"Oh yes," said Pat. "Yes, as you say, I'm acclimatized."

She tried to keep a certain forlornness out of her voice. Perhaps, she reflected, the whole world was really crooked, or was it just that she herself had been unfortunate?

She was a tall, long-legged girl, not beautiful but with a charm that was made up of vitality and a warmhearted personality. She moved well, and had lovely, gleaming chestnut-brown hair. Perhaps, from a long association with horses, she had acquired the look of a thoroughbred filly.

Crookedness in the racing world she knew about. Now, it seemed she was to encounter crookedness in the financial world. Though for all that, it seemed that her father-in-law, whom she had not yet met, was, as far as the law was concerned, a pillar of rectitude. All these people who went about boasting of "smart work" were the same: technically they always managed to be within the law. Yet it seemed to her that her Lance, whom she loved, and who had admittedly strayed outside the ringed fence in earlier days, had an honesty that these successful practitioners of the crooked lacked.

"I don't mean," said Lance, "that he's a swindler, not anything like that. But he knows how to put over a fast one."

"Sometimes," said Pat, "I feel I hate people who put over fast ones." She added, "You're fond of him." It was a statement, not a question.

Lance considered it for a moment, and then said in a surprised kind of voice:

"Do you know, darling, I believe I am."

Pat laughed. He turned his head to look at her. His eyes narrowed. What a darling she was! He loved her. The whole thing was worth it for her sake.

"In a way, you know," he said, "it's hell going back. City life. Home on the 5:18. It's not my kind of life. I'm far more at home among the down-and-outs. But one's got to settle down sometime, I suppose. And with you to hold my hand, the process may even be quite a pleasant one. And since the old boy has come round, one ought to take advantage of it. I must say I was surprised when I got his letter. . . . Percival, of all people, blotting his copybook. Percival, the good little boy. Mind you, Percy was always sly. Yes, he was always sly."

"I don't think," said Patricia Fortescue, "that I'm going to like your brother Percival."

"Don't let me put you against him. Percy and I never got on—that's all there is to it. I blew my pocket money, he saved his. I had disreputable but entertaining friends, Percy made what's called 'worthwhile contacts.' Poles apart we were, he and I. I always thought him a poor fish, and he—sometimes, you know, I think he almost hated me. I don't know why, exactly. . . ."

"I think I can see why."

"Can you, darling? You're so brainy. You know, I've always wondered—it's a fantastic thing to say—but—"

"Well? Say it."

"I've wondered if it wasn't Percival who was behind that check business—you know, when the old man kicked me out—and was mad that he'd given me a share in the firm and so couldn't disinherit me! Because the queer thing was that I never forged that check—though of course nobody would believe that after that time I swiped funds out of the till and put it on a horse. I was dead sure I could put it back, and anyway it was my own cash, in a manner of speaking. But that check business—no. I don't know why I've got the ridiculous idea that Percival did that, but I have, somehow."

"But it wouldn't have done him any good. It was paid into your account."

"I know. So it doesn't make sense, does it?"

Pat turned sharply towards him. "You mean, he did it to get you chucked out of the firm?"

"I wondered. Oh well, it's a rotten thing to say. Forget it. I wonder what old Percy will say when he sees the Prodigal returned. Those pale, boiled-gooseberry eyes of his will pop right out of his head!"

"Does he know you are coming?"

"I shouldn't be surprised if he didn't know a damned thing! The old man's got rather a funny sense of humor, you know."

"But what has your brother done to upset your father so much?"

"That's what I'd like to know. Something must have made the old man livid. Writing off to me the way he did."

"When was it you got his first letter?"

"Must be four—no, five months ago. A cagey letter, but a distinct holding out of the olive branch. 'Your elder brother has proved himself unsatisfactory in many ways.' 'You seem to have sown your wild oats and settled down.' 'I can promise you that it will be well worth your while financially.' 'Shall welcome you and your wife.' You know, darling, I think my marrying you had a lot to do with it. The old boy was impressed that I'd married into a class above me."

Pat laughed.

"What? Into the aristocratic riffraff?"

He grinned. "That's right. But riffraff didn't register and aristocracy did. You should see Percival's wife. She's the kind who says 'Pass the preserves, please' and talks about a postage stamp."

Pat did not laugh. She was considering the women of the family into which she had married. It was a point of view which Lance had not taken into account.

"And your sister?" she asked.

"Elaine? Oh, she's all right. She was pretty young when I left home. Sort of an earnest girl, but probably she's grown out of that. Very intense over things."

It did not sound very reassuring. Pat said, "She never wrote to you—after you went away?"

"I didn't leave an address. But she wouldn't have, anyway. We're not a devoted family."

"No."

He shot a quick look at her.

"Got the windup? About my family? You needn't. We're not going to live with them, or anything like that. We'll have our own little place somewhere. Horses, dogs, anything you like."

"But there will still be the 5:18."

"For me, yes. To and fro to the city all togged up. But don't worry, sweet—there are rural pockets, even round London. And lately I've felt the sap of financial affairs rising in me. After all it's in my blood, from both sides of the family."

"You hardly remember your mother, do you?"

"She always seemed to me incredibly old. She was old, of course. Nearly fifty when Elaine was born. She wore lots of clinking things and lay on the sofa and used to read me stories about knights and ladies which bored me stiff. Tennyson's *Idylls of the King*. I suppose I was fond of her. . . . She was very—colorless, you know. I realize that, looking back."

"You don't seem to have been particularly fond of anybody," said Pat disapprovingly.

Lance grasped and squeezed her arm.

"I'm fond of you," he said.

Chapter Seven

INSPECTOR NEELE was still holding the telegraph message in his hand when he heard a car drive up to the front door and stop with a careless scrunching of brakes.

Mary Dove said, "That will be Mrs. Fortescue now."

Inspector Neele moved forwards to the front door. Out of the tail of his eye, he saw Mary Dove melt unobtrusively into the background and disappear. Clearly she intended to take no part in the forthcoming scene. A remarkable display of tact and discretion, and also a rather remarkable lack of curiosity. Most women, Inspector Neele decided, would have remained. . . .

As he reached the front door he was aware of the butler, Crump, coming forward from the back of the hall. So he had heard the car.

The car was a Rolls Bentley sports model coupé. Two people got out of it and came towards the house. As they reached the door, it opened. Surprised, Adele Fortescue stared at Inspector Neele.

He realized at once that she was a very beautiful woman, and he realized, too, the force of Mary Dove's comment which had so shocked him at the time. Adele Fortescue *was* a sexy piece. In figure and type she resembled the blonde Miss Grosvenor, but whereas Miss Grosvenor was all glamour without and all respectability within, Adele Fortescue was glamour all through. Her appeal was obvious, not subtle. It said simply to every man, "Here I am. I'm a woman." She spoke and moved and breathed sex, and yet, within it all, her eyes had a shrewd, appraising quality. Adele Fortescue, he thought, liked men, but she would always like money even better.

His eyes went on behind her to the figure who carried her golf clubs. He knew the type very well. It was the type that specialized in the young wives of rich and elderly men. Mr. Vivian Dubois, if this was he, had that rather forced masculinity which is, in reality, nothing of the kind. He was the type of man who "understands" women.

"Mrs. Fortescue?"

"Yes." It was a wide blue-eyed gaze. "But I don't know—"

"I am Inspector Neele. I'm afraid I have bad news for you."

"Do you mean—a burglary—something of that kind?"

"No, nothing of that kind. It is about your husband. He was taken seriously ill this morning."

"Rex? Ill?"

"We have been trying to get in touch with you since half past eleven this morning."

"Where is he? Here? Or in the hospital?"

"He was taken to St. Jude's Hospital. I'm afraid you must prepare yourself for a shock."

"You don't mean—he isn't—dead."

She lurched forward a little and clutched his arm. Gravely, feeling like someone playing a part in a stage performance, the Inspector supported her into the hall. Crump was hovering eagerly.

"Brandy she'll be needing," he said.

The deep voice of Mr. Dubois said, "That's right, Crump. Get the brandy." To the Inspector he said, "In here."

He opened a door on the left. The procession filed in. The Inspector and Adele Fortescue, Vivian Dubois, and Crump with a decanter and two glasses.

Adele Fortescue sank onto an easy chair, her eyes covered with her hand. She accepted the glass that the Inspector offered and took a tiny sip, then pushed it away.

"I don't want it," she said. "I'm all right. But tell me, what was it? A stroke, I suppose? Poor Rex."

"It wasn't a stroke, Mrs. Fortescue."

"Did you say you were an Inspector?" It was Mr. Dubois who made the inquiry.

Neele turned to him. "That's right," he said pleasantly. "Inspector Neele of the C.I.D."

He saw the alarm grow in the dark eyes. Mr. Dubois did not like the appearance of an Inspector of the C.I.D. He didn't like it at all.

"What's up?" he said. "Something wrong, eh?"

Quite unconsciously he backed away a little towards the door. Inspector Neele noted the movement.

"I'm afraid," he said to Mrs. Fortescue, "that there will have to be an inquest."

"An inquest? Do you mean—what *do* you mean?"

"I'm afraid this is all very distressing for you, Mrs. Fortescue." The words came smoothly. "It seemed advisable to find out as soon as possible exactly what Mr. Fortescue had to eat or drink before leaving for the office this morning."

"Do you mean he might have been poisoned?"

"Well, yes, it would seem so."

"I can't believe it. Oh, you mean food poisoning." Her voice dropped half an octave on the last words.

His face wooden, his voice still smooth, Inspector Neele said, "Why, yes, madam, what did you think I meant?"

She ignored that question, hurrying on.

"But we've been all right—all of us."

"You can speak for all the members of the family?"

"Well, no—of course—I can't really."

Dubois said with a great show of consulting his watch, "I'll have to push off, Adele. Dreadfully sorry. You'll be all right, won't you? I mean, there are the maids, and the little Dove and all that—"

"Oh, Vivian, don't. Don't go."

It was quite a wail, and it affected Mr. Dubois adversely. His retreat quickened.

"Awfully sorry, old girl. Important engagement. I'm putting up at the Dormy House, by the way, Inspector. If you—er, want me for anything."

Inspector Neele nodded. He had no wish to detain Mr. Dubois. But he recognized Mr. Dubois' departure for what it was. Mr. Dubois was running away from trouble.

Adele Fortescue said, in an attempt to carry off the situation, "It's such a shock, to come back and find the police in the house."

"I'm sure it must be. But you see, it was necessary to act promptly in order to obtain the necessary specimens of foodstuffs, coffee, tea, etc."

"Tea and coffee? But they're not poisonous? I expect it's the awful bacon we sometimes get. It's quite uneatable sometimes."

"We shall find out, Mrs. Fortescue. Don't worry. You'd be surprised at some of the things that can happen. We once had a case of digitalis poisoning. It turned out that foxglove leaves had been picked in mistake for horse-radish."

"You think something like that could happen here?"

"We shall know better after the autopsy, Mrs. Fortescue."

"The autop— Oh I see." She shivered.

The Inspector went on: "You've got a lot of yew round the house, haven't you, madam? There's no possibility, I suppose, of the berries or leaves having got—mixed up in anything?"

He was watching her closely. She stared at him.

"Yew berries? Are they poisonous?"

The wonder seemed a little too wide-eyed and innocent.

"Children have been known to eat them with unfortunate results."

Adele clasped her hands to her head.

"I can't bear to talk about it any more. Must I? I want to go and lie down. I can't stand any more. Mr. Percival Fortescue will arrange everything. I can't—I can't—it isn't fair to ask me."

"We are getting in touch with Mr. Percival Fortescue as soon as possible. Unfortunately he is away in the North of England."

"Oh yes, I forgot."

"There's just one other thing, Mrs. Fortescue. There was a small quantity of grain in your husband's pocket. Could you give me some explanation of that?"

She shook her head. She appeared quite bewildered.

"Would anyone have slipped it in there as a joke?"

"I don't see why it would be a joke."

Inspector Neele did not see either. He said, "I won't trouble you any further at present, Mrs. Fortescue. Shall I send one of the maids to you? Or Miss Dove?"

"What?" The word came abstractedly. He wondered what she had been thinking about.

She fumbled with her bag and pulled out a handkerchief. Her voice trembled.

"It's so awful," she said unsteadily. "I'm only just beginning to take it in. I've really been numbed up to now. Poor Rex. Poor dear Rex."

She sobbed in a manner that was almost convincing.

Inspector Neele watched her respectfully for a moment or two. "It's been very sudden, I know," he said. "I'll send someone to you."

He went towards the door, opened it and passed through. He paused for a moment before looking into the room.

Adele Fortescue still held the handkerchief to her eyes. The ends of it hung down but did not quite obscure her mouth. On her lips was a very faint smile.

Chapter Eight

"I've got what I could, sir." So Sergeant Hay reported. "The marmalade, bit of the ham. Samples of tea, coffee and sugar, for what they're worth. Actual brews have been thrown out by now, of course, but there's one point. There was a good lot of coffee left over and they had it in the servants' hall at elevenses. That's important, I should say."

"Yes, that's important. Shows that if he took it in his coffee, it must have been slipped into the actual cup."

"By one of those present. Exactly. I've inquired, cautious like, about this yew stuff—berries or leaves—there's been none of it seen about the house. Nobody seems to know anything about the cereal in his pocket, either. . . . It just seems daft to them. Seems daft to me, too. He doesn't seem to have been one of those faddists who'll eat any mortal thing so long as it isn't cooked. My sister's husband's like that. Raw carrots, raw peas, raw turnips. But even he doesn't eat raw grain. Why, I should say it would swell up in your inside something awful."

The telephone rang, and on a nod from the Inspector, Sergeant Hay sprinted off to answer it. Following him, Neele found that it was headquarters on the line. Contact had been made with Mr. Percival Fortescue, who was returning to London immediately.

As the Inspector replaced the telephone, a car drew up at the front door. Crump went to the door and opened it. The woman who stood there had her arms full of parcels. Crump took them from her.

"Thanks, Crump. Pay the taxi, will you? I'll have tea now. Is Mrs. Fortescue or Miss Elaine in?"

The butler hesitated, looking back over his shoulder.

"We've had bad news, ma'am," he said. "About the master."

"About Mr. Fortescue?"

Neele came forward. Crump said: "This is Mrs. Percival, sir."

"What is it? What's happened? An accident?"

The Inspector looked her over as he replied. Mrs. Percival Fortescue was a plump woman with a discontented mouth. Her age he judged to be about thirty. Her questions came with a kind of eagerness. The thought flashed across his mind that she must be very bored.

"I'm sorry to have to tell you that Mr. Fortescue was taken to St. Jude's Hospital this morning seriously ill and has since died."

"Died? You mean he's dead?" The news was clearly even more sensational than she had hoped for. "Dear me, this is a surprise. My husband's away. You'll have to get in touch with him. He's in the North somewhere. I daresay they'll know at the office. He'll have to see to everything. Things always happen at the most awkward moment, don't they?"

She paused for a moment, turning things over in her mind.

"It all depends, I suppose," she said, "where they'll have the funeral. Down here, I suppose. Or will it be in London?"

"That will be for the family to say."

"Of course. I only just wondered." For the first time she took direct cognizance of the man who was speaking to her.

"Are you from the office?" she asked. "You're not a doctor, are you?"

"I'm a police officer. Mr. Fortescue's death was very sudden and—"

She interrupted him.

"Do you mean he was murdered?"

It was the first time that word had been spoken. Neele carefully surveyed her eager, questioning face.

"Now why should you think that, madam?"

"Well, people are, sometimes. You said 'sudden.' And you're police. Have you seen her about it? What did she say?"

"I don't quite understand to whom you are referring?"

"Adele, of course. I always told Val his father was crazy to go marrying a woman years younger than himself. There's no fool like an old fool. Besotted about that awful creature, he was. And now look what comes of it. . . . A nice mess we're all in. Pictures in the paper and reporters coming round."

She paused, obviously visualizing the future in a series of crude, highly-colored pictures. He thought that the prospect was still not wholly unpleasing. She turned back to him.

"What was it? Arsenic?"

In a repressive voice Inspector Neele said, "The cause of death has yet to be ascertained. There will be an autopsy and an inquest."

"But you know already, don't you? Or you wouldn't come down here."

There was a sudden shrewdness in her plump, rather foolish face.

"You've been asking about what he ate and drank, I suppose? Dinner last night. Breakfast this morning. And all the drinks, of course."

He could see her mind ranging vividly over all the possibilities. He said, with caution, "It seems possible that Mr. Fortescue's illness resulted from something he ate at breakfast."

"Breakfast?" She seemed surprised. "That's difficult. I don't see how . . ."

She paused and shook her head.

"I don't see how she could have done it then . . . unless she slipped something into the coffee when Elaine and I weren't looking . . ."

A quiet voice spoke softly beside them:

"Your tea is all ready in the library, Mrs. Val."

Mrs. Val jumped.

"Oh, thank you, Miss Dove. Yes, I could do with a cup of tea. Really, I feel quite bowled over. What about you, Mr.—Inspector—"

"Thank you, not just now."

The plump figure hesitated and then went slowly away.

As she disappeared through a doorway, Mary Dove murmured softly, "I don't think she's ever heard of the term slander."

Inspector Neele did not reply. Mary Dove went on: "Is there anything I can do for you?"

"Where can I find the housemaid, Ellen?"

"I will take you to her. She's just gone upstairs."

II

Ellen proved to be grim but unafraid. Her sour old face looked triumphantly at the Inspector.

"It's shocking business, sir. And I never thought I'd live to find myself in a house where that sort of thing has been going on. But in a way I can't say that it surprises me. I ought to have given my notice in long ago and that's a fact. I don't like the language that's used in this house, and I don't like the amount of drink that's taken, and I don't approve of the goings-on there've been. I've nothing against Mrs. Crump, but Crump and that girl Gladys just don't know what proper service is. But it's the goings-on that I mind about most."

"What goings-on do you mean exactly?"

"You'll soon hear about them if you don't know already. It's common talk all over the place. They've been seen here, there and everywhere. All this pretending to play golf—or tennis. And I've seen things with my own eyes in this house. The library door was open and there they were, kissing and canoodling."

The venom of the spinster was deadly. Neele really felt it unnecessary to say "Whom do you mean?" but he said it nevertheless.

"Who should I mean? The mistress—and that man. No shame about it, they hadn't. But if you ask me, the master had got wise to it. Put someone on to watch them, he had. Divorce, that's what it would have come to. Instead, it's come to *this*."

"When you say this, you mean—"

"You've been asking questions, sir, about what the master ate and drank and who gave it to him. They're in it together, sir, that's what I'd say. He got the stuff from somewhere, and she gave it to the master, that was the way of it, I've no doubt."

"Have you ever seen any yew berries in the house, or thrown away anywhere?"

The small eyes glinted curiously.

"Yew? Nasty, poisonous stuff. Never you touch those berries, my mother said to me when I was a child. Was that what was used, sir?"

"We don't know yet what was used."

"I've never seen her fiddling about with yew." Ellen sounded disappointed. "No, I can't say I've seen anything of that kind."

Neele questioned her about the grain found in Fortescue's pocket, but here again he drew a blank.

"No, sir. I know nothing about that."

He went on to further questions, but with no gainful result. Finally, he asked if he could see Miss Ramsbottom.

Ellen looked doubtful.

"I could ask her, but it's not everyone she'll see. She's a very old lady, you know, and she's a bit odd."

The Inspector pressed his demand, and rather unwillingly Ellen led him along a passage and up a short flight of stairs to what he thought had probably been designed as a nursery suite.

He glanced out of a passage window as he followed her and saw Sergeant Hay standing by the yew tree talking to a man who was evidently a gardener.

Ellen tapped on a door, and when she received an answer, opened it and said, "There's a police gentleman here who would like to speak to you, miss."

The answer was apparently in the affirmative, for she drew back and motioned Neele to go in.

The room he entered was almost fantastically overfurnished. The Inspector felt rather as though he had taken a step backward into not merely Edwardian but Victorian times. At a table drawn up to a gas fire an old lady was sitting laying out a patience. She wore a maroon-colored dress and her sparse gray hair was slicked down each side of her face.

Without looking up or discontinuing her game, she said impatiently, "Well, come in, come in. Sit down if you like."

The invitation was not easy to accept as every chair appeared to be covered with tracts or publications of a religious nature.

As she moved them slightly aside on the sofa, Miss Ramsbottom asked sharply, "Interested in mission work?"

"Well, I'm afraid I'm not very, ma'am."

"Wrong. You should be. That's where the Christian spirit is nowadays. Darkest Africa. Had a young clergyman here last week. Black as your hat. But a true Christian."

Inspector Neele found it a little difficult to know what to say.

The old lady further disconcerted him by snapping, "I haven't got a wireless."

"I beg your pardon?"

"Oh, I thought perhaps you came about a wireless license. Or one of these silly forms. Well, man, what is it?"

"I'm sorry to have to tell you, Miss Ramsbottom, that your brother-in-law, Mr. Fortescue, was taken seriously ill and died this morning."

Miss Ramsbottom continued with her patience without any sign of perturbation, merely remarking in a conversational way, "Struck down at last in his arrogance and sinful pride. Well, it had to come."

"I hope it's not a shock to you?"

It obviously wasn't, but the Inspector wanted to hear what she would say.

Miss Ramsbottom gave him a sharp glance over the top of her spectacles and said, "If you mean I am not distressed, that is quite right. Rex Fortescue was always a sinful man and I never liked him."

"His death was very sudden—"

"As befits the ungodly," said the old lady with satisfaction.

"It seems possible that he may have been poisoned—"

The Inspector paused to observe the effect he had made.

He did not seem to have made any. Miss Ramsbottom merely murmured, "Red seven on black eight. Now I can move up the king."

Struck apparently by the Inspector's silence, she stopped with a card poised in her hand and said sharply, "Well, what did you expect me to say? I didn't poison him if that's what you want to know."

"Have you any idea who might have done so?"

"That's a very improper question," said the old lady sharply. "Living in this house are two of my dead sister's children. I decline to believe that anybody with Ramsbottom blood in them could be guilty of murder. Because it's murder you're meaning, isn't it?"

"I didn't say so, madam."

"Of course it's murder. Plenty of people have wanted to murder Rex in their time. A very unscrupulous man. And old sins have long shadows, as the saying goes."

"Have you anyone in particular in mind?"

Miss Ramsbottom swept up the cards and rose to her feet. She was a tall woman.

"I think you'd better go now," she said.

She spoke without anger, but with a kind of cold finality.

"If you want my opinion," she went on, "it was probably one of the servants. The butler looks to me a bit of a rascal, and that parlourmaid is definitely subnormal. Good evening."

Inspector Neele found himself meekly walking out. Certainly a remarkable old lady. Nothing to be got out of her.

He came down the stairs into the square hall to find himself suddenly face to face with a tall, dark girl. She was wearing a damp mackintosh and she stared into his face with a curious blankness.

"I've just come back," she said. "And they told me—about Father—that he's dead."

"I'm afraid that's true."

She pushed out a hand behind her as though blindly seeking for support. She touched an oak chest and slowly, stiffly, she sat down on it.

"Oh no," she said. "No . . ."

Slowly two tears rolled down her cheeks.

"It's awful," she said. "I didn't think that I even liked him. . . . I thought I hated him. . . . But that can't be so, or I wouldn't mind. I do mind."

She sat there, staring in front of her, and again tears forced themselves from her eyes and down her cheeks.

Presently she spoke again, rather breathlessly.

"The awful thing is that it makes everything come right. I mean, Gerald and I can get married now. I can do everything that I want to do. But I hate it happening this way. I don't want Father to be dead. . . . Oh, I don't. Oh Daddy—Daddy . . ."

For the first time since he had come to Yewtree Lodge, Inspector Neele was startled by what seemed to be genuine grief for the dead man.

Chapter Nine

"Sounds like the wife to me," said the Assistant Commissioner. He had been listening attentively to Inspector Neele's report.

It had been an admirable précis of the case. Short, but with no relevant detail left out.

"Yes," said the A.C. "It looks like the wife. What do you think yourself, Neele, eh?"

Inspector Neele said that it looked like the wife to him, too. He reflected cynically that it usually was the wife—or the husband as the case might be.

"She had the opportunity all right. And motive?" The A.C. paused. "There is motive?"

"Oh, I think so, sir. This Mr. Dubois, you know."

"Think he was in it, too?"

"No, I shouldn't say that, sir." Inspector Neele weighed the idea. "A bit too fond of his own skin for that. He may have guessed what was in her mind, but I shouldn't imagine that he instigated it."

"No, too careful."

"Much too careful."

"Well, we mustn't jump to conclusions, but it seems a good working hypothesis. What about the other two who had opportunity?"

"That's the daughter and the daughter-in-law, sir. The daughter was mixed up with a young man whom her father didn't want her to marry. And he definitely wasn't marrying her unless she had the money. That gives her a motive. As to the daughter-in-law, I wouldn't like to say. Don't know enough about her yet. But any of the three of them could have poisoned him, and I don't see how anyone else could have done so. The parlourmaid, the butler, the cook, they all handled the breakfast or brought it in, but I don't see how any of them could have been sure of Fortescue himself getting the taxine and nobody else. That is, if it was taxine."

The A.C. said, "It was taxine all right. I've just got the preliminary report."

"That settles that, then," said Inspector Neele. "We can go ahead."

"Servants seem all right?"

"The butler and the parlourmaid both seem nervous. There's nothing uncommon about that. Often happens. The cook's fighting mad and the housemaid was grimly pleased. In fact, all quite natural and normal."

"There's nobody else whom you consider suspicious in any way?"

"No, I don't think so, sir." Involuntarily, Inspector Neele's mind went back to Mary Dove and her enigmatic smile. There had surely been a faint yet definite look of antagonism. Aloud, he said, "Now that we know it's taxine, there ought to be some evidence to be got as to how it was obtained or prepared."

"Just so. Well, go ahead, Neele. By the way, Mr. Percival Fortescue is here now. I've had a word or two with him and he's waiting to see you. We've located the other son, too. He's in Paris at the Bristol, leaving today. You'll have him met at the airport, I suppose."

"Yes, sir. That was my idea. . . ."

"Well, you'd better see Percival Fortescue now." The A.C. chuckled. "Percy Prim, that's what he is."

Mr. Percival Fortescue was a neat, fair man of thirty-odd with pale hair and eyelashes and a slightly pedantic way of speech.

"This has been a terrible shock to me, Inspector Neele, as you can well imagine."

"It must have been, Mr. Fortescue," said Inspector Neele.

"I can only say that my father was perfectly well when I left home the day before yesterday. This food poisoning, or whatever it was, must have been very sudden?"

"It was very sudden, yes. But it wasn't food poisoning, Mr. Fortescue." Percival stared and frowned.

"No? So that's why—" he broke off.

"Your father," said Inspector Neele, "was poisoned by the administration of taxine."

"Taxine? I never heard of it."

"Very few people have, I should imagine. It is a poison that takes effect very suddenly and drastically."

The frown deepened.

"Are you telling me, Inspector, that my father was deliberately poisoned by someone?"

"It would seem so, yes, sir."

"That's terrible!"

"Yes indeed, Mr. Fortescue."

Percival murmured, "I understand now their attitude in the hospital—their referring me here." He broke off. After a pause he went on, "The funeral?" He spoke interrogatively.

"The inquest is fixed for tomorrow after the postmortem. The proceedings at the inquest will be purely formal and the inquest will be adjourned."

"I understand. That is usually the case?"

"Yes, sir. Nowadays."

"May I ask have you formed any ideas, any suspicions of who could— Really, I—" Again he broke off.

"It's rather early days for that, Mr. Fortescue," murmured Neele.

"Yes, I suppose so."

"All the same it would be helpful to us, Mr. Fortescue, if you could give us some idea of your father's testamentary dispositions. Or perhaps you could put me in touch with his solicitor."

"His solicitors are Billingsley, Horsethorpe & Walters of Bedford Square. As far as his will goes I think I can more or less tell you its main dispositions."

"If you will be kind enough to do so, Mr. Fortescue. It's a routine that has to be gone through, I'm afraid."

"My father made a new will on the occasion of his marriage two years ago," said Percival precisely. "My father left the sum of £100,000 to his wife absolutely and £50,000 to my sister, Elaine. I am his residuary legatee. I am already, of course, a partner in the firm."

"There was no bequest to your brother, Lancelot Fortescue?"

"No, there is an estrangement of long standing between my father and my brother."

Neele threw a sharp glance at him—but Percival seemed quite sure of his statement.

"So as the will stands," said Inspector Neele, "the three people who stand to gain are Mrs. Fortescue, Miss Elaine Fortescue and yourself?"

"I don't think I shall be much of a gainer." Percival sighed. "There are death duties, you know, Inspector. And of late my father has been—well, all I can say is, highly injudicious in some of his financial dealings."

"You and your father have not seen eye to eye lately about the conduct of the business?" Inspector Neele threw out the question in a genial manner.

"I put my point of view to him, but alas—" Percival shrugged his shoulders.

"Put it rather forcibly, didn't you?" Neele inquired. "In fact, not to put too fine a point on it, there was quite a row about it, wasn't there?"

"I should hardly say that, Inspector." A red flush of annoyance mounted to Percival's forehead.

"Perhaps the dispute you had was about some other matter then, Mr. Fortescue."

"There was no dispute, Inspector."

"Quite sure of that, Mr. Fortescue? Well, no matter. Did I understand that your father and brother are still estranged?"

"That is so."

"Then perhaps you can tell me what this means?"

Neele handed him the telephone message Mary Dove had jotted down.

Percival read it and uttered an exclamation of surprise and annoyance. He seemed both incredulous and angry.

"I can't understand it, I really can't. I can hardly believe it."

"It seems to be true, though, Mr. Fortescue. Your brother is arriving from Paris today."

"But it's extraordinary, quite extraordinary. No, I really can't understand it."

"Your father said nothing to you about it?"

"He certainly did not. How outrageous of him. To go behind my back and send for Lance."

"You've no idea, I suppose, why he did such a thing?"

"Of course I haven't. It's all on a par with his behavior lately—crazy—unaccountable—it's got to be stopped—I—"

Percival came to an abrupt stop. The color ebbed away again from his pale face.

"I'd forgotten," he said. "For the moment I'd forgotten that my father was dead."

Inspector Neele shook his head sympathetically.

Percival Fortescue prepared to take his departure. As he picked up his hat he said, "Call upon me if there is anything I can do. But I suppose—" he paused—"you will be coming down to Yewtree Lodge?"

"Yes, Mr. Fortescue. I've got a man in charge there now."

Percival shuddered in a fastidious way.

"It will all be most unpleasant. To think such a thing should happen to us—"

He sighed and moved towards the door.

"I shall be at the office most of the day. There is a lot to be seen to here. But I shall get down to Yewtree Lodge this evening."

"Quite so, sir."

Percival Fortescue went out.

"Percy Prim," murmured Neele.

Sergeant Hay, who was sitting unobtrusively by the wall, looked up and said "Sir?" interrogatively.

Then, as Neele did not reply, he asked, "What do you make of it all, sir?"

"I don't know," said Neele. He quoted softly. " 'They're all very unpleasant people.' "

Sergeant Hay looked somewhat puzzled.

"Alice in Wonderland," said Neele. "Don't you know your Alice, Hay?"

"It's a classic, isn't it, sir?" said Hay. "Third Program stuff. I don't listen to the Third Program."

Chapter Ten

It was about five minutes after leaving Le Bourget that Lance Fortescue opened his copy of the continental *Daily Mail*. A minute or two later he uttered a startled exclamation. Pat, in the seat beside him, turned her head inquiringly.

"It's the old man," said Lance. "He's dead."

"Dead! Your father?"

"Yes, he seems to have been taken suddenly ill at the office, was taken to St. Jude's Hospital and died there soon after arrival."

"Darling, I'm so sorry. What was it, a stroke?"

"I suppose so. Sounds like it."

"Did he ever have a stroke before?"

"No. Not that I know of."

"I thought people never died from a first one."

"Poor old boy," said Lance. "I never thought I was particularly fond of him, but somehow, now that he's dead . . ."

"Of course you were fond of him."

"We haven't all got your nice nature, Pat. Oh well, it looks as though my luck's out again, doesn't it."

"Yes. It's odd that it should happen just now. Just when you were on the point of coming home."

He turned his head sharply towards her.

"Odd? What do you mean by odd, Pat?"

She looked at him with slight surprise.

"Well, a sort of coincidence."

"You mean that whatever I set out to do goes wrong?"

"No, darling, I didn't mean that. But there is such a thing as a run of bad luck."

"Yes, I suppose there is."

Pat said again, "I'm so sorry."

When they arrived at Heath Row and were waiting to disembark from the plane, an official of the air company called out in a clear voice:

"Is Mr. Lancelot Fortescue aboard?"

"Here," said Lance.

"Would you just step this way, Mr. Fortescue."

Lance and Pat followed him out of the plane, preceding the other passengers. As they passed a couple in the last seat, they heard the man whisper to his wife,

"Well-known smugglers, I expect. Caught in the act."

II

"It's fantastic," said Lance. "Quite fantastic." He stared across the table at Detective Inspector Neele.

Inspector Neele nodded his head sympathetically.

"Taxine—yewberries—the whole thing seems like some kind of melo-drama. I daresay this sort of thing seems ordinary enough to you, Inspec-tor. All in the day's work. But poisoning, in our family, seems wildly far-fetched."

"You've no idea then at all," asked Inspector Neele, "who might have poisoned your father?"

"Good Lord, no. I expect the old man's made a lot of enemies in busi-ness, lots of people who'd like to skin him alive, do him down financially—all that sort of thing. But poisoning? Anyway, I wouldn't be in the know. I've been abroad for a good many years and have known very little of what's going on at home."

"That's really what I wanted to ask you about, Mr. Fortescue. I under-stand from your brother that there was an estrangement between you and your father which had lasted for many years. Would you like to tell me the circumstances that led to your coming home at this time?"

"Certainly, Inspector. I heard from my father, let me see, it must be about—yes, six months ago now. It was soon after my marriage. My father wrote and hinted that he would like to let bygones be bygones. He suggested that I should come home and enter the firm. He was rather vague in his terms and I wasn't really sure that I wanted to do what he asked. Anyway, the upshot was that I came over to England last—yes, last August, just about three months ago. I went down to see him at Yewtree Lodge and he made me, I must say, a very advantageous offer. I told him that I'd have to think about it and I'd have to consult my wife. He quite understood that. I flew back to East Africa, talked it over with Pat. The upshot was that I decided to accept the old boy's offer. I had to wind up my affairs there, but I agreed to do so before the end of last month. I told him I would wire to him the date of my actual arrival in England."

Inspector Neele coughed.

"Your arrival back seems to have caused your brother some surprise."

Lance gave a sudden grin. His rather attractive face lit up with the spirit of pure mischief.

"Don't believe old Percy knew a thing about it," he said. "He was away on his holiday in Norway at the time. If you ask me, the old man picked that particular time on purpose. He was going behind Percy's back. In fact, I've a very shrewd suspicion that my father's offer to me was actuated by the fact that he had a blazing row with poor old Percy—or Val as he prefers to be called. Val, I think, had been more or less trying to run the old man. Well, the old man would never stand for anything of that kind.

What the exact row was about I don't know, but he was furious. And I think he thought it a jolly good idea to get me there and thereby spike poor old Val. For one thing he never liked Percy's wife much and he was rather pleased, in a snobbish kind of way, with my marriage. It would be just his idea of a good joke to get me home and suddenly confront Percy with the accomplished fact."

"How long were you at Yewtree Lodge on this occasion?"

"Oh, not more than an hour or two. He didn't ask me to stay the night. The whole idea, I'm sure, was a kind of secret offensive behind Percy's back. I don't think he even wanted the servants to report upon it. As I say, things were left that I'd think it over, talk about it to Pat and then write him my decision, which I did. I wrote giving him the approximate date of my arrival, and I finally sent him a telegram yesterday from Paris."

Inspector Neele nodded.

"A telegram which surprised your brother very much."

"I bet it did. However, as usual, Percy wins. I've arrived too late."

"Yes," said Inspector Neele thoughtfully, "you've arrived too late." He went on briskly, "On the occasion of your visit last August, did you meet any other members of the family?"

"My stepmother was there at tea."

"You had not met her previously?"

"No." He grinned suddenly. "The old boy certainly knew how to pick them. She must be thirty years younger than he, at least."

"You will excuse my asking, but did you resent your father's remarriage, or did your brother do so?"

Lance looked surprised.

"I certainly didn't, and I shouldn't think Percy did either. After all, our own mother died when we were about—oh, ten, twelve years old. What I'm really surprised at is that the old man didn't marry again before."

Inspector Neele murmured, "It may be considered taking rather a risk to marry a woman very much younger than yourself."

"Did my dear brother say that to you? It sounds rather like him. Percy is a great master of the art of insinuation. Is that the setup, Inspector? Is my stepmother suspected of poisoning my father?"

Inspector Neele's face became blank.

"It's early days to have any definite ideas about anything, Mr. Fortescue," he said pleasantly. "Now, may I ask you what your plans are?"

"Plans?" Lance considered. "I shall have to make new plans, I suppose. Where is the family? All down at Yewtree Lodge?"

"Yes."

"I'd better go down there straightaway." He turned to his wife. "You'd better go to a hotel, Pat."

She protested quickly. "No, no, Lance, I'll come with you."

"No, darling."

"But I want to."

"Really, I'd rather you didn't. Go and stay at the—oh, it's so long since I stayed in London—Barnes'. Barnes' Hotel used to be a nice, quiet sort of place. That's still going, I suppose?"

"Oh, yes, Mr. Fortescue."

"Right, Pat, I'll settle you in there if they've got a room, then I'll go on down to Yewtree Lodge."

"But why can't I come with you, Lance?"

Lance's face took suddenly a rather grim line.

"Frankly, Pat, I'm not sure of my welcome. It was Father who invited me there, but Father's dead. I don't know whom the place belongs to now. Percy, I suppose, or perhaps Adele. Anyway, I'd like to see what reception I get before I bring you there. Besides—"

"Besides what?"

"I don't want to take you to a house where there's a poisoner at large."

"Oh, what nonsense."

Lance said firmly, "Where you're concerned, Pat, I'm taking no risks."

Chapter Eleven

MR. DUBOIS was annoyed. He tore Adele Fortescue's letter angrily across and threw it into the wastepaper basket. Then, with a sudden caution, he fished out the various pieces, struck a match and watched them burn to ashes. He muttered under his breath, "Why have women got to be such damned fools? Surely common prudence . . ."

But then, Mr. Dubois reflected gloomily, women never had any prudence. Though he had profited by this lack many a time, it annoyed him now. He himself had taken every precaution. If Mrs. Fortescue rang up, they had instructions to say that he was out. Already Adele Fortescue had rung him up three times, and now she had written. On the whole, writing was far worse. He reflected for a moment or two, then went to the telephone.

"Can I speak to Mrs. Fortescue, please? Yes, Mr. Dubois." A minute or two later he heard her voice.

"Vivian, at last."

"Yes, yes, Adele, but be careful. Where are you speaking from?"

"From the library."

"Sure nobody's listening in, in the hall?"

"Why should they?"

"Well, you never know. Are the police still about the house?"

"No, they've gone for the moment, anyhow. Oh, Vivian dear, it's been awful."

"Yes, yes, it must have, I'm sure. But look here, Adele, we've got to be careful."

"Oh, of course, darling."

"Don't call me darling through the phone. It isn't safe."

"Aren't you being a little bit panicky, Vivian? After all, everybody says darling nowadays."

"Yes, yes, that's true enough. But listen. Don't telephone to me, and don't write."

"But, Vivian—"

"It's just for the present, you understand. We must be careful."

"Oh. All right." Her voice sounded offended.

"Adele, listen. My letters to you. You did burn them, didn't you?"

There was a momentary hesitation before Adele Fortescue said, "Of course. I told you I was going to do so."

"That's all right, then. Well, I'll ring off now. Don't phone and don't write. You'll hear from me in good time."

He put the receiver back on its hook. He stroked his cheek thoughtfully. He didn't like that moment's hesitation. Had Adele burnt his letters? Women were all the same. They promised to burn things and then didn't.

Letters, Mr. Dubois thought to himself. Women always wanted you to write them letters. He himself tried to be careful, but sometimes one could not get out of it. What had he said exactly in the few letters he had written to Adele Fortescue? It was the usual sort of gup, he thought, gloomily. But were there any special words—special phrases that the police could twist to make them say what they wanted them to say? He remembered the Edith Thompson case. His letters were innocent enough, he thought, but he could not be sure. His uneasiness grew. Even if Adele had not al-

ready burnt his letters, would she have the sense to burn them now? Or
had the police already got hold of them? Where did she keep them, he
wondered. Probably in the sitting-room of hers upstairs. That gimcrack little desk, probably. Sham antique Louis xiv. She had said something to
him once about there being a secret drawer in it. Secret drawer! That
would not fool the police long. But there were no police about the house
now. She had said so. They had been there that morning, and now they
had all gone away.

Up to now they had probably been busy looking for possible sources of
poison in the food. They would not, he hoped, have got round to a room-
by-room search of the house. Perhaps they would have to ask permission
or get a search warrant to do that. It was possible that if he acted now, at
once—

He visualized the house clearly in his mind's eye. It would be getting
towards dusk. Tea would be brought in, either into the library or into the
drawing-room. Everyone would be assembled downstairs and the servants
would be having tea in the servants' hall. There would be no one upstairs
on the first floor. Easy to walk up through the garden, skirting the yew
hedges that provided such admirable cover. Then there was the little door
at the side onto the terrace. That was never locked until just before
bedtime. One could slip through there and, choosing one's moment, slip
upstairs.

Vivian Dubois considered very carefully what it behooved him to do
next. If Fortescue's death had been put down to a seizure or to a stroke, as
surely it ought to have been, the position would be very different. As it
was—Dubois murmured under his breath, "Better be safe than sorry."

II

Mary Dove came slowly down the big staircase. She paused a moment at
the window on the half landing, from which she had seen Inspector
Neele arrive on the preceding day. Now, as she looked out in the half-
light, she noticed a man's figure just disappearing round the yew hedge.
She wondered if it was Lancelot Fortescue, the prodigal son. He had, perhaps, dismissed his car at the gate and was wandering round the garden,
recollecting old times there before tackling a possibly hostile family. Mary
Dove felt rather sympathetic towards Lance. A half smile on her lips, she

went on downstairs. In the hall she encountered Gladys, the maid, who jumped nervously at the sight of her.

"Was that the telephone I heard just now?" Mary asked. "Who was it?"

"Oh, that was a wrong number. Thought we were the laundry." Gladys sounded breathless and rather hurried. "And before that, it was Mr. Dubois. He wanted to speak to the mistress."

"I see."

Mary went on across the hall. Turning her head, she said, "It's teatime, I think. Haven't you brought it in yet?"

Gladys said, "I don't think it's half-past four yet, is it, miss?"

"It's twenty minutes to five. Bring it in now, will you?"

Mary Dove went on into the library where Adele Fortescue, sitting on the sofa, was staring at the fire, picking with her fingers at a small lace handkerchief. Adele said fretfully, "Where's tea?"

Mary Dove said, "It's just coming in."

A log had fallen out of the fireplace, and Mary Dove knelt down at the grate and replaced it with the tongs, adding another piece of wood and a little coal.

Gladys went out into the kitchen where Mrs. Crump raised a red and wrathful face from the kitchen table where she was mixing pastry in a large bowl.

"The library bell's been ringing and ringing. Time you took in the tea, my girl."

"All right, all right, Mrs. Crump."

"What I'll say to Crump tonight," muttered Mrs. Crump. "I'll tell him off."

Gladys went on into the pantry. She had not cut any sandwiches. Well, she jolly well wasn't going to cut sandwiches. They'd got plenty to eat without that, hadn't they? Two cakes, biscuits, and scones and honey. Fresh, black-market farm butter. Plenty without her bothering to cut tomato or *foie gras* sandwiches. She'd got other things to think about. Fair temper Mrs. Crump was in, all because Mr. Crump had gone out this afternoon. Well, it was his day out, wasn't it? Quite right of him, Gladys thought.

Mrs. Crump called out from the kitchen, "The kettle's boiling its head off. Aren't you ever going to make that tea?"

"Coming."

She jerked some tea without measuring it into the big silver pot, carried the pot into the kitchen and poured the boiling water into it. She added the teapot and the kettle to the big silver tray and carried the whole thing through to the library where she set it on the small table near the sofa. She went back hurriedly for the other tray with the eatables on it. She carried the latter as far as the hall when the sudden jarring noise of the grandfather clock preparing itself to strike made her jump.

In the library, Adele Fortescue said querulously to Mary Dove, "Where is everybody this afternoon?"

"I really don't know, Mrs. Fortescue. Miss Fortescue came in some time ago. I think Mrs. Percival's writing letters in her room."

Adele said pettishly, "Writing letters, writing letters. That woman never stops writing letters. She's like all people of her class. She takes an absolute delight in death and misfortune. Ghoulish, that's what I call it. Absolutely ghoulish."

Mary murmured tactfully, "I'll tell her that tea is ready."

Going towards the door, she drew back a little in the doorway as Elaine Fortescue came into the room.

Elaine said, "It's cold," and dropped down by the fireplace, rubbing her hands before the blaze.

Mary stood for a moment in the hall. A large tray with cakes on it was standing on one of the hall chests. Since it was getting dark in the hall, Mary switched on the light. As she did so, she thought she heard Jennifer Fortescue walking along the passage upstairs. Nobody, however, came down the stairs, and Mary went up the staircase and along the corridor.

Percival Fortescue and his wife occupied a self-contained suite in one wing of the house. Mary tapped on the sitting-room door. Mrs. Percival liked you to tap on doors, a fact which always roused Crump's scorn of her. Her voice said briskly, "Come in."

Mary opened the door and murmured, "Tea is just coming in, Mrs. Percival."

She was rather surprised to see Jennifer Fortescue with her outdoor clothes on. She was just divesting herself of a long, camel-hair coat.

"I didn't know you'd been out," said Mary.

Mrs. Percival sounded slightly out of breath.

"Oh, I was just in the garden, that's all. Just getting a little air. Really, though, it was too cold. I shall be glad to get down to the fire. The central heating here isn't as good as it might be. Somebody must speak to the gardeners about it, Miss Dove."

"I'll do so," Mary promised.

Jennifer Fortescue dropped her coat on a chair and followed Mary out of the room. She went down the stairs ahead of Mary, who drew back a little to give her precedence. In the hall, rather to Mary's surprise, she noticed the tray of eatables was still there. She was about to go out to the pantry and call to Gladys when Adele Fortescue appeared in the door to the library, saying in an irritable voice, "Aren't we ever going to have anything to eat for tea?"

Quickly Mary picked up the tray and took it into the library, disposing the various things on low tables near the fireplace. She was carrying the empty tray out to the hall again when the front doorbell rang. Setting down the tray, Mary went to the door herself. If this was the prodigal son at last, she was rather curious to see him. How unlike the rest of the Fortescues, Mary thought, as she opened the door and looked up into the dark, lean face and the faintly quizzical twist of the mouth. She said quietly, "Mr. Lancelot Fortescue?"

"Himself."

Mary peered beyond him.

"Your luggage?"

"I've paid off the taxi. This is all I've got."

He picked up a medium-sized zip bag. Some faint feeling of surprise in her mind, Mary said, "Oh, you did come in a taxi. I thought perhaps you'd walked up. And your wife?"

His face set in a rather grim line, Lance said, "My wife won't be coming. At least, not just yet."

"I see. Come this way, will you, Mr. Fortescue? Everyone is in the library, having tea."

She took him to the library door and left him there. She thought to herself that Lancelot Fortescue was a very attractive person. A second thought followed the first. Probably a great many other women thought so, too.

III

"Lance!"

Elaine came hurrying forward towards him. She flung her arms round his neck and hugged him with a schoolgirl abandon that Lance found quite surprising.

"Hullo. Here I am."

He disengaged himself gently.

"This is Jennifer?"

Jennifer Fortescue looked at him with eager curiosity.

"I'm afraid Val's been detained in town," she said. "There's so much to see to, you know. All the arrangements to make and everything. Of course it all comes on Val. He has to see to everything. You can really have no idea what we're all going through."

"It must be terrible for you," said Lance gravely.

He turned to the woman on the sofa, who was sitting with a piece of scone and honey in her hand, quietly appraising him.

"Of course," cried Jennifer, "you don't know Adele, do you?"

Lance murmured "Oh yes, I do" as he took Adele Fortescue's hand in his. As he looked down at her, her eyelids fluttered. She set down the scone she was eating with her left hand and just touched the arrangement of her hair. It was a feminine gesture. It marked her recognition of the entry to the room of a personable man. She said in her thick, soft voice, "Sit down here on the sofa beside me, Lance." She poured out a cup of tea for him. "I'm so glad you've come," she went on. "We badly need another man in the house."

Lance said, "You must let me do everything I can to help."

"You know—but perhaps you don't know—we've had the police here. They think—they think—" she broke off and cried out passionately, "Oh, it's awful! Awful!"

"I know." Lance was grave and sympathetic. "As a matter of fact, they met me at London Airport."

"The police met you?"

"Yes."

"What did they say?"

"Well," Lance was deprecating, "they told me what had happened."

"He was poisoned," said Adele, "that's what they think, what they say. Not food poisoning. Real poisoning, by someone. I believe, I really do believe they think it's one of us."

Lance gave her a sudden, quick smile.

"That's their pigeon," he said consolingly. "It's no good our worrying. What a scrumptious tea! It's a long time since I've seen a good English tea."

The others fell in with his mood soon enough. Adele said suddenly, "But your wife—haven't you got a wife, Lance?"

"I've got a wife, yes. She's in London."

"But aren't you—hadn't you better bring her down here?"

"Plenty of time to make plans," said Lance. "Pat—oh, Pat's quite all right where she is."

Elaine said sharply,

"You don't mean—you don't think—"

Lance said quickly, "What a wonderful-looking chocolate cake. I must have some." Cutting himself a slice, he asked, "Is Aunt Effie alive still?"

"Oh, yes, Lance. She won't come down and have meals with us or anything, but she's quite well. Only, she's getting very peculiar."

"She always was peculiar," said Lance. "I must go up and see her after tea."

Jennifer Fortescue murmured, "At her age one does really feel that she ought to be in some kind of a home. I mean somewhere where she will be properly looked after."

"Heaven help any old ladies' home that got Aunt Effie in their midst," said Lance. He added, "Who's the demure piece of goods who let me in?"

Adele looked surprised.

"Didn't Crump let you in? The butler? Oh no, I forgot. It's his day out today. But surely Gladys—"

Lance gave a description. "Blue eyes, hair parted in the middle, soft voice, butter wouldn't melt in the mouth. What goes on behind it all, I wouldn't like to say."

"That," said Jennifer, "would be Mary Dove."

Elaine said, "She sort of runs things for us."

"Does she, now."

Adele said, "She's really very useful."

"Yes," said Lance thoughtfully, "I should think she might be."

"But what is so nice is," said Jennifer, "that she knows her place. She never presumes, if you know what I mean."

"Clever Mary Dove," said Lance, and helped himself to another piece of chocolate cake.

Chapter Twelve

"So you've turned up again like a bad penny," said Miss Ramsbottom. Lance grinned at her. "Just as you say, Aunt Effie."

"Humph!" Miss Ramsbottom sniffed disapprovingly. "You've chosen a nice time to do it. Your father got himself murdered yesterday, the house is full of police poking about everywhere, grubbing in the dustbins, even. I've seen them out of the window." She paused, sniffed again, and asked, "Got your wife with you?"

"No. I left Pat in London."

"That shows some sense. I shouldn't bring her here if I were you. You never know what might happen."

"To her? To Pat?"

"To anybody," said Miss Ramsbottom.

Lance Fortescue looked at her thoughtfully.

"Got any ideas about it all, Aunt Effie?" he asked.

Miss Ramsbottom did not reply directly. "I had an Inspector here yesterday asking me questions. He didn't get much change out of me. But he wasn't such a fool as he looked, not by a long way." She added with some indignation, "What your grandfather would feel if he knew we had the police in the house—it's enough to make him turn in his grave. A strict Plymouth Brother he was all his life. The fuss there was when he found out I'd been attending Church of England services in the evening! And I'm sure that was harmless enough compared to murder."

Normally Lance would have smiled at this, but his long, dark face remained serious. He said, "D'you know, I'm quite in the dark after having been away so long. What's been going on here of late?"

Miss Ramsbottom raised her eyes to heaven.

"Godless doings," she said firmly.

"Yes, yes, Aunt Effie, you would say that anyway. But what gives the police the idea that Dad was killed here, in this house?"

"Adultery is one thing and murder is another," said Miss Ramsbottom. "I shouldn't like to think it of her, I shouldn't, indeed."

Lance looked alert. "Adele?" he asked.

"My lips are sealed," said Miss Ramsbottom.

"Come on, old dear," said Lance. "It's a lovely phrase, but it doesn't mean a thing. Adele had a boy friend? Adele and the boy friend fed him henbane in the morning tea. Is that the setup?"

"I'll trouble you not to joke about it."

"I wasn't really joking, you know."

"I'll tell you one thing," said Miss Ramsbottom suddenly. "I believe that girl knows something about it."

"Which girl?" Lance looked surprised.

"The one that sniffs," said Miss Ramsbottom. "The one that ought to have brought me up my tea this afternoon, but didn't. Gone out without leave, so they say. Well, shouldn't wonder if she had gone to the police. Who let you in?"

"Someone called Mary Dove, I understand. Very meek and mild, but not really. Is she the one who's gone to the police?"

"She wouldn't go to the police," said Miss Ramsbottom. "No—I mean that silly little parlourmaid. She's been twitching and jumping like a rabbit all day. 'What's the matter with you?' I said. 'Have you got a guilty conscience?' She said, 'I never did anything—I wouldn't do a thing like that.' 'I hope you wouldn't,' I said to her, 'but there's something worrying you now, isn't there?' Then she began to sniff and said she didn't want to get anybody into trouble, she was sure it must be all a mistake. I said to her, I said, 'Now, my girl, you speak the truth and shame the devil.' That's what I said. 'You go to the police,' I said, 'and tell them anything you know, because no good ever came,' I said, 'of hushing up the truth, however unpleasant it is.' Then she talked a lot of nonsense about how she couldn't go to the police, they'd never believe her and what on earth should she say? She ended up by saying anyway she didn't know anything at all."

"You don't think," Lance hesitated, "that she was just making herself important?"

"No, I don't. I think she was scared. I think she saw something or heard something that's given her some idea about the whole thing. It may be important, or it mayn't be of the least consequence."

"You don't think she herself could've had a grudge against Father and—" Lance hesitated.

Miss Ramsbottom was shaking her head decidedly.

"She's not the kind of girl your father would have taken the least notice of. No man ever will take much notice of her, poor girl. Ah, well, it's all the better for her soul, that, I dare say."

Lance took no interest in Gladys's soul. He asked, "You think she may have run along to the police station?"

Aunt Effie nodded vigorously.

"Yes. I think she mayn't like to've said anything to them in this house, in case somebody overheard her."

Lance asked, "Do you think she may have seen someone tampering with the food?"

Aunt Effie threw him a sharp glance.

"It's possible, isn't it?" she said.

"Yes, I suppose so." Then he added apologetically, "The whole thing still seems so wildly improbable. Like a detective story."

"Percival's wife is a hospital nurse," said Miss Ramsbottom.

The remark seemed so unconnected with what had gone before that Lance looked at her in a puzzled fashion.

"Hospital nurses are used to handling drugs," said Miss Ramsbottom. Lance looked doubtful.

"This stuff—taxine—is it ever used in medicine?"

"They get it from yewberries, I gather. Children eat yewberries sometimes," said Miss Ramsbottom. "Makes them very ill, too. I remember a case when I was a child. It made a great impression on me. I never forgot it. Things you remember come in useful sometimes."

Lance raised his head sharply and stared at her.

"Natural affection is one thing," said Miss Ramsbottom, "and I hope I've got as much of it as anyone. But I won't stand for wickedness. Wickedness has to be destroyed."

II

"Went off without a word to me," said Mrs. Crump, raising her red, wrathful face from the pastry she was now rolling out on the board. "Slipped out without a word to anybody. Sly, that's what it is. Sly! Afraid she'd be stopped, and I would have stopped her if I'd caught her! The idea! There's the master dead, Mr. Lance coming home that hasn't been home for years, and I said to Crump, I said, 'Day out or no day out, I know my duty. There's not going to be cold supper tonight as is usual on a Thursday, but a proper dinner. A gentleman coming home from abroad with his wife, what was formerly married in the aristocracy, things must be properly done.' You know me, miss, you know I take a pride in my work."

Mary Dove, the recipient of these confidences, nodded her head gently.

"And what does Crump say?" Mrs. Crump's voice rose angrily. " 'It's my day off and I'm goin' off,' that's what he says. 'And a fig for the aristocracy,' he says. No pride in his work, Crump hasn't. So off he goes and I tell Gladys she'll have to manage alone tonight. She just says, 'All right, Mrs. Crump,' then, when my back's turned out she sneaks. It wasn't her day out, anyway. Friday's her day. How we're going to manage now, I don't know. Thank goodness, Mr. Lance hasn't brought his wife here with him today."

"We shall manage, Mrs. Crump," Mary's voice was both soothing and authoritative, "if we just simplify the menu a little." She outlined a few suggestions. Mrs. Crump nodded unwilling acquiescence. "I shall be able to serve that quite easily," Mary concluded.

"You mean you'll wait at table yourself, miss?" Mrs. Crump sounded doubtful.

"If Gladys doesn't come back in time."

"She won't come back," said Mrs. Crump. "Gallivanting off, wasting her money somewhere in the shops. She's got a young man, you know, miss, though you wouldn't think it to look at her. Albert his name is. Going to get married next spring, so she tells me. Don't know what the married state's like, these girls don't. What I've been through with Crump." She sighed, then said in an ordinary voice, "What about tea, miss? Who's going to clear it away and wash it up?"

"I'll do that," said Mary. "I'll go and do it now."

The lights had not been turned on in the drawing-room, though Adele Fortescue was still sitting on the sofa behind the tea tray.

"Shall I switch the lights on, Mrs. Fortescue?" Mary asked. Adele did not answer.

Mary switched on the lights and went across to the window where she pulled the curtains across. It was only then that she turned her head and saw the face of the woman who had sagged back against the cushions. A half-eaten scone spread with honey was beside her and her tea cup was still half-full. Death had come to Adele Fortescue suddenly and swiftly.

III

"Well?" demanded Inspector Neele impatiently.

The doctor said promptly,

"Cyanide—potassium cyanide probably—in the tea."

"Cyanide," muttered Neele.

The doctor looked at him with slight curiosity.

"You're taking this hard. Any special reason?"

"She was cast as a murderess," said Neele.

"And she turns out to be a victim. Hm. You'll have to think again, won't you?"

Neele nodded. His face was bitter and his jaw was grimly set.

Poisoned! Right under his nose. Taxine in Rex Fortescue's breakfast coffee, cyanide in Adele Fortescue's tea. Still an intimate family affair. Or so it seemed.

Adele Fortescue, Jennifer Fortescue, Elaine Fortescue and the newly arrived Lance Fortescue had had tea together in the library. Lance had gone up to see Miss Ramsbottom, Jennifer had gone to her own sitting-room to write letters, Elaine had been the last to leave the library. According to her, Adele had then been in perfect health and had just been pouring herself out a last cup of tea.

A last cup of tea! Yes, it had indeed been her last cup of tea.

And after that a blank twenty minutes, perhaps, until Mary Dove had come into the room and discovered the body.

And during that twenty minutes—

Inspector Neele swore to himself and went out into the kitchen.

Sitting in a chair by the kitchen table, the vast figure of Mrs. Crump, her belligerence pricked like a balloon, hardly stirred as he came in.

"Where's that girl? Has she come back yet?"

"Gladys? No, she's not back. Won't be, I suspect, until eleven o'clock."

"She made the tea, you say, and took it in."

"I didn't touch it, sir, as God's my witness. And what's more, I don't believe Gladys did anything she shouldn't. She wouldn't do a thing like that —not Gladys. She's a good enough girl, sir—a bit foolish like, that's all—not wicked."

No, Neele did not think that Gladys was wicked. He did not think that Gladys was a poisoner. And in any case the cyanide had not been in the teapot.

"But what made her go off suddenly—like this? It wasn't her day out, you say."

"No, sir, tomorrow's her day out."

"Does Crump—"

Mrs. Crump's belligerence suddenly revived. Her voice rose wrathfully.

"Don't you go fastening anything on Crump. Crump's out of it. He went off at three o'clock—and thankful I am now that he did. He's as much out of it as Mr. Percival himself."

Percival Fortescue had only just returned from London—to be greeted by the astounding news of this second tragedy.

"I wasn't accusing Crump," said Neele mildly. "I just wondered if he knew anything about Gladys's plans."

"She had her best nylons on," said Mrs. Crump. "She was up to something. Don't tell me! Didn't cut any sandwiches for tea, either. Oh yes, she was up to something. I'll give her a piece of my mind when she comes back."

When she comes back—

A faint uneasiness possessed Neele. To shake it off, he went upstairs to Adele Fortescue's bedroom. A lavish apartment—all rose brocade hangings and a vast gilt bed. On one side of the room was a door into a mirror-lined bathroom with a sunken, orchid pink porcelain bath. Beyond the bathroom, reached by a communicating door, was Rex Fortescue's room. Neele went back into Adele's bedroom, and through the door on the farther side of the room into her sitting-room.

The room was furnished in Empire style with a rose pile carpet. Neele only gave it a cursory glance, for that particular room had had his close attention on the preceding day—with special attention paid to the small, elegant desk.

Now, however, he stiffened to sudden attention. On the center of the rose pile carpet was a small piece of caked mud.

Neele went over to it and picked it up. The mud was still damp.

He looked round—there were no footprints visible—only this one, isolated fragment of wet earth.

IV

Inspector Neele looked round the bedroom that belonged to Gladys Martin. It was past eleven o'clock. Crump had come in half an hour ago, but there was still no sign of Gladys. Inspector Neele looked round him. Whatever Gladys's training had been, her own natural instincts were slovenly. The bed, Inspector Neele judged, was seldom made, the windows seldom opened. Gladys's personal habits, however, were not his immediate concern. Instead, he went carefully through her possessions.

They consisted, for the most part, of cheap and rather pathetic finery. There was little that was durable or of good quality. The elderly Ellen, whom he had called upon to assist him, had not been helpful. She didn't know what clothes Gladys had or hadn't. She couldn't say what, if anything, was missing. He turned from the clothes and the underclothes to the contents of the chest of drawers. There Gladys kept her treasures. There were picture post cards and newspaper cuttings, knitting patterns, hints on beauty culture, dressmaking and fashion advice.

Inspector Neele sorted them neatly into various categories. The picture post cards consisted mainly of views of various places where he presumed Gladys had spent her holidays. Among them were three picture post cards signed "Bert." Bert he took to be the "young man" referred to by Mrs. Crump. The first post card said, in an illiterate hand, "All the best. Missing you a lot. Yours ever, Bert." The second said, "Lots of nice-looking girls here but not one that's a patch on you. Be seeing you soon. Don't forget our date. And remember after that—it's thumbs up and living happy ever after."

The third said merely, "Don't forget. I'm trusting you. Love, B."

Next, Neele looked through the newspaper cuttings and sorted them into three piles. There were the dressmaking and beauty hints, there were items about cinema stars to which Gladys had appeared greatly addicted, and she had also, it appeared, been attracted by the latest marvels of science. There were cuttings about flying saucers, about secret weapons, about truth drugs used by Russians, and claims for fantastic drugs discovered by American doctors. All the witchcraft, so Neele thought, of our twentieth century. But in all the contents of the room there was nothing to give him a clue to her disappearance. She had kept no diary, not that he had expected that. It was a remote possibility. There was no unfinished letter, no record at all of anything she might have seen in the house which could have had a bearing on Rex Fortescue's death. Whatever Gladys had seen, whatever Gladys had known, there was no record of it. It would still have to be guesswork why the second tea tray had been left in the hall, and Gladys herself had so suddenly vanished.

Sighing, Neele left the room, shutting the door behind him.

As he prepared to descend the small, winding stairs he heard a noise of running feet coming along the landing below.

The agitated face of Sergeant Hay looked up at him from the bottom of the stairs. Sergeant Hay was panting a little.

"Sir," he said urgently, "Sir! We've found her."

"Found her?"

"It was the housemaid, sir—Ellen—remembered as she hadn't brought the clothes in from where they were hanging on the line—just round the corner from the back door. So she went out with a torch to take them in and she almost fell over the body—the girl's body—strangled, she was, with a stocking round her throat—been dead for hours, I'd say. And, sir, it's a wicked kind of joke—there was a clothes peg clipped on her nose—"

Chapter Thirteen

AN ELDERLY LADY traveling by train had bought three morning papers, and each of them, as she finished it, folded it and laid it aside, showed the same headline. It was no longer a question now of a small paragraph hidden away in the corner of the papers. There were headlines with flaring announcements of Triple Tragedy at Yewtree Lodge.

The old lady sat very upright, looking out of the window of the train, her lips pursed together, an expression of distress and disapproval on her pink and white wrinkled face. Miss Marple had left St. Mary Mead by the early train, changing at the junction and going on to London where she took a Circle train to another London terminus and thence on to Baydon Heath.

At the station she signaled a taxi and asked to be taken to Yewtree Lodge. So charming, so innocent, such a fluffy and pink and white old lady was Miss Marple that she gained admittance to what was now practically a fortress in a state of siege far more easily than could have been believed possible. Though an army of reporters and photographers was being kept at bay by the police, Miss Marple was allowed to drive in without question, so impossible would it have been to believe that she was anyone but an elderly relative of the family.

Miss Marple paid off the taxi in a careful assortment of small change, and rang the front doorbell. Crump opened it and Miss Marple summed him up with an experienced glance. A shifty eye, she said to herself. Scared to death, too.

Crump saw a tall, elderly lady wearing an old-fashioned tweed coat and skirt, a couple of scarves and a small felt hat with a bird's wing. The old lady carried a capacious handbag, and an aged but good quality suitcase reposed by her feet.

Crump recognized a lady when he saw one and said, "Yes, madam?" in his best and most respectful voice.

"Could I see the mistress of the house, please?" said Miss Marple.

Crump drew back to let her in. He picked up the suitcase and put it carefully down in the hall.

"Well, madam," he said rather dubiously, "I don't know who exactly—" Miss Marple helped him out.

"I have come," she said, "to speak about the poor girl who was killed. Gladys Martin."

"Oh, I see, madam. Well, in that case—" he broke off and looked towards the library door from which a tall young woman had just emerged. "This is Mrs. Lance Fortescue, madam," he said.

Pat came forward, and she and Miss Marple looked at each other. Miss Marple was aware of a faint feeling of surprise. She had not expected to see someone like Patricia Fortescue in this particular house. Its interior was much as she had pictured it, but Pat did not somehow match with that interior.

"It's about Gladys, madam," said Crump helpfully.

Pat said rather hesitatingly, "Will you come in here? We shall be quite alone."

She led the way into the library and Miss Marple followed her.

"There wasn't anyone specially you wanted to see, was there?" said Pat. "Because perhaps I shan't be much good. You see, my husband and I only came back from Africa a few days ago. We don't really know anything about the household. But I can fetch my sister-in-law or my brother-in-law's wife."

Miss Marple looked at the girl and liked her. She liked her gravity and her simplicity. For some strange reason she felt sorry for her. A background of shabby chintz and horses and dogs, Miss Marple felt vaguely, would have been much more suitable than this richly furnished interior décor. At the pony show and gymkhanas held locally round St. Mary Mead, Miss Marple had met many Pats and knew them well. She felt at home with this rather unhappy-looking girl.

"It's very simple, really," said Miss Marple, taking off her gloves carefully and smoothing out the fingers of them. "I read in the paper, you see, about Gladys Martin having been killed. And of course I know all about her. She comes from my part of the country. I trained her, in fact, for domestic service. And since this terrible thing has happened to her, I felt—well, I felt that I ought to come and see if there was anything I could do about it."

"Yes," said Pat. "Of course. I see."

And she did see. Miss Marple's action appeared to her natural and inevitable.

"I think it's a very good thing you have come," said Pat. "Nobody seems to know very much about her. I mean relations and all that."

"No," said Miss Marple, "of course not. She hadn't got any relations. She came to me from the orphanage. St. Faith's. A very well-run place, though sadly short of funds. We do our best for the girls there, try to give them a good training and all that. Gladys came to me when she was seventeen, and I taught her how to wait at table and keep the silver and everything like that. Of course, she didn't stay long. They never do. As soon as she got a little experience, she went and took a job in a café. The girls nearly always want to do that. They think it's freer, you know, and a gayer life. Perhaps it may be. I really don't know."

"I never even saw her," said Pat. "Was she a pretty girl?"

"Oh, no," said Miss Marple, "not at all. Adenoids, and a good many spots. She was rather pathetically stupid, too. I don't suppose," went on Miss Marple thoughtfully, "that she ever made many friends anywhere. She was very keen on men, poor girl. But men didn't take much notice of her, and other girls rather made use of her."

"It sounds rather cruel," said Pat.

"Yes, my dear," said Miss Marple, "life is cruel, I'm afraid. One doesn't really know what to do with the Gladyses. They enjoy going to the pictures and all that, but they're always thinking of impossible things that can't possibly happen to them. Perhaps that's happiness of a kind. But they get disappointed. I think Gladys was disappointed in café and restaurant life. Nothing very glamorous or interesting happened to her and it was just hard on the feet. Probably that's why she came back into private service. Do you know how long she'd been here?"

Pat shook her head.

"Not very long, I should think. Only a month or two." Pat paused and then went on, "It seems so horrible and futile that she should have been caught up in this thing. I suppose she'd seen something or noticed something."

"It was the clothes peg that really worried me," said Miss Marple in her gentle voice.

"The clothes peg?"

"Yes. I read about it in the papers. I suppose it is true? That when she was found there was a clothes peg clipped onto her nose."

Pat nodded. The color rose to Miss Marple's pink cheeks.

"That's what made me so very angry, if you can understand, my dear. It was such a cruel, contemptuous gesture. It gave me a kind of picture of the murderer. To do a thing like that! It's very wicked, you know, to affront human dignity. Particularly if you've already killed."

Pat said slowly,

"I think I see what you mean." She got up. "I think you'd better come and see Inspector Neele. He's in charge of the case, and he's here now. You'll like him, I think. He's a very human person." She gave a sudden, quick shiver. "The whole thing is such a horrible nightmare. Pointless. Mad. Without rhyme or reason in it."

"I wouldn't say that, you know," said Miss Marple. "No, I wouldn't say that."

Inspector Neele was looking tired and haggard. Three deaths, and the press of the whole country whooping down the trail. A case that seemed to be shaping in well-known fashion had gone suddenly haywire. Adele Fortescue, the appropriate suspect, was now the second victim of an incomprehensible murder case. At the close of that fatal day the Assistant Commissioner had sent for Neele, and the two men had talked far into the night.

In spite of his dismay, or rather behind it, Inspector Neele had felt a faint inward satisfaction. That pattern of the wife and the lover. It had been too slick, too easy. He had always mistrusted it. And now that mistrust of his was justified.

"The whole thing takes on an entirely different aspect," the A.C. had said, striding up and down his room and frowning. "It looks to me, Neele, as though we'd got someone mentally unhinged to deal with. First the husband, then the wife. But the very circumstances of the case seem to show that it's an inside job. It's all there, in the family. Someone who sat down to breakfast with Fortescue put taxine in his coffee or on his food. Someone who had tea with the family that day put potassium cyanide in Adele Fortescue's cup of tea. Someone trusted, unnoticed, one of the family. Which of 'em, Neele?"

Neele said dryly,

"Percival wasn't there, so that lets him out again. That lets him out again," Inspector Neele repeated.

The A.C. looked at him sharply. Something in the repetition had attracted his attention.

"What's the idea, Neele? Out with it, man."

Inspector Neele looked stolid.

"Nothing sir. Not so much as an idea. All I say is it was very convenient for him."

"A bit too convenient, eh?" The A.C. reflected and shook his head. "You think he might have managed it somehow? Can't see how, Neele. No, I can't see how."

He added, "And he's a cautious type, too."

"But quite intelligent, sir."

"You don't fancy the women. Is that it? Yet the women are indicated. Elaine Fortescue and Percival's wife. They were at breakfast and they were at tea that day. Either of them could have done it. No signs of anything abnormal about them? Well, it doesn't always show. There might be something in their past medical record."

Inspector Neele did not answer. He was thinking of Mary Dove. He had no definite reason for suspecting her, but that was the way his thoughts lay. There was something unexplained about her, unsatisfactory. A faint, amused antagonism. That had been her attitude after the death of Rex Fortescue. What was her attitude now? Her behavior and manner were, as always, exemplary. There was no longer, he thought, amusement. Perhaps not even antagonism, but he wondered whether, once or twice, he had not seen a trace of fear. He had been to blame, culpably to blame, in the matter of Gladys Martin. That slight, guilty confusion of hers he had put down to no more than a natural nervousness of the police. He had come across that guilty nervousness so often. In this case it had been something more. Gladys had seen or heard something which had aroused her suspicions. It was probably, he thought, some quite small thing, something so vague and indefinite that she had hardly liked to speak about it. And now, poor little rabbit, she would never speak.

Inspector Neele looked with some interest at the mild, earnest face of the old lady who confronted him now at Yewtree Lodge. He had been in two minds at first how to treat her, but he quickly made up his mind. Miss Marple would be useful to him. She was upright, of unimpeachable rectitude and she had, like most old ladies, time on her hands and an old maid's nose for scenting bits of gossip. She'd get things out of servants and out of the women of the Fortescue family, perhaps, that he and his policemen would never get. Talk, conjecture, reminiscences, repetitions of things said and done, out of them all she would pick the salient facts. So Inspector Neele was gracious.

"It's uncommonly good of you to have come here, Miss Marple," he said.

"It was my duty, Inspector Neele. The girl had lived in my house. I feel, in a sense, responsible for her. She was a very silly girl, you know."

Inspector Neele looked at her appreciatively.

"Yes," he said, "just so."

She had gone, he felt, to the heart of the matter.

"She wouldn't know," said Miss Marple, "what she ought to do. If, I mean, something came up. Oh, dear, I'm expressing myself very badly."

Inspector Neele said that he understood.

"She hadn't got good judgment as to what was important or not, that's what you mean, isn't it?"

"Oh yes, exactly, Inspector."

"When you say she was silly—" Inspector Neele broke off.

Miss Marple took up the theme.

"She was the credulous type. She was the sort of girl who would have given her savings to a swindler, if she'd had any savings. Of course, she never did have any savings because she always spent her money on most unsuitable clothes."

"What about men?" asked the Inspector.

"She wanted a young man badly," said Miss Marple. "In fact, that's really, I think, why she left St. Mary Mead. The competition there is very keen. So few men. She did have hopes of the young man who delivered the fish. Young Fred had a pleasant word for all the girls, but of course he didn't mean anything by it. That upset poor Gladys quite a lot. Still, I gather she did get herself a young man in the end?"

Inspector Neele nodded.

"It seems so. Albert Evans, I gather, his name was. She seems to have met him at some holiday camp. He didn't give her a ring or anything, so maybe she made it all up. He was a mining engineer, so she told the cook."

"That seems most unlikely," said Miss Marple, "but I dare say it's what he told her. As I say, she'd believe anything. You don't connect him with this business at all?"

Inspector Neele shook his head.

"No. I don't think there are any complications of that kind. He never seems to have visited her. He sent her a post card from time to time, usually from a seaport. Probably Fourth Engineer on a boat on the Baltic run."

"Well," said Miss Marple, "I'm glad she had her little romance. Since her life has been cut short in this way—" She tightened her lips. "You know, Inspector, it makes me very, very angry." And she added, as she had said to Pat Fortescue, "Especially the clothes peg. That, Inspector, was really wicked."

Inspector Neele looked at her with interest.

"I know just what you mean, Miss Marple," he said.

Miss Marple coughed apologetically.

"I wonder—I suppose it would be great presumption on my part—if only could assist you in my very humble and, I'm afraid, very feminine way.

This is a wicked murderer, Inspector Neele, and the wicked should not go unpunished."

"That's an unfashionable belief nowadays, Miss Marple," Inspector Neele said rather grimly. "Not that I don't agree with you."

"There is a hotel near the station, or there's the Golf Hotel," said Miss Marple tentatively, "and I believe there's a Miss Ramsbottom in this house who is interested in foreign missions."

Inspector Neele looked at Miss Marple appraisingly.

"Yes," he said. "You've got something there, maybe. I can't say that I've had great success with the lady."

"It's really very kind of you, Inspector Neele," said Miss Marple. "I'm so glad you don't think I'm just a sensation hunter."

Inspector Neele gave a sudden, rather unexpected smile. He was thinking to himself that Miss Marple was very unlike the popular idea of an avenging fury. And yet, he thought, that was perhaps exactly what she was.

"Newspapers," said Miss Marple, "are often so sensational in their accounts. But hardly, I fear, as accurate as one might wish." She looked inquiringly at Inspector Neele. "If one could be sure of having just the sober facts."

"They're not particularly sober," said Neele. "Shorn of undue sensation, they're as follows. Mr. Fortescue died in his office as a result of taxine poisoning. Taxine is obtained from the berries and leaves of yew trees."

"Very convenient," Miss Marple said.

"Possibly," said Inspector Neele, "but we've no evidence as to that. As yet, that is." He stressed the point because it was here that he thought Miss Marple might be useful. If any brew or concoction of yewberries had been made in the house, Miss Marple was quite likely to come upon traces of it. She was the sort of old pussy who would make homemade liquors cordials and herb teas herself. She would know methods of making and methods of disposal.

"And Mrs. Fortescue?"

"Mrs. Fortescue had tea with the family in the library. The last person to leave the room and the tea table was Miss Elaine Fortescue, her step-daughter. She states that as she left the room Mrs. Fortescue was pouring herself out another cup of tea. Some twenty minutes or half-hour late Miss Dove, who acts as housekeeper, went in to remove the tea tray. Mrs Fortescue was still sitting on the sofa, dead. Beside her was a tea cup quarter full, and in the dregs of it was potassium cyanide."

"Which is almost immediate in its action, I believe," said Miss Marple.
"Exactly."

"Such dangerous stuff," murmured Miss Marple. "One has it to take wasps' nests but I'm always very, very careful."

"You're quite right," said Inspector Neele. "There was a packet of it in the gardener's shed here."

"Again very convenient," said Miss Marple. She added, "Was Mrs. Fortescue eating anything?"

"Oh, yes. They'd had tea."

"Cake, I suppose? Bread and butter? Scones, perhaps? Jam? Honey?"

"Yes, there were honey and scones, chocolate cake and swiss roll and various other plates of things." He looked at her curiously. "The potassium cyanide was in the tea, Miss Marple."

"Oh, yes, yes. I quite understand that. I was just getting the whole picture, so to speak. Rather significant, don't you think?"

He looked at her in a slightly puzzled fashion. Her cheeks were pink, her eyes were bright.

"And the third death, Inspector Neele?"

"Well, the facts there seem clear enough, too. The girl, Gladys, took the tea tray, then she brought the next tray into the hall, but left it there. She'd been rather absentminded all the day, apparently. After that no one saw her. The cook, Mrs. Crump, jumped to the conclusion that the girl had gone out without telling anybody. She based her belief, I think, on the fact that the girl was wearing a good pair of nylon stockings and her best shoes. There, however, she was proved quite wrong. The girl had obviously remembered suddenly that she had not taken in some clothes that were drying outside on the clothesline. She ran out to fetch them in, had taken down half of them apparently, when somebody took her unawares by slipping a stocking round her neck and—well, that was that."

"Someone from outside?" said Miss Marple.

"Perhaps," said Inspector Neele. "But perhaps someone from inside. Someone who'd been waiting his or her opportunity to get the girl alone. The girl was upset, nervous, when we first questioned her, but I'm afraid we didn't quite appreciate the importance of that."

"Oh, but how could you?" cried Miss Marple. "People so often do look guilty and embarrassed when they are questioned by the police."

"That's just it. But this time, Miss Marple, it was rather more than that. I think the girl Gladys had seen someone performing some action that seemed to her needed explanation. It can't, I think, have been anything very definite. Otherwise she would have spoken out. But I think she did betray the fact to the person in question. That person realized that Gladys was a danger."

"And so Gladys was strangled and a clothes peg clipped on her nose," murmured Miss Marple to herself.

"Yes, that's a nasty touch. A nasty, sneering sort of touch. Just a nasty bit of unnecessary bravado."

Miss Marple shook her head.

"Hardly unnecessary. It does all make a pattern, doesn't it?"

Inspector Neele looked at her curiously.

"I don't quite follow you, Miss Marple. What do you mean by a pattern?"

Miss Marple immediately became flustered.

"Well, I mean it does seem—I mean, regarded as a sequence, if you understand—well, one can't get away from facts, can one?"

"I don't think I quite understand."

"Well, I mean—first we have Mr. Fortescue. Rex Fortescue. Killed in his office in the city. And then we have Mrs. Fortescue, sitting here in the library and having tea. There were scones and honey. And then poor Gladys with the clothes peg on her nose. Just to point the whole thing. That very charming Mrs. Lance Fortescue said to me that there didn't seem to be any rhyme or reason in it, but I couldn't agree with her, because it's the rhyme that strikes one, isn't it?"

Inspector Neele said slowly, "I don't think—"

Miss Marple went on quickly, "I expect you're about thirty-five or thirty-six, aren't you, Inspector Neele? I think there was rather a reaction just then, when you were a little boy, I mean, against nursery rhymes. But if one has been brought up on Mother Goose—I mean it is really highly significant, isn't it? What I wondered was," Miss Marple paused, then appearing to take her courage in her hands, went on bravely, "Of course, it is great impertinence I know, on my part, saying this sort of thing to you."

"Please say anything you like, Miss Marple."

"Well, that's very kind of you. I shall. Though, as I say, I do it with the utmost diffidence because I know I am very old and rather muddleheaded, and I dare say my idea is of no value at all. But what I mean to say is: have you gone into the question of blackbirds?"

Chapter Fourteen

For about ten seconds Inspector Neele stared at Miss Marple with the utmost bewilderment. His first idea was that the old lady had gone off her head.

"Blackbirds?" he repeated.

Miss Marple nodded her head vigorously.

"Yes," she said, and forthwith recited,

> "Sing a song of sixpence, a pocketful of rye,
> Four and twenty blackbirds baked in a pie.
> When the pie was opened the birds began to sing.
> Wasn't that a dainty dish to set before the king?
>
> The king was in his counting house, counting out his money,
> The queen was in the parlour eating bread and honey,
> The maid was in the garden hanging out the clothes,
> When there came a little dickey bird and nipped off her nose."

"Good Lord," Inspector Neele said.

"I mean, it does fit," said Miss Marple. "It was rye in his pocket, wasn't it? One newspaper said so. The others just said cereal, which might mean anything. Farmer's Glory or Cornflakes—or even maize—but it was rye—"

Inspector Neele nodded.

"There you are," said Miss Marple, triumphantly. "Rex Fortescue. Rex means King. In his Counting House. And Mrs. Fortescue, the Queen in the parlour, eating bread and honey. And so, of course, the murderer had to put that clothes peg on poor Gladys's nose."

Inspector Neele said, "You mean the whole set up is crazy?"

"Well, one mustn't jump to conclusions, but it is certainly very odd. But you really must make inquiries about blackbirds. Because there must be blackbirds!"

It was at this point that Sergeant Hay came into the room, saying urgently, "Sir."

He broke off at the sight of Miss Marple.

Inspector Neele, recovering himself, said, "Thank you, Miss Marple. I'll look into the matter. Since you are interested in the girl, perhaps you would care to look over the things from her room. Sergeant Hay will show you them presently."

Miss Marple, accepting her dismissal, twittered her way out.

"Blackbirds!" murmured Inspector Neele to himself.

Sergeant Hay stared.

"Yes, Hay, what is it?"

"Sir," said Sergeant Hay urgently again. "Look at this."

He produced an article wrapped in a somewhat grubby handkerchief.

"Found it in the shrubbery," said Sergeant Hay. "Could have been chucked there from one of the back windows."

He tipped the object down on the desk in front of the Inspector, who leaned forward and inspected it with rising excitement. The exhibit was a nearly full pot of marmalade.

The Inspector stared at it without speech. His face assumed a peculiarly wooden and stupid appearance. In actual fact, this meant that Inspector Neele's mind was racing once more round an imaginary track. A moving picture was enacting itself before the eyes of his mind. He saw a new pot of marmalade, he saw hands carefully removing its cover, he saw a small quantity of marmalade removed, mixed with a preparation of taxine and replaced in the pot, the top smoothed over and the lid carefully replaced.

He broke off at this point to ask Sergeant Hay, "They don't take marmalade out of the pot and put it in fancy pots?"

"No, sir. Got into the way of serving it in its own pot during the war when things were scarce, and it's gone on like that ever since."

Neele murmured, "That made it easier, of course."

"What's more," said Sergeant Hay, "Mr. Fortescue was the only one that took marmalade for breakfast (and Mr. Percival when he was at home). The others had jam or honey."

Neele nodded.

"Yes," he said. "That made it very simple, didn't it?"

After a slight gap the moving picture went on in his mind. It was the breakfast table now. Rex Fortescue stretching out his hand for the marmalade pot, taking out a spoonful of marmalade and spreading it on his toast and butter. Easier, far easier that way than the risk and difficulty of insinuating it into his coffee cup. A foolproof method of administering the poison! And afterwards? Another gap and a picture that was not quite so clear. The replacing of that pot of marmalade by another with exactly the same amount taken from it. And then an open window. A hand and an arm flinging out that pot into the shrubbery. Whose hand and arm?

Whoever had tampered with that pot of marmalade need not have been present at the breakfast table. . . .

Inspector Neele said in a business-like voice,

"Well, we'll have of course to get this analyzed. See if there are any traces of taxine. We can't jump to conclusions."

"No, sir. There may be fingerprints, too."

"Probably not the ones we want," said Inspector Neele gloomily. "There'll be Gladys's, of course, and Crump's and Fortescue's own. Then probably Mrs. Crump's, the grocer's assistant and a few others! If anyone put taxine in here, they'd take care not to go playing about with their own fingers all over the pot. Anyway, as I say, we mustn't jump to conclusions. How do they order marmalade and where is it kept?"

The industrious Sergeant Hay had his answer pat for all these questions.

"Marmalade and jams come in in batches of six at a time. A new pot would be taken into the pantry when the old one was getting low."

"That means," said Neele, "that it could have been tampered with several days before it was actually brought onto the breakfast table. And anyone who was in the house or had access to the house could have tampered with it."

The term "access to the house" puzzled Sergeant Hay slightly. He did not see in what way his superior's mind was working.

But Neele was postulating what seemed to him a logical assumption.

If the marmalade had been tampered with beforehand, then surely that ruled out those persons who were actually at the breakfast table on the fatal morning.

Which opened up some interesting new possibilities.

He planned in his mind interviews with various people—this time with rather a different angle of approach.

He'd keep an open mind. . . .

He'd even consider seriously that old Miss What's-her-name's suggestions about the nursery rhyme. Because there was no doubt that that nursery rhyme fitted in a rather startling way. It fitted with a point that had worried him from the beginning. The pocket full of rye.

"Blackbirds?" murmured Inspector Neele to himself.

Sergeant Hay stared.

"It's not blackberry jelly, sir," he said. "It's marmalade."

II

Inspector Neele went in search of Mary Dove.

He found her in one of the bedrooms on the first floor, superintending Ellen, who was denuding the bed of what seemed to be clean sheets. A little pile of clean towels lay on a chair.

Inspector Neele looked puzzled.

"Somebody coming to stay?" he asked.

Mary Dove smiled at him. In contrast to Ellen, who looked grim and truculent, Mary was her usual imperturbable self.

"Actually," she said, "the opposite is the case."

Neele looked inquiringly at her.

"This is the guest room we had prepared for Mr. Gerald Wright."

"Gerald Wright? Who is he?"

"He's a friend of Miss Elaine Fortescue's." Mary's voice was carefully devoid of inflection.

"He was coming here—when?"

"I believe he arrived at the Golf Hotel the day after Mr. Fortescue's death."

"The day after."

"So Miss Fortescue said." Mary's voice was still impersonal. "She told me she wanted him to come and stay in the house, so I had a room prepared. Now, after these other two—tragedies—it seems more suitable that he should remain at the hotel."

"The Golf Hotel?"

"Yes."

"Quite," said Inspector Neele.

Ellen gathered up the sheets and towels and went out of the room.

Mary Dove looked inquiringly at Neele.

"You wanted to see me about something?"

Neele said pleasantly, "It's becoming important to get exact times very clearly stated. Members of the family all seem a little vague about time—perhaps understandably. You, on the other hand, Miss Dove, I have found extremely accurate in your statements as to times."

"Again understandably!"

"Yes—perhaps—I must certainly congratulate you on the way you have kept this house going in spite of the—well, panic—these last deaths must have caused." He paused and then asked curiously: "How did you do it?"

He had realized, astutely, that the one chink in the armor of Mary Dove's inscrutability was her pleasure in her own efficiency. She unbent slightly now as she answered.

"The Crumps wanted to leave at once, of course."

"We couldn't have allowed that."

"I know. But I also told them that Mr. Percival Fortescue would be more likely to be—well—generous—to those who had spared him inconvenience."

"And Ellen?"

"Ellen does not wish to leave."

"Ellen does not wish to leave," Neele repeated. "She has good nerves."

"She enjoys disasters," said Mary Dove. "Like Mrs. Percival, she finds in disaster a kind of pleasurable drama."

"Interesting—do you think Mrs. Percival has—enjoyed the tragedies?"

"No—of course not. That is going too far. I would merely say that it has enabled her to—well—stand up to them."

"And how have you yourself been affected, Miss Dove?"

Mary Dove shrugged her shoulders.

"It has not been a pleasant experience," she said dryly.

Inspector Neele felt again a longing to break down this cool young woman's defenses—to find out what was really going on behind the careful and efficient understatement of her whole attitude.

He merely said brusquely, "Now, to recapitulate times and places: the last time you saw Gladys Martin was in the hall before tea, and that was at twenty minutes to five?"

"Yes, I told her to bring in tea."

"You yourself were coming from where?"

"From upstairs. I thought I had heard the telephone a few minutes before."

"Gladys, presumably, had answered the telephone?"

"Yes. It was a wrong number. Someone who wanted the Baydon Heath Laundry."

"And that was the last time you saw her?"

"She brought the tea tray into the library about ten minutes or so later."

"After that Miss Elaine Fortescue came in?"

"Yes, about three or four minutes later. Then I went up to tell Mrs. Percival tea was ready."

"Did you usually do that?"

"Oh, no. People came in to tea when they pleased, but Mrs. Fortescue asked where everybody was. I thought I heard Mrs. Percival coming down, but that was a mistake—"

Neele interrupted. Here was something new.

"You mean you heard someone upstairs moving about?"

"Yes, at the head of the stairs, I thought. But no one came down so I went up. Mrs. Percival was in her bedroom. She had just come in. She had been out for a walk."

"Out for a walk—I see. The time being then—"

"Oh, nearly five o'clock, I think."

"And Mr. Lancelot Fortescue arrived—when?"

"A few minutes after I came downstairs again. I thought he had arrived earlier, but—"

Inspector Neele interrupted:

"Why did you think he had arrived earlier?"

"Because I thought I had caught sight of him through the landing window."

"In the garden, you mean?"

"Yes, I caught a glimpse of someone through the yew hedge, and I thought it would probably be he."

"This was when you were coming down, after telling Mrs. Percival Fortescue tea was ready?"

Mary corrected him.

"No, not then. It was earlier—when I came down the first time."

Inspector Neele stared.

"Are you sure about that, Miss Dove?"

"Yes, I'm perfectly sure. That's why I was surprised to see him—when he actually did ring the bell."

Inspector Neele shook his head. He kept his inner excitement out of his voice as he said, "It couldn't have been Lancelot Fortescue you saw. His train—which was due at 4:28—was nine minutes late. He arrived at Baydon Heath Station at 4:37. He had to wait a few minutes for a taxi—that train is always very full. It was actually nearly a quarter to five (five minutes after you had seen the man in the garden) when he left the station and it is a ten minutes' drive. He paid off the taxi at the gate here at about five minutes to five at the earliest. No, it wasn't Lancelot Fortescue you saw."

"I'm sure I did see someone."

"Yes, you saw someone. It was getting dark. You couldn't have seen the man clearly?"

"Oh no, I couldn't see his face or anything like that—just his build—tall and slender. We were expecting Lancelot Fortescue, so I jumped to the conclusion that that's who it was."

"He was going—which way?"

"Along behind the yew hedge towards the east side of the house."

"There is a side door there. Is it kept locked?"

"Not until the house is locked up for the night."

"Anyone could have come in by that side door without being observed by any of the household."

Mary Dove considered.

"I think so. Yes." She added quickly, "You mean, the person I heard later upstairs could have come in that way? Could have been hiding—upstairs?"

"Something of the kind."

"But who—?"

"That remains to be seen. Thank you, Miss Dove."

As he turned to go away Inspector Neele said in a casual voice, "By the way, you can't tell me anything about blackbirds, I suppose?"

For the first time, so it seemed, Mary Dove was taken aback. She turned back sharply.

"I—what did you say?"

"I was just asking you about blackbirds."

"Do you mean—"

"Blackbirds," said Inspector Neele.

He had on his most stupid expression.

"You mean that silly business last summer? But surely that can't . . ." She broke off.

Inspector Neele said pleasantly, "There's been a bit of talk about it, but I was sure I'd get a clear account from you."

Mary Dove was her calm, practical self again.

"It must, I think, have been some silly, spiteful joke," she said. "Four dead blackbirds were on Mr. Fortescue's desk in his study here. It was summer and the windows were open, and we rather thought it must have been the gardener's boy, though he insisted he'd never done anything of the kind. But they were actually blackbirds the gardener had shot, which had been hanging up by the fruit bushes."

"And somebody had cut them down and put them on Mr. Fortescue's desk?"

"Yes."

"Any sort of reason behind it—any association with blackbirds?"

Mary shook her head.

"I don't think so."

"How did Mr. Fortescue take it? Was he annoyed?

"Naturally he was annoyed."

"But not upset in any way?"

"I really can't remember."

"I see," said Inspector Neele.

He said no more. Mary Dove once more turned away, but this time, he thought, she went rather unwillingly, as though she would have liked to know more of what was in his mind. Ungratefully, all that Inspector Neele felt was annoyance with Miss Marple. She had suggested to him that there would be blackbirds and sure enough, there the blackbirds were! Not four and twenty of them, that was true. What might be called a token consignment.

That had been as long ago as last summer, and where it fitted in Inspector Neele could not imagine. He was not going to let this blackbird bogy divert him from the logical and sober investigation of murder by a sane murderer for a sane reason, but he would be forced from now on to keep the crazier possibilities of the case in mind.

Chapter Fifteen

"I'm sorry, Miss Fortescue, to bother you again, but I want to be quite, quite clear about this. As far as we know you were the last person—or rather the last person but one—to see Mrs. Fortescue alive. It was about twenty past five when you left the drawing-room?"

"About then," said Elaine, "I can't say exactly." She added defensively, "One doesn't look at clocks the whole time."

"No, of course not. During the time that you were alone with Mrs. Fortescue after the others had left, what did you talk about?"

"Does it matter what we talked about?"

"Probably not," said Inspector Neele, "but it might give me some clue as to what was in Mrs. Fortescue's mind."

"You mean—you think she might have done it herself?"

Inspector Neele noticed the brightening of her face. It would certainly be a very convenient solution as far as the family was concerned. Inspector Neele did not think it was true for a moment. Adele Fortescue was not, to his mind, a suicidal type. Even if she had poisoned her husband and was convinced the crime was about to be brought home to her, she would not, he thought, have ever thought of killing herself. She would have been optimistically sure that even if she were tried for murder she would be sure to be acquitted. He was not, however, averse to Elaine Fortescue's entertaining the hypothesis. He said, therefore, quite truthfully,

"There's a possibility of it, at least, Miss Fortescue. Now perhaps you'll tell me just what your conversation was about."

"Well, it was really about my affairs." Elaine hesitated.

"Your affairs being . . . ?" He paused questioningly with a general expression.

"I—a friend of mine had just arrived in the neighborhood, and I was asking Adele if she would have any objection to—to my asking him to stay here at the house."

"Ah. And who is this friend?"

"It's a Mr. Gerald Wright. He's a schoolmaster. He—he's staying at the Golf Hotel."

"A very close friend, perhaps?"

Inspector Neele gave an avuncular beam which added at least fifteen years to his age.

"We may expect an interesting announcement shortly, perhaps?"

He felt almost compunction as he saw the awkward gesture of the girl's hand and the flush on her face. She was in love with the fellow all right.

"We—we're not actually engaged and of course we couldn't have it announced just now, but—well, yes, I think we do—I mean we are going to get married."

"Congratulations," said Inspector Neele pleasantly. "Mr. Wright is staying at the Golf Hotel, isn't he? How long has he been there?"

"I wired him when Father died."

"And he came at once. I see," said Inspector Neele.

He used this favorite phrase of his in a friendly and reassuring way.

"What did Mrs. Fortescue say when you asked her about his coming here?"

"Oh, she said, all right, I could have anybody I pleased."

"She was nice about it then?"

"Not exactly nice. I mean she said—"

"Yes, what else did she say?"

Again Elaine flushed.

"Oh, something stupid about my being able to do a lot better for myself now. It was the sort of thing Adele would say."

"Ah, well," said Inspector Neele soothingly, "relations say these sort of things."

"Yes, yes, they do. But people often find it difficult to—to appreciate Gerald properly. He's an intellectual, you see, and he's got a lot of unconventional and progressive ideas that people don't like."

"That's why he didn't get on with your father?"

Elaine flushed hotly.

"Father was very prejudiced and unjust. He hurt Gerald's feelings. In fact, Gerald was so upset by my father's attitude that he went off and I didn't hear from him for weeks."

And probably wouldn't have heard from him now if your father hadn't died and left you a packet of money, Inspector Neele thought. Aloud he said, "Was there any more conversation between you and Mrs. Fortescue?"

"No. No, I don't think so."

"And that was about twenty-five past five, and Mrs. Fortescue was found dead at five minutes to six. You didn't return to the room during that half hour?"

"No."

"What were you doing?"

"I—I went out for a short walk."

"To the Golf Hotel?"

"I—well, yes, but Gerald wasn't in."

Inspector Neele said "I see" again, but this time with a rather dismissive effect.

Elaine Fortescue got up and said, "Is that all?"

"That's all, thank you, Miss Fortescue."

As she got up to go, Neele said casually, "You can't tell me anything about blackbirds, can you?"

She stared at him.

"Blackbirds? You mean the ones in the pie?"

They would be in the pie, the Inspector thought to himself. He merely said, "When was this?"

"Oh, three or four months ago—and there were some on Father's desk, too. He was furious."

"Furious, was he? Did he ask a lot of questions?"

"Yes, of course. But we couldn't find out who put them there."

"Have you any idea why he was so angry?"

"Well, it was rather a horrid thing to do, wasn't it?"

Neele looked thoughtfully at her, but he did not see any signs of evasion in her face. He said, "Oh, just one more thing, Miss Fortescue. Do you know if your stepmother made a will at any time?"

Elaine shook her head.

"I've no idea. I suppose so. People usually do, don't they?"

"They should do, but it doesn't always follow. Have you made a will yourself, Miss Fortescue?"

"No—no—I haven't—up to now I haven't had anything to leave. Now, of course—"

He saw the realization of the changed position come into her eyes.

"Yes," he said. "Fifty thousand pounds is quite a responsibility. It changes a lot of things, Miss Fortescue."

II

For some minutes after Elaine Fortescue left the room, Inspector Neele sat staring in front of him thoughtfully. He had, indeed, new food for thought. Mary Dove's statement that she had seen a man in the garden at approximately 4:35 opened up certain new possibilities. That is, of course, if Mary Dove was speaking the truth. It was never Inspector Neele's habit to assume that anyone was speaking the truth. But, examine her statement as he might, he could see no real reason why she should have lied. He was inclined to think that Mary Dove was speaking the truth when she spoke of having seen a man in the garden. It was quite clear that the man could not have been Lancelot Fortescue, although her reason for assuming that it was he was quite natural under the circumstances. It had not been Lancelot Fortescue, but it had been a man about the height and build of Lancelot Fortescue, and if there had been a man in the garden at that particular time, moreover a man moving furtively, as it seemed, to judge from the way he had crept behind the yew hedges, then that certainly opened up a line of thought.

Added to this statement of hers, there had been the further statement that she had heard someone moving about upstairs. That, in its turn, tied up with something else. The small piece of mud he had found on the floor of Adele Fortescue's boudoir. Inspector Neele's mind dwelt on the small dainty desk in that room. Pretty little sham antique with a rather obvious secret drawer in it. There had been three letters in that drawer, letters written by Vivian Dubois to Adele Fortescue. A great many love letters of one kind or another had passed through Inspector Neele's hands in the course of his career. He was acquainted with passionate letters, foolish letters, sentimental letters and nagging letters. There had also been cautious letters. Inspector Neele was inclined to classify these three as of the latter kind. Even if read in the divorce court, they could pass as inspired by a merely platonic friendship. Though in this case—"Platonic friendship, my foot!" thought the Inspector inelegantly.

Neele, when he had found the letters, had sent them up at once to the Yard since, at that time, the main question was whether the Public Prosecutor's office thought that there was sufficient evidence to proceed with the case against Adele Fortescue or Adele Fortescue and Vivian Dubois together. Everything had pointed towards Rex Fortescue having been poisoned by his wife with or without her lover's connivance. These letters, though cautious, made it fairly clear that Vivian Dubois was her lover, but there had not been in the wording, so far as Inspector Neele could see, any signs of incitement to crime. There might have been incitement of a spoken kind, but Vivian Dubois would be far too cautious to put anything of that kind down on paper.

Inspector Neele surmised accurately that Vivian Dubois had asked Adele Fortescue to destroy his letters and that Adele Fortescue had told him she had done so.

Well, now they had two more deaths on their hands. And that meant, or should mean, that Adele Fortescue had not killed her husband.

Unless, that is—Inspector Neele considered a new hypothesis. Adele Fortescue had wanted to marry Vivian Dubois and Vivian Dubois had wanted, not Adele Fortescue, but Adele Fortescue's hundred thousand pounds which would come to her on the death of her husband. He had assumed, perhaps, that Rex Fortescue's death would be put down to natural causes. Some kind of seizure or stroke. After all, everybody seemed to be worried over Rex Fortescue's health during the last year. (Parenthetically, Inspector Neele said to himself that he must look into that question. He had a subconscious feeling that it might be important in some way.) To continue: Rex Fortescue's death had not gone according to plan. It had been diagnosed, without loss of time, as poisoning and the correct poison named.

Supposing that Adele Fortescue and Vivian Dubois had been guilty, what state would they be in then? Vivian Dubois would have been scared and Adele Fortescue would have lost her head. She might have done or said foolish things. She might have rung up Dubois on the telephone, talking indiscreetly in a way that he would have realized might have been overheard in Yewtree Lodge. What would Vivian Dubois have done next?

It was early as yet to try and answer that question, but Inspector Neele proposed very shortly to make inquiries at the Golf Hotel as to whether Dubois had been in or out of the hotel between the hours of 4:15 and 6 o'clock. Vivian Dubois was tall and dark like Lance Fortescue. He might have slipped through the garden to the side door, made his way upstairs, and then what? Looked for the letters and found them gone? Waited there, perhaps, till the coast was clear, then come down into the library when tea was over and Adele Fortescue was alone?

But all this was going too fast—

Neele had questioned Mary Dove and Elaine Fortescue; he must see now what Percival Fortescue's wife had to say.

Chapter Sixteen

INSPECTOR NEELE found Mrs. Percival in her own sitting-room upstairs, writing letters. She got up rather nervously when he came in.

"Is there anything—what—are there—"

"Please sit down, Mrs. Fortescue. There are only just a few more questions I would like to ask you."

"Oh, yes. Yes, of course, Inspector. It's all so dreadful, isn't it? So very dreadful."

She sat down rather nervously in an armchair. Inspector Neele sat down in the small, straight chair near her. He studied her rather more carefully than he had done heretofore. In some ways a mediocre type of woman, he thought—and thought also that she was not very happy. Restless, unsatisfied, limited in mental outlook, yet he thought she might have been efficient and skilled in her own profession of hospital nurse. Though she had achieved leisure by her marriage with a well-to-do man, leisure had not satisfied her. She bought clothes, read novels and ate sweets, but he remembered her avid excitement on the night of Rex

Fortescue's death, and he saw in it not so much a ghoulish satisfaction but rather a revelation of the arid deserts of boredom which encompassed her life. Her eyelids fluttered and fell before his searching glance. They gave her the appearance of being both nervous and guilty, but he could not be sure that that was really the case.

"I'm afraid," he said soothingly, "we have to ask people questions again and again. It must be very tiresome for you all. I do appreciate that, but so much hangs, you understand, on the exact timing of events. You came down to tea rather late, I understand? In fact, Miss Dove came up and fetched you."

"Yes. Yes, she did. She came in and said tea was in. I had no idea it was so late. I'd been writing letters."

Inspector Neele just glanced over at the writing desk.

"I see," he said. "Somehow, or other, I thought you'd been out for a walk."

"Did she say so? Yes, now I believe you're right. I had been writing letters; then it was so stuffy and my head ached so I went out and—er—went for a walk. Only round the garden."

"I see. You didn't meet anyone?"

"Meet anyone?" She stared at him. "What do you mean?"

"Just wondered if you'd seen anybody or anybody had seen you during this walk of yours."

"I saw the gardener in the distance, that's all." She was looking at him suspiciously.

"Then you came in, came up here to your room and you were just taking your things off when Miss Dove came to tell you that tea was ready?"

"Yes. Yes, and so I came down."

"And who was there?"

"Adele and Elaine, and a minute or two later Lance arrived. My brother-in-law, you know. The one who's back from Kenya."

"And then you all had tea?"

"Yes, we had tea. Then Lance went up to see Aunt Effie and I came up here to finish my letters. I left Elaine there with Adele."

He nodded reassuringly.

"Yes. Miss Fortescue seems to have been with Mrs. Fortescue for quite five or ten minutes after you left. Your husband hadn't come home yet?"

"Oh no. Percy—Val—didn't get home until about half-past six or seven. He'd been kept up in town."

"He came by train?"

"Yes. He took a taxi from the station."

"Was it unusual for him to come back by train?"

"He does sometimes. Not very often. I think he'd been to places in the city where it's rather difficult to park the car. It was easier for him to take a train home from Cannon Street."

"I see," said Inspector Neele. He went on, "I asked your husband if Mrs. Fortescue had made a will before she died. He said he thought not. I suppose you don't happen to have any idea?"

To his surprise Jennifer Fortescue nodded vigorously.

"Oh, yes," she said. "Adele made a will. She told me so."

"Indeed! When was this?"

"Oh, it wasn't very long ago. About a month ago, I think."

"That's very interesting," said Inspector Neele.

Mrs. Percival leant forward eagerly. Her face now was all animation. She clearly enjoyed exhibiting her superior knowledge.

"Val didn't know about it," she said. "Nobody knew. It just happened that I found out about it. I was in the street. I had just come out of the stationer's; then I saw Adele coming out of the solicitor's office. Ansell and Worrall's, you know. In the High Street."

"Ah," said Neele, "the local solicitors?"

"Yes. And I said to Adele, 'Whatever have you been doing there?' And she laughed and said, 'Wouldn't you like to know?' And then as we walked along together she said, 'I'll tell you, Jennifer. I've been making my will.' 'Well,' I said. 'Why are you doing that, Adele? You're not ill or anything, are you?' And she said no, of course she wasn't ill. She'd never felt better. But everyone ought to make a will. She said she wasn't going to those stuck-up family solicitors in London, Mr. Billingsley. She said the old sneak would go round and tell the family. 'No,' she said. 'My will's my own business, Jennifer, and I'll make it my own way and nobody's going to know about it.' 'Well, Adele,' I said, 'I shan't tell anybody.' She said, 'It doesn't matter if you do. You won't know what's in it.' But I didn't tell anyone. No, not even Percy. I do think women ought to stick together, don't you, Inspector Neele?"

"I'm sure that's a very nice feeling on your part, Mrs. Fortescue," said Inspector Neele diplomatically.

"I'm sure I'm never ill-natured," said Jennifer. "I didn't particularly care for Adele, if you know what I mean. I always thought she was the kind of woman who would stick at nothing in order to get what she wanted. Now she's dead, perhaps I misjudged her, poor soul."

"Well, thank you very much, Mrs. Fortescue, for being so helpful to me."

"You're welcome, I'm sure. I'm only too glad to do anything I can. It's all so very terrible, isn't it? Who is the old lady who's arrived this morning?"

"She's a Miss Marple. She very kindly came here to give us what information she could about the girl Gladys. It seems Gladys Martin was once in service with her."

"Really? How interesting."

"There's one other thing, Mrs. Percival. Do you know anything about blackbirds?"

Jennifer Fortescue started violently. She dropped her handbag on the floor and bent to pick it up.

"Blackbirds, Inspector? Blackbirds? What kind of blackbirds?" Her voice was rather breathless.

Smiling a little, Inspector Neele said, "Just blackbirds. Alive or dead or even, shall we say, symbolical?"

Jennifer Fortescue said sharply, "I don't know what you mean. I don't know what you're talking about."

"You don't know anything about blackbirds, then, Mrs. Fortescue?"

She said slowly, "I suppose you mean the ones last summer in the pie. All very silly."

"There were some left on the library table, too, weren't there?"

"It was all a very silly practical joke. I don't know who's been talking to you about it. Mr. Fortescue, my father-in-law, was very much annoyed by it."

"Just annoyed? Nothing more?"

"Oh, I see what you mean. Yes, I suppose—yes, it's true. He asked us if there were any strangers about the place."

"Strangers!" Inspector Neele raised his eyebrows.

"Well, that's what he said," said Mrs. Percival defensively.

"Strangers," repeated Inspector Neele thoughtfully. Then he asked, "Did he seem afraid in any way?"

"Afraid? I don't know what you mean."

"Nervous. About strangers, I mean."

"Yes. Yes, he did, rather. Of course, I don't remember very well. It was several months ago, you know. I don't think it was anything except a silly practical joke. Crump perhaps. I really do think that Crump is a very unbalanced man, and I'm perfectly certain that he drinks. He's really very insolent in his manner sometimes. I've sometimes wondered if he could have had a grudge against Mr. Fortescue. Do you think that's possible, Inspector?"

"Anything's possible," said Inspector Neele and went away.

II

Percival Fortescue was in London, but Inspector Neele found Lancelot sitting with his wife in the library. They were playing chess together.

"I don't want to interrupt you," said Neele apologetically.

"We're only killing time, Inspector, aren't we, Pat?"

Pat nodded.

"I expect you'll think it's rather a foolish question I'm asking you," said Neele. "Do you know anything about blackbirds, Mr. Fortescue?"

"Blackbirds?" Lance looked amused. "What kind of blackbirds? Do you mean genuine birds, or the slave trade?"

Inspector Neele said with a sudden, disarming smile, "I'm not sure what I mean, Mr. Fortescue. It's just that a mention of blackbirds has turned up."

"Good Lord." Lancelot looked suddenly alert. "Not the old Blackbird Mine, I suppose?"

Inspector Neele said sharply,

"The Blackbird Mine? What was that?"

Lance frowned in a puzzled fashion.

"The trouble is, Inspector, that I can't really remember much myself. I just have a vague idea about some shady transaction in my papa's past. Something on the West Coast of Africa. Aunt Effie, I believe, once threw it in his teeth, but I can't remember anything definite about it."

"Aunt Effie? That will be Miss Ramsbottom, won't it?"

"Yes."

"I'll go and ask her about it," said Inspector Neele. He added ruefully, "She's rather a formidable old lady, Mr. Fortescue. Always makes me feel quite nervous."

Lance laughed.

"Yes. Aunt Effie is certainly a character, but she may be helpful to you, Inspector, if you get on the right side of her. Especially if you're delving into the past. She's got an excellent memory; she takes a positive pleasure in remembering anything that's detrimental in any way." He added thoughtfully, "There's something else. I went up to see her, you know, soon after I got back here. Immediately after tea that day, as a matter of fact. And she was talking about Gladys. The maid who got killed. Not that we knew she was dead then, of course. But Aunt Effie was saying she was quite convinced that Gladys knew something that she hadn't told the police."

"That seems fairly certain," said Inspector Neele. "She'll never tell it now, poor girl."

"No. It seems Aunt Effie had given her good advice as to spilling anything she knew. Pity the girl didn't take it."

Inspector Neele nodded. Bracing himself for the encounter, he penetrated to Miss Ramsbottom's fortress. Rather to his surprise, he found Miss Marple there. The two ladies appeared to be discussing foreign missions.

"I'll go away, Inspector." Miss Marple rose hurriedly to her feet.

"No need, madam," said Inspector Neele.

"I've asked Miss Marple to come and stay in the house," said Miss Ramsbottom. "No sense in spending money in that ridiculous Golf Hotel. A wicked nest of profiteers, that is. Drinking and card-playing all the evening. She'd better come and stay in a decent Christian household. There's a room next door to mine. Dr. Mary Peters, the missionary, had it last."

"It's very, very kind of you," said Miss Marple, "but I really think I mustn't intrude in a house of mourning."

"Mourning? Fiddlesticks," said Miss Ramsbottom. "Who'll weep for Rex in this house? Or Adele either? Or is it the police you're worried about? Any objections, Inspector?"

"None from me, madam."

"There you are," said Miss Ramsbottom.

"It's very kind of you," said Miss Marple gratefully. "I'll go and telephone to the hotel to cancel my booking." She left the room.

Miss Ramsbottom said sharply to the Inspector, "Well, and what do you want?"

"I wondered if you could tell me anything about the Blackbird Mine, ma'am."

Miss Ramsbottom uttered a sudden, shrill cackle of laughter.

"Ha. You've got on to that, have you! Took the hint I gave you the other day. Well, what do you want to know about it?"

"Anything you can tell me, madam."

"I can't tell you much. It's a long time ago now—oh, twenty to twenty-five years, maybe. Some concession or other in East Africa. My brother-in-

law went into it with a man called MacKenzie. They went out there to investigate the mine together, and MacKenzie died out there of fever. Rex
came home and said the claim or the concession or whatever you call it
was worthless. That's all I know."

"I think you know a little more than that, ma'am," said Neele persuasively.

"Anything else is hearsay. You don't like hearsay in the law, so I've
been told."

"We're not in court yet, ma'am."

"Well, I can't tell you anything. The MacKenzies kicked up a fuss.
That's all I know. They insisted that Rex had swindled MacKenzie. I
daresay he did. He was a clever, unscrupulous fellow, but I've no doubt
whatever he did it was all legal. They couldn't prove anything. Mrs.
MacKenzie was an unbalanced sort of woman. She came here and made a
lot of threats of revenge. Said Rex had murdered her husband. Silly, melodramatic fuss! I think she was a bit off her head—in fact, I believe she
went into an asylum not long after. Came here dragging along a couple of
young children who looked scared to death. Said she'd bring up her children to have revenge. Something like that. Tomfoolery, all of it. Well,
that's all I can tell you. And mind you, the Blackbird Mine wasn't the
only swindle that Rex put over in his lifetime. You'll find a good many
more if you look for them. What put you on to the Blackbird? Did you come
across some trail leading to the MacKenzies?"

"You don't know what became of the family, ma'am?"

"No idea," said Miss Ramsbottom. "Mind you, I don't think Rex would
have actually murdered MacKenzie, but he might have left him to die.
The same thing before the Lord, but not the same thing before the law. If
he did, retribution's caught up with him. The mills of God grind slowly,
but they grind exceedingly small. You'd better go away now. I can't tell
you any more and it's no good your asking."

"Thank you very much for what you have told me," said Inspector
Neele.

"Send that Marple woman back," Miss Ramsbottom called after him.
"She's frivolous, like all Church of England people, but she knows how to
run a charity in a sensible way."

Inspector Neele made a couple of telephone calls, the first to Ansell and
Worrall and the second to the Golf Hotel. Then he summoned Sergeant
Hay and told him that he was leaving the house for a short period.

"I've a short call to pay at a solicitor's office; after that, you can get me
at the Golf Hotel if anything urgent turns up."

"Yes, sir."

"And find out anything you can about blackbirds," added Neele over his shoulder.

"Blackbirds, sir?" Sergeant Hay repeated, thoroughly mystified.

"That's what I said—not blackberry jelly—blackbirds."

"Very good, sir," said Sergeant Hay bewilderedly.

Chapter Seventeen

INSPECTOR NEELE found Mr. Ansell the type of solicitor who was more easily intimidated than intimidating. A member of a small and not very prosperous firm, he was anxious not to stand upon his rights but instead to assist the police in every way possible.

Yes, he said, he had made a will for the late Mrs. Adele Fortescue. She had called at his office about five weeks previously. It had seemed to him rather a peculiar business, but naturally he had not said anything. Peculiar things did happen in a solicitor's business, and of course the Inspector would understand that discretion, etc., etc. The Inspector nodded to show he understood. He had already discovered Mr. Ansell had not transacted any legal business previously for Mrs. Fortescue or for any of the Fortescue family.

"Naturally," said Mr. Ansell, "she didn't want to go to her husband's firm of lawyers about this."

Shorn of verbiage, the facts were simple. Adele Fortescue had made a will leaving everything of which she died possessed to Vivian Dubois.

"But I gathered," said Mr. Ansell, looking at Neele in an interrogating manner, "that she hadn't actually much to leave."

Inspector Neele nodded. At the time Adele Fortescue made her will that was true enough. But since then Rex Fortescue had died, and Adele Fortescue had inherited £100,000 and presumably that £100,000 (less death duties) now belonged to Vivian Edward Dubois.

II

At the Golf Hotel, Inspector Neele found Vivian Dubois nervously await-ing his arrival. Dubois had been on the point of leaving, indeed his bags were packed, when he had received over the telephone a civil request from Inspector Neele to remain. Inspector Neele had been very pleasant about it, quite apologetic. But behind the conventional words the request had been an order. Vivian Dubois had demurred, but not too much.

He said now, "I do hope you realize, Inspector Neele, that it is very in-convenient for me to have to stay on. I really have urgent business that needs attending to."

"I didn't know you were in business, Mr. Dubois," said Inspector Neele genially.

"I'm afraid none of us can be as leisured as we would like to appear to be nowadays."

"Mrs. Fortescue's death must have been a great shock to you, Mr. Dubois. You were great friends, were you not?"

"Yes," said Dubois. "She was a charming woman. We played golf quite often together."

"I expect you'll miss her very much."

"Yes, indeed." Dubois sighed. "The whole thing is really quite, quite terrible."

"You actually telephoned her, I believe, on the afternoon of her death?"

"Did I? I really cannot remember now."

"About four o'clock, I understand."

"Yes, I believe I did."

"Don't you remember what your conversation was about, Mr. Dubois?"

"It wasn't of any significance. I think I asked her how she was feeling and if there was any further news about her husband's death—a more or less conventional inquiry."

"I see," said Inspector Neele. He added, "And then you went out for a walk?"

"Eh—yes—yes, I—I did, I think. At least, not a walk, I played a few holes of golf."

Inspector Neele said gently, "I think not, Mr. Dubois. . . . Not that particular day. . . . The porter here noticed you walking down the road towards Yewtree Lodge."

Dubois' eyes met his, then shied away again nervously.

"I'm afraid I can't remember, Inspector."

"Perhaps you actually went to call upon Mrs. Fortescue?"

Dubois said sharply, "No. No, I didn't do that. I never went near the house."

"Where did you go, then?"

"Oh, I—went on down the road, down as far as the Three Pigeons and then I turned around and came back by the links."

"You're quite sure you didn't go to Yewtree Lodge?"

"Quite sure, Inspector."

The Inspector shook his head.

"Come, now, Mr. Dubois," he said, "it's much better to be frank with us, you know. You may have had some quite innocent reason for going there."

"I tell you I never went up to see Mrs. Fortescue that day."

The Inspector stood up.

"You know, Mr. Dubois," he said pleasantly, "I think we'll have to ask you for a statement and you'll be well advised and quite within your rights in having a solicitor present when you are making your statement."

The color fled from Mr. Dubois' face, leaving it a sickly greenish color.

"You're threatening me," he said. "You're threatening me."

"No, no, nothing of the kind." Inspector Neele spoke in a shocked voice. "We're not allowed to do anything of that sort. Quite the contrary. I'm actually pointing out to you that you have certain rights."

"I had nothing to do with it all, I tell you! Nothing to do with it."

"Come now, Mr. Dubois, you were at Yewtree Lodge round half-past four on that day. Somebody looked out of the window, you know, and saw you."

"I was only in the garden. I didn't go into the house."

"Didn't you?" said Inspector Neele. "Are you sure? Didn't you go in by the side door, and up the stairs to Mrs. Fortescue's sitting-room on the first floor? You were looking for something, weren't you, in the desk there?"

"You've got them, I suppose," said Dubois sullenly. "That fool Adele kept them, then she swore she burnt them. But they don't mean what you think they mean."

"You're not denying, are you, Mr. Dubois, that you were a very close friend of Mrs. Fortescue's?"

"No, of course I'm not. How can I when you've got the letters? All I say is, there's no need to go reading any sinister meaning into them. Don't think for a moment that we—that she—ever thought of getting rid of Rex Fortescue. Good God, I'm not that kind of man!"

"But perhaps she was that kind of woman?"

"Nonsense," cried Vivian Dubois, "wasn't she killed, too?"

"Oh yes, yes."

"Well, isn't it natural to believe that the same person who killed her husband killed her?"

"It might be. It certainly might be. But there are other solutions. For instance (this is quite a hypothetical case, Mr. Dubois), it's possible that Mrs. Fortescue got rid of her husband, and that after his death she became somewhat of a danger to someone else. Someone who had, perhaps, not helped her in what she had done but who had at least encouraged her and provided, shall we say, the motive for the deed. She might be, you know, a danger to that particular person."

Dubois stammered, "You c-c-can't build up a case against me. You can't."

"She made a will, you know," said Inspector Neele. "She left all her money to you. Everything she possessed."

"I don't want the money. I don't want a penny of it."

"Of course, it isn't very much really," said Inspector Neele. "There's jewelry and some furs, but I imagine very little actual cash."

Dubois stared at him, his jaw dropping.

"But I thought her husband—"

He stopped dead.

"Did you, Mr. Dubois?" said Inspector Neele, and there was steel now in his voice. "That's very interesting. I wondered if you knew the terms of Rex Fortescue's will."

III

Inspector Neele's second interview at the Golf Hotel was with Mr. Gerald Wright. Mr. Gerald Wright was a thin, intellectual and very superior young man. He was, Inspector Neele noted, not unlike Vivian Dubois in build.

"What can I do for you, Inspector Neele?" he asked.

"I thought you might be able to help us with a little information, Mr. Wright."

"Information? Really? It seems very unlikely."

"It's in connection with the recent events at Yewtree Lodge. You've heard of them, of course?"

Inspector Neele put a little irony into the question. Mr. Wright smiled patronizingly.

"Heard of them," he said, "is hardly the right word. The newspapers appear to be full of nothing else. How incredibly bloodthirsty our public press is! What an age we live in! On one side the manufacture of atom bombs, on the other our newspapers delight in reporting brutal murders! But you said you had some questions to ask. Really, I cannot see what they can be. I know nothing about this Yewtree Lodge affair. I was actually in the Isle of Man when Mr. Fortescue was killed."

"You arrived here very shortly afterwards, didn't you, Mr. Wright? You had a telegram, I believe, from Miss Elaine Fortescue."

"Our police know everything, do they not? Yes, Elaine sent for me. I came, of course, at once."

"And you are, I understand, shortly to be married?"

"Quite right, Inspector Neele. You have no objections, I hope."

"It is entirely Miss Fortescue's business. I understand the attachment between you dates from some time back? Six or seven months ago, in fact?"

"Quite correct."

"You and Miss Fortescue became engaged to be married, but Mr. Fortescue refused to give his consent and informed you that if his daughter married against his wishes he did not propose to give her an income of any kind. Whereupon, I understand, you broke off the engagement and departed."

Gerald Wright smiled rather pityingly.

"A very crude way of putting things, Inspector Neele. Actually, I was victimized for my political opinions. Rex Fortescue was the worst type of capitalist. Naturally, I could not sacrifice my political beliefs and convictions for money."

"But you have no objections to marrying a wife who has just inherited £50,000?"

Gerald Wright gave a thin, satisfied smile.

"Not at all, Inspector Neele. The money will be used for the benefit of the community. But surely you did not come here to discuss with me either my financial circumstances—or my political convictions?"

"No, Mr. Wright. I wanted to talk to you about a simple question of fact. As you are aware, Mrs. Adele Fortescue died as a result of cyanide poisoning on the afternoon of November first. Since you were in the neighborhood of Yewtree Lodge on that afternoon I thought it possible that you might have seen or heard something that had a bearing on the case."

"And what leads you to believe that I was, as you call it, in the neighborhood of Yewtree Lodge at the time?"

"You left this hotel at a quarter-past four on that particular afternoon, Mr. Wright. On leaving the hotel you walked down the road in the direction of Yewtree Lodge. It seems natural to suppose that you were going there."

"I thought of it," said Gerald Wright, "but I considered that it would be a rather pointless thing to do. I already had an arrangement to meet Miss Fortescue—Elaine—at the hotel at six o'clock. I went for a walk along a lane that branches off from the main road and returned to the Golf Hotel just before six o'clock. Elaine did not keep her appointment. Quite naturally, under the circumstances."

"Anybody see you on this walk of yours, Mr. Wright?"

"A few cars passed me, I think, on the road. I did not see anyone I know, if that's what you mean. The lane was little more than a cart track and too muddy for cars."

"So, between the time you left the hotel at a quarter-past four until six o'clock when you arrived back again, I've only your word for it as to where you were?"

Gerald Wright continued to smile in a superior fashion.

"Very distressing for us both, Inspector, but there it is."

Inspector Neele said softly, "Then if someone said they looked out of a landing window and saw you in the garden of Yewtree Lodge at about 4:35—" He paused and left the sentence unfinished.

Gerald Wright raised his eyebrows and shook his head.

"Visibility must have been very bad by then," he said. "I think it would be difficult for anyone to be sure."

"Are you acquainted with Mr. Vivian Dubois, who is also staying here?"

"Dubois. Dubois? No, I don't think so. Is that the tall, dark man with a pretty taste in suede shoes?"

"Yes. He also was out for a walk that afternoon, and he also left the hotel and walked past Yewtree Lodge. You did not notice him in the road by any chance?"

"No. No. I can't say I did."

Gerald Wright looked for the first time faintly worried.

Inspector Neele said thoughtfully, "It wasn't really a very nice afternoon for walking, especially after dark in a muddy lane. Curious how energetic everyone seems to have felt."

IV

On Inspector Neele's return to the house he was greeted by Sergeant Hay with an air of satisfaction.

"I've found out about the blackbirds for you, sir," he said.

"You have, have you?"

"Yes, sir, in a pie they were. Cold pie was left out for Sunday night's supper. Somebody got at that pie in the larder or somewhere. They'd taken off the crust and they'd taken out the veal and 'am what was inside it, and what d'you think they put in, instead? Some stinkin' blackbirds they got out of the gardener's shed. Nasty sort of trick to play, wasn't it?"

" 'Wasn't that a dainty dish to set before the king?' " said Inspector Neele.

He left Sergeant Hay staring after him.

Chapter Eighteen

"JUST WAIT a minute," said Miss Ramsbottom. "This patience is going to come out."

She transferred a king and his various impedimenta into an empty space, put a red seven on a black eight, built up the four, five and six of spades on her foundation heap, made a few more rapid transfers of cards and then leaned back with a sigh of satisfaction.

"That's the double jester," she said. "It doesn't often come out."

She leaned back in a satisfied fashion, then raised her eyes at the girl standing by the fireplace.

"So you're Lance's wife," she said.

Pat, who had been summoned upstairs to Miss Ramsbottom's presence, nodded her head.

"Yes," she said.

"You're a tall girl," said Miss Ramsbottom, "and you look healthy."

"I'm very healthy."

Miss Ramsbottom nodded in a satisfied manner.

"Percival's wife is pasty," she said. "Eats too many sweets and doesn't take enough exercise. Well, sit down, child, sit down. Where did you meet my nephew?"

"I met him out in Kenya when I was staying there with some friends."

"You've been married before, I understand."

"Yes. Twice."

Miss Ramsbottom gave a profound sniff.

"Divorce, I suppose."

"No," said Pat. Her voice trembled a little. "They both—died. My first husband was a fighter pilot. He was killed in the war."

"And your second husband? Let me see—somebody told me. Shot himself, didn't he?"

Pat nodded.

"Your fault?"

"No," said Pat. "It wasn't my fault."

"Racing man, wasn't he?"

"Yes."

"I've never been on a race course in my life," said Miss Ramsbottom. "Betting and card-playing—all devices of the devil!"

Pat did not reply.

"I wouldn't go inside a theater or a cinema," said Miss Ramsbottom. "Ah, well, it's a wicked world nowadays. A lot of wickedness was going on in the house, but the Lord struck them down."

Pat still found it difficult to say anything. She wondered if Lance's Aunt Effie was really quite all there. She was, however, a trifle disconcerted by the old lady's shrewd glance at her.

"How much," demanded Aunt Effie, "do you know about the family you've married into?"

"I suppose," said Pat, "as much as one ever knows of the family one marries into."

"H'm, something in that, something in that. Well, I'll tell you this. My sister was a fool, my brother-in-law was a rogue, Percival is a sneak, and your Lance was always the bad boy of the family."

"I think that's all nonsense," said Pat robustly.

"Maybe you're right," said Miss Ramsbottom unexpectedly. "You can't just stick labels on people. But don't underestimate Percival. There's a tendency to believe that those who are labeled good are also stupid. Percival isn't the least bit stupid. He's quite clever in a sanctimonious kind of way. I've never cared for him. Mind you, I don't trust Lance and I don't approve of him, but I can't help being fond of him. . . . He's a reckless sort of fellow—always has been. You've got to look after him and see he doesn't go too far. Tell him not to underestimate Percival, my dear. Tell him not to believe everything that Percival says. They're all liars in this house." The old lady added with satisfaction, "Fire and brimstone shall be their portion."

II

Inspector Neele was finishing a telephone conversation with Scotland Yard.

The Assistant Commissioner at the other end said, "We ought to be able to get that information for you—by circularizing the various private sanatoriums. Of course, she may be dead."

"Probably is. It's a long time ago."

Old sins cast long shadows. Miss Ramsbottom had said that—said it with significance, too, as though she was giving him a hint.

"It's a fantastic theory," said the A.C.

"Don't I know it, sir. But I don't feel we can ignore it altogether. Too much fits in."

"Yes—yes—rye—blackbirds—the man's Christian name."

Neele said, "I'm concentrating on the other lines too. Dubois is a possibility. So is Wright. The girl Gladys could have caught sight of either of them outside the side door. She could have left the tea tray in the hall and gone out to see who it was and what they were doing. Whoever it was could have strangled her then and there and carried her body round to the clothesline and put the peg on her nose—"

"A crazy thing to do in all conscience! A nasty one, too."

"Yes, sir. That's what upset the old lady—Miss Marple, I mean. Nice old lady—and very shrewd. She's moved into the house to be near old Miss Ramsbottom, and I've no doubt she'll get to hear anything that's going."

"What's your next move, Neele?"

"I've an appointment with the London solicitors. I want to find out a little more about Rex Fortescue's affairs. And though it's old history, I want to hear a little more about the Blackbird Mine."

III

Mr. Billingsley, of Billingsley, Horsethorpe & Walters, was an urbane man whose discretion was concealed habitually by a misleadingly forthcoming manner. It was the second interview that Inspector Neele had had with him, and on this occasion, Mr. Billingsley's discretion was less noticeable than it had been on the former one. The triple tragedy at Yewtree Lodge had shaken Mr. Billingsley out of his professional reserve. He was now only too anxious to put all the facts he could before the police.

"Most extraordinary business, this whole thing," he said. "A most extraordinary business. I don't remember anything like it in all my professional career."

"Frankly, Mr. Billingsley," said Inspector Neele, "we need all the help we can get."

"You can count on me, my dear sir. I shall be only too happy to assist you in every way I can."

"First let me ask you how well you knew the late Mr. Fortescue, and how well do you know the affairs of his firm?"

"I knew Rex Fortescue fairly well. That is to say I've known him for a period of, well, sixteen years, I should say. Mind you, we are not the only firm of solicitors he employed, not by a long way."

Inspector Neele nodded. He knew that. Billingsley, Horsethorpe & Walters were what one might describe as Rex Fortescue's reputable solicitors. For his less reputable dealings he had employed several different and slightly less scrupulous firms.

"Now what do you want to know?" continued Mr. Billingsley. "I've told you about his will. Percival Fortescue is the residuary legatee."

"I'm interested now," said Inspector Neele, "in the will of his widow. On Mr. Fortescue's death she came into the sum of one hundred thousand pounds, I understand?"

Billingsley nodded his head.

"A considerable sum of money," he said, "and I may tell you in confidence, Inspector, that it is one the firm could ill have afforded to pay out."

"The firm, then, is not prosperous?"

"Frankly," said Mr. Billingsley, "and strictly between ourselves, it's drifting on the rocks and has been for the last year and a half."

"For any particular reason?"

"Why, yes, I should say the reason was Rex Fortescue himself. For the last year Rex Fortescue's been acting like a madman. Selling good stock here, buying speculative stuff there, talking big about it all the time in the most extraordinary way. Wouldn't listen to advice. Percival—the son, you know—he came here urging me to use my influence with his father. He'd tried, apparently, and been swept aside. Well, I did what I could, but Fortescue wouldn't listen to reason. Really, he seems to have been a changed man."

"But not, I gather, a depressed man," said Inspector Neele.

"No, no. Quite the contrary. Flamboyant, bombastic."

Inspector Neele nodded. An idea which had already taken form in his mind was strengthened. He thought he was beginning to understand some of the causes of friction between Percival and his father. Mr. Billingsley was continuing.

"But it's no good asking me about the wife's will. I didn't make any will for her."

"No. I know that," said Neele. "I'm merely verifying that she had something to leave. In short, a hundred thousand pounds."

Mr. Billingsley was shaking his head violently.

"No, no, my dear sir. You're wrong there."

"Do you mean the hundred thousand pounds was only left to her for her lifetime?"

"No—no—it was left to her outright. But there was a clause in the will governing that bequest. That is to say, Fortescue's wife did not inherit the sum unless she survived him for one month. That, I may say, is a clause fairly common nowadays. It has come into operation owing to the uncertainties of air travel. If two people are killed in an air accident, it becomes exceedingly difficult to say who was the survivor and a lot of curious problems arise."

Inspector Neele was staring at him.

"Then Adele Fortescue had not got a hundred thousand pounds to leave. What happened to that money?"

"It goes back into the firm. Or rather, I should say, it goes to the residuary legatee."

"And the residuary legatee is Mr. Percival Fortescue."

"That's right," said Billingsley, "it goes to Percival Fortescue. And with the state the firm's affairs are in," he added unguardedly, "I should say that he'll need it!"

IV

"The things you policemen want to know," said Inspector Neele's doctor friend.

"Come on, Bob, spill it."

"Well, as we're alone together you can't quote me, fortunately! But I should say, you know, that your idea's dead right. General Paralysis of the Insane, by the sound of it all. The family suspected it and wanted to get him to see a doctor. He wouldn't. It acts just in the way you describe. Loss of judgment, megalomania, violent fits of irritation and anger, boastfulness, delusions of grandeur—of being a great financial genius. Anyone suffering from that would soon put a solvent firm on the rocks, unless he could be restrained, and that's not so easy to do, especially if the man himself has an idea of what you're after. Yes, I should say it was a bit of luck for your friends that he died."

"They're no friends of mine," said Neele. He repeated what he had once said before:

"They're all very unpleasant people. . . ."

Chapter Nineteen

IN THE DRAWING-ROOM at Yewtree Lodge, the whole Fortescue family was assembled. Percival Fortescue, leaning against the mantelpiece, was addressing the meeting.

"It's all very well," said Percival. "But the whole position is most unsatisfactory. The police come and go and don't tell us anything. One supposes they're pursuing some line of research. In the meantime, everything's at a standstill. One can't make plans, one can't arrange things for the future."

"It's all so inconsiderate," said Jennifer. "And so stupid."

"There still seems to be this ban against anyone leaving the house," went on Percival. "Still, I think among ourselves we might discuss future plans. What about you, Elaine? I gather you're going to marry—what's-his-name—Gerald Wright? Have you any idea when?"

"As soon as possible," said Elaine.

Percival frowned.

"You mean, in about six months' time?"

"No, I don't. Why should we wait six months?"

"I think it would be more decent," said Percival.

"Rubbish," said Elaine. "A month. That's the longest we'll wait."

"Well, it's for you to say," said Percival. "And what are your plans when you are married, if you have any?"

"We're thinking of starting a school."

Percival shook his head.

"That's a very risky speculation in these times. What with the shortage of domestic labor, the difficulty of getting an adequate teaching staff— really, Elaine, it sounds all right. But I should think twice about it if I were you."

"We have thought. Gerald feels that the whole future of this country lies in right education."

"I am seeing Mr. Billingsley the day after tomorrow," said Percival. "We've got to go into various questions of finance. He was suggesting that you might like to make this money that's been left to you by Father into a trust for yourself and your children. It's a very sound thing to do nowadays."

"I don't want to do that," said Elaine. "We shall need the money to start up our school. There's a very suitable house we've heard of for sale. It's in Cornwall. Beautiful grounds and quite a good house. It would have to be built onto a good deal—several wings added."

"You mean—you mean you're going to take all your money out of the business? Really, Elaine, I don't think you're wise."

"Much wiser to take it out than leave it in, I should say," said Elaine. "Businesses are going phut all over the place. You said yourself, Val, before Father died, that things were getting into a pretty bad state."

"One says that sort of thing," said Percival vaguely, "but I must say, Elaine, to take out all your capital and sink it in the buying, equipping and running of a school is crazy. If it's not a success, look what happens? You're left without a penny."

"It will be a success," said Elaine doggedly.

"I'm with you." Lance, lying sprawled out in a chair, spoke up encouragingly. "Have a crack at it, Elaine. In my opinion it'll be a damned odd sort of school, but it's what you want to do—you and Gerald. If you lose your money you'll at any rate have had the satisfaction of doing what you wanted to do."

"Just what one might have expected you to say, Lance," said Percival acidly.

"I know, I know," said Lance. "I'm the spendthrift prodigal son. But I still think I've had more fun out of life than you have, Percy, old boy."

"It depends on what you call fun," said Percival acidly. "Which brings us to your own plans, Lance. I suppose you'll be off again back to Kenya— or Canada—or climbing Mount Everest or something fairly fantastic?"

"Now what makes you think that?" said Lance.

"Well, you've never had much use for a stay-at-home life in England, have you?"

"One changes as one gets older," said Lance. "One settles down. D'you know, Percy my boy, I'm quite looking forward to having a crack at being a sober business man."

"Do you mean . . . ?"

"I mean I'm coming into the firm with you, old boy." Lance grinned. "Oh, you're the senior partner, of course. You've got the lion's share. I'm only a very junior partner. But I have got a holding in it that gives me the right to be in on things, doesn't it?"

"Well—yes—of course, if you put it that way. But I can assure you, my dear boy, you'll be very, very bored."

"I wonder now. I don't believe I shall be bored."

Percival frowned.

"You don't seriously mean, Lance, that you're coming into the business?"

"Having a finger in the pie? Yes, that's exactly what I am doing."

Percival shook his head.

"Things are in a very bad way, you know. You'll find that out. It's going to be about all we can do to pay out Elaine her share, if she insists on having it paid out."

"There you are, Elaine," said Lance. "You see how wise you were to insist on grabbing your money while it's there to grab."

"Really, Lance." Percival spoke angrily, "these jokes of yours are in very bad taste."

"I do think, Lance, you might be more careful what you say," said Jennifer.

Sitting a little way away near the window, Pat studied them one by one. If this was what Lance had meant by twisting Percival's tail, she could see that he was achieving his object. Percival's neat impassivity was quite ruffled. He snapped again, angrily:

"Are you serious, Lance?"

"Dead serious."

"It won't work, you know. You'll soon get fed up."

"Not me. Think what a lovely change it'll be for me. A city office, typists running and going. I shall have a blonde secretary like Miss Grosvenor —is it Grosvenor? I suppose you've snaffled her. But I shall get one just the same. 'Yes, Mr. Lancelot, no, Mr. Lancelot. Your tea, Mr. Lancelot.'"

"Oh, don't play the fool," snapped Percival.

"Why are you so angry, my dear brother? Don't you look forward to having me share your city cares?"

"You haven't the least conception of the mess everything's in."

"No. You'll have to put me wise to all that."

"First, you've got to understand that for the last six months—no, more, a year—Father's not been himself. He's done the most incredibly foolish things, financially. Sold out good stock, acquired various wildcat holdings. Sometimes he's really thrown away money hand over fist. Just, one might say, for the fun of spending it."

"In fact," said Lance, "it's just as well for the family that he had taxine in his tea."

"That's a very ugly way of putting it, but in essence you're quite right. It's about the only thing that saved us from bankruptcy. But we shall have to be extremely conservative and go very cautiously for a bit."

Lance shook his head.

"I don't agree with you. Caution never does anyone any good. You must take a few risks, strike out. You must go for something big."

"I don't agree," said Percy. "Caution and economy. Those are our watchwords."

"Not mine," said Lance.

"You're only the junior partner, remember," said Percival.

"All right, all right. But I've got a little say-so all the same."

Percival walked up and down the room agitatedly.

"It's no good, Lance. I'm fond of you and all that—"

"Are you?" Lance interpolated. Percival did not appear to hear him.

". . . But I really don't think we're going to pull together at all. Our outlooks are totally different."

"That may be an advantage," said Lance.

"The only sensible thing," said Percival, "is to dissolve the partnership."

"You're going to buy me out—is that the idea?"

"My dear boy, it's the only sensible thing to do, with our ideas so different."

"If you find it hard to pay Elaine out her legacy, how are you going to manage to pay me my share?"

"Well, I didn't mean in cash," said Percival. "We could—er—divide up the holdings."

"With you taking the gilt-edged and me taking the worst of the speculative off you, I suppose?"

"They seem to be what you prefer," said Percival.

Lance grinned suddenly.

"You're right in a way, Percy, old boy. But I can't indulge my own taste entirely. I've got Pat here to think of."

Both men looked towards her. Pat opened her mouth, then shut it again. Whatever game Lance was playing, it was best that she should not interfere. That Lance was driving at something special, she was quite sure, but she was still a little uncertain as to what his actual object was.

"Line 'em up, Percy," said Lance, laughing. "Bogus Diamond Mines, Inaccessible Rubies, the Oil Concessions where no oil is. Do you think I'm quite as big a fool as I look?"

Percival said:

"Of course, some of these holdings are highly speculative, but remember, they may turn out immensely valuable."

"Changed your tune, haven't you?" said Lance, grinning. "Going to offer me Father's latest wildcat acquisitions as well as the old Blackbird Mine and things of that kind. By the way, has the Inspector been asking you about this Blackbird Mine?"

Percival frowned.

"Yes, he did. I can't imagine what he wanted to know about it. I couldn't tell him much. You and I were children at the time. I just remember vaguely that Father went out there and came back saying the whole thing was no good."

"What was it—a gold mine?"

"I believe so. Father came back pretty certain that there was no gold there. And, mind you, he wasn't the sort of man to be mistaken."

"Who got him into it? A man called MacKenzie, wasn't it?"

"Yes. MacKenzie died out there."

"MacKenzie died out there," said Lance thoughtfully. "Wasn't there a terrific scene? I seem to remember. . . . Mrs. MacKenzie, wasn't it? Came here. Ranted and stormed at Father. Hurled down curses on his head. She accused him, if I remember rightly, of murdering her husband."

"Really," said Percival repressively. "I can't recollect anything of the kind."

"I remember it, though," said Lance. "I was a good bit younger than you, of course. Perhaps that's why it appealed to me. As a child it struck me as full of drama. Where was Blackbird? West Africa, wasn't it?"

"Yes, I think so."

"I must look up the concession sometime," said Lance, "when I'm at the office."

"You can be quite sure," said Percival, "that Father made no mistake. If he came back saying there was no gold, there was no gold."

"You're probably right there," said Lance. "Poor Mrs. MacKenzie. I wonder what happened to her and to those two kids she brought along. Funny—they must be grown up by now."

Chapter Twenty

AT THE PINEWOOD PRIVATE SANATORIUM, Inspector Neele, sitting in the visitors' parlor, was facing a gray-haired, elderly lady. Helen MacKenzie was sixty-three, though she looked younger. She had pale blue, rather vacant-looking eyes, and a weak, indeterminate chin. She had a long upper lip which occasionally twitched. She held a large book in her lap and was looking down at it as Inspector Neele talked to her. In Inspector Neele's mind was the conversation he had just had with Doctor Crosbie, the head of the establishment.

"She's a voluntary patient, of course," said Doctor Crosbie, "not certified."

"She's not dangerous, then?"

"Oh, no. Most of the time she's as sane to talk to as you or I. It's one of her good periods now so that you'll be able to have a perfectly normal conversation with her."

Bearing this in mind, Inspector Neele started his first conversation essay.

"It's very kind of you to see me, madam," he said. "My name is Neele. I've come to see you about a Mr. Fortescue who has recently died. A Mr. Fortescue. I expect you know the name."

Mrs. MacKenzie's eyes were fixed on her book. She said: "I don't know what you're talking about."

"Mr. Fortescue, madam. Mr. Rex Fortescue."

"No," said Mrs. MacKenzie. "No. Certainly not."

Inspector Neele was slightly taken aback. He wondered whether this was what Doctor Crosbie called being completely normal.

"I think, Mrs. MacKenzie, you knew him a good many years ago."

"Not really," said Mrs. MacKenzie. "It was yesterday."

"I see," said Inspector Neele, falling back upon his formula rather uncertainly. "I believe," he went on, "that you paid him a visit many years ago at his residence, Yewtree Lodge."

"A very ostentatious house," said Mrs. MacKenzie.

"Yes. Yes, you might call it that. He had been connected with your husband, I believe, over a certain mine in Africa. The Blackbird Mine, I believe it was called."

"I have to read my book," said Mrs. MacKenzie. "There's not much time and I have to read my book."

"Yes, madam. Yes, I quite see that." There was a pause, then Inspector Neele went on, "Mr. MacKenzie and Mr. Fortescue went out together to Africa to survey the mine."

"It was my husband's mine," said Mrs. MacKenzie. "He found it and staked a claim to it. He wanted money to capitalize it. He went to Rex Fortescue. If I'd been wiser, if I'd known more, I wouldn't have let him do it."

"No, I see that. As it was, they went out together to Africa, and there your husband died of fever."

"I must read my book," said Mrs. MacKenzie.

"Do you think Mr. Fortescue swindled your husband over the Blackbird Mine, Mrs. MacKenzie?"

Without raising her eyes from the book, Mrs. MacKenzie said, "How stupid you are."

"Yes, yes, I dare say. . . . But you see, it's all a long time ago and making inquiries about a thing that is over a long time ago is rather difficult."

"Who said it was over?"

"I see. You don't think it is over?"

" 'No question is ever settled until it is settled right.' Kipling said that. Nobody reads Kipling nowadays, but he was a great man."

"Do you think the question will be settled right one of these days?"

"Rex Fortescue is dead, isn't he? You said so."

"He was poisoned," said Inspector Neele.

Rather disconcertingly, Mrs. MacKenzie laughed.

"What nonsense," she said, "he died of fever."

"I'm talking about Mr. Rex Fortescue."

"So am I." She looked up suddenly and her pale blue eyes fixed his. "Come now," she said, "he died in his bed, didn't he? He died in his bed?"

"He died in St. Jude's Hospital," said Inspector Neele.

"Nobody knows where my husband died," said Mrs. MacKenzie. "Nobody knows how he died or where he was buried. . . . All anyone knows is what Rex Fortescue said. And Rex Fortescue was a liar!"

"Do you think there may have been foul play?"

"Foul play, foul play, fowls lay eggs, don't they?"

"You think that Rex Fortescue was responsible for your husband's death?"

"I had an egg for breakfast this morning," said Mrs. MacKenzie. "Quite fresh, too. Surprising, isn't it, when one thinks that it was thirty years ago?"

Neele drew a deep breath. It seemed unlikely that he was ever going to get anywhere at this rate, but he persevered. "Somebody put dead blackbirds on Rex Fortescue's desk about a month or two before he died."

"That's interesting. That's very, very interesting."

"Have you any idea, madam, who might have done that?"

"Ideas aren't any help to one. One has to have action. I brought them up for that, you know, to take action."

"You're talking about your children?"

She nodded her head rapidly.

"Yes. Donald and Ruby. They were nine and seven and left without a father. I told them. I told them every day. I made them swear it every night."

Inspector Neele leant forward.

"What did you make them swear?"

"That they'd kill him, of course."

"I see."

Inspector Neele spoke as though it was the most reasonable remark in the world.

"Did they?"

"Donald went to Dunkirk. He never came back. They sent me a wire saying he was dead. 'Deeply regret killed in action.' Action, you see, the wrong kind of action."

"I'm sorry to hear that, madam. What about your daughter?"

"I haven't got a daughter," said Mrs. Mackenzie.

"You spoke of her just now," said Neele. "Your daughter Ruby."

"Ruby. Yes, Ruby." She leaned forward. "Do you know what I've done to Ruby?"

"No, madam. What have you done to her?"

She whispered suddenly,

"Look here at the Book.'

He saw then that what she was holding in her lap was a Bible. It was a very old Bible and as she opened it, on the front page, Inspector Neele saw various names had been written. It was obviously a family Bible in which the old-fashioned custom had been continued of entering each new birth. Mrs. MacKenzie's thin finger pointed to the two last names. "Donald MacKenzie" with the date of his birth, and "Ruby MacKenzie" with the date of hers. But a thick line was drawn through Ruby MacKenzie's name.

"You see?" said Mrs. MacKenzie. "I struck her out of the Book. I cut her off forever! The Recording Angel won't find her name there."

"You cut her name out of the Book? Now, why, madam?"

Mrs. MacKenzie looked at him cunningly.

"You know why," she said.

"But I don't. Really, madam, I don't."

"She didn't keep faith. You know she didn't keep faith."

"Where is your daughter now, madam?"

"I've told you. I have no daughter. There isn't such a person as Ruby MacKenzie any longer."

"You mean she's dead?"

"Dead?" The woman laughed suddenly. "It would be much better for her if she were dead. Much better. Much, much better." She sighed and turned restlessly in her seat. Then, her manner reverting to a kind of formal courtesy, she said, "I'm so sorry, but really I'm afraid I can't talk to you any longer. You see, the time is getting very short, and I must read my book."

To Inspector Neele's further remarks Mrs. MacKenzie returned no reply. She merely made a faint gesture of annoyance and continued to read her Bible with her finger following the line of the verse she was reading.

Neele got up and left. He had another brief interview with the Superintendent.

"Do any of her relations come to see her?" he asked. "A daughter, for instance?"

"I believe a daughter did come to see her in my predecessor's time, but her visit agitated the patient so much that he advised her not to come again. Since then everything is arranged through solicitors."

"And you've no idea where this Ruby MacKenzie is now?"

The Superintendent shook his head.

"No idea whatsoever."

"You've no idea whether she's married, for instance?"

"I don't know. All I can do is to give you the address of the solicitors who deal with us."

Inspector Neele had already tracked down those solicitors. They were unable, or said they were unable, to tell him anything. A trust fund had been established for Mrs. MacKenzie, which they managed. These arrangements had been made some years previously, and they had not seen Miss MacKenzie since.

Inspector Neele tried to get a description of Ruby MacKenzie, but the results were not encouraging. So many relations came to visit patients that after a lapse of years they were bound to be remembered dimly, with the appearance of one mixed up with the appearance of another. The Matron, who had been there for many years, seemed to remember that Miss MacKenzie was small and dark. The only other nurse who had been there for any length of time recalled that she was heavily built and fair.

"So there we are, sir," said Inspector Neele as he reported to the Assistant Commissioner. "There's a whole crazy setup and it fits together. It must mean something."

The A.C. nodded thoughtfully.

"The blackbirds in the pie tying up with the Blackbird Mine, rye in the dead man's pocket, bread and honey with Adele Fortescue's tea (not that that is conclusive. After all, anyone might have had bread and honey for tea!). The third murder, that girl strangled with a stocking and a clothes peg nipped onto her nose. Yes, crazy as the setup is, it certainly can't be ignored."

"Half a minute, sir," said Inspector Neele.

"What is it?"

Neele was frowning.

"You know, what you've just said. It didn't ring true. It was wrong somewhere." He shook his head and sighed. "No. I can't place it."

Chapter Twenty-one

LANCE AND PAT WANDERED round the well-kept grounds surrounding Yewtree Lodge.

"I hope I'm not hurting your feelings, Lance," Pat murmured, "if I say this is quite the nastiest garden I've been in."

"It won't hurt my feelings," said Lance. "Is it? Really I don't know. It seems to have three gardeners working on it very industriously."

Pat said, "Probably that's what's wrong with it. No expense spared, no signs of individual taste. All the right rhododendrons and all the right bedding out, done in the proper season, I expect."

"Well, what would you put in an English garden, Pat, if you had one?"

"My garden," said Pat, "would have hollyhocks, larkspurs and Canterbury bells, no bedding out and none of these horrible yews."

She glanced up at the dark yew hedges disparagingly.

"Association of ideas," said Lance easily.

"There's something awfully frightening about a poisoner," said Pat. "I mean, it must be a horrid, brooding, revengeful mind."

"So that's how you see it? Funny! I just think of it as businesslike and cold-blooded."

"I suppose one could look at it that way." She resumed, with a slight shiver, "All the same, to do three murders. . . . Whoever did it must be mad."

"Yes," said Lance, in a low voice. "I'm afraid so." Then, breaking out sharply, he said, "For God's sake, Pat, do go away from here. Go back to London. Go down to Devonshire or up to the Lakes. Go to Stratford on

Avon or go and look at the Norfolk Broads. The police wouldn't mind your going—you had nothing to do with this. You were in Paris when the old man was killed and in London when the other two died. I tell you it worries me to death to have you here."

Pat paused a moment before saying quietly:

"You know who it is, don't you?"

"No, I don't."

"But you think you know. . . . That's why you're frightened for me. I wish you'd tell me."

"I can't tell you. I don't know anything. But I wish to God you'd go away from here."

"Darling," said Pat, "I'm not going. I'm staying here. For better, for worse. That's how I feel about it." She added, with a sudden catch in her voice, "Only with me it's always for worse."

"What on earth do you mean, Pat?"

"I bring bad luck. That's what I mean. I bring bad luck to anybody I come in contact with."

"My dear, adorable nitwit, you haven't brought bad luck to me. Look how after I married you the old man sent for me to come home and make friends with him."

"Yes, and what happened when you did come home? I tell you, I'm unlucky to people."

"Look here, my sweet, you've got a thing about all this. It's superstition, pure and simple."

"I can't help it. Some people do bring bad luck. I'm one of them."

Lance took her by the shoulders and shook her violently. "You're my Pat and to be married to you is the greatest luck in the world. So get that into your silly head." Then, calming down, he said in a more sober voice, "But seriously, Pat, do be very careful. If there is someone unhinged round here, I don't want you to be the one who stops the bullet or drinks the henbane."

"Or drinks the henbane, as you say."

"When I'm not around, stick to that old lady. What's-her-name Marple. Why do you think Aunt Effie asked her to stay here?"

"Goodness knows why Aunt Effie does anything. Lance, how long are we going to stay here?"

Lance shrugged his shoulders.

"Difficult to say."

"I don't think," said Pat, "that we're really awfully welcome." She hesitated as she spoke the words. "The house belongs to your brother now, I suppose? He doesn't really want us here, does he?"

Lance chuckled suddenly.

"Not he, but he's got to stick us for the present, at any rate."

"And afterwards? What are we going to do, Lance? Are we going back to East Africa, or what?"

"Is that what you'd like to do, Pat?"

She nodded vigorously.

"That's lucky," said Lance, "because it's what I'd like to do, too. I don't take much to this country nowadays."

Pat's face brightened.

"How lovely. From what you said the other day, I was afraid you might want to stop here."

A devilish glint appeared in Lance's eyes.

"You're to hold your tongue about our plans, Pat," he said. "I have it in my mind to twist dear brother Percival's tail a bit."

"Oh, Lance, do be careful."

"I'll be careful, my sweet, but I don't see why old Percy should get away with everything."

II

With her head a little on one side, looking like an amiable cockatoo, Miss Marple sat in the large drawing-room listening to Mrs. Percival Fortescue. Miss Marple looked particularly incongruous in the drawing-room. Her light, spare figure was alien to the vast, brocaded sofa in which she sat, with its many-hued cushions strewn around her. Miss Marple sat very upright because she had been taught to use a back-board as a girl, and not to loll. In a large armchair beside her, dressed in elaborate black, was Mrs. Percival, talking away volubly at nineteen to the dozen. "Exactly," thought Miss Marple, "like poor Mrs. Emmett, the bank manager's wife." She remembered how one day Mrs. Emmett had come to call and talk about the selling arrangements for Poppy Day, and how after the preliminary business had been settled, Mrs. Emmett had suddenly begun to talk and talk and talk. Mrs. Emmett occupied rather a difficult position in St. Mary Mead. She did not belong to the old guard of ladies in reduced circumstances who lived in neat houses round the church, and who knew intimately all the ramifications of the County families, even though they might not be strictly county themselves. Mr. Emmett, the bank manager, had undeniably married beneath him and the result was that his wife was in a position of great loneliness since she could not, of course, associate with the wives of trades people. Snobbery here raised its hideous head and marooned Mrs. Emmett on a permanent island of loneliness.

The necessity to talk grew upon Mrs. Emmett, and on that particular day it had burst its bounds, and Miss Marple had received the full flood of the torrent. She had been sorry for Mrs. Emmett then, and today she was rather sorry for Mrs. Percival Fortescue.

Mrs. Percival had had a lot of grievances to bear and the relief of airing them to a more or less total stranger was enormous.

"Of course, I never want to complain," said Mrs. Percival. "I've never been of the complaining kind. What I always say is that one must put up with things. What can't be cured must be endured and I'm sure I've never said a word to anyone. It's really difficult to know whom I could have spoken to. In some ways one is very isolated here—very isolated. It's very convenient, of course, and a great saving of expense to have our own set of rooms in this house. But, of course, it's not at all like having a place of your own. I'm sure you agree."

Miss Marple said she agreed.

"Fortunately, our new house is almost ready to move into. It is a question really of getting the painters and decorators out. These men are so slow. My husband, of course, has been quite satisfied living here. But then it's different for a man. That's what I always say—it's so different for a man. Don't you agree?"

Miss Marple agreed that it was very different for a man. She could say this without a qualm as it was what she really believed. "The gentlemen" were, in Miss Marple's mind, in a totally different category from her own sex. They required two eggs plus bacon for breakfast, three good nourishing meals a day, and were never to be contradicted or argued with before dinner. Mrs. Percival went on:

"My husband, you see, is away all day in the city. When he comes home he's just tired and wants to sit down and read. But I, on the contrary, am alone here all day with no congenial company at all. I've been perfectly comfortable and all that. Excellent food. But what I do feel one needs is a really pleasant social circle. The people round here are really not my kind. Part of them are what I call a flashy, bridge-playing lot. Not nice bridge. I like a hand of bridge myself as well as anybody, but of course they're all very rich down here. They play for enormously high stakes, and there's a great deal of drinking. In fact, the sort of life that I call really fast society. Then, of course, there's a sprinkling of—well, you can only call them old pussies who love to potter round with a trowel and do gardening."

Miss Marple looked slightly guilty, since she was herself an inveterate gardener.

"I don't want to say anything against the dead," resumed Mrs. Percy rapidly, "but there's no doubt about it, Mr. Fortescue, my father-in-law, I mean, made a very foolish second marriage. My—well, I can't call her my mother-in-law, she was the same age as I am. The real truth of it is she was man-mad. Absolutely man-mad. And the way she spent money! My father-in-law was an absolute fool about her. Didn't care what bills she ran up. It vexed Percy very much, very much indeed. Percy is always so careful about money matters. He hates waste. And then what with Mr. Fortescue being so peculiar and so bad-tempered, flashing out in these terrible rages, spending money like water, backing wildcat schemes. Well—it wasn't at all nice."

Miss Marple ventured upon making a remark.

"That must have worried your husband, too?"

"Oh yes, it did. For the last year Percy's been very worried, indeed. It's really made him quite different. His manner, you know, changed even towards me. Sometimes when I talked to him he used not to answer." Mrs. Percy sighed, then went on, "Then Elaine, my sister-in-law, you know, she's a very odd sort of girl. Very out-of-doors and all that. Not exactly unfriendly but not sympathetic, you know. She never wanted to go up to London to shop, or go to a matinée or anything of that kind. She wasn't even interested in clothes." Mrs. Percival sighed again and murmured, "But, of course, I don't want to complain in any way." A qualm of compunction came over her. She said, hurriedly: "You must think it most odd, talking to you like this when you are a comparative stranger. But really, what with all the strain and shock—I think really it's the shock that matters most. Delayed shock. I feel so nervous, you know, that I really—well, I really must speak to someone. You remind me so much of a dear old lady, Miss Trefusis James. She fractured her femur when she was seventy-five. It was a very long business nursing her, and we became great friends. She gave me a fox fur cape when I left and I did think it was kind of her."

"I know just how you feel," said Miss Marple.

And this again was true. Mrs. Percival's husband was obviously bored by her and paid very little attention to her, and the poor woman had managed to make no local friends. Running up to London and shopping, matinées and a luxurious house to live in did not make up for the lack of humanity in her relations with her husband's family.

"I hope it's not rude of me to say so," said Miss Marple in a gentle, old lady's voice, "but I really feel that the late Mr. Fortescue cannot have been a very nice man."

"He wasn't," said his daughter-in-law. "Quite frankly, my dear, between you and me, he was a detestable old man. I don't wonder—I really don't—that someone put him out of the way."

"You've no idea at all who—" began Miss Marple and broke off. "Oh dear, perhaps this is a question I should not ask—not even an idea who—who—well, who it might have been?"

"Oh, I think it was that horrible man, Crump," said Mrs. Percival. "I've always disliked him very much. He's got a manner, not really rude, you know, but yet it is rude. Impertinent, that's more it."

"Still, there would have to be a motive, I suppose."

"I really don't know that that sort of person requires much motive. I daresay Mr. Fortescue ticked him off about something, and I rather suspect that sometimes he drinks too much. But what I really think is that he's a bit unbalanced, you know. Like that footman, or butler, whoever it was, who went round the house shooting everybody. Of course, to be quite honest with you, I did suspect that it was Adele who poisoned Mr. Fortescue. But now, of course, one can't suspect that since she's been poisoned herself. She may have accused Crump, you know. And then he lost his head and perhaps managed to put something in the sandwiches and Gladys saw him do it and so he killed her too. I think it's really dangerous having him in the house at all. Oh dear, I wish I could get away, but I suppose these horrible policemen won't let one do anything of the kind." She leant forward impulsively and put a plump hand on Miss Marple's arm. "Sometimes I feel I must get away—that if it doesn't all stop soon I shall—I shall actually run away—"

She leant back studying Miss Marple's face.

"But perhaps—that wouldn't be wise?"

"No, I don't think it would be very wise. The police could soon find you, you know."

"Could they? Could they really? You think they're clever enough for that?"

"It is very foolish to underestimate the police. Inspector Neele strikes me as a particularly intelligent man."

"Oh! I thought he was rather stupid."

Miss Marple shook her head.

"I can't help feeling—" Jennifer Fortescue hesitated—"that it's dangerous to stay here."

"Dangerous for you, you mean?"

"Ye-es—well, yes—"

"Because of something you—know?"

Mrs. Percival seemed to take breath.

"Oh no, of course. I don't know anything. What should I know? It's just—just that I'm nervous. That man Crump—"

But it was not, Miss Marple thought, of Crump that Mrs. Percival Fortescue was thinking, watching the clenching and unclenching of Jennifer's hands. Miss Marple thought that for some reason Jennifer Fortescue was very badly frightened indeed.

Chapter Twenty-two

IT WAS GROWING DARK. Miss Marple had taken her knitting over to the window in the library. Looking out of the glass pane, she saw Pat Fortescue walking up and down the terrace outside. Miss Marple unlatched the window and called through it.

"Come in, my dear. Do come in. I'm sure it's much too cold and damp for you to be out there without a coat on."

Pat obeyed the summons. She came in and shut the window and turned on two of the lamps.

"Yes," she said, "it's not a very nice afternoon." She sat down on the sofa by Miss Marple. "What are you knitting?"

"Oh, just a little matinée coat, dear. For a baby, you know. I always say young mothers can't have too many matinée coats for their babies. It's the second size. I always knit the second size. Babies so soon grow out of the first size."

Pat stretched out long legs towards the fire.

"It's nice in here today," she said. "With the fire and the lamps and you knitting things for babies. It all seems cozy and homely and as England ought to be."

"It's as England is," said Miss Marple. "There are not so many Yewtree Lodges, my dear."

"I think that's a good thing," said Pat. "I don't believe this was ever a happy house. I don't believe anybody was ever happy in it, in spite of all the money they spent and the things they had."

"No," Miss Marple agreed. "I shouldn't say it had been a happy house."

"I suppose Adele may have been happy," said Pat. "I never met her, of course, so I don't know, but Jennifer is pretty miserable and Elaine's been eating her heart out over a young man who she probably knows in her heart of hearts doesn't care for her. Oh, how I want to get away from here!" She looked at Miss Marple and smiled suddenly. "D'you know," she said, "that Lance told me to stick as close to you as I could? He seemed to think I should be safe that way."

"Your husband's no fool," said Miss Marple.

"No. Lance isn't a fool. At least, he is in some ways. But I wish he'd tell me exactly what he's afraid of. One thing seems clear enough. Somebody in this house is mad, and madness is always frightening because you don't know how mad people's minds will work. You don't know what they'll do next."

"My poor child," said Miss Marple.

"Oh, I'm all right, really. I ought to be tough enough by now."

Miss Marple said gently, "You've had a good deal of unhappiness, haven't you, my dear?"

"Oh, I've had some very good times, too. I had a lovely childhood in Ireland, riding, hunting, and a great big, bare draughty house with lots and lots of sun in it. If you've had a happy childhood, nobody can take that away from you, can they? It was afterwards—when I grew up—that things seemed always to go wrong. To begin with, I suppose, it was the war."

"Your husband was a fighter pilot, wasn't he?"

"Yes. We'd only been married a month when Don was shot down." She stared ahead of her into the fire. "I thought at first I wanted to die, too. It seemed so unfair, so cruel. And yet—in the end—I almost began to see that it had been the best thing. Don was wonderful in the war. Brave and reckless and gay. He had all the qualities that are needed, wanted in a war. But I don't believe, somehow, peace would have suited him. He had a kind of—oh, how shall I put it?—arrogant insubordination. He wouldn't have fitted in or settled down. He'd have fought against things. He was, well, antisocial in a way. No, he wouldn't have fitted in."

"It's wise of you to see that, my dear." Miss Marple bent over her knitting, picked up a stitch, counted under her breath, "Three plain, two purl, slip one, knit two together," and then said, aloud, "And your second husband, my dear?"

"Freddy? Freddy shot himself."

"Oh dear. How very sad. What a tragedy."

"We were very happy together," said Pat. "I began to realize, about two years ago after we were married, that Freddy wasn't—well, wasn't always straight. I began to find out the sort of things that were going on. But it didn't seem to matter, between us two, that is. Because, you see, Freddy loved me and I loved him. I tried not to know what was going on. That was cowardly of me, I suppose, but I couldn't have changed him, you know. You can't change people."

"No," said Miss Marple, "you can't change people."

"I'd taken him and loved him and married him for what he was, and I sort of felt that I just had to—put up with it. Then things went wrong and he couldn't face it, and he shot himself. After he died I went out to Kenya to stay with some friends there. I couldn't stop on in England and go on meeting all—all the old crowd that knew about it all. And out in Kenya I met Lance." Her face changed and softened. She went on looking into the fire, and Miss Marple looked at her. Presently Pat turned her head and said, "Tell me, Miss Marple, what do you really think of Percival?"

"Well, I've not seen very much of him. Just at breakfast, usually. That's all. I don't think he very much likes my being here."

Pat laughed suddenly.

"He's mean, you know. Terribly mean about money. Lance says he always was. Jennifer complains of it, too. Goes over the housekeeping accounts with Miss Dove. Complaining of every item. But Miss Dove manages to hold her own. She's rather a wonderful person. Don't you think so?"

"Yes, indeed. She reminds me of Mrs. Latimer in my own village, St. Mary Mead. She ran the Women's Voluntary Services, you know, and the Girl Guides, and indeed, she ran practically everything there. It wasn't for quite five years that we discovered that—oh, but I mustn't gossip. Nothing is more boring than people talking to you about places and people whom you've never seen and know nothing about. You must forgive me, my dear."

"Is St. Mary Mead a very nice village?"

"Well, I don't quite know what you would call a nice village, my dear.

It's quite a pretty village. There are some nice people living in it and some extremely unpleasant people as well. Very curious things go on there just as in any other village. Human nature is much the same everywhere, is it not?"

"You go up and see Miss Ramsbottom a good deal, don't you?" said Pat. "Now, she really frightens me."

"Frightens you? Why?"

"Because I think she's crazy. I think she's got religious mania. You don't think she could be—really—mad, do you?"

"In what way mad?"

"Oh, you know what I mean, Miss Marple, well enough. She sits up there and never goes out, and broods about sin. Well, she might have felt in the end that it was her mission in life to execute judgment."

"Is that what your husband thinks?"

"I don't know what Lance thinks. He won't tell me. But I'm quite sure of one thing—that he believes that it's someone who's mad, and it's someone in the family. Well, Percival's sane enough, I should say. Jennifer's just stupid and rather pathetic. She's a bit nervy, but that's all, and Elaine is one of those queer, tempestuous, tense girls. She's desperately in love with this young man of hers and she'll never admit to herself for a moment that he's marrying her for her money."

"You think he is marrying her for money?"

"Yes, I do. Don't you think so?"

"I should say so quite certainly," said Miss Marple. "Like young Ellis who married Marion Bates, the rich ironmonger's daughter. She was a very plain girl and absolutely besotted about him. However, it turned out quite well. People like young Ellis and this Gerald Wright are only really disagreeable when they've married a poor girl for love. They are so annoyed with themselves for doing it that they take it out on the girl. But if they marry a rich girl they continue to respect her."

"I don't see," went on Pat, frowning, "how it can be anyone from outside. And so—and so that accounts for the atmosphere that is here. Everyone watching everybody else. Only something's got to happen soon—"

"There won't be any more deaths," said Miss Marple. "At least, I shouldn't think so."

"You can't be sure of that."

"Well, as a matter of fact, I am fairly sure. The murderer's accomplished his purpose, you see."

"His?"

"Well, his or her. One says his for convenience."

"You say his or her purpose. What sort of purpose?"

Miss Marple shook her head—she was not yet quite sure herself.

Chapter Twenty-three

ONCE AGAIN Miss Somers had just made tea in the typists' room, and once again the kettle had not been boiling when Miss Somers poured the water onto the tea. History repeats itself. Miss Griffith, accepting her cup, thought to herself, I really must speak to Mr. Percival about Somers. I'm sure we can do better. But with all this terrible business going on, one doesn't like to bother him over office details.

As so often before, Miss Griffith said sharply, "Water not boiling again, Somers."

Miss Somers, going pink, replied in her usual formula, "Oh, dear, I was sure it was boiling this time."

Further developments on the same line were interrupted by the entrance of Lance Fortescue. He looked round him somewhat vaguely, and Miss Griffith, jumping up, came forward to meet him.

"Mr. Lance!" she exclaimed.

He swung round towards her and his face lit up in a smile.

"Hullo. Why, it's Miss Griffith."

Miss Griffith was delighted. Eleven years since he had seen her and he knew her name. She said in a confused voice, "Fancy your remembering."

And Lance said easily, with all his charm to the fore, "Of course I remember."

A flicker of excitement was running round the typists' room. Miss Somers' troubles over the tea were forgotten. She was gaping at Lance with her mouth slightly open. Miss Bell gazed eagerly over the top of her typewriter and Miss Chase unobtrusively drew out her compact and powdered her nose. Lance Fortescue looked round him.

"So everything's still going on just the same here," he said.

"Not many changes, Mr. Lance. How brown you look and how well! I suppose you must have had a very interesting life abroad."

"You could call it that," said Lance, "but perhaps I am now going to try and have an interesting life in London."

"You're coming back here to the office?"

"Maybe."

"Oh, but how delightful."

"You'll find me very rusty," said Lance. "You'll have to show me all the ropes, Miss Griffith."

Miss Griffith laughed delightedly.

"It will be very nice to have you back, Mr. Lance. Very nice indeed."

Lance threw her an appreciative glance.

"That's sweet of you," he said. "That's very sweet of you."

"We never believed—none of us thought . . ." Miss Griffith broke off and flushed.

Lance patted her on the arm.

"You didn't believe the devil was as black as he was painted? Well, perhaps he wasn't. But that's all old history now. There's no good going back over it. The future's the thing." He added, "Is my brother here?"

"He's in the inner office, I think."

Lance nodded easily and passed on. In the anteroom to the inner sanctum a hard-faced woman of middle age rose behind a desk and said forbiddingly, "Your name and business, please?"

Lance looked at her doubtfully.

"Are you—Miss Grosvenor?" he asked.

Miss Grosvenor had been described to him as a glamorous blonde. She had, indeed, appeared so in the pictures that had been published in the newspapers reporting the inquest on Rex Fortescue. This, surely, could not be Miss Grosvenor.

"Miss Grosvenor left last week. I am Mrs. Hardcastle, Mr. Percival Fortescue's personal secretary."

How like old Percy, thought Lance. To get rid of a glamorous blonde and take on a Gorgon instead. I wonder why? Was it safety or was it because this one comes cheaper? Aloud he said easily, "I'm Lancelot Fortescue. You haven't met me yet."

"Oh, I'm sorry, Mr. Lancelot," Mrs. Hardcastle apologized. "This is the first time, I think, you've been to the office?"

"The first time but not the last," said Lance, smiling.

He crossed the room and opened the door of what had been his father's private office. Somewhat to his surprise, it was not Percival who was sitting behind the desk there, but Inspector Neele. Inspector Neele looked up from a large wad of papers which he was sorting, and nodded his head.

"Good morning, Mr. Fortescue, you've come to take up your duties, I suppose."

"So you've heard I decided to come into the firm?"

"Your brother told me so."

"He did, did he? With enthusiasm?"

Inspector Neele endeavored to conceal a smile.

"The enthusiasm was not marked," he said gravely.

"Poor Percy," commented Lance.

Inspector Neele looked at him curiously.

"Are you really going to become a City man?"

"You don't think it's likely, Inspector Neele?"

"It doesn't seem quite in character, Mr. Fortescue."

"Why not? I'm my father's son."

"And your mother's."

Lance shook his head.

"You haven't got anything there, Inspector. My mother was a Victorian romantic. Her favorite reading was the *Idylls of the King*, as indeed you may have deduced from our curious Christian names. She was an invalid and always, I should imagine, out of touch with reality. I'm not like that at all. I have no sentiment, very little sense of romance, and I'm a realist first and last."

"People aren't always what they think themselves to be," Inspector Neele pointed out.

"No, I suppose that's true," said Lance.

He sat down in a chair and stretched his long legs out in his own characteristic fashion. He was smiling to himself. Then he said unexpectedly, "You're shrewder than my brother, Inspector."

"In what way, Mr. Fortescue?"

"I've put the wind up Percy, all right. He thinks he's going to have my fingers fiddling about in his pie. He thinks I'll launch out and spend the firm's money and try and embroil him in wildcat schemes. It would be almost worth doing just for the fun of it! Almost, but not quite. I couldn't really stand an office life, Inspector. I like the open air and some possibilities of adventure. I'd stifle in a place like this." He added quickly, "This is off the record, mind. Don't give me away to Percy, will you?"

"I don't suppose the subject will arise, Mr. Fortescue."

"I must have my bit of fun with Percy," said Lance. "I want to make him sweat a bit. I've got to get a bit of my own back."

"That's rather a curious phrase, Mr. Fortescue," said Neele. "Your own back—for what?"

Lance shrugged his shoulders.

"Oh, it's old history now. Not worth going back over."

"There was a little matter of a check, I understand, in the past. Would that be what you're referring to?"

"How much you know, Inspector!"

"There was no question of prosecution, I understand," said Neele. "Your father wouldn't have done that."

"No. He just kicked me out, that's all."

Inspector Neele eyed him speculatively, but it was not Lance Fortescue of whom he was thinking, but of Percival. The honest, industrious, parsimonious Percival. It seemed to him that wherever he got in the case he was always coming up against the enigma of Percival Fortescue, a man of whom everybody knew the outer aspects, but whose inner personality was much harder to gauge. One would have said from observing him, a somewhat colorless and insignificant character, a man who had been very much under his father's thumb. Percy Prim, in fact, as the A.C. had once said. Neele was trying now, through Lance, to get a closer appreciation of Percival's personality. He murmured in a tentative manner:

"Your brother seems always to have been very much—well, how shall I put it—under your father's thumb."

"I wonder." Lance seemed definitely to be considering the point. "I wonder. Yes, that would be the effect, I think, given. But I'm not sure that it was really the truth. It's astonishing, you know, when I look back through life, to see how Percy always got his own way without seeming to do so, if you know what I mean."

Yes, Inspector Neele thought, it was indeed astonishing. He sorted through the papers in front of him, fished out a letter and shoved it across the desk towards Lance.

"This is a letter you wrote last August, isn't it, Mr. Fortescue?"

Lance took it, glanced at it and returned it.

"Yes," he said, "I wrote it after I got back to Kenya last summer. Dad kept it, did he? Where was it—here in the office?"

"No, Mr. Fortescue, it was among your father's papers in Yewtree Lodge."

The Inspector considered it speculatively as it lay on the desk in front of him. It was not a long letter.

"Dear Dad, I've talked things over with Pat and I agree to your proposition. It will take me a little time to get things fixed up here, say about the end of October or beginning of November. I'll let you know nearer the time. I hope we'll pull together better than we used to do. Anyway, I'll do my best. I can't say more. Look after yourself. Yours, Lance."

"Where did you address this letter, Mr. Fortescue? To the office or Yew-tree Lodge?"

Lance frowned in an effort of recollection.

"It's difficult. I can't remember. You see, it's almost three months now. The office, I think. Yes, I'm almost sure. Here to the office." He paused a moment before asking with frank curiosity, "Why?"

"I wondered," said Inspector Neele. "Your father did not put it in the file here among his private papers. He took it back with him to Yewtree Lodge, and I found it in his desk there. I wondered why he should have done that."

Lance laughed.

"To keep it out of Percy's way, I suppose."

"Yes," said Inspector Neele, "it would seem so. Your brother, then, had access to your father's private papers here?"

"Well," Lance hesitated and frowned, "not exactly. I mean, I suppose he could have looked through them at any time if he liked, but he wouldn't be . . ."

Inspector Neele finished the sentence for him.

"Wouldn't be supposed to do so?"

Lance grinned broadly. "That's right. Frankly, it would have been snooping. But Percy, I should imagine, always did snoop."

Inspector Neele nodded. He, also, thought it probable that Percival Fortescue snooped. It would be in keeping with what the Inspector was beginning to learn of his character.

"And talk of the devil," murmured Lance, as at that moment the door opened and Percival Fortescue came in. About to speak to the Inspector, he stopped, frowning, as he saw Lance.

"Hallo," he said. "You here? You didn't tell me you were coming here today."

"I felt a kind of zeal for work coming over me," said Lance, "so here I am ready to make myself useful. What do you want me to do?"

Percival said testily, "Nothing at present. Nothing at all. We shall have to come to some kind of arrangement as to what side of the business you're going to look after. We shall have to arrange an office for you."

Lance inquired, with a grin:

"By the way, why did you get rid of glamorous Grosvenor, old boy, and replace her by Horse-faced Hetty out there?"

"Really, Lance," Percival protested sharply.

"Definitely a change for the worse," said Lance. "I've been looking forward to the glamorous Grosvenor. Why did you sack her? Thought she knew a bit too much?"

"Of course not. What an idea!" Percy spoke angrily, a flush mounting his pale face. He turned to the Inspector. "You mustn't pay any attention to my brother," he said coldly. "He has a rather peculiar sense of humor." He added, "I never had a very high opinion of Miss Grosvenor's intelligence. Mrs. Hardcastle has excellent references and is most capable, besides very moderate in her terms."

"Very moderate in her terms," murmured Lance, casting his eyes towards the ceiling. "You know, Percy, I don't really approve of skimping over the office personnel. By the way, considering how loyally the staff has stood by us during these last tragic weeks, don't you think we ought to raise their salaries all round?"

"Certainly not," snapped Percival Fortescue. "Quite uncalled for and unnecessary."

Inspector Neele noticed the gleam of devilry in Lance's eyes. Percival, however, was far too upset to notice it.

"You always had the most extraordinarily extravagant ideas," he stuttered. "In the state in which this firm has been left, economy is our only hope."

Inspector Neele coughed apologetically.

"That's one of the things I wanted to talk to you about, Mr. Fortescue," he said to Percival.

"Yes, Inspector?" Percival switched his attention to Neele.

"I want to put certain suggestions before you, Mr. Fortescue. I understand that for the past six months or longer, possibly a year, your father's general behavior and conduct have been a source of increasing anxiety to you."

"He wasn't well," said Percival with finality. "He certainly wasn't at all well."

"You tried to induce him to see a doctor but you failed. He refused categorically?"

"That is so."

"May I ask you if you suspected that your father was suffering from what is familiarly referred to as G.P.I., General Paralysis of the Insane, a condition with signs of megalomania and irritability, which terminates sooner or later in hopeless insanity?"

Percival looked surprised. "It is remarkably astute of you, Inspector. That is exactly what I did fear. That is why I was so anxious for my father to submit to medical treatment."

Neele went on:

"In the meantime, until you could persuade your father to do that, he was capable of causing great havoc to the business?"

"He certainly was," Percival agreed.

"A very unfortunate state of affairs," said the Inspector.

"Quite terrible. No one knows the anxiety I have been through."

Neele said gently, "From the business point of view, your father's death was an extremely fortunate circumstance."

Percival said sharply, "You can hardly think I would regard my father's death in that light."

"It is not a question of how you regard it, Mr. Fortescue. I'm speaking merely of a question of fact. Your father died before his finances were completely on the rocks."

Percival said impatiently, "Yes, yes. As a matter of actual fact, you are right."

"It was a fortunate occurrence for your whole family, since they are dependent on this business."

"Yes. But really, Inspector, I don't see what you're driving at . . ." Percival broke off.

"Oh, I'm not driving at anything, Mr. Fortescue," said Neele. "I just like getting my facts straight. Now, there's another thing. I understood you to say that you'd had no communication of any kind with your brother here since he left England many years ago."

"Quite so," said Percival.

"Yes, but it isn't quite so, is it, Mr. Fortescue? I mean that last summer when you were so worried about your father's health, you actually wrote to your brother in Africa, told him of your anxiety about your father's behavior. You wanted, I think, your brother to combine with you in getting your father medically examined and put under restraint, if necessary."

"I—I—really, I don't see . . ."

Percival was badly shaken.

"That is so, isn't it, Mr. Fortescue?"

"Well, actually, I thought it only right. After all, Lancelot was a junior partner."

Inspector Neele transferred his gaze to Lance. Lance was grinning.

"You received that letter?" Inspector Neele asked.

Lance Fortescue nodded.

"What did you reply to it?"

Lance's grin widened.

"I told Percy to go and boil his head and to let the old man alone. I said the old man probably knew what he was doing quite well."

Inspector Neele's gaze went back again to Percival.

"Were those the terms of your brother's answer?"

"I—I—well, I suppose roughly, yes. Far more offensively couched, however."

"I thought the Inspector had better have a bowdlerized version," said Lance. He went on, "Frankly, Inspector Neele, that is one of the reasons why, when I got a letter from my father, I came home to see for myself what I thought. In the short interview I had with my father, frankly, I couldn't see anything much wrong with him. He was slightly excitable, that was all. He appeared to me perfectly capable of managing his own affairs. Anyway, after I got back to Africa and had talked things over with Pat, I decided that I'd come home and—what shall we say?—see fair play."

He shot a glance at Percival as he spoke.

"I object," said Percival Fortescue. "I object strongly to what you are suggesting. I was not intending to victimize my father. I was concerned for his health. I admit that I was also concerned . . ." he paused.

Lance filled the pause quickly.

"You were also concerned for your pocket, eh? For Percy's little pocket." He got up and all of a sudden his manner changed. "All right, Percy, I'm through. I was going to string you along a bit by pretending to work here. I wasn't going to let you have things all your own sweet way, but I'm damned if I'm going on with it. Frankly, it makes me sick to be in the same room with you. You've always been a dirty, mean, little skunk all your life. Prying and snooping and lying and making trouble. I'll tell you another thing. I can't prove it, but I've always believed it was you who forged that check there was all the row about, that got me shot out of here. For one thing, it was a damn bad forgery, a forgery that drew attention to itself in letters a foot high. My record was too bad for me to be able to protest effectively, but I often wondered that the old boy didn't realize that if I had forged his name I could have made a much better job of it than that."

Lance swept on, his voice rising, "Well, Percy, I'm not going on with the silly game. I'm sick of this country, and of the City. I'm sick of little men like you with their pinstripe trousers and their black coats and their mincing voices and their mean, shoddy, financial deals. We'll share out as you suggested, and I'll get back with Pat to a different country—a country where there's room to breathe and move about. You can make your own list of securities. Keep the gilt-edged and the conservative ones, keep the safe 2 per cent and 3 per cent and 3½ per cent. Give me father's latest wildcat speculations, as you call them. Most of them are probably duds. But I'll bet that one or two of them will pay better in the end than all your playing safe with 3 per cent Trustee stocks will do. Father was a shrewd old devil. He took chances, plenty of them. Some of those chances paid five and six and 700 per cent. I'll back his judgment and his luck. As for you, you little worm . . ."

Lance advanced towards his brother, who retreated rapidly round the end of the desk towards Inspector Neele. "All right," said Lance, "I'm not going to touch you. You wanted me out of here, you're getting me out of here. You ought to be satisfied." He added as he strode towards the door, "You can throw in the old Blackbird Mine concession too, if you like. If you've got the murdering MacKenzies on our trail, I'll draw them off to Africa." He added, as he swung through the doorway, "Revenge—after all these years—scarcely seems credible. But Inspector Neele seems to take it seriously, don't you, Inspector?"

"Nonsense," said Percival. "Such a thing is impossible!"

"Ask him," said Lance. "Ask him why he's making all these inquiries into blackbirds and rye in father's pocket."

Gently stroking his upper lip, Inspector Neele said, "You remember the blackbirds last summer, Mr. Fortescue. There are certain grounds for inquiry."

"Nonsense," said Percival again. "Nobody's heard of the MacKenzies for years."

"And yet," said Lance, "I'd almost dare to swear that there's a MacKenzie in our midst. I rather imagine the Inspector thinks so, too."

II

Inspector Neele caught up Lancelot Fortescue as the latter emerged into the street below.

Lance grinned at him rather sheepishly.

"I didn't mean to do that," he said. "But I suddenly lost my temper. Oh, well, it would have come to the same before long. I'm meeting Pat at the Savoy. Are you coming my way, Inspector?"

"No, I'm returning to Baydon Heath. But there's just something I'd like to ask you, Mr. Fortescue."

"Yes?"

"When you came into the inner office and saw me there, you were surprised. Why?"

"Because I didn't expect to see you, I suppose. I thought I'd find Percy there."

"You weren't told that he'd gone out?"

Lance looked at him curiously.

"No. They said he was in his office."

"I see. Nobody knew he'd gone out. There's no second door out of the inner office, but there is a door leading straight into the corridor from the little antechamber. I suppose your brother went out that way, but I'm surprised Mrs. Hardcastle didn't tell you so."

Lance laughed.

"She'd probably been to collect her cup of tea."

"Yes, yes—quite so."

Lance looked at him. "What's the idea, Inspector?"

"Just puzzling over a few little things, that's all, Mr. Fortescue."

Chapter Twenty-four

IN THE TRAIN on the way down to Baydon Heath, Inspector Neele had singularly little success doing the *Times* crossword. His mind was distracted by various possibilities. In the same way, he read the news with only half his brain taking it in. He read of an earthquake in Japan, of the discovery of uranium deposits in Tanganyika, of the body of a merchant seaman washed up near Southampton, and of the imminent strike among the dockers. He read of the latest victims of the cosh and of a new drug that had achieved wonders in advanced cases of tuberculosis.

All these items made a queer kind of pattern in the back of his mind. Presently he returned to the crossword puzzle and was able to put down three clues in rapid succession.

When he reached Yewtree Lodge he had come to a certain decision. He said to Sergeant Hay, "Where's that old lady? Is she still here?"

"Miss Marple? Oh, yes, she's here still. Great buddies with the old lady upstairs."

"I see." Neele paused for a moment and then said, "Where is she now? I'd like to see her."

Miss Marple arrived in a few minutes' time, looking rather flushed, and breathing fast.

"You want to see me, Inspector Neele? I do hope I haven't kept you waiting. Sergeant Hay couldn't find me at first. I was in the kitchen, talking to Mrs. Crump. I was congratulating her on her pastry and how light her hand is, and telling her how delicious the soufflé was last night. I always think, you know, it's better to approach a subject gradually, don't you? At least, I suppose it isn't so easy for you. You more or less have to come almost straightaway to the questions you want to ask. But, of course, for an old lady like me who has all the time in the world, as you might say, it's really expected of her that there should be a great deal of unnecessary talk. And the way to a cook's heart, as they say, is through her pastry."

"What you really wanted to talk to her about," said Inspector Neele, "was Gladys Martin."

Miss Marple nodded.

"Yes. Gladys. You see, Mrs. Crump could really tell me a lot about the girl. Not in connection with the murder. I don't mean that. But about her spirits lately and the odd things she said. I don't mean odd in the sense of peculiar. I mean just the odds and ends of conversation."

"Did you find it helpful?" asked Inspector Neele.

"Yes," said Miss Marple. "I found it very helpful indeed. I really think, you know, that things are becoming very much clearer, don't you?"

"I do and I don't," said Inspector Neele.

Sergeant Hay, he noticed, had left the room. He was glad of it because what he was about to do and say now was, to say the least of it, slightly unorthodox.

"Look here, Miss Marple," he said, "I want to talk to you seriously."

"Yes, Inspector Neele?"

"In a way," said Inspector Neele, "you and I represent different points of view. I admit, Miss Marple, that I've heard something about you at the Yard." He said, "It seems you're fairly well known there."

"I don't know how it is," fluttered Miss Marple, "but I so often seem to get mixed up in things that are really no concern of mine. Crimes, I mean, and peculiar happenings."

"You've got a reputation," said Inspector Neele.

"Sir Henry Clithering, of course," said Miss Marple, "is a very old friend of mine."

"As I said before," Neele went on, "you and I represent opposite points of view. One might almost call them sanity and insanity."

Miss Marple put her head a little on one side.

"Now what exactly do you mean by that, I wonder, Inspector?"

"Well, Miss Marple, there's a sane way of looking at things. This murder benefits certain people. One person, I may say, in particular. The second murder benefits the same person. The third murder one might call a murder for safety."

"But which do you call the third murder?" Miss Marple asked.

Her eyes, a very bright china blue, looked shrewdly at the Inspector. He nodded.

"Yes. You've got something there, perhaps. You know, the other day when the A.C. was speaking to me of these murders, something that he said seemed to me to be wrong. That was it. I was thinking, of course, of the nursery rhyme. The king in his counting house, the queen in the parlor and the maid hanging out the clothes."

"Exactly," said Miss Marple. "A sequence in that order, but actually Gladys must have been murdered before Mrs. Fortescue, mustn't she?"

"I think so," said Neele. "I take it it's quite certainly so. Her body wasn't discovered till late that night, and of course it was difficult then to say exactly how long she'd been dead. But I think myself that she must almost certainly have been murdered round about five o'clock, because otherwise . . ."

Miss Marple cut in. "Because otherwise she would certainly have taken the second tray into the drawing-room?"

"Quite so. She took one tray in with the tea on it, she brought the second tray into the hall, and then something happened. She saw something or she heard something. The question is what that something was. It might have been Dubois coming down the stairs from Mrs. Fortescue's room. It might have been Elaine Fortescue's young man, Gerald Wright, coming in at the side door. Whoever it was lured her away from the tea tray and out into the garden. And once that had happened, I don't see any possibility of her death being long delayed. It was cold out and she was wearing only her thin uniform."

"Of course you're quite right," said Miss Marple. "I mean it was never a case of 'the maid was in the garden hanging up the clothes.' She wouldn't be hanging up clothes at that time of the evening and she wouldn't go out to the clothesline without putting a coat on. That was all camouflage, like the clothes peg, to make the thing fit in with the rhyme."

"Exactly," said Inspector Neele, "crazy. That's where I can't see eye to eye with you. I can't—I simply can't swallow this nursery rhyme business."

"But it fits, Inspector. You must agree it fits."

"It fits," said Neele heavily, "but all the same the sequence is wrong. I mean the rhyme definitely suggests that the maid was the third murder. But we know that the Queen was the third murder. Adele Fortescue was not killed until between twenty-five past five and five minutes to six. By then Gladys must already have been dead."

"And that's all wrong, isn't it?" said Miss Marple. "All wrong for the nursery rhyme—that's very significant, isn't it?"

Inspector Neele shrugged his shoulders.

"It's probably splitting hairs. The deaths fulfill the conditions of the rhyme, and I suppose that's all that was needed. But I'm talking now as though I were on your side. I'm going to outline my side of the case now, Miss Marple. I'm washing out the blackbirds and the rye and all the rest of it. I'm going by sober facts and common sense and the reasons for which sane people do murders. First, the death of Rex Fortescue, and whom his death benefits. Well, it benefits quite a lot of people, but most of all it benefits his son, Percival. His son Percival wasn't at Yewtree Lodge that morning. He couldn't have put poison in his father's coffee or in anything that he ate for breakfast. Or that's what we thought at first."

"Ah," Miss Marple's eyes brightened. "So there was a method, was there? I've been thinking about it, you know, a good deal, and I've had several ideas. But, of course, no evidence or proof."

"There's no harm in my letting you know," said Inspector Neele. "Taxine was added to a new jar of marmalade. That jar of marmalade was placed on the breakfast table and the top layer of it was eaten by Mr. Fortescue at breakfast. Later that jar of marmalade was thrown out into the bushes and a similar jar with a similar amount taken out of it was placed in the pantry. The jar in the bushes was found, and I've just had the result of the analysis. It shows definite evidence of taxine."

"So that was it," murmured Miss Marple. "So simple and easy to do."

"Consolidated Investments," Neele went on, "was in a bad way. If the firm had had to pay out a hundred thousand pounds to Adele Fortescue under her husband's will, it would, I think, have crashed. If Mrs. Fortescue had survived her husband for a month, that money would have had to be paid out to her. She would have had no feeling for the firm or its difficulties. But she didn't survive her husband for a month. She died, and as a result of her death the gainer was the residuary legatee of Rex Fortescue's will. In other words, Percival Fortescue again.

"Always Percival Fortescue," the Inspector continued bitterly. "And though he could have tampered with the marmalade, he couldn't have poisoned his stepmother or strangled Gladys. According to his secretary, he was in his city office at five o'clock that afternoon, and he didn't arrive back here until nearly seven."

"That makes it very difficult, doesn't it?" said Miss Marple.

"It makes it impossible," said Inspector Neele gloomily. "In other words, Percival is out." Abandoning restraint and prudence, he spoke with some bitterness, almost unaware of his listener. "Wherever I go, wherever I turn, I always come up against the same person. Percival Fortescue! Yet it can't be Percival Fortescue." Calming himself a little he said, "Oh, there are other possibilities, other people who had a perfectly good motive."

"Mr. Dubois, of course," said Miss Marple sharply. "And that young Mr. Wright. I do so agree with you, Inspector. Wherever there is a question of gain, one has to be very suspicious. The great thing to avoid is having in any way a trustful mind."

In spite of himself, Neele smiled.

"Always think the worst, eh?" he asked.

It seemed a curious doctrine to be proceeding from this charming and fragile-looking old lady.

"Oh yes," said Miss Marple fervently. "I always believe the worst. What is so sad is that one is usually justified in doing so."

"All right," said Neele, "let's think the worst. Dubois could have done it, Gerald Wright could have done it (that is to say, if he'd been acting in collusion with Elaine Fortescue and she tampered with the marmalade), Mrs. Percival could have done it, I suppose. She was on the spot. But none of the people I have mentioned tie up with the crazy angle. They don't tie up with blackbirds and pockets full of rye. That's your theory and it may be that you're right. If so, it boils down to one person, doesn't it? Mrs. MacKenzie's in a mental home and has been for a good number of years. She hasn't been messing about with marmalade pots or putting cyanide in the drawing-room afternoon tea. Her son Donald was killed at Dunkirk. That leaves the daughter Ruby MacKenzie. And if your theory is correct, if this whole series of murders arises out of the old Blackbird Mine business, then Ruby MacKenzie must be here in this house, and there's only one person that Ruby MacKenzie could be."

"I think, you know," said Miss Marple, "that you're being a little too dogmatic."

Inspector Neele paid no attention.

"Just one person," he said grimly.

He got up and went out of the room.

II

Mary Dove was in her own sitting-room. It was a small, rather austerely furnished room, but comfortable. When Inspector Neele tapped at the door, Mary Dove raised her head, which had been bent over a pile of tradesmen's books, and said in her clear voice:

"Come in."

The Inspector entered.

"Do sit down, Inspector." Miss Dove indicated a chair. "Could you wait just one moment? The total of the fishmonger's account does not seem to be correct, and I must check it."

Inspector Neele sat in silence, watching her as she totted up the column. How wonderfully calm and self-possessed the girl was, he thought. He was intrigued, as so often before, by the personality that underlay that self-assured manner. He tried to trace in her features any resemblance to those of the woman he had talked to at the Pinewood Sanatorium. The coloring was not unlike, but he could detect no real facial resemblance. Presently Mary Dove raised her head from her accounts and said:

"Yes, Inspector? What can I do for you?"

Inspector Neele said quietly, "You know, Miss Dove, there are certain very peculiar features about this case."

"Yes?"

"To begin with, there is the odd circumstance of the rye found in Mr. Fortescue's pocket."

"That was very extraordinary," Mary Dove agreed. "You know, I really cannot think of any explanation for that."

"Then there is the curious circumstance of the blackbirds. Those four blackbirds on Mr. Fortescue's desk last summer, and also the incident of the blackbirds being substituted for the veal and ham in the pie. You were here, I think, Miss Dove, at the time of both those occurrences?"

"Yes, I was. I remember now. It was most upsetting. It seemed such a very purposeless, spiteful thing to do, especially at the time."

"Perhaps not entirely purposeless. What do you know, Miss Dove, about the Blackbird Mine?"

"I don't think I've ever heard of the Blackbird Mine."

"Your name, you told me, is Mary Dove. Is that your real name, Miss Dove?"

Mary Dove raised her eyebrows. Inspector Neele was almost sure that a wary expression had come into her blue eyes.

"What an extraordinary question, Inspector. Are you suggesting that my name is not Mary Dove?"

"That is exactly what I am suggesting. I'm suggesting," said Neele pleasantly, "that your name is Ruby MacKenzie."

She stared at him. For a moment her face was entirely blank, with neither protest on it nor surprise. There was, Inspector Neele thought, a very definite effect of calculation. After a minute or two she said in a quiet, colorless voice, "What do you expect me to say?"

"Please answer me. Is your name Ruby MacKenzie?"

"I have told you my name is Mary Dove."

"Yes, but have you proof of that, Miss Dove?"

"What do you want to see? My birth certificate?"

"That might be helpful or it might not. You might, I mean, be in possession of the birth certificate of a Mary Dove. That Mary Dove might be a friend of yours or might be someone who had died."

"Yes, there are a lot of possibilities, aren't there?" Amusement had crept back into Mary Dove's voice. "It's really quite a dilemma for you, isn't it, Inspector?"

"They might possibly be able to recognize you at Pinewood Sanatorium," said Neele.

"Pinewood Sanatorium!" Mary raised her eyebrows. "What or where is Pinewood Sanatorium?"

"I think you know very well, Miss Dove."

"I assure you I am quite in the dark."

"And you deny categorically that you are Ruby MacKenzie?"

"I shouldn't really like to deny anything. I think, you know, Inspector, that it's up to you to prove I am this Ruby MacKenzie, whoever she is." There was definite amusement now in her blue eyes, amusement and challenge. Looking him straight in the eyes, Mary Dove said, "Yes, it's up to you, Inspector. Prove that I'm Ruby MacKenzie, if you can."

Chapter Twenty-five

"The old tabby's looking for you, sir," said Sergeant Hay in a conspiratorial whisper, as Inspector Neele descended the stairs. "It appears as how she's got a lot more to say to you."

"Hell and damnation," said Inspector Neele.

"Yes, sir," said Sergeant Hay, not a muscle of his face moving.

He was about to move away when Neele called him back.

"Go over those notes given us by Miss Dove, Hay, notes as to her former employment and situations. Check up on them—and, yes, there are just one or two other things that I would like to know. Put these inquiries in hand, will you?"

He jotted down a few lines on a sheet of paper and gave them to Sergeant Hay who said, "I'll get on to it at once, sir."

Hearing a murmur of voices in the library as he passed, Inspector Neele looked in. Whether Miss Marple had been looking for him or not, she was now fully engaged talking to Mrs. Percival Fortescue while her knitting needles clicked busily. The middle of the sentence which Inspector Neele caught was:

". . . I have really always thought it was a vocation you needed for nursing. It certainly is very noble work."

Inspector Neele withdrew quietly. Miss Marple had noticed him, he thought, but she had taken no notice of his presence.

She went on in her gentle, soft voice:

"I had such a charming nurse looking after me when I once broke my wrist. She went on from me to nurse Mrs. Sparrow's son, a very nice young naval officer. Quite a romance, really, because they became engaged. So romantic I thought it. They were married and were very happy and had two dear little children." Miss Marple sighed sentimentally. "It was pneumonia, you know. So much depends on nursing in pneumonia, does it not?"

"Oh, yes," said Jennifer Fortescue, "nursing is nearly everything in pneumonia, though, of course, nowadays M and B Sulfa works wonders, and it's not the long, protracted battle it used to be."

"I'm sure you must have been an excellent nurse, my dear," said Miss Marple. "That was the beginning of your romance, was it not? I mean, you came here to nurse Mr. Percival Fortescue, did you not?"

"Yes," said Jennifer. "Yes, yes—that's how it did happen."

Her voice was not encouraging, but Miss Marple seemed to take no notice.

"I understand. One should not listen to servants' gossip, of course, but I'm afraid an old lady like myself is always interested to hear about the people in the house. Now, what was I saying? Oh, yes. There was another nurse at first, was there not? and she got sent away—something like that. Carelessness, I believe."

"I don't think it was carelessness," said Jennifer. "I believe her father or someone was desperately ill, and so I came to replace her."

"I see," said Miss Marple. "And you fell in love and that was that. Yes, very nice indeed, very nice."

"I'm not so sure about that," said Jennifer Fortescue. "I often wish," her voice trembled, "I often wish I was back in the wards again."

"Yes, yes, I understand. You were keen on your profession."

"I wasn't so much at the time, but now when I think of it—life's so monotonous, you know. Day after day with nothing to do, and Val so absorbed in business."

Miss Marple shook her head.

"Gentlemen have to work so hard nowadays," she said. "There really doesn't seem any leisure, no matter how much money there is."

"Yes, it makes it very lonely and dull for a wife sometimes. I often wish I'd never come here," said Jennifer. "Oh, well, I dare say it serves me right. I ought never to have done it."

"Ought never to have done what, my dear?"

"I ought never to have married Val. Oh, well—" she sighed abruptly. "Don't let's talk of it any more."

Obligingly, Miss Marple began to talk about the new skirts that were being worn in Paris.

II

"So kind of you not to interrupt just now," said Miss Marple when, having tapped at the door of the study, Inspector Neele had told her to come in. "There were just one or two little points, you know, that I wanted to verify." She added reproachfully, "We didn't really finish our little talk just now."

"I'm so sorry, Miss Marple." Inspector Neele summoned up a charming smile. "I'm afraid I was rather rude. I summoned you to a consultation and did all the talking myself."

"Oh, that's quite all right," said Miss Marple immediately, "because, you see, I wasn't really quite ready then to put all my cards on the table. I mean, I wouldn't like to make any accusation unless I was absolutely sure about it. Sure, that is, in my own mind. And I am sure, now."

"You're sure about what, Miss Marple?"

"Well, certainly about who killed Mr. Fortescue. What you told me about the marmalade, I mean, just clinches the matter. Showing how, I mean, as well as who, and well within the mental capacity."

Inspector Neele blinked a little.

"I'm so sorry," said Miss Marple, perceiving this reaction on his part. "I'm afraid I find it difficult sometimes to make myself perfectly clear."

"I'm not quite sure yet, Miss Marple, what we're talking about."

"Well, perhaps," said Miss Marple, "we'd better begin all over again. I mean, if you could spare the time. I would rather like to put my own point of view before you. You see, I've talked a good deal to people, to old Miss Ramsbottom and to Mrs. Crump and to her husband. He, of course, is a liar, but that doesn't really matter because if you know liars are liars, it comes to the same thing. But I did want to get the telephone calls clear and the nylon stockings and all that."

Inspector Neele blinked again and wondered what he had let himself in for and why he had ever thought that Miss Marple might be a desirable and clear-headed colleague. Still, he thought to himself, however muddle-headed she was, she might have picked up some useful bits of information. All Inspector Neele's successes in his profession had come from listening well. He was prepared to listen now.

"Please tell me all about it, Miss Marple," he said, "but start at the beginning, won't you?"

"Yes, of course," said Miss Marple, "and the beginning is Gladys. I mean I came here because of Gladys. And you very kindly let me look through all her things. And what with that and the nylon stockings and the telephone calls and one thing and another, it did come out perfectly clear. I mean about Mr. Fortescue and the taxine."

"You have a theory," asked Inspector Neele, "as to who put the taxine into Mr. Fortescue's marmalade?"

"It isn't a theory," said Miss Marple. "I know."

For the third time Inspector Neele blinked.

"It was Gladys, of course," said Miss Marple.

Chapter Twenty-six

INSPECTOR NEELE stared at Miss Marple and slowly shook his head.

"Are you saying," he said incredulously, "that Gladys Martin deliberately murdered Rex Fortescue? I'm sorry, Miss Marple, but I simply don't believe it."

"No, of course she didn't mean to murder him," said Miss Marple, "but she did it all the same! You said yourself that she was nervous and upset when you questioned her. And that she looked guilty."

"Yes, but not guilty of murder."

"Oh, no, I agree. As I say, she didn't mean to murder anybody, but she put the taxine in the marmalade. She didn't think it was poison, of course."

"What did she think it was?" Inspector Neele's voice still sounded incredulous.

"I rather imagine she thought it was a truth drug," said Miss Marple. "It's very interesting, you know, and very instructive—the things these girls cut out of papers and keep. It's always been the same, you know, all through the ages. Recipes for beauty, for attracting the man you love. And witchcraft and charms and marvelous happenings. Nowadays they're mostly lumped together under the heading of Science. Nobody believes in magicians any more, nobody believes that anyone can come along and wave a wand and turn you into a frog. But if you read in the paper that by injecting certain glands scientists can alter your vital tissues and you'll develop froglike characteristics, well, everybody would believe that. And having read in the papers about truth drugs, of course Gladys would believe it absolutely when he told her that that's what it was."

"When who told her?" asked Inspector Neele.

"Albert Evans," said Miss Marple. "Not, of course, that that is really his name. But, anyway, he met her last summer at a holiday camp, and he flattered her up and made love to her, and I should imagine, told her some story of injustice or persecution, or something like that. Anyway, the point was that Rex Fortescue had to be made to confess what he had done and make restitution. I don't know this, of course, Inspector Neele, but I'm pretty sure about it. He got her to take a post here, and it's really very easy nowadays, with the shortage of domestic staff, to obtain a post where you want one. Staffs are changing the whole time. Then they arranged a date together. You remember on that last post card he said, 'Remember our date.' That was to be the great day they were working for. Gladys would put the drug that he gave her into the top of the marmalade, so that Mr. Fortescue would eat it at breakfast, and she would also put the rye in his pocket. I don't know what story he told her to account for the rye, but as I told you from the beginning, Inspector Neele, Gladys Martin was a very credulous girl. In fact, there's hardly anything she wouldn't believe if a personable young man put it to her the right way."

"Go on," said Inspector Neele in a dazed voice.

"The idea probably was," continued Miss Marple, "that Albert was going to call upon him at the office that day, and that by that time the truth drug would have worked, and that Mr. Fortescue would have confessed everything and so on and so on. You can imagine the poor girl's feelings when she hears that Mr. Fortescue is dead."

"But, surely," Inspector Neele objected, "she would have told?"

Miss Marple asked sharply, "What was the first thing she said to you when you questioned her?"

"She said 'I didn't do it,'" Inspector Neele said.

"Exactly," said Miss Marple triumphantly. "Don't you see that's exactly what she would say? If she broke an ornament, you know, Gladys would always say, 'I didn't do it, Miss Marple. I can't think how it happened.' They can't help it, poor dears. They're very upset at what they've done and their great idea is to avoid blame. You don't think that a nervous young woman who had murdered someone when she didn't mean to murder him is going to admit it, do you? That would have been quite out of character."

"Yes," Neele said, "I suppose it would."

He ran his mind back over his interview with Gladys. Nervous, upset, guilty, shifty-eyed, all those things. They might have had small significance or a big one. He could not really blame himself for having failed to come to the right conclusion.

"Her first idea, as I say," went on Miss Marple, "would be to deny it all. Then, in a confused way, she would try to sort it all out in her mind.

Perhaps Albert hadn't known how strong the stuff was, or he'd made a mistake and given her too much of it. She'd think of excuses for him and explanations. She'd hope he'd get in touch with her, which, of course, he did. By telephone."

"Do you know that?" asked Neele sharply.

Miss Marple shook her head.

"No. I admit I'm assuming it. But there were calls that day. That is to say, people rang up, and when Crump, or Mrs. Crump answered, the phone was hung up. That's what he'd do, you know. Ring up and wait until Gladys answered the phone, and then he'd make an appointment with her to meet him."

"I see," said Neele. "You mean she had an appointment to meet him on the day she died."

Miss Marple nodded vigorously.

"Yes, that was indicated. Mrs. Crump was right about one thing. The girl had on her best nylon stockings and her good shoes. She was going to meet someone. Only, she wasn't going out to meet him. He was coming to Yewtree Lodge. That's why she was on the lookout that day and flustered and late with tea. Then, as she brought the second tray into the hall, I think she looked along the passage to the side door, and saw him there, beckoning to her. She put the tray down and went out to meet him."

"And then he strangled her," said Neele.

Miss Marple pursed her lips together. "It would only take a minute," she said, "but he couldn't risk her talking. She had to die, poor, silly, credulous girl. And then—he put a clothes peg on her nose!" Stern anger vibrated the old lady's voice. "To make it fit in with the rhyme. The rye, the blackbirds, the counting house, the bread and honey, and the clothes peg—the nearest he could get to a little dickey bird that nipped off her nose."

"And I suppose at the end of it all he'll go to Broadmoor, and we shan't be able to hang him because he's crazy!" said Neele slowly.

"I think you'll hang him all right," said Miss Marple. "And he's not crazy, Inspector, not for a moment!"

Inspector Neele looked hard at her.

"Now see here, Miss Marple, you've outlined a theory to me. Yes, yes—although you say you know, it's only a theory. You're saying that a man is responsible for these crimes, who called himself Albert Evans, who picked up the girl Gladys at a holiday camp and used her for his own purposes. This Albert Evans was someone who wanted revenge for the old Blackbird Mine business. You're suggesting, aren't you, that Mrs. MacKenzie's son, Don MacKenzie, didn't die at Dunkirk. That he's still alive, that he's behind all this?"

But to Inspector Neele's surprise, Miss Marple was shaking her head violently.

"Oh no!" she said, "oh no! I'm not suggesting that at all. Don't you see, Inspector Neele, all this blackbird business is really a complete fake? It was used, that was all, used by somebody who heard about the blackbirds —the ones in the library and in the pie. The blackbirds were genuine enough. They were put there by someone who knew about the old business, who wanted revenge for it. But only the revenge of trying to frighten Mr. Fortescue or to make him uncomfortable. I don't believe, you know, Inspector Neele, that children can really be brought up and taught to wait and brood and carry out revenge. Children, after all, have got a lot of sense. But anyone whose father had been swindled and perhaps left to die might be willing to play a malicious trick on the person who was supposed to have done it. That's what happened, I think. And the killer used it."

"The killer," said Inspector Neele. "Come now, Miss Marple, let's have your ideas about the killer. Who was he?"

"You won't be surprised," said Miss Marple. "Not really. Because you'll see, as soon as I tell you who he is or rather who I think he is, for one must be accurate, must one not? You'll see that he's just the type of person who would commit these murders. He's sane, brilliant and quite unscrupulous. And he did it, of course, for money, probably for a good deal of money."

"Percival Fortescue?" Inspector Neele spoke almost imploringly, but he knew as he spoke that he was wrong. The picture of the man that Miss Marple had built up for him had no resemblance to Percival Fortescue.

"Oh, no," said Miss Marple. "Not Percival. Lance."

Chapter Twenty-seven

"IT'S IMPOSSIBLE," said Inspector Neele.

He leaned back in his chair and watched Miss Marple with fascinated eyes. As Miss Marple had said, he was not surprised. His words were a denial not of probability, but of possibility. Lance Fortescue fitted the description: Miss Marple had outlined it well enough. But Inspector Neele simply could not see how Lance could be the answer.

Miss Marple leaned forward in her chair and gently, persuasively, and rather in the manner of someone explaining the simple facts of arithmetic to a small child, outlined her theory.

"He's always been like that, you see. I mean, he's always been bad. Bad all through, although with it he's always been attractive. Especially attractive to women. He's got a brilliant mind and he'll take risks. He's always taken risks, and because of his charm people have always believed the best and not the worst about him. He came home in the summer to see his father. I don't believe for a moment that his father wrote to him or sent for him—unless, of course, you've got actual evidence to that effect." She paused inquiringly.

Neele shook his head. "No," he said, "I've no evidence of his father sending for him. I've got a letter that Lance is supposed to have written to him. But Lance could quite easily have slipped that among his father's papers in the study here the day he arrived."

"Sharp of him," said Miss Marple, nodding her head. "Well, as I say, he probably flew over here and attempted a reconciliation with his father, but Mr. Fortescue wouldn't have it. You see, Lance had recently got married, and the small pittance he was living on, and which he had doubtless been supplementing in various dishonest ways, was not enough for him any more. He was very much in love with Pat (who is a dear, sweet girl) and he wanted a respectable, settled life with her—nothing shifty. And that, from his point of view, meant having a lot of money. When he was at Yewtree Lodge, he must have heard about these blackbirds. Perhaps his father mentioned them. Perhaps Adele did. He jumped to the conclusion that MacKenzie's daughter was established in the house, and it occurred to him that she would make a very good scapegoat for murder. Because, you see, when he realized that he couldn't get his father to do what he wanted, he must have cold-bloodedly decided that murder it would have to be. He may have realized that his father wasn't—er—very well—and have feared that by the time his father died there would have been a complete crash."

"He knew about his father's health all right," said the Inspector.

"Ah—that explains a good deal. Perhaps the coincidence of his father's Christian name being Rex together with the blackbird incident suggested the idea of the nursery rhyme. Make a crazy business of the whole thing—and tie it up with that old revenge threat of the MacKenzies. Then, you see, he could dispose of Adele, too, and that hundred thousand pounds going out of the firm. But there would have to be a third character, the 'maid in the garden hanging up the clothes'—and I suppose that suggested the whole wicked plan to him. An innocent accomplice whom he could silence before she could talk. And that would give him what he wanted—a genuine alibi for the first murder.

"The rest was easy. He arrived here from the station just before five o'clock, which was the time when Gladys brought the second tray into the hall. He came to the side door, saw her and beckoned to her. Strangling her and carrying her body round the house to where the clotheslines were would only have taken three or four minutes. Then he rang the front doorbell, was admitted to the house, and joined the family for tea. After tea he went up to see Miss Ramsbottom. When he came down, he slipped into the drawing-room, found Adele alone there drinking a last cup of tea and sat down by her on the sofa, and while he was talking to her, he managed to slip the cyanide into her tea. It wouldn't be difficult, you know. A little piece of white stuff, like sugar. He might have stretched out his hand to the sugar basin and taken a lump and apparently dropped it into her cup. He'd laugh and say, 'Look, I've dropped more sugar into your tea.' She'd say she didn't mind, stir it and drink it. It would be as easy and audacious as that. Yes, he's an audacious fellow."

Inspector Neele said slowly, "It's actually possible—yes. But I cannot see—really, Miss Marple, I cannot see—what he stood to gain by it. Granted that unless old Fortescue died the business would soon be on the rocks, is Lance's share big enough to cause him to plan three murders? I don't think so. I really don't think so."

"That is a little difficult," admitted Miss Marple. "Yes, I agree with you. That does present difficulties. I suppose . . ." She hesitated, looking at the Inspector. "I suppose—I am so very ignorant in financial matters—but I suppose it is really true that the Blackbird Mine is worthless?"

Neele reflected. Various scraps fitted together in his mind. Lance's willingness to take the various speculative or worthless shares off Percival's hands. His parting words today in London that Percival had better get rid of the Blackbird and its hoodoo. A gold mine. A worthless gold mine. But perhaps the mine had not been worthless. And yet, somehow, that seemed unlikely. Old Rex Fortescue was hardly likely to have made a mistake on that point, although of course there might have been soundings recently. Where was the mine? West Africa, Lance had said. Yes, but somebody else—was it Miss Ramsbottom—had said it was in East Africa. Had Lance been deliberately misleading when he said West instead of East? Miss

Ramsbottom was old and forgetful, and yet she might have been right and not Lance. East Africa. Lance had just come from East Africa. Had he perhaps some recent knowledge?

Suddenly with a click another piece fitted into the Inspector's puzzle. Sitting in the train, reading the *Times*. *Uranium deposits found in Tanganyika*. Supposing that the uranium deposits were on the site of the old Blackbird? That would explain everything. Lance had come to have knowledge of that, being on the spot, and with uranium deposits there, there was a fortune to be grasped. An enormous fortune! He sighed. He looked at Miss Marple.

"How do you think," he asked reproachfully, "that I'm ever going to be able to prove all this?"

Miss Marple nodded at him encouragingly as an aunt might have encouraged a bright nephew who was going in for a scholarship exam.

"You'll prove it," she said. "You're a very, very clever man, Inspector Neele. I've seen that from the first. Now you know who it is, you ought to be able to get the evidence. At that holiday camp, for instance, they'll recognize his photograph. He'll find it hard to explain why he stayed there for a week calling himself Albert Evans."

Yes, Inspector Neele thought, Lance Fortescue was brilliant and unscrupulous, but he was foolhardy, too. The risks he took were just a little too great.

Neele thought to himself, "I'll get him!" Then, doubt sweeping over him, he looked at Miss Marple.

"It's all pure assumption, you know," he said.

"Yes—but you are sure, aren't you?"

"I suppose so. After all, I've known his kind before."

The old lady nodded.

"Yes—that matters so much—that's really why I'm sure."

Neele looked at her playfully.

"Because of your knowledge of criminals."

"Oh, no, of course not. Because of Pat—a dear girl—and the kind that always marries a bad lot. That's really what drew my attention to him at the start."

"I may be sure—in my own mind," said the Inspector, "but there's a lot that needs explaining—the Ruby MacKenzie business for instance. I could swear that—"

Miss Marple interrupted, "And you're quite right. But you've been thinking of the wrong person. Go and talk to Mrs. Percy."

II

"Mrs. Fortescue," said Inspector Neele, "do you mind telling me your name before you were married?"

"Oh!" Jennifer gasped. She looked frightened.

"You needn't be nervous, madam," said Inspector Neele, "but it's much better to come out with the truth. I'm right, I think, in saying that your name before you were married was Ruby MacKenzie?"

"My—well, oh well—oh dear—well, why shouldn't it be?" said Mrs. Percival Fortescue.

"No reason at all," said Inspector Neele gently, and added, "I was talking to your mother a few days ago at Pinewood Sanatorium."

"She's very angry with me," said Jennifer. "I never go and see her now because it only upsets her. Poor Mumsy, she was so devoted to Dad, you know."

"And she brought you up to have very melodramatic ideas of revenge?"

"Yes," said Jennifer. "She kept making us swear on the Bible that we'd never forget and that we'd kill him one day. Of course, once I'd gone into hospital and started my training, I began to realize that her mental balance wasn't what it should be."

"You yourself must have felt revengeful though, Mrs. Fortescue?"

"Well, of course I did. Rex Fortescue practically murdered my father! I don't mean he actually shot him, or knifed him or anything like that. But I'm quite certain that he did leave Father to die. That's the same thing, isn't it?"

"It's the same thing morally—yes."

"So I did want to pay him back," said Jennifer. "When a friend of mine came to nurse his son I got her to leave and to propose my replacing her. I don't know exactly what I meant to do. . . . I didn't, really I didn't, Inspector, I never meant to kill Mr. Fortescue. I had some idea, I think, of nursing his son so badly that the son would die. But, of course, if you are a nurse by profession, you can't do that sort of thing. Actually, I had quite a job pulling Val through. And then he got fond of me and asked me to marry him and I thought, Well, really, that's a far more sensible revenge than anything else. I mean, to marry Mr. Fortescue's eldest son and get the money he swindled Father out of back that way. I think it was a far more sensible way."

"Yes, indeed," said Inspector Neele, "far more sensible." He added, "It was you, I suppose, who put the blackbirds on the desk and in the pie?"

Mrs. Percival flushed.

"Yes. I suppose it was silly of me really. . . . But Mr. Fortescue had been talking about suckers one day and boasting of how he'd swindled people—got the best of them. Oh, in quite a legal way. And I thought I'd just like to give him—well, a kind of fright. And it did give him a fright! He was awfully upset." She added anxiously, "But I didn't do anything else! I didn't really, Inspector. You don't—you don't honestly think I would murder anyone, do you?"

Inspector Neele smiled.

"No," he said, "I don't." He added, "By the way, have you given Miss Dove any money lately?"

Jennifer's jaw dropped.

"How did you know?"

"We know a lot of things," said Inspector Neele and added to himself, "And guess a good many, too."

Jennifer continued, speaking rapidly.

"She came to me and said that you'd accused her of being Ruby Mac-Kenzie. She said if I'd get hold of five hundred pounds she'd let you go on thinking so. She said if you knew that I was Ruby MacKenzie, I'd be suspected of murdering Mr. Fortescue and my stepmother. I had an awful job getting the money because, of course, I couldn't tell Percival. He doesn't know about me. I had to sell my diamond engagement ring and a very beautiful necklace Mr. Fortescue gave me."

"Don't worry, Mrs. Percival," said Inspector Neele, "I think we can get your money back for you."

III

It was on the following day that Inspector Neele had another interview with Miss Dove.

"I wonder, Miss Dove," he said, "if you'd give me a check for five hundred pounds payable to Mrs. Percival Fortescue."

He had the pleasure of seeing Mary Dove lose countenance for once.

"The silly fool told you, I suppose," she said.

"Yes. Blackmail, Miss Dove, is rather a serious charge."

"It wasn't exactly blackmail, Inspector. I think you'd find it hard to make out a case of blackmail against me. I was just doing Mrs. Percival a special service to oblige her."

"Well, if you'll give me that check, Miss Dove, we'll leave it like that." Mary Dove got her checkbook and took out her fountain pen.

"It's very annoying," she said with a sigh. "I'm particularly hard up at the moment."

"You'll be looking for another job soon, I suppose?"

"Yes. This one hasn't turned out quite according to plan. It's all been very unfortunate from my point of view."

Inspector Neele agreed.

"Yes, it put you in rather a difficult position, didn't it? I mean, it was quite likely that any moment we might have to look into your antecedents."

Mary Dove, cool once more, allowed her eyebrows to rise.

"Really, Inspector, my past is quite blameless, I assure you."

"Yes, it is," Inspector Neele agreed cheerfully. "We've nothing against you at all, Miss Dove. It's a curious coincidence, though, that in the last three places which you have filled so admirably, there have happened to be robberies about three months after you left. The thieves have seemed remarkably well informed as to where mink coats, jewels, et cetera, were kept. Curious coincidence, isn't it?"

"Coincidences do happen, Inspector."

"Oh, yes," said Neele. "They happen. But they mustn't happen too often, Miss Dove. I daresay," he added, "that we may meet again in the future."

"I hope," said Mary Dove, "I don't mean to be rude, Inspector Neele— but I hope we don't."

Chapter Twenty-eight

Miss Marple smoothed over the top of her suitcase, tucked in an end of woolly shawl and shut the lid down. She looked round her bedroom. No, she had left nothing behind. Crump came in to fetch down her luggage. Miss Marple went into the next room to say good-by to Miss Ramsbottom.

"I'm afraid," said Miss Marple, "that I've made a very poor return for your hospitality. I hope you will be able to forgive me some day."

"Hah," said Miss Ramsbottom.

She was as usual playing patience.

"Black knave, red queen," she observed, then she darted a shrewd, sideways glance at Miss Marple. "You found out what you wanted to, I suppose," she said.

"Yes."

"And I suppose you've told that police inspector all about it? Will he be able to prove a case?"

"I'm almost sure he will," said Miss Marple. "It may take a little time."

"I'm not asking you any questions," said Miss Ramsbottom. "You're a shrewd woman. I knew that as soon as I saw you. I don't blame you for what you've done. Wickedness is wickedness and has got to be punished. There's a bad streak in this family. It didn't come from our side, I'm thankful to say. Elvira, my sister, was a fool. Nothing worse.

"Black knave," repeated Miss Ramsbottom, fingering the card. "Handsome, but a black heart. Yes, I was afraid of it. Ah, well, you can't always help loving a sinner. The boy always had a way with him. Even got round me. . . . Told a lie about the time he left me that day. I didn't contradict him, but I wondered. . . . I've wondered ever since. But he was Elvira's boy—I couldn't bring myself to say anything. Ah, well, you're a righteous woman, Jane Marple, and right must prevail. I'm sorry for his wife, though."

"So am I," said Miss Marple.

In the hall Pat Fortescue was waiting to say good-by.

"I wish you weren't going," she said. "I shall miss you."

"It's time for me to go," said Miss Marple. "I've finished what I came here to do. It hasn't been—altogether pleasant. But it's important, you know, that wickedness shouldn't triumph."

Pat looked puzzled.

"I don't understand."

"No, my dear. But perhaps you will someday. If I might venture to advise, if anything ever—goes wrong in your life—I think the happiest thing for you would be to go back to where you were happy as a child. Go back to Ireland, my dear. Horses and dogs. All that."

Pat nodded.

"Sometimes I wish I'd done just that when Freddy died. But if I had," her voice changed and softened, "I'd never have met Lance."

Miss Marple sighed.

"We're not staying here, you know," said Pat. "We're going back to East Africa as soon as everything's cleared up. I'm so glad."

"God bless you, dear child," said Miss Marple. "One needs a great deal of courage to get through life. I think you have it."

She patted the girl's hand and, releasing it, went through the front door to the waiting taxi.

II

Miss Marple reached home late that evening.

Kitty, the latest graduate from St. Faith's Home, let her in and greeted her with a beaming face.

"I've got a herring for your supper, miss. I'm so glad to see you home. You'll find everything very nice in the house. Regular spring cleaning I've had."

"That's very nice, Kitty. I'm glad to be home."

Six spider webs on the cornice, Miss Marple noted. These girls never raised their heads! She was none the less too kind to say so.

"Your letters is on the hall table, miss. And there's one as went to Daisymead by mistake. Always doing that, aren't they? Does look a bit alike, Dane and Daisy, and the writing's so bad I don't wonder this time. They've been away there and the house shut up. They only got back and sent it round today. Said as how they hoped it wasn't important."

Miss Marple picked up her correspondence. The letter to which Kitty had referred was on top of the others. A faint chord of remembrance stirred in Miss Marple's mind at the sight of the blotted scrawled hand-writing. She tore it open.

Dear Madam,

I hope as you'll forgive me writing this but I really don't know what to do indeed I don't and I never meant no harm. Dear madam, you'll have seen the newspapers it was murder they say but it wasn't me that did it, not really because I would never do anything wicked like that and I know was how he woun't either. Albert, I mean. I'm telling this badly, but you see we met last summer and was going to be married only Bert hadn't got his rights, he'd been done out of them, swindled by this Mr. Fortescue who's dead. And Mr. Fortescue he just denied everything and of course everybody believed him and not Bert because he was rich and Bert was poor. But Bert had a friend who works in a place where they make these new drugs and there's what they call a truth drug you've read about it per-haps in the paper and it makes people speak the truth whether they want to or not. Bert was going to see Mr. Fortescue in his office on Oct. 31st, and taking a lawyer with him and I was to be sure to give him the drug at breakfast that morning and then it would work just right for when they came and he'd admit as all what Bert said was quite true. Well, madam, I put it in the marmalade but now he's dead and I think as how it must have been too strong but it wasn't Bert's fault because Bert would never do a thing like that but I can't tell the police because maybe they'd think Bert did it on purpose which I know he didn't. Oh, madam, I don't know what to do or what to say and the police are here in the house and it's awful and they ask you questions and look at you so stern and I don't know what to do and I haven't heard from Bert. Oh, madam, I don't like to ask it of you but if you could only come here and help me they'd listen to you and you were always so kind to me and, I didn't mean anything wrong and Bert didn't either. If you could only help us.

Yours respectfully,
Gladys Martin

P.S. I'm enclosing a snap of Bert and me. One of the boys took it at the camp and give it me. Bert doesn't know I've got it—he hates being snapped. But you can see, madam, what a nice boy he is.

Miss Marple, her lips pursed together, stared down at the photograph. The pair pictured there were looking at each other. Miss Marple's eyes went from Gladys's pathetic, adoring face, the mouth slightly open, to the other face—the dark, handsome, smiling face of Lance Fortescue.

The last words of the pathetic letter echoed in her mind:

You can see what a nice boy he is.

The tears rose in Miss Marple's eyes. Succeeding pity, there came anger —anger against a heartless killer.

And then, displacing both these emotions, there came a surge of triumph—the triumph some specialist might feel who has successfully reconstructed an extinct animal from a fragment of jawbone and a couple of teeth.

At Bertram's Hotel

Chapter One

In THE heart of the West End, there are many quiet pockets, unknown to almost all but taxi drivers who traverse them with expert knowledge, and arrive triumphantly thereby at Park Lane, Berkeley Square or South Audley Street.

If you turn off an unpretentious street from the Park, and turn left and right once or twice, you will find yourself in a quiet street with Bertram's Hotel on the right hand side. Bertram's Hotel has been there a long time. During the war, houses were demolished on the right of it, and a little farther down on the left of it, but Bertram's itself remained unscathed. Naturally it could not escape being, as house agents would say, scratched, bruised and marked, but by the expenditure of only a reasonable amount of money it was restored to its original condition. By 1955 it looked precisely as it had looked in 1939—dignified, unostentatious, and quietly expensive.

Such was Bertram's, patronized over a long stretch of years by the higher echelons of the clergy, dowager ladies of the aristocracy up from the country, girls on their way home for the holidays from expensive finishing schools. ("So few places where a girl can stay alone in London but of course it is *quite* all right at Bertram's. We have stayed there for years.")

There had, of course, been many other hotels on the model of Bertram's. Some still existed, but nearly all had felt the wind of change. They had had necessarily to modernize themselves, to cater for a different clientele. Bertram's, too, had had to change, but it had been done so cleverly that it was not at all apparent at the first casual glance.

Outside the steps that led up to the big swing doors stood what at first sight appeared to be no less than a Field-Marshal. Gold braid and medal ribbons adorned a broad and manly chest. His deportment was perfect. He received you with tender concern as you emerged with rheumatic difficulty from a taxi or a car, guided you carefully up the steps and piloted you through the silently swinging doorway.

Inside, if this was the first time you had visited Bertram's, you felt, almost with alarm, that you had re-entered a vanished world. Time had gone back. You were in Edwardian England once more.

There was, of course, central heating, but it was not apparent. As there had always been, in the big central lounge, there were two magnificent coal fires; beside them big brass coal scuttles shone in the way they used to shine when Edwardian housemaids polished them, and they were filled with exactly the right sized lumps of coal. There was a general appearance of rich red velvet and plushy cosiness. The arm-chairs were not of this time and age. They were well above the level of the floor, so that rheumatic old ladies had not to struggle in an undignified manner in order to get to their feet. The seats of the chairs did not, as in so many modern high-priced arm-chairs, stop half-way between the thigh and the knee, thereby inflicting agony on those suffering from arthritis and sciatica; and they were not all of a pattern. There were straight backs and reclining backs, different widths to accommodate the slender and the obese. People of almost any dimension could find a comfortable chair at Bertram's.

Since it was now the tea hour, the lounge hall was full. Not that the lounge hall was the only place where you could have tea. There was a drawing-room (chintzy), a smoking-room, (by some hidden influence reserved for gentlemen only) where the vast chairs were of fine leather, two writing-rooms, where you could take a special friend and have a cosy little gossip in a quiet corner—and even write a letter if you wanted to. Besides these amenities of the Edwardian age, there were other retreats, not in any way publicized, but known to those who wanted them. There was a double bar, with two bar attendants, an American barman to make the Americans feel at home and to provide them with bourbon, rye, and every kind of cocktail, and an English one to deal with sherries and Pimms No. 1, and to talk knowledgeably about the runners at Ascot and Newbury to the middle-aged men who stayed at Bertram's for the more serious race meetings. There was also, tucked down a passage, in a secretive way, a television room for those who asked for it.

But the big entrance lounge was the favourite place for the afternoon tea drinking. The elderly ladies enjoyed seeing who came in and out, recognizing old friends, and commenting unfavourably on how these had aged. There were also American visitors fascinated by seeing the titled

English really getting down to their traditional afternoon tea. For afternoon tea was quite a feature of Bertram's.

It was nothing less than splendid. Presiding over the ritual was Henry, a large and magnificent figure, a ripe fifty, avuncular, sympathetic, and with the courtly manners of that long-vanished species: the perfect butler. Slim youths performed the actual work under Henry's austere direction. There were large crested silver trays, and Georgian silver teapots. The china, if not actually Rockingham and Davenport, looked like it. The Blind Earl services were particular favourites. The tea was the best Indian, Ceylon, Darjeeling, Lapsang, etc. As for eatables, you could ask for anything you liked—and get it!

On this particular day, November the 17th, Lady Selina Hazy, sixty-five, up from Leicestershire, was eating delicious well-buttered muffins with all an elderly lady's relish.

Her absorption with muffins, however, was not so great that she failed to look up sharply every time the inner pair of swing doors opened to admit a newcomer.

So it was that she smiled and nodded to welcome Colonel Luscombe—erect, soldierly, race glasses hanging round his neck. Like the old autocrat that she was, she beckoned imperiously and in a minute or two, Luscombe came over to her.

"Hallo, Selina, what brings you up to Town?"

"Dentist," said Lady Selina, rather indistinctly, owing to muffin. "And I thought as I *was* up, I might as well go and see that man in Harley Street about my arthritis. You know whom I mean."

Although Harley Street contained several hundreds of fashionable practitioners for all and every ailment, Luscombe did know whom she meant.

"Do you any good?" he asked.

"I rather think he did," said Lady Selina grudgingly. "Extraordinary fellow. Took me by the neck when I wasn't expecting it, and wrung it like a chicken." She moved her neck gingerly.

"Hurt you?"

"It must have done, twisting it like that, but really I hadn't time to know." She continued to move her neck gingerly. "Feels all right. Can look over my right shoulder for the first time in years."

She put this to a practical test and exclaimed.

"Why I do believe that's old Jane Marple. Thought she was dead years ago. Looks a hundred."

Colonel Luscombe threw a glance in the direction of Jane Marple thus resurrected, but without much interest: Bertram's always had a sprinkling of what he called fluffy old pussies.

Lady Selina was continuing.

"Only place in London you can still get muffins. Real muffins. Do you know when I went to America last year they had something *called* muffins on the breakfast menu. Not real muffins at all. Kind of teacake with raisins in them. I mean, why call them muffins?"

She pushed in the last buttery morsel and looked round vaguely. Henry materialized immediately. Not quickly or hurriedly. It seemed that, just suddenly, he was there.

"Anything further I can get you, my lady? Cake of any kind?"

"Cake?" Lady Selina thought about it, was doubtful.

"We are serving very good seed cake, my lady. I can recommend it."

"Seed cake? I haven't eaten seed cake for *years*. It is *real* seed cake?"

"Oh yes, my lady. The cook has had the receipt for years. You'll enjoy it, I'm sure."

Henry gave a glance at one of his retinue, and the lad departed in search of seed cake.

"I suppose you've been at Newbury, Derek?"

"Yes. Darned cold, I didn't wait for the last two races. Disastrous day. That filly of Harry's was no good at all."

"Didn't think she would be. What about Swanhilda?"

"Finished fourth." Luscombe rose. "Got to see about my room."

He walked across the lounge to the reception desk. As he went he noted the tables and their occupants. Astonishing number of people having tea here. Quite like old days. Tea as a meal had rather gone out of fashion since the war. But evidently not at Bertram's. Who *were* all these people? Two Canons and the Dean of Chislehampton. Yes, and another pair of gaitered legs over in the corner, a Bishop, no less! Mere Vicars were scarce. "Have to be at least a Canon to afford Bertram's," he thought. The rank and file of the clergy certainly couldn't, poor devils. As far as that went, he wondered how on earth people like old Selina Hazy could. She'd only got twopence or so a year to bless herself with. And there was old Lady Berry, and Mrs. Posselthwaite from Somerset, and Sybil Kerr—all poor as church mice.

Still thinking about this he arrived at the desk and was pleasantly greeted by Miss Gorringe the receptionist. Miss Gorringe was an old friend. She knew every one of the clientele and, like Royalty, never forgot a face. She looked frumpy but respectable. Frizzled yellowish hair (old-fashioned tongs, it suggested), black silk dress, a high bosom on which reposed a large gold locket and a cameo brooch.

"Number fourteen," said Miss Gorringe. "I think you had fourteen last time, Colonel Luscombe, and liked it. It's quiet."

"How you always manage to remember these things, I can't imagine, Miss Gorringe."

"We like to make our old friends comfortable."

"Takes me back a long way, coming in here. Nothing seems to have changed."

He broke off as Mr. Humfries came out from an inner sanctum to greet him.

Mr. Humfries was often taken by the uninitiated to be Mr. Bertram in person. Who the actual Mr. Bertram was, or indeed, if there ever *had* been a Mr. Bertram was now lost in the mists of antiquity. Bertram's had existed since about 1840, but nobody had taken any interest in tracing its past history. It was just there, solid, a fact. When addressed as Mr. Bertram, Mr. Humfries never corrected the impression. If they wanted him to be Mr. Bertram he would be Mr. Bertram. Colonel Luscombe knew his name, though he didn't know if Humfries was the manager or the owner. He rather fancied the latter.

Mr. Humfries was a man of about fifty. He had very good manners, and the presence of a Junior Minister. He could, at any moment, be all things to all people. He could talk racing shop, cricket, foreign politics, tell anecdotes of Royalty, give Motor Show information, knew the most interesting plays on at present—advise on places Americans ought to see in England however short their stay. He had knowledgeable information about where it would suit persons of all incomes and tastes to dine. With all this, he did not make himself too cheap. He was not on tap all the time. Miss Gorringe had all the same facts at her fingertips and could retail them efficiently. At brief intervals Mr. Humfries, like the sun, made his appearance above the horizon and flattered someone by his personal attention.

This time it was Colonel Luscombe who was so honoured. They exchanged a few racing platitudes, but Colonel Luscombe was absorbed by his problem. And here was the man who could give him the answer.

"Tell me, Humfries, how do all these old dears manage to come and stay here?"

"Oh, you've been wondering about that?" Mr. Humfries seemed amused. "Well, the answer's simple. They couldn't afford it. Unless—"

He paused.

"Unless you make special prices for them? Is that it?"

"More or less. They don't know, usually, that they *are* special prices, or if they do realize it, they think it's because they're old customers."

"And it isn't just that?"

"Well, Colonel Luscombe, I *am* running a hotel. I couldn't afford actually to lose money."

"But how can that pay you?"

"It's a question of atmosphere . . . Strangers coming to this country (Americans, in particular, because they are the ones who have the money) have their own rather queer ideas of what England is like. I'm not talking, you understand, of the rich business tycoons who are always crossing the Atlantic. They usually go to the Savoy or the Dorchester. They want modern décor, American food, all the things that will make them feel at home. But there are a lot of people who come abroad at rare intervals and who expect this country to be—well, I won't go back as far as Dickens, but they've read *Cranford* and Henry James, and they don't want to find this country just the same as their own! So they go back home afterwards and say: 'There's a wonderful place in London: Bertram's Hotel, it's called. It's just like stepping back a hundred years. It just *is* old England! And the people who stay there! People you'd never come across anywhere else. Wonderful old Duchesses. They serve all the old English dishes, there's a marvellous old-fashioned beefsteak pudding! You've never tasted anything like it; and great sirloins of beef and saddles of mutton, and an old-fashioned English tea and a wonderful English breakfast. And of course all the usual things as well. And it's wonderfully comfortable. *And* warm. Great log fires.'"

Mr. Humfries ceased his impersonation and permitted himself something nearly approaching a grin.

"I see," said Luscombe thoughtfully. "These people; decayed aristocrats, impoverished members of the old County families, they are all so much *mise en scène?*"

Mr. Humfries nodded agreement.

"I really wonder no one else has thought of it. Of course I found Bertram's ready made, so to speak. All it needed was some rather expensive restoration. All the people who come here think it's something that they've discovered for themselves, that no one else knows about."

"I suppose," said Luscombe, "that the restoration *was* quite expensive?"

"Oh yes. The place has got to *look* Edwardian, but it's got to have the modern comforts that we take for granted in these days. Our old dears—if you will forgive me referring to them as that—have got to feel that nothing has changed since the turn of the century, and our travelling clients have got to feel they can have period surroundings, and still have what they are used to having at home, and can't really live without!"

"Bit difficult sometimes?" suggested Luscombe.

"Not really. Take central heating for instance. Americans require—need, I should say—at least ten degrees Fahrenheit higher than English people do. We actually have two quite different sets of bedrooms. The English we put in one lot, the Americans in the other. The rooms all look alike, but they are full of actual differences—electric razors, and showers as well as tubs in some of the bathrooms, and if you want an American breakfast, it's there—cereals and iced orange juice and all—or if you prefer you can have the English breakfast."

"Eggs and bacon?"

"As you say—but a good deal more than that if you want it. Kippers, kidney and bacon, cold grouse, York ham. Oxford marmalade."

"I must remember all that tomorrow morning. Don't get that sort of thing any more at home."

Humfries smiled.

"Most gentlemen only ask for eggs and bacon. They've—well, they've got out of the way of thinking about the things there used to be."

"Yes, yes . . . I remember when I was a child . . . Sideboards groaning with hot dishes. Yes, it was a luxurious way of life."

"We endeavour to give people anything they ask for."

"Including seed cake and muffins—yes, I see. To each according to his need—I see . . . Quite Marxian."

"I beg your pardon?"

"Just a thought, Humfries. Extremes meet."

Colonel Luscombe turned away, taking the key Miss Gorringe offered him. A page-boy sprang to attention and conducted him to the lift. He saw in passing that Lady Selina Hazy was now sitting with her friend Jane Something or other.

Chapter Two

"AND I suppose you're still living at that dear St. Mary Mead?" Lady Selina was asking. "Such a sweet unspoilt village. I often think about it. Just the same as ever, I suppose?"

"Well, not quite." Miss Marple reflected on certain aspects of her place of residence. The new Building Estate. The additions to the Village Hall, the altered appearance of the High Street with its up-to-date shop fronts— She sighed. "One has to accept change, I suppose."

"Progress," said Lady Selina vaguely. "Though it often seems to me that it isn't progress. All these smart plumbing fixtures they have nowadays. Every shade of colour and superb what they call 'finish'—but do any of them really *pull*? Or *push*, when they're that kind. Every time you go to a friend's house, you find some kind of a notice in the Loo— 'Press sharply and release,' 'Pull to the *left*,' 'Release *quickly*.' But in the old days, one just pulled up a handle *any* kind of way, and cataracts of water came *at once*— There's the dear Bishop of Medmenham," Lady Selina broke off to say, as a handsome, elderly cleric passed by. "Practically quite blind, I believe. But such a splendid *militant* priest."

A little clerical talk was indulged in, interspersed by Lady Selina's recognition of various friends and acquaintances, many of whom were not the people she thought they were. She and Miss Marple talked a little of "old days", though Miss Marple's upbringing, of course, had been quite different from Lady Selina's, and their reminiscences were mainly confined to the few years when Lady Selina, a recent widow of severely straitened means, had taken a small house in the village of St. Mary Mead during the time her second son had been stationed at an airfield near-by.

"Do you always stay here when you come up, Jane? Odd I haven't seen you here before."

"Oh no, indeed. I couldn't afford to, and anyway, I hardly ever leave home these days. No, it was a very kind niece of mine who thought it would be a treat for me to have a short visit to London. Joan is a very kind girl—at least perhaps hardly a girl." Miss Marple reflected with a qualm that Joan must now be close on fifty. "She is a painter, you know. Quite a well-known painter. Joan West. She had an exhibition not long ago."

Lady Selina had little interest in painters, or indeed in anything artistic. She regarded writers, artists and musicians as a species of clever performing animals; she was prepared to feel indulgent towards them, but to wonder privately why they wanted to do what they did.

"This modern stuff, I suppose," she said, her eyes wandering. "There's Cicely Longhurst—dyed her hair again, I see."

"I'm afraid dear Joan *is* rather modern."

Here Miss Marple was quite wrong. Joan West had been modern about twenty years ago, but was now regarded by the young *arriviste* artists as completely old-fashioned.

Casting a brief glance at Cicely Longhurst's hair, Miss Marple relapsed into a pleasant remembrance of how kind Joan had been. Joan had actually said to her husband, "I wish we could do something for poor old Aunt Jane. She never gets away from home. Do you think she'd like to go to Bournemouth for a week or two?"

"Good idea," said Raymond West. His last book was doing very well indeed, and he felt in a generous mood.

"She enjoyed her trip to the West Indies, I think, though it was a pity she had to get mixed up in a murder case. Quite the wrong thing at her age."

"That sort of thing seems to happen to her."

Raymond was very fond of his old aunt and was constantly devising treats for her, and sending her books that he thought might interest her. He was surprised when she often politely declined the treats, and though she always said the books were "so interesting" he sometimes suspected that she had not read them. But then, of course, her eyes were failing.

In this last he was wrong. Miss Marple had remarkable eyesight for her age, and was at this moment taking in everything that was going on round her with keen interest and pleasure.

To Joan's proffer of a week or two at one of Bournemouth's best hotels, she had hesitated, murmured, "It's very, very kind of you, my dear, but I really don't think—"

"But it's *good* for you, Aunt Jane. Good to get away from home sometimes. It gives you new ideas, and new things to think about."

"Oh yes, you are quite right there, and I *would* like a little visit somewhere for a change. Not, perhaps, Bournemouth."

Joan was slightly surprised. She had thought Bournemouth would have been Aunt Jane's Mecca.

"Eastbourne? Or Torquay?"

"What I would really like—" Miss Marple hesitated.

"Yes?"

"I dare say you will think it rather silly of me."

"No, I'm sure I shan't." (Where *did* the old dear want to go?)

"I would really like to go to Bertram's Hotel—in London."

"Bertram's Hotel?" The name was vaguely familiar.

Words came from Miss Marple in a rush.

"I stayed there once—when I was fourteen. With my uncle and aunt, Uncle Thomas, that was, he was Canon of Ely. And I've never forgotten it. If I could stay there—a week would be quite enough—two weeks might be too expensive."

"Oh, that's all right. Of course you shall go. I ought to have thought that you might want to go to London—the shops and everything. We'll fix it up—if Bertram's Hotel still exists. So many hotels have vanished, sometimes bombed in the war and sometimes just given up."

"No, I happen to know Bertram's Hotel is still going. I had a letter from there—from my American friend Amy McAllister of Boston. She and her husband were staying there."

"Good, then I'll go ahead and fix it up." She added gently, "I'm afraid you may find it's changed a good deal from the days when you knew it. So don't be disappointed."

But Bertram's Hotel had not changed. It was just as it had always been. Quite miraculously so, in Miss Marple's opinion. In fact, she wondered . . .

It really seemed too good to be true. She knew quite well with her usual clear-eyed common sense, that what she wanted was simply to refurbish her memories of the past in their old original colours. Much of her life had, perforce, to be spent recalling past pleasures. If you could find someone to remember them with, that was indeed happiness. Nowadays that was not easy to do; she had outlived most of her contemporaries. But she still sat and remembered. In a queer way, it made her come to life again—Jane Marple, that pink and white eager young girl . . . Such a silly girl in many ways . . . now who was that very unsuitable young man whose name—oh dear, she couldn't even remember it now! How wise her mother had been to nip that friendship so firmly in the bud. She had come across him years later—and really he was quite dreadful! At the time she had cried herself to sleep for at least a week!

Nowadays, of course—she considered nowadays . . . These poor young things. Some of them had mothers, but never mothers who seemed to be any good—mothers who were quite incapable of protecting their daughters from silly affairs, illegitimate babies, and early and unfortunate marriages. It was all very sad.

Her friend's voice interrupted these meditations.

"Well, I never. Is it—yes, it is—Bess Sedgwick over there! Of all the unlikely places—"

Miss Marple had been listening with only half an ear to Lady Selina's comments on her surroundings. She and Miss Marple moved in entirely different circles, so that Miss Marple had been unable to exchange scandalous titbits about the various friends or acquaintances that Lady Selina recognized or thought she recognized.

But Bess Sedgwick was different. Bess Sedgwick was a name that almost everyone in England knew. For over thirty years now, Bess Sedgwick had been reported by the Press as doing this or that outrageous or extraordinary thing. For a good part of the war she had been a member of the French Resistance, and was said to have six notches on her gun representing dead Germans. She had flown solo across the Atlantic years ago, had ridden on horseback across Europe and fetched up at Lake Van. She had driven racing cars, had once saved two children from a burning house, had several marriages to her credit and discredit and was said to be the second best-dressed woman in Europe. It was also said that she had successfully smuggled herself on board a nuclear submarine on its test voyage.

It was therefore with the most intense interest that Miss Marple sat up and indulged in a frankly avid stare.

Whatever she had expected of Bertram's Hotel, it was not to find Bess Sedgwick there. An expensive night club, or a lorry drivers' pull up—either of those would be quite in keeping with Bess Sedgwick's range of interests. But this highly respectable and old world hostelry seemed strangely alien.

Still there she was—no doubt of it. Hardly a month passed without Bess Sedgwick's face appearing in the fashion magazines or the popular Press. Here she was in the flesh, smoking a cigarette in a quite impatient manner and looking in a surprised way at the large tea tray in front of her as though she had never seen one before. She had ordered—Miss Marple screwed up her eyes and peered—it was rather far away—yes, *doughnuts*. Very interesting.

As she watched, Bess Sedgwick stubbed out her cigarette in her saucer, lifted a doughnut and took an immense bite. Rich red real strawberry jam gushed out over her chin. Bess threw back her head and laughed, one of the loudest and gayest sounds to have been heard in the lounge of Bertram's Hotel for some time.

Henry was immediately beside her, a small delicate napkin proffered. She took it, scrubbed her chin with the vigour of a schoolboy, exclaiming: "That's what I call a *real* doughnut. Gorgeous."

She dropped the napkin on the tray and stood up. As usual every eye was on her. She was used to that. Perhaps she liked it, perhaps she no longer noticed it. She was worth looking at—a striking woman rather than a beautiful one. The palest of platinum hair fell sleek and smooth to her shoulders. The bones of her head and face were exquisite. Her nose was faintly aquiline, her eyes deep set and a real grey in colour. She had the wide mouth of a natural comedian. Her dress was of such simplicity that it puzzled most men. It looked like the coarsest kind of sacking, had no ornamentation of any kind, and no apparent fastening or seams. But women knew better. Even the provincial old dears in Bertram's knew, quite certainly, that it had cost the earth!

Striding across the lounge towards the lift, she passed quite close to Lady Selina and Miss Marple, and she nodded to the former.

"Hallo, Lady Selina. Haven't seen you since Crufts. How are the Borzois?"

"What on earth are you doing here, Bess?"

"Just staying here. I've just driven up from Land's End. Four hours and three quarters. Not bad."

"You'll kill yourself one of these days. Or someone else."

"Oh I hope not."

"But why are you staying *here?*"

Bess Sedgwick threw a swift glance round. She seemed to see the point and acknowledged it with an ironic smile.

"Someone told me I ought to try it. I think they're right. I've just had the most marvellous doughnut."

"My dear, they have *real* muffins too."

"Muffins," said Lady Sedgwick thoughtfully. "Yes . . ." She seemed to concede the point. "Muffins!"

She nodded and went on towards the lift.

"Extraordinary girl," said Lady Selina. To her, like to Miss Marple, every woman under sixty was a girl. "Known her ever since she was a child. Nobody could do anything with her. Ran away with an Irish groom when she was sixteen. They managed to get her back in time—or perhaps not in time. Anyway they bought him off and got her safely married to old Coniston—thirty years older than she was, awful old rip, quite dotty about her. *That* didn't last long. She went off with Johnnie Sedgwick. That *might* have stuck if he hadn't broken his neck steeplechasing. After that she married Ridgway Becker, an American yacht owner. He divorced her three years ago and I hear she's taken up with some Racing Motor Driver —a Pole or something. I don't know whether she's actually married him or not. After the American divorce she went back to calling herself Sedgwick. She goes about with *the* most extraordinary people. They *say* she takes drugs. . . . I don't know, I'm sure."

"One wonders if she is happy," said Miss Marple.

Lady Selina, who had clearly never wondered anything of the kind, looked rather startled.

"She's got packets of money, I suppose," she said doubtfully. "Alimony and all that. Of course that isn't everything . . ."

"No, indeed."

"And she's usually got a man—or several men—in tow."

"Yes?"

"Of course when some women get to that age, that's all they want . . . But somehow—"

She paused.

"No," said Miss Marple. "*I* don't think so either."

There were people who would have smiled in gentle derision at this pronouncement on the part of an old-fashioned old lady who could hardly be expected to be an authority on nymphomania, and indeed it was not a word that Miss Marple would have used—her own phrase would have been "always too fond of men." But Lady Selina accepted her opinion as a confirmation of her own.

"There have been a lot of men in her life," she pointed out.

"Oh yes, but I should say, wouldn't you, that men were an adventure to her, not a need?"

And would any woman, Miss Marple wondered, come to Bertram's Hotel for an assignation with a man? Bertram's was very definitely not that sort of place. But possibly that could be, to someone of Bess Sedgwick's disposition, the very reason for choosing it.

She sighed, looked up at the handsome grandfather clock decorously ticking in the corner, and rose with the careful effort of the rheumatic to her feet. She walked slowly towards the lift. Lady Selina cast a glance around her and pounced upon an elderly gentleman of military appearance who was reading the *Spectator*.

"How nice to see you again. Er—it is General Arlington, isn't it?"

But with great courtesy the old gentleman declined being General Arlington. Lady Selina apologized, but was not unduly discomposed. She combined short sight with optimism and since the thing she enjoyed most was meeting old friends and acquaintances, she was always making this kind of mistake. Many other people did the same, since the lights were pleasantly dim and heavily shaded. But nobody ever took offence—usually indeed it seemed to give them pleasure.

Miss Marple smiled to herself as she waited for the lift to come down. So like Selina! Always convinced that she knew everybody. She herself could not compete. Her solitary achievement in that line had been the handsome and well-gaitered Bishop of Westchester whom she had addressed affectionately as "dear Robbie" and who had responded with equal affection and with memories of himself as a child in a Hampshire village calling out lustily "Be a crocodile now, Aunty Jane. Be a crocodile and eat me."

The lift came down, the uniformed middle-aged man threw open the door. Rather to Miss Marple's surprise the alighting passenger was Bess Sedgwick whom she had seen go up only a minute or two before.

And then, one foot poised, Bess Sedgwick stopped dead, with a suddenness that surprised Miss Marple and made her own forward step falter. Bess Sedgwick was staring over Miss Marple's shoulder with such concentration that the old lady turned her own head.

The commissionaire had just pushed open the two swing doors of the entrance and was holding them to let two women pass through into the lounge. One of them was a fussy looking middle-aged lady wearing a rather unfortunate flowered violet hat, the other was a tall, simply but smartly dressed, girl of perhaps seventeen or eighteen with long straight flaxen hair.

Bess Sedgwick pulled herself together, wheeled round abruptly and re-entered the lift. As Miss Marple followed her in, she turned to her and apologized.

"I'm so sorry. I nearly ran into you." She had a warm, friendly voice. "I just remembered I'd forgotten something—which sounds nonsense but isn't really."

"Second floor?" said the operator. Miss Marple smiled and nodded in acknowledgement of the apology, got out and walked slowly along to her room, pleasurably turning over sundry little unimportant problems in her mind as was so often her custom.

For instance what Lady Sedgwick had said wasn't true. She had only just gone up to her room, and it must have been then that she "remembered she had forgotten something" (if there had been any truth in that statement at all) and had come down to find it. Or had she perhaps come down to meet someone or look for someone? But if so, what she had seen as the lift door opened had startled and upset her, and she had immediately swung round into the lift again and gone up so as *not* to meet whoever it was she had seen.

It must have been the two newcomers. The middle-aged woman and the girl. Mother and daughter? No, Miss Marple thought, *not* mother and daughter.

Even at Bertram's, thought Miss Marple, happily, interesting things could happen . . .

Chapter Three

"Er—is Colonel Luscombe—?"

The woman in the violet hat was at the desk. Miss Gorringe smiled in a welcoming manner and a page, who had been standing at the ready, was immediately dispatched but had no need to fulfil his errand, as Colonel Luscombe himself entered the lounge at that moment and came quickly across to the desk.

"How do you do, Mrs. Carpenter." He shook hands politely, then turned to the girl. "My dear Elvira." He took both her hands affectionately in his. "Well, well, this *is* nice. Splendid—splendid. Come and let's sit down." He led them to chairs, established them. "Well, well," he repeated, "this is nice."

The effort he made was somewhat palpable as was his lack of ease. He could hardly go on saying how nice this was. The two ladies were not very helpful. Elvira smiled very sweetly. Mrs. Carpenter gave a meaningless little laugh, and smoothed her gloves.

"A good journey, eh?"

"Yes, thank you," said Elvira.

"No fog. Nothing like that?"

"Oh no."

"Our flight was five minutes ahead of time," said Mrs. Carpenter.

"Yes, yes. Good, very good." He took a pull upon himself. "I hope this place will be all right for you?"

"Oh, I'm sure it's *very* nice," said Mrs. Carpenter warmly, glancing round her. "Very comfortable."

"Rather old-fashioned, I'm afraid," said the Colonel apologetically. "Rather a lot of old fogies. No—er—dancing, anything like that."

"No, I suppose not," agreed Elvira.

She glanced round in an expressionless manner. It certainly seemed impossible to connect Bertram's with dancing.

"Lot of old fogies here, I'm afraid," said Colonel Luscombe, repeating himself. "Ought, perhaps, to have taken you somewhere more modern. Not very well up in these things, you see."

"This is very nice," said Elvira politely.

"It's only for a couple of nights," went on Colonel Luscombe. "I thought we'd go to a show this evening. A musical—" he said the word rather doubtfully, as though not sure he was using the right term. "*Let Down Your Hair Girls.* I hope that will be all right?"

"How delightful," exclaimed Mrs. Carpenter. "That will be a treat, won't it, Elvira?"

"Lovely," said Elvira, tonelessly.

"And then supper afterwards? At the Savoy?"

Fresh exclamations from Mrs. Carpenter. Colonel Luscombe, stealing a glance at Elvira, cheered up a little. He thought that Elvira was pleased, though quite determined to express nothing more than polite approval in front of Mrs. Carpenter. "And I don't blame her," he said to himself.

He said to Mrs. Carpenter,

"Perhaps you'd like to see your rooms—see they're all right and all that—"

"Oh, I'm sure they will be."

"Well, if there's anything you don't like about them, we'll make them change it. They know me here very well."

Miss Gorringe, in charge at the desk, was pleasantly welcoming. Nos. 28 and 29 on the second floor with an adjoining bathroom.

"I'll go up and get things unpacked," said Mrs. Carpenter. "Perhaps, Elvira, you and Colonel Luscombe would like to have a little gossip."

Tact, thought Colonel Luscombe. A bit obvious, perhaps, but anyway it would get rid of her for a bit. Though what he was going to gossip about to Elvira, he really didn't know. A very nice-mannered girl, but he wasn't used to girls. His wife had died in childbirth and the baby, a boy, had been brought up by his wife's family whilst an elder sister had come to keep house for him. His son had married and gone to live in Kenya, and his grandchildren were eleven, five and two and a half and had been entertained on their last visit by football and space science talk, electric trains, and a ride on his foot. Easy! But young girls!

He asked Elvira if she would like a drink. He was about to propose a bitter lemon, ginger ale, or orangeade, but Elvira forestalled him.

"Thank you. I should like a gin and vermouth."

Colonel Luscombe looked at her rather doubtfully. He supposed girls of —what was she?—sixteen? seventeen?—did drink gin and vermouth. But he reassured himself that Elvira knew, so to speak, correct Greenwich social time. He ordered a gin and vermouth and a dry sherry.

He cleared his throat and asked:

"How was Italy?"

"Very nice, thank you."

"And that place you were at, the Contessa what's-her-name? Not too grim?"

"She is rather strict. But I didn't let that worry me."

He looked at her, not quite sure whether the reply was not slightly ambiguous.

He said, stammering a little, but with a more natural manner than he had been able to manage before:

"I'm afraid we don't know each other as well as we ought to, seeing I'm your guardian as well as your godfather. Difficult for me, you know— difficult for a man who's an old buffer like me—to know what a girl wants —at least—I mean to know what a girl ought to have. Schools and then after schools—what they used to call finishing in my day. But now, I suppose it's all more serious. Careers eh? Jobs? All that? We'll have to have a talk about all that sometime. Anything in particular you want to do?"

"I suppose I shall take a secretarial course," said Elvira without enthusiasm.

"Oh. You want to be a secretary?"

"Not particularly."

"Oh—well, then—"

"It's just what you start with," Elvira explained.

Colonel Luscombe had an odd feeling of being relegated to his place.

"These cousins of mine, the Melfords. You think you'll like living with them? If not—"

"Oh I think so. I like Nancy quite well. And Cousin Mildred is rather a dear."

"That's all right then?"

"Quite, for the present."

Luscombe did not know what to say to that. Whilst he was considering what next to say, Elvira spoke. Her words were simple and direct.

"Have I any money?"

Again he took his time before answering, studying her thoughtfully. Then he said:

"Yes. You've got quite a lot of money. That is to say, you will have when you are twenty-one."

"Who has got it now?"

He smiled. "It's held in trust for you; a certain amount is deducted each year from the income to pay for your maintenance and education."

"And you are the trustee?"

"One of them. There are three."

"What happens if I die?"

"Come, come, Elvira, you're not going to die. What nonsense!"

"I hope not—but one never knows, does one? An airliner crashed only last week and everyone was killed."

"Well, it's not going to happen to you," said Luscombe firmly.

"You can't really know that," said Elvira. "I was just wondering who would get my money if I died?"

"I haven't the least idea," said the Colonel irritably. "Why do you ask?"

"It might be interesting," said Elvira thoughtfully. "I wondered if it would be worth anyone's while to kill me."

"Really, Elvira! This is a most unprofitable conversation. I can't understand why your mind dwells on such things."

"Oh, just ideas. One wants to know what the facts really are."

"You're not thinking of the *Mafia*—or something like that?"

"Oh no. That would be silly. Who would get my money if I was married?"

"Your husband, I suppose. But really—"

"Are you sure of that?"

"No, I'm not in the least sure. It depends on the wording of the Trust. But you're not married, so why worry?"

Elvira did not reply. She seemed lost in thought. Finally she came out of her trance and asked:

"Do you ever see my mother?"

"Sometimes. Not very often."

"Where is she now?"

"Oh—abroad."

"Where abroad?"

"France—Portugal. I don't really know."

"Does she ever want to see me?"

Her limpid gaze met his. He didn't know what to reply. Was this a moment for truth? Or for vagueness? Or for a good thumping lie? What could you say to a girl who asked a question of such simplicity, when the answer was of great complexity? He said unhappily,

"I don't know."

Her eyes searched him gravely. Luscombe felt thoroughly ill at ease. He was making a mess of this. The girl must wonder—clearly was wondering. Any girl would.

He said, "You mustn't think—I mean it's difficult to explain. Your mother is, well, rather different from—" Elvira was nodding energetically.

"I know. I'm always reading about her in the papers. She's something rather special, isn't she? In fact, she's rather a wonderful person."

"Yes," agreed the Colonel. "That's exactly right. She's a wonderful person." He paused and then went on. "But a wonderful person is very often—" He stopped and started again—"it's not always a happy thing to have a wonderful person for a mother. You can take that from me because it's the truth."

"You don't like speaking the truth very much, do you? But I think what you've just said *is* the truth."

They both sat staring towards the big brass-bound swing doors that led to the world outside.

Suddenly the doors were pushed open with violence—a violence quite unusual in Bertram's Hotel—and a young man strode in and went straight across to the desk. He wore a black leather jacket. His vitality was such that Bertram's Hotel took on the atmosphere of a museum by way of contrast. The people were the dust encrusted relics of a past age. He bent towards Miss Gorringe and asked,

"Is Lady Sedgwick staying here?"

Miss Gorringe on this occasion had no welcoming smile. Her eyes were flinty. She said,

"Yes." Then, with definite unwillingness, she stretched out her hand towards the telephone. "Do you want to—?"

"No," said the young man. "I just wanted to leave a note for her."

He produced it from a pocket of his leather coat and slid it across the mahogany counter.

"I only wanted to be sure this was the right hotel."

There might have been some slight incredulity in his voice as he looked round him, then turned back towards the entrance. His eyes passed indifferently over the people sitting round him. They passed over Luscombe and Elvira in the same way, and Luscombe felt a sudden unsuspected anger. "Dammit all," he thought to himself, "Elvira's a pretty girl. When I was a young chap I'd have noticed a pretty girl, especially among all these fossils." But the young man semed to have no interested eyes to spare for pretty girls. He turned back to the desk and asked, raising his voice slightly as though to call Miss Gorringe's attention,

"What's the telephone number here? 1129 isn't it?"

"No," said Miss Gorringe, "3925."

"Regent?"

"No. Mayfair."

He nodded. Then swiftly he strode across to the door and passed out, swinging the doors to behind him with something of the same explosive quality he had shown on entering.

Everybody seemed to draw a deep breath; to find difficulty in resuming their interrupted conversations.

"Well," said Colonel Luscombe, rather inadequately, as if at a loss for words. "Well, really! These young fellows nowadays . . ."

Elvira was smiling.

"You recognized him, didn't you?" she said. "You know who he is?" She spoke in a slightly awed voice. She proceeded to enlighten him. "Ladislaus Malinowski."

"Oh, that chap." The name was indeed faintly familiar to Colonel Luscombe. "Racing driver."

"Yes. He was world champion two years running. He had a bad crash a year ago. Broke lots of things. But I believe he's driving again now." She raised her head to listen. "That's a racing car he's driving now."

The roar of the engine had penetrated through to Bertram's Hotel from the street outside. Colonel Luscombe perceived that Ladislaus Malinowski was one of Elvira's heroes. "Well," he thought to himself, "better that than one of those pop singers or crooners or long-haired Beatles or whatever they call themselves." Luscombe was old-fashioned in his views of young men.

The swing doors opened again. Both Elvira and Colonel Luscombe looked at them expectantly but Bertram's Hotel had reverted to normal. It was merely a white-haired elderly cleric who came in. He stood for a moment looking round him with a slightly puzzled air as of one who fails to understand where he was or how he had come there. Such an experience was no novelty to Canon Pennyfather. It came to him in trains when he did not remember where he had come from, where he was going, or why!

It came to him when he was walking along the street, it came to him when he found himself sitting on a committee. It had come to him before now when he was in his cathedral stall, and did not know whether he had already preached his sermon or was about to do so.

"I believe I know that old boy," said Luscombe, peering at him. "Who is he now? Stays here fairly often, I believe. Abercrombie? Archdeacon Abercrombie—no, it's not Abercrombie, though he's rather like Abercrombie."

Elvira glanced round at Canon Pennyfather without interest. Compared with a racing driver he had no appeal at all. She was not interested in ecclesiastics of any kind although, since being in Italy, she admitted to a mild admiration for Cardinals whom she considered as at any rate properly picturesque.

Canon Pennyfather's face cleared and he nodded his head appreciatively. He had recognized where he was. In Bertram's Hotel, of course; where he was going to spend the night on his way to—now where was he on his way to? Chadminster? No, no, he had just *come* from Chadminster. He was going to—of course—to the Congress at Lucerne. He stepped forward, beaming, to the reception desk and was greeted warmly by Miss Gorringe.

"So glad to see you, Canon Pennyfather. How well you are looking."

"Thank you—thank you—I had a severe cold last week but I've got over it now. You have a room for me. I *did* write?"

Miss Gorringe reassured him.

"Oh yes, Canon Pennyfather, we got your letter. We've reserved No. 19 for you, the room you had last time."

"Thank you—thank you. For—let me see—I shall want it for four days. Actually I am going to Lucerne and shall be away for one night, but please keep the room. I shall leave most of my things here and only take a small bag to Switzerland. There won't be any difficulty over that?"

Again Miss Gorringe reassured him.

"Everything's going to be quite all right. You explained very clearly in your letter."

Other people might not have used the word "clearly". "Fully" would have been better, since he had certainly written at length.

All anxieties set at rest, Canon Pennyfather breathed a sigh of relief and was conveyed, together with his baggage, to Room 19.

In Room 28 Mrs. Carpenter had removed her crown of violets from her head and was carefully adjusting her nightdress on the pillow of her bed. She looked up as Elvira entered.

"Ah, there you are, my dear. Would you like me to help you with your unpacking?"

"No, thank you," said Elvira politely. "I shan't unpack very much, you know."

"Which of the bedrooms would you like to have? The bathroom is between them. I told them to put your luggage in the far one. I thought this room might be a little noisy."

"That was very kind of you," said Elvira in her expressionless voice.

"You're sure you wouldn't like me to help you?"

"No, thanks, really I wouldn't. I think I might perhaps have a bath."

"Yes, I think that's a very good idea. Would you like to have the first bath? I'd rather finish putting my things away."

Elvira nodded. She went into the adjoining bathroom, shut the door behind her and pushed the bolts across. She went into her own room, opened her suitcase and flung a few things on the bed. Then she undressed, put on a dressing-gown, went into the bathroom and turned the taps on. She went back into her own room and sat down on the bed by the telephone. She listened a moment or two in case of interruptions, then lifted the receiver.

"This is Room 29. Can you give me Regent 1129 please?"

Chapter Four

WITHIN the confines of Scotland Yard a conference was in progress. It was by way of being an informal conference. Six or seven men were sitting easily round a table and each of those six men was a man of some importance in his own line. The subject that occupied the attention of these guardians of the law was a subject that had grown terrifically in importance during the last two or three years. It concerned a branch of crime whose success had been overwhelmingly disquieting. Robbery on a big scale was increasing. Bank hold-ups, snatches of pay-rolls, thefts of consignments of jewels sent through the mail, train robberies. Hardly a month passed but some daring and stupendous coup was attempted and brought off successfully.

Sir Ronald Graves, Assistant Commissioner of Scotland Yard, was presiding at the head of the table. According to his usual custom he did more listening than talking. No formal reports were being presented on this occasion. All that belonged to the ordinary routine of CID work. This was a high level consultation, a general pooling of ideas between men looking at affairs from slightly different points of view. Sir Ronald Graves's eyes went slowly round his little group, then he nodded his head to a man at the end of the table.

"Well, Father," he said, "let's hear a few homely wisecracks from you."

The man addressed as "Father" was Chief-Inspector Fred Davy. His retirement lay not long ahead and he appeared to be even more elderly than he was. Hence his nickname of "Father". He had a comfortable spreading presence, and such a benign and kindly manner that many criminals had been disagreeably surprised to find him a less genial and gullible man than he had seemed to be.

"Yes, Father, let's hear your views," said another Chief-Inspector.

"It's big," said Chief-Inspector Davy with a deep sigh. "Yes, it's big. Maybe it's growing."

"When you say big, do you mean numerically?"

"Yes, I do."

Another man, Comstock, with a sharp, foxy face and alert eyes, broke in to say,

"Would you say that was an advantage to them?"

"Yes and no," said Father. "It *could* be a disaster. But so far, devil take it, they've got it all well under control."

Superintendent Andrews, a fair, slight, dreamy-looking man, said thoughtfully,

"I've always thought there's a lot more to size than people realize. Take a little one-man business. If that's well run and if it's the right size, it's a sure and certain winner. Branch out, make it bigger, increase personnel, and perhaps you'll get it suddenly to the *wrong* size and down the hill it goes. The same way with a great big chain of stores. An empire in industry. If that's *big* enough it will succeed. If it's *not* big enough it just won't manage it. Everything has got its right size. When it is its right size and well run it's the tops."

"How big do you think this show is?" Sir Ronald barked.

"Bigger than we thought at first," said Comstock.

A tough looking man, Inspector McNeill, said,

"It's growing, I'd say. Father's right. Growing all the time."

"That may be a good thing," said Davy. "It may grow a bit *too* fast, and then it'll get out of hand."

"The question is, Sir Ronald," said McNeill, "who we pull in and when?"

"There's a round dozen or so we could pull in," said Comstock. "The Harris lot are mixed up in it, we know that. There's a nice little pocket down Luton way. There's a garage at Epsom, there's a pub near Maidenhead, and there's a farm on the Great North Road."

"Any of them worth pulling in?"

"I don't think so. Small fry all of them. Links. Just links here and there in the chain. A spot where cars are converted, and turned over quickly; a respectable pub where messages get passed; a second-hand clothes shop where appearance can be altered, a theatrical costumier in the East End, also very useful. They're paid, these people. Quite well paid but they don't really *know* anything!"

The dreamy Superintendent Andrews said again,

"We're up against some good brains. We haven't got near them yet. We know some of their affiliations and that's all. As I say, the Harris crowd are in it and Marks is in on the financial end. The foreign contacts are in touch with Weber but he's only an agent. We've nothing actually *on* any of these people. We know that they all have ways of maintaining contact with each other, and with the different branches of the concern, but we don't know exactly how they do it. We watch them and follow them, and they know we're watching them. *Somewhere* there's a great central exchange. What we want to get at is the planners."

Comstock said,

"It's like a giant network. I agree that there must be an operational headquarters somewhere. A place where each operation is planned and detailed and dovetailed completely. Somewhere, someone plots it all, and produces a working blueprint of Operation Mailbag or Operation Payroll. Those are the people we're out to get."

"Possibly they are not even in this country," said Father quietly.

"No, I dare say that's true. Perhaps they're in an igloo somewhere, or in a tent in Morocco or in a chalet in Switzerland."

"I don't believe in these master-minds," said McNeill, shaking his head. "They sound all right in a story. There's got to *be* a head, of course, but I don't believe in a Master Criminal. I'd say there was a very clever little Board of Directors behind this. Centrally planned, with a Chairman. They've got on to something good, and they're improving their technique all the time. All the same—"

"Yes?" said Sir Ronald encouragingly.

"Even in a right tight little team, there are probably expendables. What I call the Russian Sledge principle. From time to time, if they think we might be getting hot on the scent, they throw off one of them, the one they think they can best afford."

"Would they dare to do that? Wouldn't it be rather risky?"

"I dare say it could be done in such a way that whoever it was wouldn't even know he *had* been pushed off the sledge. He'd just think he'd fallen off. He'd keep quiet because he'd think it was worth his while to keep quiet. So it would be, of course. They've got plenty of money to play with, and they can afford to be generous. Family looked after, if he's got one, whilst he's in prison. Possibly an escape engineered."

"There's been too much of that," said Comstock.

"I think, you know," said Sir Ronald, "that it's not much good going over and over our speculations again. We always say much the same thing."

McNeill laughed.

"What is it you really wanted us for, sir?"

"Well—" Sir Ronald thought a moment, "we're all agreed on the main things," he said slowly. "We're agreed on our main policy, on what we're trying to do. I think it *might* be profitable to have a look around for some of the small things, the things that don't matter much, that are just a bit out of the usual run. It's hard to explain what I mean, but like that business some years ago in the Culver case. An ink stain. Do you remember? An ink stain round a mouse-hole. Now why on earth should a man empty a bottle of ink into a mouse-hole? It didn't seem important. It was hard to get at the answer. But when we did hit on the answer, it led somewhere. That's—roughly—the sort of thing I was thinking about. Odd things. Don't mind saying if you come across something that strikes you as a bit out of the usual. Petty if you like, but irritating, because it doesn't quite fit in. I see Father's nodding his head."

"Couldn't agree with you more," said Chief-Inspector Davy. "Come on, boys, try to come up with something. Even if it's only a man wearing a funny hat."

There was no immediate response. Everyone looked a little uncertain and doubtful.

"Come on," said Father. "I'll stick my neck out first. It's just a funny story, really, but you might as well have it for what it's worth. The London and Metropolitan Bank holdup. Carmolly Street Branch. Remember it? A whole list of car numbers and car colours and makes. We appealed to people to come forward and they responded—how they responded! About a hundred and fifty pieces of misleading information! Got it sorted out in the end to about seven cars that had been seen in the neighbourhood, any one of which *might* have been concerned in the robbery."

"Yes," said Sir Ronald, "go on."

"There were one or two we couldn't get tags on. Looked as though the numbers might have been changed. Nothing out of the way in that. It's often done. Most of them got tracked down in the end. I'll just bring up one instance. Morris Oxford, black saloon, number CMG 256, reported by a probation officer. He said it was being driven by Mr. Justice Ludgrove."

He looked round. They were listening to him, but without any manifest interest.

"I know," he said, "wrong as usual. Mr. Justice Ludgrove is a rather noticeable old boy, ugly as sin for one thing. Well, it wasn't Mr. Justice Ludgrove because at that exact time he was actually in Court. He *has* got a Morris Oxford, but its number isn't CMG 256." He looked round. "All right. All right. So there's no point in it, you'll say. But do you know what the number *was*? CMG 265. Near enough, eh? Just the sort of mistake one does make when you're trying to remember a car number."

"I'm sorry," said Sir Ronald, "I don't quite see—"

"No," said Chief-Inspector Davy, "there's nothing *to* see really, is there? Only—it was very like the actual car number, wasn't it? 265—256 CMG. Really rather a coincidence that there should be a Morris Oxford car of the right colour with the number just one digit wrong, and with a man in it closely resembling the owner of the car."

"Do you mean—?"

"Just one little digit difference. Today's 'deliberate mistake.' It almost seems like that."

"Sorry, Davy. I still don't get it."

"Oh, I don't suppose there's anything *to* get. There's a Morris Oxford car, CMG 265, proceeding along the street two and a half minutes after the bank snatch. In it, the probation officer recognizes Mr. Justice Ludgrove."

"Are you suggesting it really *was* Mr. Justice Ludgrove? Come now, Davy."

"No, I'm not suggesting that it was Mr. Justice Ludgrove and that he was mixed up in a bank robbery. He was staying at Bertram's Hotel in Pond Street, and he was at the Law Courts at that exact time. All proved up to the hilt. I'm saying the car number and make and the identification by a probation officer who knows old Ludgrove quite well by sight is the kind of coincidence that *ought* to mean something. Apparently it doesn't. Too bad."

Comstock stirred uneasily.

"There was another case a bit like that in connection with the Jewellery business at Brighton. Some old Admiral or other. I've forgotten his name now. Some woman identified him most positively as having been on the scene."

"And he wasn't?"

"No, he'd been in London that night. Went up for some naval dinner or other, I think."

"Staying at his club?"

"No, he was staying at a hotel—I believe it was that one you mentioned just now, Father, Bertram's, isn't it? Quiet place. A lot of old service geezers go there, I believe."

"Bertram's Hotel," said Chief-Inspector Davy, thoughtfully.

Chapter Five

MISS MARPLE awoke early because she always woke early. She was appreciative of her bed. Most comfortable.

She pattered across to the window and pulled the curtains, admitting a little pallid London daylight. As yet, however, she did not try to dispense with the electric light. A very nice bedroom they had given her, again quite in the tradition of Bertram's. A rose-flowered wallpaper, a large well-polished mahogany chest of drawers—a dressing-table to correspond. Two upright chairs, one easy chair of a reasonable height from the ground. A connecting door led to a bathroom which was modern but which had a tiled wallpaper of roses and so avoided any suggestion of over-frigid hygiene.

Miss Marple got back into bed, plumped her pillows up, glanced at her clock, half-past seven, picked up the small devotional book that always accompanied her, and read as usual the page and a half allotted to the day. Then she picked up her knitting and began to knit, slowly at first, since her fingers were stiff and rheumatic when she first awoke, but very soon her pace grew faster, and her fingers lost their painful stiffness.

"Another day," said Miss Marple to herself, greeting the fact with her usual gentle pleasure. Another day—and who knew what it might bring forth?

She relaxed, and abandoning her knitting, let thoughts pass in an idle stream through her head . . . Selina Hazy . . . what a pretty cottage she had had in St. Mary Mead's—and now someone had put on that ugly green roof . . . Muffins . . . very wasteful in butter . . . but very good . . . And fancy serving old-fashioned seed cake! She had never expected, not for a moment, that things would be as much like they used to be . . . because, after all, Time didn't stand still . . . And to have made it stand still in this way must really have cost a lot of money . . . Not a bit of plastic in the place! . . . It must pay them, she supposed. The out-of-date returns in due course as the picturesque . . . Look how people wanted old-fashioned roses now, and scorned hybrid teas! . . . None of this place seemed real at all . . . well, why should it? . . . It was fifty—no, nearer sixty years since she had stayed here. And it didn't seem real to her because she was now acclimatized in this present year of Our Lord—Really, the whole thing opened up a very interesting set of problems . . . The atmosphere and the *people* . . . Miss Marple's fingers pushed her knitting farther away from her.

"Pockets," she said aloud . . . "Pockets, I suppose . . . And quite difficult to find . . ."

Would that account for that curious feeling of uneasiness she had had last night? That feeling that something was wrong . . .

All those elderly people—really very much like those she remembered when she had stayed here fifty years ago. They had been natural then—but they weren't very natural now. Elderly people nowadays weren't like elderly people then—they had that worried harried look of domestic anxieties with which they are too tired to cope, or they rushed round to committees and tried to appear bustling and competent, or they dyed their hair gentian blue, or wore wigs, and their hands were not the hands she remembered, tapering, delicate hands—they were harsh from washing up and detergents . . .

And so—well, so these people didn't look real. But the point was that they *were* real. Selina Hazy was real. And that rather handsome old military man in the corner was real—she had met him once, although she did not recall his name—and the Bishop (dear Robbie!) was dead.

Miss Marple glanced at her little clock. It was eight-thirty. Time for her breakfast.

She examined the instructions given by the hotel— Splendid big print so that it wasn't necessary to put one's spectacles on.

Meals could be ordered through the telephone by asking for Room Service, or you could press the bell labelled Chambermaid.

Miss Marple did the latter. Talking to Room Service always flustered her.

The result was excellent. In no time at all there was a tap on the door and a highly satisfactory chambermaid appeared. A real chambermaid looking unreal, wearing a striped lavender print dress and actually a *cap*, a freshly laundered cap. A smiling, rosy, positively *countrified* face. (Where did they *find* these people?)

Miss Marple ordered her breakfast. Tea, poached eggs, fresh rolls. So adept was the chambermaid that she did not even mention cereals or orange juice.

Five minutes later breakfast came. A comfortable tray with a big pot-bellied teapot, creamy-looking milk, a silver hot water jug. Two beautifully poached eggs on toast, poached the proper way, not little round hard bullets shaped in tin cups, a good-sized round of butter stamped with a thistle. Marmalade, honey and strawberry jam. Delicious-looking rolls, not the hard kind with papery interiors—they *smelt* of fresh bread (the most delicious smell in the world!). There were also an apple, a pear and a banana.

Miss Marple inserted a knife gingerly but with confidence. She was not disappointed. Rich deep yellow yolk oozed out, thick and creamy. *Proper* eggs!

Everything piping hot. A *real* breakfast. She could have cooked it herself but she hadn't had to! It was brought to her as if—no, not as though she were a queen—as though she were a middle-aged lady staying in a good but not unduly expensive hotel. In fact—back to 1909. Miss Marple expressed appreciation to the chambermaid who replied smiling,

"Oh, yes, Madam, the Chef is very particular about his breakfasts."

Miss Marple studied her appraisingly. Bertram's Hotel could certainly produce marvels. A *real* housemaid. She pinched her left arm surreptitiously.

"Have you been here long?" she asked.

"Just over three years, Madam."

"And before that?"

"I was in a hotel at Eastbourne. Very modern and up-to-date—but I prefer an old-fashioned place like this."

Miss Marple took a sip of tea. She found herself humming in a vague way—words fitting themselves to a long forgotten song.

"Oh where have you been all my life . . ."

The chambermaid was looking slightly startled.

"I was just remembering an old song," twittered Miss Marple apologetically. "Very popular at one time."

Again she sang softly. "Oh where have you been all my life . . ."

"Perhaps you know it?" she asked.

"Well—" The chambermaid looked rather apologetic.

"Too long ago for you," said Miss Marple. "Ah well, one gets to remembering things—in a place like this."

"Yes, Madam, a lot of the ladies who stay here feel like that, I think."

"It's partly why they come, I expect," said Miss Marple.

The chambermaid went out. She was obviously used to old ladies who twittered and reminisced.

Miss Marple finished her breakfast, and got up in a pleasant leisurely fashion. She had a plan ready made for a delightful morning of shopping. Not too much—to overtire herself. Oxford Street today, perhaps. And tomorrow Knightsbridge. She planned ahead happily.

It was about ten o'clock when she emerged from her room fully equipped: hat, gloves, umbrella—just in case, though it looked fine—handbag—her smartest shopping bag—

The door next but one on the corridor opened sharply and someone looked out. It was Bess Sedgwick. She withdrew back into the room and closed the door sharply.

Miss Marple wondered as she went down the stairs. She preferred the stairs to the lift first thing in the morning. It limbered her up. Her steps grew slower and slower . . . she stopped.

II

As Colonel Luscombe strode along the passage from his room, a door at the top of the stairs opened sharply and Lady Sedgwick spoke to him.

"There you are at last! I've been on the look-out for you—waiting to pounce. Where can we go and talk? That is to say without falling over some old pussy every second."

"Well, really, Bess, I'm not quite sure—I think on the mezzanine floor there's a sort of writing-room."

"You'd better come in here. Quick now, before the chambermaid gets peculiar ideas about us."

Rather unwillingly, Colonel Luscombe stepped across the threshold and had the door shut firmly behind him.

"I'd no idea you would be staying here, Bess, I hadn't the faintest idea of it."

"I don't suppose you had."

"I mean—I would never have brought Elvira here. I *have* got Elvira here, you know?"

"Yes, I saw her with you last night."

"But I really didn't know that you were here. It seemed such an unlikely place for you."

"I don't see why," said Bess Sedgwick, coldly. "It's far and away the most comfortable hotel in London. Why shouldn't I stay here?"

"You must understand that I hadn't any idea of . . . I mean—"

She looked at him and laughed. She was dressed ready to go out in a well cut dark suit and a shirt of bright emerald green. She looked gay and very much alive. Beside her, Colonel Luscombe looked rather old and faded.

"Darling Derek, don't look so worried. I'm not accusing you of trying to stage a mother and daughter sentimental meeting. It's just one of those things that happen; where people meet each other in unsuspected places. But you *must* get Elvira out of here, Derek. You must get her out of it at once—today."

"Oh, she's going. I mean, I only brought her here just for a couple of nights. Do a show—that sort of thing. She's going down to the Melfords tomorrow."

"Poor girl, that'll be boring for her."

Luscombe looked at her with concern. "Do you think she will be very bored?"

Bess took pity on him.

"Probably not after duress in Italy. She might even think it wildly thrilling."

Luscombe took his courage in both hands.

"Look here, Bess, I was startled to find you here, but don't you think it

—well, you know, it might be *meant* in a way. I mean that it might be an opportunity—I don't think you really know how—well, how the girl might feel."

"What are you trying to say, Derek?"

"Well, you *are* her mother, you know."

"Of course I'm her mother. She's my daughter. And what good has that fact ever been to either of us, or ever will be?"

"You can't be sure. I think—I think she feels it."

"What gives you that idea?" said Bess Sedgwick sharply.

"Something she said yesterday. She asked where you were, what you were doing."

Bess Sedgwick walked across the room to the window. She stood there a moment tapping on the pane.

"You're so nice, Derek," she said. "You have such nice ideas. But they don't work, my poor angel. That's what you've got to say to yourself. They don't work and they might be dangerous."

"Oh come now, Bess. Dangerous?"

"Yes, yes, yes. Dangerous. *I'm* dangerous. I've always been dangerous."

"When I think of some of the things you've done," said Colonel Luscombe.

"That's my own business," said Bess Sedgwick. "Running into danger has become a kind of habit with me. No, I wouldn't say habit. More an addiction. Like a drug. Like that nice little dollop of heroin addicts have to have every so often to make life seem bright coloured and worth living. Well, that's all right. That's my funeral—or not—as the case may be. I've never taken drugs—never needed them— Danger has been my drug. But people who live as I do can be a source of harm to others. Now don't be an obstinate old fool, Derek. You keep that girl well away from me. I can do her no good. Only harm. If possible, don't even let her know I was staying in the same hotel. Ring up the Melfords and take her down there *today*. Make some excuse about a sudden emergency—"

Colonel Luscombe hesitated, pulling his moustache.

"I think you're making a mistake, Bess." He sighed. "She asked where you were. I told her you were abroad."

"Well, I shall be in another twelve hours, so that all fits very nicely."

She came up to him, kissed him on the point of his chin, turned him smartly around as though they were about to play Blind Man's Buff, opened the door, gave him a gentle little propelling shove out of it. As the door shut behind him, Colonel Luscombe noticed an old lady turning the corner from the stairs. She was muttering to herself as she looked into her handbag. "Dear, dear me. I suppose I must have left it in my room. Oh dear."

She passed Colonel Luscombe without paying much attention to him apparently, but as he went on down the stairs Miss Marple paused by her room door and directed a piercing glance after him. Then she looked towards Bess Sedgwick's door. "So that's who she was waiting for," said Miss Marple to herself. "I wonder why."

III

Canon Pennyfather, fortified by breakfast, wandered across the lounge, remembered to leave his key at the desk, pushed his way through the swinging doors, and was neatly inserted into a taxi by the Irish commissionaire who existed for this purpose.

"Where to, sir?"

"Oh dear," said Canon Pennyfather in sudden dismay. "Now let me see—where *was* I going?"

The traffic in Pond Street was held up for some minutes whilst Canon Pennyfather and the commissionaire debated this knotty point.

Finally Canon Pennyfather had a brainwave and the taxi was directed to go to the British Museum.

The commissionaire was left on the pavement with a broad grin on his face, and since no other exits seemed to be taking place, he strolled a little way along the façade of the hotel whistling an old tune in a muted manner.

One of the windows on the ground floor of Bertram's was flung up—but the commissionaire did not even turn his head until a voice spoke unexpectedly through the open window.

"So this is where you've landed up, Micky. What on earth brought you to this place?"

He swung round, startled—and stared.

Lady Sedgwick thrust her head through the open window.

"Don't you know me?" she demanded.

A sudden gleam of recognition came across the man's face.

"Why, if it isn't little Bessie now! Fancy that! After all these years. Little Bessie."

"Nobody but you ever called me Bessie. It's a revolting name. What have you been doing all these years?"

"This and that," said Micky with some reserve. "I've not been in the news like you have. I've read of your doings in the paper time and again."

Bess Sedgwick laughed. "Anyway, I've worn better than you have," she said. "You drink too much. You always did."

"You've worn well because you've always been in the money."

"Money wouldn't have done you any good. You'd have drunk even more and gone to the dogs completely. Oh yes, you would! What brought you *here*? That's what I want to know. How did you ever get taken on at this place?"

"I wanted a job. I had these—" his hand flicked over the row of medals.

"Yes, I see." She was thoughtful. "All genuine too, aren't they?"

"Sure they're genuine. Why shouldn't they be?"

"Oh I believe you. You always had courage. You've always been a good fighter. Yes, the army suited you. I'm sure of that."

"The army's all right in time of war, but it's no good in peace time."

"So you took to this stuff. I hadn't the least idea—" she stopped.

"You hadn't the least idea what, Bessie?"

"Nothing. It's queer seeing you again after all these years."

"I haven't forgotten," said the man. "I've never forgotten you, little Bessie. Ah! a lovely girl you were! A lovely slip of a girl."

"A damn' fool of a girl, that's what I was," said Lady Sedgwick.

"That's true now. You hadn't much sense. If you had, you wouldn't have taken up with me. What hands you had for a horse. Do you remember that mare—what was her name now?—Molly O'Flynn. Ah, she was a wicked devil that one was."

"You were the only one that could ride her," said Lady Sedgwick.

"She'd have had me off if she could! When she found she couldn't, she gave in. Ah, she was a beauty, now. But talking of sitting a horse, there wasn't one lady in those parts better than you. A lovely seat you had, lovely hands. Never any fear in you, not for a minute! And it's been the same ever since, so I judge. Aeroplanes, racing cars."

Bess Sedgwick laughed.

"I must get on with my letters."

She drew back from the window.

Micky leaned over the railing. "I've not forgotten Ballygowlan," he said with meaning. "Sometimes I've thought of writing to you—"

Bess Sedgwick's voice came out harshly.

"And what do you mean by that, Mick Gorman?"

"I was just saying as I haven't forgotten—anything. I was just—reminding you like."

Bess Sedgwick's voice still held its harsh note.

"If you mean what I think you mean, I'll give you a piece of advice. Any trouble from you, and I'd shoot you as easily as I'd shoot a rat. I've shot men before—"

"In foreign parts, maybe—"

"Foreign parts or here—it's all the same to me."

"Ah, good lord, now, and I believe you would do just that!" His voice held admiration. "In Ballygowlan—"

"In Ballygowlan," she cut in, "they paid you to keep your mouth shut and paid you well. You took the money. You'll get no more from me so don't think it."

"It would be a nice romantic story for the Sunday papers . . ."

"You heard what I said."

"Ah," he laughed, "I'm not serious. I was just joking. I'd never do anything to hurt my little Bessie. I'll keep my mouth shut."

"Mind you do," said Lady Sedgwick.

She shut down the window. Staring down at the desk in front of her she looked at her unfinished letter on the blotting paper. She picked it up, looked at it, crumpled it into a ball and slung it into the waste-paper basket. Then abruptly she got up from her seat and walked out of the room. She did not even cast a glance around her before she went.

The smaller writing-rooms at Bertram's often had an appearance of being empty even when they were not. Two well-appointed desks stood in the windows, there was a table on the right that held a few magazines, on the left were two very high-backed arm-chairs turned towards the fire. These were favourite spots in the afternoon for elderly military or naval gentlemen to ensconce themselves and fall happily asleep until tea-time. Anyone coming in to write a letter did not usually even notice them. The chairs were not so much in demand during the morning.

As it happened, however, they were on this particular morning both occupied. An old lady was in one and a young girl in the other. The young girl rose to her feet. She stood a moment looking uncertainly towards the door through which Lady Sedgwick had passed out, then she moved slowly towards it. Elvira Blake's face was deadly pale.

It was another five minutes before the old lady moved. Then Miss Marple decided that the little rest which she always took after dressing and coming downstairs had lasted quite long enough. It was time to go out and enjoy the pleasures of London. She might walk as far as Piccadilly, and take a No. 9 bus to High Street, Kensington, or she might walk along to Bond Street and take a 25 bus to Marshall & Snelgrove's or she might take a 25 the other way which as far as she remembered would land her up at the Army & Navy Stores. Passing through the swing doors she was still savouring these delights in her mind. The Irish commissionaire, back on duty, made up her mind for her.

"You'll be wanting a taxi, Ma'am," he said with firmness.

"I don't think I do," said Miss Marple. "I think there's a 25 bus I could take quite near here—or a 2 from Park Lane."

"You'll not be wanting a bus," said the commissionaire firmly. "It's very dangerous springing on a bus when you're getting on in life. The way they start and stop and go on again. Jerk you off your feet, they do. No heart at all, these fellows, nowadays. I'll whistle you along a taxi and you'll go to wherever you want to like a queen."

Miss Marple considered and fell.

"Very well then," she said, "perhaps I *had* better have a taxi."

The commissionaire had no need even to whistle. He merely clicked his thumb and a taxi appeared like magic. Miss Marple was helped into it with every possible care and decided on the spur of the moment to go to Robinson & Cleaver's and look at their splendid offer of real linen sheets. She sat happily in her taxi feeling indeed as the commissionaire had promised her, just like a queen. Her mind was filled with pleasurable anticipation of linen sheets, linen pillow cases and proper glass- and kitchen-cloths without pictures of bananas, figs or performing dogs and other pictorial distractions to annoy you when you were washing up.

Lady Sedgwick came up to the Reception desk.

"Mr. Humfries in his office?"

"Yes, Lady Sedgwick." Miss Gorringe looked startled.

Lady Sedgwick passed behind the desk, tapped on the door and went in without waiting for any response.

Mr. Humfries looked up startled.

"What—?"

"Who engaged that man Michael Gorman?"

Mr. Humfries spluttered a little.

"Parfitt left—he had a car accident a month ago. We had to replace him quickly. This man seemed all right. References OK—ex-army—quite good record—Not very bright perhaps—but that's all the better sometimes—you don't know anything against him, do you?"

"Enough not to want him here."

"If you insist," Humfries said slowly, "we'll give him his notice—"

"No," said Lady Sedgwick slowly. "No—it's too late for that— Never mind."

Chapter Six

"ELVIRA."

"Hallo, Bridget."

The Hon. Elvira Blake pushed her way through the front door of 180 Onslow Square, which her friend Bridget had rushed down to open for her, having been watching through the window.

"Let's go upstairs," said Elvira.

"Yes, we'd better. Otherwise we'll get entangled by Mummy."

The two girls rushed up the stairs, thereby circumventing Bridget's mother, who came out on to the landing from her own bedroom just too late.

"You really are lucky not to have a mother," said Bridget, rather breathlessly, as she took her friend into her bedroom and shut the door firmly. "I mean, Mummy's quite a pet and all that, but the *questions* she asks! Morning, noon and night. Where are you going, and who have you met? And are they cousins of somebody else of the same name in Yorkshire? I mean, the *futility* of it all."

"I suppose they have nothing else to think about," said Elvira vaguely. "Look here, Bridget, there's something terribly important I've got to do, and you've got to help me."

"Well, I will if I can. What is it—a man?"

"No, it isn't, as a matter of fact." Bridget looked disappointed. "I've got to get away to Ireland for twenty-four hours or perhaps longer, and you've got to cover up for me."

"To Ireland? Why?"

"I can't tell you all about it now. There's no time. I've got to meet my guardian, Colonel Luscombe, at Prunier's for lunch at half-past one."

"What have you done with the Carpenter?"

"Gave her the slip in Debenham's."

Bridget giggled.

"And after lunch they're taking me down to the Melfords. I'm going to live with them until I'm twenty-one."

"How ghastly!"

"I expect I shall manage. Cousin Mildred is fearfully easy to deceive. It's arranged. I'm to come up for classes and things. There's a place called World of Today. They take you to lectures and to Museums and to Picture Galleries and the House of Lords, and all that. The whole point is that nobody will know whether you're where you ought to be or not! We'll manage lots of things."

"I expect we will." Bridget giggled. "We managed in Italy, didn't we? Old Macaroni thought she was so strict. Little did she know what we got up to when we tried."

Both girls laughed in the pleasant consciousness of successful wickedness.

"Still, it did need a lot of planning," said Elvira.

"And some splendid lying," said Bridget. "Have you heard from Guido?"

"Oh yes, he wrote me a long letter signed Ginevra as though he was a girl-friend. But I do wish you'd stop talking so much, Bridget. We've got a lot to do and only about an hour and a half to do it in. Now first of all just *listen*. I'm coming up tomorrow for an appointment with the dentist. That's easy, I can put it off by telephone—or you can from here. Then, about midday, you can ring up the Melfords pretending to be your mother and explain that the dentist wants to see me again the next day and so I'm staying over with you here."

"That ought to go down all right. They'll say how very kind and gush. But supposing you're *not* back the next day?"

"Then you'll have to do some more ringing up."

Bridget looked doubtful.

"We'll have lots of time to think up something before then," said Elvira impatiently. "What's worrying me now is *money*. You haven't got any, I suppose?" Elvira spoke without much hope.

"Only about two pounds."

"That's no good. I've got to buy my air ticket. I've looked up the flights. It only takes about two hours. A lot depends upon how long it takes me when I get there."

"Can't you tell me what you're going to do?"

"No, I can't. But it's terribly, terribly important."

Elvira's voice was so different that Bridget looked at her in some surprise.

"Is anything really the matter, Elvira?"

"Yes, it is."

"Is it something nobody's got to know about?"

"Yes, that's the sort of thing. It's frightfully, frightfully secret. I've got
to find out if something is really true or not. It's a bore about the money.
What's maddening is that I'm really quite rich. My guardian told me so.
But all they give me is a measly dress allowance. And that seems to go as
soon as I get it."

"Wouldn't your guardian—Colonel Thingummybob lend you some
money?"

"That wouldn't do at all. He'd ask a lot of questions and want to know
what I wanted it for."

"Oh dear, I suppose he would. I can't think why everybody wants to
ask so many questions. Do you know that if somebody rings me up,
Mummy has to ask *who it is?* When it really is *no* business of hers!"

Elvira agreed, but her mind was on another tack.

"Have you ever pawned anything, Bridget?"

"Never. I don't think I'd know how to."

"It's quite easy, I believe," said Elvira. "You go to the sort of jeweller
who has three balls over the door, isn't that right?"

"I don't think I've got anything that would be any good taking to a
pawnbroker," said Bridget.

"Hasn't your mother got some jewellery somewhere?"

"I don't think we'd better ask her to help."

"No, perhaps not— But we could pinch something perhaps."

"Oh, I don't think we could do that," said Bridget, shocked.

"No? Well, perhaps you're right. But I bet she wouldn't notice. We
could get it back before she missed it. I know. We'll go to Mr. Bollard."

"Who's Mr. Bollard?"

"Oh, he's a sort of family jeweller. I take my watch there always to
have it mended. He's known me ever since I was six. Come on, Bridget,
we'll go there right away. We'll just have time."

"We'd better go out the back way," said Bridget, "and then Mummy
won't ask us where we're going."

Outside the old established business of Bollard and Whitley in Bond
Street the two girls made their final arrangements.

"Are you sure you understand, Bridget?"

"I think so," said Bridget in a far from happy voice.

"First," said Elvira, "we synchronize our watches."

Bridget brightened up a little. This familiar literary phrase had a heartening effect. They solemnly synchronized their watches, Bridget adjusting hers by one minute.

"Zero hour will be twenty-five past exactly," said Elvira. "That will give me plenty of time. Perhaps even more than I need, but it's better that way about."

"But supposing—?" began Bridget.

"Supposing what?" asked Elvira.

"Well, I mean, supposing I *really* got run over?"

"Of course you won't get run over," said Elvira. "You know how nippy you are on your feet, and all London traffic is used to pulling up suddenly. It'll be all right."

Bridget looked far from convinced.

"You won't let me down, Bridget, will you?"

"All right," said Bridget, "I won't let you down."

"Good," said Elvira.

Bridget crossed to the other side of Bond Street and Elvira pushed open the doors of Messrs. Bollard and Whitley, old established jewellers and watchmakers. Inside there was a beautiful and hushed atmosphere. A frock-coated nobleman came forward and asked Elvira what he could do for her.

"Could I see Mr. Bollard?"

"Mr. Bollard. What name shall I say?"

"Miss Elvira Blake."

The nobleman disappeared and Elvira drifted to a counter where, below plate glass, brooches, rings and bracelets showed off their jewelled proportions against suitable shades of velvet. In a very few moments Mr. Bollard made his appearance. He was the senior partner of the firm, an elderly man of sixty odd. He greeted Elvira with warm friendliness.

"Ah, Miss Blake, so you are in London. It's a great pleasure to see you. Now what can I do for you?"

Elvira produced a dainty little evening wrist-watch.

"This watch doesn't go properly," said Elvira. "Could you do something to it?"

"Oh yes, of course. There's no difficulty about *that*." Mr. Bollard took it from her. "What address shall I send it to?"

Elvira gave the address.

"And there's another thing," she said. "My guardian—Colonel Luscombe you know—"

"Yes, yes of course."

"He asked me what I'd like for a Christmas present," said Elvira. "He suggested I should come in here and look at some different things. He said would I like him to come with me, and I said I'd rather come along first—because I always think it's rather embarrassing, don't you? I mean, prices and all that."

"Well, that's certainly one aspect," said Mr. Bollard, beaming in an avuncular manner. "Now what had you in mind, Miss Blake? A brooch, bracelet—a ring?"

"I think really brooches are more useful," said Elvira. "But I wonder—could I look at a *lot* of things?" She looked up at him appealingly. He smiled sympathetically.

"Of course, of course. No pleasure at all if one has to make up one's mind too quickly, is it?"

The next five or six minutes were spent very agreeably. Nothing was too much trouble for Mr. Bollard. He fetched things from one case and another, brooches and bracelets piled up on the piece of velvet spread in front of Elvira. Occasionally she turned aside to look at herself in a mirror, trying the effect of a brooch or a pendant. Finally, rather uncertainly, a pretty little bangle, a small diamond wrist-watch and two brooches were laid aside.

"We'll make a note of these," said Mr. Bollard, "and then when Colonel Luscombe is in London next, perhaps he'll come in and see what he decides himself he'd like to give you."

"I think that way will be very nice," said Elvira. "Then he'll feel more that he's chosen my present himself, won't he?" Her limpid blue gaze was raised to the jeweller's face. That same blue gaze had registered a moment earlier that the time was now exactly twenty-five minutes past the hour.

Outside there was the squealing of brakes and a girl's loud scream. Inevitably the eyes of everyone in the shop turned towards the windows of the shop giving on Bond Street. The movement of Elvira's hand on the counter in front of her and then to the pocket of her neat tailor-made coat and skirt was so rapid and unobtrusive as to be almost unnoticeable, even if anybody had been looking.

"Tcha, tcha," said Mr. Bollard, turning back from where he had been peering out into the street. "Very nearly an accident. Silly girl! Rushing across the road like that."

Elvira was already moving towards the door. She looked at her wrist-watch and uttered an exclamation.

"Oh dear, I've been far too long in here. I shall miss my train back to the country. Thank you *so* much, Mr. Bollard, and you won't forget which the four things are, will you?"

In another minute she was out of the door. Turning rapidly to the left and then to the left again, she stopped in the arcade of a shoe shop until Bridget, rather breathless, rejoined her.

"Oh," said Bridget, "I was terrified. I thought I was going to be killed. And I've torn a hole in my stocking, too."

"Never mind," said Elvira and walked her friend rapidly along the street and round yet another corner to the right. "Come on."

"Is it—was it—all right?"

Elvira's hand slipped into her pocket and out again, showing the diamond and sapphire bracelet in her palm.

"Oh, Elvira, how you dared!"

"Now, Bridget, you've got to get along to that pawnshop we marked down. Go in and see how much you can get for this. Ask for a hundred."

"Do you think—supposing they say—I mean—I mean, it might be on a list of stolen things—"

"Don't be silly. How could it be on a list so soon? They haven't even noticed it's gone yet."

"But Elvira, when they *do* notice it's gone, they'll think—perhaps they'll know—that you must have taken it."

"They *might* think so—if they discover it soon."

"Well, then they'll go to the police and—"

She stopped as Elvira shook her head slowly, her pale yellow hair swinging to and fro and a faint enigmatic smile curving up the corners of her mouth.

"They won't go to the police, Bridget. Certainly not if they think *I* took it."

"Why—you mean—?"

"As I told you, I'm going to have a lot of money when I'm twenty-one. I shall be able to buy lots of jewels from them. *They* won't make a scandal. Go on and get the money quick. Then go to Aer Lingus and book the ticket—I must take a taxi to Prunier's. I'm already ten minutes late. I'll be with you tomorrow morning by half-past ten."

"Oh Elvira, I wish you wouldn't take such frightful risks," moaned Bridget.

But Elvira had hailed a taxi.

II

Miss Marple had a very enjoyable time at Robinson & Cleaver's. Besides purchasing expensive but delicious sheets—she loved linen sheets with their texture and their coolness—she also indulged in a purchase of good quality red-bordered glass-cloths. Really the difficulty in getting proper glass-cloths nowadays! Instead, you were offered things that might as well have been ornamental table-cloths, decorated with radishes or lobsters or the *Tour Eiffel* or Trafalgar Square, or else littered with lemons and oranges. Having given her address in St. Mary Mead, Miss Marple found a convenient bus which took her to the Army & Navy Stores.

The Army & Navy Stores had been a haunt of Miss Marple's aunt in days long gone. It was not, of course, quite the same nowadays. Miss Marple cast her thoughts back to Aunt Helen seeking out her own special man in the grocery department, settling herself comfortably in a chair, wearing a bonnet and what she always called her "black poplin" mantle. Then there would ensue a long hour with nobody in a hurry and Aunt Helen thinking of every conceivable grocery that could be purchased and stored up for future use. Christmas was provided for, and there was even a far-off look towards Easter. The young Jane had fidgeted somewhat, and had been told to go and look at the glass department by way of amusement.

Having finished her purchases, Aunt Helen would then proceed to lengthy inquiries about her chosen shop-assistant's mother, wife, second boy and crippled sister-in-law. Having had a thoroughly pleasant morning, Aunt Helen would say in the playful manner of those times, "And how would a little girl feel about some luncheon?" Whereupon they went up in the lift to the fourth floor and had luncheon which always finished with a strawberry ice. After that, they bought half a pound of coffee chocolate creams and went to a matinée in a four wheeler.

Of course, the Army & Navy Stores had had a good many face lifts since those days. In fact, it was now quite unrecognizable from the old times. It was gayer and much brighter. Miss Marple, though throwing a kindly and indulgent smile at the past, did not object to the amenities of the present. There was still a restaurant, and there she repaired to order her lunch.

As she was looking carefully down the menu and deciding what to have, she looked across the room and her eyebrows went up a little. How extraordinary coincidence was! Here was a woman she had never seen till the day before, though she had seen plenty of newspaper photographs of her—at race meetings, in Bermuda, or standing by her own plane or car. Yesterday, for the first time, she had seen her in the flesh. And now, as was so often the case, there was the coincidence of running into her again in a most unlikely place. For somehow she did not connect lunch at the Army & Navy Stores with Bess Sedgwick. She would not have been surprised to see Bess Sedgwick emerging from a den in Soho, or stepping out of Covent Garden Opera House in evening dress with a diamond tiara on her head. But somehow, not in the Army & Navy Stores which in Miss Marple's mind was, and always would be, connected with the armed forces, their wives, daughters, aunts and grandmothers. Still, there Bess Sedgwick was, looking as usual very smart, in her dark suit and her emerald shirt, lunching at a table with a man. A young man with a lean hawklike face, wearing a black leather jacket. They were leaning forward talking earnestly together, forking in mouthfuls of food as though they were quite unaware what they were eating.

An assignation, perhaps? Yes, probably an assignation. The man must be fifteen or twenty years younger than she was—but Bess Sedgwick was a magnetically attractive woman.

Miss Marple looked at the young man consideringly and decided that he was what she called a "handsome fellow". She also decided that she didn't like him very much. "Just like Harry Russell," said Miss Marple to herself, dredging up a prototype as usual from the past. "Never up to any good. Never did any woman who had anything to do with him any good either."

"She wouldn't take advice from me," thought Miss Marple, "but I could give her some." However, other people's love affairs were no concern of hers, and Bess Sedgwick, by all accounts, could take care of herself very well when it came to love affairs.

Miss Marple sighed, ate her lunch, and meditated a visit to the stationery department.

Curiosity, or what she preferred herself to call "taking an interest" in other people's affairs, was undoubtedly one of Miss Marple's characteristics.

Deliberately leaving her gloves on the table, she rose and crossed the floor to the cash desk, taking a route that passed close to Lady Sedgwick's table. Having paid her bill she "discovered" the absence of her gloves and returned to get them—unfortunately dropping her handbag on the return route. It came open and spilled various oddments. A waitress rushed to assist her in picking them up, and Miss Marple was forced to show a great shakiness and dropped coppers and keys a second time.

She did not get very much by these subterfuges but they were not entirely in vain—and it was interesting that neither of the two objects of her curiosity spared as much as a glance for the dithery old lady who kept dropping things.

As Miss Marple waited for the lift down she memorized such scraps as she had heard.

"*What about the weather forecast?*"

"*OK. No fog.*"

"*All set for Lucerne?*"

"*Yes. Plane leaves 9.40.*"

That was all she had got the first time. On the way back it had lasted a little longer.

Bess Sedgwick had been speaking angrily.

"*What possessed you to come to Bertram's yesterday—you shouldn't have come near the place.*"

"*It's all right. I asked if you were staying there and everyone knows we're close friends—*"

"*That's not the point. Bertram's is all right for me— Not for you. You stick out like a sore thumb. Everyone stares at you.*"

"*Let them!*"

"*You really are an idiot. Why—why? What reasons did you have? You had a reason—I know you . . .*"

"*Calm down, Bess.*"

"*You're such a liar!*"

That was all she had been able to hear. She found it interesting.

Chapter Seven

On the evening of 19th November Canon Pennyfather had finished an early dinner at the Athenæum, he had nodded to one or two friends, had

had a pleasant acrimonious discussion on some crucial points of the dating of the Dead Sea scrolls and now, glancing at his watch, saw that it was time to leave to catch his plane to Lucerne. As he passed through the hall he was greeted by one more friend: Dr. Whittaker, of the SOAS, who said cheerfully:

"How are you, Pennyfather? Haven't seen you for a long time. How did you get on at the Congress? Any points of interest come up?"

"I am sure there will be."

"Just come back from it, haven't you?"

"No, no, I am on my way there. I'm catching a plane this evening."

"Oh I see." Whittaker looked slightly puzzled. "Somehow or other I thought the Congress was today."

"No, no. Tomorrow, the 19th."

Canon Pennyfather passed out through the door while his friend, looking after him, was just saying,

"But my dear chap, *today* is the 19th, isn't it?"

Canon Pennyfather, however, had gone beyond earshot. He picked up a taxi in Pall Mall, and was driven to the air terminal in Kensington. There was quite a fair crowd this evening. Presenting himself at the desk it at last came to his turn. He managed to produce ticket and passport and other necessities for the journey. The girl behind the desk, about to stamp these credentials, paused abruptly.

"I beg your pardon, sir, this seems to be the wrong ticket."

"The wrong ticket? No, no, that is quite right. Flight one hundred and —well, I can't really read without my glasses—one hundred and something to Lucerne."

"It's the date, sir. This is dated Wednesday the 18th."

"No, no, surely. At least—I mean—today is Wednesday the 18th."

"I'm sorry, sir. Today is the 19th."

"The 19th!" The Canon was dismayed. He fished out a small diary, turning the pages eagerly. In the end he had to be convinced. Today *was* the 19th. The plane he had meant to catch had gone yesterday.

"Then that means—that means—dear me, it means the Congress at Lucerne has taken place *today*."

He stared in deep dismay across the counter; but there were many others travelling; the Canon and his perplexities were elbowed aside. He stood sadly, holding the useless ticket in his hand. His mind ranged over various possibilities. Perhaps his ticket could be changed? But that would be no use—no indeed—what time was it now? Going on for 9 o'clock? The conference had actually taken place; starting at 10 o'clock this morning. Of course, that was what Whittaker had meant at the Athenæum. He thought Canon Pennyfather had already *been* to the Congress.

"Oh dear, oh dear," said Canon Pennyfather, to himself. *"What* a muddle I have made of it all!" He wandered sadly and silently into the Cromwell Road, not at its best a very cheerful place.

He walked slowly along the street carrying his bag and revolving perplexities in his mind. When at last he had worked out to his satisfaction the various reasons for which he had made a mistake in the day, he shook his head sadly.

"Now, I suppose," he said to himself, "I suppose—let me see, it's after nine o'clock, yes, I suppose I had better have something to eat."

It was curious, he thought, that he did not feel hungry.

Wandering disconsolately along the Cromwell Road he finally settled upon a small restaurant which served Indian curries. It seemed to him that though he was not quite as hungry as he ought to be, he had better keep his spirits up by having a meal, and after that he must find a hotel and—but no, there was no need to do *that*. He had a hotel! Of course. He was staying at Bertram's; and had reserved his room for four days. What a piece of luck! What a splendid piece of luck! So his room was there, waiting for him. He had only to ask for his key at the desk and—here another reminiscence assailed him. Something heavy in his pocket?

He dipped his hand in and brought out one of those large and solid keys with which hotels try and discourage their vaguer guests from taking them away in their pockets. It had not prevented the Canon from doing so!

"No. 19," said the Canon, in happy recognition. "That's right. It's very fortunate that I haven't got to go and find a room in a hotel. They say they're very crowded just now. Yes, Edmunds was saying so at the Athenæum this evening. He had a terrible job finding a room."

Somewhat pleased with himself and the care he had taken over his travelling arrangements by booking a hotel beforehand, the Canon abandoned his curry, remembered to pay for it, and strode out once more into the Cromwell Road.

It seemed a little tame to go home just like this when he ought to have been dining in Lucerne and talking about all sorts of interesting and fascinating problems. His eye was caught by a cinema. *Walls of Jericho*. It seemed an eminently suitable title. It would be interesting to see if biblical accuracy had been preserved.

He bought himself a seat and stumbled into the darkness. He enjoyed the film, though it seemed to him to have no relationship to the biblical story whatsoever. Even Joshua seemed to have been left out. The walls of Jericho seemed to be a symbolical way of referring to a certain lady's marriage vows. When they had tumbled down several times, the beautiful star met the dour and uncouth hero whom she had secretly loved all along and between them they proposed to build up the walls in a way that would stand the test of time better. It was not a film destined particularly to appeal to an elderly clergyman; but Canon Pennyfather enjoyed it very much. It was not the sort of film he often saw and he felt it was enlarging his knowledge of life. The film ended, the lights went up, the National Anthem was played and Canon Pennyfather stumbled out into the lights of London, slightly consoled for the sad events of earlier in the evening.

It was a fine night and he walked home to Bertram's Hotel after first getting into a bus which took him in the opposite direction. It was midnight when he got in and Bertram's Hotel at midnight usually preserved a decorous appearance of everyone having gone to bed. The lift was on a higher floor so the Canon walked up the stairs. He came to his room, inserted the key in the lock, threw the door open and entered!

Good gracious, was he seeing things? But who—how—he saw the upraised arm too late . . .

Stars exploded in a kind of Guy Fawkes' display within his head . . .

Chapter Eight

THE IRISH MAIL rushed through the night. Or, more correctly through the darkness of the early morning hours.

At intervals the diesel engine gave its weird banshee warning cry. It was travelling at well over eighty miles an hour. It was on time.

Then, with some suddenness, the pace slackened as the brakes came on. The wheels screamed as they gripped the metals. Slower . . . slower . . . The guard put his head out of the window, noting the red signal ahead as the train came to a final halt. Some of the passengers woke up. Most did not.

One elderly lady, alarmed by the suddenness of the deceleration, opened the door and looked out along the corridor. A little way along one of the doors to the line was open. An elderly cleric with a thatch of thick white hair was climbing up from the permanent way. She presumed he had previously climbed down to the line to investigate.

The morning air was distinctly chilly. Someone at the end of the corridor said: "Only a signal." The elderly lady withdrew into her compartment and tried to go to sleep again.

Farther up the line, a man waving a lantern was running towards the train from a signal box. The fireman climbed down from the engine. The guard who had descended from the train came along to join him. The man with the lantern arrived, rather short of breath, and spoke in a series of gasps.

"Bad crash ahead . . . Goods train derailed . . ."

The engine driver looked out of his cab, then climbed down also to join the others.

At the rear of the train, six men who had just climbed up the embankment boarded the train through a door left open for them in the last coach. Six passengers from different coaches met them. With well rehearsed speed, they proceeded to take charge of the postal van, isolating it from the rest of the train. Two men in Balaclava helmets at front and rear of the compartment stood on guard, coshes in hand.

A man in railway uniform went forward along the corridor of the stationary train, uttering explanations to such as demanded them.

"Block on the line ahead. Ten minutes' delay, maybe, not much more . . ." It sounded friendly and reassuring.

By the engine, the driver and the fireman lay neatly gagged and trussed up. The man with the lantern called out:

"Everything OK here."

The guard lay by the embankment, similarly gagged and tied.

The expert cracksmen in the postal van had done their work. Two more neatly trussed bodies lay on the floor. The special mailbags sailed out to where other men on the embankment awaited them.

In their compartments, passengers grumbled to each other that the railways were not what they used to be.

Then, as they settled themselves to sleep again, there came through the darkness the roar of an exhaust.

"Goodness," murmured a woman. "Is that a jet plane?"

"Racing car, I should say."

The roar died away.

On the Bedhampton Motorway, nine miles away, a steady stream of night lorries was grinding its way north. A big white racing car flashed past them.

Ten minutes later, it turned off the motorway.

The garage on the corner of the B road bore the sign CLOSED. But the big doors swung open and the white car was driven straight in, the doors closing again behind it. Three men worked at lightning speed. A fresh set of number plates were attached. The driver changed his coat and cap. He had worn white sheepskin before. Now he wore black leather. He drove out again. Three minutes after his departure, an old Morris Oxford, driven by a clergyman, chugged out on to the road and proceeded to take a route through various turning and twisting country lanes.

A station wagon, driven along a country road, slowed up as it came upon an old Morris Oxford stationary by the hedge, with an elderly man standing over it.

The driver of the station wagon put out a head.

"Having trouble? Can I help?"

"Very good of you. It's my lights."

The two drivers approached each other—listened. "All clear."

Various expensive American-style cases were transferred from the Morris Oxford to the station wagon.

A mile or two farther on, the station wagon turned off on what looked like a rough track but which presently turned out to be the back way to a large and opulent mansion. In what had been a stableyard, a big white Mercedes car was standing. The driver of the station wagon opened its boot with a key, transferred the cases to the boot, and drove away again in the station wagon.

In a near-by farmyard a cock crowed noisily.

Chapter Nine

ELVIRA BLAKE looked up at the sky, noted that it was a fine morning and went into a telephone box. She dialled Bridget's number in Onslow Square. Satisfied by the response, she said,

"Hallo? Bridget?"

"Oh Elvira, is that you?" Bridget's voice sounded agitated.

"Yes. Has everything been all right?"

"Oh no. It's been *awful*. Your cousin, Mrs. Melford, rang up Mummy yesterday afternoon."

"What, about me?"

"Yes. I thought I'd done it so well when I rang her up at lunch-time. But it seems she got worried about your teeth. Thought there might be something really wrong with them. Abscesses or something. So she rang up the dentist herself and found, of course, that you'd never been there at all. So then she rang up Mummy and unfortunately Mummy was right there by the telephone. So I couldn't get there first. And naturally Mummy said *she* didn't know anything about it, and that you certainly weren't staying *here*. I didn't know *what* to do."

"What *did* you do?"

"Pretended I knew nothing about it. I did say that I thought you'd said something about going to see some friends at Wimbledon."

"Why Wimbledon?"

"It was the first place came into my head."

Elvira sighed. "Oh well, I suppose I'll have to cook up something. An old governess, perhaps, who lives at Wimbledon. All this fussing does make things so *complicated*. I hope Cousin Mildred doesn't make a real fool of herself and ring up the police or something like that?"

"Are you going down there now?"

"Not till this evening. I've got a lot to do first."

"You got to Ireland. Was it—all right?"

"I found out what I wanted to know."

"You sound—sort of grim."

"I'm feeling grim."

"Can't I help you, Elvira? Do anything?"

"Nobody can help me really . . . It's a thing I have to do myself. I hoped something wasn't true, but it *is* true. I don't know quite what to do about it."

"Are you in danger, Elvira?"

"Don't be melodramatic, Bridget. I'll have to be careful that's all. I'll have to be very careful."

"Then you *are* in danger."

Elvira said after a moment's pause, "I expect I'm just imagining things, that's all."

"Elvira, what are you going to do about that bracelet?"

"Oh, that's all right. I've arranged to get some money from someone, so I can go and—what's the word?—redeem it. Then just take it back to Bollards."

"D'you think they'll be all right about it?—No, Mummy, it's just the laundry. They say we never sent that sheet. Yes, Mummy, yes, I'll tell the manageress. All right then."

At the other end of the line Elvira grinned and put down the receiver. She opened her purse, sorted through her money, counted out the coins she needed and arranged them in front of her and proceeded to put through a call. When she got the number she wanted she put in the necessary coins, pressed Button A and spoke in a small rather breathless voice.

"Hallo, Cousin Mildred. Yes, it's me . . . I'm terribly sorry . . . Yes, I know . . . well I was going to . . . yes it was dear old Maddy, you know our old Mademoiselle . . . yes I wrote a postcard, then I forgot to post it. It's still in my pocket now . . . well, you see she was ill and there was no one to look after her and so I just stopped to see she was all right. Yes, I *was* going to Bridget's but this changed things . . . I don't understand about the message you got. Someone must have jumbled it up . . . Yes, I'll explain it all to you when I get back . . . yes, this afternoon. No, I shall just wait and see the nurse who's coming to look after old Maddy— well, not really a nurse. You know one of those—er—practical aid nurses or something like that. No, she would hate to go to hospital . . . But I *am* sorry, Cousin Mildred, I really am very, very sorry." She put down the receiver and sighed in an exasperated manner. "If only," she murmured to herself, "one didn't have to tell so many lies to everybody."

She came out of the telephone box, noting as she did so the big newspaper placards—BIG TRAIN ROBBERY. IRISH MAIL ATTACKED BY BANDITS.

II

Mr. Bollard was serving a customer when the shop door opened. He looked up to see the Honourable Elvira Blake entering.

"No," she said to an assistant who came forward to her. "I'd rather wait until Mr. Bollard is free."

Presently Mr. Bollard's customer's business was concluded and Elvira moved into the vacant place.

"Good morning, Mr. Bollard," she said.

"I'm afraid your watch isn't done quite as soon as this, Miss Elvira," said Mr. Bollard.

"Oh, it's not the watch," said Elvira. "I've come to apologize. A dreadful thing happened." She opened her bag and took out a small box. From it she extracted the sapphire and diamond bracelet. "You will remember when I came in with my watch to be repaired that I was looking at things for a Christmas present and there was an accident outside in the street. Somebody was run over I think, or nearly run over. I suppose I must have had the bracelet in my hand and put it into the pocket of my suit without thinking, although I only found it this morning. So I rushed along *at once* to bring it back. I'm so terribly sorry, Mr. Bollard, I don't know how I came to do such an idiotic thing."

"Why, that's quite all right, Miss Elvira," said Mr. Bollard, slowly.

"I suppose you thought someone had stolen it," said Elvira.

Her limpid blue eyes met his.

"We *had* discovered its loss," said Mr. Bollard. "Thank you very much, Miss Elvira, for bringing it back so promptly."

"I felt simply awful about it when I found it," said Elvira. "Well, thank you very much, Mr. Bollard, for being so nice about it."

"A lot of strange mistakes do occur," said Mr. Bollard. He smiled at her in an avuncular manner. "We won't think of it any more. But don't do it again, though." He laughed with the air of one making a genial little joke.

"Oh no," said Elvira, "I shall be terribly careful in future."

She smiled at him, turned and left the shop.

"Now I wonder," said Mr. Bollard to himself, "I really do wonder . . ."

One of his partners, who had been standing near, moved nearer to him.

"So she *did* take it?" he said.

"Yes. She took it all right," said Mr. Bollard.

"But she brought it back," his partner pointed out.

"She brought it back," agreed Mr. Bollard. "I didn't actually expect that."

"You mean you didn't expect her to bring it back?"

"No, not if it was she who'd taken it."

"Do you think her story is true?" his partner inquired curiously. "I mean, that she slipped it into her pocket by accident?"

"I suppose it's possible," said Bollard, thoughtfully.

"Or it *could* be kleptomania, I suppose."

"Or it could be kleptomania," agreed Bollard. "It's more likely that she took it on purpose . . . But if so, why did she bring it back so soon? It's curious—"

"Just as well we didn't notify the police. I admit *I* wanted to."

"I know, I know. You haven't got as much experience as I have. In this case, it was definitely better not." He added softly to himself, "The thing's interesting, though. Quite interesting. I wonder how old she is? Seventeen or eighteen I suppose. She might have got herself in a jam of some kind."

"I thought you said she was rolling in money."

"You may be an heiress and rolling in money," said Bollard, "but at seventeen you can't always get your hands on it. The funny thing is, you know, they keep heiresses much shorter of cash than they keep the more impecunious. It's not always a good idea. Well, I don't suppose we shall ever know the truth of it."

He put the bracelet back in its place in the display case and shut down the lid.

Chapter Ten

THE OFFICES of Egerton, Forbes & Willborough were in Bloomsbury, in one of those imposing and dignified squares which have as yet not felt the wind of change. Their brass plate was suitably worn down to illegibility. The firm had been going for over a hundred years and a good proportion of the landed gentry of England were their clients. There was no Forbes in the firm any more and no Willborough. Instead there were Atkinsons, father and son, and a Welsh Lloyd and a Scottish MacAllister. There was, however, still an Egerton, descendant of the original Egerton. This particular Egerton was a man of fifty-two and he was adviser to several families which had in their day been advised by his grandfather, his uncle, and his father.

At this moment he was sitting behind a large mahogany desk in his handsome room on the first floor, speaking kindly but firmly to a dejected looking client. Richard Egerton was a handsome man, tall, dark with a touch of grey at the temples and very shrewd grey eyes. His advice was always good advice, but he seldom minced his words.

"Quite frankly you haven't got a leg to stand upon, Freddie," he was saying. "Not with those letters you've written."

"You don't think—" Freddie murmured dejectedly.

"No, I don't," said Egerton. "The only hope is to settle out of court. It

might even be held that you've rendered yourself liable to criminal prosecution."

"Oh look here, Richard, that's carrying things a bit far."

There was a small discreet buzz on Egerton's desk. He picked up the
telephone receiver with a frown.

"I thought I said I wasn't to be disturbed."

There was a murmur at the other end. Egerton said, "Oh. Yes— Yes, I
see. Ask her to wait, will you."

He replaced the receiver and turned once more to his unhappy looking
client.

"Look here, Freddie," he said, "I know the law and you don't. You're in
a nasty jam. I'll do my best to get you out of it, but it's going to cost you a
bit. I doubt if they'd settle for less than twelve thousand."

"Twelve thousand!" The unfortunate Freddie was aghast. "Oh, I say! I
haven't got it, Richard."

"Well, you'll have to raise it then. There are always ways and means. If
she'll settle for twelve thousand, you'll be lucky, and if you fight the case
it'll cost you a lot more."

"You lawyers!" said Freddie. "Sharks, all of you!"

He rose to his feet. "Well," he said, "do your bloody best for me, Richard old boy."

He took his departure, shaking his head sadly. Richard Egerton put
Freddie and his affairs out of his mind, and thought about his next client.
He said softly to himself, "The Honourable Elvira Blake. I wonder what
she's like . . ." He lifted the receiver. "Lord Frederick's gone. Send up
Miss Blake, will you."

As he waited he made little calculations on his desk pad. How many
years since—? She must be fifteen—seventeen—perhaps even more than
that. Time went so fast. "Coniston's daughter," he thought, "and Bess's
daughter. I wonder which of them she takes after?"

The door opened, the clerk announced Miss Elvira Blake and the girl
walked into the room. Egerton rose from his chair and came towards her.
In appearance, he thought, she did not resemble either of her parents.
Tall, slim, very fair, Bess's colouring but none of Bess's vitality, with an
old-fashioned air about her; though that was difficult to be sure of, since
the fashion in dress happened at the moment to be ruffles and baby
bodices.

"Well, well," he said, as he shook hands with her. "This is a surprise.
Last time I saw you, you were eleven years old. Come and sit here." He
pulled forward a chair and she sat down.

"I suppose," said Elvira, a little uncertainly, "that I ought to have written first. Written and made an appointment. Something like that, but I really made up my mind very suddenly and it seemed an opportunity, since I was in London."

"And what are you doing in London?"

"Having my teeth seen to."

"Beastly things, teeth," said Egerton. "Give us trouble from the cradle to the grave. But I am grateful for the teeth, if it gives me an opportunity of seeing you. Let me see now; you've been in Italy, haven't you, finishing your education there at one of these places all girls go to nowadays?"

"Yes," said Elvira, "the Contessa Martinelli. But I've left there now for good. I'm living with the Melfords in Kent until I make up my mind if there's anything I'd like to do."

"Well, I hope you'll find something satisfactory. You're not thinking of a university or anything like that?"

"No," said Elvira, "I don't think I'd be clever enough for that." She paused before saying, "I suppose *you*'d have to agree to anything if I did want to do it?"

Egerton's keen eyes focused sharply.

"I am one of your guardians, and a trustee under your father's will, yes," he said. "Therefore, you have a perfect right to approach me at any time."

Elvira said "Thank you" politely. Egerton asked:

"Is there anything worrying you?"

"No. Not really. But you see, I don't *know* anything. Nobody's ever told me things. One doesn't always like to ask."

He looked at her attentively.

"You mean things about yourself?"

"Yes," said Elvira. "It's kind of you to understand. Uncle Derek—" she hesitated.

"Derek Luscombe, you mean?"

"Yes. I've always called him uncle."

"I see."

"He's very kind," said Elvira, "but he's not the sort of person who ever tells you anything. He just arranges things, and looks a little worried in case they mightn't be what I'd like. Of course he listens to a lot of people —women, I mean—who tell him things. Like Contessa Martinelli. He arranges for me to go to schools or to finishing places."

"And they haven't been where you wanted to go?"

"No, I didn't mean that. They've been quite all right. I mean they've been more or less where everyone else goes."

"I see."

"But I don't know anything about *myself*. I mean what money I've got, and how much, and what I could do with it if I wanted."

"In fact," said Egerton, with his attractive smile, "you want to talk business. Is that it? Well, I think you're quite right. Let's see. How old are you? Sixteen—seventeen?"

"I'm nearly twenty."

"Oh dear. I'd no idea."

"You see," explained Elvira, "I feel all the time that I'm being shielded and sheltered. It's nice in a way, but it can get very irritating."

"It's an attitude that's gone out of date," agreed Egerton, "but I can quite see that it would appeal to Derek Luscombe."

"He's a dear," said Elvira, "but very difficult, somehow, to talk to seriously."

"Yes, I can see that that might be so. Well, how much *do* you know about yourself, Elvira? About your family circumstances?"

"I know that my father died when I was five and that my mother had run away from him with someone when I was about two, I don't remember her at all. I barely remember my father. He was very old and had his leg up on a chair. He used to swear. I was rather scared of him. After he died I lived first with an aunt or a cousin or something of my father's, until *she* died, and then I lived with Uncle Derek and his sister. But then she died and I went to Italy. Uncle Derek has arranged for me, now, to live with the Melfords, who are his cousins, and very kind and nice and have two daughters about my age."

"You're happy there?"

"I don't know yet. I've barely got there. They're all very dull. I really wanted to know how much money I've got."

"So it's financial information you really want?"

"Yes," said Elvira. "I've got *some* money, I know. Is it a lot?"

Egerton was serious now.

"Yes," he said. "You've got a lot of money. Your father was a very rich man. You were his only child. When he died, the title and the estate went to a cousin. He didn't like the cousin, so he left all his personal property, which was considerable, to his daughter—to you, Elvira. You're a very rich woman, or will be, when you are twenty-one."

"You mean I am not rich *now*?"

"Yes," said Egerton, "you're rich now, but the money is not yours to dispose of until you are twenty-one or marry. Until that time it is in the hands of your trustees. Luscombe, myself and another." He smiled at her. "We haven't embezzled it or anything like that. It's still there. In fact, we've increased your capital considerably by investments."

"How much will I have?"

"At the age of twenty-one or upon your marriage, you will come into a sum which at a rough estimate would amount to six or seven hundred thousand pounds."

"That *is* a lot," said Elvira, impressed.

"Yes, it is a lot. Probably it is because it is such a lot that nobody has ever talked to you about it much."

He watched her as she reflected upon this. Quite an interesting girl, he thought. Looked an unbelievably milk-and-water Miss, but she was more than that. A good deal more. He said, with a faintly ironic smile:

"Does that satisfy you?"

She gave him a sudden smile.

"It ought to, oughtn't it?"

"Rather better than winning the pools," he suggested.

She nodded, but her mind was elsewhere. Then she came out abruptly with a question.

"Who gets it if I die?"

"As things stand now, it would go to your next of kin."

"I mean—I couldn't make a will now, could I? Not until I was twenty-one. That's what someone told me."

"They were quite right."

"That's really rather annoying. If I was married and died I suppose my husband would get the money?"

"Yes."

"And if I wasn't married my mother would be my next of kin and get it. I really seem to have very few relations—I don't even know my mother. What is she like?"

"She's a very remarkable woman," said Egerton shortly. "Everybody would agree to that."

"Didn't she ever *want* to see me?"

"She may have done . . . I think it's very possible that she did. But having made—in certain ways—rather a mess of her own life, she may have thought that it was better for you that you should be brought up quite apart from her."

"Do you actually *know* that she thinks that?"

"No. I don't really know anything about it."

Elvira got up.

"Thank you," she said. "It's very kind of you to tell me all this."

"I think perhaps you ought to have been told more about things before," said Egerton.

"It's rather humiliating *not* to know things," said Elvira. "Uncle Derek, of course, thinks I'm just a *child*."

"Well, he's not a very young man himself. He and I, you know, are well advanced in years. You must make allowances for us when we look at things from the point of view of our advanced age."

Elvira stood looking at him for a moment or two.

"But *you* don't think I'm really a child, do you?" she said shrewdly, and added, "I expect you know rather more about girls than Uncle Derek does. He just lived with his sister." Then she stretched out her hand and said, very prettily, "Thank you so much. I hope I haven't interrupted some important work you had to do," and went out.

Egerton stood looking at the door that had closed behind her. He pursed up his lips, whistled a moment, shook his head and sat down again, picked up a pen and tapped thoughtfully on his desk. He drew some papers towards him, then thrust them back and picked up his telephone.

"Miss Cordell, get me Colonel Luscombe, will you? Try his club first. And then the Shropshire address."

He put back the receiver. Again he drew his papers towards him and started reading them but his mind was not on what he was doing. Presently his buzzer went.

"Colonel Luscombe is on the wire now, Mr. Egerton."

"Right. Put him through. Hallo, Derek. Richard Egerton here. How are you? I've just been having a visit from someone you know. A visit from your ward."

"From Elvira?" Derek Luscombe sounded very surprised.

"Yes."

"But why—what on earth—what did she come to you for? Not in any trouble?"

"No, I wouldn't say so. On the contrary, she seemed rather—well, pleased with herself. She wanted to know all about her financial position."

"You didn't tell her, I hope?" said Colonel Luscombe, in alarm.

"Why not? What's the point of secrecy?"

"Well, I can't help feeling it's a little unwise for a girl to know that she is going to come into such a large amount of money."

"Somebody else will tell her that, if we don't. She's got to be prepared, you know. Money is a responsibility."

"Yes, but she's so much of a child still."

"Are you sure of that?"

"What do you mean? Of course she's a child."

"I wouldn't describe her as such. Who's the boy-friend?"

"I beg your pardon."

"I said who's the boy-friend? There *is* a boy-friend in the offing, isn't there?"

"No, indeed. Nothing of the sort. What on earth makes you think that?"

"Nothing that she actually said. But I've got some experience, you know. I think you'll find there *is* a boy-friend."

"Well, I can assure you you're quite wrong. I mean, she's been most carefully brought up, she's been at very strict schools, she's been in a very select finishing establishment in Italy. I should know if there was anything of that kind going on. I dare say she's met one or two pleasant young fellows and all that, but I'm sure there's been nothing of the kind you suggest."

"Well, my diagnosis is a boy-friend—and probably an undesirable one."

"But why, Richard, why? What do *you* know about young girls?"

"Quite a lot," said Egerton dryly. "I've had three clients in the last year, two of whom were made wards of court and the third one managed to bully her parents into agreeing to an almost certainly disastrous marriage. Girls don't get looked after the way they used to be. Conditions are such that it's very difficult to look after them at all—"

"But I assure you Elvira has been most carefully looked after."

"The ingenuity of the young female of the species is beyond anything you could conjecture! You keep an eye on her, Derek. Make a few inquiries as to what she's been up to."

"Nonsense. She's just a sweet simple girl."

"What you don't know about sweet simple girls would fill an album! Her mother ran away and caused a scandal—remember?—when she was younger than Elvira is today. As for old Coniston, he was one of the worst rips in England."

"You upset me, Richard. You upset me very much."

"You might as well be warned. What I didn't quite like was one of her other questions. Why is she so anxious to know who'd inherit her money if she dies?"

"It's queer your saying that, because she asked me that same question."

"Did she now? Why should her mind run on early death? She asked me about her mother, by the way."

Colonel Luscombe's voice sounded worried as he said: "I wish Bess would get in touch with the girl."

"Have you been talking to her on the subject—to Bess, I mean?"

"Well, yes . . . Yes I did. I ran across her by chance. We were staying in the same hotel, as a matter of fact. I urged Bess to make some arrangements to see the girl."

"What did she say?" asked Egerton curiously.

"Refused point blank. She more or less said that she wasn't a safe person for the girl to know."

"Looked at from one point of view I don't suppose she is," said Egerton. "She's mixed up with that racing fellow, isn't she?"

"I've heard rumours."

"Yes, I've heard them too. I don't know if there's much in it really. There might be, I suppose. That could be why she feels as she does. Bess's friends are strong meat from time to time! But what a woman she is, eh Derek? What a woman."

"Always been her own worst enemy," said Derek Luscombe, gruffly.

"A really nice conventional remark," said Egerton. "Well, sorry I bothered you, Derek, but keep a look-out for undesirables in the background. Don't say you haven't been warned."

He replaced the receiver and drew the pages on his desk towards him once more. This time he was able to put his whole attention on what he was doing.

Chapter Eleven

Mrs. McCrae, Canon Pennyfather's housekeeper, had ordered a Dover sole for the evening of his return. The advantages attached to a good Dover sole were manifold. It need not be introduced to the grill or frying pan until the Canon was safely in the house. It could be kept until the next day if necessary. Canon Pennyfather was fond of Dover sole; and, if a telephone call or telegram arrived saying that the Canon would after all be elsewhere on this particular evening, Mrs. McCrae was fond of a good Dover sole herself. All therefore was in good trim for the Canon's return. The Dover sole would be followed by pancakes. The sole sat on the kitchen table, the batter for the pancakes was ready in a bowl. All was in readiness. The brass shone, the silver sparkled, not a minuscule of dust showed anywhere. There was only one thing lacking. The Canon himself.

The Canon was scheduled to return on the train arriving at 6.30 from London.

At 7 o'clock he had not returned. No doubt the train was late. At 7.30 he still had not returned. Mrs. McCrae gave a sigh of vexation. She suspected that this was going to be another of these things. Eight o'clock came and no Canon. Mrs. McCrae gave a long, exasperated sigh. Soon, no doubt, she would get a telephone call, though it was quite within the bounds of possibility that there would not be even a telephone call. He might have written to her. No doubt he had written, but he had probably omitted to post the letter.

"Dear, dear!" said Mrs. McCrae.

At 9 o'clock she made herself three pancakes with the pancake batter. The sole she put carefully away in the Frigidaire. "I wonder where the good man's got to now," she said to herself. She knew by experience that he might be anywhere. The odds were that he would discover his mistake in time to telegraph her or telephone her before she retired to bed. "I shall sit up until 11 o'clock but no longer," said Mrs. McCrae. Ten-thirty was her bed-time, and extension to eleven she considered her duty, but if at eleven there was nothing, no word from the Canon, then Mrs. McCrae would duly lock up the house and betake herself to bed.

It cannot be said that she was worried. This sort of thing had happened before. There was nothing to be done but wait for news of some kind. The possibilities were numerous. Canon Pennyfather might have got on the wrong train and failed to discover his mistake until he was at Land's End or John o' Groats, or he might still be in London having made some mistake in the date, and was therefore convinced he was not returning until tomorrow. He might have met a friend or friends at this foreign conference he was going to and been induced to stay out there perhaps over the weekend. He would have meant to let her know but had entirely forgotten to do so. So, as has been already said, she was not worried. The day after tomorrow his old friend, Archdeacon Simmons, was coming to stay. That was the sort of thing the Canon *did* remember, so no doubt he himself or a telegram from him would arrive tomorrow and at latest he would be home on the day after, or there would be a letter.

The morning of the day after, however, arrived without a word from him. For the first time Mrs. McCrae began to be uneasy. Between 9 a.m. and 1 p.m. she eyed the telephone in a doubtful manner. Mrs. McCrae had her own fixed views about the telephone. She used it and recognized its convenience but she was not fond of the telephone. Some of her household shopping was done by telephone, though she much preferred to do it in person owing to a fixed belief that if you did not see what you were being given, a shopkeeper was sure to try and cheat you. Still, telephones were useful for domestic matters. She occasionally, though rarely, telephoned her friends or relations in the near neighbourhood. To make a call of any distance, or a London call, upset her severely. It was a shameful waste of money. Nevertheless, she began to meditate facing that problem.

Finally, when yet another day dawned without any news of him she decided to act. She knew where the Canon was staying in London. Bertram's Hotel. A nice old-fashioned place. It might be as well, perhaps, if she rang up and made certain inquiries. They would probably know where the Canon was. It was not an ordinary hotel. She would ask to be put through to Miss Gorringe. Miss Gorringe was always efficient and thoughtful. The Canon might, of course, return by the twelve-thirty. If so he would be here any minute now.

But the minutes passed and there was no Canon. Mrs. McCrae took a deep breath, nerved herself and asked for a call to London. She waited, biting her lips and holding the receiver clamped firmly to her ear.

"Bertram's Hotel, at your service," said a voice.

"I would like, if you please, to speak to Miss Gorringe," said Mrs. McCrae.

"Just a moment. What name shall I say?"

"It's Canon Pennyfather's housekeeper. Mrs. McCrae."

"Just a moment please."

Presently the calm and efficient voice of Miss Gorringe came through.

"Miss Gorringe here. Did you say Canon Pennyfather's housekeeper?"

"That's right. Mrs. McCrae."

"Oh yes. Of course. What can I do for you, Mrs. McCrae?"

"Is Canon Pennyfather staying at the hotel still?"

"I'm glad you've rung up," said Miss Gorringe. "We have been rather worried as to what exactly to do."

"Do you mean something's happened to Canon Pennyfather? Has he had an accident?"

"No, no, nothing of that kind. But we expected him back from Lucerne on Friday or Saturday."

"Eh—that'd be right."

"But he didn't arrive. Well, of course that wasn't really surprising. He had booked his room on—booked it, that is, until yesterday. He didn't come back yesterday or send any word and his things are still here. The major part of his baggage. We hadn't been quite sure what to do about it. Of course," Miss Gorringe went on hastily, "we know the Canon is, well—somewhat forgetful sometimes."

"You may well say that!"

"It makes it a little difficult for us. We are so fully booked up. His room is actually booked for another guest." She added: "You have no idea where he is?"

With bitterness Mrs. McCrae said,

"The man might be anywhere!" She pulled herself together. "Well, thank you, Miss Gorringe."

"Anything I can do—" Miss Gorringe suggested helpfully.

"I dare say I'll hear soon enough," said Mrs. McCrae. She thanked Miss Gorringe again and rang off.

She sat by the telephone, looking upset. She did not fear for the Canon's personal safety. If he had an accident she would by now have been notified. She felt sure of that. On the whole the Canon was not what one would call accident prone. He was what Mrs. McCrae called to herself "one of the scatty ones", and the scatty ones seemed always to be looked after by a special providence. Whilst taking no care or thought, they could still survive even a Panda crossing. No, she did not visualize Canon Pennyfather as lying groaning in a hospital. He was *somewhere*, no doubt innocently and happily prattling with some friend or other. Maybe he was abroad still. The difficulty was that Archdeacon Simmons would expect to find a host to receive him. She couldn't put Archdeacon Simmons off because she didn't know where he was. It was all very difficult, but it had, like most difficulties, its bright spot. Its bright spot was Archdeacon Simmons. Archdeacon Simmons would know what to do. She would place the matter in his hands.

Archdeacon Simmons was a complete contrast to her employer. He knew where he was going, and what he was doing, and was always cheerfully sure of knowing the right thing to be done and doing it. A confident cleric. Archdeacon Simmons, when he arrived, to be met by Mrs. McCrae's explanations, apologies and perturbation, was a tower of strength. He, too, was not alarmed.

"Now don't you worry, Mrs. McCrae," he said in his genial fashion, as he sat down to the meal she had prepared for his arrival. "We'll hunt the absent-minded fellow down. Ever heard that story about Chesterton? G. K. Chesterton, you know, the writer. Wired to his wife when he'd gone on a lecture tour 'Am at Crewe Station. Where ought I to be?'"

He laughed. Mrs. McCrae smiled dutifully. She did not think it was very funny because it was so exactly the sort of thing that Canon Penny-father might have done.

"Ah," said Archdeacon Simmons, with appreciation, "one of your excellent veal cutlets! You're a marvellous cook, Mrs. McCrae. I hope my old friend appreciates you."

Veal cutlets having been succeeded by some small castle puddings with a blackberry sauce which Mrs. McCrae had remembered was one of the Archdeacon's favourite sweets, the good man applied himself in earnest to the tracking down of his missing friend. He addressed himself to the telephone with vigour and a complete disregard for expense, which made Mrs. McCrae purse her lips anxiously, although not really disapproving, because definitely her master had got to be tracked down.

Having first dutifully tried the Canon's sister who took little notice of her brother's goings and comings and as usual had not the faintest idea where he was or might be, the Archdeacon spread his net farther afield. He addressed himself once more to Bertram's Hotel and got details as precisely as possible. The Canon had definitely left there on the early evening of the 19th. He had with him a small BEA handbag, but his other luggage had remained behind in his room, which he had duly retained. He had mentioned that he was going to a conference of some kind at Lucerne. He had not gone direct to the airport from the hotel. The commissionaire, who knew him well by sight, had put him into a taxi and had directed it, as told by the Canon, to the Athenæum Club. That was the last time that anyone at Bertram's Hotel had seen Canon Pennyfather. Oh yes, a small detail—he had omitted to leave his key behind but had taken it with him. It was not the first time that that had happened.

Archdeacon Simmons paused for a few minutes' consideration before the next call. He could ring up the air station in London. That would no doubt take some time. There might be a short cut. He rang up Dr. Weiss-garten, a learned Hebrew scholar who was almost certain to have been at the conference.

Dr. Weissgarten was at his home. As soon as he heard who was speaking to him he launched out into a torrent of verbiage consisting mostly of disparaging criticism of two papers that had been read at the conference in Lucerne.

"Most unsound, that fellow Hogarov," he said, "most unsound. How he gets away with it I don't know! Fellow isn't a scholar at all. Do you know what he actually said?"

The Archdeacon sighed and had to be firm with him. Otherwise there was a good chance that the rest of the evening would be spent in listening to criticism of fellow scholars at the Lucerne Conference. With some reluctance Dr. Weissgarten was pinned down to more personal matters.

"Pennyfather?" he said, "Pennyfather? He ought to have been there. Can't think why he wasn't there. Said he was going. Told me so only a week before when I saw him in the Athenæum."

"You mean he wasn't at the conference at all?"

"That's what I've just said. He *ought* to have been there."

"Do you know *why* he wasn't there? Did he send an excuse?"

"How should I know? He certainly talked about being there. Yes, now I remember. He was expected. Several people remarked on his absence. Thought he might have had a chill or something. Very treacherous weather." He was about to revert to his criticisms of his fellow scholars but Archdeacon Simmons rang off.

He had got a fact but it was a fact that for the first time awoke in him an uneasy feeling. Canon Pennyfather had not been at the Lucerne Conference. He had meant to go to that conference. It seemed very extraordinary to the Archdeacon that he had not been there. He might, of course, have taken the wrong plane, though on the whole BEA were pretty careful of you and shepherded you away from such possibilities. Could Canon Pennyfather have forgotten the actual day that he was going to the conference? It was always possible, he supposed. But if so where had he gone instead?

He addressed himself now to the air terminal. It involved a great deal of patient waiting and being transferred from department to department. In the end he got a definite fact. Canon Pennyfather had booked as a passenger on the 21.40 plane to Lucerne on the 18th but he had not been on the plane.

"We're getting on," said Archdeacon Simmons to Mrs. McCrae, who was hovering in the background. "Now, let me see. Who shall I try next?"

"All this telephoning will cost a fearful lot of money," said Mrs. McCrae.

"I'm afraid so. I'm afraid so," said Archdeacon Simmons. "But we've got to get on his track, you know. He's not a very young man."

"Oh, sir, you don't think there's anything could really have happened to him?"

"Well I hope not . . . I don't think so, because I think you'd have heard if so. He—er—always had his name and address on him, didn't he?"

"Oh yes, sir, he had cards on him. He'd have letters too, and all sorts of things in his wallet."

"Well, I don't think he's in a hospital then," said the Archdeacon. "Let me see. When he left the hotel he took a taxi to the Athenæum. I'll ring them up next."

Here he got some definite information. Canon Pennyfather, who was well known there, had dined there at seven-thirty on the evening of the 19th. It was then that the Archdeacon was struck by something he had overlooked until then. The aeroplane ticket had been for the 18th but the Canon had left Bertram's Hotel by taxi to the Athenæum, having mentioned he was going to the Lucerne Conference, on the 19th. Light began to break. "Silly old ass," thought Archdeacon Simmons to himself, but careful not to say it aloud in front of Mrs. McCrae. "Got his dates wrong. The conference was on the 19th. I'm sure of it. He must have thought that he was leaving on the 18th. He was one day wrong."

He went over the next bit carefully. The Canon would have gone to the Athenæum, he would have dined, he would have gone on to Kensington Air Station. There, no doubt, it would have been pointed out to him that his ticket was for the day before and he would then have realized that the conference he was going to attend was now over.

"That's what happened," said Archdeacon Simmons, "depend upon it." He explained it to Mrs. McCrae, who agreed that it was likely enough. "Then what would he do?"

"Go back to his hotel," said Mrs. McCrae.

"He wouldn't have come straight down here—gone straight to the station, I mean."

"Not if his luggage was at the hotel. At any rate, he would have called there for his luggage."

"True enough," said Simmons. "All right. We'll think of it like this. He left the airport with his little bag and he went back to the hotel, or started for the hotel at all events. He might have had dinner perhaps—no, he'd dined at the Athenæum. All right, he went back to the hotel. *But* he never arrived there." He paused a moment or two and then said doubtfully, "Or did he? Nobody seems to have seen him there. So what happened to him on the way?"

"He could have met someone," said Mrs. McCrae, doubtfully.

"Yes. Of course that's perfectly possible. Some old friend he hadn't seen for a long time . . . He could have gone off with a friend to the friend's hotel or the friend's house, but he wouldn't have stayed there three days, would he? He wouldn't have forgotten for three whole days that his luggage was at the hotel. He'd have rung up about it, he'd have called for it, or in a supreme fit of absent-mindedness he might have come straight home. Three days' silence. That's what's so inexplicable."

"If he had an accident—"

"Yes, Mrs. McCrae, of course that's possible. We can try the hospitals. You say he had plenty of papers on him to identify him? Hm—I think there's only one thing for it."

Mrs. McCrae looked at him apprehensively.

"I think, you know," said the Archdeacon gently, "that we've got to go to the police."

Chapter Twelve

MISS MARPLE had found no difficulty in enjoying her stay in London. She did a lot of the things that she had not had the time to do in her hitherto brief visits to the capital. It has to be regretfully noted that she did not avail herself of the wide cultural activities that would have been possible to her. She visited no picture galleries and no museums. The idea of patronizing a dress show of any kind would not even have occurred to her. What she did visit were the glass and china departments of the large stores, and the household linen departments, and she also availed herself of some marked down lines in furnishing fabrics. Having spent what she considered a reasonable sum upon these household investments, she indulged in various excursions of her own. She went to places and shops she remembered from her young days, sometimes merely with the curiosity of seeing whether they were still there. It was not a pursuit that she had ever had time for before, and she enjoyed it very much. After a nice little nap after lunch, she would go out, and, avoiding the attentions of the commissionaire if possible, because he was so firmly imbued with the idea that a lady of her age and frailty should always go in a taxi, she walked towards a bus stop, or tube station. She had bought a small guide to buses and their routes—and an Underground Transport Map; and she would plan her excursion carefully. One afternoon she could be seen walking happily and nostalgically round Evelyn Gardens or Onslow Square murmuring softly, "Yes, that was Mrs. Van Dylan's house. Of course it looks *quite* different now. They seem to have remodelled it. Dear me, I see it's got four bells. Four flats, I suppose. Such a nice old-fashioned square this always was."

Rather shamefacedly she paid a visit to Madame Tussaud's, a well-remembered delight of her childhood. In Westbourne Grove she looked in vain for Bradley's. Aunt Helen had always gone to Bradley's about her sealskin jacket.

Window shopping in the general sense did not interest Miss Marple, but she had a splendid time rounding up knitting patterns, new varieties of knitting wool, and such-like delights. She made a special expedition to Richmond to see the house that had been occupied by Great-Uncle Thomas, the retired admiral. The handsome terrace was still there but here again each house seemed to be turned into flats. Much more painful was the house in Lowndes Square where a distant cousin, Lady Marridew, had lived in some style. Here a vast skyscraper building of modernistic design appeared to have arisen. Miss Marple shook her head sadly and said firmly to herself, "There must *be* progress I suppose. If Cousin Ethel knew, she'd turn in her grave, I'm sure."

It was on one particularly mild and pleasant afternoon that Miss Marple embarked on a bus that took her over Battersea Bridge. She was going to combine the double pleasure of taking a sentimental look at Princes Terrace Mansions where an old governess of hers had once lived, and visiting Battersea Park. The first part of her quest was abortive. Miss Ledbury's former home had vanished without trace and had been replaced by a great deal of gleaming concrete. Miss Marple turned into Battersea Park. She had always been a good walker but had to admit that nowadays her walking powers were not what they were. Half a mile was quite enough to tire her. She could manage, she thought, to cross the Park and go out over Chelsea Bridge and find herself once more on a convenient bus route, but her steps grew gradually slower and slower, and she was pleased to come upon a tea enclosure situated on the edge of the lake.

Teas were still being served there in spite of the autumn chill. There were not many people today, a certain amount of mothers and prams, and a few pairs of young lovers. Miss Marple collected a tray with tea and two sponge cakes. She carried her tray carefully to a table and sat down. The tea was just what she needed. Hot, strong and very reviving. Revived, she looked round her, and her eyes stopping suddenly at a particular table, she sat up very straight in her chair. Really, a very strange coincidence, very strange indeed! First the Army & Navy Stores and now here. Very unusual places those particular two people chose! But no! She was wrong. Miss Marple took a second and stronger pair of glasses from her bag. Yes, she had been mistaken. There was a certain similarity, of course. That long straight blonde hair; but this was not Bess Sedgwick. It was someone years younger. Of course! It was the daughter! The young girl who had come into Bertram's with Lady Selina Hazy's friend, Colonel Luscombe. But the man was the same man who had been lunching with Lady Sedgwick in the Army & Navy Stores. No doubt about it, the same handsome, hawk-like look, the same leanness, the same predatory toughness and—yes, the same strong virile attraction.

"Bad!" said Miss Marple. "Bad all through! Cruel! Unscrupulous. I don't *like* seeing this. First the mother, now the daughter. What does it mean?"

It meant no good. Miss Marple was sure of that. Miss Marple seldom gave anyone the benefit of the doubt; she invariably thought the worst, and nine times out of ten, so she insisted, she was right in so doing. Both these meetings, she was sure, were more or less secret meetings. She observed now the way these two bent forward over the table until their heads nearly touched; and the earnestness with which they talked. The girl's face—Miss Marple took off her spectacles, rubbed the lenses carefully, then put them on again. Yes, this girl was in love. Desperately in love, as only the young can be in love. But what were her guardians about to let her run about London and have these clandestine assignments in Battersea Park? A nicely brought up, well-behaved girl like that. *Too* nicely brought up, no doubt! Her people probably believed her to be in some quite other spot. She had to tell lies.

On her way out Miss Marple passed the table where they were sitting, slowing down as much as she could without its being too obvious. Unfortunately, their voices were so low that she could not hear what they said. The man was speaking, the girl was listening, half pleased, half afraid. "Planning to run away together, perhaps?" thought Miss Marple "She's still under age."

Miss Marple passed through the small gate in the fence that led to the side-walk of the park. There were cars parked along there and presently she stopped beside one particular car. Miss Marple was not particularly knowledgeable over cars but such cars as this one did not come her way very often, so she had noted and remembered it. She had acquired a little information about cars of this style from an enthusiastic great-nephew. It was a racing car. Some foreign make—she couldn't remember the name now. Not only that, she had seen this car or one exactly like it, seen it only yesterday in a side street close to Bertram's Hotel. She had noticed it not only because of its size and its powerful and unusual appearance but because the number had awakened some vague memory, some trace of association in her memory. FAN 2266. It had made her think of her cousin Fanny Godfrey. Poor Fanny who stuttered, who had said "I have got t-t-t-t-wo s-s-s-potz . . ."

She walked along and looked at the number of this car. Yes, she was quite right. FAN 2266. It was the same car. Miss Marple, her footsteps growing more painful every moment, arrived deep in thought at the other side of Chelsea Bridge and by then was so exhausted that she hailed the first taxi she saw with decision. She was worried by the feeling that there was something she ought to do about things. But what things and what to do about them? It was all so indefinite. She fixed her eyes absently on some newsboards.

"Sensational developments in train robbery," they ran. "Engine driver's story," said another one. Really! Miss Marple thought to herself, every day here seemed to be a bank hold-up or a train robbery or a wage pay snatch.

Crime seemed to have got above itself.

Chapter Thirteen

VAGUELY reminiscent of a large bumble bee, Chief-Inspector Fred Davy wandered around the confines of the Criminal Investigation Department, humming to himself. It was a well-known idiosyncrasy of his, and caused no particular notice except to give rise to the remark that "Father was on the prowl again."

His prowling led him at last to the room where Inspector Campbell was sitting behind a desk with a bored expression. Inspector Campbell was an ambitious young man and he found much of his occupation tedious in the extreme. Nevertheless, he coped with the duties appointed to him and achieved a very fair measure of success in so doing. The powers that be approved of him, thought he should do well and doled out from time to time a few words of encouraging commendation.

"Good morning, sir," said Inspector Campbell, respectfully, when Father entered his domain. Naturally he called Chief-Inspector Davy "Father" behind his back as everyone else did; but he was not yet of sufficient seniority to do such a thing to his face.

"Anything I can do for you, sir?" he inquired.

"La, la, boom, boom," hummed the Chief-Inspector, slightly off key. "Why must they call me Mary when my name's Miss Gibbs?" After this rather unexpected resurrection of a by-gone musical comedy, he drew up a chair and sat down.

"Busy?" he asked.

"Moderately so."

"Got some disappearance case or other on, haven't you, to do with some hotel or other. What's the name of it now? Bertram's. Is that it?"

"Yes, that's right, sir. Bertram's Hotel."

"Contravening the licensing hours? Call girls?"

"Oh no, sir," said Inspector Campbell, slightly shocked at hearing Bertram's Hotel being referred to in such a connection. "Very nice, quiet, old fashioned place."

"Is it now?" said Father. "Yes, is it now? Well, that's interesting, really."

Inspector Campbell wondered why it was interesting. He did not like to ask, as tempers in the upper hierarchy were notoriously short since the mail train robbery which had been a spectacular success for the criminals. He looked at Father's large, heavy, bovine face and wondered as he had once or twice wondered before, how Chief-Inspector Davy had reached his present rank and why he was so highly thought of in the department. "All right in his day, I suppose," thought Inspector Campbell, "but there are plenty of go-ahead chaps about who could do with some promotion, once the deadwood is cleared away." But the deadwood had begun another song, partly hummed, with an occasional word or two here and there.

"*Tell me, gentle stranger, are there any more at home like you?*" intoned Father and then in a sudden falsetto, "*A few, kind sir, and nice girls you never knew*. No, let's see, I've got the sexes mixed up. *Floradora*. That was a good show, too."

"I believe I've heard of it, sir," said Inspector Campbell.

"Your mother sang you to sleep in the cradle with it, I expect," said Chief-Inspector Davy. "Now then, what's been going on at Bertram Hotel? Who has disappeared and how and why?"

"A Canon Pennyfather, sir. Elderly clergyman."

"Dull case, eh?"

Inspector Campbell smiled.

"Yes, sir, it *is* rather dull in a way."

"What did he look like?"

"Canon Pennyfather?"

"Yes—you've got a description, I suppose?"

"Of course." Campbell shuffled papers and read: "Height 5 ft. 8. Large thatch of white hair—stoops . . ."

"And he disappeared from Bertram's Hotel—when?"

"About a week ago—November 19th."

"And they've just reported it. Took their time about it, didn't they?"

"Well, I think there was a general idea that he'd turn up."

"Any idea what's behind it?" asked Father. "Has a decent God-fearing man suddenly gone off with one of the churchwardens' wives? Or does he do a bit of secret drinking, or has he embezzled the church funds? Or is he the sort of absent-minded old chap who goes in for this sort of thing?"

"Well, from all I can hear, sir, I should say the latter. He's done it before."

"What—disappeared from a respectable West End hotel?"

"No, not exactly that, but he's not always returned home when he was expected. Occasionally he's turned up to stay with friends on a day when they haven't asked him, or not turned up on the date when they *had* asked him. That sort of thing."

"Yes," said Father. "Yes. Well, that sounds very nice and natural and according to plan, doesn't it? When exactly did you say he disappeared?"

"Thursday. November 19th. He was supposed to be attending a congress at—" He bent down and studied some papers on his desk. "—Oh yes, Lucerne. Society of Biblical Historical Studies. That's the English translation of it. I think it's actually a German society."

"And it was held at Lucerne? The old boy—I suppose he *is* an old boy?"

"Sixty-three, sir, I understand."

"The old boy didn't turn up, is that it?"

Inspector Campbell drew his papers towards him and gave Father the ascertainable facts in so far as they had been ascertained.

"Doesn't sound as if he'd gone off with a choirboy," observed Chief-Inspector Davy.

"I expect he'll turn up all right," said Campbell, "but we're looking into it, of course. Are you—er—particularly interested in the case, sir?" He could hardly restrain his curiosity on this point.

"No," said Davy thoughtfully. "No, I'm not interested in the *case*. I don't see anything to be interested about in it."

There was a pause, a pause which clearly contained the words "Well, then?" with a question mark after it from Inspector Campbell, which he was too well trained to utter in audible tones.

"What I'm *really* interested in," said Father, "is the date. And Bertram's Hotel, of course."

"It's always been very well conducted, sir. No trouble there."

"That's very nice, I'm sure," said Father. He added thoughtfully, "I'd rather like to have a look at the place."

"Of course, sir," said Inspector Campbell. "Any time you like. I was thinking of going round there myself."

"I might as well come along with you," said Father. "Not to butt in, nothing like that. But I'd just rather like to have a look at the place, and this disappearing Archdeacon of yours, or whatever he is, makes rather a good excuse. No need to call me 'sir' when we're there—you throw your weight about. I'll just be your stooge."

Inspector Campbell became interested.

"Do you think there's something that might tie in there, sir, something that might tie in with something else?"

"There's no reason to believe so, so far," said Father. "But you know how it is. One gets—I don't know what to call them—whims, do you think? Bertram's Hotel, somehow, sounds almost too good to be true."

He resumed his impersonation of a bumble bee with a rendering of "Let's All Go Down the Strand."

The two detective officers went off together, Campbell looking smart in a lounge suit, (he had an excellent figure), and Chief-Inspector Davy carrying with him a tweedy air of being up from the country. They fitted in quite well. Only the astute eye of Miss Gorringe, as she raised it from her ledgers, singled them out and appreciated them for what they were. Since she had reported the disappearance of Canon Pennyfather herself and had already had a word with a lesser personage in the police force, she had been expecting something of this kind.

A faint murmur to the earnest-looking girl assistant whom she kept handy in the background enabled the latter to come forward and deal with any ordinary inquiries or services while Miss Gorringe gently shifted herself a little farther along the counter and looked up at the two men. Inspector Campbell laid down his card on the desk in front of her and she nodded. Looking past him to the large tweed-coated figure behind him, she noted that he had turned slightly sideways, and was observing the lounge and its occupants with an apparently naïve pleasure at beholding such a well bred, upper-class world in action.

"Would you like to come into the office?" said Miss Gorringe. "We can talk better there perhaps."

"Yes, I think that would be best."

"Nice place you've got here," said the large, fat, bovine-looking man, turning his head back towards her. "Comfortable," he added, looking approvingly at the large fire. "Good old-fashioned comfort."

Miss Gorringe smiled with an air of pleasure.

"Yes indeed. We pride ourselves on making our visitors comfortable," she said. She turned to her assistant. "Will you carry on, Alice? There is the ledger. Lady Jocelyn will be arriving quite soon. She is sure to want to change her room as soon as she sees it but you must explain to her we are really full up. If necessary, you can show her number 340 on the third floor and offer her that instead. It's not a very pleasant room and I'm sure she will be content with her present one as soon as she sees that."

"Yes, Miss Gorringe. I'll do just that, Miss Gorringe."

"And remind Colonel Mortimer that his field glasses are here. He asked me to keep them for him this morning. Don't let him go off without them."

"No, Miss Gorringe."

These duties accomplished, Miss Gorringe looked at the two men, came out from behind the desk and walked along to a plain mahogany door with no legend on it. Miss Gorringe opened it and they went into a small, rather sad-looking office. All three sat down.

"The missing man is Canon Pennyfather, I understand," said Inspector Campbell. He looked at his notes. "I've got Sergeant Wadell's report. Perhaps you'll tell me in your own words just what occurred."

"I don't think that Canon Pennyfather has really disappeared in the sense in which one would usually use that word," said Miss Gorringe. "I think, you know, that he's just met someone somewhere, some old friend or something like that, and has perhaps gone off with him to some scholarly meeting or reunion or something of that kind, on the Continent— He is so very vague."

"You've known him for a long time?"

"Oh yes, he's been coming here to stay for—let me see—oh five or six years at least, I should think."

"You've been here some time yourself, ma'am," said Chief-Inspector Davy, suddenly putting in a word.

"I have been here, let me think, fourteen years," said Miss Gorringe.

"It's a nice place," repeated Davy again. "And Canon Pennyfather usually stayed here when he was in London? Is that right?"

"Yes. He always came to us. He wrote well beforehand to retain his room. He was much less vague on paper than he was in real life. He asked for a room from the 17th to the 21st. During that time he expected to be away for one or two nights, and he explained that he wished to keep his room on while he was away. He quite often did that."

"When did you begin to get worried about him?" asked Campbell.

"Well, I didn't really. Of course it was awkward. You see, his room was let on from the 23rd and when I realized—I didn't at first—that he hadn't come back from Lugano—"

"I've got Lucerne here in my notes," said Campbell.

"Yes, yes, I think it *was* Lucerne. Some Archæological Congress or other. Anyway, when I realized he hadn't come back here and that his baggage was still here waiting in his room, it made things rather awkward. You see, we are very booked up at this time of year and I had someone else coming into his room. The Honourable Mrs. Saunders, who lives at Lyme Regis. She always has that room. And then his housekeeper rang up. She was worried."

"The housekeeper's name is Mrs. McCrae, so I understand from Archdeacon Simmons. Do you know her?"

"Not personally, no, but I have spoken to her on the telephone once or twice. She is, I think, a very reliable woman and has been with Canon Pennyfather for some years. She was worried naturally. I believe she and Archdeacon Simmons got in touch with near friends and relations but they knew nothing of Canon Pennyfather's movements. And since he was expecting the Archdeacon to stay with him it certainly seemed very odd— in fact it still does—that the Canon should not have returned home."

"Is this Canon usually as absent-minded as that?" asked Father.

Miss Gorringe ignored him. This large man, presumably the accompanying sergeant, seemed to her to be pushing himself forward a little too much.

"And now I understand," continued Miss Gorringe, in an annoyed voice, "and now I understand from Archdeacon Simmons that the Canon never even went to this conference in Lucerne."

"Did he send any message to say he wouldn't go?"

"I don't think so—not from here. No telegram or anything like that. I really know nothing about Lucerne—I am really only concerned with *our* side of the matter. It has got into the evening papers, I see—the fact that he is missing, I mean. They haven't mentioned he was staying *here*. I hope they won't. We don't want the Press here, our visitors wouldn't like that at all. If you can keep them off us, Inspector Campbell, we should be very grateful. I mean it's not as if he had disappeared from *here*."

"His luggage is still here?"

"Yes. In the baggage room. If he didn't go to Lucerne, have you considered the possibility of his being run over? Something like that?"

"Nothing like that has happened to him."

"It really does seem very, very curious," said Miss Gorringe, a faint flicker of interest appearing in her manner, to replace the annoyance. "I mean, it does make one wonder where he *could* have gone and why?"

Father looked at her comprehendingly.

"Of course," he said. "You've only been thinking of it from the hotel angle. Very natural."

"I understand," said Inspector Campbell, referring once more to his notes, "that Canon Pennyfather left here about six-thirty on the evening of Thursday the 19th. He had with him a small overnight bag and he left here in a taxi, directing the commissionaire to tell the driver to drive to the Athenæum Club."

Miss Gorringe nodded her head.

"Yes, he dined at the Athenæum Club—Archdeacon Simmons told me that *that* was the place he was last seen."

There was a firmness in Miss Gorringe's voice as she transferred the responsibility of seeing the Canon last from Bertram's Hotel to the Athenæum Club.

"Well, it's nice to get the facts straight," said Father in a gentle rumbling voice. "We've got 'em straight now. He went off with his little blue BOAC bag or whatever he'd got with him—it *was* a blue BOAC bag, yes? He went off and he didn't come back, and that's that."

"So you see, really I cannot help you," said Miss Gorringe, showing a disposition to rise to her feet and get back to work.

"It doesn't *seem* as if you could help us," said Father, "but someone else might be able to," he added.

"Someone else?"

"Why, yes," said Father. "One of the staff perhaps."

"I don't think anyone knows *anything*; or they would certainly have reported it to me."

"Well, perhaps they might. Perhaps they mightn't. What I mean is, they'd have told you if they'd distinctly *known* anything. But I was thinking more of something he might have *said*."

"What sort of thing?" said Miss Gorringe, looking perplexed.

"Oh, just some chance word that might give one a clue. Something like

'I'm going to see an old friend tonight that I haven't seen since we met in Arizona.' Something like that. Or 'I'm going to stay next week with a niece of mine for her daughter's confirmation.' With absent-minded people, you know, clues like that are a great help. They show what was in the person's mind. It may be that after his dinner at the Athenæum, he gets into a taxi and thinks 'Now where am I going?' and having got—say—the confirmation in his mind—thinks he's going off there."

"Well, I see what you mean," said Miss Gorringe doubtfully. "It seems a little unlikely."

"Oh, one never knows one's luck," said Father cheerfully. "There are the various guests here. I suppose Canon Pennyfather knew some of them since he came here fairly often."

"Oh yes," said Miss Gorringe. "Let me see now. I've seen him talking to—yes, Lady Selina Hazy. Then there was the Bishop of Norwich. They're old friends, I believe. They were at Oxford together. And Mrs. Jameson and her daughters. They come from the same part of the world. Oh yes, quite a lot of people."

"You see," said Father, "he might have talked to one of *them*. He might have just mentioned some little thing that would give us a clue. Is there anyone staying here now that the Canon knew fairly well?"

Miss Gorringe frowned in thought.

"Well, I think General Radley is here still. And there's an old lady who came up from the country—who used to stay here as a girl, so she told me. Let me see, I can't remember her name at the moment, but I can find it for you. Oh yes, Miss Marple, that's her name. I believe she knew him."

"Well, we could make a start with those two. And there'd be a chambermaid, I suppose."

"Oh yes," said Miss Gorringe. "But she has been interviewed already by Sergeant Wadell."

"I know. But not perhaps from this angle. What about the waiter who attended on his table. Or the head waiter?"

"There's Henry, of course," said Miss Gorringe.

"Who's Henry?" asked Father.

Miss Gorringe looked almost shocked. It was to her impossible that anyone should not know Henry.

"Henry has been here for more years than I can say," she said. "You must have noticed him serving teas as you came in."

"Kind of personality," said Davy. "I remember noticing him."

"I don't know what we should do without Henry," said Miss Gorringe with feeling. "He really is wonderful. He sets the tone of the place, you know."

"Perhaps he might like to serve some tea to me," said Chief-Inspector Davy. "Muffins, I saw he'd got there. I'd like a good muffin again."

"Certainly if you like," said Miss Gorringe, rather coldly. "Shall I order two teas to be served to you in the lounge?" she added, turning to Inspector Campbell.

"That would—" the inspector began, when suddenly the door opened and Mr. Humfries appeared in his Olympian manner.

He looked slightly taken aback, then looked inquiringly at Miss Gorringe. Miss Gorringe explained.

"These are two gentlemen from Scotland Yard, Mr. Humfries," she said.

"Detective-Inspector Campbell," said Campbell.

"Oh yes. Yes, of course," said Mr. Humfries. "The matter of Canon Pennyfather, I suppose? Most extraordinary business. I hope nothing's happened to him, poor old chap."

"So do I," said Miss Gorringe. "Such a dear old man."

"One of the old school," said Mr. Humfries approvingly.

"You seem to have quite a lot of the old school here," observed Chief-Inspector Davy.

"I suppose we do, I suppose we do," said Mr. Humfries. "Yes, in many ways we are quite a survival."

"We have our regulars you know," said Miss Gorringe. She spoke proudly. "The same people come back year after year. We have a lot of Americans. People from Boston, and Washington. Very quiet, nice people."

"They like our English atmosphere," said Mr. Humfries, showing his very white teeth in a smile.

Father looked at him thoughtfully. Inspector Campbell said,

"You're quite sure that no message came here from the Canon? I mean it might have been taken by someone who forgot to write it down or to pass it on."

"Telephone messages are always taken down *most* carefully," said Miss Gorringe with ice in her voice. "I cannot conceive it possible that a message would not have been passed on to me or to the appropriate person on duty."

She glared at him.

Inspector Campbell looked momentarily taken aback.

"We've really answered all these questions before, you know," said Mr.

Humfries, also with a touch of ice in his voice. "We gave all the information at our disposal to your sergeant—I can't remember his name for the moment."

Father stirred a little and said, in a kind of homely way,

"Well you see, things have begun to look rather more serious. It looks like a bit more than absent-mindedness. That's why, I think, it would be a good thing if we could have a word or two with those two people you mentioned—General Radley and Miss Marple."

"You want me to—to arrange an interview with them?" Mr. Humfries looked rather unhappy. "General Radley's very deaf."

"I don't think it will be necessary to make it too formal," said Chief-Inspector Davy. "We don't want to worry people. You can leave it quite safely to us. Just point out those two you mentioned. There is just a chance, you know, that Canon Pennyfather *might* have mentioned some plan of his, or some person he was going to meet at Lucerne or who was going with him to Lucerne. Anyway, it's worth trying."

Mr. Humfries looked somewhat relieved.

"Nothing more we can do for you?" he asked. "I'm sure you understand that we wish to help you in every way, only you do understand how we feel about any Press publicity."

"Quite," said Inspector Campbell.

"And I'll just have a word with the chambermaid," said Father.

"Certainly, if you like. I doubt very much whether she can tell you anything."

"Probably not. But there might be some detail—some remark the Canon made about a letter or an appointment. One never knows."

Mr. Humfries glanced at his watch.

"She'll be on duty at six," he said. "Second floor. Perhaps, in the meantime, you'd care for tea?"

"Suits me," said Father promptly.

They left the office together.

Miss Gorringe said, "General Radley will be in the smoking-room. The first room down that passage on the left. He'll be in front of the fire there with *The Times*. I think," she added discreetly, "he might be asleep. You're sure you don't want me to—"

"No, no, I'll see to it," said Father. "And what about the other one—the old lady?"

"She's sitting over there, by the fireplace," said Miss Gorringe.

"The one with white fluffy hair and the knitting?" said Father, taking a look. "Might almost be on the stage, mightn't she? Everybody's universal great-aunt."

"Great-aunts aren't much like that nowadays," said Miss Gorringe, "nor grandmothers nor great-grandmothers, if it comes to that. We had the Marchioness of Barlowe in yesterday. She's a great-grandmother. Honestly, I didn't know her when she came in. Just back from Paris. Her face a mask of pink and white and her hair platinum blonde and I suppose an entirely false figure, but it looked wonderful."

"Ah," said Father, "I prefer the old-fashioned kind myself. Well, thank you, ma'am." He turned to Campbell. "I'll look after it, shall I, sir? I know you've got an important appointment."

"That's right," said Campbell, taking his cue. "I don't suppose anything much will come of it, but it's worth trying."

Mr. Humfries disappeared into his inner sanctum, saying as he did so: "Miss Gorringe—just a moment, please."

Miss Gorringe followed him in and shut the door behind her.

Humfries was walking up and down. He demanded sharply,

"What do they want to see Rose for? Wadell asked all the necessary questions."

"I suppose it's just routine," said Miss Gorringe, doubtfully.

"You'd better have a word with her first."

Miss Gorringe looked a little startled.

"But surely Inspector Campbell—"

"Oh, I'm not worried about Campbell. It's the other one. Do you know who he is?"

"I don't think he gave his name. Sergeant of some kind, I suppose. He looks rather a yokel."

"Yokel my foot," said Mr. Humfries, abandoning his elegance. "That's Chief-Inspector Davy, an old fox if there ever was one. They think a lot of him at the Yard. I'd like to know what *he's* doing here, nosing about and playing the genial hick. I don't like it at all."

"You can't think—"

"I don't know what to think. But I tell you I don't like it. Did he ask to see anyone else besides Rose?"

"I think he's going to have a word with Henry."

Mr. Humfries laughed. Miss Gorringe laughed too.

"We needn't worry about Henry."

"No, indeed."

"And the visitors who knew Canon Pennyfather?"

Mr. Humfries laughed again.

"I wish him joy of old Radley. He'll have to shout the place down and then he won't get anything worth having. He's welcome to Radley and that funny old hen, Miss Marple. All the same, I don't much like his poking his nose in . . ."

Chapter Fourteen

"You KNOW," said Chief-Inspector Davy thoughtfully, "I don't much like that chap Humfries."

"Think there's something wrong with him?" asked Campbell.

"Well—" Father sounded apologetic, "you know the sort of feeling one gets. Smarmy sort of chap. I wonder if he's the owner or only the manager."

"I could ask him." Campbell took a step back towards the desk.

"No, don't ask him," said Father. "Just find out—quietly."

Campbell looked at him curiously.

"What's on your mind, sir?"

"Nothing in particular," said Father. "I just think I'd like to have a good deal more information about this place. I'd have to know who is behind it, what its financial status is. All that sort of thing."

Campbell shook his head.

"I should have said if there was one place in London that was absolutely above suspicion—"

"I know, I know," said Father. "And what a useful thing it is to have that reputation!"

Campbell shook his head and left. Father went down the passage to the smoking-room. General Radley was just waking up. *The Times* had slipped from his knees and disintegrated slightly. Father picked it up and reassembled the sheets and handed it to him.

"Thank ye, sir. Very kind," said General Radley gruffly.

"General Radley?"

"Yes."

"You'll excuse me," said Father, raising his voice, "but I want to speak to you about Canon Pennyfather."

"Eh—what's that?" The General approached a hand to his ear.

"Canon Pennyfather," bellowed Father.

"My father? Dead years ago."

"Canon *Penny*-father."

"Oh. What about him? Saw him the other day. He was staying here."

"There was an address he was going to give me. Said he'd leave it with you."

This was rather more difficult to get over but he succeeded in the end.

"Never gave me any address. Must have mixed me up with somebody else. Muddle-headed old fool. Always was. Scholarly sort of chap, you know. They're always absent-minded."

Father persevered for a little longer but soon decided that conversation with General Radley was practically impossible and almost certainly unprofitable. He went and sat down in the lounge at a table adjacent to that of Miss Jane Marple.

"Tea, sir?"

Father looked up. He was impressed, as everyone was impressed by Henry's personality. Though such a large and portly man he had appeared, as it were, like some vast travesty of Ariel who could materialize and vanish at will. Father ordered tea.

"Did I see you've got muffins here?" he asked.

Henry smiled benignly.

"Yes, sir. Very good indeed our muffins are, if I may say so. Everyone enjoys them. Shall I order you muffins, sir? Indian or China tea?"

"Indian," said Father. "Or Ceylon if you've got it."

"Certainly we have Ceylon, sir."

Henry made the faintest gesture with a finger and the pale young man who was his minion departed in search of Ceylon tea and muffins. Henry moved graciously elsewhere.

"You're *Someone*, you are," thought Father. "I wonder where they got hold of you and what they pay you. A packet, I bet, *and* you'd be worth it." He watched Henry bending in a fatherly manner over an elderly lady. He wondered what Henry thought, if he thought anything, about Father. Father considered that he fitted into Bertram's Hotel reasonably well. He might have been a prosperous gentleman farmer or he might have been a peer of the realm with a resemblance to a bookmaker. Father knew two peers who were very like that. On the whole, he thought, he passed muster, but he also thought it possible that he had not deceived Henry. "Yes, you're *Someone* you are," Father thought again.

Tea came and the muffins. Father bit deeply. Butter ran down his chin.

He wiped it off with a large handkerchief. He drank two cups of tea with plenty of sugar. Then he leaned forward and spoke to the lady sitting in the chair next to him.

"Excuse me," he said, "but aren't you Miss Jane Marple?"

Miss Marple transferred her gaze from her knitting to Chief Detective-Inspector Davy.

"Yes," she said, "I am Miss Marple."

"I hope you don't mind my speaking to you. As a matter of fact I am a police officer."

"Indeed? Nothing seriously wrong here, I hope?"

Father hastened to reassure her in his best paternal fashion.

"Now, don't you worry, Miss Marple," he said. "It's not the sort of thing you mean at all. No burglary or anything like that. Just a little difficulty about an absent-minded clergyman, that's all. I think he's a friend of yours. Canon Pennyfather."

"Oh, Canon Pennyfather. He was here only the other day. Yes, I've known him slightly for many years. As you say, he *is* very absent-minded." She added, with some interest, "What has he done now?"

"Well, as you might say in a manner of speaking, he's lost himself."

"Oh dear," said Miss Marple. "Where ought he to be?"

"Back home in his Cathedral Close," said Father, "but he isn't."

"He told *me*," said Miss Marple, "he was going to a conference at Lucerne. Something to do with the Dead Sea scrolls, I believe. He's a great Hebrew and Aramaic scholar, you know."

"Yes," said Father. "You're quite right. That's where he—well, that's where he was supposed to be going."

"Do you mean he didn't turn up there?"

"No," said Father, "he didn't turn up."

"Oh, well," said Miss Marple, "I expect he got his dates wrong."

"Very likely, very likely."

"I'm afraid," said Miss Marple, "that that's not the first time that that's happened. I went to have tea with him in Chadminster once. He was actually absent from home. His housekeeper told me then how very absent-minded he was."

"He didn't say anything to you when he was staying here that might give us a clue, I suppose?" asked Father, speaking in an easy and confidential way. "You know the sort of thing I mean, any old friend he'd met or any plans he'd made apart from this Lucerne Conference?"

"Oh no. He just mentioned the Lucerne Conference. I think he said it was on the 19th. Is that right?"

"That was the date of the Lucerne Conference, yes."

"I didn't notice the date particularly. I mean—" like most old ladies, Miss Marple here became slightly involved—"I *thought* he said the 19th and he *might* have said the 19th, but at the same time he might have *meant* the 19th and it might really have been the 20*th*. I mean, he may have thought the 20th *was* the 19th or he may have thought the 19th was the 20th."

"Well—" said Father, slightly dazed.

"I'm putting it badly," said Miss Marple, "but I mean people like Canon Pennyfather, if they say they're going somewhere on a Thursday, one is quite prepared to find that they didn't mean Thursday, it may be Wednesday or Friday they really mean. Usually they find out in time but sometimes they just don't. I thought at the time that something like that must have happened."

Father looked slightly puzzled.

"You speak as though you knew already, Miss Marple, that Canon Pennyfather hadn't gone to Lucerne."

"I knew he wasn't in Lucerne on *Thursday*," said Miss Marple. "He was here all day—or most of the day. That's why I thought, of course, that though he may have said Thursday to me, it was really Friday he meant. He certainly left here on Thursday evening carrying his BEA bag."

"Quite so."

"I took it he was going off to the airport then," said Miss Marple. "That's why I was so surprised to see he was back again."

"I beg your pardon, what do you mean by 'back again'?"

"Well, that he was back here again, I mean."

"Now, let's get this quite clear," said Father, careful to speak in an agreeable and reminiscent voice, and not as though it was really important. "You saw the old idio—you saw the Canon, that is to say, leave as you thought for the airport with his overnight bag, fairly early in the evening. Is that right?"

"Yes. About half-past six, I would say, or quarter to seven."

"But you say he came *back*."

"Perhaps he missed the plane. That would account for it."

"*When* did he come back?"

"Well, I don't really know. I didn't see him come back."

"Oh," said Father, taken aback. "I thought you said you *did* see him."

"Oh, I did see him *later*," said Miss Marple, "I meant I didn't see him actually come into the hotel."

"You saw him later? When?"

Miss Marple thought.

"Let me see. It was about 3 a.m. I couldn't sleep very well. Something woke me up. Some sound. There are so many queer noises in London. I looked at my little clock, it was ten minutes past three. For some reason— I'm not quite sure what—I felt uneasy. Footsteps, perhaps, outside my door. Living in the country, if one hears footsteps in the middle of the night it makes one nervous. So I just opened my door and looked out. There was Canon Pennyfather leaving his room—it's next door to mine— and going off down the stairs wearing his overcoat."

"He came out of his room wearing his overcoat and went down the stairs at 3 a.m. in the morning?"

"Yes," said Miss Marple, and added: "I thought it odd at the time."

Father looked at her for some moments.

"Miss Marple," he said, "why haven't you told anyone this before?"

"Nobody asked me," said Miss Marple simply.

Chapter Fifteen

FATHER drew a deep breath.

"No," he said. "No, I suppose nobody would ask you. It's as simple as that."

He relapsed into silence again.

"You think something has happened to him, don't you?" asked Miss Marple.

"It's over a week now," said Father. "He didn't have a stroke and fall down in the street. He's not in a hospital as a result of an accident. So where *is* he? His disappearance has been reported in the Press, but nobody's come forward with any information yet."

"They may not have seen it. *I* didn't."

"It looks—it really looks—" Father was following out his own line of thought—"as though he *meant* to disappear. Leaving this place like that in the middle of the night. You're quite sure about it, aren't you?" he demanded sharply. "You didn't dream it?"

"I am absolutely sure," said Miss Marple with finality.

Father heaved himself to his feet.

"I'd better go and see that chambermaid," he said.

Father found Rose Sheldon on duty and ran an approving eye over her pleasant person.

"I'm sorry to bother you," he said. "I know you've seen our sergeant already. But it's about that missing gentleman, Canon Pennyfather."

"Oh yes, sir, a very nice gentleman. He often stays here."

"Absent-minded," said Father.

Rose Sheldon permitted a discreet smile to appear on her respectful mask of a face.

"Now let me see." Father pretended to consult some notes. "The last time you saw Canon Pennyfather—was—"

"On the Thursday morning, sir. Thursday the 19th. He told me that he would not be back that night and possibly not the next either. He was going, I think, to Geneva. Somewhere in Switzerland, anyway. He gave me two shirts he wanted washed and I said they would be ready for him on the morning of the following day."

"And that's the last you saw of him, eh?"

"Yes, sir. You see, I'm not on duty in the afternoons. I come back again at 6 o'clock. By then he must have left, or at any rate he was downstairs. Not in his room. He had left two suitcases behind."

"That's right," said Father. The contents of the suitcases had been examined, but had given no useful lead. He went on: "Did you call him the next morning?"

"Call him? No, sir, he was away."

"What did you do ordinarily—take him early tea? Breakfast?"

"Early tea, sir. He breakfasted downstairs always."

"So you didn't go into his room at all the next day?"

"Oh yes, sir." Rose sounded shocked. "I went into his room as usual. I took his shirts in for one thing. And of course I dusted the room. We dust all the rooms every day."

"Had the bed been slept in?"

She stared at him. "The bed, sir? Oh no."

"Was it rumpled—creased in any way?"

She shook her head.

"What about the bathroom?"

"There was a damp hand towel, sir, that had been used, I presume that would be the evening before. He may have washed his hands last thing before going off."

"And there was nothing to show that he had come back into the room—perhaps quite late—after midnight?"

She stared at him with an air of bewilderment. Father opened his mouth, then shut it again. Either she knew nothing about the Canon's return or she was a highly accomplished actress.

"What about his clothes—suits. Were they packed up in his suitcases?"

"No, sir, they were hanging up in the cupboards. He was keeping his room on, you see, sir."

"Who did pack them up?"

"Miss Gorringe gave orders, sir. When the room was wanted for the new lady coming in."

A straightforward coherent account. But if that old lady was correct in stating that she saw Canon Pennyfather leaving his room at 3 a.m. on Friday morning, then he must have come back to that room sometime. Nobody had seen him enter the hotel. Had he, for some reason, deliberately avoided being seen? He had left no traces in the room. He hadn't even lain down on the bed. Had Miss Marple dreamed the whole thing? At her age it was possible enough. An idea struck him.

"What about his airport bag?"

"I beg your pardon, sir?"

"A small bag, dark blue—a BEA or BOAC bag—you must have seen it?"

"Oh that—yes, sir. But of course he'd take that with him abroad."

"But he didn't go abroad. He never went to Switzerland after all. So he must have left it behind. Or else he came back and left it here with his other luggage."

"Yes—yes—I think—I'm not quite sure—I believe he did."

Quite unsolicited, the thought raced into Father's mind: *They didn't brief you on that, did they?*

Rose Sheldon had been calm and competent up till now. But that question had rattled her. She hadn't known the right answer to it. *But she ougʻit to have known.*

The Canon had taken his bag to the airport, had been turned away from the airport. If he had come back to Bertram's, the bag would have been with him. *But Miss Marple had made no mention of it when she had described the Canon leaving his room and going down the stairs.*

Presumably it was left in the bedroom, but it had not been put in the baggage room with the suitcases. Why not? *Because the Canon was supposed to have gone to Switzerland?*

He thanked Rose genially and went downstairs again.

Canon Pennyfather! Something of an enigma, Canon Pennyfather.

Talked a lot about going to Switzerland, muddled up things so that he didn't go to Switzerland, came back to his hotel so secretly that nobody saw him, left it again in the early hours of the morning. (To go where? To do what?)

Could absent-mindedness account for all this?

If not, then what was Canon Pennyfather up to? And more important, where was he?

From the staircase, Father cast a jaundiced eye over the occupants of the lounge, and wondered whether *anyone* was what they seemed to be. He had got to that stage! Elderly people, middle-aged people (nobody very young), nice old-fashioned people, nearly all well-to-do, all highly respectable. Service people, lawyers, clergymen; American husband and wife near the door, a French family near the fireplace. Nobody flashy, nobody out of place; most of them enjoying an old-fashioned English afternoon tea. Could there really be anything seriously wrong with a place that served old-fashioned afternoon teas?

The Frenchman made a remark to his wife that fitted in appositively enough.

"*Le Five o'clock*," he was saying. "*C'est bien Anglais ça, n'est-ce pas?*" He looked round him with approval.

"Le Five o'clock," thought Davy as he passed through the swing doors to the street. "That chap doesn't know that 'le Five o'clock' is as dead as the Dodo!"

Outside, various vast American wardrobe cases and suitcases were being loaded on to a taxi. It seemed that Mr. and Mrs. Elmer Cabot were on their way to the Hotel Vendôme, Paris.

Beside him on the kerb, Mrs. Elmer Cabot was expressing her views to her husband.

"The Pendleburys were quite right about this place, Elmer. It just *is* old England. So beautifully Edwardian. I just feel Edward the Seventh could walk right in any moment and sit down there for his afternoon tea. I mean to come back here next year—I really do."

"If we've got a million dollars or so to spare," said her husband dryly.

"Now, Elmer, it wasn't as bad as all *that*."

The baggage was loaded, the tall commissionaire helped them in, murmuring "Thank you, sir" as Mr. Cabot made the expected gesture. The taxi drove off. The commissionaire transferred his attention to Father.

"Taxi, sir?"

Father looked up at him.

Over six feet. Good-looking chap. A bit run to seed. Ex-army. Lots of medals—genuine, probably. A bit shifty? Drinks too much.

Aloud he said: "Ex-army man?"

"Yes, sir. Irish Guards."

"Military Medal, I see. Where did you get that?"

"Burma."

"What's your name?"

"Michael Gorman. Sergeant."

"Good job here?"

"It's a peaceful spot."

"Wouldn't you prefer the Hilton?"

"I would not. I like it here. Nice people come here, and quite a lot of racing gentlemen—for Ascot and Newbury. I've had good tips from them now and again."

"Ah, so you're an Irishman and a gambler, is that it?"

"Och! now, what would life be like without a gamble?"

"Peaceful and dull," said Chief-Inspector Davy, "like mine."

"Indeed, sir?"

"Can you guess what my profession is?" asked Father.

The Irishman grinned.

"No offence to you, sir, but if I may guess I'd say you were a cop."

"Right first time," said Chief-Inspector Davy. "You remember Canon Pennyfather?"

"Canon Pennyfather now, I don't seem to mind the name—"

"Elderly clergyman."

Michael Gorman laughed.

"Ah now, clergymen are as thick as peas in a pod in there."

"This one disappeared from here."

"Oh, *that* one!" The commissionaire seemed slightly taken aback.

"Did you know him?"

"I wouldn't remember him if it hadn't been for people asking me questions about him. All I know is, I put him into a taxi and he went to the Athenæum Club. That's the last I saw of him. Somebody told me he'd gone to Switzerland, but I hear he never got there. Lost himself, it seems."

"You didn't see him later that day?"

"Later— No, indeed."

"What time do you go off duty?"

"Eleven-thirty."

Chief-Inspector Davy nodded, refused a taxi and moved slowly away along Pond Street. A car roared past him close to the kerb, and pulled up outside Bertram's Hotel, with a scream of brakes. Chief-Inspector Davy turned his head soberly and noted the number plate. FAN 2266. There was something reminiscent about that number, though he couldn't for the moment place it.

Slowly he retraced his steps. He had barely reached the entrance before the driver of the car, who had gone through the doors a moment or two before, came out again. He and the car matched each other. It was a racing model, white with long gleaming lines. The young man had the same eager greyhound look with a handsome face and a body with not a superfluous inch of flesh on it.

The commissionaire held the car door open, the young man jumped in, tossed a coin to the commissionaire and drove off with a burst of powerful engine.

"You know who *he* is?" said Michael Gorman to Father.

"A dangerous driver, anyway."

"Ladislaus Malinowski. Won the Grand Prix two years ago—world champion he was. Had a bad smash last year. They say he's all right again now."

"Don't tell me *he's* staying at Bertram's. Highly unsuitable."

Michael Gorman grinned.

"He's not staying here, no. But a friend of his is—" He winked.

A porter in a striped apron came out with more American luxury travel equipment.

Father stood absent-mindedly watching them being ensconced in a Daimler Hire Car whilst he tried to remember what he knew about Ladislaus Malinowski. A reckless fellow—said to be tied up with some well known woman—what was her name now? Still staring at a smart wardrobe case, he was just turning away when he changed his mind and re-entered the hotel again.

He went to the desk and asked Miss Gorringe for the hotel register. Miss Gorringe was busy with departing Americans, and pushed the book along the counter towards him. He turned the pages. Lady Selina Hazy, Little Cottage, Merryfield, Hants. Mr. and Mrs. Hennessey King, Elderberries, Essex. Sir John Woodstock, 5 Beaumont Crescent, Cheltenham. Lady Sedgwick, Hurstings House, Northumberland. Mr. and Mrs. Elmer Cabot, Connecticut. General Radley, 14, The Green, Chichester. Mr. and Mrs. Woolmer Pickington, Marble Head, Connecticut. La Comtesse de Beauville, Les Sapins, St. Germain en Laye. Miss Jane Marple, St. Mary Mead, Much Benham. Colonel Luscombe, Little Green, Suffolk. Mrs. Carpenter, The Hon. Elvira Blake. Canon Pennyfather, The Close, Chadminster. Mrs. Holding, Miss Holding, Miss Audrey Holding, The Manor House, Carmanton. Mr. and Mrs. Rysville, Valley Forge, Pennsylvania. The Duke of Barnstable, Doone Castle, N. Devon . . . A cross section of the kind of people who stayed at Bertram's Hotel. They formed, he thought, a kind of pattern . . .

As he shut the book, a name on an earlier page caught his eye. Sir William Ludgrove.

Mr. Justice Ludgrove who had been recognized by a probation officer near the scene of a bank robbery. Mr. Justice Ludgrove—Canon Penny-father—both patrons of Bertram's Hotel . . .

"I hope you enjoyed your tea, sir?" It was Henry, standing at his elbow. He spoke courteously, and with the slight anxiety of the perfect host.

"The best tea I've had for years," said Chief-Inspector Davy.

He remembered he hadn't paid for it. He attempted to do so, but Henry raised a deprecating hand.

"Oh no, sir. I was given to understand that your tea was on the house. Mr. Humfries' orders."

Henry moved away. Father was left uncertain whether he ought to have offered Henry a tip or not. It was galling to think that Henry knew the answer to that social problem much better than he did!

As he moved away along the street, he stopped suddenly. He took out his note-book and put down a name and an address—no time to lose. He went into a telephone box. He was going to stick out his neck. Come hell or high water, he was going all out on a hunch.

Chapter Sixteen

IT WAS the wardrobe that worried Canon Pennyfather. It worried him before he was quite awake. Then he forgot it and he fell asleep again. But when his eyes opened once more, there the wardrobe still was in the wrong place. He was lying on his left side facing the window and the wardrobe ought to have been there between him and the window on the left wall. But it wasn't. It was on the right. It worried him. It worried him so much that it made him feel tired. He was conscious of his head aching badly, and on top of that, to have the wardrobe in the wrong place . . . At this point once more his eyes closed.

There was rather more light in the room the next time he woke. It was not daylight yet. Only the faint light of dawn. "Dear me," said Canon Pennyfather to himself, suddenly solving the problem of the wardrobe. "How stupid I am! Of course, I'm not at home."

He moved gingerly. No, this wasn't his own bed. He was away from home. He was—where was he? Oh, of course. He'd gone to London, hadn't he? He was in Bertram's Hotel and—but no, he *wasn't* in Bertram's Hotel. In Bertram's Hotel his bed was facing the window. So that was wrong, too.

"Dear me, where can I be?" said Canon Pennyfather.

Then he remembered that he was going to Lucerne. "Of course," he said to himself, "I'm in Lucerne." He began thinking about the paper he was going to read. He didn't think about it long. Thinking about his paper seemed to make his head ache so he went to sleep again.

The next time he woke his head was a great deal clearer. Also there was a good deal more light in the room. He was not at home, he was not at Bertram's Hotel and he was fairly sure that he was not in Lucerne. This wasn't a hotel bedroom at all. He studied it fairly closely. It was an entirely strange room with very little furniture in it. A kind of cupboard (what he'd taken for the wardrobe) and a window with flowered curtains through which the light came. A chair and a table and a chest of drawers. Really, that was about all.

"Dear me," said Canon Pennyfather, "this is *most* odd. Where am I?" He was thinking of getting up to investigate but when he sat up in bed his headache began again so he lay down.

"I must have been ill," decided Canon Pennyfather. "Yes, definitely I must have been ill." He thought a minute or two and then said to himself, "As a matter of fact, I think perhaps I'm still ill. Influenza, perhaps?" Influenza, people often said, came on very suddenly. Perhaps—perhaps it had come on at dinner at the Athenæum. Yes, that was right. He remembered that he had dined at the Athenæum.

There were sounds of moving about in the house. Perhaps they'd taken him to a nursing home. But no, he didn't think this was a nursing home. With the increased light it showed itself as a rather shabby and ill-furnished small bedroom. Sounds of movement went on. From downstairs a voice called out, "Goodbye, ducks. Sausage and mash this evening."

Canon Pennyfather considered this. Sausage and mash. The words had a faintly agreeable quality.

"I believe," he said to himself, "I'm *hungry*."

The door opened. A middle-aged woman came in, went across to the curtains, pulled them back a little and turned towards the bed.

"Ah, you're awake now," she said. "And how are you feeling?"

"Really," said Canon Pennyfather, rather feebly, "I'm not quite sure."

"Ah, I expect not. You've been quite bad, you know. Something hit you a nasty crack, so the doctor said. These motorists! Not even stopping after they'd knocked you down."

"Have I had an accident?" said Canon Pennyfather. "A motor accident?"

"That's right," said the woman. "Found you by the side of the road when we come home. Thought you was drunk at first." She chuckled pleasantly at the reminiscence. "Then my husband said he'd better take a look. It may have been an accident, he said. There wasn't no smell of drink or anything. No blood or anything neither. Anyway, there you was, out like a log. So my husband said 'we can't leave him here lying like that' and he carried you in here. See?"

"Ah," said Canon Pennyfather, faintly, somewhat overcome by all these revelations. "A good Samaritan."

"And he saw you were a clergyman so my husband said 'it's all quite respectable'. Then he said he'd better not call the police because being a clergyman and all that you mightn't like it. That's if you was drunk, in spite of there being no smell of drink. So then we hit upon getting Dr. Stokes to come and have a look at you. We still call him Dr. Stokes although he's been struck off. A very nice man he is, embittered a bit, of course, by being struck off. It was only his kind heart really, helping a lot of girls who were no better than they should be. Anyway, he's a good enough doctor and we got him to come and take a look at you. He says you've come to no real harm, says it's mild concussion. All we'd got to do was to keep you lying flat and quiet in a dark room. 'Mind you,' he said, 'I'm not giving an opinion or anything like that. This is unofficial. I've no right to prescribe or to say anything. By rights I dare say you ought to report it to the police, but if you don't want to, why should you?' Give the poor old geezer a chance, that's what he said. Excuse me if I'm speaking disrespectful. He's a rough and ready speaker, the doctor is. Now what about a drop of soup or some hot bread and milk?"

"Either," said Canon Pennyfather faintly, "would be very welcome."

He relapsed on to his pillows. An accident? So *that* was it. An accident, and he couldn't remember a thing about it! A few minutes later the good woman returned bearing a tray with a steaming bowl on it.

"You'll feel better after this," she said. "I'd like to have put a drop of whisky or a drop of brandy in it but the doctor said you wasn't to have nothing like that."

"Certainly not," said Canon Pennyfather, "not with concussion. No. It would have been unadvisable."

"I'll put another pillow behind your back, shall I, ducks? There, is that all right?"

Canon Pennyfather was a little startled by being addressed as "ducks". He told himself that it was kindly meant.

"Upsydaisy," said the woman, "there we are."

"Yes, but where are we?" said Canon Pennyfather. "I mean, where am I? Where is this place?"

"Milton St. John," said the woman. "Didn't you know?"

"Milton St. John?" said Canon Pennyfather. He shook his head. "I never heard the name before."

"Oh well, it's not much of a place. Only a village."

"You have been very kind," said Canon Pennyfather. "May I ask your name?"

"Mrs. Wheeling. Emma Wheeling."

"You are most kind," said Canon Pennyfather again. "But this accident now. I simply cannot remember—"

"You put yourself outside that, luv, and you'll feel better and up to remembering things."

"Milton St. John," said Canon Pennyfather to himself, in a tone of wonder. "The name means nothing to me *at all*. How very extraordinary!"

Chapter Seventeen

SIR RONALD GRAVES drew a cat upon his blotting pad. He looked at the large portly figure of Chief-Inspector Davy sitting opposite him and drew a bulldog.

"Ladislaus Malinowski?" he said. "Could be. Got any evidence?"

"No. He'd fit the bill, would he?"

"A daredevil. No nerves. Won the World Championship. Bad crash about a year ago. Bad reputation with women. Sources of income doubtful. Spends money here and abroad very freely. Always going to and fro to the Continent. Have you got some idea that he's the man behind these big organized robberies and hold-ups?"

"I don't think he's the planner. But I think he's in with them."

"Why?"

"For one thing, he runs a Mercedes-Otto car. Racing model. A car answering to that description was seen near Bedhampton on the morning of the mail robbery. Different number plates—but we're used to that. And it's the same stunt—unlike, but not too unlike. FAN 2299 instead of 2266. There aren't so many Mercedes-Otto models of that type about. Lady Sedgwick has one and young Lord Merrivale."

"You don't think Malinowski runs the show?"

"No—I think there are better brains than his at the top. But he's in it. I've looked back over the files. Take the hold-up at the Midland and West London. Three vans happened—just happened—to block a certain street. A Mercedes-Otto that was on the scene got clear away owing to that block."

"It was stopped later."

"Yes. And given a clear bill of health. Especially as the people who'd reported it weren't sure of the correct number. It was reported as FAM 3366 —Malinowski's registration number is FAN 2266— It's all the same picture."

"And you persist in tying it up with Bertram's Hotel. They dug up some stuff about Bertram's for you—"

Father tapped his pocket.

"Got it here. Properly registered company. Balance—paid up capitals— directors—etcetera, etcetera, etcetera. Doesn't mean a thing! These financial shows are all the same—just a lot of snakes swallowing each other! Companies, and holding companies—makes your brain reel!"

"Come now, Father. That's just a way they have in the City. Has to do with taxation—"

"What I want is the real dope. If you'll give me a chit, sir, I'd like to go and see some top brass."

The A.C. stared at him.

"And what exactly do you mean by top brass?"

Father mentioned a name.

The A.C. looked upset. "I don't know about that. I hardly think we dare approach *him*."

"It might be very helpful."

There was a pause. The two men looked at each other. Father looked bovine, placid, and patient. The A.C. gave in.

"You're a stubborn old devil, Fred," he said. "Have it your own way. Go and worry the top brains behind the international financiers of Europe."

"*He'll* know," said Chief-Inspectory Davy. "He'll *know*. And if he doesn't, he can find out by pressing one buzzer on his desk or making one telephone call."

"I don't know that he'll be pleased."

"Probably not," said Father, "but it won't take much of his time. I've got to have authority behind me, though."

"You're really serious about this place, Bertram's, aren't you? But what have you got to go on? It's well run, has a good respectable clientele—no trouble with the licensing laws."

"I know—I know. No drinks, no drugs, no gambling, no accommodation for criminals. All pure as the driven snow. No beatniks, no thugs, no juvenile delinquents. Just sober Victorian-Edwardian old ladies, county families, visiting travellers from Boston and the more respectable parts of the USA. All the same, a respectable Canon of the church is seen to leave it at 3 a.m. in the morning in a somewhat surreptitious manner—"

"Who saw that?"

"An old lady."

"How did she manage to see him? Why wasn't she in bed and asleep?"

"Old ladies are like that, sir."

"You're not talking of—what's his name—Canon Pennyfather?"

"That's right, sir. His disappearance was reported and Campbell has been looking into it."

"Funny coincidence—his name's just come up in connection with the mail robbery at Bedhampton."

"Indeed? In what way, sir?"

"Another old lady—or middle-aged anyway. When the train was stopped by that signal that had been tampered with, a good many people woke up and looked out into the corridor. This woman, who lives in Chadminster and knows Canon Pennyfather by sight, says she saw him entering the train by one of the doors. She thought he'd got out to see what was wrong and was getting in again. We were going to follow it up because of his disappearance being reported—"

"Let's see—the train was stopped at 5.30 a.m. Canon Pennyfather left Bertram's Hotel not long after 3 a.m. Yes, it could be done. If he were driven there—say—in a racing car . . ."

"So we're back again to Ladislaus Malinowski!"

The A.C. looked at his blotting pad doodles. "What a bulldog you are, Fred," he said.

Half an hour later Chief-Inspector Davy was entering a quiet and rather shabby office.

The large man behind the desk rose and put forward a hand.

"Chief-Inspector Davy? Do sit down," he said. "Do you care for a cigar?"

Chief-Inspector Davy shook his head.

"I must apologize," he said, in his deep countryman's voice, "for wasting your valuable time."

Mr. Robinson smiled. He was a fat man and very well dressed. He had a yellow face, his eyes were dark and sad looking and his mouth was large and generous. He frequently smiled to display over-large teeth. "The better to eat you with," thought Chief-Inspector Davy irrelevantly. His English was perfect and without accent but he was not an Englishman. Father wondered, as many others had wondered before him, what nationality Mr. Robinson really was.

"Well, what can I do for you?"

"I'd like to know," said Chief-Inspector Davy, "who owns Bertram's Hotel."

The expression on Mrs. Robinson's face did not change. He showed no surprise at hearing the name nor did he show recognition. He said thoughtfully,

"You want to know who owns Bertram's Hotel. That, I think, is in Pond Street, off Piccadilly."

"Quite right, sir."

"I have occasionally stayed there myself. A quiet place. Well run."

"Yes," said Father, "particularly well run."

"And you want to know who owns it? Surely that is easy to ascertain?"

There was a faint irony behind his smile.

"Through the usual channels, you mean? Oh yes." Father took a small piece of paper from his pocket and read out three or four names and addresses.

"I see," said Mr. Robinson, "someone has taken quite a lot of trouble. Interesting. And you come to me?"

"If anyone knows, you would, sir."

"Actually I do not know. But it is true that I have ways of obtaining information. One has—" he shrugged his very large, fat shoulders—"one has contacts."

"Yes, sir," said Father with an impassive face.

Mr. Robinson looked at him, then he picked up the telephone on his desk.

"Sonia? Get me Carlos." He waited a minute or two then spoke again. "Carlos?" He spoke rapidly half a dozen sentences in a foreign language. It was not a language that Father could even recognize.

Father could converse in good British French. He had a smattering of Italian and he could make a guess at plain travellers' German. He knew the sounds of Spanish, Russian and Arabic, though he could not understand them. This language was none of those. At a faint guess he hazarded it might be Turkish or Persian or Armenian, but even of that he was by no means sure. Mr. Robinson replaced the receiver.

"I do not think," he said genially, "that we shall have long to wait. I am interested, you know. Very much interested. I have occasionally wondered myself—"

Father looked inquiring.

"About Bertram's Hotel," said Mr. Robinson. "Financially, you know. One wonders how it can pay. However, it has never been any of my business. And one appreciates—" He shrugged his shoulders, "—a comfortable hostelry with an unusually talented personnel and staff . . . Yes, I have wondered." He looked at Father. "You know how and why?"

"Not yet," said Father, "but I mean to."

"There are several possibilities," said Mr. Robinson, thoughtfully. "It is like music, you know. Only so many notes to the octave, yet one can combine them in—what is it—several million different ways? A musician told me once that you do not get the same tune twice. Most interesting."

There was a slight buzz on his desk and he picked up the receiver once more.

"Yes? Yes, you have been very prompt. I am pleased. I see. Oh! Amsterdam, yes . . . Ah . . . Thank you . . . Yes. You will spell that? Good."

He wrote rapidly on a pad at his elbow.

"I hope this will be useful to you," he said, as he tore off the sheet and passed it across the table to Father, who read the name out loud. "Wilhelm Hoffman."

"Nationality Swiss," said Mr. Robinson. "Though not, I would say, born in Switzerland. Has a good deal of influence in Banking circles and though keeping strictly on the right side of the law, he has been behind a great many—questionable deals. He operates solely on the Continent, not in this country."

"Oh."

"But he has a brother," said Mr. Robinson. "Robert Hoffman. Living in London—a diamond merchant—most respectable business— His wife is Dutch— He also has offices in Amsterdam— Your people may know about him. As I say, he deals mainly in diamonds, but he is a very rich man, and he owns a lot of property, not usually in his own name. Yes, he is behind quite a lot of enterprises. He and his brother are the real owners of Bertram's Hotel."

"Thank you, sir." Chief-Inspector Davy rose to his feet. "I needn't tell you that I'm much obliged to you. It's wonderful," he added, allowing himself to show more enthusiasm than was normal.

"That I should know?" inquired Mr. Robinson, giving one of his larger smiles. "But that is one of my specialties. Information. I like to know. That is why you came to me, is it not?"

"Well," said Chief-Inspector Davy, "we do know about you. The Home Office. The Special Branch and all the rest of it." He added almost naïvely, "It took a bit of nerve on my part to approach you."

Again Mr. Robinson smiled.

"I find you an interesting personality, Chief-Inspector Davy," he said. "I wish you success in whatever you are undertaking."

"Thank you, sir. I think I shall need it. By the way, these two brothers, would you say they were violent men?"

"Certainly not," said Mr. Robinson. "It would be quite against their policy. The brothers Hoffman do not apply violence in business matters. They have other methods that serve them better. Year by year, I would say, they get steadily richer, or so my information from Swiss Banking circles tells me."

"It's a useful place, Switzerland," said Chief-Inspector Davy.

"Yes, indeed. What we should all do without it I do not know! So much rectitude. Such a fine business sense! Yes, we business men must all be very grateful to Switzerland. I myself," he added, "have also a high opinion of Amsterdam." He looked hard at Davy, then smiled again, and the Chief-Inspector left.

When he got back to headquarters again, he found a note awaiting him.

Canon Pennyfather has turned up—safe if not sound. Apparently was knocked down by a car at Milton St. John and has concussion.

Chapter Eighteen

CANON PENNYFATHER looked at Chief-Inspector Davy and Inspector Campbell, and Chief-Inspector Davy and Inspector Campbell looked at him. Canon Pennyfather was at home again. Sitting in the big arm-chair in his library, a pillow behind his head and his feet up on a pouffe, with a rug over his knees to emphasize his invalid status.

"I'm afraid," he was saying politely, "that I simply cannot remember anything at all."

"You can't remember the accident when the car hit you?"

"I'm really afraid not."

"Then how did you know a car hit you?" demanded Inspector Campbell acutely.

"The woman there, Mrs.—Mrs.—was her name Wheeling?—told me about it."

"And how did she know?"

Canon Pennyfather looked puzzled.

"Dear me, you are quite right. She couldn't have known, could she? I suppose she thought it was what must have happened."

"And you really cannot remember *anything?* How did you come to be in Milton St. John?"

"I've no idea," said Canon Pennyfather. "Even the name is quite unfamiliar to me."

Inspector Campbell's exasperation was mounting, but Chief-Inspector Davy said in his soothing, homely voice,

"Just tell us again the last thing you do remember, sir."

Canon Pennyfather turned to him with relief. The inspector's dry scepticism had made him uncomfortable.

"I was going to Lucerne to a congress. I took a taxi to the airport—at least to Kensington Air Station."

"Yes. And then?"

"That's all. I can't remember any more. The next thing I remember is the wardrobe."

"What wardrobe?" demanded Inspector Campbell.

"It was in the wrong place."

Inspector Campbell was tempted to go into this question of a wardrobe in the wrong place. Chief-Inspector Davy cut in.

"Do you remember arriving at the air station, sir?"

"I suppose so," said Canon Pennyfather, with the air of one who has a great deal of doubt on the matter.

"And you duly flew to Lucerne."

"Did I? I don't remember anything about it if so."

"Do you remember arriving back at Bertram's Hotel that night?"

"No."

"You do remember Bertram's Hotel?"

"Of course. I was staying there. Very comfortable. I kept my room on."

"Do you remember travelling in a train?"

"A train? No, I can't recall a train."

"There was a hold-up. The train was robbed. Surely, Canon Penny-father, you can remember *that*."

"I ought to, oughtn't I?" said Canon Pennyfather. "But somehow—" he spoke apologetically, "—I don't." He looked from one to the other of the officers with a bland gentle smile.

"Then your story is that you remember nothing after going in a taxi to the air station until you woke up in the Wheelings' cottage at Milton St. John."

"There is nothing unusual in that," the Canon assured him. "It happens quite often in cases of concussion."

"What did you think had happened to you when you woke up?"

"I had such a headache I really couldn't think. Then of course I began to wonder where I was and Mrs. Wheeling explained and brought me some excellent soup. She called me 'love' and 'dearie', and 'ducks'," said the Canon with slight distaste, "but she was very kind. Very kind indeed."

"She ought to have reported the accident to the police. Then you would have been taken to hospital and properly looked after," said Campbell.

"She looked after me very well," the Canon protested, with spirit, "and I understand that with concussion there is very little you *can* do except keep the patient quiet."

"If you should remember anything more, Canon Pennyfather—"

The Canon interrupted him.

"Four whole days I seem to have lost out of my life," he said. "Very curious. Really very curious indeed. I wonder so much where I was and what I was doing. The doctor tells me it may all come back to me. On the other hand it may not. Possibly I shall never know what happened to me during those days." His eyelids flickered. "You'll excuse me. I think I am rather tired."

"That's quite enough now," said Mrs. McCrae, who had been hovering by the door, ready to intervene if she thought it necessary. She advanced upon them. "Doctor says he wasn't to be worried," she said firmly.

The policemen rose and moved towards the door. Mrs. McCrae shepherded them out into the hall rather in the manner of a conscientious sheepdog. The Canon murmured something and Chief-Inspector Davy who was the last to pass through the door wheeled round at once.

"What was that?" he asked, but the Canon's eyes were now closed.

"What did you think he said?" said Campbell as they left the house after refusing Mrs. McCrae's lukewarm offer of refreshment.

Father said thoughtfully,

"I thought he said 'the walls of Jericho'."

"What could he mean by that?"

"It sounds biblical," said Father.

"Do you think we'll ever know," asked Campbell, "how that old boy got from the Cromwell Road to Milton St. John?"

"It doesn't seem as if we shall get much help from him," agreed Davy.

"That woman who says she saw him on the train after the hold-up. Can he possibly be right? Can he be mixed up in some way with these robberies? It seems impossible. He's such a thoroughly respectable old boy. Can't very well suspect a Canon of Chadminster Cathedral of being mixed up with a train robbery, can one?"

"No," said Father thoughtfully, "no. No more than one can imagine Mr. Justice Ludgrove being mixed up with a bank hold-up."

Inspector Campbell looked at his superior officer curiously.

The expedition to Chadminster concluded with a short and unprofitable interview with Dr. Stokes.

Dr. Stokes was aggressive, unco-operative and rude.

"I've known the Wheelings quite a while. They're by way of being neighbours of mine. They'd picked some old chap up off the road. Didn't know whether he was dead drunk, or ill. Asked me in to have a look. I told them he wasn't drunk—that it was concussion—"

"And you treated him for that."

"Not at all. I didn't treat him, or prescribe for him or attend him. I'm not a doctor—I was once, but I'm not now—I told them what they ought to do was ring up the police. Whether they did or not I don't know. Not my business. They're a bit dumb, both of them—but kindly folk."

"You didn't think of ringing up the police yourself?"

"No, I did not. I'm not a doctor. Nothing to do with me. As a human being I told them not to pour whisky down his throat and to keep him quiet and flat until the police came."

He glared at them and, reluctantly, they had to leave it at that.

Chapter Nineteen

MR. HOFFMAN was a big solid-looking man. He gave the appearance of being carved out of wood—preferably teak.

His face was so expressionless as to give rise to surmise—could such a man be capable of thinking—of feeling emotion? It seemed impossible.

His manner was highly correct.

He rose, bowed, and held out a wedge-like hand.

"Chief-Inspector Davy? It is some years since I had the pleasure—you may not even remember—"

"Oh yes I do, Mr. Hoffman. The Aaronberg Diamond Case. You were a witness for the Crown—a most excellent witness, let me say. The Defence was quite unable to shake you."

"I am not easily shaken," said Mr. Hoffman gravely.

He did not look a man who would easily be shaken.

"What can I do for you?" he went on. "No trouble, I hope—I always want to agree well with the police. I have the greatest admiration for your superb police force."

"Oh! there is no trouble. It is just that we wanted you to confirm a little information."

"I shall be delighted to help you in any way I can. As I say, I have the highest opinion of your London Police Force. You have such a splendid class of men. So full of integrity, so fair, so just."

"You'll make me embarrassed," said Father.

"I am at your service. What is it that you want to know?"

"I was just going to ask you to give me a little dope about Bertram Hotel."

Mr. Hoffman's face did not change. It was possible that his entire att tude became for a moment or two even more static than it had been before —that was all.

"Bertram's Hotel?" he said. His voice was inquiring, slightly puzzled. It might have been that he had never heard of Bertram's Hotel or that he could not quite remember whether he knew Bertram's Hotel or not.

"You have a connection with it, have you not, Mr. Hoffman?"

Mr. Hoffman moved his shoulders.

"There are so many things," he said. "One cannot remember them all. So much business—so much—it keeps me very busy."

"You have your fingers in a lot of pies, I know that."

"Yes," Mr. Hoffman smiled a wooden smile. "I pull out many plums, that is what you think? And so you believe I have a connection with this— Bertram's Hotel?"

"I shouldn't have said a connection. As a matter of fact, you own it, don't you?" said Father genially.

This time, Mr. Hoffman definitely did stiffen.

"Now who told you *that,* I wonder?" he said softly.

"Well, it's true, isn't it?" said Chief-Inspector Davy, cheerfully. "Very nice place to own, I should say. In fact, you must be quite proud of it."

"Oh yes," said Hoffman. "For the moment—I could not quite remember —you see—" he smiled deprecatingly, "—I own quite a lot of property in London. It is a good investment—property. If something comes on the market in what I think is a good position, and there is a chance of snapping it up cheap, I invest."

"And was Bertram's Hotel going cheap?"

"As a running concern, it had gone down the hill," said Mr. Hoffman, shaking his head.

"Well, it's on its feet now," said Father. "I was in there just the other day. I was very much struck with the atmosphere there. Nice old-fashioned clientele, comfortable, old-fashioned premises, nothing rackety about it, a lot of luxury without looking luxurious."

"I know very little about it personally," explained Mr. Hoffman. "It is just one of my investments—but I believe it is doing well."

"Yes, you seem to have a first-class fellow running it. What is his name? Humfries? Yes, Humfries."

"An excellent man," said Mr. Hoffman. "I leave everything to him. I look at the balance sheet once a year to see that all is well."

"The place was thick with titles," said Father. "Rich travelling Americans, too." He shook his head thoughtfully. "Wonderful combination."

"You say you were in there the other day?" Mr. Hoffman inquired. "Not—not officially, I hope?"

"Nothing serious. Just trying to clear up a little mystery."

"A mystery? In Bertram's Hotel?"

"So it seems. The Case of the Disappearing Clergyman, you might label it."

"That is a joke," Mr. Hoffman said. "That is your Sherlock Holmes language."

"This clergyman walked out of the place one evening and was never seen again."

"Peculiar," said Mr. Hoffman, "but such things happen. I remember many, many years ago now, a great sensation. Colonel—now let me think of his name—Colonel Fergusson I think, one of the equerries of Queen Mary. He walked out of his club one night and he, too, was never seen again."

"Of course," said Father, with a sigh, "a lot of these disappearances are voluntary."

"You know more about that than I do, my dear Chief-Inspector," said Mr. Hoffman. He added, "I hope they gave you every assistance at Bertram's Hotel?"

"They couldn't have been nicer," Father assured him. "That Miss Gorringe, she has been with you some time, I believe?"

"Possibly. I really know so very little about it. I take no *personal* interest, you understand. In fact—" he smiled disarmingly, "—I was surprised that you even knew it belonged to me."

It was not quite a question; but once more there was a slight uneasiness in his eyes. Father noted it without seeming to. "The ramifications that go on in the City are like a gigantic jigsaw," he said. "It would make my head ache if I had to deal with that side of things. I gather that a company—Mayfair Holding Trust or some name like that—is the registered owner. They're owned by another company and so on and so on. The real truth of the matter is that it belongs to *you*. Simple as that. I'm right, aren't I?"

"I and my fellow directors are what I dare say you'd call behind it, yes," admitted Mr. Hoffman rather reluctantly.

"Your fellow directors. And who might they be? Yourself and, I believe, a brother of yours?"

"My brother Wilhelm is associated with me in this venture. You must understand that Bertram's is only a part of a chain of various hotels, offices, clubs and other London properties."

"Any other directors?"

"Lord Pomfret, Abel Isaacstein." Hoffman's voice was suddenly edged. "Do you really need to know all these things? Just because you are looking into the Case of the Disappearing Clergyman?"

Father shook his head and looked apologetic.

"I suppose it's really curiosity. Looking for my disappearing clergyman was what took me to Bertram's, but then I got—well, interested if you understand what I mean. One thing leads to another sometimes, doesn't it?"

"I suppose that could be so, yes. And now?" he smiled, "your curiosity is satisfied?"

"Nothing like coming to the horse's mouth when you want information, is there?" said Father, genially. He rose to his feet. "There's only one thing I'd really like to know—and I don't suppose you'll tell me that."

"Yes, Chief-Inspector?" Hoffman's voice was wary.

"Where do Bertram's get hold of their staff? Wonderful! That fellow what's-his-name—Henry. The one that looks like an Archduke or an Archbishop, I'm not sure which. Anyway, he serves you tea and muffins—most wonderful muffins! An unforgettable experience."

"You like muffins with much butter, yes?" Mr. Hoffman's eyes rested for a moment on the rotundity of Father's figure with disapprobation.

"I expect you can see I do," said Father. "Well, I mustn't be keeping you. I expect you're pretty busy taking over takeover bids, or something like that."

"Ah. It amuses you to pretend to be ignorant of all these things. No, I am not busy. I do not let business absorb me too much. My tastes are simple. I live simply, with leisure, with growing of roses, and my family to whom I am devoted."

"Sounds ideal," said Father. "Wish I could live like that."

Mr. Hoffman smiled and rose ponderously to shake hands with him.

"I hope you will find your disappearing clergyman very soon."

"Oh! that's all right. I'm sorry I didn't make myself clear. He's found— disappointing case, really. Had a car accident and got concussion—simple as that."

Father went to the door, then turned and asked:

"By the way, is Lady Sedgwick a director of your company?"

"Lady Sedgwick?" Hoffman took a moment or two. "No. Why should she be?"

"Oh well, one hears things— Just a shareholder?"

"I—yes."

"Well, goodbye, Mr. Hoffman. Thanks very much."

Father went back to the Yard and straight to the A.C.

"The two Hoffman brothers are the ones behind Bertram's Hotel—financially."

"What? Those scoundrels?" demanded Sir Ronald.

"Yes."

"They've kept it very dark."

"Yes—and Robert Hoffman didn't half like our finding it out. It was a shock to him."

"What did he say?"

"Oh, we kept it all very formal and polite. He tried, not too obviously, to learn how I had found out about it."

"And you didn't oblige him with that information, I suppose."

"I certainly did not."

"What excuse did you give for going to see him?"

"I didn't give any," said Father.

"Didn't he think that a bit odd?"

"I expect he did. On the whole I thought that was a good way to play it, sir."

"If the Hoffmans are behind all this, it accounts for a lot. They're never concerned in anything crooked themselves—oh no! *They* don't organize crime—they finance it though!

"Wilhelm deals with the banking side from Switzerland. He was behind those foreign currency rackets just after the war—we knew it—but we couldn't prove it. Those two brothers control a great deal of money and they use it for backing all kinds of enterprises—some legitimate—some not. But they're careful—they know every trick of the trade. Robert's diamond broking is straightforward enough—but it makes a suggestive picture—diamonds—banking interests, and property—clubs, cultural foundations, office buildings, restaurants, hotels—all apparently owned by somebody else."

"Do you think Hoffman is the planner of these organized robberies?"

"No, I think those two deal only with finance. No, you'll have to look elsewhere for your planner. Somewhere there's a first-class brain at work."

Chapter Twenty

THE FOG had come down over London suddenly that evening. Chief-Inspector Davy pulled up his coat collar and turned into Pond Street. Walking slowly like a man who was thinking of something else, he did not look particularly purposeful but anyone who knew him well would realize that his mind was wholly alert. He was prowling as a cat prowls before the moment comes for it to pounce on its prey.

Pond Street was quiet tonight. There were few cars about. The fog had been patchy to begin with, had almost cleared, then had deepened again. The noise of the traffic from Park Lane was muted to the level of a suburban side road. Most of the buses had given up. Only from time to time individual cars went on their way with determined optimism. Chief-Inspector Davy turned up a cul-de-sac, went to the end of it and came back again. He turned again, aimlessly as it seemed, first one way, then the other, but he was not aimless. Actually his cat prowl was taking him in a circle round one particular building. Bertram's Hotel. He was appraising carefully just what lay to the east of it, to the west of it, to the north of it and to the south of it. He examined the cars that were parked by the pavement, he examined the cars that were in the cul-de-sac. He examined a mews with special care. One car in particular interested him and he stopped. He pursed up his lips and said softly, "So you're here again, you beauty." He checked the number and nodded to himself. "FAN 2266 tonight, are you?" He bent down and ran his fingers over the number plate delicately, then nodded approval. "Good job they made of it," he said under his breath.

He went on, came out at the other end of the mews, turned right and right again and came out in Pond Street once more, fifty yards from the entrance of Bertram's Hotel. Once again he paused, admiring the handsome lines of yet another racing car.

"You're a beauty, too," said Chief-Inspector Davy. "Your number plate's the same as the last time I saw you. I rather fancy your number plate always *is* the same. And that should mean—" he broke off "—or should it?"

he muttered. He looked up towards what could have been the sky. "Fog's getting thicker," he said to himself.

Outside the door to Bertram's, the Irish commissionaire was standing swinging his arms backwards and forwards with some violence to keep himself warm. Chief-Inspector Davy said good evening to him.

"Good evening, sir. Nasty night."

"Yes. I shouldn't think anyone would want to go out tonight who hadn't got to."

The swing doors were pushed open and a middle-aged lady came out and paused uncertainly on the step.

"Want a taxi, ma'am?"

"Oh dear. I meant to walk."

"I wouldn't if I were you, ma'am. It's very nasty, this fog. Even in a taxi it won't be too easy."

"Do you think you could find me a taxi?" said the lady doubtfully.

"I'll do my best. You go inside now, and keep warm and I'll come in and tell you if I've got one." His voice changed, modulated to a persuasive tone. "Unless you *have* to, ma'am, I wouldn't go out tonight at all."

"Oh dear. Perhaps you're right. But I'm expected at some friends in Chelsea. I don't know. It might be very difficult getting back here. What do you think?"

Michael Gorman took charge.

"If I were you, ma'am," he said firmly, "I'd go in and telephone to your friends. It's not nice for a lady like you to be out on a foggy night like this."

"Well—really—yes, well, perhaps you're right."

She went back in again.

"I have to look after them," said Micky Gorman turning in an explanatory manner to Father. "That kind would get her bag snatched, she would. Going out this time of night in a fog and wandering about Chelsea or West Kensington or wherever she's trying to go."

"I suppose you've had a good deal of experience of dealing with elderly ladies?" said Davy.

"Ah yes, indeed. This place is a home from home to them, bless their ageing hearts. How about you, sir? Were you wanting a taxi?"

"Don't suppose you could get me one if I did," said Father. "There don't seem to be many about in this. And I don't blame them."

"Ah, now, I might lay my hand on one for you. There's a place round the corner where there's usually a taxi driver got his cab parked, having a warm up and a drop of something to keep the cold out."

"A taxi's no good to me," said Father with a sigh.

He jerked his thumb towards Bertram's Hotel.

"I've got to go inside. I've got a job to do."

"Indeed now? Would it be still the missing Canon?"

"Not exactly. He's been found."

"Found?" The man stared at him. "Found where?"

"Wandering about with concussion after an accident."

"Ah, that's just what one might expect of him. Crossed the road without looking, I expect."

"That seems to be the idea," said Father.

He nodded, and pushed through the doors into the hotel. There were not very many people in the lounge this evening. He saw Miss Marple sitting in a chair near the fire and Miss Marple saw him. She made, however, no sign of recognition. He went towards the desk. Miss Gorringe, as usual, was behind her books. She was, he thought, faintly discomposed to see him. It was a very slight reaction, but he noted the fact.

"You remember me, Miss Gorringe," he said. "I came here the other day."

"Yes, of course I remember you, Chief-Inspector. Is there anything more you want to know? Do you want to see Mr. Humfries?"

"No thank you. I don't think that'll be necessary. I'd just like one more look at your register if I may."

"Of course." She pushed it along to him.

He opened it and looked slowly down the pages. To Miss Gorringe he gave the appearance of a man looking for one particular entry. In actuality this was not the case. Father had an accomplishment which he had learnt early in life and had developed into a highly skilled art. He could remember names and addresses with a perfect and photographic memory. That memory would remain with him for twenty-four or even forty-eight hours. He shook his head as he shut the book and returned it to her.

"Canon Pennyfather hasn't been in, I suppose?" he said in a light voice.

"Canon Pennyfather?"

"You know he's turned up again?"

"No indeed. Nobody has told *me*. Where?"

"Some place in the country. Car accident it seems. Wasn't reported to us. Some good Samaritan just picked him up and looked after him."

"Oh! I am pleased. Yes, I really am very pleased. I was worried about him."

"So were his friends," said Father. "Actually I was looking to see if one of them might be staying here now. Archdeacon—Archdeacon—I can't remember his name now, but I'd know it if I saw it."

"Tomlinson?" said Miss Gorringe helpfully. "He is due next week. From Salisbury."

"No, not Tomlinson. Well, it doesn't matter." He turned away.

It was quiet in the lounge tonight.

An ascetic looking middle-aged man was reading through a badly typed thesis, occasionally writing a comment in the margin in such small crabbed handwriting as to be almost illegible. Every time he did this, he smiled in vinegary satisfaction.

There were one or two married couples of long standing who had little need to talk to each other. Occasionally two or three people were gathered together in the name of the weather conditions, discussing anxiously how they or their families were going to get where they wanted to be.

"—I rang up and begged Susan not to come by car . . . it means the M1 and always so dangerous in fog—"

"They say it's clearer in the Midlands . . ."

Chief-Inspector Davy noted them as he passed. Without haste, and with no seeming purpose, he arrived at his objective.

Miss Marple was sitting near the fire and observing his approach.

"So you're still here, Miss Marple. I'm glad."

"I go tomorrow," said Miss Marple.

That fact had, somehow, been implicit in her attitude. She had sat, not relaxed, but upright, as one sits in an airport lounge, or a railway waiting-room. Her luggage, he was sure, would be packed, only toilet things and night wear to be added.

"It is the end of my fortnight's holiday," she explained.

"You've enjoyed it, I hope?"

Miss Marple did not answer at once.

"In a way—yes . . ." She stopped.

"And in another way, no?"

"It's difficult to explain what I mean—"

"Aren't you, perhaps, a little too near the fire? Rather hot, here. Wouldn't you like to move—into that corner perhaps."

Miss Marple looked at the corner indicated, then she looked at Chief-Inspector Davy.

"I think you are quite right," she said.

He gave her a hand up, carried her handbag and her book for her and established her in the quiet corner he had indicated.

"All right?"

"Quite all right."

"You know why I suggested it?"

"You thought—very kindly—that it was too hot for me by the fire. Besides," she added, "our conversation cannot be overheard here."

"Have you got something you want to tell me, Miss Marple?"

"Now why should you think that?"

"You looked as though you had," said Davy.

"I'm sorry I showed it so plainly," said Miss Marple. "I didn't mean to."

"Well, what about it?"

"I don't know if I ought to do so. I would like you to believe, Inspector, that I am not really fond of interfering. I am against interference. Though often well meant, it can cause a great deal of harm."

"It's like that, is it? I see. Yes, it's quite a problem for you."

"Sometimes one sees people doing things that seem to one unwise—even dangerous. But has one any right to interfere? Usually not, I think."

"Is this Canon Pennyfather you're talking about?"

"Canon Pennyfather?" Miss Marple sounded very surprised. "Oh no. Oh dear me no, nothing whatever to do with him. It concerns—a girl."

"A girl, indeed? And you thought I could help?"

"I don't know," said Miss Marple. "I simply don't know. But I'm worried, very worried."

Father did not press her. He sat there looking large and comfortable and rather stupid. He let her take her time. She had been willing to do her best to help him, and he was quite prepared to do anything he could to help her. He was not, perhaps, particularly interested. On the other hand, one never knew.

"One reads in the papers," said Miss Marple in a low clear voice, "accounts of proceedings in court, of young people, children or girls 'in need of care and protection'. It's just a sort of legal phrase, I suppose, but it could mean something real."

"This girl you mentioned, you feel she is in need of care and protection?"

"Yes. Yes I do."

"Alone in the world?"

"Oh no," said Miss Marple. "Very much not so, if I may put it that way. She is to all outward appearances very heavily protected and very well cared for."

"Sounds interesting," said Father.

"She was staying in this hotel," said Miss Marple, "with a Mrs. Carpenter, I think. I looked in the register to see the name. The girl's name is Elvira Blake."

Father looked up with a quick air of interest.

"She was a lovely girl. Very young, very much as I say, sheltered and protected. Her guardian was a Colonel Luscombe, a very nice man. Quite charming. Elderly of course, and I am afraid terribly innocent."

"The guardian or the girl?"

"I meant the guardian," said Miss Marple. "I don't know about the girl. But I do think she is in danger. I came across her quite by chance in Battersea Park. She was sitting at a refreshment place there with a young man."

"Oh, that's it, is it?" said Father. "Undesirable, I suppose. Beatnik—spiv —thug—"

"A very handsome man," said Miss Marple. "Not so very young. Thirty-odd, the kind of man that I should say is very attractive to women, but his face is a bad face. Cruel, hawklike, predatory."

"He mayn't be as bad as he looks," said Father soothingly.

"If anything he is worse than he looks," said Miss Marple. "I am convinced of it. He drives a large racing car."

Father looked up quickly.

"Racing car?"

"Yes. Once or twice I've seen it standing near this hotel."

"You don't remember the number, do you?"

"Yes, indeed I do. FAN 2266. I had a cousin who stuttered," Miss Marple explained. "That's how I remember it."

Father looked puzzled.

"Do you know who he is?" demanded Miss Marple.

"As a matter of fact I do," said Father slowly. "Half French, half Polish. Very well known racing driver, he was world champion three years ago. His name is Ladislaus Malinowski. You're quite right in some of your views about him. He has a bad reputation where women are concerned. That is to say, he is not a suitable friend for a young girl. But it's not easy to do anything about that sort of thing. I suppose she is meeting him on the sly, is that it?"

"Almost certainly," said Miss Marple.

"Did you approach her guardian?"

"I don't know him," said Miss Marple. "I've only just been introduced to him once by a mutual friend. I don't like the idea of going to him in a tale-bearing way. I wondered if perhaps in some way *you* could do something about it."

"I can try," said Father. "By the way, I thought you might like to know that your friend, Canon Pennyfather, has turned up all right."

"Indeed!" Miss Marple looked animated. "Where?"

"A place called Milton St. John."

"How very odd. What was he doing there? Did he know?"

"*Apparently*—" Chief-Inspector Davy stressed the word. "—He had had an accident."

"What kind of an accident?"

"Knocked down by a car—concussed—or else, of course, he might have been conked on the head."

"Oh! I see." Miss Marple considered the point. "Doesn't he know himself?"

"He *says*—" again the Chief-Inspector stressed the word, "—that he does not know anything."

"Very remarkable."

"Isn't it? The last thing he remembers is driving in a taxi to Kensington Air Station."

Miss Marple shook her head perplexedly.

"I know it does happen that way in concussion," she murmured. "Didn't he say anything—useful?"

"He murmured something about the Walls of Jericho."

"Joshua?" hazarded Miss Marple, "or Archæology—excavations?—or I remember, long ago, a play—by Mr. Sutro, I think."

"And all this week north of the Thames, Gaumont Cinemas—*The Walls of Jericho*, featuring Olga Radbourne and Bart Levinne," said Father.

Miss Marple looked at him suspiciously.

"He could have gone to that film in the Cromwell Road. He could have come out about eleven and come back here—though if so, someone ought to have seen him—it would be well before midnight—"

"Took the wrong bus," Miss Marple suggested. "Something like that—"

"Say he got back here *after* midnight," Father said, "—he *could* have walked up to his room without anyone seeing him— But if so, what happened then—and why did he go out again three hours later?"

Miss Marple groped for a word.

"The only idea that occurs to me is—oh!"

She jumped as a report sounded from the street outside.

"Car backfiring," said Father soothingly.

"I'm sorry to be so jumpy—I am nervous tonight—that feeling one has—"

"That something's going to happen? I don't think you need worry."

"I have never liked fog."

"I wanted to tell you," said Chief-Inspector Davy, "that you've given me a lot of help. The things you've noticed here—just little things—they've added up."

"So there *was* something wrong with this place?"

"There was and is everything wrong with it."

Miss Marple sighed.

"It seemed wonderful at first—unchanged you know—like stepping back into the past—to the part of the past that one had loved and enjoyed."

She paused.

"But of course, it wasn't really like that. I learned (what I suppose I really knew already) that one can never go back, that one should not ever try to go back—that the essence of life is going forward. Life is really a One Way Street, isn't it?"

"Something of the sort," agreed Father.

"I remember," said Miss Marple, diverging from her main topic in a characteristic way, "I remember being in Paris with my mother and my grandmother, and we went to have tea at the Elysée Hotel. And my grandmother looked round, and she said suddenly, 'Clara, I do believe I am the only woman here in a *bonnet!*' And she was, too! When she got home she packed up all her bonnets, and her beaded mantles too—and sent them off—"

"To the Jumble Sale?" inquired Father, sympathetically.

"Oh no. Nobody would have wanted them at a jumble sale. She sent them to a theatrical Repertory Company. They appreciated them very much. But let me see—" Miss Marple recovered her direction. "—Where was I?"

"Summing up this place."

"Yes. It seemed all right—but it wasn't. It was mixed up—real people and people who weren't real. One couldn't always tell them apart."

"What do you mean by not real?"

"There were retired military men, but there were also what seemed to be military men but who had never been in the army. And clergymen who weren't clergymen. And admirals and sea captains who've never been in the navy. My friend, Selina Hazy—it amused me at first how she was always so anxious to recognize people she knew (quite natural, of course) and how often she was mistaken and they weren't the people she thought they were. But it happened too often. And so—I began to wonder. Even Rose, the chambermaid—so nice—but I began to think that perhaps *she* wasn't real, either."

"If it interests you to know, she's an ex-actress. A good one. Gets a better salary here than she ever drew on the stage."

"But—why?"

"Mainly, as part of the décor. Perhaps there's more than that to it."

"I'm glad to be leaving here," said Miss Marple. She gave a little shiver. "Before anything happens."

Chief-Inspector Davy looked at her curiously.

"What do you expect to happen?" he asked.

"Evil of some kind," said Miss Marple.

"Evil is rather a big word—"

"You think it is too melodramatic? But I have some experience—I seem to have been—so often—in contact with murder."

"Murder?" Chief-Inspector Davy shook his head. "I'm not suspecting murder. Just a nice cosy round up of some remarkably clever criminals—"

"That's not the same thing. Murder—the wish to do murder—is something quite different. It—how shall I say—it defies God."

He looked at her and shook his head gently and reassuringly.

"There won't be any murders," he said.

A sharp report, louder than the former one, came from outside. It was followed by a scream and another report.

Chief-Inspector Davy was on his feet, moving with a speed surprising in such a bulky man. In a few seconds he was through the swing doors and out in the street.

II

The screaming—a woman's—was piercing the mist with a note of terror. Chief-Inspector Davy raced down Pond Street in the direction of the screams. He could dimly visualize a woman's figure backed against a railing. In a dozen strides he had reached her. She wore a long pale fur coat, and her shining blonde hair hung down each side of her face. He thought for a moment that he knew who she was, then he realized that this was only a slip of a girl. Sprawled on the pavement at her feet was the body of a man in uniform. Chief-Inspector Davy recognized him. It was Michael Gorman.

As Davy came up to the girl, she clutched at him, shivering all over, stammering out broken phrases.

"Someone tried to kill me . . . Someone . . . they shot at me . . . If it hadn't been for *him*—" she pointed down at the motionless figure at her feet. "He pushed me back and got in front of me—and then the second shot came . . . and he fell . . . He saved my life. I think he's hurt—badly hurt . . ."

Chief-Inspector Davy went down on one knee. His torch came out. The tall Irish commissionaire had fallen like a soldier. The left hand side of his tunic showed a wet patch that was growing wetter as the blood oozed out into the cloth. Davy rolled up an eyelid, touched a wrist. He rose to his feet again.

"He's had it all right," he said.

The girl gave a sharp cry. "Do you mean he's *dead?* Oh no, no! He can't be *dead.*"

"Who was it shot at you?"

"I don't know . . . I'd left my car just round the corner and was feeling my way along by the railings—I was going to Bertram's Hotel. And then suddenly there was a shot—and a bullet went past my cheek and then—he —the porter from Bertram's—came running down the street towards me, and shoved me behind him, and then another shot came . . . I think—I think whoever it was must have been hiding in that area there."

Chief-Inspector Davy looked where she pointed. At this end of Bertram's Hotel there was an old-fashioned area below the level of the street, with a gate and some steps down to it. Since it gave only on some store-rooms it was not much used. But a man could have hidden there easily enough.

"You didn't see him?"

"Not properly. He rushed past me like a shadow. It was all thick fog." Davy nodded.

The girl began to sob hysterically.

"But who could possibly want to kill me? Why should anyone want to kill me? That's the second time. I don't understand . . . why . . ."

One arm round the girl, Chief-Inspector Davy fumbled in his pocket with the other hand.

The shrill notes of a police whistle penetrated the mist.

III

In the lounge of Bertram's Hotel, Miss Gorringe had looked up sharply from the desk.

One or two of the visitors had looked up also. The older and deafer did not look up.

Henry, about to lower a glass of old brandy to a table, stopped poised with it still in his hand.

Miss Marple sat forward, clutching the arms of her chair. A retired admiral said decisively,

"Accident! Cars collided in the fog, I expect."

The swing doors from the street were pushed open. Through them came what seemed like an outsize policeman, looking a good deal larger than life.

He was supporting a girl in a pale fur coat. She seemed hardly able to walk. The policeman looked round for help with some embarrassment.

Miss Gorringe came out from behind the desk, prepared to cope. But at that moment the lift came down. A tall figure emerged, and the girl shook herself free from the policeman's support, and ran frantically across the lounge.

"Mother," she cried. "Oh *Mother, Mother . . .*" and threw herself, sobbing, into Bess Sedgwick's arms.

Chapter Twenty-one

CHIEF-INSPECTOR DAVY settled himself back in his chair and looked at the two women sitting opposite him. It was past midnight. Police officials had come and gone. There had been doctors, fingerprint men, an ambulance to remove the body; and now everything had narrowed to this one room dedicated for the purposes of the Law by Bertram's Hotel. Chief-Inspector

Davy sat one side of the table. Bess Sedgwick and Elvira sat the other side. Against the wall a policeman sat unobtrusively writing. Detective-Sergeant Wadell sat near the door.

Father looked thoughtfully at the two women facing him. Mother and daughter. There was, he noted, a strong superficial likeness between them. He could understand how for one moment in the fog he had taken Elvira Blake for Bess Sedgwick. But now, looking at them, he was more struck by the points of difference than the points of resemblance. They were not really alike save in colouring, yet the impression persisted that here he had a positive and a negative version of the same personality. Everything about Bess Sedgwick was positive. Her vitality, her energy, her magnetic attraction. He admired Lady Sedgwick. He always had admired her. He had admired her courage and had always been excited over her exploits; had said, reading his Sunday papers: "She'll never get away with *that*," and invariably she had got away with it! He had not thought it possible that she would reach journey's end and she had reached journey's end. He admired particularly the indestructible quality of her. She had had one air crash, several car crashes, had been thrown badly twice from her horse, but at the end of it here she was. Vibrant, alive, a personality one could not ignore for a moment. He took off his hat to her mentally. Some day, of course, she would come a cropper. You could only bear a charmed life for so long. His eyes went from mother to daughter. He wondered. He wondered very much.

In Elvira Blake, he thought, everything had been driven inward. Bess Sedgwick had got through life by imposing her will on it. Elvira, he guessed, had a different way of getting through life. She submitted, he thought. She obeyed. She smiled in compliance and behind that, he thought, she slipped away through your fingers. "Sly," he said to himself, appraising that fact. "That's the only way she can manage, I expect. She can never brazen things out or impose herself. That's why, I expect, the people who've looked after her have never had the least idea of what she might be up to."

He wondered what she had been doing slipping along the street to Bertram's Hotel on a late foggy evening. He was going to ask her presently. He thought it highly probable that the answer he would get would not be the true one. "That's the way," he thought, "that the poor child defends herself." Had she come here to meet her mother or to find her mother? It was perfectly possible, but he didn't think so. Not for a moment. Instead he thought of the big sports car tucked away round the corner—the car with the number plate FAN 2266. Ladislaus Malinowski must be some-where in the neighbourhood since his car was there.

"Well," said Father, addressing Elvira in his most kindly and father-like manner, "well, and how are you feeling now?"

"I'm quite all right," said Elvira.

"Good. I'd like you to answer a few questions if you feel up to it; be-cause, you see, time is usually the essence of these things. You were shot at twice and a man was killed. We want as many clues as we can get to the person who killed him."

"I'll tell you everything I can, but it all came so suddenly. And you can't *see* anything in a fog. I've no idea myself who it could have been—or even what he looked like. That's what was so frightening."

"You said this was the second time somebody had tried to kill you. Does that mean there was an attempt on your life before?"

"Did I say that? I can't remember." Her eyes moved uneasily. "I don't think I said that."

"Oh, but you did, you know," said Father.

"I expect I was just being—being hysterical."

"No," said Father, "I don't think you were. I think you meant just what you said."

"I might have been imagining things," said Elvira. Her eyes shifted again.

Bess Sedgwick moved. She said quietly:

"You'd better tell him, Elvira."

Elvira shot a quick, uneasy look at her mother.

"You needn't worry," said Father, reassuringly. "We know quite well in the police force that girls don't tell their mothers or their guardians every-thing. We don't take those things too seriously, but we've got to *know* about them, because, you see, it all helps."

Bess Sedgwick said,

"Was it in Italy?"

"Yes," said Elvira.

Father said: "That's where you've been at school, isn't it, or to a finish-ing place or whatever they call it nowadays?"

"Yes. I was at Contessa Martinelli's. There were about eighteen or twenty of us."

"And you thought that somebody tried to kill you. How was that?"

"Well, a big box of chocolates and sweets and things came for me. There was a card with it written in Italian in a flowery hand. The sort of thing they say, you know, "To the bellissima Signorina." Something like that. And my friends and I—well—we laughed about it a bit, and wondered who'd sent it."

"Did it come by post?"

"No. No, it couldn't have come by post. It was just there in my room. Someone must have put it there."

"I see. Bribed one of the servants, I suppose. I am to take it that you didn't let the Contessa whoever-it-was in on this?"

A faint smile appeared on Elvira's face. "No. No. We certainly didn't. Anyway we opened the box and they were lovely chocolates. Different kinds, you know, but there were some violet creams. That's the sort of chocolate that has a crystallized violet on top. My favourite. So of course I ate one or two of those first. And then afterwards, in the night, I felt terribly ill. I didn't think it was the chocolates, I just thought it was something perhaps that I'd eaten at dinner."

"Anybody else ill?"

"No. Only me. Well, I was very sick and all that, but I felt all right by the end of the next day. Then a day or two later I ate another of the same chocolates, and the same thing happened. So I talked to Bridget about it. Bridget was my special friend. And we looked at the chocolates, and we found that the violet creams had got a sort of hole in the bottom that had been filled up again, so we thought that someone had put some poison in and they'd only put it in the violet creams so that I would be the one who ate them."

"Nobody else was ill?"

"No."

"So presumably nobody else ate the violet creams?"

"No. I don't think they could have. You see, it was my present and they knew I liked the violet ones, so they'd leave them for me."

"The chap took a risk, whoever he was," said Father. "The whole place might have been poisoned."

"It's absurd," said Lady Sedgwick sharply. "Utterly absurd! I never heard of anything so crude."

Chief-Inspector Davy made a slight gesture with his hand. "Please," he said, then went on to Elvira: "Now I find that very interesting, Miss Blake. And you still didn't tell the Contessa?"

"Oh no, we didn't. She'd have made a terrible fuss."

"What did you do with the chocolates?"

"We threw them away," said Elvira. "They were lovely chocolates," she added, with a tone of slight grief.

"You didn't try and find out who sent them?"

Elvira looked embarrassed.

"Well, you see, I thought it might have been Guido."

"Yes?" said Chief-Inspector Davy, cheerfully. "And who is Guido?"

"Oh, Guido . . ." Elvira paused. She looked at her mother.

"Don't be stupid," said Bess Sedgwick. "Tell Chief-Inspector Davy about Guido, whoever he is. Every girl of your age has a Guido in her life. You met him out there, I suppose?"

"Yes. When we were taken to the opera. He spoke to me there. He was nice. Very attractive. I used to see him sometimes when we went to classes. He used to pass me notes."

"And I suppose," said Bess Sedgwick, "that you told a lot of lies and made plans with some friends and you managed to get out and meet him? Is that it?"

Elvira looked relieved by this short cut to confession.

"Yes. Bridget and I sometimes went out together. Sometimes Guido managed to—"

"What was Guido's other name?"

"I don't know," said Elvira. "He never told me."

Chief-Inspector Davy smiled at her.

"You mean you're not going to tell? Never mind. I dare say we'll be able to find out quite all right without your help, if it should really matter. But why should you think that this young man, who was presumably fond of you, should want to kill you?"

"Oh, because he used to threaten things like that. I mean, we used to have rows now and then. He'd bring some of his friends with him, and I'd pretend to like them better than him, and then he'd get very, very wild and angry. He said I'd better be careful what I did. I couldn't give him up just like that! That if I wasn't faithful to him he'd kill me! I just thought he was being melodramatic and theatrical."

Elvira smiled suddenly and unexpectedly. "But it was all rather fun. I didn't think it was *real* or *serious*."

"Well," said Chief-Inspector Davy, "I don't think it *does* seem very likely that a young man such as you describe would really poison chocolates and send them to you."

"Well, I don't think so really either," said Elvira, "but it must have been him because I can't see that there's anyone else. It worried me. And then, when I came back here, I got a note—" She stopped.

"What sort of a note?"

"It just came in an envelope and was printed. It said, 'Be on your guard. Somebody wants to kill you'."

Chief-Inspector Davy's eyebrows went up.

"Indeed? Very curious. Yes, very curious. And it worried you. You were frightened?"

"Yes. I began to—to wonder who could possibly want me out of the way. That's why I tried to find out if I was really very rich."

"Go on."

"And the other day in London something else happened. I was in the tube and there were a lot of people on the platform. I thought someone tried to push me on to the line."

"My dear child!" said Bess Sedgwick. "Don't romance."

Again Father made that slight gesture of his hand.

"Yes," said Elvira apologetically. "I expect I *have* been imagining it all but—I don't know—I mean, after what happened this evening it seems, doesn't it, as though it might all be true?" She turned suddenly to Bess Sedgwick, speaking with urgency, "*Mother! You* might know. *Does* anyone want to kill me? *Could* there be anyone? Have I got an enemy?"

"Of course you've not got an enemy," said Bess Sedgwick, impatiently. "Don't be an idiot. Nobody wants to kill you. Why should they?"

"Then who shot at me tonight?"

"In that fog," said Bess Sedgwick, "you might have been mistaken for someone else. That's possible, don't you think?" she said, turning to Father.

"Yes, I think it might be quite possible," said Chief-Inspector Davy.

Bess Sedgwick was looking at him very intently. He almost fancied the motion of her lips saying "later."

"Well," he said cheerfully, "we'd better get down to some more facts now. Where had you come from tonight? What were you doing walking along Pond Street on such a foggy evening?"

"I came up for an Art class at the Tate this morning. Then I went to lunch with my friend Bridget. She lives in Onslow Square. We went to a film and when we came out, there was this fog—quite thick and getting worse, and I thought perhaps I'd better not drive home."

"You drive a car, do you?"

"Yes. I took my driving test last summer. Only, I'm not a very good driver and I hate driving in fog. So Bridget's mother said I could stay the night, so I rang up Cousin Mildred—that's where I live in Kent—"

Father nodded.

"—and I said I was going to stay up over-night. She said that was very wise."

"And what happened next?" asked Father.

"And then the fog seemed lighter suddenly. You know how patchy fogs are. So I said I would drive down to Kent after all. I said goodbye to Bridget and started off. But then it began to come down again. I didn't like it very much. I ran into a very thick patch of it and I lost my way and I didn't know where I was. Then after a bit I realized I was at Hyde Park Corner and I thought 'I really *can't* go down to Kent in this.' At first, I thought I'd go back to Bridget's but then I remembered how I'd lost my way already. And then I realized that I was quite close to this nice hotel where Uncle Derek took me, when I came back from Italy, and I thought, 'I'll go there and I'm sure they can find me a room.' That was fairly easy, I found a place to leave the car and then I walked back up the street towards the hotel."

"Did you meet anyone or did you hear anyone walking near you?"

"It's funny you saying that, because I did think I heard someone walking behind me. Of course, there must be lots of people walking about in London. Only in a fog like this, it gives you a nervous feeling. I waited and listened but I didn't hear any footsteps and I thought I'd imagined them. I was quite close to the hotel by then."

"And then?"

"And then quite suddenly there was a shot. As I told you, it seemed to go right past my ear. The commissionaire man who stands outside the hotel came running down towards me and he pushed me behind him and then—then—the other shot came . . . He—he fell down and I screamed." She was shaking now. Her mother spoke to her.

"Steady, girl," said Bess in a low, firm voice. "Steady now." It was the voice Bess Sedgwick used for her horses and it was quite as efficacious when used on her daughter. Elvira blinked at her, drew herself up a little, and became calm again.

"Good girl," Bess said.

"And then *you* came," said Elvira to Father. "You blew your whistle, you told the policeman to take me into the hotel. And as soon as I got in, I saw—I saw Mother." She turned and looked at Bess Sedgwick.

"And that brings us more or less up to date," said Father. He shifted his bulk a little in the chair.

"Do you know a man called Ladislaus Malinowski?" he asked. His tone was even, casual, without any direct inflection. He did not look at the girl, but he was aware, since his ears were functioning at full attention, of a quick little gasp she gave. His eyes were not on the daughter but on the mother.

"No," said Elvira, having waited just a shade too long to say it. "No, I don't."

"Oh," said Father. "I thought you might. I thought he might have been here this evening."

"Oh? Why should he be here?"

"Well, his car is here," said Father. "That's why I thought he might be."

"I don't know him," said Elvira.

"My mistake," said Father. "You do, of course?" he turned his head towards Bess Sedgwick.

"Naturally," said Bess Sedgwick. "Known him for many years." She added, smiling slightly, "He's a madman, you know. Drives like an angel or a devil—he'll break his neck one of these days. Had a bad smash eighteen months ago."

"Yes, I remember reading about it," said Father. "Not racing again yet, is he?"

"No, not yet. Perhaps he never will."

"Do you think I could go to bed now?" asked Elvira, plaintively. "I'm—really terribly tired."

"Of course. You must be," said Father. "You've told us all you can remember?"

"Oh. Yes."

"I'll go up with you," said Bess.

Mother and daughter went out together.

"*She* knows him all right," said Father.

"Do you really think so?" asked Sergeant Wadell.

"I know it. She had tea with him in Battersea Park only a day or two ago."

"How did you find that out?"

"Old lady told me—distressed. Didn't think he was a nice friend for a young girl. He isn't of course."

"Especially if he and the mother—" Wadell broke off delicately. "It's pretty general gossip—"

"Yes. May be true, may not. Probably *is*."

"In that case which one is he really after?"

Father ignored that point. He said:

"I want him picked up. I want him badly. His car's here—just round the corner."

"Do you think he might be actually staying in this hotel?"

"Don't think so. It wouldn't fit into the picture. He's not supposed to be here. *If* he came here, he came to meet the girl. She definitely came to meet him, I'd say."

The door opened and Bess Sedgwick reappeared.

"I came back," she said, "because I wanted to speak to you."

She looked from him to the other two men.

"I wonder if I could speak to you alone? I've given you all the information I have, such as it is; but I would like a word or two with you in private."

"I don't see any reason why not," said Chief-Inspector Davy. He motioned with his head, and the young detective-constable took his note-book and went out. Wadell went with him. "Well?" said Chief-Inspector Davy.

Lady Sedgwick sat down again opposite him.

"That silly story about poisoned chocolates," she said. "It's nonsense. Absolutely ridiculous. I don't believe anything of the kind ever happened."

"You don't, eh?"

"Do you?"

Father shook his head doubtfully. "You think your daughter cooked it up?"

"Yes. But why?"

"Well, if you don't know why," said Chief-Inspector Davy, "how should I know? She's your daughter. Presumably you know her better than I do."

"I don't know her at all," said Bess Sedgwick bitterly. "I've not seen her or had anything to do with her since she was two years old, when I ran away from my husband."

"Oh yes. I know all that. I find it curious. You see, Lady Sedgwick, courts usually give the mother, even if she is a guilty party in a divorce, custody of a young child if she asks for it. Presumably then you didn't ask for it? You didn't want it."

"I thought it—better not."

"Why?"

"I didn't think it was—safe for her."

"On moral grounds?"

"No. Not on moral grounds. Plenty of adultery nowadays. Children have to learn about it, have to grow up with it. No. It's just that *I* am not really a safe person to be with. The life I'd lead wouldn't be a safe life. You can't help the way you're born. I was born to live dangerously. I'm not law-abiding or conventional. I thought it would be better for Elvira, happier, to have a proper English conventional bringing-up. Shielded, looked after . . ."

"But minus a mother's love?"

"I thought if she learned to love me it might bring sorrow to her. Oh, you mayn't believe me, but that's what I felt."

"I see. Do you still think you were right?"

"No," said Bess. "I don't. I think now I may have been entirely wrong."

"*Does* your daughter know Ladislaus Malinowski?"

"I'm sure she doesn't. She said so. You heard her."

"I heard her, yes."

"Well, then?"

"She was afraid, you know, when she was sitting here. In our profession we get to know fear when we meet up with it. She was afraid—why? Chocolates or no chocolates, her life has been attempted. That tube story may be true enough—"

"It was ridiculous. Like a thriller—"

"Perhaps. But that sort of thing does happen, Lady Sedgwick. Oftener than you'd think. Can you give me any idea who might want to kill your daughter?"

"Nobody—nobody at all!"

She spoke vehemently.

Chief-Inspector Davy sighed and shook his head.

Chapter Twenty-two

CHIEF-INSPECTOR DAVY waited patiently until Mrs. Melford had finished talking. It had been a singularly unprofitable interview. Cousin Mildred had been incoherent, unbelieving and generally feather-headed. Or that was Father's private view. Accounts of Elvira's sweet manners, nice nature, troubles with her teeth, odd excuses told through the telephone, had led on to serious doubts whether Elvira's friend Bridget was really a suitable friend for her. All these matters had been presented to the Chief-Inspector in a kind of general hasty pudding. Mrs. Melford knew nothing, had heard nothing, had seen nothing and had apparently deduced very little.

A short telephone call to Elvira's guardian, Colonel Luscombe, had been even more unproductive, though fortunately less wordy. "More Chinese monkeys," he muttered to his sergeant as he put down the receiver. "See no evil, hear no evil, speak no evil.

"The trouble is that everyone who's had anything to do with this girl has been far too nice—if you get my meaning. Too many nice people who don't know anything about evil. Not like my old lady."

"The Bertram's Hotel one?"

"Yes, that's the one. She's had a long life of experience in noticing evil, fancying evil, suspecting evil and going forth to do battle with evil. Let's see what we can get out of the girl friend Bridget."

The difficulties in this interview were represented first, last, and most of the time by Bridget's mamma. To talk to Bridget without the assistance of her mother took all Chief-Inspector Davy's adroitness and cajolery. He was, it must be admitted, ably seconded by Bridget. After a certain amount of stereotyped questions and answers and expressions of horror on the part of Bridget's mother at hearing of Elvira's narrow escape from death, Bridget said, "You know it's time for that committee meeting, Mum. You said it was very important."

"Oh dear, dear," said Bridget's mother.

"You know they'll get into a frightful mess without you, Mummy."

"Oh they will, they certainly will. But perhaps I ought—"

"Now that's quite all right, Madam," said Chief-Inspector Davy, putting on his kindly old father look. "You don't want to worry. Just you get off. I've finished all the important things. You've told me really everything I wanted to know. I've just one or two routine inquiries about people in Italy which I think your daughter, Miss Bridget, might be able to help me with."

"Well, if you think you could manage, Bridget—"

"Oh, I can manage, Mummy," said Bridget.

Finally, with a great deal of fuss, Bridget's mother went off to her committee.

"Oh dear," said Bridget, sighing, as she came back after closing the front door. "Really! I do think mothers are *difficult.*"

"So they tell me," said Chief-Inspector Davy. "A lot of young ladies I come across have a lot of trouble with their mothers."

"I'd have thought you'd put it the other way round," said Bridget.

"Oh I do, I do," said Davy. "But that's not how the young ladies see it. Now you can tell me a little more."

"I couldn't really speak frankly in front of Mummy," explained Bridget. "But I do feel, of course, that it is really important that you should know as much as possible about all this. I do know Elvira was terribly worried about something and *afraid*. She wouldn't exactly admit she was in danger, but she was."

"I thought that might have been so. Of course I didn't like to ask you too much in front of your mother."

"Oh no," said Bridget, "we don't want *Mummy* to hear about it. She gets in such a frightful state about things and she'd go and *tell* everyone. I mean, if Elvira doesn't want things like this to be known . . ."

"First of all," said Chief-Inspector Davy, "I want to know about a box of chocolates in Italy. I gather there was some idea that a box was sent to her which might have been poisoned."

Bridget's eyes opened wide. "Poisoned," she said. "Oh no. I don't think so. At least . . ."

"There was something?"

"Oh yes. A box of chocolates came and Elvira did eat a lot of them and she was rather sick that night. Quite ill."

"But she didn't suspect poison?"

"No. At least—oh yes, she did say that someone was trying to poison one of us and we looked at the chocolates to see, you know, if anything had been injected into them."

"And had it?"

"No, it hadn't," said Bridget. "At least, not as far as we could see."

"But perhaps your friend, Miss Elvira, might still have thought so?"

"Well, she might—but she didn't *say* any more."

"But you think she was afraid of someone?"

"I didn't think so at the time or notice anything. It was only here, later."

"What about this man, Guido?"

Bridget giggled.

"He had a terrific crush on Elvira," she said.

"And you and your friend used to meet him places?"

"Well, I don't mind telling *you*," said Bridget. "After all you're the police. It isn't important to you, that sort of thing, and I expect you understand. Countess Martinelli was frightfully strict—or thought she was. And of course we had all sorts of dodges and things. We all stood in with each other. You know."

"And told the right lies, I suppose?"

"Well, I'm afraid so," said Bridget. "But what can one do when anyone is so suspicious?"

"So you did meet Guido and all that. And used he to threaten Elvira?"

"Oh, not seriously, I don't think."

"Then perhaps there was someone else she used to meet?"

"Oh—that—well, I don't know."

"Please tell me, Miss Bridget. It might be—vital, you know."

"Yes. Yes I can see that. Well there was *someone*. I don't know who it was, but there was someone else—she really minded about. She was deadly serious. I mean it was a really *important* thing."

"She used to meet him?"

"I think so. I mean she'd *say* she was meeting Guido but it wasn't always Guido. It was this other man."

"Any idea who it was?"

"No." Bridget sounded a little uncertain.

"It wouldn't be a racing motorist called Ladislaus Malinowski?"

Bridget gaped at him.

"So you *know*?"

"Am I right?"

"Yes—I think so. She'd got a photograph of him torn out of a paper. She kept it under her stockings."

"That might have been just a pin-up hero, mightn't it?"

"Well it *might*, of course, but I don't think it was."

"Did she meet him here in this country, do you know?"

"I don't know. You see I don't know really what she's been doing since she came back from Italy."

"She came up to London to the dentist," Davy prompted her. "Or so she said. Instead she came to you. She rang up Mrs. Melford with some story about an old governess."

A faint giggle came from Bridget.

"That wasn't true, was it?" said the Chief-Inspector, smiling. "Where did she really go?"

Bridget hesitated and then said, "She went to Ireland."

"She went to Ireland, did she? Why?"

"She wouldn't tell me. She said there was something she had to find out."

"Do you know where she went in Ireland?"

"Not exactly. She mentioned a name. Bally something. Ballygowlan, I think it was."

"I see. You're sure she went to Ireland?"

"I saw her off at Kensington Airport. She went by Aer Lingus."

"She came back when?"

"The following day."

"Also by air?"

"Yes."

"You're quite sure, are you, that she came back by air?"

"Well—I suppose she did!"

"Had she taken a return ticket?"

"No. No, she didn't. I remember."

"She might have come back another way, mightn't she?"

"Yes, I suppose so."

"She might have come back for instance by the Irish Mail?"

"She didn't say she had."

"But she didn't *say* she'd come by air, did she?"

"No," Bridget agreed. "But why should she come back by boat and train instead of by air?"

"Well, if she had found out what she wanted to know and had had nowhere to stay, she might think it would be easier to come back by the Night Mail."

"Why, I suppose she *might*."

Davy smiled faintly.

"I don't suppose you young ladies," he said, "think of going anywhere except in terms of flying, do you, nowadays?"

"I suppose we don't really," agreed Bridget.

"Anyway, she came back to England. Then what happened? Did she come to you or ring you up?"

"She rang up."

"What time of day?"

"Oh, in the morning some time. Yes, it must have been about eleven or twelve o'clock, I think."

"And she said, what?"

"Well, she just asked if everything was all right."

"And was it?"

"No, it wasn't, because, you see, Mrs. Melford had rung up and Mummy had answered the phone and things had been very difficult and I hadn't known what to say. So Elvira said she would not come to Onslow Square, but that she'd ring up her cousin Mildred and try to fix up some story or other."

"And that's all you can remember?"

"That's all," said Bridget, making certain reservations. She thought of Mr. Bollard and the bracelet. That was certainly a thing she was not going to tell Chief-Inspector Davy. Father knew quite well that something was being kept from him. He could only hope that it was not something pertinent to his inquiry. He asked again:

"You think your friend was really frightened of someone or something?"

"Yes I do."

"Did she mention it to you or did you mention it to her?"

"Oh, I asked her outright. At first she said no and then she admitted that she *was* frightened. And I know she was," went on Bridget violently. "She was in danger. She was quite sure of it. But I don't know why or how or anything about it."

"Your surety on this point relates to that particular morning, does it, the morning she had come back from Ireland?"

"Yes. Yes, that's when I was so sure about it."

"On the morning when she *might* have come back on the Irish Mail?"

"I don't think it's very likely that she did. Why don't you ask her?"

"I probably shall do in the end. But I don't want to call attention to that point. Not at the moment. It might just possibly make things more dangerous for her."

Bridget opened round eyes.

"What do you mean?"

"You may not remember it, Miss Bridget, but that was the night, or rather the early morning, of the Irish Mail robbery."

"Do you mean that Elvira was in *that* and never told me a thing about it?"

"I agree it's unlikely," said Father. "But it just occurred to me that she might have seen something or someone, or some incident might have occurred connected with the Irish Mail. She might have seen someone she knew, for instance, and that might have put her in danger."

"Oh!" said Bridget. She thought it over. "You mean—someone she knew was mixed up in the robbery."

Chief-Inspector Davy got up.

"I think that's all," he said. "Sure there's nothing more you can tell me? Nowhere where your friend went that day? Or the day before?"

Again visions of Mr. Bollard and the Bond Street shop rose before Bridget's eyes.

"No," she said.

"I think there is something you haven't told me," said Chief-Inspector Davy.

Bridget grasped thankfully at a straw.

"Oh, I forgot," she said. "Yes. I mean she did go to some lawyers. Lawyers who were trustees, to find out something."

"Oh, she went to some lawyers who were her trustees. I don't suppose you know their name?"

"Their name was Egerton—Forbes Egerton and Something," said Bridget. "Lots of names. I think that's more or less right."

"I see. And she wanted to find out something, did she?"

"She wanted to know how much money she'd got," said Bridget.

Inspector Davy's eyebrows rose.

"Indeed!" he said. "Interesting. Why didn't she know herself?"

"Oh, because people never told her anything about money," said Bridget. "They seem to think it's bad for you to know actually how much money you have."

"And she wanted to know badly, did she?"

"Yes," said Bridget. "I think she thought it was important."

"Well, thank you," said Chief-Inspector Davy. "You've helped me a good deal."

Chapter Twenty-three

RICHARD EGERTON looked again at the official card in front of him, then up into the Chief-Inspector's face.

"Curious business," he said.

"Yes, sir," said Chief-Inspector Davy, "a very curious business."

"Bertram's Hotel," said Egerton, "in the fog. Yes, it was a bad fog last night. I suppose you get a lot of that sort of thing in fogs, don't you? Snatch and grab—handbags—that sort of thing?"

"It wasn't quite like that," said Father. "Nobody attempted to snatch anything from Miss Blake."

"Where did the shot come from?"

"Owing to the fog we can't be sure. She wasn't sure herself. But we think—it seems the best idea—that the man may have been standing in the area."

"He shot at her twice, you say?"

"Yes. The first shot missed. The commissionaire rushed along from where he was standing outside the hotel door and shoved her behind him just before the second shot."

"So that he got hit instead, eh?"

"Yes."

"Quite a brave chap."

"Yes. He was brave," said the Chief-Inspector. "His military record was very good. An Irishman."

"What's his name?"

"Gorman. Michael Gorman."

"Michael Gorman." Egerton frowned for a minute. "No," he said. "For a moment I thought the name meant something."

"It's a very common name, of course. Anyway, he saved the girl's life."

"And why exactly have you come to me, Chief-Inspector?"

"I hoped for a little information. We always like full information, you know, about the victim of a murderous assault."

"Oh, naturally, naturally. But really, I've only seen Elvira twice since he was a child."

"You saw her when she came to call upon you about a week ago, didn't you?"

"Yes, that's quite right. What exactly do you want to know? If it's anything about her personally, who her friends were or about boy-friends, or lovers' quarrels—all that sort of thing—you'd do better to go to one of the women. There's a Mrs. Carpenter who brought her back from Italy, I believe, and there's Mrs. Melford with whom she lives in Sussex."

"I've seen Mrs. Melford."

"Oh."

"No good. Absolutely no good at all, sir. And I don't so much want to know about the girl personally—after all, I've seen her for myself and I've heard what she can tell me—or rather what she's willing to tell me—"

At a quick movement of Egerton's eyebrows he saw that the other had appreciated the point of the word "willing".

"I've been told that she was worried, upset, or afraid about something, and convinced that her life was in danger. Was that your impression when she came to see you?"

"No," said Egerton, slowly, "no, I wouldn't go as far as that; though she did say one or two things that struck me as curious."

"Such as?"

"Well, she wanted to know who would benefit if she were to die suddenly."

"Ah," said Chief-Inspector Davy, "so she had that possibility in her mind, did she? That she might die suddenly. Interesting."

"She'd got something in her head but I didn't know what it was. She also wanted to know how much money she had—or would have when she was twenty-one. That, perhaps, is more understandable."

"It's a lot of money I believe."

"It's a very large fortune, Chief-Inspector."

"Why do you think she wanted to know?"

"About the money?"

"Yes, and about who would inherit it?"

"I don't know," said Egerton. "I don't know at all. She also brought up the subject of marriage—"

"Did you form the impression that there was a man in the case?"

"I've no evidence—but—yes, I did think just that. I felt sure there was a boy-friend somewhere in the offing. There usually is! Luscombe—that's Colonel Luscombe, her guardian, doesn't seem to know anything about a boy-friend. But then dear old Derek Luscombe wouldn't. He was quite upset when I suggested that there was such a thing in the background and probably an unsuitable one at that."

"He is unsuitable," said Chief-Inspector Davy.

"Oh. Then you know who he is?"

"I can have a very good guess at it. Ladislaus Malinowski."

"The racing motorist? Really! A handsome daredevil. Women fall for him easily. I wonder how he came across Elvira. I don't see very well where their orbits would meet except—yes, I believe he was in Rome a couple of months ago. Possible she met him there."

"Very possibly. Or she could have met him through her mother?"

"What, through Bess? I wouldn't say that was at all likely."

Davy coughed.

"Lady Sedgwick and Malinowski are said to be close friends, sir."

"Oh yes, yes, I know that's the gossip. May be true, may not. They are close friends—thrown together constantly by their way of life. Bess has had her affairs, of course; though, mind you, she's not the nymphomaniac type. People are ready enough to say that about a woman, but it's not true in Bess's case. Anyway, as far as I know, Bess and her daughter are practically not even acquainted with each other."

"That's what Lady Sedgwick told me. And you agree?"

Egerton nodded.

"What other relatives has Miss Blake got?"

"For all intents and purposes, none. Her mother's two brothers were killed in the war—and she was old Coniston's only child. Mrs. Melford, though the girl calls her 'Cousin Mildred,' is actually a cousin of Colonel Luscombe's. Luscombe's done his best for the girl in his conscientious old-fashioned way—but it's difficult . . . for a man."

"Miss Blake brought up the subject of marriage, you say? There's no possibility, I suppose, that she may actually already *be* married—"

"She's well under age—she'd have to have the assent of her guardian and trustees."

"Technically yes, yes. But they don't always wait for that," said Father.

"I know. Most regrettable. One has to go through all the machinery of making them Wards of Court, and all the rest of it. And even that has its difficulties."

"And once they're married, they're married," said Father. "I suppose, if she *were* married, and died suddenly, her husband would inherit?"

"This idea of marriage is most unlikely. She has been most carefully looked after and . . ." He stopped, reacting to Chief-Inspector Davy's cynical smile.

However carefully Elvira had been looked after, she seemed to have succeeded in making the acquaintance of the highly unsuitable Ladislaus Malinowski.

He said dubiously, "Her mother bolted, it's true."

"Her mother bolted, yes—that's what she would do—but Miss Blake's a different type. She's just as set on getting her own way, but she'd go about it differently."

"You don't really think—"

"I don't think anything—*yet*," said Chief-Inspector Davy.

Chapter Twenty-four

LADISLAUS MALINOWSKI looked from one to the other of the two police officers and flung back his head and laughed.

"It is very amusing!" he said. "You look solemn as owls. It is ridiculous that you should ask me to come here and wish to ask me questions. You have nothing against me, nothing."

"We think you may be able to assist us in our inquiries, Mr. Malinowski." Chief-Inspector Davy spoke with official smoothness. "You own a car, Mercedes-Otto, registration number FAN 2266."

"Is there any reason why I should not own such a car?"

"No reason at all, sir. There's just a little uncertainty as to the correct number. Your car was on a motor road, M7, and the registration plate on that occasion was a different one."

"Nonsense. It must have been some other car."

"There aren't so many of that make. We have checked up on those there are."

"You believe everything, I suppose, that your traffic police tell you! It is laughable! Where was all this?"

"The place where the police stopped you and asked to see your license is not very far from Bedhampton. It was on the night of the Irish Mail robbery."

"You really do amuse me," said Ladislaus Malinowski.

"You have a revolver?"

"Certainly, I have a revolver and an automatic pistol. I have proper licences for them."

"Quite so. They are both still in your possession?"

"Certainly."

"I have already warned you, Mr. Malinowski."

"The famous policeman's warning! Anything you say will be taken down and used against you at your trial."

"That's not quite the wording," said Father mildly. "Used, yes. Against, no. You don't want to qualify that statement of yours?"

"No, I do not."

"And you are sure you don't want your solicitor here?"

"I do not like solicitors."

"Some people don't. Where are those firearms now?"

"I think you know very well where they are, Chief-Inspector. The small pistol is in the pocket of my car, the Mercedes-Otto whose registered number is, as I have said, FAN 2266. The revolver is in a drawer in my flat."

"You're quite right about the one in the drawer in your flat," said Father, "but the other—the pistol—is not in your car."

"Yes, it is. It is in the left hand pocket."

Father shook his head. "It may have been once. It isn't now. Is this it, Mr. Malinowski?"

He passed a small automatic pistol across the table. Ladislaus Malinowski, with an air of great surprise, picked it up.

"Ah-ha, yes. This is it. So it was *you* who took it from my car?"

"No," said Father, "we didn't take it from your car. It was not in your car. We found it somewhere else."

"Where did you find it?"

"We found it," said Father, "in an area in Pond Street which—as you no doubt know—is a street near Park Lane. It could have been dropped by a man walking down that street—or running perhaps."

Ladislaus Malinowski shrugged his shoulders. "That is nothing to do with me—I did not put it there. It was in my car a day or two ago. One does not continually look to see if a thing is still where one has put it. One assumes it will be."

"Do you know, Mr. Malinowski, that this is the pistol which was used to shoot Michael Gorman on the night of November 26th?"

"Michael Gorman? I do not know a Michael Gorman."

"The commissionaire from Bertram's Hotel."

"Ah yes, the one who was shot. I read about it. And you say *my* pistol shot him? Nonsense!"

"It's not nonsense. The ballistic experts have examined it. You know enough of firearms to be aware that their evidence is reliable."

"You are trying to frame me. I know what you police do!"

"I think you know the police of this country better than that, Mr. Malinowski."

"Are you suggesting that I shot Michael Gorman?"

"So far we are only asking for a statement. No charge has been made."

"But this is what you think—that I shot that ridiculous dressed-up military figure. Why should I? I didn't owe him money, I had no grudge against him."

"It was a young lady who was shot at. Gorman ran to protect her and received the second bullet in his chest."

"A young lady?"

"A young lady whom I think you know. Miss Elvira Blake."

"Do you say someone tried to shoot Elvira with *my* pistol?"

He sounded incredulous.

"It could be that you had had a disagreement."

"You mean that I quarrelled with Elvira and shot her? What madness! Why should I shoot the girl I am going to marry?"

"Is that part of your statement? That you are going to marry Miss El-vira Blake?"

Just for a moment or two Ladislaus hesitated. Then he said, shrugging his shoulders,

"She is still very young. It remains to be discussed."

"Perhaps she had promised to marry you, and then—she changed her mind. There was *someone* she was afraid of. Was it you, Mr. Mali-nowski?"

"Why should *I* want her to die? I am in love with her and want to marry her or if I do not want to marry her I need not marry her. It is as simple as that. So why should I kill her?"

"There aren't many people close enough to her to want to kill her." Davy waited a moment and then said, almost casually: "There's her mother, of course."

"What!" Malinowski sprang up. *"Bess?* Bess kill her own daughter? You are mad! Why should Bess kill Elvira?"

"Possibly because, as next of kin, she might inherit an enormous for-tune."

"Bess? You mean Bess would kill for money? She has plenty of money from her American husband. Enough, anyway."

"Enough is not the same as a great fortune," said Father. "People do do murder for a large fortune, mothers have been known to kill their chil-dren, and children have killed their mothers."

"I tell you, you are mad!"

"You say that you may be going to marry Miss Blake. Perhaps you have already married her? If so, then *you* would be the one to inherit a vast for-tune."

"What more crazy, stupid things can you say! No, I am not married to Elvira. She is a pretty girl. I like her, and she is in love with me. Yes, I admit it. I met her in Italy. We had fun—but that is all. No more, do you understand?"

"Indeed? Just now, Mr. Malinowski, you said quite definitely that she was the girl you were going to marry."

"Oh that."

"Yes—that. Was it true?"

"I said it because—it sounded more respectable that way. You are so— prudish in this country—"

"That seems to me an unlikely explanation."

"You do not understand anything at all. The mother and I—we are lovers—I did not wish to say so—so I suggest instead that the daughter and

I—we are engaged to be married. That sounds very English and proper."

"It sounds to me even more far-fetched. You're rather badly in need of money, aren't you, Mr. Malinowski?"

"My dear Chief-Inspector, I am always in need of money. It is very sad."

"And yet a few months ago I understand you were flinging money about in a very carefree way."

"Ah. I had had a lucky flutter. I am a gambler. I admit it."

"I find that quite easy to believe. Where did you have this 'flutter'?"

"That I do not tell. You can hardly expect it."

"I don't expect it."

"Is that all you have to ask me?"

"For the moment, yes. You have identified the pistol as yours. That will be very helpful."

"I don't understand—I can't conceive—" he broke off and stretched out his hand. "Give it me please."

"I'm afraid we'll have to keep it for the present, so I'll write you out a receipt for it."

He did so and handed it to Malinowski.

The latter went out slamming the door.

"Temperamental chap," said Father.

"You didn't press him on the matter of the false number plate and Bedhampton?"

"No. I wanted him rattled. But not too badly rattled. We'll give him one thing to worry about at a time— And he *is* worried."

"The Old Man wanted to see you, sir, as soon as you were through."

Chief-Inspector Davy nodded and made his way to Sir Ronald's room.

"Ah! Father. Making progress?"

"Yes. Getting along nicely—quite a lot of fish in the net. Small fry mostly. But we're closing in on the big fellows. Everything's in train—"

"Good show, Fred," said the A.C.

Chapter Twenty-five

Miss Marple got out of her train at Paddington and saw the burly figure of Chief-Inspector Davy standing on the platform waiting for her.

He said, "Very good of you, Miss Marple," put his hand under her elbow and piloted her through the barrier to where a car was waiting. The driver opened the door, Miss Marple got in, Chief-Inspector Davy followed her and the car drove off.

"Where are you taking me, Chief-Inspector Davy?"

"To Bertram's Hotel."

"Dear me, Bertram's Hotel again. Why?"

"The official reply is: because the police think you can assist them in their inquiries."

"That sounds familiar, but surely rather sinister? So often the prelude to an arrest, is it not?"

"I am not going to arrest you, Miss Marple." Father smiled. "You have an alibi."

Miss Marple digested this in silence. Then she said, "I see."

They drove to Bertram's Hotel in silence. Miss Gorringe looked up from the desk as they entered, but Chief-Inspector Davy piloted Miss Marple straight to the lift.

"Second floor."

The lift ascended, stopped, and Father led the way along the corridor. As he opened the door of No. 18 Miss Marple said,

"This is the same room I had when I was staying here before."

"Yes," said Father.

Miss Marple sat down in the arm-chair.

"A very comfortable room," she observed, looking round with a slight sigh.

"They certainly know what comfort is here," Father agreed.

"You look tired, Chief-Inspector," said Miss Marple unexpectedly.

"I've had to get round a bit. As a matter of fact I've just got back from Ireland."

"Indeed. From Ballygowlan?"

"Now how the devil did *you* know about Ballygowlan? I'm sorry—I beg your pardon."

Miss Marple smiled forgiveness.

"I suppose Michael Gorman happened to tell you he came from there—was that it?"

"No, not exactly," said Miss Marple.

"Then how, if you'll excuse me asking you, *did* you know?"

"Oh dear," said Miss Marple, "it's really very embarrassing. It was just something I—happened to overhear."

"Oh, I see."

"I wasn't eavesdropping. It was in a public room—at least technically a public room. Quite frankly, I enjoy listening to people talking. One does. Especially when one is old and doesn't get about very much. I mean, if people are talking near you, you listen."

"Well, that seems to me quite natural," said Father.

"Up to a point, yes," said Miss Marple. "If people do not choose to lower their voices, one must assume that they are prepared to be overheard. But of course matters may develop. The situation sometimes arises when you realize that though it *is* a public room, other people talking do not realize that there is anyone else in it. And then one has to decide what to do about it. Get up and cough, or just stay quite quiet and hope they won't realize you've been there. Either way is embarrassing."

Chief-Inspector Davy glanced at his watch.

"Look here," he said, "I want to hear more about this—but I've got Canon Pennyfather arriving at any moment. I must go and collect him. You don't mind?"

Miss Marple said she didn't mind. Chief-Inspector Davy left the room.

II

Canon Pennyfather came through the swing doors into the hall of Bertram's Hotel. He frowned slightly, wondering what it was that seemed a little different about Bertram's today. Perhaps it had been painted or done up in some way? He shook his head. That was not it, but there was *something*. It did not occur to him that it was the difference between a six foot commissionaire with blue eyes and dark hair and a five foot seven commissionaire with sloping shoulders, freckles and a sandy thatch of hair bulging out under his commissionaire's cap. He just knew something was different. In his usual vague way he wandered up to the desk. Miss Gorringe was there and greeted him.

"Canon Pennyfather. How nice to see you. Have you come to fetch your baggage? It's all ready for you. If you'd only let us know we could have sent it to you to any address you like."

"Thank you," said Canon Pennyfather, "thank you very much. You're always most kind, Miss Gorringe. But as I had to come up to London anyway today I thought I might as well call for it."

"We were so worried about you," said Miss Gorringe. "Being missing, you know. Nobody able to find you. You had a car accident, I hear?"

"Yes," said Canon Pennyfather. "Yes. People drive much too fast nowadays. Most dangerous. Not that I can remember much about it. It affected my head. Concussion, the doctor says. Oh well, as one is getting on in life, one's memory—" he shook his head sadly. "And how are you, Miss Gorringe?"

"Oh, I'm very well," said Miss Gorringe.

At that moment it struck Canon Pennyfather that Miss Gorringe also was different. He peered at her, trying to analyse where the difference lay. Her hair? That was the same as usual. Perhaps even a little frizzier. Black dress, large locket, cameo brooch. All there as usual. But there was a difference. Was she perhaps a little thinner? Or was it—yes, surely, she looked *worried*. It was not often that Canon Pennyfather noticed whether people looked worried, he was not the kind of man who noticed emotion in the faces of others, but it struck him today, perhaps because Miss Gorringe had so invariably presented exactly the same countenance to guests for so many years.

"You've not been ill, I hope?" he asked solicitously. "You look a little thinner."

"Well, we've had a good deal of worry, Canon Pennyfather."

"Indeed. Indeed. I'm sorry to hear it. Not due to my disappearance, I hope?"

"Oh no," said Miss Gorringe. "We were worried, of course, about that, but as soon as we heard that you were all right—" She broke off and said, "No. No—it's this—well, perhaps you haven't read about it in the papers. Gorman, our outside porter, got killed."

"Oh yes," said Canon Pennyfather. "I remember now. I did see it mentioned in the paper—that you had had a murder here."

Miss Gorringe shuddered at this blunt mention of the word murder. The shudder went all up her black dress.

"Terrible," she said, "terrible. Such a thing has *never* happened at Bertram's. I mean, we're not the sort of hotel where murders happen."

"No, no, indeed," said Canon Pennyfather quickly. "I'm sure you're not. I mean it would never have occurred to me that anything like that could happen *here*."

"Of course it wasn't *inside* the hotel," said Miss Gorringe, cheering up a little as this aspect of the affair struck her. "It was outside in the street."

"So really nothing to do with you at all," said the Canon, helpfully.

That apparently was not quite the right thing to say.

"But it was connected with Bertram's. We had to have the police here questioning people, since it was our commissionaire who was shot."

"So that's a new man you have outside. D'you know, I thought somehow things looked a little strange."

"Yes, I don't know that he's very satisfactory. I mean, not quite the style we're used to here. But of course we had to get someone quickly."

"I remember all about it now," said Canon Pennyfather, assembling some rather dim memories of what he had read in the paper a week ago. "But I thought it was a *girl* who was shot."

"You mean Lady Sedgwick's daughter? I expect you remember seeing her here with her guardian, Colonel Luscombe. Apparently she was attacked by someone in the fog. I expect they wanted to snatch her bag. Anyway they fired a shot at her and then Gorman, who of course had been a soldier and was a man with a lot of presence of mind, rushed down, got in front of her and got shot himself, poor fellow."

"Very sad, very sad," said the Canon, shaking his head.

"It makes everything terribly difficult," complained Miss Gorringe. "I mean, the police constantly in and out. I suppose that's to be expected, but we don't *like* it here, though I must say Chief-Inspector Davy and Sergeant Wadell are very respectable looking. Plain clothes, and very good style, not the sort with boots and macintoshes like one sees on films. Almost like one of *us*."

"Er—yes," said Canon Pennyfather.

"Did you have to go to hospital?" inquired Miss Gorringe.

"No," said the Canon, "some very nice people, really good Samaritans—a market gardener, I believe—picked me up and his wife nursed me back to health. I'm most grateful, most grateful. It is refreshing to find that there is still human kindness in the world. Don't you think so?"

Miss Gorringe said she thought it was very refreshing. "After all one reads about the increase in crime," she added, "all those dreadful young men and girls holding up banks and robbing trains and ambushing people." She looked up and said, "There's Chief-Inspector Davy coming down the stairs now. I think he wants to speak to you."

"I don't know why he should want to speak to me," said Canon Penny-father, puzzled. "He's already been to see me, you know," he said, "at Chadminster. He was very disappointed, I think, that I couldn't tell him anything useful."

"You couldn't?"

The Canon shook his head sorrowfully.

"I couldn't remember. The accident took place somewhere near a place called Bedhampton and really I don't understand *what* I can have been doing there. The Chief-Inspector kept asking me why I was there and I couldn't tell him. Very odd, isn't it? He seemed to think I'd been driving a car from somewhere near a railway station to a vicarage."

"That sounds very possible," said Miss Gorringe.

"It doesn't seem possible at all," said Canon Pennyfather. "I mean, why should I be driving about in a part of the world that I don't really know?"

Chief-Inspector Davy had come up to them.

"So here you are, Canon Pennyfather," he said. "Feeling quite yourself again?"

"Oh, I feel quite well now," said the Canon, "but rather inclined to have headaches still. And I've been told not to do too much. But I still don't seem to remember what I ought to remember and the doctor says it may never come back."

"Oh well," said Chief-Inspector Davy, "we mustn't give up hope." He led the Canon away from the desk. "There's a little experiment I want you to try," he said. "You don't mind helping me, do you?"

III

When Chief-Inspector Davy opened the door of Number 18 Miss Marple was still sitting in the arm-chair by the window.

"A good many people in the street today," she observed. "More than usual."

"Oh well—this is a way through to Berkeley Square and Shepherd's Market."

"I didn't mean only passers-by. Men doing things—road repairs, a tele-phone repair van—a meat trolley—a couple of private cars—"

"And what—may I ask—do you deduce from that?"

"I didn't say that I deduced anything."

Father gave her a look. Then he said,

"I want you to help me."

"Of course. That is why I am here. What do you want me to do?"

"I want you to do exactly what you did on the night of November 19th. You were asleep—you woke up—possibly awakened by some unusual noise. You switched on the light, looked at the time, got out of bed, opened the door and looked out. Can you repeat those actions?"

"Certainly," said Miss Marple. She got up and went across to the bed. "Just a moment."

Chief-Inspector Davy went and tapped on the connecting walls of the next room.

"You'll have to do that louder," said Miss Marple. "This place is very well built."

The Chief-Inspector redoubled the force of his knuckles.

"I told Canon Pennyfather to count ten," he said, looking at his watch. "Now then, off you go."

Miss Marple touched the electric lamp, looked at an imaginary clock, got up, walked to the door, opened it and looked out. To her right, just leaving his room, walking to the top of the stairs, was Canon Pennyfather. He arrived at the top of the stairs and started down them. Miss Marple gave a slight catch of her breath. She turned back.

"Well?" said Chief-Inspector Davy.

"The man I saw that night can't have been Canon Pennyfather," said Miss Marple. "Not if that's Canon Pennyfather now."

"I thought you said—"

"I know. He looked like Canon Pennyfather. His hair and his clothes and everything. But he didn't walk the same way. I think—I think he must have been a younger man. I'm sorry, very sorry, to have misled you, but it wasn't Canon Pennyfather that I saw that night. I'm quite sure of it."

"You really are quite sure this time, Miss Marple."

"Yes," said Miss Marple. "I'm sorry," she added again, "to have misled you."

"You were very nearly right. Canon Pennyfather did come back to the hotel that night. Nobody saw him come in—but that wasn't remarkable. He came in after midnight. He came up the stairs, he opened the door of his room next door and he went in. What he saw or what happened next we don't know, because he can't or won't tell us. If there was only some way we could jog his memory . . ."

"There's that German word of course," said Miss Marple, thoughtfully.

"What German word?"

"Dear me, I've forgotten it now, but—"

There was a knock at the door.

"May I come in?" said Canon Pennyfather. He entered. "Was it satisfactory?"

"Most satisfactory," said Father. "I was just telling Miss Marple—you know Miss Marple?"

"Oh yes," said Canon Pennyfather, really slightly uncertain as to whether he did or not.

"I was just telling Miss Marple how we have traced your movements. You came back to the hotel that night after midnight. You came upstairs and you opened the door of your room and went in—" He paused.

Miss Marple gave an exclamation.

"I remember now," she said, "what that German word is. *Doppelganger!*"

Canon Pennyfather uttered an exclamation. "But of course," he said, "of *course!* How could I have forgotten? You're quite right, you know. After that film, *The Walls of Jericho* I came back here and I came upstairs and I opened my room and I saw—extraordinary, I distinctly saw *myself* sitting in a chair facing me. As you say, dear lady, a *doppelganger.* How very remarkable! And then—let me see—" He raised his eyes, trying to think.

"And then," said Father, "startled out of their lives to see you, when they thought you were safely in Lucerne, somebody hit you on the head."

Chapter Twenty-six

Canon Pennyfather had been sent on his way in a taxi to the British Museum. Miss Marple had been ensconced in the lounge by the Chief-Inspector. Would she mind waiting for him there for about ten minutes?

Miss Marple had not minded. She welcomed the opportunity to sit and look around her and think.

Bertram's Hotel. So many memories . . . The past fused itself with the present. A French phrase came back to her, *Plus ça change, plus c'est la même chose.* She reversed the wording. *Plus c'est la même chose, plus ça change.* Both true, she thought.

She felt sad—for Bertram's Hotel and for herself. She wondered what Chief-Inspector Davy wanted of her next. She sensed in him the excitement of purpose. He was a man whose plans were at last coming to fruition. It was Chief-Inspector Davy's D-Day.

The life of Bertram's went on as usual. No, Miss Marple decided, *not* as usual. There was a difference, though she could not have defined where the difference lay. An underlying uneasiness, perhaps?

The doors swung open once more and this time the big bovine-looking countryman came through them and across to where Miss Marple sat.

"All set?" he inquired genially.

"Where are you taking me now?"

"We're going to pay a call on Lady Sedgwick."

"Is she staying here?"

"Yes. With her daughter."

Miss Marple rose to her feet. She cast a glance round her and murmured: "Poor Bertram's."

"What do you mean—poor Bertram's?"

"I think you know quite well what I mean."

"Well—looking at it from your point of view, perhaps I do."

"It is always sad when a work of art has to be destroyed."

"You call this place a work of art?"

"Certainly I do. So do you."

"I see what you mean," admitted Father.

"It is like when you get ground elder really badly in a border. There's nothing else you can do about it—except dig the whole thing up."

"I don't know much about gardens. But change the metaphor to dry rot and I'd agree."

They went up in the lift and along a passage to where Lady Sedgwick and her daughter had a corner suite.

Chief-Inspector Davy knocked on the door, a voice said Come in, and he entered with Miss Marple behind him.

Bess Sedgwick was sitting in a high-backed chair near the window. She had a book on her knee which she was not reading.

"So it's you again, Chief-Inspector." Her eyes went past him towards Miss Marple and she looked slightly surprised.

"This is Miss Marple," explained Chief-Inspector Davy. "Miss Marple—Lady Sedgwick."

"I've met you before," said Bess Sedgwick. "You were with Selina Hazy the other day, weren't you? Do sit down," she added. Then she turned towards Chief-Inspector Davy again. "Have you any news of the man who shot at Elvira?"

"Not actually what you'd call *news*."

"I doubt if you ever will have. In a fog like that, predatory creatures come out and prowl around looking for women walking alone."

"True up to a point," said Father. "How is your daughter?"

"Oh, Elvira is quite all right again."

"You've got her here with you?"

"Yes. I rang up Colonel Luscombe—her guardian. He was delighted that I was willing to take charge." She gave a sudden laugh. "Dear old boy. He's always been urging a mother-and-daughter reunion act!"

"He may be right at that," said Father.

"Oh no, he isn't. Just at the moment, yes, I think it is the best thing." She turned her head to look out of the window and spoke in a changed voice. "I hear you've arrested a friend of mine—Ladislaus Malinowski. On what charge?"

"Not *arrested*," Chief-Inspector Davy corrected her. "He's just assisting us with our inquiries."

"I've sent my solicitor to look after him."

"Very wise," said Father approvingly. "Anyone who's having a little difficulty with the police is very wise to have a solicitor. Otherwise they may so easily say the wrong thing."

"Even if completely innocent?"

"Possibly it's even more necessary in that case," said Father.

"You're quite a cynic, aren't you? What are you questioning him about, may I ask? Or mayn't I?"

"For one thing we'd like to know just exactly what his movements were on the night when Michael Gorman died."

Bess Sedgwick sat up sharply in her chair.

"Have you got some ridiculous idea that *Ladislaus* fired those shots at Elvira? They didn't even know each other."

"He could have done it. His car was just round the corner."

"Rubbish," said Lady Sedgwick robustly.

"How much did that shooting business the other night upset you, Lady Sedgwick?"

She looked faintly surprised.

"Naturally I was upset when my daughter had a narrow escape of her life. What do you expect?"

"I didn't mean that. I mean how much did the death of Michael Gorman upset you?"

"I was very sorry about it. He was a brave man."

"Is that all?"

"What more would you expect me to say?"

"You knew him, didn't you?"

"Of course. He worked here."

"You knew him a little better than that, though, didn't you?"

"What do you mean?"

"Come, Lady Sedgwick. He was your husband, wasn't he?"

She did not answer for a moment or two, though she displayed no signs of agitation or surprise.

"You know a good deal, don't you, Chief-Inspector?" She sighed and sat back in her chair. "I hadn't seen him for—let me see—a great many years. Twenty—more than twenty. And then I looked out of a window one day, and suddenly recognized Micky."

"And he recognized you?"

"Quite surprising that we did recognize each other," said Bess Sedgwick. "We were only together for about a week. Then my family caught up with us, paid Micky off, and took me home in disgrace."

She sighed.

"I was very young when I ran away with him. I knew very little. Just a fool of a girl with a head full of romantic notions. He was a hero to me, mainly because of the way he rode a horse. He didn't know what fear was. And he was handsome and gay with an Irishman's tongue! I suppose really I ran away with *him!* I doubt if he'd have thought of it himself! But I was wild and headstrong and madly in love!" She shook her head. "It didn't last long . . . The first twenty-four hours were enough to disillusion me. He drank and he was coarse and brutal. When my family turned up and took me back with them, I was thankful. I never wanted to see him or hear of him again."

"Did your family know that you were married to him?"

"No."

"You didn't tell them?"

"I didn't think I *was* married."

"How did that come about?"

"We were married in Ballygowlan, but when my people turned up, Micky came to me and told me the marriage had been a fake. He and his friends had cooked it up between them, he said. By that time it seemed to me quite a natural thing for him to have done. Whether he wanted the money that was being offered him, or whether he was afraid he'd committed a breach of law by marrying me when I wasn't of age, I don't know. Anyway, I didn't doubt for a moment that what he said was true—not then."

"And later?"

She seemed lost in her thoughts. "It wasn't until—oh, quite a number of years afterwards, when I knew a little more of life, and of legal matters, that it suddenly occurred to me that probably I was married to Micky Gorman after all!"

"In actual fact, then, when you married Lord Coniston, you committed bigamy."

"And when I married Johnnie Sedgwick, and again when I married my American husband, Ridgeway Becker." She looked at Chief-Inspector Davy and laughed with what seemed like genuine amusement.

"So much bigamy," she said. "It really does seem very ridiculous."

"Did you never think of getting a divorce?"

She shrugged her shoulders. "It all seemed like a silly dream. Why rake it up? I'd told Johnnie, of course." Her voice softened and mellowed as she said his name.

"And what did he say?"

"He didn't care. Neither Johnnie nor I were ever very law-abiding."

"Bigamy carries certain penalties, Lady Sedgwick."

She looked at him and laughed.

"Who was ever going to worry about something that had happened in Ireland years ago? The whole thing was over and done with. Micky had taken his money and gone off. Oh don't you understand? It seemed just a silly little incident. An incident I wanted to forget. I put it aside with the things—the very many things—that don't matter in life."

"And then," said Father, in a tranquil voice, "one day in November, Michael Gorman turned up again and blackmailed you?"

"Nonsense! Who said he blackmailed me?"

Slowly Father's eyes went round to the old lady sitting quietly, very upright, in her chair.

"You." Bess Sedgwick stared at Miss Marple. "What can *you* know about it?"

Her voice was more curious than accusing.

"The arm-chairs in this hotel have very high backs," said Miss Marple. "Very comfortable they are. I was sitting in one in front of the fire in the writing-room. Just resting before I went out one morning. You came in to write a letter. I suppose you didn't realize there was anyone else in the room. And so—I heard your conversation with this man Gorman."

"You listened?"

"Naturally," said Miss Marple. "Why not? It was a public room. When you threw up the window and called to the man outside, I had no idea that it was going to be a private conversation."

Bess stared at her for a moment, then she nodded her head slowly.

"Fair enough," she said. "Yes, I see. But all the same you misunderstood what you heard. Micky didn't blackmail me. He might have thought of it —but I warned him off before he could try!" Her lips curled up again in that wide generous smile that made her face so attractive. "I frightened him off."

"Yes," agreed Miss Marple. "I think you probably did. You threatened to shoot him. You handled it—if you won't think it impertinent of me to say so—very very well indeed."

Bess Sedgwick's eyebrows rose in some amusement.

"But I wasn't the only person to hear you," Miss Marple went on.

"Good gracious! Was the whole hotel listening?"

"The other arm-chair was also occupied."

"By whom?"

Miss Marple closed her lips. She looked at Chief-Inspector Davy, and it was almost a pleading glance. "If it *must* be done, *you* do it," the glance said, "but I can't . . ."

"Your daughter was in the other chair," said Chief-Inspector Davy.

"Oh, no!" The cry came out sharply. "Oh *no*. Not Elvira! I see—yes, I see. She must have thought—"

"She thought seriously enough of what she had overheard to go to Ireland and search for the truth. It wasn't difficult to discover."

Again Bess Sedgwick said softly: "Oh no . . ." And then: "Poor child! . . . Even now, she's never asked me a thing. She's kept it all to herself. Bottled up inside herself. If she'd only told me I could have explained it all to her—showed her how it didn't matter."

"She mightn't have agreed with you there," said Chief-Inspector Davy. "It's a funny thing, you know," he went on, in a reminiscent, almost gossipy manner, looking like an old farmer discussing his stock and his land, "I've learnt after a great many years' trial and error—I've learned to distrust a pattern when it's simple. Simple patterns are often too good to be true. The pattern of this murder the other night was like that. Girl says someone shot at her and missed. The commissionaire came running to save her, and copped it with a second bullet. That may be all true enough. That may be the way the girl saw it. But actually behind the appearances, things might be rather different.

"You said pretty vehemently just now, Lady Sedgwick, that there could be no reason for Ladislaus Malinowski to attempt your daughter's life. Well, I'll agree with you. I don't think there was. He's the sort of young man who might have a row with a woman, pull out a knife and stick it into her. But I don't think he'd hide in an area, and wait cold-bloodedly to shoot her. But supposing he wanted to shoot *someone else*. Screams and shots—but what actually has happened is that *Michael Gorman* is dead. Suppose that was actually what was *meant* to happen. Malinowski plans it very carefully. He chooses a foggy night, hides in the area and waits until your daughter comes up the street. He knows she's coming because he has managed to arrange it that way. He fires a shot. It's not meant to hit the girl. He's careful not to let the bullet go anywhere near her, but *she* thinks it's aimed at her all right. She screams. The porter from the hotel, hearing the shot and the scream, comes rushing down the street *and then Malinowski shoots the person he's come to shoot. Michael Gorman.*"

"I don't believe a word of it! Why on earth should Ladislaus want to shoot Micky Gorman?"

"A little matter of blackmail, perhaps," said Father.

"Do you mean that Micky was blackmailing *Ladislaus*? What about?"

"Perhaps," said Father, "about the things that go on at Bertram's Hotel. Michael Gorman might have found out quite a lot about that."

"Things that go on at Bertram's Hotel? What *do* you mean?"

"It's been a good racket," said Father. "Well planned, beautifully executed. But nothing lasts forever. Miss Marple here asked me the other day what was wrong with this place. Well, I'll answer that question now. Bertram's Hotel is to all intents and purposes the headquarters of one of the best and biggest crime syndicates that's been known for years."

Chapter Twenty-seven

THERE WAS silence for about a minute and a half. Then Miss Marple spoke.

"How *very* interesting," she said conversationally.

Bess Sedgwick turned on her. "You don't seem surprised, Miss Marple."

"I'm not. Not really. There were so many curious things that didn't seem quite to fit in. It was all too good to be true—if you know what I mean. What they call in theatrical circles, a beautiful performance. But it *was* a performance—not real.

"And there were a lot of little things, people claiming a friend or an acquaintance—and turning out to be wrong."

"These things happen," said Chief-Inspector Davy, "but they happened too often. Is that right, Miss Marple?"

"Yes," agreed Miss Marple. "People like Selina Hazy do make that kind of mistake. But there were so many other people doing it too. One couldn't help *noticing* it."

"She notices a lot," said Chief-Inspector Davy, speaking to Bess Sedgwick as though Miss Marple was his pet performing dog.

Bess Sedgwick turned on him sharply.

"What did you mean when you said this place was the headquarters of a Crime Syndicate? I should have said that Bertram's Hotel was the most respectable place in the world."

"Naturally," said Father. "It would have to be. A lot of money, time, and thought has been spent on making it just what it is. The genuine and the phony are mixed up very cleverly. You've got a superb actor manager running the show in Henry. You've got that chap, Humfries, wonderfully plausible. He hasn't got a record in this country but he's been mixed up in some rather curious hotel dealings abroad. There are some very good character actors playing various parts here. I'll admit, if you like, that I can't help feeling a good deal of admiration for the whole set-up. It has cost this country a mint of money. It's given the CID and the provincial police forces constant headaches. Every time we seemed to be getting somewhere, and put our finger on some particular incident—it turned out to be the kind of incident that had nothing to do with anything else. But we've gone on working on it, a piece there, a piece here. A garage where stacks of number plates were kept, transferable at a moment's notice to certain cars. A firm of furniture vans, a butcher's van, a grocer's van, even one or two phony postal vans. A racing driver with a racing car covering incredible distances in incredibly few minutes, and at the other end of the scale an old clergyman jogging along in his old Morris Oxford. A cottage with a market gardener in it who lends first aid if necessary and who is in touch with a useful doctor. I needn't go into it all. The ramifications seem unending. That's one half of it. The foreign visitors who come to Bertram's are the other half. Mostly from America, or from the Dominions. Rich people above suspicion, coming here with a good lot of luxury luggage, leaving here with a good lot of luxury luggage which looks the same but isn't. Rich tourists arriving in France and not worried unduly by the Customs because the Customs don't worry tourists when they're bringing money into the country. Not the same tourists too many times. The pitcher mustn't go to the well too often. None of it's going to be easy to prove or to tie up, but it will all tie up in the end. We've made a beginning. The Cabots, for instance—"

"What about the Cabots?" asked Bess sharply.

"You remember them? Very nice Americans. Very nice indeed. They stayed here last year and they've been here again this year. They wouldn't have come a third time. Nobody ever comes here more than twice on the same racket. Yes, we arrested them when they arrived at Calais. Very well made job, that wardrobe case they had with them. It had over three hundred thousand pounds neatly stashed. Proceeds of the Bedhampton train robbery. Of course, that's only a drop in the ocean.

"Bertram's Hotel, let me tell you, is the headquarters of the whole thing! Half the staff are in on it. Some of the guests are in on it. Some of the guests are who they say they are—some are not. The real Cabots, for instance, are in Yucatan just now. Then there was the identification racket. Take Mr. Justice Ludgrove. A familiar face, bulbous nose and a wart. Quite easy to impersonate. Canon Pennyfather. A mild country clergyman, with a great white thatch of hair and notable absent-minded behaviour. His mannerisms, his way of peering over his spectacles—all very easily imitated by a good character actor."

"But what was the use of all that?" asked Bess.

"Are you really asking me? Isn't it obvious? Mr. Justice Ludgrove is seen near the scene of a bank hold-up. Someone recognizes him, mentions it. We go into it. It's all a mistake. He was somewhere else at the time.

But it wasn't for a while that we realized that these were all what is sometimes called 'deliberate mistakes'. Nobody's bothered about the man who had looked so like him. And doesn't look particularly like him really. He takes off his make-up and stops acting his part. The whole thing brings about confusion. At one time we had a High Court judge, an Archdeacon, an Admiral, a Major-General, all seen near the scene of a crime.

"After the Bedhampton train robbery at least four vehicles were concerned before the loot arrived in London. A racing car driven by Malinowski took part in it, a false Metal Box lorry, an old-fashioned Daimler with an admiral in it, and an old clergyman with a thatch of white hair in a Morris Oxford. The whole thing was a splendid operation, beautifully planned.

"And then one day the gang had a bit of bad luck. That muddleheaded old ecclesiastic, Canon Pennyfather, went off to catch his plane on the wrong day, they turned him away from the air station, he wandered out into Cromwell Road, went to a film, arrived back here after midnight, came up to his room of which he had the key in his pocket, opened the door, and walked in to get the shock of his life when he saw what appeared to be *himself* sitting in a chair facing him! The last thing the gang expected was to see the real Canon Pennyfather, supposed to be safely in Lucerne, walk in! His double was just getting ready to start off to play his part at Bedhampton when in walked the real man. They didn't know what to do but there was a quick reflex action from one member of the party. Humfries, I suspect. He hit the old man on the head, and he went down unconscious. Somebody, I think, was angry over that. Very angry. However, they examined the old boy, decided he was only knocked out, and would probably come round later and they went on with their plans. The false Canon Pennyfather left his room, went out of the hotel, and drove to the scene of activities where he was to play his part in the relay race. What they did with the real Canon Pennyfather I don't know. I can only guess. I presume he too was moved later that night, driven down in a car, taken to the market gardener's cottage which was at a spot not too far from where the train was to be held up and where a doctor could attend to him. Then, if reports came through about Canon Pennyfather having been seen in that neighbourhood, it would all fit in. It must have been an anxious moment for all concerned until he regained consciousness and they found that at least three days had been knocked out of his remembrance."

"Would they have killed him otherwise?" asked Miss Marple.

"No," said Father. "I don't think they would have killed him. Someone wouldn't have let that happen. It has seemed very clear all along that whoever ran this show had an objection to murder."

"It sounds fantastic," said Bess Sedgwick. "Utterly fantastic! And I don't believe you have any evidence whatever to link Ladislaus Malinowski with this rigmarole."

"I've got plenty of evidence against Ladislaus Malinowski," said Father. "He's careless, you know. He hung around here when he shouldn't have. On the first occasion he came to establish connection with your daughter. They had a code arranged."

"Nonsense. She told you herself that she didn't know him."

"She may have told me that but it wasn't true. She's in love with him. She wants the fellow to marry her."

"I don't believe it!"

"You're not in a position to know," Chief-Inspector Davy pointed out. "Malinowski isn't the sort of person who tells all his secrets and your daughter you don't know at all. You admitted as much. You were angry, weren't you, when you found out Malinowski had come to Bertram's Hotel."

"Why should I be angry?"

"*Because you're the brains of the show*," said Father. "You and Henry. The financial side was run by the Hoffman brothers. They made all the arrangements with the continental banks and accounts and that sort of thing, but the boss of the syndicate, the brains that run it, and plan it, are your brains, Lady Sedgwick."

Bess looked at him and laughed. "I never heard anything so ridiculous!" she said.

"Oh no, it's not ridiculous at all. You've got brains, courage and daring. You've tried most things; you thought you'd turn your hand to crime. Plenty of excitement in it, plenty of risk. It wasn't the money that attracted you, I'd say, it was the fun of the whole thing. But you wouldn't stand for murder, or for undue violence. There were no killings, no brutal assaults, only nice quiet scientific taps on the head if necessary. You're a very interesting woman, you know. One of the few really interesting great criminals."

There was silence for some few minutes. Then Bess Sedgwick rose to her feet.

"I think you must be mad." She put her hand out to the telephone.

"Going to ring up your solicitor? Quite the right thing to do before you say too much."

With a sharp gesture she slammed the receiver back on the hook.

"On second thoughts I hate solicitors . . . All right. Have it your own way. Yes, I ran this show. You're quite correct when you say it was fun. I loved every minute of it. It was fun scooping money from banks, trains and post offices and so-called security vans! It was fun planning and deciding; glorious fun and I'm glad I had it. The pitcher goes to the well once too often? That's what you said just now, wasn't it? I suppose it's true. Well, I've had a good run for my money! But you're wrong about Ladislaus Malinowski shooting Michael Gorman! He didn't. *I did.*" She laughed a sudden high, excited laugh. "Never mind what it was he did, what he threatened . . . I told him I'd shoot him—Miss Marple heard me —and I *did* shoot him. I did very much what you suggested Ladislaus did. I hid in that area. When Elvira passed, I fired one shot wild, and when she screamed and Micky came running down the street, I'd got him where I wanted him, and I let him have it! I've got keys to all the hotel entrances, of course. I just slipped in through the area door and up to my room. It never occurred to me you'd trace the pistol to Ladislaus—or would even suspect him. I'd pinched it from his car without his knowing. But not, I can assure you, with any idea of throwing suspicion on *him.*"

She swept round on Miss Marple. "You're a witness to what I've said, remember. *I killed Gorman.*"

"Or perhaps you are saying so because you're in love with Malinowski," suggested Davy.

"I'm not." Her retort came sharply. "I'm his good friend, that's all. Oh yes, we've been lovers in a casual kind of way, but I'm not in love with him. In all my life, I've only loved one person—John Sedgwick." Her voice changed and softened as she pronounced the name.

"But Ladislaus is my friend. I don't want him railroaded for something he didn't do. *I killed Michael Gorman.* I've said so, and Miss Marple has heard me . . . And now, dear Chief-Inspector Davy—" Her voice rose excitedly, and her laughter rang out—"*Catch me if you can.*"

With a sweep of her arm, she smashed the window with the heavy telephone set, and before Father could get to his feet, she was out of the window and edging her way rapidly along the narrow parapet. With surprising quickness in spite of his bulk, Davy had moved to the other window and flung up the sash. At the same time he blew the whistle he had taken from his pocket.

Miss Marple, getting to her feet with rather more difficulty a moment or two later, joined him. Together they stared out along the façade of Bertram's Hotel.

"She'll fall. She's climbing up a drainpipe," Miss Marple exclaimed. "But why *up?*"

"Going to the roof. It's her only chance and she knows it. Good God, look at her. Climbs like a cat. She looks like a fly on the side of the wall. The risks she's taking!"

Miss Marple murmured, her eyes half closing, "She'll fall. She can't do it . . ."

The woman they were watching disappeared from sight. Father drew back a little into the room.

Miss Marple asked,

"Don't you want to go and—?"

Father shook his head. "What good am I with my bulk? I've got my men posted ready for something like this. They know what to do. In a few minutes we shall know . . . I wouldn't put it past her to beat the lot of them! She's a woman in a thousand, you know." He sighed. "One of the wild ones. Oh, we've some of them in every generation. You can't tame them, you can't bring them into the community and make them live in law and order. They go their own way. If they're saints they go and tend lepers or something, or get themselves martyred in jungles. If they're bad lots they commit the atrocities that you don't like hearing about. And sometimes—they're just wild! They'd have been all right, I suppose, born in another age when it was everyone's hand for himself, everyone fighting to keep life in their veins. Hazards at every turn, danger all round them, and they themselves perforce dangerous to others. That world would have suited them; they'd have been at home in it. This one doesn't."

"Did you know what she was going to do?"

"Not really. That's one of her gifts. The unexpected. She must have thought this out, you know. She knew what was coming. So she sat look-ing at us—keeping the ball rolling—and thinking. Thinking and planning hard. I expect—ah—" He broke off as there came the sudden roar of a car's exhaust, the screaming of wheels, and the sound of a big racing engine. He leaned out. "She's made it, she's got to her car."

There was more screaming as the car came round the corner on two wheels, a great roar, and the beautiful white monster came tearing up the street.

"She'll kill someone," said Father, "she'll kill a lot of people . . . even if she doesn't kill herself."

"I wonder," said Miss Marple.

"She's a good driver, of course. A damn' good driver. Whoof, that was a near one!"

They heard the roar of the car racing away with the horn blaring, heard it grow fainter. Heard cries, shouts, the sound of brakes, cars hooting and pulling up and finally a great scream of tyres and a roaring exhaust and—

"She's crashed," said Father.

He stood there very quietly waiting with the patience that was characteristic of his whole big patient form. Miss Marple stood silent beside him. Then, like a relay race, word came down along the street. A man on the pavement opposite looked up at Chief-Inspector Davy and made rapid signs with his hands.

"She's had it," said Father heavily. "Dead! Went about ninety miles an hour into the park railings. No other casualties bar a few slight collisions. Magnificent driving. Yes, she's dead." He turned back into the room and said heavily, "Well, she told her story first. You heard her."

"Yes," said Miss Marple. "I heard her." There was a pause. "It wasn't true, of course," said Miss Marple quietly.

Father looked at her. "You didn't believe her, eh?"

"Did you?"

"No," said Father. "No, it wasn't the right story. She thought it out so that it would meet the case exactly, but it wasn't true. She didn't shoot Michael Gorman. D'you happen to know who did?"

"Of course I know," said Miss Marple. "The girl."

"Ah! When did you begin to think that?"

"I always wondered," said Miss Marple.

"So did I," said Father. "She was full of fear that night. And the lies she told were poor lies. But I couldn't see a motive at first."

"That puzzled me," said Miss Marple. "She had found out her mother's marriage was bigamous, but would a girl do murder for that? Not nowadays! I suppose—there was a money side to it?"

"Yes, it was money," said Chief-Inspector Davy. "Her father left her a colossal fortune. When she found out that her mother was married to Michael Gorman she realized that the marriage to Coniston hadn't been legal. She thought that meant that the money wouldn't come to her because, though she was his daughter, she wasn't legitimate. She was wrong, you know. We had a case something like that before. Depends on the terms of a will. Coniston left it quite clearly to her, naming her by name. She'd get it all right, but she didn't know that. And she wasn't going to let go of the cash."

"Why did she need it so badly?"

Chief-Inspector Davy said grimly, "To buy Ladislaus Malinowski. He would have married her for her money. He wouldn't have married her without it. She wasn't a fool, that girl. She knew that. But she wanted him on any terms. She was desperately in love with him."

"I know," said Miss Marple. She explained: "I saw her face that day in Battersea Park . . ."

"She knew that with the money she'd get him, and without the money she'd lose him," said Father. "And so she planned a cold-blooded murder. She didn't hide in the area, of course. There was nobody in the area. She just stood by the railings and fired a shot and screamed, and when Michael Gorman came racing down the street from the hotel, she shot him at close quarters. Then she went on screaming. She was a cool hand. She'd no idea of incriminating young Ladislaus. She pinched his pistol because it was the only way she could get hold of one easily; and she never dreamed that he would be suspected of the crime, or that he would be anywhere in the neighbourhood that night. She thought it would be put down to some thug taking advantage of the fog. Yes, she was a cool hand. But she was afraid that night—afterwards! And her mother was afraid for her . . ."

"And now—what will you do?"

"I know she did it," said Father, "but I've no evidence. Maybe she'll have beginner's luck . . . Even the law seems to go on the principle now of allowing a dog to have one bite—translated into human terms. An experienced counsel could make great play with the sob stuff—so young a girl, unfortunate upbringing—and she's beautiful, you know."

"Yes," said Miss Marple. "The children of Lucifer are often beautiful— And as we know, they flourish like the green bay tree."

"But, as I tell you, it probably won't even come to that—there's no evidence—take yourself—you'll be called as a witness—a witness to what her mother said—to her mother's confession of the crime."

"I know," said Miss Marple. "She impressed it on me, didn't she? She chose death for herself, at the price of her daughter going free. She forced it on me as a dying request . . ."

The connecting door to the bedroom opened. Elvira Blake came through. She was wearing a straight shift dress of pale blue. Her fair hair fell down each side of her face. She looked like one of the angels in an early primitive Italian painting. She looked from one to the other of them. She said,

"I heard a car and a crash and people shouting . . . Has there been an accident?"

"I'm sorry to tell you, Miss Blake," said Chief-Inspector Davy formally, "that your mother is dead."

Elvira gave a little gasp. "Oh no," she said. It was a faint uncertain protest.

"Before she made her escape," said Chief-Inspector Davy, "because it *was* an escape—she confessed to the murder of Michael Gorman."

"You mean—she said—that it was *she—*"

"Yes," said Father. "That is what she *said*. Have you anything to add?"

Elvira looked for a long time at him. Very faintly she shook her head.

"No," she said, "I haven't anything to add."

Then she turned and went out of the room.

"Well," said Miss Marple. "Are you going to let her get away with it?"

There was a pause, then Father brought down his fist with a crash on the table.

"No," he roared— "No, by God I'm not!"

Miss Marple nodded her head slowly and gravely.

"May God have mercy on her soul," she said.

The Moving Finger

Chapter One

WHEN AT LAST I was taken out of the plaster, and the doctors had pulled me about to their hearts' content, and nurses had wheedled me into cautiously using my limbs, and I had been nauseated by their practically using baby talk to me, Marcus Kent told me I was to go and live in the country.

"Good air, quiet life, nothing to do—that's the prescription for you. That sister of yours will look after you. Eat, sleep and imitate the vegetable kingdom as far as possible."

I didn't ask him if I'd ever be able to fly again. There are questions that you don't ask because you're afraid of the answers to them. In the same way during the last five months I'd never asked if I was going to be condemned to lie on my back all my life. I was afraid of a bright hypocritical reassurance from Sister. "Come now, *what* a question to ask! We don't let our patients go talking in *that* way!"

So I hadn't asked—and it had been all right. I wasn't to be a helpless cripple. I could move my legs, stand on them, finally walk a few steps—and if I did feel rather like an adventurous baby learning to toddle, with wobbly knees and cotton wool soles to my feet—well, that was only weakness and disuse and would pass.

Marcus Kent, who is the right kind of doctor, answered what I hadn't said.

"You're going to recover completely," he said. "We weren't sure until last Tuesday when you had that final overhaul, but I can tell you so authoritatively now. But—it's going to be a long business. A long and, if I may say so, a wearisome business. When it's a question of healing nerves and muscles, the brain must help the body. Any impatience, any fretting, will throw you back. And whatever you do, don't 'will yourself to get well quickly.' Anything of that kind and you'll find yourself back in a nursing home. You've got to take life slowly and easily, the *tempo* is marked *Legato*. Not only has your body got to recover, but your nerves have been weakened by the necessity of keeping you under drugs for so long.

"That's why I say, go down to the country, take a house, get interested in local politics, in local scandal, in village gossip. Take an inquisitive and violent interest in your neighbours. If I may make a suggestion, go to a part of the world where you haven't got any friends scattered about."

I nodded. "I had already," I said, "thought of that."

I could think of nothing more insufferable than members of one's own gang dropping in full of sympathy and their own affairs.

"But Jerry, you're looking marvellous—isn't he? Absolutely. Darling, I must tell you—What do you think Buster has done now?"

No, none of that for me. Dogs are wise. They crawl away into a quiet corner and lick their wounds and do not rejoin the world until they are whole once more.

So it came about that Joanna and I, sorting wildly through house-agents' glowing eulogies of properties all over the British Isles, selected Little Furze, Lymstock, as one of the "possibles" to be viewed, mainly because we had never been to Lymstock, and knew no one in that neighbourhood.

And when Joanna saw Little Furze she decided at once that it was just the house we wanted.

It lay about half a mile out of Lymstock on the road leading up to the moors. It was a prim low white house, with a sloping Victorian veranda painted a faded green. It had a pleasant view over a slope of heather-covered land with the church spire of Lymstock down below to the left.

It had belonged to a family of maiden ladies, the Misses Barton, of whom only one was left, the youngest, Miss Emily.

Miss Emily Barton was a charming little old lady who matched her house in an incredible way. In a soft apologetic voice she explained to Joanna that she had never let her house before, indeed would never have thought of doing so, "but you see, my dear, things are so different now-adays—*taxation*, of course, and then my stocks and shares, so *safe*, as I always imagined, and indeed the bank manager *himself* recommended some of them, but they seem to be paying *nothing* at all these days—*foreign*, of course! And really it makes it all so *difficult*. One does not (I'm sure you will understand me, my dear, and not take offence, you look so kind) *like* the idea of letting one's house to strangers—but something must be done, and really, having seen you, I shall be quite *glad* to think of you being here—it needs, you know, *young life*. And I must confess I did shrink from the idea of having *Men* here!"

At this point, Joanna had to break the news of me. Miss Emily rallied well.

"Oh dear, I see. How sad! A flying accident? So brave, these young men. Still, your brother will be practically an invalid——"

The thought seemed to soothe the gentle little lady. Presumably I should not be indulging in those grosser masculine activities which Emily Barton feared. She inquired diffidently if I smoked.

"Like a chimney," said Joanna. "But then," she pointed out, "so do I."

"Of course, of course. So stupid of me. I'm afraid, you know, I haven't moved with the times. My sisters were all older than myself, and my dear mother lived to be ninety-seven—just fancy!—and was most particular. Yes, yes, everyone smokes now. The only thing is, there are no ash-trays in the house."

Joanna said that we would bring lots of ash-trays, and she added with a smile, "We won't put down cigarette ends on your nice furniture, that I do promise you. Nothing makes me so mad myself as to see people do that."

So it was settled and we took Little Furze for a period of six months, with an option of another three, and Emily Barton explained to Joanna that she herself was going to be very comfortable because she was going into rooms kept by an old parlourmaid, "my faithful Florence," who had married "after being with us for fifteen years. *Such* a nice girl, and her husband is in the building trade. They have a nice house in the High Street and two beautiful rooms on the top floor where I shall be *most* comfortable, and Florence so pleased to have me."

So everything seemed to be most satisfactory, and the agreement was signed and in due course Joanna and I arrived and settled in, and Miss Emily Barton's maid Partridge having consented to remain, we were well looked after with the assistance of a "girl" who came in every morning and who seemed to be half-witted but amiable.

Partridge, a gaunt, dour female of middle age, cooked admirably, and though disapproving of late dinner (it having been Miss Emily's custom to dine lightly off a boiled egg) nevertheless accommodated herself to our ways and went so far as to admit that she could see I needed my strength building up.

When we had settled in and been at Little Furze a week Miss Emily

Barton came solemnly and left cards. Her example was followed by Mrs. Symmington, the lawyer's wife, Miss Griffith, the doctor's sister, Mrs. Dane Calthrop, the vicar's wife, and Mr. Pye of Prior's End.

Joanna was much impressed.

"I didn't know," she said in an awestruck voice, "that people really *called*—with *cards*."

"That is because, my child," I said, "you know nothing about the country."

"Nonsense. I've stayed away for heaps of week-ends with people."

"That is not all the same thing," I said.

I am five years older than Joanna. I can remember as a child the big white shabby untidy house we had with the fields running down to the river. I can remember creeping under the nets of raspberry canes unseen by the gardener, and the smell of white dust in the stable yard and an orange cat crossing it, and the sound of horse hoofs kicking something in the stables.

But when I was seven and Joanna two, we went to live in London with an aunt, and thereafter our Christmas and Easter holidays were spent there with pantomimes and theatres and cinemas and excursions to Kensington Gardens with boats, and later to skating rinks. In August we were taken to an hotel by the seaside somewhere.

Reflecting on this, I said thoughtfully to Joanna, and with a feeling of compunction as I realised what a selfish, self-centred invalid I had become:

"This is going to be pretty frightful for you, I'm afraid. You'll miss everything so."

For Joanna is very pretty and very gay, and she likes dancing and cocktails, and love affairs and rushing about in high-powered cars.

Joanna laughed and said she didn't mind at all.

"As a matter of fact, I'm glad to get away from it all. I really was fed up with the whole crowd, and although you won't be sympathetic, I was really very cut up about Paul. It will take me a long time to get over it."

I was sceptical over this. Joanna's love affairs always run the same course. She has a mad infatuation for some completely spineless young man who is a misunderstood genius. She listens to his endless complaints and works like anything to get him recognition. Then, when he is ungrateful, she is deeply wounded and says her heart is broken—until the next gloomy young man comes along, which is usually about three weeks later!

So I did not take Joanna's broken heart very seriously. But I did see that living in the country was like a new game to my attractive sister.

"At any rate," she said, "I look all right, don't I?"

I studied her critically and was not able to agree.

Joanna was dressed (by Mirotin) for *le Sport*. That is to say she was wearing a skirt of outrageous and preposterous checks. It was skin-tight, and on her upper half she had a ridiculous little short-sleeved jersey with a Tyrolean effect. She had sheer silk stockings and some irreproachable but brand new brogues.

"No," I said, "you're all wrong. You ought to be wearing a very old tweed skirt, preferably of dirty green or faded brown. You'd wear a nice cashmere jumper matching it, and perhaps a cardigan coat, and you'd have a felt hat and thick stockings and old shoes. Then, and only then you'd sink into the background of Lymstock High Street, and not stand out as you do at present." I added: "Your face is all wrong, too."

"What's wrong with that? I've got on my Country Tan Make-up No. 2."

"Exactly," I said. "If you lived in Lymstock, you would have on just a little powder to take the shine off the nose, and possibly a *soupçon* of lipstick—not very well applied—and you would almost certainly be wearing all your eyebrows instead of only a quarter of them."

Joanna gurgled and seemed much amused.

"Do you think they'll think I'm awful?" she said.

"No," I said. "Just queer."

Joanna had resumed her study of the cards left by our callers. Only the vicar's wife had been so fortunate, or possibly unfortunate, as to catch Joanna at home.

Joanna murmured:

"It's rather like Happy Families, isn't it? Mrs. Legal the lawyer's wife, Miss Dose the doctor's daughter, etc." She added with enthusiasm: "I do think this is a nice place, Jerry! So sweet and funny and old-world. You just can't think of anything nasty happening here, can you?"

And although I knew what she said was really nonsense, I agreed with her. In a place like Lymstock nothing could happen. It is odd to think that it was just a week later that we got the first letter.

II

I see that I have begun badly. I have given no description of Lymstock and without understanding what Lymstock is like, it is impossible to understand my story.

To begin with, Lymstock has its roots in the past. Somewhere about the time of the Norman Conquest, Lymstock was a place of importance. That importance was chiefly ecclesiastical. Lymstock had a priory, and it had a long succession of ambitious and powerful priors. Lords and barons in the surrounding countryside made themselves right with Heaven by leaving certain of their lands to the priory. Lymstock Priory waxed rich and important and was a power in the land for many centuries. In due course, however, Henry the Eighth caused it to share the fate of its contemporaries. From then on a castle dominated the town. It was still important. It had rights and privileges and wealth.

And then, somewhere in seventeen hundred and something, the tide of progress swept Lymstock into a backwater. The castle crumbled. Neither railways nor main roads came near Lymstock. It turned into a little provincial market town, unimportant and forgotten, with a sweep of moorland rising behind it, and placid farms and fields ringing it round.

A market was held there once a week, on which day one was apt to encounter cattle in the lanes and roads. It had a small race meeting twice a year which only the most obscure horses attended. It had a charming High Street with dignified houses set flat back, looking slightly incongruous with their ground-floor windows displaying buns or vegetables or fruit. It had a long straggling draper's shop, a large and portentous ironmonger's, a pretentious post office, and a row of straggly indeterminate shops, two rival butchers and an International Stores. It had a doctor, a firm of solicitors, Messrs. Galbraith, Galbraith and Symmington, a beautiful and unexpectedly large church dating from fourteen hundred and twenty, with some Saxon remains incorporated in it, a new and hideous school, and two pubs.

Such was Lymstock, and urged on by Emily Barton, anybody who was anybody came to call upon us, and in due course Joanna, having bought a pair of gloves and assumed a velvet beret rather the worse for wear, sallied forth to return them.

To us, it was all quite novel and entertaining. We were not there for life. It was, for us, an interlude. I prepared to obey my doctor's instructions and get interested in my neighbours.

Joanna and I found it all great fun.

I remembered, I suppose, Marcus Kent's instructions to enjoy the local scandals. I certainly didn't suspect how those scandals were going to be introduced to my notice.

The odd part of it was that the letter, when it came, amused us more than anything else.

It arrived, I remember, at breakfast. I turned it over, in the idle way one does when time goes slowly and every event must be spun out to its full extent. It was, I saw, a local letter with a typewritten address.

I opened it before the two with London postmarks, since one of them was a bill and the other from a rather tiresome cousin.

Inside, printed words and letters had been cut out and gummed to a sheet of paper. For a minute or two I stared at the words without taking them in. Then I gasped.

Joanna, who was frowning over some bills, looked up.

"Hallo," she said, "what is it? You look quite startled."

The letter, using terms of the coarsest character, expressed the writer's opinion that Joanna and I were not brother and sister.

"It's a particularly foul anonymous letter," I said.

I was still suffering from shock. Somehow one didn't expect that kind of thing in the placid backwater of Lymstock.

Joanna at once displayed lively interest.

"No? What does it say?"

In novels, I have noticed, anonymous letters of a foul and disgusting character are never shown, if possible, to women. It is implied that women must at all cost be shielded from the shock it might give their delicate nervous systems.

I am sorry to say it never occurred to me not to show the letter to Joanna. I handed it to her at once.

She vindicated my belief in her toughness by displaying no emotion but that of amusement.

"What an awful bit of dirt! I've always heard about anonymous letters, but I've never seen one before. Are they always like this?"

"I can't tell you," I said. "It's my first experience, too."

Joanna began to giggle.

"You must have been right about my make-up, Jerry. I suppose they think I just *must* be an abandoned female!"

"That," I said, "coupled with the fact that our father was a tall, dark lantern-jawed man and our mother a fair-haired blue-eyed little creature, and that I take after him and you take after her."

Joanna nodded thoughtfully.

"Yes, we're not a bit alike. Nobody would take us for brother and sister."

"Somebody certainly hasn't," I said with feeling.

Joanna said she thought it was frightfully funny.

She dangled the letter thoughtfully by one corner and asked what we were to do with it.

"The correct procedure, I believe," I said, "is to drop it into the fire with a sharp exclamation of disgust."

I suited the action to the word, and Joanna applauded.

"You did that beautifully," she added. "You ought to have been on the stage. It's lucky we still have fires, isn't it?"

"The waste-paper basket would have been much less dramatic," I agreed. "I could, of course, have set light to it with a match and slowly watched it burn—or watched it slowly burn."

"Things never burn when you want them to," said Joanna. "They go out. You'd probably have had to strike match after match."

She got up and went towards the window. Then, standing there, she turned her head sharply.

"I wonder," she said, "who wrote it?"

"We're never likely to know," I said.

"No—I suppose not." She was silent a moment, and then said: "I don't know when I come to think of it that it is so funny after all. You know, I thought they—they *liked* us down here."

"So they do," I said. "This is just some half-crazy brain on the border-line."

"I suppose so. Ugh—— Nasty!"

As she went out into the sunshine I thought to myself as I smoked my after-breakfast cigarette that she was quite right. It was nasty. Someone resented our coming here—someone resented Joanna's bright young sophisticated beauty—someone wanted to *hurt*. To take it with a laugh was perhaps the best way—but deep down it wasn't funny. . . .

Dr. Griffith came that morning. I had fixed up for him to give me a weekly overhaul. I liked Owen Griffith. He was dark, ungainly, with awkward ways of moving and deft, very gentle hands. He had a jerky way of talking and was rather shy.

He reported progress to be encouraging. Then he added:

"You're feeling all right, aren't you? Is it my fancy, or are you a bit under the weather this morning?"

"Not really," I said. "A particularly scurrilous anonymous letter arrived with the morning coffee, and it's left rather a nasty taste in the mouth."

He dropped his bag on the floor. His thin dark face was excited.

"Do you mean to say that *you've* had one of them?"

I was interested.

"They've been going about, then?"

"Yes. For some time."

"Oh," I said, "I see. I was under the impression that our presence as strangers was resented here."

"No, no, it's nothing to do with that. It's just——" He paused and then asked, "What did it say? At least——" he turned suddenly red and embarrassed—"perhaps I oughtn't to ask?"

"I'll tell you with pleasure," I said. "It just said that the fancy tart I'd brought down with me wasn't my sister—not 'alf! And that, I may say, is a Bowdlerized version."

His dark face flushed angrily.

"How damnable! Your sister didn't—she's not upset, I hope?"

"Joanna," I said, "looks a little like the angel off the top of the Christmas tree, but she's eminently modern and quite tough. She found it highly entertaining. Such things haven't come her way before."

"I should hope not, indeed," said Griffith warmly.

"And anyway," I said firmly, "that's the best way to take it, I think. As something utterly ridiculous."

"Yes," said Owen Griffith. "Only——"

He stopped, and I chimed in quickly:

"Quite so," I said. "Only is the word!"

"The trouble is," he said, "that this sort of thing, once it starts, grows."

"So I should imagine."

"It's pathological, of course."

I nodded. "Any idea who's behind it?" I asked.

"No, I wish I had. You see, the anonymous letter pest arises from one of two causes. Either it's *particular*—directed at one particular person or set of people, that is to say it's *motivated*, it's someone who's got a definite grudge (or thinks they have) and who chooses a particularly nasty and underhand way of working it off. It's mean and disgusting but it's not necessarily crazy, and it's usually fairly easy to trace the writer—a discharged servant, a jealous woman—and so on. But if it's *general*, and not particular, then it's more serious. The letters are sent indiscriminately and serve the purpose of working off some frustration in the writer's mind. As I say, it's definitely pathological. And the craze grows. In the end, of course, you track down the person in question—it's often someone extremely unlikely, and that's that. There was a bad outburst of the kind over the other side of the county last year—turned out to be the head of the millinery department in a big draper's establishment. Quiet, refined woman—had been there for years. I remember something of the same kind in my last practice up north—but that turned out to be purely personal spite. Still, as I say, I've seen something of this kind of thing, and, quite frankly, it frightens me!"

"Has it been going on long?" I asked.

"I don't think so. Hard to say, of course, because people who get these letters don't go round advertising the fact. They put them in the fire."

He paused.

"I've had one myself. Symmington, the solicitor, he's had one. And one or two of my poorer patients have told me about them."

"All much the same sort of thing?"

"Oh yes. A definite harping on the sex theme. That's always a feature." He grinned. "Symmington was accused of illicit relations with his lady clerk—poor old Miss Ginch, who's forty at least, with pince-nez and teeth like a rabbit. Symmington took it straight to the police. My letters accused me of violating professional decorum with my lady patients, stressing the details. They're all quite childish and absurd, but horribly venomous." His face changed, grew grave. "But all the same, I'm *afraid*. These things can be dangerous, you know."

"I suppose they can."

"You see," he said, "crude, childish spite though it is, sooner or later one of these letters will hit the mark. And then, God knows what may happen! I'm afraid, too, of the effect upon the slow, suspicious, uneducated mind. If they see a thing written, they believe it's true. All sorts of complications may arise."

"It was an illiterate sort of letter," I said thoughtfully, "written by somebody practically illiterate, I should say."

"Was it?" said Owen, and went away.

Thinking it over afterwards, I found that "Was it?" rather disturbing.

Chapter Two

I AM NOT going to pretend that the arrival of our anonymous letter did not leave a nasty taste in the mouth. It did. At the same time, it soon passed out of my mind. I did not, you see, at that point, take it seriously. I think I remember saying to myself that these things probably happen fairly often in out-of-the-way villages. Some hysterical woman with a taste for dramatising herself was probably at the bottom of it. Anyway, if the letters were as childish and silly as the one we had got, they couldn't do much harm.

The next *incident*, if I may put it so, occurred about a week later, when Partridge, her lips set tightly together, informed me, that Beatrice, the daily help, would not be coming to-day.

"I gather, sir," said Partridge, "that the girl has been Upset."

I was not very sure what Partridge was implying, but I diagnosed (wrongly) some stomachic trouble to which Partridge was too delicate to allude more directly. I said I was sorry and hoped she would soon be better.

"The girl is perfectly well, sir," said Partridge. "She is Upset in her Feelings."

"Oh," I said rather doubtfully.

"Owing," went on Partridge, "to a letter she has received. Making, I understand, Insinuations."

The grimness of Partridge's eye, coupled with the obvious capital I of Insinuations, made me apprehensive that the insinuations were concerned with me. Since I would hardly have recognised Beatrice by sight if I had met her in the town, so unaware of her had I been—I felt a not unnatural annoyance. An invalid hobbling about on two sticks is hardly cast for the role of deceiver of village girls. I said irritably:

"What nonsense!"

"My very words, sir, to the girl's mother," said Partridge. "'Goings On in this house,' I said to her, 'there never have been and never will be while I am in charge. As to Beatrice,' I said, 'girls are different nowadays, and as to Goings On elsewhere I can say nothing.' But the truth is, sir, that Beatrice's friend from the garage as she walks out with got one of them nasty letters too, and he isn't acting reasonable at all."

"I have never heard anything so preposterous in my life," I said angrily.

"It's my opinion, sir," said Partridge, "that we're well rid of the girl. What I say is, she wouldn't take on so if there wasn't *something* she didn't want found out. No smoke without fire, that's what I say."

I had no idea how horribly tired I was going to get of that particular phrase.

II

That morning, by way of adventure, I was to walk down to the village. (Joanna and I always called it the village, although technically we were incorrect, and Lymstock would have been annoyed to hear us.)

The sun was shining, the air was cool and crisp with the sweetness of spring in it. I assembled my sticks and started off, firmly refusing to permit Joanna to accompany me.

"No," I said, "I will not have a guardian angel teetering along beside me and uttering encouraging chirrups. A man travels fastest who travels alone, remember. I have much business to transact. I shall go to Galbraith, Galbraith and Symmington, and sign that transfer of shares, I shall call in at the baker's and complain about the currant loaf, and I shall return that book we borrowed. I have to go to the bank, too. Let me away, woman, the morning is all too short."

It was arranged that Joanna should pick me up with the car and drive me back up the hill in time for lunch.

"That ought to give you time to pass the time of day with everyone in Lymstock."

"I have no doubt," I said, "that I shall have seen anybody who is anybody by then."

For morning in the High Street was a kind of rendezvous for shoppers, when news was exchanged.

I did not, after all, walk down to the town unaccompanied. I had gone about two hundred yards, when I heard a bicycle bell behind me, then a scrunching of brakes, and then Megan Hunter more or less fell off her machine at my feet.

"Hallo," she said breathlessly as she rose and dusted herself off.

I rather liked Megan and always felt oddly sorry for her.

She was Symmington the lawyer's step-daughter, Mrs. Symmington's daughter by a first marriage. Nobody talked much about Mr. (or Captain) Hunter, and I gathered that he was considered best forgotten. He was reported to have treated Mrs. Symmington very badly. She had divorced him a year or two after the marriage. She was a woman with means of her own and had settled down with her little daughter in Lymstock "to forget," and had eventually married the only eligible bachelor in the place, Richard Symmington. There were two boys of the second marriage to whom their parents were devoted, and I fancied that Megan sometimes felt odd man out in the establishment. She certainly did not resemble her mother, who was a small anæmic woman, fadedly pretty, who talked in a thin melancholy voice of servant difficulties and her health.

Megan was a tall awkward girl, and although she was actually twenty, she looked more like a schoolgirlish sixteen. She had a shock of untidy brown hair, hazel green eyes, a thin bony face, and an unexpected charming one-sided smile. Her clothes were drab and unattractive and she usually had on lisle thread stockings with holes in them.

She looked, I decided this morning, much more like a horse than a human being. In fact she would have been a very nice horse with a little grooming.

She spoke, as usual, in a kind of breathless rush.

"I've been up to the farm—you know, Lasher's—to see if they'd got any duck's eggs. They've got an awfully nice lot of little pigs. Sweet! Do you like pigs? I do. I even like the smell."

"Well-kept pigs shouldn't smell," I said.

"Shouldn't they? They all do round here. Are you walking down to the town? I saw you were alone, so I thought I'd stop and walk with you, only I stopped rather suddenly."

"You've torn your stocking," I said.

Megan looked rather ruefully at her right leg.

"So I have. But it's got two holes already, so it doesn't matter very much, does it?"

"Don't you ever mend your stockings, Megan?"

"Rather. When Mummy catches me. But she doesn't notice awfully what I do—so it's lucky in a way. isn't it?"

"You don't seem to realise you're grown up," I said.

"You mean I ought to be more like your sister? All dolled up?"

I rather resented this description of Joanna.

"She looks clean and tidy and pleasing to the eye," I said.

"She's awfully pretty," said Megan. "She isn't a bit like you, is she? Why not?"

"Brothers and sisters aren't always alike."

"No. Of course I'm not very like Brian or Colin. And Brian and Colin aren't like eath other." She paused and said, "It's very rum, isn't it?"

"What is?"

Megan replied briefly: "Families."

I said thoughtfully, "I suppose they are."

I wondered just what was passing in her mind. We walked on in silence for a moment or two, then Megan said in a rather shy voice:

"You fly, don't you?"

"Yes."

"That's how you got hurt?"

"Yes, I crashed."

Megan said:

"Nobody down here flies."

"No," I said. "I suppose not. Would you like to fly, Megan?"

"Me?" Megan seemed surprised. "Goodness, no. I should be sick. I'm sick in a train even."

She paused, and then asked with that directness which only a child usually displays:

"Will you get all right and be able to fly again, or will you always be a bit of a crock?"

"My doctor says I shall be quite all right."

"Yes, but is he the kind of man who tells lies?"

"I don't think so," I replied. "In fact, I'm quite sure of it. I trust him."

"That's all right then. But a lot of people do tell lies."

I accepted this undeniable statement of fact in silence.

Megan said in a detached judicial kind of way:

"I'm glad. I was afraid you looked bad tempered because you were crocked up for life—but if it's just natural, it's different."

"I'm not bad tempered," I said coldly.

"Well, irritable, then."

"I'm irritable because I'm in a hurry to get fit again—and these things can't be hurried."

"Then why fuss?"

I began to laugh.

"My dear girl, aren't you ever in a hurry for things to happen?"

Megan considered the question. She said:

"No. Why should I be? There's nothing to be in a hurry about. Nothing ever happens."

I was struck by something forlorn in the words. I said gently: "What do you do with yourself down here?"

She shrugged her shoulders.

"What is there to do?"

"Haven't you got any hobbies? Do you play games? Have you got friends round about?"

"I'm stupid at games. And I don't like them much. There aren't many girls round here, and the ones there are I don't like. They think I'm awful."

"Nonsense. Why should they?"

Megan shook her head.

"Didn't you go to school at all?"

"Yes, I came back a year ago."

"Did you enjoy school?"

"It wasn't bad. They taught you things in an awfully silly way, though."

"How do you mean?"

"Well—just bits and pieces. Chopping and changing from one thing to the other. It was a cheap school, you know, and the teachers weren't very good. They could never answer questions properly."

"Very few teachers can," I said.

"Why not? They ought to."

I agreed.

"Of course I'm pretty stupid," said Megan. "And such a lot of things seem to me such rot. History, for instance. Why, it's quite different out of different books!"

"That is its real interest," I said.

"And grammar," went on Megan. "And silly compositions. And all the blathering stuff Shelley wrote, twittering on about skylarks, and Wordsworth going all potty over some silly daffodils. And Shakespeare."

"What's wrong with Shakespeare?" I inquired with interest.

"Twisting himself up to say things in such a difficult way that you can't get at what he means. Still, I like *some* Shakespeare."

"He would be gratified to know that, I'm sure," I said.

Megan suspected no sarcasm. She said, her face lighting up:

"I like Goneril and Regan, for instance."

"Why these two?"

"Oh, I don't know. They're *satisfactory*, somehow. Why do you think they were like that?"

"Like what?"

"Like they were. I mean *something* must have made them like that?"

For the first time I wondered. I had always accepted Lear's elder daughters as two nasty bits of goods and had let it go at that. But Megan's demand for a first cause interested me.

"I'll think about it," I said.

"Oh, it doesn't really matter. I just wondered. Anyway, it's only English Literature, isn't it?"

"Quite, quite. Wasn't there any subject you enjoyed?"

"Only Maths."

"Maths?" I said, rather surprised.

Megan's face had lit up.

"I loved Maths. But it wasn't awfully well taught. I'd like to be taught Maths really well. It's heavenly. I think there's something heavenly about numbers, anyway, don't you?"

"I've never felt it," I said truthfully.

We were now entering the High Street. Megan said sharply:

"Here's Miss Griffith. Hateful woman."

"Don't you like her?"

"I loathe her. She's always at me to join her foul Guides. I hate Guides. Why dress yourself up and go about in clumps, and put badges on yourself for something you haven't really learnt to do properly. I think it's all rot."

On the whole, I rather agreed with Megan. But Miss Griffith had descended on us before I could voice my assent.

The doctor's sister, who rejoiced in the singularly inappropriate name of Aimée, had all the positive assurance that her brother lacked. She was a handsome woman in a masculine weather-beaten way, with a deep hearty voice.

"Hallo, you two," she bayed at us. "Gorgeous morning, isn't it? Megan, you're just the person I wanted to see. I want some help addressing envelopes for the Conservative Association."

Megan muttered something elusive, propped up her bicycle against the curb and dived in a purposeful way into the International Stores.

"Extraordinary child," said Miss Griffith, looking after her. "Bone lazy.

Spends her time mooning about. Must be a great trial to poor Mrs. Symmington. I know her mother's tried more than once to get her to take up something—shorthand-typing, you know, or cookery, or keeping Angora rabbits. She needs an *interest* in life."

I thought that was probably true, but felt that in Megan's place I should have withstood firmly any of Aimée Griffith's suggestions for the simple reason that her aggressive personality would have put my back up.

"I don't believe in idleness," went on Miss Griffith. "And certainly not for young people. It's not as though Megan was pretty or attractive or anything like that. Sometimes I think the girl's half-witted. A great disappointment to her mother. The father, you know," she lowered her voice slightly, "was definitely a wrong 'un. Afraid the child takes after him. Painful for her mother. Oh, well, it takes all sorts to make a world, that's what I say."

"Fortunately," I responded.

Aimée Griffith gave a "jolly" laugh.

"Yes, it wouldn't do if we were all made to one pattern. But I don't like to see any one not getting all they can out of life. I enjoy life myself and I want everyone to enjoy it too. People say to me you must be bored to death living down there in the country all the year round. Not a bit of it, I say. I'm always busy, always happy! There's always something going on in the country. My time's taken up, what with my Guides, and the Institute and various committees—to say nothing of looking after Owen."

At this minute, Miss Griffith saw an acquaintance on the other side of the street, and uttering a bay of recognition she leaped across the road, leaving me free to pursue my course to the bank.

I always found Miss Griffith rather overwhelming, though I admired her energy and vitality, and it was pleasant to see the beaming contentment with her lot in life which she always displayed, and which was a pleasant contrast to the subdued complaining murmurs of so many women.

My business at the bank transacted satisfactorily, I went on to the offices of Messrs. Galbraith, Galbraith and Symmington. I don't know if there were any Galbraiths extant. I never saw any. I was shown into Richard Symmington's inner office which had the agreeable mustiness of a long-established legal firm.

Vast numbers of deed boxes, labelled Lady Hope, Sir Everard Carr, William Yatesby-Hoares, Esq., Deceased, etc., gave the required atmosphere of decorous county families and legitimate long-established business.

Studying Mr. Symmington as he bent over the documents I had brought, it occurred to me that if Mrs. Symmington had encountered disaster in her first marriage, she had certainly played it safe in her second. Richard Symmington was the acme of calm respectability, the sort of man who would never give his wife a moment's anxiety. A long neck with a pronounced Adam's apple, a slightly cadaverous face and a long thin nose. A kindly man, no doubt, a good husband and father, but not one to set the pulses madly racing.

Presently Mr. Symmington began to speak. He spoke clearly and slowly, delivering himself of much good sense and shrewd acumen. We settled the matter in hand and I rose to go, remarking as I did so:

"I walked down the hill with your step-daughter."

For a moment Mr. Symmington looked as though he did not know who his step-daughter was, then he smiled.

"Oh yes, of course, Megan. She—er—has been back from school some time. We're thinking about finding her something to do—yes, to do. But of course she's very young still. And backward for her age, so they say. Yes, so they tell me."

I went out. In the outer office was a very old man on a stool writing slowly and laboriously, a small cheeky looking boy and a middle-aged woman with frizzy hair and pince-nez who was typing with some speed and dash.

If this was Miss Ginch I agreed with Owen Griffith that tender passages between her and her employer were exceedingly unlikely.

I went into the baker's and said my piece about the currant loaf. It was received with the exclamations and incredulity proper to the occasion, and a new currant loaf was thrust upon me in replacement—"fresh from the oven this minute" —as its indecent heat pressed against my chest proclaimed to be no less than truth.

I came out of the shop and looked up and down the street hoping to see Joanna with the car. The walk had tired me a good deal and it was awkward getting along with my sticks and the currant loaf.

But there was no sign of Joanna as yet.

Suddenly my eyes were held in glad and incredulous surprise.

Along the pavement towards me there came floating a goddess. There is really no other word for it.

The perfect features, the crisply curling golden hair, the tall exquisitely shaped body! And she walked like a goddess, without effort, seeming to swim nearer and nearer. A glorious, an incredible, a breath-taking girl!

In my intense excitement something had to go. What went was the currant loaf. It slipped from my clutches. I made a dive after it and lost my stick, which clattered to the pavement, and I slipped and nearly fell myself.

It was the strong arm of the goddess that caught and held me. I began to stammer:

"Th-thanks awfully, I'm f-f-frightfully sorry."

She had retrieved the currant loaf and handed it to me together with the stick. And then she smiled kindly and said cheerfully:

"Don't mention it. No trouble, I assure you," and the magic died completely before the flat competent voice.

A nice healthy-looking well set-up girl, no more.

I fell to reflecting what would have happened if the Gods had given Helen of Troy exactly those flat accents. How strange that a girl could trouble your inmost soul so long as she kept her mouth shut, and that the moment she spoke the glamour could vanish as though it had never been.

I had known the reverse happen, though. I had seen a little sad monkey-faced woman whom no one would turn to look at twice. Then she had opened her mouth and suddenly enchantment had lived and bloomed and Cleopatra had cast her spell anew.

Joanna had drawn up at the curb beside me without my noticing her arrival. She asked if there was anything the matter.

"Nothing," I said, pulling myself together. "I was reflecting on Helen of Troy and others."

"What a funny place to do it," said Joanna. "You looked *most* odd, standing there clasping currant bread to your breast with your mouth wide open."

"I've had a shock," I said. "I have been transplanted to Ilium and back again."

"Do you know who that is?" I added, indicating a retreating back that was swimming gracefully away.

Peering after the girl Joanna said that it was the Symmingtons' nursery governess.

"Is that what struck you all of a heap?" she asked. "She's good-looking, but a bit of a wet fish."

"I know," I said. "Just a nice kind girl. And I'd been thinking her Aphrodite."

Joanna opened the door of the car and I got in.

"It's funny, isn't it?" she said. "Some people have lots of looks and absolutely no S.A. That girl has. It seems such a pity."

I said that if she was a nursery governess it was probably just as well.

Chapter Three

THAT AFTERNOON we went to tea with Mr. Pye.

Mr. Pye was an extremely ladylike plump little man, devoted to his *petit point* chairs, his Dresden shepherdesses and his collection of bric-à-brac. He lived at Prior's Lodge in the grounds of which were the ruins of the old Priory.

Prior's Lodge was certainly a very exquisite house and under Mr. Pye's loving care it showed to its best advantage. Every piece of furniture was polished and set in the exact place most suited to it. The curtains and cushions were of exquisite tone and colour, and of the most expensive silks.

It was hardly a man's house, and it did strike me that to live there would be rather like taking up one's abode in a Period room at a museum. Mr. Pye's principal enjoyment in life was taking people round his house. Even those completely insensitive to their surroundings could not escape. Even if you were so hardened as to consider the essentials of living a radio, a cocktail bar, a bath and a bed surrounded by the necessary walls, Mr. Pye did not despair of leading you to better things.

His small plump hands quivered with sensibility as he described his treasures, and his voice rose to a falsetto squeak as he narrated the exciting circumstances under which he had brought his Italian bedstead home from Verona.

Joanna and I being both fond of antiquities and of period furniture, met with approval.

"It is really a pleasure, a great pleasure, to have such an acquisition to our little community. The dear good people down here, you know, so painfully bucolic—not to say *provincial*. They don't know anything. Vandals—absolute vandals! And the inside of their houses—it would make you weep, dear lady, I assure you it would make you weep. Perhaps it has done so?"

Joanna said that she hadn't gone quite as far as that.

"But you see what I mean? They mix things so terribly! I've seen with my own eyes a most delightful little Sheraton piece—delicate, perfect—a collector's piece, absolutely—and next to it a Victorian occasional table, or quite possibly a fumed oak revolving bookcase—yes, even that—*fumed oak.*"

He shuddered—and murmured plaintively:

"Why are people so blind? You agree—I'm sure you agree, that beauty is the only thing worth living for."

Hypnotised by his earnestness, Joanna said, yes, yes, that was so.

"Then why," demanded Mr. Pye, "do people surround themselves with ugliness?"

Joanna said it was very odd.

"Odd? It's *criminal!* That's what I call it—criminal! And the excuses they give! They say something is *comfortable.* Or that it is *quaint.* Quaint! Such a horrible word.

"The house you have taken," went on Mr. Pye, "Miss Emily Barton's house. Now that is charming, and she has some quite nice pieces. Quite nice. One or two of them are really first class. And she has taste, too—although I'm not quite so sure of that as I was. Sometimes, I am afraid, I think it's really sentiment. She likes to keep things as they were—but not for *le bon motif*—not because of the resultant harmony—but because it is the way her mother had them."

He transferred his attention to me, and his voice changed. It altered from that of the rapt artist to that of the born gossip.

"You didn't know the family at all? No, quite so—yes, through house agents. But, my dears, you *ought* to have known that family! When I came here the old mother was still alive. An incredible person—quite incredible! A *monster,* if you know what I mean. Positively a monster. The old-fashioned Victorian monster, devouring her young. Yes, that's what it amounted to. She was monumental, you know, must have weighed seventeen stone, and all the five daughters revolved round her. 'The girls'! that's how she always spoke of them. The girls! And the eldest was well over sixty then. 'Those stupid girls!' she used to call them sometimes. Black slaves, that's all they were, fetching and carrying and agreeing with her. Ten o'clock they had to go to bed and they weren't allowed a fire in their bedroom, and as for asking their own friends to the house, that would have been unheard of. She despised them, you know, for not getting married, and yet so arranged their lives that it was practically impossible for them to meet anybody. I believe Emily, or perhaps it was Agnes, did have some kind of affair with a curate. But his family wasn't good enough and Mamma soon put a stop to *that!*"

"It sounds like a novel," said Joanna.

"Oh, my dear, it was. And then the dreadful old woman died, but of course it was far too late *then*. They just went on living there and talking in hushed voices about what poor Mamma would have wished. Even repapering her bedroom they felt to be quite sacrilegious. Still they did enjoy themselves in the parish in a quiet way. . . . But none of them had much stamina, and they just died off one by one. Influenza took off Edith, and Minnie had an operation and didn't recover and poor Mabel had a stroke—Emily looked after her in the most devoted manner. Really that poor woman has done nothing but nursing for the last ten years. A charming creature, don't you think. Like a piece of Dresden. So sad for her having financial anxieties—but of course all investments have depreciated."

"We feel rather awful being in her house," said Joanna.

"No, no, my dear young lady. You mustn't feel that way. Her dear good Florence is devoted to her and she told me herself how happy she was to have got such nice tenants." Here Mr. Pye made a little bow. "She told me she thought she had been most fortunate."

"The house," I said, "has a very soothing atmosphere."

Mr. Pye darted a quick glance at me.

"Really? You feel that? Now, that's very interesting. I wondered, you know. Yes, I wondered."

"What do you mean, Mr. Pye?" asked Joanna.

Mr. Pye spread out his plump hands.

"Nothing, nothing. One wondered, that is all. I do believe in atmosphere, you know. People's thoughts and feelings. They give their impression to the walls and the furniture."

I did not speak for a moment or two. I was looking round me and wondering how I would describe the atmosphere of Prior's Lodge. It seemed to me that the curious thing was that it hadn't any atmosphere! That was really very remarkable.

I reflected on this point so long that I heard nothing of the conversation going on between Joanna and her host. I was recalled to myself, however, by hearing Joanna uttering farewell preliminaries. I came out of my dream and added my quota.

We all went out into the hall. As we came towards the front door a letter came through the box and fell on the mat.

"Afternoon post," murmured Mr. Pye as he picked it up. "Now, my dear young people, you will come again, won't you? Such a pleasure to meet some broader minds, if you understand me. Someone with an appreciation of Art. Really you know, these dear good people down here, if you mention the Ballet, it conveys to them pirouetting toes, and *tulle* skirts and old gentlemen with opera glasses in the Naughty Nineties. It does indeed. Fifty years behind the times—that's what I put them down as. A wonderful country, England. It has, you know, *pockets*. Lymstock is one of them. Interesting from a collector's point of view—I always feel I have voluntarily put myself under a glass shade when I am here. The peaceful backwater where nothing ever happens."

Shaking hands with us twice over, he helped me with exaggerated care into the car. Joanna took the wheel, she negotiated with some care the circular sweep round a plot of unblemished grass, then with a straight drive ahead, she raised a hand to wave good-bye to our host where he stood on the steps of the house. I leaned forward to do the same.

But our gesture of farewell went unheeded. Mr. Pye had opened his mail.

He was standing staring down at the open sheet in his hand.

Joanna has described him once as a plump pink cherub. He was still plump, but he was not looking like a cherub now. His face was a dark congested purple, contorted with rage and surprise.

And at that moment I realised that there had been something familiar about the look of that envelope. I had not realised it at the time—indeed it had been one of those things that you note unconsciously without knowing that you do note them.

"Goodness," said Joanna. "What's bitten the poor pet?"

"I rather fancy," I said, "that it's the Hidden Hand again."

She turned an astonished face towards me and the car swerved.

"Careful, wench," I said.

Joanna refixed her attention on the road. She was frowning.

"You mean a letter like the one you got?"

"That's my guess."

"What is this place?" asked Joanna. "It looks the most innocent sleepy harmless little bit of England you can imagine——"

"Where to quote Mr. Pye, nothing ever happens," I cut in. "He chose the wrong minute to say that. Something has happened."

"But who writes these things, Jerry?"

I shrugged my shoulders.

"My dear girl, how should I know? Some local nitwit with a screw loose, I suppose."

"But why? It seems so idiotic."

"You must read Freud and Jung and that lot to find out. Or ask our Dr. Owen."

Joanna tossed her head.

"Dr. Owen doesn't like me."

"He's hardly seen you."

"He's seen quite enough, apparently, to make him cross over if he sees me coming along the High Street."

"A most unusual reaction," I said sympathetically. "And one you're not used to."

Joanna was frowning again.

"No, but seriously, Jerry, why *do* people write anonymous letters?"

"As I say, they've got a screw loose. It satisfies some urge, I suppose. If you've been snubbed, or ignored, or frustrated, and your life's pretty drab and empty, I suppose you get a sense of power from stabbing in the dark at people who are happy and enjoying themselves."

Joanna shivered. "Not nice."

"No, not nice. I should imagine the people in these country places tend to be inbred—and so you would get a fair amount of queers."

"Somebody, I suppose, quite uneducated and inarticulate? With better education——"

Joanna did not finish her sentence, and I said nothing. I have never been able to accept the easy belief that education is a panacea for every ill.

As we drove through the town before climbing up the hill road, I looked curiously at the few figures abroad in the High Street. Was one of those sturdy country-women going about with a load of spite and malice behind her placid brow, planning perhaps even now a further outpouring of vindictive spleen?

But I still did not take the thing seriously.

II

Two days later we went to a bridge party at the Symmingtons'.

It was a Saturday afternoon—the Symmingtons always had their bridge parties on a Saturday, because the office was shut then.

There were two tables. The players were the Symmingtons, ourselves, Miss Griffith, Mr. Pye, Miss Barton and a Colonel Appleton whom we had not yet met and who lived at Combeacre, a village some seven miles distant. He was a perfect specimen of the Blimp type, about sixty years of age, liked playing what he called a "plucky game" (which usually resulted in enormous sums above the line being scored by his opponents) and was so intrigued by Joanna that he practically never took his eyes off her the whole afternoon.

I was forced to admit that my sister was probably the most attractive thing that had been seen in Lymstock for many a long day.

When we arrived, Elsie Holland, the children's governess, was hunting for some extra bridge scorers in an ornate writing desk. She glided across the floor with them in the same celestial way I had first noticed, but the spell could not be cast a second time. Exasperating that it should be so—a waste of a perfectly lovely form and face. But I noticed now only too clearly the exceptionally large white teeth like tombstones, and the way she showed her gums when she laughed. She was, unfortunately, one of your prattling girls.

"Are these the ones, Mrs. Symmington? It's ever so stupid of me not to remember where we put them away last time. It's my fault, too, I'm afraid. I had them in my hand and then Brian called out his engine had got caught, and I ran out and what with one thing and another I must have just stuffed them in somewhere stupid. These aren't the right ones, I see now, they're a bit yellow at the edges. Shall I tell Agnes tea at five? I'm taking the kiddies to Long Barrow so there won't be any noise."

A nice kind bright girl. I caught Joanna's eye. She was laughing. I stared at her coldly. Joanna always knows what is passing in my mind, curse her.

We settled down to bridge.

I was soon to know to a nicety the bridge status of everyone in Lymstock. Mrs. Symmington was an exceedingly good bridge player and was quite a devotee of the game. Like many definitely unintellectual women, she was not stupid and had a considerable natural shrewdness. Her husband was a good sound player, slightly over-cautious. Mr. Pye can best be described as brilliant. He had an uncanny flair for psychic bidding. Joanna and I, since the party was in our honour, played at a table with Mrs. Symmington and Mr. Pye. It was Symmington's task to pour oil on troubled waters and by the exercise of tact to reconcile the three other players at his table. Colonel Appleton, as I have said, was wont to play "a plucky game." Little Miss Barton was without exception the worst bridge player I have ever come across and always enjoyed herself enormously.

She did manage to follow suit, but had the wildest ideas as to the strength of her hand, never knew the score, repeatedly led out of the wrong hand and was quite unable to count trumps and often forgot what they were. Aimée Griffith's play can be summed up in her own words. "I like a good game of bridge with no nonsense—and I don't play any of these rubbishy conventions. I say what I mean. And no postmortems! After all, it's only a game!" It will be seen, therefore, that their host had not too easy a task.

Play proceeded fairly harmoniously, however, with occasional forgetfulness on the part of Colonel Appleton as he stared across at Joanna.

Tea was laid in the dining-room, round a big table. As we were finishing, two hot and excited little boys rushed in and were introduced, Mrs. Symmington beaming with maternal pride, as was their father.

Then, just as we were finishing, a shadow darkened my plate, and I turned my head to see Megan standing in the french window.

"Oh," said her mother. "Here's Megan."

Her voice held a faintly surprised note, as though she had forgotten that Megan existed.

The girl came in and shook hands, awkwardly and without any grace.

"I'm afraid I forgot about your tea, dear," said Mrs. Symmington. "Miss Holland and the boys took theirs out with them, so there's no nursery tea to-day. I forgot you weren't with them."

Megan nodded.

"That's all right. I'll go to the kitchen."

She slouched out of the room. She was untidily dressed as usual and there were potatoes in both heels.

Mrs. Symmington said with a little apologetic laugh:

"My poor Megan. She's just at that awkward age, you know. Girls are always shy and awkward when they've just left school before they're properly grown up."

I saw Joanna's fair head jerk backwards in what I knew to be a warlike gesture.

"But Megan's twenty, isn't she?" she said.

"Oh, yes, yes. She is. But of course she's very young for her age. Quite a child still. It's so nice, I think, when girls don't grow up too quickly." She laughed again. "I expect all mothers want their children to remain babies."

"I can't think why," said Joanna. "After all, it would be a bit awkward if one had a child who remained mentally six while his body grew up."

"Oh, you mustn't take things so literally, Miss Burton," said Mrs. Symmington.

It occurred to me at that moment that I did not much care for Mrs. Symmington. That anæmic, slighted, faded prettiness concealed, I thought, a selfish and grasping nature. She said, and I disliked her a little more still:

"My poor Megan. She's rather a difficult child, I'm afraid. I've been trying to find something for her to do—I believe there are several things one can learn by correspondence. Designing and dressmaking—or she might try and learn shorthand and typing."

The red glint was still in Joanna's eye. She said as we sat down again at the bridge table:

"I suppose she'll be going to parties and all that sort of thing. Are you going to give a dance for her?"

"A dance?" Mrs. Symmington seemed surprised and amused. "Oh, no, we don't do things like that down here."

"I see. Just tennis parties and things like that."

"Our tennis court has not been played on for years. Neither Richard nor I play. I suppose, later, when the boys grow up—Oh, Megan will find plenty to do. She's quite happy just pottering about, you know. Let me see, did I deal? Two No Trumps."

As we drove home, Joanna said with a vicious pressure on the accelerator pedal that made the car leap forward:

"I feel awfully sorry for that girl."

"Megan?"

"Yes. Her mother doesn't like her."

"Oh, come now, Joanna, it's not as bad as that."

"Yes, it is. Lots of mothers don't like their children. Megan, I should imagine, is an awkward sort of creature to have about the house. She disturbs the pattern—the Symmington pattern. It's a complete unit without her—and that's a most unhappy feeling for a sensitive creature to have—and she *is* sensitive."

"Yes," I said, "I think she is."

I was silent for a moment.

Joanna suddenly laughed mischievously.

"Bad luck for you about the governess."

"I don't know what you mean," I said with dignity.

"Nonsense. Masculine chagrin was written on your face every time you looked at her. I agree with you. It is a waste."

"I don't know what you're talking about."

"But I'm delighted, all the same. It's the first sign of reviving life. I was quite worried about you at the nursing home. You never even looked at that remarkably pretty nurse you had. An attractive minx, too—absolutely God's gift to a sick man."

"Your conversation, Joanna, I find definitely low."

My sister continued without paying the least attention to my remarks.

"So I was much relieved to see you'd still got an eye for a nice bit of skirt. She *is* a good looker. Funny that the S.A. should have been left out so completely. It is odd, you know, Jerry. What *is* the thing that some women have and others haven't. What is it that makes one woman, even if she only says 'Foul weather' so attractive that every man within range wants to come over and talk about the weather with her? I suppose Providence makes a mistake every now and then when sending out the parcel. One Aphrodite face and form, one temperament ditto. And something goes astray and the Aphrodite temperament goes to some little plain-faced creature, and then all the other women go simply mad and say, 'I can't think what the men see in her. She isn't even good-looking!'"

"Have you quite finished, Joanna?"

"Well, you do agree, don't you?"

I grinned. "I'll admit to disappointment."

"And I don't see who else there is here for you. You'll have to fall back upon Aimée Griffith."

"God forbid," I said.

"She's quite good-looking, you know."

"Too much of an Amazon for me."

"She seems to enjoy her life all right," said Joanna. "Absolutely disgustingly hearty, isn't she? I shouldn't be at all surprised if she had a cold bath every morning."

"And what are you going to do for yourself?" I asked.

"Me?"

"Yes. You'll need a little distraction down here if I know you."

"Who's being low now? Besides, you forget Paul." Joanna heaved up a not very convincing sigh.

"I shan't forget him nearly as quickly as you will. In about ten days you'll be saying, 'Paul? Paul Who? I never knew a Paul.'"

"You think I'm completely fickle," said Joanna.

"When people like Paul are in question, I'm only too glad that you should be."

"You never did like him. But he really was a bit of a genius."

"Possibly, though I doubt it. Anyway, from all I've heard, geniuses are people to be heartily disliked. One thing, you won't find any geniuses down here."

Joanna considered for a moment, her head on one side.

"I'm afraid not," she said regretfully.

"You'll have to fall back upon Owen Griffith," I said. "He's the only unattached male in the place. Unless you count old Colonel Appleton. He was looking at you like a hungry bloodhound most of the afternoon."

Joanna laughed.

"He was, wasn't he? It was quite embarrassing."

"Don't pretend. You're never embarrassed."

Joanna drove in silence through the gate and round to the garage. She said then:

"There may be something in that idea of yours."

"What idea?"

Joanna replied:

"I don't see why any man should deliberately cross the street to avoid me. It's rude, apart from anything else."

"I see," I said. "You're going to hunt the man down in cold blood."

"Well, I don't like being avoided."

I got slowly and carefully out of the car, and balanced my sticks. Then I offered my sister a piece of advice.

"Let me tell you this, girl. Owen Griffith isn't any of your tame whining artistic young men. Unless you're careful you'll stir up a hornet's nest about your ears. That man could be dangerous."

"Oo, do you think so?" demanded Joanna with every symptom of pleasure at the prospect.

"Leave the poor devil alone," I said sternly.

"How dare he cross the street when he saw me coming?"

"All you women are alike. You harp on one theme. You'll have Sister Aimée gunning for you, too, if I'm not mistaken."

"She dislikes me already," said Joanna. She spoke meditatively, but with a certain satisfaction.

"We have come down here," I said sternly, "for peace and quiet, and I mean to see we get it."

But peace and quiet were the last things we were to have.

Chapter Four

I⟶ WAS, I think, about a week later, that Partridge informed me that Mrs. Baker would like to speak to me for a minute or two if I would be so kind.

The name Mrs. Baker conveyed nothing at all to me.

"Who is Mrs. Baker?" I said, bewildered—"Can't she see Miss Joanna?"

But it appeared that I was the person with whom an interview was desired. It further transpired that Mrs. Baker was the mother of the girl Beatrice.

I had forgotten Beatrice. For a fortnight now, I had been conscious of a middle-aged woman with wisps of grey hair, usually on her knees retreating crablike from bathroom and stairs and passages when I appeared, and I knew, I suppose, that she was our new Daily Woman. Otherwise the Beatrice complication had faded from my mind.

I could not very well refuse to see Beatrice's mother, especially as I learned that Joanna was out, but I was, I must confess, a little nervous at the prospect. I sincerely hoped that I was not going to be accused of having trifled with Beatrice's affections. I cursed the mischievous activities of anonymous letter writers to myself at the same time as, aloud, I commanded that Beatrice's mother should be brought to my presence.

Mrs. Baker was a big broad weather-beaten woman with a rapid flow of speech. I was relieved to notice no signs of anger or accusation.

"I hope, sir," she said, beginning at once when the door had closed behind Partridge, "that you'll excuse the liberty I've taken in coming to see you. But I thought, sir, as you was the proper person to come to, and I should be thankful if you could see your way to telling me what I ought to do in the circumstances, because in my opinion, sir, something ought to be done, and I've never been one to let the grass grow under my feet, and what I say is, no use moaning and groaning, but 'Up and doing' as vicar said in his sermon only the week before last."

I felt slightly bewildered and as though I had missed something essential in the conversation.

"Certainly," I said. "Won't you—er—sit down, Mrs. Baker? I'm sure I shall be glad to—er help you in any way I can——"

I paused expectantly.

"Thank you, sir." Mrs. Baker sat down on the edge of a chair. "It's very good of you, I'm sure. And glad I am that I came to you, I said to Beatrice, I said, and her howling and crying on her bed, Mr. Burton will know what to do, I said, being a London gentleman. And something must be done, what with young men being so hot-headed and not listening to reason the way they are, and not listening to a word a girl says, and anyway, if it was *me*, I says to Beatrice I'd give him as good as I got, and what about that girl down at the mill?"

I felt more than ever bewildered.

"I'm sorry," I said. "But I don't quite understand. What has happened?"

"It's the letters, sir. Wicked letters—indecent, too, using such words and all. Worse than I've even seen in the Bible, even."

Passing over an interesting side-line here, I said desperately:

"Has your daughter been having more letters?"

"Not her, sir. She had just the one. That one as was the occasion of her leaving here."

"There was absolutely no reason——" I began, but Mrs. Baker firmly and respectfully interrupted me:

"There is no need to tell me, sir, that what was wrote was all wicked lies. I had Miss Partridge's word for that—and indeed I would have known it for myself. You aren't that type of gentleman, sir, that I well know, and you an invalid and all. Wicked untruthful lies it was, but all the same I says to Beatrice as she'd better leave because you know what talk is, sir. No smoke without fire, that's what people say. And a girl can't be too careful. And besides the girl herself felt bashful like after what had been written, so I says, 'Quite right,' to Beatrice when she said she wasn't coming up here again, though I'm sure we both regretted the inconvenience being such——"

Unable to find her way out of this sentence, Mrs. Baker took a deep breath and began again.

"And that, I hoped, would be the end of any nasty talk. But now George, down at the garage, him what Beatrice is going with, he's got one of them. Saying awful things about our Beatrice, and how she's going on with Fred Ledbetter's Tom—and I can assure you, sir, the girl has been no more than civil to him and passing the time of day so to speak."

My head was now reeling under this new complication of Mr. Ledbetter's Tom.

"Let me get this straight," I said. "Beatrice's—er—young man has had an anonymous letter making accusations about her and another young man?"

"That's right, sir, and not nicely put at all—horrible words used, and it drove young George mad with rage, it did, and he came round and told Beatrice he wasn't going to put up with that sort of thing from her, and he wasn't going to have her go behind his back with other chaps—and she says it's all a lie—and he says no smoke without fire, he says, and rushes off being hot-like in his temper, and Beatrice she took on ever so, poor girl, and I said I'll put my hat on and come straight up to you, sir."

Mrs. Baker paused and looked at me expectantly, like a dog waiting for reward after doing a particularly clever trick.

"But why come to me?" I demanded.

"I understood, sir, that you'd had one of these nasty letters yourself, and I thought, sir, that being a London gentleman, you'd know what to do about them."

"If I were you," I said, "I should go to the police. This sort of thing ought to be stopped."

Mrs. Baker looked deeply shocked.

"Oh, no, sir, I couldn't go to the police."

"Why not?"

"I've never been mixed up with the police, sir. None of us ever have."

"Probably not. But the police are the only people who can deal with this sort of thing. It's their business."

"Go to Bert Rundle?"

Bert Rundle was the constable, I knew.

"There's a sergeant, or an inspector, surely, at the police station."

"Me, go into the police station?"

Mrs. Baker's voice expressed reproach and incredulity. I began to feel annoyed.

"That's the only advice I can give you."

Mrs. Baker was silent, obviously quite unconvinced. She said wistfully and earnestly:

"These letters ought to be stopped, sir, they did ought to be stopped. There'll be mischief done sooner or later."

"It seems to me there is mischief done now," I said.

"I meant *violence*, sir. These young fellows, they get violent in their feelings—and so do the older ones."

I asked:

"Are a good many of these letters going about?"

Mrs. Baker nodded.

"It's getting worse and worse, sir. Mr. and Mrs. Beadle at the Blue Boar—very happy they've always been—and now these letters comes and it sets him thinking things—things that aren't so, sir."

I leaned forward:

"Mrs. Baker," I said, "have you any idea, any idea at all, who is writing these abominable letters?"

To my great surprise she nodded her head.

"We've got our idea, sir. Yes, we've all got a very fair idea."

"Who is it?"

I had fancied she might be reluctant to mention a name, but she replied promptly:

"'Tis Mrs. Cleat—that's what we all think, sir. 'Tis Mrs. Cleat for sure."

I had heard so many names this morning that I was quite bewildered. I asked:

"Who is Mrs. Cleat?"

Mrs. Cleat, I discovered, was the wife of an elderly jobbing gardener. She lived in a cottage on the road leading down to the Mill. My further questions only brought unsatisfactory answers. Questioned as to why Mrs. Cleat should write these letters, Mrs. Baker would only say vaguely that "'Twould be like her."

In the end, I let her go, reiterating once more my advice to go to the police, advice which I could see Mrs. Baker was not going to act upon. I was left with the impression that I had disappointed her.

I thought over what she had said. Vague as the evidence was, I decided that if the village was all agreed that Mrs. Cleat was the culprit, then it was probably true. I decided to go and consult Griffith about the whole thing. Presumably he would know this Cleat woman. If he thought advisable, he or I might suggest to the police that she was at the bottom of this growing annoyance.

I timed my arrival for about the moment I fancied Griffith would have finished his "Surgery." When the last patient had left, I went into the surgery.

"Hallo, it's you, Burton."

"Yes. I want to talk to you."

I outlined my conversation with Mrs. Baker, and passed on to him the conviction that this Mrs. Cleat was responsible. Rather to my disappointment, Griffith shook his head.

"It's not so simple as that," he said.

"You don't think this Cleat woman is at the bottom of it?"

"She may be. But I should think it most unlikely."

"Then why do they all think it is her?"

He smiled.

"Oh," he said, "you don't understand. Mrs. Cleat is the local witch."

"Good gracious!" I exclaimed.

"Yes, sounds rather strange nowadays, nevertheless that's what it amounts to. The feeling lingers you know, that there are certain people, certain families, for instance, whom it isn't wise to offend. Mrs. Cleat came from a family of 'wise women.' And I'm afraid she's taken pains to cultivate the legend. She's a queer woman with a bitter and sardonic sense of humour. It's been easy enough for her, if a child cuts its finger, or had a bad fall, or sickened with mumps, to nod her head and say, 'Yes, he stole my apples last week' or 'He pulled my cat's tail.' Soon enough mothers pulled their children away, and other women brought honey or a cake they'd baked to give to Mrs. Cleat so as to keep on the right side of her so that she shouldn't 'ill wish' them. It's superstitious and silly, but it happens. So naturally, now, they think she's at the bottom of this."

"But she isn't?"

"Oh, no. She isn't the type. It's—it's not so simple as that."

"Have you any idea?" I looked at him curiously.

He shook his head, but his eyes were absent.

"No," he said. "I don't know at all. But I don't like it, Burton—some harm is going to come of this."

II

When I got back to the house I found Megan sitting on the veranda steps, her chin resting on her knees.

She greeted me with her usual lack of ceremony.

"Hallo," she said. "Do you think I could come to lunch?"

"Certainly," I said.

"If it's chops, or anything difficult like that and they won't go round, just tell me," shouted Megan as I went round to apprise Partridge of the fact that there would be three to lunch.

I fancy that Partridge sniffed. She certainly managed to convey without saying a word of any kind, that she didn't think much of that Miss Megan.

I went back to the veranda.

"Is it quite all right?" asked Megan anxiously.

"Quite all right," I said. "Irish stew."

"Oh well, that's rather like dogs' dinner anyway, isn't it? I mean it's mostly potato and flavour."

"Quite," I said.

I took out my cigarette case and offered it to Megan. She flushed.

"How nice of you."

"Won't you have one?"

"No, I don't think I will, but it was very nice of you to offer it to me—just as though I was a real person."

"Aren't you a real person?" I said, amused.

Megan shook her head, then, changing the subject, she stretched out a long dusty leg for my inspection.

"I've darned my stockings," she announced proudly.

I am not an authority on darning, but it did occur to me that the strange puckered blot of violently contrasting wool was perhaps not quite a success.

"It's much more uncomfortable than the hole," said Megan.

"It looks as though it might be," I agreed.

"Does your sister darn well?"

I tried to think if I had ever observed any of Joanna's handiwork in this direction.

"I don't know," I had to confess.

"Well, what does she do when she gets a hole in her stocking?"

"I rather think," I said reluctantly, "that she throws them away and buys another pair."

"Very sensible," said Megan. "But I can't do that. I get an allowance now—forty pounds a year. You can't do much on that."

I agreed.

"If only I wore black stockings, I could ink my legs," said Megan sadly. "That's what I always did at school. Miss Batworthy, the mistress who looked after our mending was like her name—blind as a bat. It was awfully useful."

"It must have been," I said.

We were silent while I smoked my pipe. It was quite a companionable silence.

Megan broke it by saying suddenly and violently:

"I suppose you think I'm awful, like everyone else?"

I was so startled that my pipe fell out of my mouth. It was a meer-schaum, just colouring nicely, and it broke. I said angrily to Megan:

"Now, see what you've done."

That most unaccountable of children, instead of being upset, merely grinned broadly.

"I do like you," she said.

It was a most warming remark. It is the remark that one fancies, per-haps erroneously, that one's dog would say if he could talk. It occurred to me that Megan, for all she looked like a horse had the disposition of a dog. She was certainly not quite human.

"What did you say before the catastrophe?" I asked, carefully picking up the fragments of my cherished pipe.

"I said I supposed you thought me awful," said Megan, but not at all in the same tone she had said it before.

"Why should I?"

Megan said gravely:

"Because I am."

I said sharply:

"Don't be stupid."

Megan shook her head.

"That's just it. I'm not really stupid. People think I am. They don't know that inside I know just what they're like, and that all the time I'm hating them."

"*Hating* them?"

"Yes," said Megan.

Her eyes, those melancholy, unchildlike eyes stared straight into mine, without blinking. It was a long mournful gaze.

"You would hate people if you were like me," she said. "If you weren't wanted."

"Don't you think you're being rather morbid?" I asked.

"Yes," said Megan. "That's what people always say when you're saying the truth. And it is true. I'm not wanted and I can quite see why. Mum-mie dosen't like me a bit. I remind her, I think, of my father, who was cruel to her and pretty dreadful from all I can hear. Only mothers can't say they don't want their children and just go away. Or eat them. Cats eat the kittens they don't like. Awfully sensible, I think. No waste or mess. But human mothers have to keep their children, and look after them. It hasn't been so bad while I could be sent away to school—but you see what Mummie would really like is to be just herself and my stepfather and the boys."

I said slowly:

"I still think you're morbid, Megan, but accepting some of what you say as true, why don't you go away and have a life of your own?"

She gave me an unchildlike smile.

"You mean take up a career. Earn my living?"

"Yes."

"What at?"

"You could train for something, I suppose. Shorthand typing—book-keeping."

"I don't believe I could. I am stupid about doing things. And be-sides——"

"Well?"

She had turned her face away, now she turned it slowly back again. It was crimson and there were tears in her eyes. She spoke now with all the childishness back in her voice.

"Why should I go away? And be made to go away? They don't want me, but I'll *stay*. I'll stay and make everyone sorry. I'll make them all sorry. Hateful pigs! I hate everyone here in Lymstock. They all think I'm stupid and ugly. I'll show them. I'll show them. I'll——"

It was a childish, oddly pathetic rage.

I heard a step on the gravel round the corner of the house.

"Get up," I said savagely. "Go into the house through the drawing-room. Go up to the first floor to the bathroom. End of the passage. Wash your face. Quick."

She sprang awkwardly to her feet and darted through the window as Joanna came round the corner of the house.

"Gosh, I'm hot," she called out. She sat down beside me and fanned her face with the Tyrolean scarf that had been round her head. "Still I think I'm educating these damned brogues now. I've walked miles. I've learnt one thing, you shouldn't have these fancy holes in your brogues. The gorse prickles go through. Do you know, Jerry, I think we ought to have a dog?"

"So do I," I said. "By the way, Megan is coming to lunch."

"Is she? Good."

"You like her?" I asked.

"I think she's a changeling," said Joanna. "Something left on a doorstep, you know, while the fairies take the right one away. It's very interesting to meet a changeling. Oof, I must go up and wash."

"You can't yet," I said, "Megan is washing."

"Oh, she's been foot-slogging too, has she?"

Joanna took out her mirror and looked at her face long and earnestly. "I don't think I like this lipstick," she announced presently.

Megan came out through the window. She was composed, moderately clean, and showed no signs of the recent storm. She looked doubtfully at Joanna.

"Hallo," said Joanna, still preoccupied by her face. "I'm so glad you've come to lunch. Good gracious, I've got a freckle on my nose. I must do something about it. Freckles are so earnest and Scottish."

Partridge came out and said coldly that luncheon was served.

"Come on," said Joanna, getting up. "I'm starving."

She put her arm through Megan's and they went into the house together.

Chapter Five

I SEE THAT THERE has been one omission in my story. So far I have made little or no mention of Mrs. Dane Calthrop, or indeed of the Rev. Caleb Dane Calthrop.

And yet both the vicar and his wife were distinct personalities. Dane Calthrop himself was perhaps a being more remote from everyday life than any one I have ever met. His existence was in his books and in his study, and in his intimate knowledge of early Church history. Mrs. Dane Calthrop, on the other hand, was quite terrifyingly on the spot. I have perhaps purposely put off mentioning her, because I was from the first a little afraid of her. She was a woman of character and of almost Olympian knowledge. She was not in the least the typical vicar's wife—but that, as I set it down, makes me ask myself, what do I know of vicars' wives?

The only one I remember well was a quiet nondescript creature, devoted to a big strong husband with a magnetic way of preaching, she had so little general conversation that it was a puzzle to know how to sustain a conversation with her.

Otherwise I was depending on the fictional presentment of vicars' wives, caricatures of females poking their noses everywhere, and uttering platitudes. Probably no such type exists.

Mrs. Dane Calthrop never poked her nose in anywhere, yet she had an uncanny power of knowing things and I soon discovered that almost everyone in the village was slightly afraid of her. She gave no advice and never interfered, yet she represented, to any uneasy conscience, the Deity personified.

I have never seen a woman more indifferent to her material surroundings. On hot days she would stride about clad in Harris tweed, and in rain or even sleet, I have seen her absent-mindedly race down the village street in a cotton dress of printed poppies. She had a long thin well-bred face like a greyhound, and a most devastating sincerity of speech.

She stopped me in the High Street the day after Megan had come to lunch. I had the usual feeling of surprise, because Mrs. Dane Calthrop's progress resembled coursing more than walking, and her eyes were always fixed on the distant horizon so that you felt sure her real objective was about a mile and a half away.

"Oh," she said, "Mr. Burton!"

She said it rather triumphantly, as someone might who had solved a particularly clever puzzle.

I admitted that I was Mr. Burton and Mrs. Dane Calthrop stopped focusing on the horizon and seemed to be trying to focus on me instead.

"Now what," she said, "did I want to see you about?"

I could not help her there. She stood frowning, deeply perplexed.

"Something rather nasty," she said.

"I'm sorry about that," I said, startled.

"Ah," cried Mrs. Dane Calthrop. "I hate my love with an A. That's it. Anonymous letters! What's this story you've brought down here about anonymous letters?"

"I didn't bring it," I said. "It was here already."

"Nobody got any until you came, though," said Mrs. Dane Calthrop accusingly.

"But they did, Mrs. Dane Calthrop. The trouble had already started."

"Oh dear," said Mrs. Dane Calthrop. "I don't like that."

She stood there, her eyes absent and far away again. She said:

"I can't help feeling it's all *wrong*. We're not like that here. Envy, of course, and malice, and all the mean spiteful little sins—but I didn't think there was any one who would do that—No, I really didn't. And it distresses me, you see, because I ought to know."

Her fine eyes came back from the horizon and met mine. They were worried, and seemed to hold the honest bewilderment of a child.

"How should you know?" I said.

"I usually do. I've always felt that's my function. Caleb preaches good sound doctrine and administers the sacraments. That's a priest's duty, but if you admit marriage at all for a priest, then I think his wife's duty is to know what people are feeling and thinking, even if she can't do anything about it. And I haven't the least idea whose mind is——"

She broke off, adding absently:

"They are such silly letters, too."

"Have you—er—had any yourself?"

I was a little diffident of asking, but Mrs. Dane Calthrop replied perfectly naturally, her eyes opening a little wider:

"Oh yes, two—no, three. I forget exactly what they said. Something very silly about Caleb and the school-mistress, I think. Quite absurd, because Caleb has absolutely no taste for fornication. He never has had. So lucky, being a clergyman."

"Quite," I said, "Oh, quite."

"Caleb would have been a saint," said Mrs. Dane Calthrop, "if he hadn't been just a little too intellectual."

I did not feel qualified to answer this criticism, and anyway Mrs. Dane Calthrop went on, leaping back from her husband to the letters in rather a puzzling way.

"There are so many things the letters might say, but don't. That's what is so curious."

"I should hardly have thought they erred on the side of restraint," I said bitterly.

"But they don't seem to know anything. None of the real things."

"You mean?"

Those fine vague eyes met mine.

"Well, of course. There's plenty of adultery here—and everything else. Any amount of shameful secrets. Why doesn't the writer use those?" She paused and then asked abruptly, "What did they say in your letter?"

"They suggested that my sister wasn't my sister."

"And she is?"

Mrs. Dane Calthrop asked the question with unembarrassed friendly interest.

"Certainly Joanna is my sister."

Mrs. Dane Calthrop nodded her head.

"That just shows you what I mean. I dare say there are other things——"

Her clear uninterested eyes looked at me thoughtfully, and I suddenly understood why Lymstock was afraid of Mrs. Dane Calthrop.

In everybody's life there are hidden chapters which they hope may never be known. I felt that Mrs. Dane Calthrop knew them.

For once in my life, I was positively delighted when Aimée Griffith's hearty boice boomed out:

"Hallo, Maud. Glad I've just caught you. I want to suggest an alteration of date for the Sale of Work. Morning, Mr. Burton."

She went on:

"I must just pop into the grocer's and leave my order, then I'll come along to the Institute if that suits you?"

"Yes, yes, that will do quite well," said Mrs. Dane Calthrop.

Aimée Griffith went into the International Stores.

Mrs. Dane Calthrop said: "Poor thing."

I was puzzled. Surely she could not be pitying Aimée?

She went on, however:

"You know, Mr. Burton, I'm rather afraid——"

"About this letter business?"

"Yes, you see it means—it must mean——" She paused lost in thought, her eyes screwed up. Then she said slowly, as one who solves a problem, "Blind hatred . . . yes, blind hatred. But even a blind man might stab to the heart by pure chance. . . . And what would happen then, Mr. Burton?"

We were to know that before another day had passed.

II

It was Partridge who brought the news of the tragedy. Partridge enjoys calamity. Her nose always twitches ecstatically when she has to break bad news of any kind.

She came into Joanna's room with her nose working overtime, her eyes bright, and her mouth pulled down into an exaggerated gloom. "There's terrible news, this morning, miss," she observed as she drew up the blinds.

It takes a minute or two for Joanna, with her London habits, to become fully conscious in the morning. She said, "Er ah," and rolled over without real interest.

Partridge placed her early tea beside her and began again.

"Terrible it is. Shocking! I couldn't hardly believe it when I heard."

"What's terrible?" said Joanna, struggling into wakefulness.

"Poor Mrs. Symmington." She paused dramatically. "Dead."

"Dead?" Joanna sat up in bed, now wide awake.

"Yes, miss, yesterday afternoon, and what's worse, took her own life."

"Oh no, Partridge?"

Joanna was really shocked—Mrs. Symmington was not, somehow, the sort of person you associated with tragedies.

"Yes, miss, it's the truth. Did it deliberate. Not but what she was drove to it, poor soul."

"Drove to it?" Joanna had an inkling of the truth then. "Not——?"

Her eyes questioned Partridge and Partridge nodded.

"That's right, miss. One of them nasty letters!"

"What did it say?"

But that, to Partridge's regret, she had not succeeded in learning.

"They're beastly things," said Joanna. "But I don't see why they should make one want to kill oneself."

Partridge sniffed and then said with meaning:

"Not unless they were *true*, miss."

"Oh," said Joanna.

She drank her tea after Partridge had left the room, then she threw on a dressing-gown and came in to me to tell me the news.

I thought of what Owen Griffith had said. Sooner or later the shot in the dark went home. It had done with Mrs. Symmington. She, apparently the most unlikely of women, had had a secret. . . . It was true, I reflected, that for all her shrewdness she was not a woman of much stamina. She was the anæmic clinging type that crumples easily.

Joanna nudged me and asked me what I was thinking about.

I repeated to her what Owen had said.

"Of course," said Joanna waspishly, "he would know all about it. That man thinks he knows everything."

"He's clever," I said.

"He's conceited," said Joanna. She added, "Abominably conceited!"

After a minute or two she said:

"How awful for her husband—and for the girl. What do you think Megan will feel about it?"

I hadn't the slightest idea and said so. It was curious that one could never gauge what Megan would think or feel.

Joanna nodded and said:

"No, one never does know with changelings."

After a minute or two she said:

"Do you think—would you like—I wonder if she'd like to come and stay with us for a day or two? It's rather a shock for a girl that age."

"We might go along and suggest it," I agreed.

"The children are all right," said Joanna. "They've got that governess woman. But I expect she's just the sort of creature who would drive someone like Megan mad."

I thought that was very possible. I could imagine Elsie Holland uttering platitude after platitude and suggesting innumerable cups of tea. A kindly creature, but not, I thought, the person for a sensitive girl.

I had thought myself of bringing Megan away, and I was glad that Joanna had thought of it spontaneously without prompting from me.

We went down to the Symmingtons' house after breakfast.

We were a little nervous, both of us. Our arrival might look like sheer ghoulish curiosity. Luckily we met Owen Griffith just coming out through the gate. He looked worried and preoccupied.

He greeted me, however, with some warmth.

"Oh, hallo, Burton. I'm glad to see you. What I was afraid would happen sooner or later has happened. A damnable business!"

"Good morning, Dr. Griffith," said Joanna, using the voice she keeps for one of our deafer aunts.

Griffith started and flushed.

"Oh—oh, good morning, Miss Burton."

"I thought perhaps," said Joanna, "that you didn't see me."

Owen Griffith got redder still. His shyness enveloped him like a mantle.

"I'm—I'm so sorry—preoccupied—I didn't."

Joanna went on mercilessly: "After all, I *am* life size."

"Merely kit-kat," I said in a stern aside to her. Then I went on:

"My sister and I, Griffith, wondered whether it would be a good thing if the girl came and stopped with us for a day or two? What do you think? I don't want to butt in—but it must be rather grim for the poor child. What would Symmington feel about it, do you think?"

Griffith turned the idea over in his mind for a moment ot two.

"I think it would be an excellent thing," he said at last. "She's a queer nervy sort of girl, and it would be good for her to get away from the whole thing. Miss Holland is doing wonders—she's an excellent head on her shoulders, but she really has quite enough to do with the two children and Symmington himself. He's quite broken up—bewildered."

"It was——" I hesitated—"suicide?"

Griffith nodded.

"Oh yes. No question of accident. She wrote, 'I can't go on' on a scrap of paper. The letter must have come by yesterday afternoon's post. The envelope was down on the floor by her chair and the letter itself was screwed up into a ball and thrown into the fireplace."

"What did——"

I stopped, rather horrified at myself.

"I beg your pardon," I said.

Griffith gave a quick unhappy smile.

"You needn't mind asking. That letter will have to be read at the inquest. No getting out of it, more's the pity. It was the usual kind of thing—couched in the same foul style. The specific accusation was that the second boy, Colin, was not Symmington's child."

"Do you think that was true?" I exclaimed incredulously.

Griffith shrugged his shoulders.

"I've no means of forming a judgment. I've only been here five years. As far as I've ever seen, the Symmingtons were a placid, happy couple devoted to each other and their children. It's true that the boy doesn't particularly resemble his parents—he's got bright red hair, for one thing—but a child often throws back in appearance to a grandfather or grandmother."

"That lack of resemblance might have been what prompted the particular accusation. A foul and quite uncalled-for bow at a venture."

"Very likely. In fact, probably. There's not been much accurate knowledge behind these poison pen letters, just unbridled spite and malice."

"But it happened to hit the bull's eye," said Joanna. "After all, she wouldn't have killed herself otherwise, would she?"

Griffith said doubtfully:

"I'm not quite sure. She's been ailing in health for some time, neurotic, hysterical. I've been treating her for a nervous condition. It's possible, I think, that the shock of receiving such a letter, couched in those terms, may have induced such a state of panic and despondency that she may have decided to take her life. She may have worked herself up to feel that her husband might not believe her if she denied the story, and the general shame and disgust might have worked upon her so powerfully as to temporarily unbalance her judgment."

"Suicide whilst of unsound mind," said Joanna.

"Exactly. I shall be quite justified, I think, in putting forward that point of view at the inquest."

"I see," said Joanna.

There was something in her voice which made Owen say:

"Perfectly justified!" in an angry voice. He added. "You don't agree, Miss Burton?"

"Oh yes, I do," said Joanna. "I'd do exactly the same in your place."

Owen looked at her doubtfully, then moved slowly away down the street. Joanna and I went on into the house.

The front door was open and it seemed easier than ringing the bell, especially as we heard Elsie Holland's voice inside.

She was talking to Mr. Symmington who, huddled in a chair, was looking completely dazed.

"No, but really, Mr. Symmington, you must take something. You haven't had any breakfast, not what I call a proper breakfast, and nothing to eat last night, and what with the shock and all, you'll be getting ill yourself, and you'll need all your strength. The doctor said so before he left."

Symmington said in a toneless voice:

"You're very kind, Miss Holland, but——"

"A nice cup of hot tea," said Elsie Holland, thrusting the beverage on him firmly.

Personally I should have given the poor devil a stiff whisky and soda. He looked as though he needed it. However, he accepted the tea, and looking up at Elsie Holland:

"I can't thank you for all you've done and are doing, Miss Holland. You've been perfectly splendid."

The girl flushed and looked pleased.

"It's nice of you to say that, Mr. Symmington. You must let me do all I can to help. Don't worry about the children—I'll see to them, and I've got the servants calmed down, and if there's anything I can do, letter-writing or telephoning, don't hesitate to ask me."

"You're very kind," Symmington said again.

Elsie Holland, turning, caught sight of us and came hurrying out into the hall.

"Isn't it terrible?" she said in a hushed whisper.

I thought, as I looked at her, that she was really a very nice girl. Kind, competent, practical in an emergency. Her magnificent blue eyes were just faintly rimmed with pink, showing that she had been soft-hearted enough to shed tears for her employer's death.

"Can we speak to you a minute?" asked Joanna. "We don't want to disturb Mr. Symmington."

Elsie Holland nodded comprehendingly and led the way into the dining-room on the other side of the hall.

"It's been awful for him," she said. "Such a shock. Who ever would have thought a thing like this could happen? But of course, I do realise now that she had been queer for some time. Awfully nervy and weepy. I thought it was her health, though Dr. Griffith always said there was nothing really wrong with her. But she was snappy and irritable and some days you wouldn't know just how to take her."

"What we really came for," said Joanna, "was to know whether we could have Megan for a few days—that is, if she'd like to come."

Elsie Holland looked rather surprised.

"Megan?" she said doubtfully. "I don't know, I'm sure. I mean, it's ever so kind of you, but she's such a queer girl. One never knows what she's going to say or feel about things."

Joanna said rather vaguely:

"We thought it might be a help, perhaps."

"Oh well, as far as that goes, it would. I mean, I've got the boys to look after (they're with cook just now) and poor Mr. Symmington—he really needs looking after as much as any one, and such a lot to do and see to. I really haven't had time to see much of Megan. I think she's upstairs in the old nursery at the top of the house. She seems to want to get away from everyone. I don't know if——"

Joanna gave me the faintest of looks. I slipped quickly out of the room and upstairs.

The old nursery was at the top of the house. I opened the door and went in. The room downstairs had given on to the garden behind and the blinds had not been down there. But in this room which faced the road they were decorously drawn down.

Through a dim grey gloom I saw Megan. She was crouching on a divan set against the far wall, and I was reminded at once of some terrified animal, hiding. She looked petrified with fear.

"Megan," I said.

I came forward, and unconsciously I adopted the tone one does adopt when you want to reassure a frightened animal. I'm really surprised I didn't hold out a carrot or a piece of sugar. I felt like that.

She stared at me, but she did not move, and her expression did not alter.

"Megan," I said again. "Joanna and I have come to ask you if you would like to come and stay with us for a little."

Her voice came hollowly out of the dim twilight.

"Stay with you? In your house?"

"Yes."

"You mean, you'll take me away from here?"

"Yes, my dear."

Suddenly she began to shake all over. It was frightening and very moving.

"Oh, do take me away! Please do. It's so awful, being here, and feeling so wicked."

I came over to her and her hands fastened on my coat sleeve.

"I'm an awful coward. I didn't know what a coward I was."

"It's all right, funny face," I said. "These things are a bit shattering. Come along."

"Can we go at once? Without waiting a minute?"

"Well, you'll have to put a few things together, I suppose."

"What sort of things? Why?"

"My dear girl," I said. "We can provide you with a bed and a bath and the rest of it, but I'm damned if I lend you my toothbrush."

She gave a very faint weak little laugh.

"I see. I think I'm stupid to-day. You mustn't mind. I'll go and pack some things. You—you won't go away? You'll wait for me?"

"I'll be on the mat."

"Thank you. Thank you very much. I'm sorry I'm so stupid. But you see it's rather dreadful when your mother dies."

"I know," I said.

I gave her a friendly pat on the back and she flashed me a grateful look and disappeared into a bedroom. I went on downstairs.

"I found Megan," I said. "She's coming."

"Oh now, that *is* a good thing," exclaimed Elsie Holland. "It will take her out of herself. She's rather a nervy girl, you know. Difficult. It will be a great relief to feel I haven't got her on my mind as well as everything else. It's very kind of you, Miss Burton. I hope she won't be a nuisance. Oh dear, there's the telephone. I must go and answer it. Mr. Symmington isn't fit."

She hurried out of the room. Joanna said:

"Quite the ministering angel!"

"You said that rather nastily," I observed. "She's a nice kind girl, and obviously most capable."

"Most. And she knows it."

"This is unworthy of you, Joanna," I said.

"Meaning why shouldn't the girl do her stuff?"

"Exactly."

"I never can stand seeing people pleased with themselves," said Joanna. "It arouses all my worst instincts. How did you find Megan?"

"Crouching in a darkened room looking rather like a stricken gazelle."

"Poor kid. She was quite willing to come?"

"She leapt at it."

A series of thuds out in the hall announced the descent of Megan and her suitcase. I went out and took it from her. Joanna, behind me, said urgently:

"Come on. I've already refused some nice hot tea twice."

We went out to the car. It annoyed me that Joanna had to sling the suitcase in. I could get along with one stick now, but I couldn't do any athletic feats.

"Get in," I said to Megan.

She got in, I followed her. Joanna started the car and we drove off.

We got to Little Furze and went into the drawing-room.

Megan dropped into a chair and burst into tears. She cried with the hearty fervour of a child—bawled, I think, is the right word. I left the room in search of a remedy. Joanna stood by feeling rather helpless, I think.

Presently I heard Megan say in a thick choked voice:

"I'm sorry for doing this. It seems idiotic."

Joanna said kindly, "Not at all. Have another handkerchief."

I gather she supplied the necessary article. I re-entered the room and handed Megan a brimming glass.

"What is it?"

"A cocktail," I said.

"Is it? Is it really?" Megan's tears were instantly dried. "I've never drunk a cocktail."

"Everything has to have a beginning," I said.

Megan sipped her drink gingerly, then a beaming smile spread over her face, she tilted her head back and gulped it down at a draught.

"It's lovely," she said. "Can I have another?"

"No," I said.

"Why not?"

"In about ten minutes you'll probably know."

"Oh!"

Megan transferred her attention to Joanna.

"I really am awfully sorry for having made such a nuisance of myself howling away like that. I can't think why. It seems awfully silly when I'm so glad to be here."

"That's all right," said Joanna. "We're very pleased to have you."

"You can't be, really. It's just kindness on your part. But I am grateful."

"Please don't be grateful," said Joanna. "It will embarrass me. I was speaking the truth when I said we should be glad to have you. Jerry and I have used up all our conversation. We can't think of any more things to say to each other."

"But now," I said, "we shall be able to have all sorts of interesting discussions—about Goneril and Regan and things like that."

Megan's face lit up.

"I've been thinking about that, and I think I know the answer. It was because that awful old father of theirs always insisted on such a lot of sucking up. When you've always got to be saying thank you and how kind and all the rest of it, it would make you go a bit rotten and queer inside, and you'd just long to be able to be beastly for a change—and when you got the chance, you'd probably find it went to your head and you'd go too far. Old Lear was pretty awful, wasn't he? I mean, he did deserve the snub Cordelia gave him."

"I can see," I said, "that we are going to have many interesting discussions about Shakespeare."

"I can see you two are going to be very highbrow," said Joanna. "I'm afraid I always find Shakespeare terribly dreary. All those long scenes where everybody is drunk and it's supposed to be funny."

"Talking of drink," I said turning to Megan. "How are you feeling?"

"Quite all right, thank you."

"Not at all giddy? You don't see two of Joanna or anything like that?"

"No. I just feel as though I'd like to talk rather a lot."

"Splendid," I said. "Obviously you are one of our natural drinkers. That is to say, if that really was your first cocktail."

"Oh, it was."

"A good strong head is an asset to any human being," I said.

Joanna took Megan upstairs to unpack.

Partridge came in, looking sour, and said she had made two cup custards for lunch and what should she do about it?

Chapter Six

THE INQUEST was held three days later. It was all done as decorously as possible, but there was a large attendance and, as Joanna observed, the beady bonnets were wagging.

The time of Mrs. Symmington's death was put at between three and four o'clock. She was alone in the house, Symmington was at his office, the maids were having their day out, Elsie Holland and the children were out walking and Megan had gone for a bicycle ride.

The letter must have come by the afternoon post. Mrs. Symmington must have taken it out of the box, read it—and then in a state of agitation she had gone to the potting shed, fetched some of the cyanide kept there for taking wasps' nests, dissolved it in water and drunk it after writing those last agitated words, "I can't go on . . ."

Owen Griffith gave medical evidence and stressed the view he had outlined to us of Mrs. Symmington's nervous condition and poor stamina. The coroner was suave and discreet. He spoke with bitter condemnation of people who write those despicable things, anonymous letters. Whoever had written that wicked, and lying letter was morally guilty of murder, he said. He hoped the police would soon discover the culprit and take action against him or her. Such a dastardly and malicious piece of spite deserved to be punished with the utmost rigour of the law. Directed by him, the jury brought in the inevitable verdict. Suicide whilst temporarily insane.

The coroner had done his best—Owen Griffith also, but afterwards, jammed in the crowd of eager village women, I heard the same hateful sibilant whisper I had begun to know so well, "No smoke without fire, that's what *I* say!" "Must 'a been something in it for certain sure. She wouldn't never have done it otherwise . . ."

Just for a moment I hated Lymstock and its narrow boundaries, and its gossiping whispering women.

II

It is difficult to remember things in their exact chronological order. The next landmark of importance, of course, was Superintendent Nash's visit. But it was before that, I think, that we received calls from various members of the community, each of which was interesting in its way and shed some light on the characters and personalities of the people involved.

Aimée Griffith came on the morning after the inquest. She was looking, as always, radiant with health and vigour and succeeded, also as usual, in putting my back up almost immediately. Joanna and Megan were out, so I did the honours.

"Good morning," said Miss Griffith. "I hear you've got Megan Hunter here?"

"We have."

"Very good of you, I'm sure. It must be rather a nuisance to you. I came up to say she can come to us if you like. I dare say I can find ways of making her useful about the house."

I looked at Aimée Griffith with a good deal of distaste.

"How good of you," I said. "But we like having her. She potters about quite happily."

"I dare say. Much too fond of pottering, that child. Still, I suppose she can't help it, being practically half-witted."

"I think she's rather an intelligent girl," I said.

Aimée Griffith gave me a hard stare.

"First time I've ever heard any one say that of her," she remarked. "Why, when you talk to her, she looks through you as though she doesn't understand what you are saying!"

"She probably just isn't interested," I said.

"If so, she's extremely rude," said Aimée Griffith.

"That may be. But not half-witted."

Miss Griffith declared sharply:

"At best, it's wool-gathering. What Megan needs is good hard work—something to give her an interest in life. You've no idea what a difference that makes to a girl. I know a lot about girls. You'd be surprised at the difference even becoming a Guide makes to a girl. Megan's much too old to spend her time lounging about and doing nothing."

"It's been rather difficult for her to do anything else so far," I said. "Mrs. Symmington always seemed under the impression that Megan was about twelve years old."

Miss Griffith snorted.

"I know. I had no patience with that attitude of hers. Of course she's dead now, poor woman, so one doesn't want to say much, but she was a perfect example of what I call the unintelligent domestic type. Bridge and gossip and her children—and even there that Holland girl did all the looking after them. I'm afraid I never thought very much of Mrs. Symmington, although of course I never suspected the truth."

"The truth?" I said sharply.

Miss Griffith flushed.

"I was terribly sorry for Dick Symmington, its all having to come out as it did at the inquest," she said. "It was awful for him."

"But surely you heard him say that there was not a word of truth in that letter—that he was quite sure of that?"

"Of course he *said* so. Quite right. A man's got to stick up for his wife. Dick would." She paused and then explained:

"You see, I've known Dick Symmington a long time."

I was a little surprised.

"Really?" I said. "I understood from your brother that he only bought this practice a few years ago."

"Oh yes, but Dick Symmington used to come and stay in our part of the world up north. I've known him for years."

Women jump to conclusions that men do not. Nevertheless, the suddenly softened tone of Aimée Griffith's voice put, as our old nurse would have expressed it, ideas into my head.

I looked at Aimée curiously. She went on—still in that softened tone:

"I know Dick very well. . . . He's a proud man, and very reserved. But he's the sort of man who could be very jealous."

"That would explain," I said deliberately, "why Mrs. Symmington was afraid to show him or tell him about the letter. She was afraid that, being a jealous man, he might not believe her denials."

Miss Griffith looked at me angrily and scornfully.

"Good Lord," she said, "do you think any woman would go and swallow a lot of cyanide of potassium for an accusation that wasn't true?"

"The coroner seemed to think it was possible. Your brother, too——"

Aimée interrupted me.

"Men are all alike. All for preserving the decencies. But don't catch *me*

believing that stuff. If an innocent woman gets some foul anonymous letter, she laughs and chucks it away. That's what I——" she paused suddenly, and then finished, "would do."

But I had noticed the pause. I was almost sure that what she had been
about to say was "That's what I did."

I decided to take the war into the enemy's country.

"I see," I said pleasantly, "so you've had one, too?"

Aimée Griffith was the type of woman who scorns to lie. She paused a
minute—flushed, then said:

"Well, yes. But I didn't let it worry me!"

"Nasty?" I inquired, sypathetically, as a fellow-sufferer.

"Naturally. These things always are. The ravings of a lunatic. I read a
few words of it, realised what it was and chucked it straight into the
waste-paper basket."

"You didn't think of taking it to the police?"

"Not then. Least said soonest mended—that's what I felt."

An urge came over me to say solemnly: "No smoke without fire!" but I
restrained myself. To avoid temptation I reverted to Megan.

"Have you any idea of Megan's financial position?" I asked. "It's not
idle curiosity on my part. I wondered if it would actually be necessary for
her to earn her living."

"I don't think it's strictly *necessary*. Her grandmother, her father's
mother, left her a small income, I believe. And in any case Dick Symmington would always give her a home and provide for her, even if her
mother hasn't left her anything outright. No, it's the *principle* of the
thing."

"What principle?"

"Work, Mr. Burton. There's nothing like work, for men and women.
The one unforgivable sin is idleness."

"Sir Edward Grey," I said, "afterwards our foreign minister, was sent
down from Oxford for incorrigible idleness. The Duke of Wellington, I
have heard, was both dull and inattentive at his books. And has it ever occurred to you, Miss Griffith, that you would probably not be able to take a
good express train to London if little Georgie Stephenson had been out
with his youth movement instead of lolling about, bored, in his mother's
kitchen until the curious behaviour of the kettle lid attracted the attention
of his idle mind?"

Aimée merely snorted.

"It is a theory of mine," I said, warming to my theme, "that we owe most of our great inventions and most of the achievements of genius to idleness—either enforced or voluntary. The human mind prefers to be spoon-fed with the thoughts of others, but deprived of such nourishment it will reluctantly, begin to think for itself—and such thinking, remember, is original thinking and may have valuable results.

"Besides," I went on, before Aimée could get in another sniff, "there is the artistic side."

I got up and took from my desk where it always accompanied me a photograph of my favourite Chinese picture. It represents an old man sitting beneath a tree playing cat's cradle with a piece of string on his fingers and toes.

"It was in the Chinese exhibition," I said. "It fascinated me. Allow me to introduce you. It is called 'Old Man enjoying the Pleasures of Idleness.'"

Aimée Griffith was unimpressed by my lovely picture. She said: "Oh well, we all know what the Chinese are like!"

"It doesn't appeal to you?" I asked.

"Frankly, no. I'm not very interested in art, I'm afraid. Your attitude, Mr. Burton, is typical of that of most men. You dislike the idea of women working—of their competing——"

I was taken aback. I had come up against the Feminist. Aimée was well away, her cheeks flushed.

"It is incredible to you that women should want a career. It was incredible to my parents. I was anxious to study for a doctor. They would not hear of paying the fees. But they paid them readily for Owen. Yet I should have made a far better doctor than my brother."

"I'm sorry about that," I said. "It was tough on you. If one wants to do a thing——"

She went on quickly:

"Oh, I've got over it now. I've plenty of will-power. My life is busy and active. I'm one of the happiest people in Lymstock. Plenty to do. But I do go up in arms against the silly old-fashioned prejudice that women's place is always the home."

"I'm sorry if I offended you," I said. "And that wasn't really my point. I don't see Megan in a domestic role at all."

"No, poor child. She'll be a misfit anywhere, I'm afraid." Aimée had calmed down. She was speaking quite normally again. "Her father, you know——"

She paused and I said bluntly: "I *don't* know. Everyone says 'her father' and drops their voice, and that is that. What did the man *do?* Is he alive still?"

"I really don't know. And I'm rather vague myself, I'm afraid. But he was definitely a bad lot. Prison, I believe. And a streak of very strong abnormality. That's why it wouldn't surprise me if Megan was a bit 'wanting.'"

"Megan," I said, "is in full possession of her senses, and as I said before, I consider her an intelligent girl. My sister thinks so too. Joanna is very fond of her."

Aimée said:

"I'm afraid your sister must find it very dull down here."

And as she said it, I learnt something else. Aimée Griffith disliked my sister. It was there in the smooth conventional tones of her voice.

"We've all wondered how you could both bear to bury yourselves in such an out-of-the-way spot."

It was a question and I answered it.

"Doctor's orders. I was to come somewhere very quiet where nothing ever happened." I paused and added, "Not quite true of Lymstock now."

"No, no, indeed."

She sounded worried and got up to go. She said then:

"You know—it's got to be put a stop to—all this beastliness! We can't have it going on."

"Aren't the police doing anything?"

"I suppose so. But I think we ought to take it in hand *ourselves.*"

"We're not as well equipped as they are."

"Nonsense! We probably have far more sense and intelligence! A little determination is all that is needed."

She said good-bye abruptly and went away.

When Joanna and Megan came back from their walk I showed Megan my Chinese picture. Her face lighted up. She said, "It's heavenly, isn't it?"

"That *is* rather my opinion."

Her forehead was crinkling in the way I knew so well.

"But it would be difficult, wouldn't it?"

"To be idle."

"No, not to be idle—but to enjoy the pleasures of it. You'd have to be very old——"

She paused. I said: "He *is* an old man."

"I don't mean old that way. Not *age.* I mean old in—in . . ."

"You mean," I said, "that one would have to attain a very high state of civilisation for the thing to present itself to you in that way—a fine point of sophistication? I think I shall complete your education, Megan, by reading to you one hundred poems translated from the Chinese."

III

I met Symmington in the town later in the day.

"Is it quite all right for Megan to stay on with us for a bit?" I asked. "It's company for Joanna—she's rather lonely sometimes with none of her own friends."

"Oh—er—Megan? Oh yes, very good of you."

I took a dislike to Symmington then which I never quite overcame. He had so obviously forgotten all about Megan. I wouldn't have minded if he had actively disliked the girl—a man may sometimes be jealous of a first husband's child—but he didn't dislike her, he just hardly noticed her. He felt towards her much as a man who doesn't care much for dogs would feel about a dog in the house. You notice it when you fall over it and swear at it, and you give it a vague pat sometimes when it presents itself to be patted. Symmington's complete indifference to his stepdaughter annoyed me very much.

I said, "What are you planning to do with her?"

"With Megan?" He seemed rather startled. "Well, she'll go on living at home. I mean, naturally, it is her home."

My grandmother, of whom I had been very fond, used to sing old-fashioned songs to her guitar. One of them, I remembered, ended thus:

> *Oh maid, most dear, I am not here*
> *I have no place, no part,*
> *No dwelling more, by sea nor shore,*
> *But only in your heart.*

I went home humming it.

IV

Emily Barton came just after tea had been cleared away.

She wanted to talk about the garden. We talked garden for about half an hour. Then we turned back towards the house.

It was then that lowering her voice, she murmured:

"I do hope that that child—that she hasn't been too much *upset* by all this dreadful business?"

"Her mother's death, you mean?"

"That, of course. But I really meant, the—the unpleasantness *behind* it."

I was curious. I wanted Miss Barton's reaction.

"What do you think about that? Was it true?"

"Oh, no, no, surely not. I'm quite sure that Mrs. Symmington never—that he wasn't"—little Emily Barton was pink and confused—"I mean it's quite untrue—although of course it may have been a judgment."

"A judgment?" I said, staring.

Emily Barton was very pink, very dresden china shepherdess-like.

"I cannot help feeling that all these dreadful letters, all the sorrow and pain they have caused, may have been sent for a *purpose*."

"They were sent for a purpose, certainly," I said grimly.

"No, no, Mr. Burton, you misunderstand me. I'm not talking of the misguided creature who wrote them—someone quite abandoned that must be. I mean that they have been permitted—by Providence! To awaken us to a sense of our shortcomings."

"Surely," I said, "the Almighty could choose a less unsavoury weapon."

Miss Emily murmured that God moved in a mysterious way.

"No," I said. "There's too much tendency to attribute to God the evils that man does of his own free will. I might concede you the Devil. God doesn't really need to punish us, Miss Barton. We're so very busy punishing ourselves."

"What I can't make out is *why* should any one want to do such a thing?"

I shrugged my shoulders.

"A warped mentality."

"It seems very sad."

"It doesn't seem to me sad. It seems to me just damnable. And I don't apologise for the word. I mean just that."

The pink had gone out of Miss Barton's cheeks. They were very white.

"But why, Mr. Burton, *why?* What pleasure can any one get out of it?"

"Nothing you and I can understand, thank goodness."

Emily Barton lowered her voice.

"They say that *Mrs. Cleat*—but I really cannot believe it."

I shook my head. She went on in an agitated manner:

"Nothing of this kind has ever happened before—never in my memory. It has been such a happy little community. What would my dear mother have said? Well, one must be thankful that she has been spared."

I thought from all I had heard that old Mrs. Barton had been sufficiently tough to have taken anything, and would probably have enjoyed this sensation.

Emily went on:

"It distresses me deeply."

"You've not—er—had anything yourself?"

She flushed crimson.

"Oh, no—oh, no, indeed. Oh! that would be dreadful."

I apologised hastily, but she went away looking rather upset.

I went into the house. Joanna was standing by the drawing-room fire which she had just lit, for the evenings were still chilly.

She had an open letter in her hand.

She turned her head quickly as I entered.

"Jerry! I found this in the letter box—dropped in by hand. It begins, 'You painted trollop . . .'"

"What else does it say?"

Joanna gave a wide grimace.

"Same old muck."

She dropped it on to the fire. With a quick gesture that hurt my back I jerked it off again just before it caught.

"Don't," I said. "We may need it."

"Need it?"

"For the police."

V

Superintendent Nash came to see me the following morning. From the first moment I saw him I took a great liking to him. He was the best type of C.I.D. county superintendent. Tall, soldierly, with quiet reflective eyes and a straightforward unassuming manner.

He said: "Good morning, Mr. Burton, I expect you can guess what I've come to see you about."

"Yes, I think so. This letter business."

He nodded.

"I understand you had one of them?"

"Yes, soon after we got here."

"What did it say exactly?"

I thought a minute, then conscientiously repeated the wording of the letter as closely as possible.

The superintendent listened with an immovable face, showing no signs of any kind of emotion. When I had finished, he said:

"I see. You didn't keep the letter, Mr. Burton?"

"I'm sorry. I didn't. You see, I thought it was just an isolated instance of spite against newcomers to the place."

The superintendent inclined his head comprehendingly.

He said briefly: "A pity."

"However," I said, "my sister got one yesterday. I just stopped her putting it in the fire."

"Thank you, Mr. Burton, that was thoughtful of you."

I went across to my desk and unlocked the drawer in which I had put it. It was not, I thought, very suitable for Partridge's eyes. I gave it to Nash.

He read it through. Then he looked up and asked me:

"Is this the same in appearance as the last one?"

"I think so—as far as I can remember."

"The same difference between the envelope and the text?"

"Yes," I said. "The envelope was typed. The letter itself had printed words pasted on to a sheet of paper."

Nash nodded and put it in his pocket. Then he said:

"I wonder, Mr. Burton, if you would mind coming down to the station with me? We could have a conference there and it would save a good deal of time and overlapping."

"Certainly," I said. "You would like me to come now?"

"If you don't mind."

There was a police car at the door. We drove down in it. I said:

"Do you think you'll be able to get to the bottom of this?"

Nash nodded with easy confidence.

"Oh yes, we'll get to the bottom of it all right. It's a question of time and routine. They're slow, these cases, but they're pretty sure. It's a matter of narrowing things down."

"Elimination?" I said.

"Yes. And general routine."

"Watching post boxes, examining typewriters, fingerprints, all that?"

He smiled. "As you say."

At the police station I found Symmington and Griffith were already there. I was introduced to a tall lantern-jawed man in plain clothes, Inspector Graves.

"Inspector Graves," explained Nash, "has come down from London to help us. He's an expert on anonymous letter cases."

Inspector Graves smiled mournfully. I reflected that a life spent in the pursuit of anonymous letter writers must be singularly depressing. Inspector Graves, however, showed a kind of melancholy enthusiasm.

"They're all the same, these cases," he said in a deep lugubrious voice like a depressed bloodhound. "You'd be surprised. The wording of the letters and the things they say."

"We had a case just on two years ago," said Nash. "Inspector Graves helped us then."

Some of the letters, I saw, were spread out on the table in front of Graves. He had evidently been examining them.

"Difficulty is," said Nash, "to get hold of the letters. Either people put them in the fire, or they won't admit to having received anything of the kind. Stupid, you see, and afraid of being mixed up with the police. They're a backward lot here."

"Still, we've got a fair amount to get on with," said Graves. Nash took the letter I had given him from his pocket and tossed it over to Graves.

The latter glanced through it, laid it with the others and observed approvingly:

"Very nice—very nice indeed."

It was not the way I should have chosen to describe the epistle in question, but experts, I suppose, have their own point of view. I was glad that that screed of vituperative and obscene abuse gave *somebody* pleasure.

"We've got enough, I think, to go on with," said Inspector Graves, "and I'll ask all you gentlemen, if you should get any more, to bring them along at once. Also, if you hear of someone else getting one—(you, in particular, doctor, among your patients) do your best to get them to come along here with them. I've got——" he sorted with deft fingers among his exhibits, "one to Mr. Symmington, received as far back as two months ago, one to Dr. Griffith, one to Miss Ginch, one written to Mrs. Mudge, the butcher's wife, one to Jennifer Clark, barmaid at the Three Crowns, the one received by Mrs. Symmington, this one now to Miss Burton—oh yes, and one from the bank manager."

"Quite a representative collection," I remarked.

"And not one I couldn't match from other cases! This one here is as near as nothing to one written by that milliner woman. This one is the dead spit of an outbreak we had up in Northumberland—written by a schoolgirl, they were. I can tell you, gentlemen, I'd like to see something *new* sometimes, instead of the same old treadmill."

"There is nothing new under the sun," I murmured.

"Quite so, sir. You'd know that if you were in our profession."

Nash sighed and said, "Yes, indeed."

Symmington asked:

"Have you come to any definite opinion as to the writer?"

Graves cleared his throat and delivered a small lecture.

"There are certain similarities shared by all these letters. I shall enumerate them, gentlemen, in case they suggest anything to your minds. The text of the letters is composed of words made up from individual letters cut out of a printed book. It's an old book, printed, I should say, about the year 1830. This has obviously been done to avoid the risk of recognition through handwriting which is, as most people know nowadays, a fairly easy matter . . . the so-called disguising of a hand not amounting to much when faced with expert tests. There are no fingerprints on the letters and envelopes of a distinctive character. That is to say, they have been handled by the postal authorities, the recipient, and there are other stray fingerprints, but no set common to all, showing therefore that the person who put them together was careful to wear gloves. The envelopes are typewritten by a Windsor 7 machine, well worn, with the a and the t out of alignment. Most of them have been posted locally, or put in the box of a house by hand. It is therefore evident that they are of local provenance. They were written by a woman, and in my opinion a woman of middle age or over, and probably, though not certainly, unmarried."

We maintained a respectful silence for a minute or two. Then I said:

"The typewriter's your best bet, isn't it? That oughtn't to be difficult in a little place like this."

Inspector Graves shook his head sadly and said:

"That's where you're wrong, sir."

"The typewriter," said Superintendent Nash, "is unfortunately too easy. It's an old one from Mr. Symmington's office, given by him to the Women's Institute where, I may say, it's fairly easy of access. The ladies here all often go into the Institute."

"Can't you tell something definite from the—er—the touch, don't you call it?"

Again Graves nodded.

"Yes, that can be done—but these envelopes have all been typed by someone using one finger."

"Someone then unused to the typewriter?"

"No, I wouldn't say that. Someone, say, who can type but doesn't want us to know the fact."

"Whoever writes these things has been very cunning," I said slowly.

"She is, sir, she is," said Graves. "Up to every trick of the trade."

"I shouldn't have thought one of these bucolic women down here would have had the brains," I said.

Graves coughed.

"I haven't made myself plain, I'm afraid. Those letters were written by an educated woman."

"What, by a lady?"

The word slipped out involuntarily. I hadn't used the term "lady" for years. But now it came automatically to my lips, re-echoed from days long ago, and my grandmother's faint unconsciously arrogant voice saying, "Of course, she isn't a *lady*, dear."

Nash understood at once. The word lady still meant something to him.

"Not necessarily a lady," he said. "But certainly not a village woman. They're mostly pretty illiterate down here, can't spell, and certainly can't express themselves with fluency."

I was silent, for I had had a shock. The community was so small. Unconsciously I had visualized the writer of the letters as a Mrs. Cleat or her like, some spiteful, cunning half-wit.

Symmington put my thoughts into words. He said sharply:

"But that narrows it down to about half a dozen to a dozen people in the whole place!"

"That's right."

"I can't believe it."

Then, with a slight effort, and looking straight in front of him as though the mere sound of his own words was distasteful, he said:

"You have heard what I stated at the inquest. In case you may have thought that that statement was actuated by a desire to protect my wife's memory, I should like to repeat now that I am firmly convinced that the subject matter of the letter my wife received was absolutely false. I *know* it was false. My wife was a very sensitive woman, and—er—well, you might call it *prudish* in some respects. Such a letter would have been a great shock to her, and she was in poor health."

Graves responded instantly.

"That's quite likely to be right, sir. None of these letters show any signs of intimate knowledge. They're just blind accusations. There's been no attempt to blackmail. And there doesn't seem to be any religious bias—such as we sometimes get. It's just sex and spite! And that's going to give us quite a good pointer towards the writer."

Symmington got up. Dry and unemotional as the man was, his lips were trembling.

"I hope you find the devil who writes these soon. She murdered my wife as surely as if she'd put a knife into her." He paused. "How does she feel now, I wonder?"

He went out, leaving that question unanswered.

"How does she feel, Griffith?" I asked. It seemed to me the answer was in his province.

"God knows. Remorseful, perhaps. On the other hand, it may be that she's enjoying her power. Mrs. Symmington's death may have fed her mania."

"I hope not," I said, with a slight shiver. "Because if so, she'll——"

I hesitated and Nash finished the sentence for me.

"She'll try it again? That, Mr. Burton, would be the best thing that could happen, for us. The pitcher goes to the well once too often, remember."

"She'd be mad to go on with it," I exclaimed.

"She'll go on," said Graves. "They always do. It's a vice, you know, they can't let it alone."

I shook my head with a shudder. I asked if they needed me any longer, I wanted to get out into the air. The atmosphere seemed tinged with evil.

"There's nothing more, Mr. Burton," said Nash. "Only keep your eyes open, and do as much propaganda as you can—that is to say, urge on everyone that they've got to report any letter they receive."

I nodded.

"I should think everyone in the place has had one of the foul things by now," I said.

"I wonder," said Graves. He put his sad head a little on one side and asked, "You don't know, definitely, of any one who *hasn't* had a letter?"

"What an extraordinary question! The population at large isn't likely to take me into their confidence."

"No, no, Mr. Burton, I didn't mean that. I just wondered if you knew of any one person who quite definitely, to your certain knowledge, has not received an anonymous letter."

"Well, as a matter of fact," I hesitated, "I do, in a way."

And I repeated my conversation with Emily Barton and what she had said.

Graves received the information with a wooden face and said: "Well, that may come in useful. I'll note it down."

I went out into the afternoon sunshine with Owen Griffith. Once in the street, I swore aloud.

"What kind of place is this for a man to come to to lie in the sun and heal his wounds? It's full of festering poison, this place, and it looks as peaceful and as innocent as the Garden of Eden."

"Even there," said Owen dryly, "there was one serpent."

"Look here, Griffith, do they know anything? Have they got any idea?"

"I don't know. They've got a wonderful technique, the police. They're seemingly so frank, and they tell you nothing."

"Yes. Nash is a nice fellow."

"And a very capable one."

"If anyone's batty in this place, *you* ought to know it," I said accusingly.

Griffith shook his head. He looked discouraged. But he looked more than that—he looked worried. I wondered if he had an inkling of some kind.

We had been walking along the High Street. I stopped at the door of the house agents.

"I believe my second instalment of rent is due—in advance. I've got a good mind to pay it and clear out with Joanna right away. Forfeit the rest of the tenancy."

"Don't go," said Owen.

"Why not?"

He didn't answer. He said slowly after a minute or two,

"After all—I dare say you're right. Lymstock isn't healthy just now. It might—it might harm you or—or your sister."

"Nothing harms Joanna," I said. "She's tough. I'm the weakly one. Somehow this business makes me sick."

"It makes *me* sick," said Owen.

I pushed the door of the house agents half-open.

"But I shan't go," I said. "Vulgar curiosity is stronger than pusillanimity. I want to know the solution."

I went in.

A woman who was typing got up and came towards me. She had frizzy hair and simpered, but I found her more intelligent than the spectacled youth who had previously held sway in the outer office.

A minute or two later something familiar about her penetrated through to my consciousness. It was Miss Ginch, lately Symmington's lady clerk. I commented on the fact.

"You were with Galbraith and Symmington, weren't you?" I said.

"Yes. Yes, indeed. But I thought it was better to leave. This is quite a good post, though not quite so well paid. But there are things that are more valuable than money, don't you think so?"

"Undoubtedly," I said.

"Those awful letters," breathed Miss Ginch in a sibilant whisper. "I got a dreadful one. About me and Mr. Symmington—oh, terrible it was, saying the most *awful* things! I knew my duty and I took it to the police, though of course it wasn't exactly *pleasant* for me, was it?"

"No, no, most unpleasant."

"But they thanked me and said I had done quite right. But I felt that, after that, if people were talking—and evidently they *must* have been, or where did the writer get the idea from?—then I must avoid even the appearance of evil, though there has never been anything at all *wrong* between me and Mr. Symmington."

I felt rather embarrassed.

"No, no, of course not."

"But people have such evil minds. Yes, alas, such evil minds!"

Nervously trying to avoid it, I nevertheless met her eye, and I made a most unpleasant discovery.

Miss Ginch was thoroughly enjoying herself.

Already once to-day I had come across someone who reacted pleasurably to anonymous letters. Inspector Graves's enthusiasm was professional. Miss Ginch's enjoyment I found merely suggestive and disgusting.

An idea flashed across my startled mind.

Had Miss Ginch written these letters herself?

Chapter Seven

WHEN I GOT HOME I found Mrs. Dane Calthrop sitting talking to Joanna. She looked, I thought, grey and ill.

"This has been a terrible shock to me, Mr. Burton," she said. "Poor thing, poor thing."

"Yes," I said. "It's awful to think of someone being driven to the stage of taking their own life."

"Oh, you mean Mrs. Symmington?"

"Didn't you?"

Mrs. Dane Calthrop shook her head.

"Of course one is sorry for her, but it would have been bound to happen anyway, wouldn't it?"

"Would it?" said Joanna dryly.

Mrs. Dane Calthrop turned to her.

"Oh, I think so, dear. If suicide is your idea of escape from trouble then it doesn't very much matter what the trouble is. Whenever some very unpleasant shock had to be faced, she'd have done the same thing. What it really comes down to is that she was that kind of woman. Not that one would have guessed it. She always seemed to me a selfish, rather stupid woman, with a good firm hold on life. Not the kind to panic, you would think—but I'm beginning to realise how little I really know about any one."

"I'm still curious as to whom you meant when you said 'Poor thing'," I remarked.

She stared at me.

"The woman who wrote the letters, of course."

"I don't think," I said dryly, "I shall waste sympathy on her."

Mrs. Dane Calthrop leaned forward. She laid a hand on my knee.

"But don't you realise—can't you *feel?* Use your imagination. Think how desperately, violently unhappy any one must be to sit down and write these things. How lonely, how cut off from human kind. Poisoned through and through, with a dark stream of poison that finds its outlet in this way. That's why I feel so self-reproachful. Somebody in this town has been racked with that terrible unhappiness, and I've had no idea of it. I should have had. You can't interfere with actions—I never do. But that black inward unhappiness—like a septic arm physically, all black and swollen. If you could cut it and let the poison out it would flow away harmlessly. Yes, poor soul, poor soul."

She got up to go.

I did not feel like agreeing with her. I had no sympathy for our anonymous letter writer whatsoever. But I did ask curiously:

"Have you any idea at all, Mrs. Calthrop, who this woman is?"

She turned her fine perplexed eyes on me.

"Well, I can guess," she said. "But then I might be wrong, mightn't I?"

She went swiftly out through the door, popping her head back to ask:

"Do tell me, why have you never married, Mr. Burton?"

In any one else it would have been impertinence, but with Mrs. Dane Calthrop you felt that the idea had suddenly come into her head and she had really wanted to know.

"Shall we say," I said, rallying, "that I have never met the right woman?"

"We can say so," said Mrs. Dane Calthrop, "but it wouldn't be a very good answer, because so many men have obviously married the wrong woman."

This time she really departed.

Joanna said:

"You know I really do think she's mad. But I like her. The people in the village here are afraid of her."

"So am I, a little."

"Because you never know what's coming next?"

"Yes. And there's a careless brilliancy about her guesses."

Joanna said slowly: "Do you really think whoever wrote these letters is very unhappy?"

"I don't know what the damned hag is thinking or feeling! And I don't care. It's her victims I'm sorry for."

It seems odd to me now that in our speculations about Poison Pen's frame of mind, we missed the most obvious one. Griffith had pictured her as possibly exultant. I had envisaged her as remorseful—appalled by the result of her handiwork. Mrs. Dane Calthrop had seen her as suffering.

Yet the obvious, the inevitable reaction we did not consider—or perhaps I should say, I did not consider. That reaction was Fear.

For with the death of Mrs. Symmington, the letters had passed out of one category into another. I don't know what the legal position was—Symmington knew, I suppose, but it was clear that with a death resulting, the position of the writer of the letters was much more serious. There could now be no question of passing it off as a joke if the identity of the writer was discovered. The police were active, a Scotland Yard expert called in. It was vital now for the anonymous author to remain anonymous.

And granted that Fear was the principal reaction, other things followed. Those possibilities also I was blind to. Yet surely they should have been obvious.

II

Joanna and I came down rather late to breakfast the next morning. That is to say, late by the standards of Lymstock. It was nine-thirty, an hour at which, in London, Joanna was just unclosing an eyelid, and mine would probably be still tight shut. However when Partridge had said "Breakfast at half-past eight, or nine o'clock?" neither Joanna nor I had had the nerve to suggest a later hour.

To my annoyance, Aimée Griffith was standing on the doorstep talking to Megan.

She gave tongue with her usual heartiness at the sight of us.

"Hallo, there, slackers! I've been up for hours."

That, of course, was her own business. A doctor, no doubt, has to have early breakfast, and a dutiful sister is there to pour out his tea, or coffee. But it is no excuse for coming and butting in on one's more somnolent neighbours. Nine-thirty is not the time for a morning call.

Megan slipped back into the house and into the dining-room, where I gathered she had been interrupted in her breakfast.

"I said I wouldn't come in," said Aimée Griffith—though why it is more of a merit to force people to come and speak to you on the doorstep, than to talk to them inside the house I do not know. "Just wanted to ask Miss Burton if she'd any vegetables to spare for our Red Cross stall on the main road. If so, I'd get Owen to call for them in the car."

"You're out and about very early," I said.

"The early bird catches the worm," said Aimée. "You have a better chance of finding people in this time of the day. I'm off to Mr. Pye's next. Got to go over to Brenton this afternoon. Guides."

"Your energy makes me quite tired," I said, and at that moment the telephone rang and I retired to the back of the hall to answer it, leaving Joanna murmuring rather doubtfully something about rhubarb and french beans and exposing her ignorance of the vegetable garden.

"Yes?" I said into the telephone mouthpiece.

A confused noise of deep breathing came from the other end of the wire and a doubtful female voice said "Oh!"

"Yes?" I said again encouragingly.

"Oh," said the voice again, and then it inquired adenoidally, "Is that—what I mean—is that Little Furze?"

"This is Little Furze."

"Oh!" This was clearly a stock beginning to every sentence. The voice inquired cautiously, "Could I speak to Miss Partridge just a minute?"

"Certainly," I said. "Who shall I say?"

"Oh. Tell her it's Agnes, would you? Agnes Waddle."

"Agnes Waddle?"

"That's right."

Resisting the temptation to say, "Donald Duck to you," I put down the telephone receiver and called up the stairs to where I could hear the sound of Partridge's activities overhead.

"Partridge. Partridge."

Partridge appeared at the head of the stairs, a long mop in one hand, and a look of "What is it *now?*" clearly discernible behind her invariably respectful manner.

"Yes, sir?"

"Agnes Waddle wants to speak to you on the telephone."

"I beg your pardon, sir?"

I raised my voice. "Agnes Waddle."

I have spelt the name as it presented itself to my mind. But I will now spell it as it was actually written.

"Agnes Woddell—whatever can she want now?"

Very much put out of countenance Partridge relinquished her mop and rustled down the stairs, her print dress crackling with agitation.

I beat an unobtrusive retreat into the dining-room where Megan was wolfing down kidneys and bacon. Megan, unlike Aimée Griffith, was displaying no "glorious morning face." In fact she replied very gruffly to my morning salutations and continued to eat in silence.

I opened the morning paper and a minute or two later Joanna entered looking somewhat shattered.

"Whew!" she said. "I'm so tired. And I think I've exposed my utter ignorance of what grows when. Aren't there runner beans this time of year?"

"August," said Megan.

"Well, one has them any time in London," said Joanna defensively.

"Tins, sweet fool," I said. "And cold storage on ships from the far-flung limits of empire."

"Like ivory, apes and peacocks?" asked Joanna.

"Exactly."

"I'd rather have peacocks," said Joanna thoughtfully.

"I'd like a monkey of my own as a pet," said Megan.

Meditatively peeling an orange, Joanna said:

"I wonder what it would feel like to be Aimée Griffith, all bursting with health and vigour and enjoyment of life. Do you think she's ever tired, or depressed, or—or wistful?"

I said I was quite certain Aimée Griffith was never wistful, and followed Megan out of the open french window on to the veranda.

Standing there, filling my pipe, I heard Partridge enter the dining-room from the hall and heard her voice say grimly:

"Can I speak to you a minute, miss?"

"Dear me," I thought. "I hope Partridge isn't going to give notice. Emily Barton will be very annoyed with us if so."

Partridge went on: "I must apologise, miss, for being rung up on the telephone. That is to say, the young person who did so should have known better. I have never been in the habit of using the telephone or of permitting my friends to ring me up on it, and I'm very sorry indeed that it should have occurred, and the master taking the call and everything."

"Why, that's quite all right, Partridge," said Joanna soothingly, "why shouldn't your friends use the phone if they want to speak to you?"

Partridge's face, I could feel, though I could not see it, was more dour than ever as she replied coldly:

"It is not the kind of thing that has ever been done in this house. Miss Emily would never permit it. As I say, I am sorry it occurred, but Agnes Woddell the girl who did it was upset and she's young too, and doesn't know what's fitting in a gentleman's house."

"That's one for you, Joanna," I thought gleefully.

"This Agnes who rung me up, miss," went on Partridge, "she used to be in service here under me. Sixteen she was, then, and come straight from the orphanage. And you see, not having a home, or a mother or any relations to advise her, she's been in the habit of coming to me. I can tell her what's what, you see."

"Yes?" said Joanna and waited. Clearly there was more to follow.

"So I am taking the liberty of asking you, miss, if you would allow Agnes to come here to tea this afternoon in the kitchen. It's her day out, you see, and she's got something on her mind she wants to consult me about. I wouldn't dream of suggesting such a thing in the usual way."

Joanna said bewildered:

"But why shouldn't you have any one to tea with you?"

Partridge drew herself up at this, so Joanna said afterwards and really looked most formidable, as she replied:

"It has never been the custom of This House, miss. Old Mrs. Barton never allowed visitors in the kitchen, excepting as it should be our own day out, in which case we were allowed to entertain friends here instead of going out, but otherwise, on ordinary days, no. And Miss Emily she keeps to the old ways."

Joanna is very nice to servants and most of them like her but she has never cut any ice with Partridge.

"It's no good, my girl," I said when Partridge had gone and Joanna had joined me outside. "Your sympathy and leniency are not appreciated. The good old overbearing ways for Partridge and things done the way they should be done in a gentleman's house."

"I never heard of such tyranny as not allowing them to have their friends to see them," said Joanna. "It's all very well, Jerry, but they can't *like* being treated like black slaves."

"Evidently they do," I said. "At least the Partridges of this world do."

"I can't imagine why she doesn't like me. Most people do."

"She probably despises you as an inadequate housekeeper. You never draw your hand across a shelf and examine it for traces of dust. You don't look under the mats. You don't ask what happened to the remains of the chocolate soufflé, and you never order a nice bread pudding."

"Ugh!" said Joanna.

She went on sadly. "I'm a failure all round to-day. Despised by our Aimée for ignorance of the vegetable kingdom. Snubbed by Partridge for being a human being. I shall now go out into the garden and eat worms."

"Megan's there already," I said.

For Megan had wandered away a few minutes previously and was now standing aimlessly in the middle of a patch of lawn looking not unlike a meditative bird waiting for nourishment.

She came back, however, towards us and said abruptly:

"I say, I must go home to-day."

"What?" I was dismayed.

She went on, flushing, but speaking with nervous determination.

"It's been awfully good of you having me and I expect I've been a fearful nuisance, but I have enjoyed it awfully, only now I must go back, because after all, well, it's my home and one can't stay away for ever, so I think I'll go this morning."

Both Joanna and I tried to make her change her mind, but she was quite adamant, and finally Joanna got out the car and Megan went upstairs and came down a few minutes later with her belongings packed up again.

The only person pleased seemed to be Partridge, who had almost a smile on her grim face. She had never liked Megan much.

I was standing in the middle of the lawn when Joanna returned.

She asked me if I thought I was a sundial.

"Why?"

"Standing there like a garden ornament. Only one couldn't put on you the motto of only marking the sunny hours. You looked like thunder!"

"I'm out of humour. First Aimée Griffith—('Gracious!' murmured Joanna in parentheses, 'I must speak about those vegetables!') and then Megan beetling off. I'd thought of taking her for a walk up to Legge Tor."

"With a collar and lead, I suppose," said Joanna.

"What?"

Joanna repeated loudly and clearly as she moved off round the corner of the house to the kitchen garden:

"I said, 'With a collar and lead, I suppose?' Master's lost his dog, that's what's the matter with you!"

III

I was annoyed, I must confess, at the abrupt way in which Megan had left us. Perhaps she had suddenly got bored with us.

After all, it wasn't a very amusing life for a girl. At home she'd got the kids and Elsie Holland.

I heard Joanna returning and hastily moved in case she should make more rude remarks about sundials.

Owen Griffith called in his car just before lunch-time, and the gardener was waiting for him with the necessary garden produce.

Whilst old Adams was stowing it in the car I brought Owen indoors for a drink. He wouldn't stay to lunch.

When I came in with the sherry I found Joanna had begun doing her stuff.

No signs of animosity now. She was curled up in the corner of the sofa and was positively purring, asking Owen questions about his work, if he liked being a G.P., if he wouldn't rather have specialised? She thought doctoring was one of the most fascinating things in the world.

Say what you will of her, Joanna is a lovely, a heaven-born listener. And after listening to so many would-be geniuses telling her how they had been unappreciated, listening to Owen Griffith was easy money. By the time we had got to the third glass of sherry, Griffith was telling her about some obscure reaction or lesion in such scientific terms that nobody could have understood a word of it except a fellow medico.

Joanna was looking intelligent and deeply interested.

I felt a moment's qualm. It was really too bad of Joanna. Griffith was too good a chap to be played fast and loose with. Women really were devils.

Then I caught a sideways view of Griffith, his long purposeful chin and the grim set of his lips, and I was not so sure that Joanna was going to have it her own way after all. And anyway, a man has no business to let himself be made a fool of by a woman. It's his own look-out if he does.

Then Joanna said:

"Do change your mind and stay to lunch with us, Dr. Griffith," and Griffith flushed a little and said he would, only his sister would be expecting him back——

"We'll ring her up and explain," said Joanna quickly and went out into the hall and did so.

I thought Griffith looked a little uneasy, and it crossed my mind that he was probably a little afraid of his sister.

Joanna came back smiling and said that that was all right.

And Owen Griffith stayed to lunch and seemed to enjoy himself. We talked about books and plays and world politics, and about music and painting and modern architecture.

We didn't talk about Lymstock at all, or about anonymous letters, or Mrs. Symmington's suicide.

We got right away from everything, and I think Owen Griffith was happy. His dark sad face lighted up, and he revealed an interesting mind.

When he had gone I said to Joanna:

"That fellow's too good for your tricks."

Joanna said:

"That's what you say! You men all stick together!"

"Why are you out after his hide, Joanna? Wounded vanity?"

"Perhaps," said my sister.

IV

That afternoon we were to go to tea with Miss Emily Barton at her rooms in the village.

We strolled down there on foot, for I felt strong enough now to manage the hill back again.

We must actually have allowed too much time and got there early, for the door was opened to us by a tall rawboned fierce-looking woman who told us that Miss Barton wasn't in yet.

"But she's expecting you, I know, so if you'll come up and wait, please."

This was evidently Faithful Florence.

We followed her up the stairs and she threw open a door and showed us into what was quite a comfortable sitting-room, though perhaps a little over-furnished. Some of the things, I suspected, had come from Little Furze.

The woman was clearly proud of her room.

"It's nice, isn't it?" she demanded.

"Very nice," said Joanna warmly.

"I make her as comfortable as I can. Not that I can do for her as I'd like to and in the way she ought to have. She ought to be in her own house, properly, not turned out into rooms."

Florence, who was clearly a dragon, looked from one to the other of us reproachfully. It was not, I felt, our lucky day. Joanna had been ticked off by Aimée Griffith and Partridge and now we were both being ticked off by the dragon Florence.

"Parlourmaid I was for fifteen years there," she added.

Joanna, goaded by injustice, said:

"Well, Miss Barton wanted to let the house. She put it down at the house agents."

"Forced to it," said Florence. "And she living so frugal and careful. But even then, the government can't leave her alone! Has to have its pound of flesh just the same."

I shook my head sadly.

"Plenty of money there was in the old lady's time," said Florence. "And then they all died off one by one, poor dears. Miss Emily nursing of them one after the other. Wore herself out she did, and always so patient and uncomplaining. But it told on her, and then to have worry about money on top of it all! Shares not bringing in what they used to, so she says, and why not, I should like to know? They ought to be ashamed of themselves. Doing down a lady like her who's got no head for figures and can't keep up to their tricks."

"Practically everyone has been hit that way," I said, but Florence remained unsoftened.

"It's all right for some as can look after themselves, but not for *her*. She needs looking after, and as long as she's with me I'm going to see no one imposes on her or upsets her in any way. I'd do anything for Miss Emily."

And glaring at us for some moments in order to drive that point thoroughly home, the indomitable Florence left the room, carefully shutting the door behind her.

"Do you feel like a blood-sucker, Jerry?" inquired Joanna. "Because I do. What's the matter with us?"

"We don't seem to be going down very well," I said. "Megan gets tired of us, Partridge disapproves of you, faithful Florence disapproves of both of us."

Joanna murmured: "I wonder why Megan *did* leave?"

"She got bored."

"I don't think she did at all. I wonder—do you think, Jerry, it could have been something that Aimée Griffith said?"

"You mean this morning, when they were talking on the doorstep."

"Yes. There wasn't much time, of course, but——"

I finished the sentence.

"But that woman's got the tread of a cow elephant! She might have——"

The door opened and Miss Emily came in. She was pink and a little out of breath and seemed excited. Her eyes were very blue and shining. She chirruped at us in quite a distracted manner.

"Oh dear, I'm so sorry I'm late. Just doing a little shopping in the town, and the cakes at the Blue Rose didn't seem to me quite fresh, so I went on to Mrs. Lygon's. I always like to get my cakes the last thing, then one gets the newest batch just out of the oven, and one isn't put off with the day before's. But I am so distressed to have kept you waiting—really unpardonable——"

Joanna cut in.

"It's our fault, Miss Barton. We're early. We walked down and Jerry strides along so fast now that we arrive everywhere too soon."

"Never too soon, dear. Don't say that. One cannot have too much of a good thing, you know."

And the old lady patted Joanna affectionately on the shoulder.

Joanna brightened up. At last, so it seemed, she was being a success. Emily Barton extended her smile to include me, but with a slight timidity in it, rather as one might approach a man-eating tiger guaranteed for the moment harmless.

"It's very good of you to come to such a feminine meal as tea, Mr. Burton."

Emily Barton, I think, has a mental picture of men as interminably consuming whiskies and sodas and smoking cigars, and in the intervals dropping out to do a few seductions of village maidens, or to conduct a liaison with a married woman.

When I said this to Joanna later, she replied that it was probably wishful thinking, that Emily Barton would have liked to come across such a man, but alas, had never done so.

In the meantime Miss Emily was fussing round the room, arranging Joanna and myself with little tables, and carefully providing ash-trays, and a minute later the door opened and Florence came in bearing a tray of tea with some fine Crown Derby cups on it which I gathered Miss Emily had brought with her. The tea was china and delicious and there were plates of sandwiches and thin bread and butter, and a quantity of little cakes.

Florence was beaming now, and looked at Miss Emily with a kind of maternal pleasure, as at a favourite child enjoying a doll's tea party.

Joanna and I ate far more than we wanted to, our hostess pressed us so earnestly. The little lady was clearly enjoying her tea party and I perceived that, to Emily Barton, Joanna and I were a big adventure, two people from the mysterious world of London and sophistication. Miss Barton spoke warmly of Dr. Griffith, his kindness and his cleverness as a doctor. Mr. Symmington, too, was a very clever lawyer, and had helped Miss Barton to get some money back from the income tax which she would never have known about. He was so nice to his children, too, devoted to them and to his wife—she caught herself up. "Poor Mrs. Symmington, it's so dreadfully sad, with those young children left motherless. Never, perhaps, a very strong woman—and her health had been bad of late. A brain storm, that is what it must have been. I read about such a thing in the paper. People really do not know what they are doing under those circumstances. And she can't have known what she was doing or else she would have remembered Mr. Symmington and the children."

"That anonymous letter must have shaken her up very badly," said Joanna.

Miss Barton flushed. She said, with a tinge of reproof in her voice:

"Not a very nice thing to discuss, do you think, dear? I know there have been—er—letters, but we won't talk about them. Nasty things. I think they are better just ignored."

Well, Miss Barton might be able to ignore them, but for some people it wasn't so easy. However I obediently changed the subject and we discussed Aimée Griffith.

"Wonderful, quite wonderful," said Emily Barton. "Her energy and her organising powers are really splendid. She's so good with girls too. And she's so practical and up-to-date in every way. She really runs this place. And absolutely devoted to her brother. It's very nice to see such devotion between brother and sister."

"Doesn't he ever find her a little overwhelming?" asked Joanna.

Emily Barton stared at her in a startled fashion.

"She has sacrificed a great deal for his sake," she said with a touch of reproachful dignity.

I saw a touch of Oh Yeay! in Joanna's eyes and hastened to divert the conversation to Mr. Pye.

Emily Barton was a little dubious about Mr. Pye.

All she could say was, repeated rather doubtfully, that he was very kind

—yes, very kind. Very well off, too, and most generous. He had very strange visitors sometimes, but then, of course, he had travelled a lot.

We agreed that travel not only broadened the mind, but occasionally resulted in the forming of strange acquaintances.

"I have often wished myself, to go on a cruise," said Emily Barton wistfully. "One reads about them in the papers and they sound so attractive."

"Why don't you go?" asked Joanna.

This turning of a dream into a reality seemed to alarm Miss Emily. "Oh, no, no, that would be *quite* impossible."

"But why? They're fairly cheap."

"Oh, it's not only the expense. But I shouldn't like to go alone. Travelling alone would look very peculiar, don't you think?"

"No," said Joanna.

Miss Emily looked at her doubtfully.

"And I don't know how I would manage about my luggage—and going ashore at foreign ports—and all the different currencies——"

Innumerable pitfalls seemed to rise up before the little lady's affrighted gaze, and Joanna hastened to calm her by a question about an approaching garden fête and sale of work. This led us quite naturally to Mrs. Dane Calthrop.

A faint spasm showed for a minute on Miss Barton's face.

"You know, dear," she said, "she is really a very *odd* woman. The things she says sometimes."

I asked what things.

"Oh, I don't know. Such very *unexpected* things. And the way she looks at you, as though you weren't there but somebody else was—I'm expressing it badly but it is so hard to convey the impression I mean. And then she won't—well, *interfere* at all. There are so many cases where a vicar's wife could advise and—perhaps *admonish*. Pull people up, you know, and make them mend their ways. Because people would listen to her, I'm sure of that, they're all quite in awe of her. But she insists on being aloof and far away, and has such a curious habit of feeling sorry for the most unworthy people."

"That's interesting," I said, exchanging a quick glance with Joanna.

"Still, she is a very well-bred woman. She was a Miss Farroway of Bellpath, very good family, but these old familes sometimes *are* a little peculiar, I believe. But she is devoted to her husband who is a man of very fine intellect—wasted, I am sometimes afraid, in this country circle. A good man, and most sincere, but I always find his habit of quoting Latin a little confusing."

"Hear, hear," I said fervently.

"Jerry had an expensive public school education, so he doesn't recognise Latin when he hears it," said Joanna.

This led Miss Barton to a new topic.

"The schoolmistress here is a most unpleasant young woman," she said. "Quite *Red*, I'm afraid." She lowered her voice over the word "Red."

Later, as we walked home up the hill, Joanna said to me: "She's rather sweet."

V

At dinner that night, Joanna said to Partridge that she hoped her tea party had been a success.

Partridge got rather red in the face and held herself even more stiffly.

"Thank you, miss, but Agnes never turned up after all."

"Oh, I'm sorry."

"It didn't matter to *me*," said Partridge.

She was so swelling with grievance that she condescended to pour it out to us.

"It wasn't me who thought of asking her! She rang up herself, said she'd something on her mind and could she come here, it being her day off. And I said, yes, subject to your permission which I obtained. And after that, not a sound or sign of her! And no word of apology either, though I should hope I'll get a postcard to-morrow morning. These girls nowadays—don't know their place—no idea of how to behave."

Joanna attempted to soothe Partridge's wounded feelings.

"She mayn't have felt well. You didn't ring up to find out?"

Partridge drew herself up again.

"No, I did *not*, miss. No, indeed. If Agnes likes to behave rudely that's her look-out, but I shall give her a piece of my mind when we meet."

Partridge went out of the room still stiff with indignation and Joanna and I laughed.

"Probably a case of 'Advice from Aunt Nancy's Column'," I said. " '*My boy is very cold in his manner to me, what shall I do about it?*' Failing Aunt Nancy, Partridge was to be applied to for advice, but instead there has been a reconciliation and I expect at this minute that Agnes and her boy are one of those speechless couples locked in each other's arms that you come upon suddenly standing by a dark hedge. They embarrass you horribly, but you don't embarrass them."

Joanna laughed and said she expected that was it.

We began talking of the anonymous letters and wondered how Nash and the melancholy Graves were getting on.

"It's a week to-day exactly," said Joanna, "since Mrs. Symmington's suicide. I should think they must have got on to something by now. Fingerprints, or handwriting, or *something*."

I answered her absently. Somewhere behind my conscious mind, a queer uneasiness was growing. It was connected in some way with the phrase that Joanna had used, "a week exactly."

I ought, I dare say, to have put two and two together earlier. Perhaps, unconsciously, my mind was already suspicious.

Anyway the leaven was working now. The uneasiness was growing— coming to a head.

Joanna noticed suddenly that I wasn't listening to her spirited account of a village encounter.

"What's the matter, Jerry?"

I did not answer because my mind was busy piecing things together.

Mrs. Symmington's suicide. . . . She was alone in the house that afternoon. . . . Alone in the house *because the maids were having their day out*. . . . A week ago exactly. . . .

"Jerry, what——"

I interrupted.

"Joanna, maids have days out once a week, don't they?"

"And alternate Sundays," said Joanna. "What on——"

"Never mind Sundays. They go out the same day every week?"

"Yes. That's the usual thing."

Joanna was staring at me curiously. Her mind had not taken the track mine had done.

I crossed the room and rang the bell. Partridge came.

"Tell me," I said, "this Agnes Woddell. She's in service?"

"Yes, sir. At Mrs. Symmington's. At Mr. Symmington's, I should say now."

I drew a deep breath. I glanced at the clock. It was half-past ten.

"Would she be back now, do you think?"

Partridge was looking disapproving.

"Yes, sir. The maids have to be in by ten there. They're old-fashioned."

I said: "I'm going to ring up."

I went out to the hall. Joanna and Partridge followed me. Partridge was clearly furious. Joanna was puzzled. She said, as I was trying to get the number:

"What are you going to do, Jerry?"

"I'd like to be sure that the girl has come in all right."

Partridge sniffed. Just sniffed, nothing more. But I did not care twopence about Partridge's sniffs.

Elsie Holland answered the telephone the other end.

"Sorry to ring you up," I said. "This is Jerry Burton speaking. Is—has—your maid Agnes come in?"

It was not until after I had said it that I suddenly felt a bit of a fool. For if the girl had come in and it was all right, how on earth was I going to explain my ringing up and asking. It would have been better if I had let Joanna ask the question, though even that would need a bit of explaining. I foresaw a new trail of gossip started in Lymstock, with myself and the unknown Agnes Woddell as its centre.

Elsie Holland sounded, not unnaturally, very much surprised.

"Agnes? Oh, she's sure to be in by now."

I felt a fool, but I went on with it.

"Do you mind just seeing if she has come in, Miss Holland?"

There is one thing to be said for a nursery governess; she is used to doing things when told. Hers not to reason why! Elsie Holland put down the receiver and went off obediently.

Two minutes later I heard her voice.

"Are you there, Mr. Burton?"

"Yes."

"Agnes isn't in yet, as a matter of fact."

I knew then that my hunch had been right.

I heard a noise of voices vaguely from the other end, then Symmington himself spoke.

"Hallo, Burton, what's the matter?"

"Your maid Agnes isn't back yet."

"No. Miss Holland has just been to see. What's the matter? There's not been an accident, has there?"

"Not an *accident*," I said.

"Do you mean you have reason to believe something has happened to the girl?"

I said grimly: "I shouldn't be surprised."

Chapter Eight

I SLEPT BADLY that night. I think that, even then, there were pieces of the puzzle floating about in my mind. I believe that if I had given my mind to it, I could have solved the whole thing then and there. Otherwise why did those fragments tag along so persistently?

How much do we know at any time? Much more, or so I believe, than we know we know! But we cannot break through to that subterranean knowledge. It is there, but we cannot reach it.

I lay on my bed, tossing uneasily, and only vague bits of the puzzle came to torture me.

There *was* a pattern, if only I could get hold of it. I ought to know who wrote those damned letters. There was a trail somewhere if only I could follow it. . . .

As I dropped off to sleep, words danced irritatingly through my drowsy mind.

"No smoke without fire." No fire without smoke. Smoke . . . Smoke? Smoke screen . . . No, that was the war—a war phrase. War. Scrap of paper. . . . Only a scrap of paper. Belgium—Germany. . . .

I fell asleep. I dreamt that I was taking Mrs. Dane Calthrop who had turned into a greyhound, for a walk with a collar and lead.

II

It was the ringing of the telephone that roused me. A persistent ringing.

I sat up in bed, glanced at my watch. It was half-past seven. I had not yet been called. The telephone was ringing in the hall downstairs.

I jumped out of bed, pulled on a dressing-gown, and raced down. I beat Partridge coming through the back door from the kitchen by a short head. I picked up the receiver.

"Hallo?"

"Oh——" It was a sob of relief. "It's *you!*" Megan's voice. Megan's voice indescribably forlorn and frightened. "Oh, please do come—*do* come. Oh, please do! Will you?"

"I'm coming at once," I said. "Do you hear? *At once.*"

I took the stairs two at a time and burst in on Joanna.

"Look here, Jo, I'm going off to the Symmingtons'."

Joanna lifted a curly blonde head from the pillow and rubbed her eyes like a small child.

"Why—what's happened?"

"I don't know. It was the child—Megan. She sounded all in."

"What do you think it is?"

"The girl Agnes, unless I'm very much mistaken."

As I went out of the door, Joanna called after me:

"Wait. I'll get up and drive you down."

"No need. I'll drive myself."

"You can't drive the car."

"Yes, I can."

I did, too. It hurt, but not too much. I'd washed, shaved, dressed, got the car out and driven to the Symmingtons' in half an hour. Not bad going.

Megan must have been watching for me. She came out of the house at a run and clutched me. Her poor little face was white and twitching.

"Oh, you've come—you've *come!*"

"Hold up, funny face," I said. "Yes, I've come. Now what is it?"

She began to shake. I put my arm round her.

"I—I found her."

"You found Agnes? Where?"

The trembling grew.

"Under the stairs. There's a cupboard there. It has fishing-rods and golf clubs and things. You know."

I nodded. It was the usual cupboard.

Megan went on.

"She was there—all huddled up—and—and *cold*—horribly cold. She was —she was *dead,* you know!"

I asked curiously. "What made you look there?"

"I—I don't know. You telephoned last night. And we all began wondering where Agnes was. We waited up some time, but she didn't come in, and at last we went to bed. I didn't sleep very well and I got up early.

There was only Rose (the cook, you know) about. She said she was very cross about Agnes not having come back. She said she'd been before somewhere when a girl did a flit like that. I had some milk and bread and butter in the kitchen—and then suddenly Rose came in looking queer and she said that Agnes's outdoor things were still in her room. Her best ones that she goes out in. And I began to wonder if—if she'd ever left the house, and I started looking round, and I opened the cupboard under the stairs and—and she was there . . ."

"Somebody's rung up the police, I suppose?"

"Yes, they're here now. My stepfather rang them up straightaway. And then I—I felt I couldn't bear it, and I rang *you* up. You don't mind?"

"No," I said. "I don't mind."

I looked at her curiously.

"Did anybody give you some brandy, or some coffee, or some tea after—after you found her?"

Megan shook her head.

I cursed the whole Symmington *ménage.* That stuffed shirt, Symmington, thought of nothing but the police. Neither Elsie Holland nor the cook seemed to have thought of the effect on the sensitive child who had made that gruesome discovery.

"Come on, slabface," I said. "We'll go to the kitchen."

We went round the house to the back door and into the kitchen. Rose, a plump pudding-faced woman of forty, was drinking strong tea by the kitchen fire. She greeted us with a flow of talk and her hand to her heart.

She'd come all over queer, she told me, awful the palpitations were! Just think of it, it might have been *her,* it might have been any of them, murdered in their beds they might have been.

"Dish out a good strong cup of that tea for Miss Megan," I said. "She's had a shock, you know. Remember it was she who found the body."

The mere mention of a body nearly sent Rose off again, but I quelled her with a stern eye and she poured out a cup of inky fluid.

"There you are, young woman," I said to Megan. "You drink that down. You haven't got any brandy, I suppose, Rose?"

Rose said rather doubtfully that there was a drop of cooking brandy left over from the Christmas puddings.

"That'll do," I said, and put a dollop of it into Megan's cup. I saw by Rose's eye that she thought it a good idea.

I told Megan to stay with Rose.

"I can trust you to look after Miss Megan?" I said, and Rose replied in a gratified way, "Oh yes, sir."

I went through into the house. If I knew Rose and her kind, she would soon find it necessary to keep her strength up with a little food, and that would be good for Megan too. Confound these people, why couldn't they look after the child?

Fuming inwardly I ran into Elsie Holland in the hall. She didn't seem surprised to see me. I suppose that the gruesome excitement of the discovery made one oblivious of who was coming and going. The constable, Bert Rundle, was by the front door.

Elsie Holland gasped out:

"Oh, Mr. Burton, isn't it *awful*? Whoever can have done such a dreadful thing?"

"It *was* murder, then?"

"Oh, yes. She was struck on the back of the head. It's all blood and hair —oh! it's *awful*—and bundled into that cupboard. Who can have done such a wicked thing? And *why*? Poor Agnes, I'm sure she never did anyone any harm."

"No," I said. "Somebody saw to that pretty promptly."

She stared at me. Not, I thought, a quick-witted girl. But she had good nerves. Her colour was as usual, slightly heightened by excitement, and I even fancied that in a macabre kind of way, and in spite of a naturally kind heart, she was enjoying the drama.

She said apologetically: "I must go up to the boys. Mr. Symmington is so anxious that they shouldn't get a shock. He wants me to keep them right away."

"Megan found the body, I hear," I said. "I hope somebody is looking after her?"

I will say for Elsie Holland that she looked conscience stricken.

"Oh dear," she said. "I forgot all about her. I do hope she's all right. I've been so rushed, you know, and the police and everything—but it was remiss of me. Poor girl, she must be feeling bad. I'll go and look for her at once."

I relented.

"She's all right," I said. "Rose is looking after her. You get along to the kids."

She thanked me with a flash of white tombstone teeth and hurried upstairs. After all, the boys were her job, and not Megan—Megan was nobody's job. Elsie was paid to look after Symmington's blinking brats. One could hardly blame her for doing so.

As she flashed round the corner of the stairs, I caught my breath. For a minute I caught a glimpse of a Winged Victory, deathless and incredibly beautiful, instead of a conscientious nursery governess.

Then a door opened and Superintendent Nash stepped out into the hall with Symmington behind him.

"Oh, Mr. Burton," he said. "I was just going to telephone you. I'm glad you are here."

He didn't ask me—then—why I was here.

He turned his head and said to Symmington:

"I'll use this room if I may."

It was a small morning-room with a window on the front of the house.

"Certainly, certainly."

Symmington's poise was pretty good, but he looked desperately tired. Superintendent Nash said gently:

"I should have some breakfast if I were you, Mr. Symmington. You and Miss Holland and Miss Megan will feel much better after coffee and eggs and bacon. Murder is a nasty business on an empty stomach."

He spoke in a comfortable family doctor kind of way.

Symmington gave a faint attempt at a smile and said:

"Thank you, superintendent, I'll take your advice."

I followed Nash into the little morning-room and he shut the door. He said then:

"You've got here very quickly. How did you hear?"

I told him that Megan had rung me up. I felt well disposed towards Superintendent Nash. He, at any rate, had not forgotten that Megan, too, would be in need of breakfast.

"I hear that you telephoned last night, Mr. Burton, asking about this girl? Why was that?"

I suppose it did seem odd. I told him about Agnes's telephone call to Partridge and her non-appearance. He said, "Yes, I see . . ."

He said it slowly and reflectively, rubbing his chin.

Then he sighed:

"Well," he said. "It's murder now, right enough. Direct physical action. The question is, what did the girl know? Did she say anything to this Partridge? Anything definite?"

"I don't think so. But you can ask her."

"Yes. I shall come up and see her when I've finished here."

"What happened exactly?" I asked. "Or don't you know yet?"

"Near enough. It was the maids' day out——"

"Both of them?"

"Yes, it seems that there used to be two sisters here who liked to go out together, so Mrs. Symmington arranged it that way. Then when these two came, she kept to the same arrangement. They used to leave cold supper laid out in the dining-room, and Miss Holland used to get tea."

"I see."

"It's pretty clear up to a point. The cook, Rose, comes from Nether Mickford, and in order to get there on her day out she has to catch the half-past two bus. So Agnes has to finish clearing up lunch always. Rose used to wash up the supper things in the evenings to even things up.

"That's what happened yesterday. Rose went off to catch the bus at two twenty-five, Symmington left for his office at five-and-twenty to three. Elsie Holland and the children went out at a quarter to three. Megan Hunter went out on her bicycle about five minutes later. Agnes would then be alone in the house. As far as I can make out, she normally left the house between three o'clock and half-past three."

"The house being then left empty?"

"Oh, they don't worry about that down here. There's not much locking up done in these parts. As I say, at ten minutes to three Agnes was alone in the house. That she never left it is clear, for she was in her cap and apron still when we found her body."

"I suppose you can tell roughly the time of death?"

"Doctor Griffith won't commit himself. Between two o'clock and four-thirty, is his official medical verdict."

"How was she killed?"

"She was first stunned by a blow on the back of the head. Afterwards an ordinary kitchen skewer, sharpened to a fine point, was thrust into the base of the skull, causing instantaneous death."

I lit a cigarette. It was not a nice picture.

"Pretty cold blooded," I said.

"Oh yes, yes, that was indicated."

I inhaled deeply.

"Who did it?" I said. "And why?"

"I don't suppose," said Nash slowly, "that we shall ever know exactly why. But we can guess."

"She knew something?"

"She knew something."

"She didn't give any one here a hint?"

"As far as I can make out, no. She's been upset, so the cook says, ever since Mrs. Symmington's death, and according to this Rose, she's been getting more and more worried, and kept saying she didn't know what she ought to do."

He gave a short exasperated sigh.

"It's always the way. They won't come to us. They've got that deep-seated prejudice against 'being mixed up with the police.' If she'd come along and told us what was worrying her, she'd be alive to-day."

"Didn't she give the other woman *any* hint?"

"No, or so Rose says, and I'm inclined to believe her. For if she had, Rose would have blurted it out at once with a good many fancy embellishments of her own."

"It's maddening," I said, "not to know."

"We can still guess, Mr. Burton. To begin with, it can't be anything very definite. It's got to be the sort of thing that you think over, and as you think it over, your uneasiness grows. You see what I mean?"

"Yes."

"Actually, I think I know what it was."

I looked at him with respect.

"That's good work, superintendent."

"Well, you see, Mr. Burton, I know something that you don't. On the afternoon that Mrs. Symmington committed suicide both maids were supposed to be out. It was their day out. But actually Agnes came back to the house."

"You know that?"

"Yes. Agnes has a boy friend—young Rendell from the fish shop. Wednesday is early closing and he comes along to meet Agnes and they go for a walk, or to the pictures if it's wet. That Wednesday they had a row practically as soon as they met. Our letter writer had been active, suggesting that Agnes had other fish to fry, and young Fred Rendell was all worked up. They quarrelled violently and Agnes bolted back home and said she wasn't coming out unless Fred said he was sorry."

"Well?"

"Well, Mr. Burton, the kitchen faces the back of the house but the pantry looks out where we are looking now. There's only one entrance gate. You come through it and either up to the front door, or else along the path at the side of the house to the back door."

He paused.

"Now I'll tell you something. That letter that came to Mrs. Symmington that afternoon *didn't come by post*. It had a used stamp affixed to it, and the postmark faked quite convincingly in lamp-black, so that it would seem to have been delivered by the postman with the afternoon letters. But actually *it had not been through the post*. You see what that means?"

I said slowly: "It means that it was left *by hand*, pushed through the letter box some time before the afternoon post was delivered, so that it should be amongst the other letters."

"Exactly. The afternoon post comes round about a quarter to four. My theory is this. The girl was in the pantry looking through the window (it's masked by shrubs but you can see through them quite well) watching out for her young man to turn up and apologise."

I said: *"And she saw whoever it was deliver that note?"*

"That's my guess, Mr. Burton. I may be wrong, of course."

"I don't think you are. . . . It's simple—and convincing—and it means that Agnes knew *who the anonymous letter writer was.*"

"Yes."

"But then why didn't she——?"

I paused, frowning.

Nash said quickly:

"As I see it, the girl *didn't realise what she had seen*. Not at first. Somebody had left a letter at the house, yes—but that somebody was nobody she would dream of connecting with the anonymous letters. It was somebody, from that point of view, quite above suspicion.

"But the more she thought about it, the more uneasy she grew. Ought she, perhaps, to tell someone about it? In her perplexity she thinks of Miss Barton's Partridge who, I gather, is a somewhat dominant personality and whose judgment Agnes would accept unhesitatingly. She decides to ask Partridge what she ought to do."

"Yes," I said thoughtfully. "It fits well enough. And somehow or other, Poison Pen found out. How did she find out, superintendent?"

"You're not used to living in the country, Mr. Burton. It's a kind of miracle how things get round. First of all there's the telephone call. Who overheard it your end?"

I reflected.

"I answered the telephone originally. Then I called up the stairs to Partridge."

"Mentioning the girl's name?"

"Yes—yes, I did."

"Anyone overhear you?"

"My sister or Miss Griffith might have done so."

"Ah, Miss Griffith. What was she doing up there?"

I explained.

"Was she going back to the village?"

"She was going to Mr. Pye first."

Superintendent Nash sighed.

"That's two ways it could have gone all over the place."

I was incredulous.

"Do you mean that either Miss Griffith or Mr. Pye would bother to repeat a meaningless little bit of information like that?"

"Anything's news in a place like this. You'd be surprised. If the dress-maker's mother has got a bad corn everybody hears about it! And then there is this end. Miss Holland, Rose—they could have heard what Agnes said. And there's Fred Rendell. It may have gone round through him that Agnes went back to the house that afternoon."

I gave a slight shiver. I was looking out of the window. In front of me was a neat square of grass and a path and the low prim gate.

Someone had opened the gate, had walked very correctly and quietly up to the house, and had pushed a letter through the letter box. I saw, hazily, in my mind's eye, that vague woman's shape. The face was blank—but it must be a face that I knew. . . .

Superintendent Nash was saying:

"All the same, this narrows things down. That's always the way we get 'em in the end. Steady, patient elimination. There aren't so very many people it could be now."

"You mean——?"

"It knocks out any women clerks who were at their work all yesterday afternoon. It knocks out the school-mistress. She was teaching. And the district nurse. I know where she was yesterday. Not that I ever thought it was any of *them*, but now we're *sure*. You see, Mr. Burton, we've got two definite times now on which to concentrate—yesterday afternoon, and the week before. On the day of Mrs. Symmington's death from, say, a quarter-past three (the earliest possible time at which Agnes could have been back in the house after her quarrel) and four o'clock when the post must have come (but I can get that fixed more accurately with the postman). And yesterday from ten minutes to three (when Miss Megan Hunter left the house) until half-past three or more probably a quarter-past three as Agnes hadn't begun to change."

"What do you think happened yesterday?"

Nash made a grimace.

"What do I think? I think a certain lady walked up to the front door

and rang the bell, quite calm and smiling, the afternoon caller. . . .
Maybe she asked for Miss Holland, or for Miss Megan, or perhaps she
had brought a parcel. Anyway Agnes turns round to get a salver for cards,
or to take the parcel in, and our lady-like caller bats her on the back of her
unsuspecting head."

"What with?"

Nash said:

"The ladies round here usually carry large sizes in handbags. No saying
what mightn't be inside it."

"And then stabs her through the back of the neck and bundles her into
the cupboard? Wouldn't that be a hefty job for a woman?"

Superintendent Nash looked at me with rather a queer expression.

"The woman we're after isn't normal—not by a long way—and that type
of mental instability goes with surprising strength. Agnes wasn't a big
girl."

He paused and then asked: "What made Miss Megan Hunter think of
looking in that cupboard?"

"Sheer instinct," I said.

Then I asked: "Why drag Agnes into the cupboard? What was the
point?"

"The longer it was before the body was found, the more difficult it
would be to fix the time of death accurately. If Miss Holland, for instance,
fell over the body as soon as she came in, a doctor might be able to fix it
within ten minutes or so—which might be awkward for our lady friend."

I said, frowning:

"But if Agnes were suspicious of this person——"

Nash interrupted me.

"She wasn't. Not to the pitch of definite suspicion. She just thought it
'queer.' She was a slow-witted girl, I imagine, and she was only vaguely
suspicious with a feeling that something was wrong. She certainly didn't
suspect that she was up against a woman who would do murder."

"Did you suspect that?" I asked.

Nash shook his head. He said, with feeling:

"I ought to have known. That suicide business, you see, frightened
Poison Pen. She got the wind up. Fear, Mr. Burton, is an incalculable
thing."

Yes, fear. That was the thing we ought to have foreseen. Fear—in a lunatic brain . . .

"You see," said Superintendent Nash, and somehow his words made the whole thing seem absolutely horrible, "we're up against someone who's respected and thought highly of—someone, in fact, of good social position!"

III

Presently Nash said that he was going to interview Rose once more. I asked him, rather diffidently, if I might come too. Rather to my surprise he assented cordially.

"I'm very glad of your co-operation, Mr. Burton, if I may say so."

"That sounds suspicious," I said. "In books when a detective welcomes someone's assistance, that someone is usually the murderer."

Nash laughed shortly. He said: "You're hardly the type to write anonymous letters, Mr. Burton."

He added: "Frankly, you can be useful to us."

"I'm glad, but I don't see how."

"You're a stranger down here, that's why. You've got no preconceived ideas about the people here. But at the same time, you've got the opportunity of getting to know things in what I may call a social way."

"The murderer is a person of good social position," I murmured.

"Exactly."

"I'm to be the spy within the gates?"

"Have you any objection?"

I thought it over.

"No," I said, "frankly I haven't. If there's a dangerous lunatic about driving inoffensive women to suicide and hitting miserable little maidservants on the head, then I'm not averse to doing a bit of dirty work to put that lunatic under restraint."

"That's sensible of you, sir. And let me tell you, the person we're after is dangerous. She's about as dangerous as a rattlesnake and a cobra and a black mamba rolled into one."

I gave a slight shiver. I said:

"In fact, we've got to make haste?"

"That's right. Don't think we're inactive in the force. We're not. We're working on several different lines."

He said it grimly.

I had a vision of a fine far-flung spider's web. . . .

Nash wanted to hear Rose's story again, so he explained to me, because she had already told him two different versions, and the more versions he got from her, the more likely it was that a few grains of truth might be incorporated.

We found Rose washing up breakfast, and she stopped at once and rolled her eyes and clutched her heart and explained again how she'd been coming over queer all the morning.

Nash was patient with her but firm. He'd been soothing the first time, so he told me, and peremptory the second, and he now employed a mixture of the two.

Rose enlarged pleasurably on the details of the past week, of how Agnes had gone about in deadly fear, and had shivererd and said, "Don't ask me," when Rose had urged her to say what was the matter. "It would be death if she told me," that's what she said, finished Rose, rolling her eyes happily.

Had Agnes given no hint of what was troubling her?

No, except that she went in fear of her life.

Superintendent Nash sighed and abandoned the theme, contenting himself with extracting an exact account of Rose's own activities the preceding afternoon.

This, put baldly, was that Rose had caught the 2.30 bus and had spent the afternoon and evening with her family, returning by the 8.40 bus from Nether Mickford. The recital was complicated by the extraordinary presentiments of evil Rose had had all the afternoon and how her sister had commented on it and how she hadn't been able to touch a morsel of seed cake.

From the kitchen we went in search of Elsie Holland, who was superintending the children's lessons. As always, Elsie Holland was competent and obliging. She rose and said:

"Now, Colin, you and Brian will do these three sums and have the answers ready for me when I come back."

She then led us into the night nursery. "Will this do? I thought it would be better not to talk before the children."

"Thank you, Miss Holland. Just tell me, once more, are you *quite* sure that Agnes never mentioned to you being worried over anything—since Mrs. Symmington's death, I mean?"

"No, she never said anything. She was a very quiet girl, you know, and didn't talk much."

"A change from the other one, then!"

"Yes, Rose talks much too much. I have to tell her not to be impertinent sometimes."

"Now, will you tell me exactly what happened yesterday afternoon? Everything you can remember."

"Well, we had lunch as usual. One o'clock, and we hurry just a little. I don't let the boys dawdle. Let me see. Mr. Symmington went back to the office, and I helped Agnes by laying the table for supper—the boys ran out in the garden till I was ready to take them."

"Where did you go?"

"Towards Combeacre, by the field path—the boys wanted to fish. I forgot their bait and had to go back for it."

"What time was that?"

"Let me see, we started about twenty to three—or just after. Megan was coming but changed her mind. She was going out on her bicycle. She's got quite a craze for bicycling."

"I mean what time was it when you went back for the bait? Did you go into the house?"

"No. I'd left it in the conservatory at the back. I don't know what time it was then—about ten minutes to three, perhaps."

"Did you see Megan or Agnes?"

"Megan must have started, I think. No, I didn't see Agnes. I didn't see anyone."

"And after that you went fishing?"

"Yes, we went along by the stream. We didn't catch anything. We hardly ever do, but the boys enjoy it. Brian got rather wet. I had to change his things when we got in."

"You attend to tea on Wednesdays?"

"Yes. It's all ready in the drawing-room for Mr. Symmington. I just make the tea when he comes in. The children and I have ours in the schoolroom—and Megan, of course. I have my own tea things and everything in the cupboard up there."

"What time did you get in?"

"At ten minutes to five. I took the boys up and started to lay tea. Then when Mr. Symmington came in at five I went down to make his but he said he would have it with us in the schoolroom. The boys were so pleased. We played Animal Grab afterwards. It seems so awful to think of now—with that poor girl in the cupboard all the time."

"Would anybody go to that cupboard normally?"

"Oh no, it's only used for keeping junk. The hats and coats hang in the little cloakroom to the right of the front door as you come in. No one might have gone to the other cupboard for months."

"I see. And you noticed nothing unusual, nothing abnormal at all when you came back?"

The blue eyes opened very wide.

"Oh no, inspector, nothing at all. Everything was just the same as usual. That's what was so awful about it."

"And the week before?"

"You mean the day Mrs. Symmington——"

"Yes."

"Oh, that was terrible—terrible!"

"Yes, yes, I know. You were out all that afternoon also?"

"Oh yes, I always take the boys out in the afternoon—if it's fine enough. We do lessons in the morning. We went up on the moor, I remember—quite a long way. I was afraid I was late back because as I turned in at the gate I saw Mr. Symmington coming from his office at the other end of the road, and I hadn't even put the kettle on, but it was just ten minutes to five."

"You didn't go up to Mrs. Symmington?"

"Oh no. I never did. She always rested after lunch. She had attacks of neuralgia—and they used to come on after meals. Dr. Griffith had given her some cachets to take. She used to lie down and try to sleep."

Nash said in a casual voice:

"So no one would take her up the post?"

"The afternoon post? No, I'd look in the letter box and put the letters on the hall table when I came in. But very often Mrs. Symmington used to come down and get it herself. She didn't sleep all the afternoon. She was usually up again by four."

"You didn't think anything was wrong because she wasn't up that afternoon?"

"Oh, no, I never dreamed of such a thing. Mr. Symmington was hanging up his coat in the hall and I said, 'Tea's not quite ready, but the kettle's nearly boiling,' and he nodded and called out, 'Mona, Mona!'—and then as Mrs. Symmington didn't answer he went upstairs to her bedroom, and it must have been the most terrible shock to him. He called me and I came, and he said, 'Keep the children away,' and then he phoned Dr. Griffith and we forgot all about the kettle and it burnt the bottom out! Oh dear, it *was* dreadful, and she'd been so happy and cheerful at lunch."

Nash said abruptly: "What is your own opinion of that letter she received, Miss Holland?"

Elsie Holland said firmly:

"Oh, I think it was wicked—wicked!"

"Yes, yes, I don't mean that. Did you think it was true?"

Elise Holland said firmly:

"No, indeed I don't. Mrs. Symmington was very sensitive—very sensitive indeed. She had to take all sorts of things for her nerves. And she was very—well, *particular*." Elsie flushed. "Anything of that sort—*nasty*, I mean —would have given her a great shock."

Nash was silent for a moment, then he asked:

"Have you had any of these letters, Miss Holland?"

"No. No, I haven't had any."

"Are you sure? Please"—he lifted a hand—"don't answer in a hurry. They're not pleasant things to get, I know. And sometimes people don't like to admit they've had them. But it's very important in this case that we should know. We're quite aware that the statements in them are just a tissue of lies, so you needn't feel embarrassed."

"But I haven't, superintendent. Really I haven't. Not anything of the kind."

She was indignant, almost tearful, and her denials seemed genuine enough.

When she went back to the children, Nash stood looking out of the window.

"Well," he said, "that's that! She says she hasn't received any of these letters. And she sounds as though she's speaking the truth."

"She did certainly. I'm sure she was."

"H'm," said Nash. "Then what I want to know is, why the devil hasn't she?"

He went on rather impatiently, as I stared at him.

"She's a pretty girl, isn't she?"

"Rather more than pretty."

"Exactly. As a matter of fact, she's uncommonly good looking. And she's young. In fact she's just the meat an anonymous letter writer would like. Then why has she been left out?"

I shook my head.

"It's interesting, you know. I must mention it to Graves. He asked if we could tell him definitely of any one who hadn't had one."

"She's the second person," I said. "There's Emily Barton, remember."

Nash gave a faint chuckle.

"You shouldn't believe everything you're told, Mr. Burton. Miss Barton had one all right—more than one."

"How do you know?"

"That devoted dragon she's lodging with told me—her late parlourmaid or cook. Florence Elford. Very indignant she was about it. Would like to have the writer's blood."

"Why did Miss Emily say she hadn't had any?"

"Delicacy. Their language isn't nice. Little Miss Barton has spent her life avoiding the coarse and unrefined."

"What did the letters say?"

"The usual. Quite ludicrous in her case. And incidentally insinuated that she poisoned off her old mother and most of her sisters!"

I said incredulously:

"Do you mean to say there's really this dangerous lunatic going about and we can't spot her right away?"

"We'll spot her," said Nash, and his voice was grim. "She'll write just one letter too many."

"But, my goodness, man, she won't go on writing these things—not now."

He looked at me.

"Oh yes, she will. You see, *she can't stop now*. It's a morbid craving. The letters will go on, make no mistake about that."

Chapter Nine

I WENT AND FOUND Megan before leaving the house. She was in the garden and seemed almost back to her usual self. She greeted me quite cheerfully.

I suggested that she should come back to us again for a while, but after a momentary hesitation she shook her head.

"It's nice of you—but I think I'll stay here. After all, it is—well, I suppose it's my home. And I dare say I can help with the boys a bit."

"Well," I said, "it's as you like."

"Then I think I'll stay. I could—I could——"

"Yes?" I prompted.

"If—if anything awful happened, I could ring you up, couldn't I, and you'd come."

I was touched. "Of course. But what awful thing do you think might happen?"

"Oh, I don't know." She looked vague. "Things seem rather like that just now, don't they?"

"For God's sake," I said. "Don't go nosing out any more bodies! It's not good for you."

She gave me a brief flash of a smile.

"No, it isn't. It made me feel awfully sick."

I didn't much like leaving her there, but after all, as she had said, it was her home. And I fancied that now Elsie Holland would feel more responsible for her.

Nash and I went up together to Little Furze. Whilst I gave Joanna an account of the morning's doings, Nash tackled Partridge. He rejoined us looking discouraged.

"Not much help there. According to this woman, the girl only said she was worried about something and didn't know what to do and that she'd like Miss Partridge's advice."

"Did Partridge mention the fact to any one?" asked Joanna.

Nash nodded, looking grim.

"Yes, she told Mrs. Emory—your daily woman—on the lines, as far as I can gather, that there were *some* young women who were willing to take advice from their elders and didn't think they could settle everything for themselves off-hand! Agnes mightn't be very bright, but she was a nice respectful girl and knew her manners."

"Partridge preening herself, in fact," murmured Joanna. "And Mrs. Emory could have passed it round the town?"

"That's right, Miss Burton."

"There's one thing rather surprises me," I said. "Why were my sister and I included amongst the recipients of the anonymous letters? We were strangers down here—nobody could have had a grudge against us."

"You're failing to allow for the mentality of a Poison Pen—all is grist that comes to their mill. Their grudge, you might say, is against humanity."

"I suppose," said Joanna thoughtfully, "that that is what Mrs. Dane Calthrop meant."

Nash looked at her inquiringly, but she did not enlighten him. The superintendent said:

"I don't know if you happened to look closely at the envelope of the letter you got, Miss Burton. If so, you may have noticed that it was actually addressed to Miss Barton and the *a* altered to a *u* afterwards."

That remark, properly interpreted, ought to have given us a clue to the whole business. As it was, none of us saw any significance in it.

Nash went off, and I was left with Joanna. She actually said: "You don't think that letter can really have been meant for Miss Emily, do you?"

"It would hardly have begun 'You painted trollop'," I pointed out, and Joanna agreed.

Then she suggested that I should go down to the town. "You ought to hear what everyone is saying. It will be *the* topic this morning!"

I suggested that she should come too, but rather to my surprise Joanna refused. She said she was going to mess about in the garden.

I paused in the doorway and said, lowering my voice:

"I suppose Partridge is all right?"

"Partridge!"

The amazement in Joanna's voice made me feel ashamed of my idea. I said apologetically: "I just wondered. She's rather 'queer' in some ways—a grim spinster—the sort of person who might have religious mania."

"This isn't religious mania—or so you told me Graves said."

"Well, sex mania. They're very closely tied up together, I understand. She's repressed and respectable, and has been shut up here with a lot of elderly women for years."

"What put the idea into your head?"

I said slowly:

"Well, we've only her word for it, haven't we, as to what the girl Agnes said to her? Suppose Agnes asked Partridge to tell her why Partridge came and left a note that day—and Partridge said she'd call round that afternoon and explain."

"And then camouflaged it by coming to us and asking if the girl could come here?"

"Yes."

"But Partridge never went out that afternoon."

"We don't know that. We were out ourselves, remember."

"Yes, that's true. It's possible, I suppose." Joanna turned it over in her mind. "But I don't think so, all the same. I don't think Partridge has the mentality to cover her tracks over the letters. To wipe off fingerprints, and all that. It isn't only cunning you want—it's knowledge. I don't think she's got that. I suppose——" Joanna hesitated, then said slowly, "they are sure it is a woman, aren't they?"

"You don't think it's a man?" I exclaimed incredulously.

"Not—not an ordinary man—but a certain kind of man. I'm thinking, really, of Mr. Pye."

"So Pye is your selection?"

"Don't you feel yourself that he's a possibility? He's the sort of person who might be lonely—and unhappy—and spiteful. Everyone, you see, rather laughs at him. Can't you see him secretly hating all the normal happy people, and taking a queer perverse artistic pleasure in what he was doing?"

"Graves said a middle-aged spinster."

"Mr. Pye," said Joanna, "is a middle-aged spinster."

"A misfit," I said slowly.

"Very much so. He's rich, but money doesn't help. And I do feel he might be unbalanced. He is, really, rather a *frightening* little man."

"He got a letter himself, remember."

"We don't know that," Joanna pointed out. "We only thought so. And anyway, he might have been putting on an act."

"For our benefit?"

"Yes. He's clever enough to think of that—and not to overdo it."

"He must be a first-class actor."

"But of course, Jerry, whoever is doing this *must* be a first-class actor. That's partly where the pleasure comes in."

"For God's sake, Joanna, don't speak so understandingly! You make me feel that you—that you understand the mentality."

"I think I do. I can—just—get into the mood. If I weren't Joanna Burton, if I weren't young and reasonably attractive and able to have a good time, if I were—how shall I put it?—behind bars, watching other people enjoy life, would a black evil tide rise in me, making me want to hurt, to torture—even to destroy?"

"Joanna!" I took her by the shoulders and shook her. She gave a little sigh and shiver, and smiled at me.

"I frightened you, didn't I, Jerry? But I have a feeling that that's the right way to solve this problem. You've got to be the person, knowing how they feel and what makes them act, and then—and then perhaps you'll know what they're going to do next."

"Oh, hell!" I said. "And I came down here to be a vegetable and get interested in all the dear little local scandals. Dear little local scandals! Libel, vilification, obscene language and murder!"

II

Joanna was quite right. The High Street was full of interested groups. I was determined to get everyone's reactions in turn.

I met Griffith first. He looked terribly ill and tired. So much so that I wondered. Murder is not, certainly, all in the day's work to a doctor, but his profession does equip him to face most things including suffering, the ugly side of human nature, and the fact of death.

"You look all in," I said.

"Do I?" He was vague. "Oh! I've had some worrying cases lately."

"Including our lunatic at large?"

"That, certainly." He looked away from me across the street. I saw a fine nerve twitching in his eyelid.

"You've no suspicions as to—who?"

"No. No. I wish to God I had."

He asked abruptly after Joanna, and said, hesitatingly, that he had some photographs she'd wanted to see.

I offered to take them to her.

"Oh, it doesn't matter. I shall be passing that way actually later in the morning."

I began to be afraid that Griffith had got it badly. Curse Joanna! Griffith was too good a man to be dangled as a scalp.

I let him go, for I saw his sister coming and I wanted, for once, to talk to her.

Aimée Griffith began, as it were, in the middle of a conversation.

"Absolutely shocking!" she boomed. "I hear you were there—quite early?"

There was a question in the words, and her eyes glinted as she stressed the word "early." I wasn't going to tell her that Megan had rung me up. I said instead:

"You see, I was a bit uneasy last night. The girl was due to tea at our house and didn't turn up."

"And so you feared the worst? Damned smart of you!"

"Yes," I said. "I'm quite the human bloodhound."

"It's the first murder we've ever had in Lymstock. Excitement is terrific. Hope the police can handle it all right."

"I shouldn't worry," I said. "They're an efficient body of men."

"Can't even remember what the girl looked like, although I suppose she's opened the door to me dozens of times. Quiet, insignificant little thing. Knocked on the head and then stabbed through the back of the neck, so Owen tells me. Looks like a boy friend to me. What do you think?"

"That's your solution?"

"Seems the most likely one. Had a quarrel, I expect. They're very inbred round here—bad heredity, a lot of them." She paused, and then went on, "I hear Megan Hunter found the body? Must have given her a bit of a shock."

I said shortly:

"It did."

"Not too good for her, I should imagine. In my opinion she's not too strong in the head—and a thing like this might send her completely off her onion."

I took a sudden resolution. I had to know something.

"Tell me, Miss Griffith, was it you who persuaded Megan to return home yesterday?"

"Well, I wouldn't say exactly persuaded."

I stuck to my guns.

"But you did say something to her?"

Aimée Griffith planted her feet firmly and stared at me in the eyes. She was, just slightly, on the defensive. She said:

"It's no good that young woman shirking her responsibilities. She's young and she doesn't know how tongues wag, so I felt it my duty to give her a hint."

"Tongues——?" I broke off because I was too angry to go on.

Aimée Griffith continued with that maddeningly complacent confidence in herself which was her chief characteristic:

"Oh, I dare say *you* don't hear all the gossip that goes round. I do! I know what people are saying. Mind you, I don't for a minute think there's anything in it—not for a minute! But you know what people are—if they can say something ill-natured, they do! And it's rather hard lines on the girl when she's got her living to earn."

"Her living to earn?" I said, puzzled.

Aimée went on:

"It's a difficult position for her, naturally. And I think she did the right thing. I mean, she couldn't go off at a moment's notice and leave the children with no one to look after them. She's been splendid—absolutely splendid. I say so to everybody! But there it is, it's an invidious position, and people will talk."

"Who are you talking about?" I asked.

"Elsie Holland, of course," said Aimée Griffith impatiently. "In my opinion, she's a thoroughly nice girl, and has only been doing her duty."

"And what are people saying?"

Aimée Griffith laughed. It was, I thought, rather an unpleasant laugh.

"They're saying that she's already considering the possibility of becoming Mrs. Symmington No. 2—that she's all out to console the widower and make herself indispensable."

"But, good God," I said, shocked, "Mrs. Symmington's only been dead a week!"

Aimée Griffith shrugged her shoulders.

"Of course. It's absurd! But you know what people are! The Holland girl is young and she's good looking—that's enough. And mind you, being a nursery governess isn't much of a prospect for a girl. I wouldn't blame her if she wanted a settled home and a husband and was playing her cards accordingly.

"Of course," she went on, "poor Dick Symmington hasn't the least idea of all this! He's still completely knocked out by Mona Symmington's death. But you know what men are! If the girl is always there, making him comfortable, looking after him, being obviously devoted to the children—well, he gets to be dependent on her."

I said quietly:

"So you do think that Elsie Holland is a designing hussy?"

Aimée Griffith flushed.

"Not at all. I'm sorry for the girl—with people saying nasty things! That's why I more or less told Megan that she ought to go home. It looks better than having Dick Symmington and the girl alone in the house."

I began to understand things.

Aimée Griffith gave her jolly laugh.

"You're shocked, Mr. Burton, at hearing what our gossiping little town thinks. I can tell you this—they always think the worst!"

She laughed and nodded and strode away.

III

I came upon Mr. Pye by the church. He was talking to Emily Barton, who looked pink and excited.

Mr. Pye greeted me with every evidence of delight.

"Ah, Burton, good-morning, good-morning! How is your charming sister?"

I told him that Joanna was well.

"But not joining our village parliament? We are all agog over the news. Murder! Real Sunday newspaper murder in our midst! Not the most interesting of crimes, I fear. Somewhat sordid. The brutal murder of a little serving maid. No finer points about the crime, but still undeniably, news."

Miss Barton said tremulously:

"It is shocking—quite shocking."

Mr. Pye turned to her.

"But you enjoy it, dear lady, you enjoy it. Confess it now. You disapprove, you deplore, but there *is* the thrill. I insist, there *is* the thrill!"

"Such a nice girl," said Emily Barton. "She came to me from St. Clotilde's Home. Quite a raw girl. But most teachable. She turned into such a nice little maid. Partridge was very pleased with her."

I said quickly:

"She was coming to tea with Partridge yesterday afternoon." I turned to Pye. "I expect Aimée Griffith told you."

My tone was quite casual. Pye responded apparently quite unsuspiciously: "She did mention it, yes. She said, I remember, that it was something quite new for servants to ring up on their employers' telephones."

"Partridge would never dream of doing such a thing," said Miss Emily, "and I am really surprised at Agnes doing so."

"You are behind the times, dear lady," said Mr. Pye. "My two terrors use the telephone constantly and smoked all over the house until I objected. But one daren't say too much. Prescott is a divine cook, though temperamental, and Mrs. Prescott is an admirable house-parlourmaid."

"Yes, indeed, we all think you're very lucky."

I intervened, since I did not want the conversation to become purely domestic.

"The news of the murder has got round very quickly," I said.

"Of course, of course," said Mr. Pye. "The butcher, the baker, the candlestick maker. Enter Rumour, painted full of tongues! Lymstock, alas! is going to the dogs. Anonymous letters, murders, any amount of criminal tendencies."

Emily Barton said nervously: "They don't think—there's no idea—that—that the two are connected."

Mr. Pye pounced on the idea.

"An interesting speculation. The girl knew something, therefore she was murdered. Yes, yes, most promising. How clever of you to think of it."

"I—I can't bear it."

Emily Barton spoke abruptly and turned away, walking very fast.

Pye looked after her. His cherubic face was pursed up quizzically.

He turned back to me and shook his head gently.

"A sensitive soul. A charming creature, don't you think? Absolutely a period piece. She's not, you know, of her own generation, she's of the generation before that. The mother must have been a woman of a very strong character. She kept the family ticking at about 1870, I should say. The whole family preserved under a glass case. I do like to come across that sort of thing."

I did not want to talk about period pieces.

"What do you really think about all this business?" I asked.

"Meaning by that?"

"Anonymous letters, murder . . ."

"Our local crime wave? What do you?"

"I asked you first," I said pleasantly.

Mr. Pye said gently:

"I'm a student, you know, of abnormalities. They interest me. Such apparently unlikely people do the most fantastic things. Take the case of Lizzie Borden. There's not really a reasonable explanation of that. In this case, my advice to the police would be—study *character*. Leave your fingerprints and your measuring of handwriting and your microscopes. Notice instead what people do with their hands, and their little tricks of manner, and the way they eat their food, and if they laugh sometimes for no apparent reason."

I raised my eyebrows. "Mad?" I said.

"Quite, quite mad," said Mr. Pye, and added, "but you'd never know it!"

"Who?"

His eyes met mine. He smiled.

No, no, Burton, that would be slander. We can't add slander to all the rest of it."

He fairly skipped off down the street.

IV

As I stood staring after him the church door opened and the Rev. Caleb Dane Calthrop came out.

He smiled vaguely at me.

"Good—good-morning, Mr.—er—er——"

I helped him. "Burton."

"Of course, of course, you mustn't think I don't remember you. Your name had just slipped my memory for the moment. A beautiful day."

"Yes," I said rather shortly.

He peered at me.

"But something—something—ah, yes, that poor unfortunate child who was in service at the Symmingtons'. I find it hard to believe, I must confess, that we have a murderer in our midst, Mr.—er—Burton."

"It does seem a bit fantastic," I said.

"Something else has just reached my ears." He leaned towards me. "I learn that there have been anonymous letters going about. Have you heard any rumour of such things?"

"I have heard," I said.

"Cowardly and dastardly things." He paused and quoted an enormous stream of Latin. "Those words of Horace are very applicable, don't you think?" he said.

"Absolutely," I said.

V

There didn't seem any one more I could profitably talk to, so I went home, dropping in for some tobacco and for a bottle of sherry, so as to get some of the humbler opinions on the crime.

"A narsty tramp," seemed to be the verdict.

"Come to the door, they do, and whine and ask for money, and then if it's a girl alone in the house, they turn narsty. My sister Dora, over to Combeacre, she had a narsty experience one day—Drunk, he was, and selling those little printed poems . . ."

The story went on, ending with the intrepid Dora courageously banging the door in the man's face and taking refuge and barricading herself in some vague retreat, which I gathered from the delicacy in mentioning it must be the lavatory. "And there she stayed till her lady came home!"

I reached Little Furze just a few minutes before lunch time. Joanna was standing in the drawing-room window doing nothing at all and looking as though her thoughts were miles away.

"What have you been doing with yourself?" I asked.

"Oh, I don't know. Nothing particular."

I went out on the veranda. Two chairs were drawn up to an iron table and there were two empty sherry glasses. On another chair was an object at which I looked with bewilderment for some time.

"What on earth is this?"

"Oh," said Joanna, "I think it's a photograph of a diseased spleen or something. Dr. Griffith seemed to think I'd be interested to see it."

I looked at the photograph with some interest. Every man has his own ways of courting the female sex. I should not, myself, choose to do it with photographs of spleens, diseased or otherwise. Still no doubt Joanna had asked for it!

"It looks most unpleasant," I said.

Joanna said it did, rather.

"How was Griffith?" I asked.

"He looked tired and very unhappy. I think he's got something on his mind."

"A spleen that won't yield to treatment?"

"Don't be silly. I mean something real."

"I should say the man's got *you* on his mind. I wish you'd lay off him, Joanna."

"Oh, do shut up. I haven't done anything."

"Women always say that."

Joanna whirled angrily out of the room.

The diseased spleen was beginning to curl up in the sun. I took it by one corner and brought it into the drawing-room. I had no affection for it myself, but I presumed it was one of Griffith's treasures.

I stooped down and pulled out a heavy book from the bottom shelf of the bookcase in order to press the photograph flat again between its leaves. It was a ponderous volume of somebody's sermons.

The book came open in my hand in rather a surprising way. In another minute I saw why. *From the middle of it a number of pages had been neatly cut out.*

VI

I stood staring at it. I looked at the title page. It had been published in 1840.

There could be no doubt at all. I was looking at the book from the pages of which the anonymous letters had been put together. Who had cut them out?

Well, to begin with, it could be Emily Barton herself. She was, perhaps, the obvious person to think of. Or it could have been Partridge.

But there were other possibilities. The pages could have been cut out by anyone who had been alone in this room, any visitor, for instance, who had sat there waiting for Miss Emily. Or even anyone who called on business.

No, that wasn't so likely. I had noticed that when, one day, a clerk from the bank had come to see me, Partridge had shown him into the little study at the back of the house. That was clearly the house routine.

A visitor, then? Someone "of good social position." Mr. Pye? Aimée Griffith? Mrs. Dane Calthrop?

VII

The gong sounded and I went in to lunch. Afterwards, in the drawing-room I showed Joanna my find.

We discussed it from every aspect. Then I took it down to the police station.

They were elated at the find, and I was patted on the back for what was, after all, the sheerest piece of luck.

Graves was not there, but Nash was, and rang up the other man. They would test the book for fingerprints, though Nash was not hopeful of finding anything. I may say that he did not. There were mine, Partridge's and nobody else's, merely showing that Partridge dusted conscientiously.

Nash walked back with me up the hill. I asked how he was getting on. "We're narrowing it down, Mr. Burton. We've eliminated the people it couldn't be."

"Ah," I said. "And who remains?"

"Miss Ginch. She was to meet a client at a house yesterday afternoon by appointment. The house was situated not far along the Combeacre Road, that's the road that goes past the Symmingtons'. She would have to pass the house both going and coming . . . the week before, the day the anonymous letter was delivered, and Mrs. Symmington committed suicide, was her last day at Symmington's office. Mr. Symmington thought at first she had not left the office at all that afternoon. He had Sir Henry Lushington with him all the afternoon and rang several times for Miss Ginch. I find, however, that she did leave the office between three and four. She went out to get some high denomination of stamp of which they had run short. The office boy could have gone, but Miss Ginch elected to go, saying she had a headache and would like the air. She was not gone long."

"But long enough?"

"Yes, long enough to hurry along to the other end of the village, slip the letter in the box and hurry back. I must say, however, that I cannot find anybody who saw her near the Symmingtons' house."

"Would they notice?"

"They might and they might not."

"Who else is in your bag?"

Nash looked very straight ahead of him.

"You'll understand that we can't exclude anybody—anybody at all."

"No," I said. "I see that."

He said gravely: "Miss Griffith went to Brenton for a meeting of Girl Guides yesterday. She arrived rather late."

"You don't think——"

"No, I don't think. But I don't *know*. Miss Griffith seems an eminently sane healthy-minded woman—but I say, I don't *know*."

"What about the previous week? Could she have slipped the letter in the box?"

"It's possible. She was shopping in the town that afternoon." He paused. "The same applies to Miss Emily Barton. She was out shopping early yesterday afternoon and she went for a walk to see some friends on the road past the Symmingtons' house the week before."

I shook my head unbelievingly. Finding the cut book in Little Furze was bound, I knew, to direct attention to the owner of that house, but when I remembered Miss Emily coming in yesterday so bright and happy and excited . . .

Damn it all—excited . . . Yes, excited—pink cheeks—shining eyes— surely not because—not because——

I said thickly: "This business is bad for one! One sees things—one imagines things——"

"Yes, it isn't very pleasant to look upon the fellow creatures one meets as possible criminal lunatics."

He paused for a moment, then went on:

"And there's Mr. Pye——"

I said sharply: "So you have considered him?"

Nash smiled.

"Oh, yes, we've considered him all right. A very curious character—not, I should say, a very nice character. He's got no alibi. He was in his garden, alone, on both occasions."

"So you're not only suspecting women?"

"I don't think a man wrote the letters—in fact I'm sure of it—and so is Graves—always excepting our Mr. Pye, that is to say, who's got an abnormally female streak in his character. But we've checked up on *everybody* for yesterday afternoon. That's a murder case, you see. *You're* all right," he grinned, "and so's your sister, and Mr. Symmington didn't leave his office after he got there and Dr. Griffith was on a round in the other direction, and I've checked up on his visits."

He paused, smiled again, and said, "You see, we *are* thorough."

I said slowly, "So your case is eliminated down to those four—Miss Ginch, Mr. Pye, Miss Griffith and little Miss Barton?"

"Oh, no, we've got a couple more—besides the vicar's lady."

"You've thought of *her?*"

"We've thought of *everybody*, but Mrs. Dane Calthrop is a little too openly mad, if you know what I mean. Still, she *could* have done it. She was in a wood watching birds yesterday afternoon—and the birds can't speak for her."

He turned sharply as Owen Griffith came into the police station.

"Hallo, Nash. I heard you were round asking for me this morning. Anything important?"

"Inquest on Friday, if that suits you, Dr. Griffith."

"Right. Moresby and I are doing the P.M. to-night."

Nash said:

"There's just one other thing, Dr. Griffith. Mrs. Symmington was taking some cachets, powders or something, that you prescribed for her——"

He paused. Owen Griffith said interrogatively:

"Yes?"

"Would an overdose of those cachets have been fatal?"

Griffith said dryly:

"Certainly not. Not unless she'd taken about twenty-five of them!"

"But you once warned her about exceeding the dose, so Miss Holland tells me."

"Oh that, yes. Mrs. Symmington was the sort of woman who would go and overdo anything she was given—fancy that to take twice as much would do her twice as much good, and you don't want anyone to overdo even phenacetin or aspirin—bad for the heart. And anyway there's absolutely no doubt about the cause of death. It was cyanide."

"Oh, I know that—you don't get my meaning. I only thought that when committing suicide you'd prefer to take an overdose of a soporific rather than to feed yourself prussic acid."

"Oh quite. On the other hand, prussic acid is more dramatic and is pretty certain to do the trick. With barbiturates, for instance, you can bring the victim round if only a short time has elapsed."

"I see, thank you, Dr. Griffith."

Griffith departed, and I said good-bye to Nash. I went slowly up the hill home. Joanna was out—at least there was no sign of her, and there was an enigmatical memorandum scribbled on the telephone block presumably for the guidance of either Partridge or myself.

If Dr. Griffith rings up, I can't go on Tuesday, but could manage Wednesday or Thursday.

I raised my eyebrows and went into the drawing-room. I sat down in the most comfortable arm-chair—(none of them were very comfortable, they tended to have straight backs and were reminiscent of the late Mrs. Barton)—stretched out my legs and tried to think the whole thing out.

With sudden annoyance I remembered that Owen's arrival had interrupted my conversation with the inspector, and that he had just mentioned two other people as being possibilities.

I wondered who they were.

Partridge, perhaps, for one? After all, the cut book had been found in this house. And Agnes could have been struck down quite unsuspecting by her guide and mentor. No, you couldn't eliminate Partridge.

But who was the other?

Somebody, perhaps, that I didn't know? Mrs. Cleat? The original local suspect?

I closed my eyes. I considered four people, strangely unlikely people, in turn. Gentle, frail little Emily Barton? What points were there actually against her? A starved life? Dominated and repressed from early childhood? Too many sacrifices asked of her? Her curious horror of discussing anything "not quite nice"? Was that actually a sign of inner preoccupation with just these themes? Was I getting too horribly Freudian? I remembered a doctor once telling me that the mutterings of gentle maiden ladies when going off under an anæsthetic were a revelation. "You wouldn't think they knew such words!"

Aimée Griffith?

Surely nothing repressed or "inhibited" about her. Cheery, mannish, successful. A full, busy life. Yet Mrs. Dane Calthrop had said, "Poor thing!"

And there was something—something—some remembrance . . . Ah! I'd got it. Owen Griffith saying something like, "We had an outbreak of anonymous letters up North where I had a practice."

Had that been Aimée Griffith's work too? Surely rather a coincidence. Two outbreaks of the same thing.

Stop a minute, they'd tracked down the author of those. Griffith had said so. A schoolgirl.

Cold it was suddenly—must be a draught, from the window. I turned uncomfortably in my chair. Why did I suddenly feel so queer and upset?

Go on thinking . . . Aimée Griffith? Perhaps it was Aimée Griffith, *not* that other girl? And Aimée had come down here and started her tricks again. And that was why Owen Griffith was looking so unhappy and hag ridden. He suspected. Yes, he suspected . . .

Mr. Pye? Not, somehow, a very nice little man. I could imagine him staging the whole business . . . laughing . . .

That telephone message on the telephone pad in the hall . . . why did I keep thinking of it? Griffith and Joanna—he was falling for her. . . . No, that wasn't why the message worried me. It was something else . . .

My senses were swimming, sleep was very near. I repeated idiotically to myself, "No smoke without fire. No smoke without fire. . . . That's it . . . it all links up together . . ."

And then I was walking down the street with Megan and Elsie Holland passed. She was dressed as a bride, and people were murmuring: "She's going to marry Dr. Griffith at last. Of course they've been engaged secretly for years . . ."

There we were, in the church, and Dane Calthrop was reading the service in Latin.

And in the middle of it Mrs. Dane Calthrop jumped up and cried energetically:

"It's got to be stopped, I tell you. It's got to be stopped!"

For a minute or two I didn't know whether I was asleep or awake. Then my brain cleared, and I realised I was in the drawing-room of Little Furze and that Mrs. Dane Calthrop had just come through the window and was standing in front of me saying with nervous violence:

"It has got to be *stopped*, I tell you."

I jumped up. I said: "I beg your pardon. I'm afraid I was asleep. What did you say?"

Mrs. Dane Calthrop beat one fist fiercely on the palm of her other hand.

"It's got to be stopped. These letters! Murder! You can't go on having poor innocent children like Agnes Woddell *killed!*"

"You're quite right," I said, "but how do you propose to set about it?"

Mrs. Dane Calthrop said:

"We've got to do something!"

I smiled, perhaps in rather a superior fashion.

"And what do you suggest that we should do?"

"Get the whole thing cleared up! I said this wasn't a wicked place. I was wrong. It is."

I felt annoyed. I said, not too politely:

"Yes, my dear woman, but what are you going to *do?*"

Mrs. Dane Calthrop said: "Put a stop to it all, of course."

"The police are doing their best."

"If Agnes could be killed yesterday, their best isn't good enough."

"So you know better than they do?"

"Not at all. *I* don't know anything at all. That's why I'm going to call in an expert."

I shook my head.

"You can't do that. Scotland Yard will only take over on a demand from the chief constable of the county. Actually they *have* sent Graves."

"I don't mean *that* kind of an expert. I don't mean someone who knows about anonymous letters or even about murder. I mean someone who knows *people*. Don't you see? We want someone who knows a great deal about *wickedness!*"

It was a queer point of view. But it was, somehow, stimulating.

Before I could say anything more, Mrs. Dane Calthrop nodded her head at me and said in a quick, confident tone:

"I'm going to see about it right away."

And she went out of the window again.

Chapter Ten

THE NEXT WEEK, I think, was one of the queerest times I have ever passed through. It had an odd dream quality. Nothing seemed real.

The inquest on Agnes Woddell was held and the curious of Lymstock attended *en masse*. No new facts came to light and the only possible verdict was returned, "Murder by person or persons unknown."

So poor little Agnes Woddell, having had her hour of limelight, was duly buried in the quiet old churchyard and life in Lymstock went on as before.

No, that last statement is untrue. Not as before . . .

There was a half-scared, half-avid gleam in almost everybody's eye. Neighbour looked at neighbour. One thing had been brought out clearly at the inquest—it was most unlikely that any stranger had killed Agnes Woddell. No tramps nor unknown men had been noticed or reported in the district. Somewhere, then, in Lymstock, walking down the High Street, shopping, passing the time of day, was a person who had cracked a defenceless girl's skull and driven a sharp skewer home to her brain.

And no one knew who that person was.

As I say, the days went by in a kind of dream. I looked at everyone I met in a new light, the light of a possible murderer. It was not an agreeable sensation!

And in the evenings, with the curtain drawn, Joanna and I sat talking, talking, arguing, going over in turn all the various possibilities that still seemed so fantastic and incredible.

Joanna held firm to her theory of Mr. Pye. I, after wavering a little, had gone back to my original suspect, Miss Ginch. But we went over the possible names again and again.

Mr. Pye?

Miss Ginch?

Mrs. Dane Calthrop?

Aimée Griffith?

Emily Barton?

Partridge?

And all the time, nervously, apprehensively, we waited for something to happen.

But nothing did happen. Nobody, so far as we knew, received any more letters. Nash made periodic appearances in the town but what he was doing and what traps the police were setting, I had no idea. Graves had gone again.

Emily Barton came to tea. Megan came to lunch. Owen Griffith went about his practice. We went and drank sherry with Mr. Pye. And we went to tea at the vicarage.

I was glad to find Mrs. Dane Calthrop displayed none of the militant ferocity she had shown on the occasion of our last meeting. I think she had forgotten all about it.

She seemed principally concerned with the destruction of white butterflies so as to preserve cauliflower and cabbage plants.

Our afternoon at the vicarage was really one of the most peaceful we had spent. It was an attractive old house and had a big shabby comfortable drawing-room with faded rose cretonne. The Dane Calthrops had a guest staying with them, an amiable elderly lady who was knitting something with white fleecy wool. We had very good hot scones for tea, the vicar came in, and beamed placidly on us whilst he pursued his gentle erudite conversation. It was very pleasant.

I don't mean that we got away from the topic of the murder, because we didn't.

Miss Marple, the guest, was naturally thrilled by the subject. As she said apologetically: "We have so little to talk about in the country!" She had made up her mind that the dead girl must have been just like her Edith.

"Such a nice little maid, and so willing, but sometimes just a *little* slow to take in things."

Miss Marple also had a cousin whose niece's sister-in-law had a great deal of annoyance and trouble over some anonymous letters, so the letters, also, were very interesting to the charming old lady.

"But tell me, dear," she said to Mrs. Dane Calthrop, "what do the village people—I mean the townspeople—say? What do *they* think?"

"Mrs. Cleat still, I suppose," said Joanna.

"Oh no," said Mrs. Dane Calthrop. "Not *now*."

Miss Marple asked who Mrs. Cleat was.

Joanna said she was the village witch.

"That's right, isn't it, Mrs. Dane Calthrop?"

The vicar murmured a long Latin quotation about, I think, the evil power of witches, to which we all listened in respectful and uncomprehending silence.

"She's a very silly woman," said his wife. "Likes to show off. Goes out to gather herbs and things at the full of the moon and takes care that everybody in the place knows about it."

"And silly girls go and consult her, I suppose?" said Miss Marple.

I saw the vicar getting ready to unload more Latin on us and I asked hastily: "But why shouldn't people suspect her of the murder now? They thought the letters were her doing."

Miss Marple said: "Oh! But the girl was killed with a *skewer*, so I hear —(very unpleasant!). Well, naturally, that takes *all* suspicion away from this Mrs. Cleat. Because, you see, she could ill-wish her, so that the girl would waste away and die from natural causes."

"Strange how those old beliefs linger," said the vicar. "In early Christian times, local superstitions were wisely incorporated with Christian doctrines and their more unpleasant attributes gradually eliminated."

"It isn't superstition we've got to deal with here," said Mrs. Dane Calthrop, "but *facts*."

"And very unpleasant facts," I said.

"As you say, Mr. Burton," said Miss Marple. "Now *you*—excuse me if I am being too personal—are a stranger here, and have a knowledge of the world and of various aspects of life. It seems to me that you ought to be able to find a solution to this distasteful problem."

I smiled. "The best solution I have had was a dream. In my dream it all fitted in and panned out beautifully. Unfortunately when I woke up the whole thing was nonsense!"

"How interesting, though. Do tell me how the nonsense went?"

"Oh, it all started with the silly phrase, 'No smoke without fire.' People have been saying that *ad nauseam*. And then I got it mixed up with war terms. Smoke screen, scrap of paper, telephone messages—No, that was another dream."

"And what was that dream?"

The old lady was so eager about it, that I felt sure she was a secret reader of Napoleon's Book of Dreams, which had been the great stand-by of my old nurse.

"Oh! only Elsie Holland—the Symmingtons' nursery governess, you know, was getting married to Dr. Griffith and the vicar here was reading the service in Latin— ('Very appropriate, dear,' murmured Mrs. Dane Calthrop to her spouse) and then Mrs. Dane Calthrop got up and forbade the banns and said it had got to be stopped!"

"But that part," I added with a smile, "was true. I woke up and found you standing over me saying it."

"And I was quite right," said Mrs. Dane Calthrop—but quite mildly, I was glad to note.

"But where did a telephone message come in?" asked Miss Marple, crinkling her brows.

"I'm afraid I'm being rather stupid. That wasn't in the dream. It was just before it. I came through the hall and noticed Joanna had written down a message to be given to someone if they rang up. . . ."

Miss Marple leaned forward. There was a pink spot in each cheek. "Will you think me *very* inquisitive and *very* rude if I ask just what that message was?" She cast a glance at Joanna. "I *do* apologise, my dear."

Joanna, however, was highly entertained.

"Oh, I don't mind," she assured the old lady. "I can't remember anything about it myself, but perhaps Jerry can. It must have been something quite trivial."

Solemnly I repeated the message as best I could remember it, enormously tickled at the old lady's rapt attention.

I was afraid the actual words were going to disappoint her, but perhaps she had some sentimental idea of a romance, for she nodded her head and smiled and seemed pleased.

"I see," she said. "I thought it might be something like that."

Mrs. Dane Calthrop said sharply: "Like what, Jane?"

"Something quite ordinary," said Miss Marple.

She looked at me thoughtfully for a moment or two, then she said unexpectedly:

"I can see you are a very clever young man—but not quite enough confidence in yourself. You ought to have!"

Joanna gave a loud hoot.

"For goodness' sake don't encourage him to feel like that. He thinks quite enough of himself as it is."

"Be quiet, Joanna," I said. "Miss Marple understands me."

Miss Marple had resumed her fleecy knitting. "You know," she observed pensively. "To commit a successful murder must be very much like bringing off a conjuring trick."

"The quickness of the hand deceives the eye?"

"Not only that. You've got to make people look at the wrong thing and in the wrong place—Misdirection, they call it, I believe."

"Well," I remarked. "So far everybody seems to have looked in the wrong place for our lunatic at large."

"I should be inclined, myself," said Miss Marple, "to look for somebody very sane."

"Yes," I said thoughtfully. "That's what Nash said. I remember he stressed respectability too."

"Yes," agreed Miss Marple. "That's *very* important."

Well, we all seemed agreed.

I addressed Mrs. Calthrop. "Nash thinks," I said, "that there will be more anonymous letters. What do you think?"

She said slowly: "There may be, I suppose."

"If the police think that, there will have to be, no doubt," said Miss Marple.

I went on doggedly to Mrs. Dane Calthrop.

"Are you still sorry for the writer?"

She flushed. "Why not?"

"I don't think I agree with you, dear," said Miss Marple. "Not in this case."

I said hotly: "They've driven one woman to suicide, and caused untold misery and heartburnings!"

"Have you had one, Miss Burton?" asked Miss Marple of Joanna.

Joanna gurgled, "Oh yes! It said the most frightful things."

"I'm afraid," said Miss Marple, "that the people who are young and pretty are apt to be singled out by the writer."

"That's why I certainly think it's odd that Elsie Holland hasn't had any," I said.

"Let me see," said Miss Marple. "Is that the Symmingtons' nursery governess—the one you dreamt about, Mr. Burton?"

"Yes."

"She's probably had one and won't say so," said Joanna.

"No," I said, "I believe her. So does Nash."

"Dear me," said Miss Marple. "Now that's *very* interesting. That's the most interesting thing I've heard yet."

II

As we were going home Joanna told me that I ought not to have repeated what Nash said about letters coming.

"Why not?"

"Because Mrs. Dane Calthrop might be It."

"You don't really believe that!"

"I'm not sure. She's a queer woman."

We began our discussion of probables all over again.

It was two nights later that I was coming back in the car from Exhampton. I had had dinner there and then started back and it was already dark before I got into Lymstock.

Something was wrong with the car lights, and after slowing up and switching them on and off, I finally got out to see what I could do. I was some time fiddling, but I managed to fix them up finally.

The road was quite deserted. Nobody in Lymstock is about after dark. The first few houses were just ahead, amongst them the ugly gabled building of the Women's Institute. It loomed up in the dim starlight and something impelled me to go and have a look at it. I don't know whether I had caught a faint glimpse of a stealthy figure flitting through the gate—if so, it must have been so indeterminate that it did not register in my conscious mind, but I did suddenly feel a kind of overweening curiosity about the place.

The gate was slightly ajar, and I pushed it open and walked in. A short path and four steps led up to the door.

I stood there a moment hesitating. What was I really doing there? I didn't know, and then, suddenly, just near at hand, I caught the sound of a rustle. It sounded like a woman's dress. I took a sharp turn and went round the corner of the building towards where the sound had come from.

I couldn't see anybody. I went on and again turned a corner. I was at the back of the house now and suddenly I saw, only two feet away from me, an open window.

I crept up to it and listened. I could hear nothing, but somehow or other I felt convinced that there was someone inside.

My back wasn't too good for acrobatics as yet, but I managed to hoist myself up and drop over the sill inside. I made rather a noise unfortunately.

I stood just inside the window listening. Then I walked forward, my hands outstretched. I heard then the faintest sound ahead of me to my right.

I had a torch in my pocket and I switched it on.

Immediately a low, sharp voice said: "Put that out."

I obeyed instantly, for in that brief second I had recognized Superintendent Nash.

I felt him take my arm and propel me through a door and into a passage. Here, where there was no window to betray our presence to anyone outside, he switched on a lamp and looked at me more in sorrow than in anger.

"You *would* have to butt in just that minute, Mr. Burton."

"Sorry," I apologised. "But I got a hunch that I was on to something."

"And so you were probably. Did you see anyone?"

I hesitated. "I'm not sure," I said slowly. "I've got a vague feeling I saw someone sneak in through the front gate but I didn't really *see* anyone. Then I heard a rustle round the side of the house."

Nash nodded.

"That's right. Somebody came round the house before you. They hesitated by the window, then went on quickly—heard *you*, I expect."

I apologised again. "What's the big idea?" I asked.

Nash said:

"I'm banking on the fact that an anonymous letter writer can't stop writing letters. She may know it's dangerous, but she'll have to do it. It's like a craving for drink or drugs."

I nodded.

"Now you see, Mr. Burton, I fancy whoever it is will want to keep the letters looking the same as much as possible. She's got the cut-out pages of that book, and can go on using letters and words cut out of them. But the envelopes present a difficulty. She'll want to type them on the same machine. She can't risk using another typewriter or her own handwriting."

"Do you really think she'll go on with the game?" I asked incredulously.

"Yes, I do. And I'll bet you anything you like she's full of confidence.

They're always vain as hell, these people! Well, then, I figured out that whoever it was would come to the Institute after dark so as to get at the typewriter."

"Miss Ginch," I said.

"Maybe."

"You don't know yet?"

"I don't *know.*"

"But you suspect?"

"Yes. But somebody's very cunning, Mr. Burton. Somebody knows all the tricks of the game."

I could imagine some of the network that Nash had spread abroad. I had no doubt that every letter written by a suspect and posted or left by hand was immediately inspected. Sooner or later the criminal would slip up, would grow careless.

For the third time I apologised for my zealous and unwanted presence.

"Oh well," said Nash philosophically. "It can't be helped. Better luck next time."

I went out into the night. A dim figure was standing beside my car. To my astonishment I recognised Megan.

"Hallo!" she said. "I thought this was your car. What have you been doing?"

"What are you doing is much more to the point?" I said.

"I'm out for a walk. I like walking at night. Nobody stops you and says silly things, and I like the stars, and things smell better, and everyday things look all mysterious."

"All of that I grant you freely," I said. "But only cats and witches walk in the dark. They'll wonder about you at home."

"No, they won't. They never wonder where I am or what *I'm* doing."

"How are you getting on?" I asked.

"All right, I suppose."

"Miss Holland look after you and all that?"

"Elsie's all right. She can't help being a perfect fool."

"Unkind—but probably true," I said. "Hop in and I'll drive you home."

It was not quite true that Megan was never missed.

Symmington was standing on the doorstep as we drove up.

He peered towards us. "Hallo, is Megan there?"

"Yes," I said. "I've brought her home."

Symmington said sharply:

"You mustn't go off like this without telling us, Megan. Miss Holland has been quite worried about you."

Megan muttered something and went past him into the house. Symmington sighed.

"A grown-up girl is a great responsibility with no mother to look after her. She's too old for school, I suppose."

He looked towards me rather suspiciously.

"I suppose you took her for a drive?"

I thought it best to leave it like that.

Chapter Eleven

ON THE FOLLOWING DAY I went mad. Looking back on it, that is really the only explanation I can find.

I was due for my monthly visit to Marcus Kent. . . . I went up by train. To my intense surprise Joanna elected to stay behind. As a rule she was eager to come and we usually stayed up for a couple of days.

This time, however, I proposed to return the same day by the evening train, but even so I was astonished at Joanna. She merely said enigmatically that she'd got plenty to do, and why spend hours in a nasty stuffy train when it was a lovely day in the country?

That, of course, was undeniable, but sounded very unlike Joanna.

She said she didn't want the car, so I was to drive it to the station and leave it parked there against my return.

The station of Lymstock is situated, for some obscure reason known to railway companies only, quite half a mile from Lymstock itself. Half-way along the road I overtook Megan shuffling along in an aimless manner. I pulled up.

"Hallo, what are you doing?"

"Just out for a walk."

"But not what is called a good brisk walk, I gather. You were crawling along like a dispirited crab."

"Well, I wasn't going anywhere particular."

"Then you'd better come and see me off at the station." I opened the door of the car and Megan jumped in.

"Where are you going?" she asked.

"London. To see my doctor."

"Your back's not worse, is it?"

"No, it's practically all right again. I'm expecting him to be very pleased about it."

Megan nodded.

We drew up at the station. I parked the car and went in and bought my ticket at the booking office. There were very few people on the platform and nobody I knew.

"You wouldn't like to lend me a penny, would you?" said Megan. "Then I'd get a bit of chocolate out of the slot machine."

"Here you are, baby," I said, handing her the coin in question. "Sure you wouldn't like some clear gums or some throat pastilles as well?"

"I like chocolate best," said Megan without suspecting sarcasm.

She went off to the chocolate machine, and I looked after her with a feeling of mounting irritation.

She was wearing trodden over shoes, and coarse unattractive stockings and a particularly shapeless jumper and skirt. I don't know why all this should have infuriated me, but it did.

I said angrily as she came back:

"Why do you wear those disgusting stockings?"

Megan looked down at them, surprised.

"What's the matter with them?"

"Everything's the matter with them. They're loathsome. And why wear a pullover like a decayed cabbage?"

"It's all right, isn't it? I've had it for years."

"So I should imagine. And why do you——"

At this minute the train came in and interrupted my angry lecture.

I got into an empty first-class carriage, let down the window and leaned out to continue the conversation.

Megan stood below me, her face upturned. She asked me why I was so cross.

"I'm not cross," I said untruly. "It just infuriates me to see you so slack, and not caring how you look."

"I couldn't look nice, anyway, so what does it matter?"

"My God," I said. "I'd like to see you turned out properly. I'd like to take you to London and outfit you from tip to toe."

"I wish you could," said Megan.

The train began to move. I looked down into Megan's upturned, wistful face.

And then, as I have said, madness came upon me.

I opened the door, grabbed Megan with one arm and fairly hauled her into the carriage.

There was an outraged shout from a porter, but all he could do was dexterously to bang shut the door again. I pulled Megan up from the floor where my impetuous action had landed her.

"What on earth did you do that for?" she demanded, rubbing one knee.

"Shut up," I said. "You're coming to London with me and when I've done with you you won't know yourself. I'll show you what you can look like if you try. I'm tired of seeing you mouch about down at heel and all anyhow."

"Oh!" said Megan in an ecstatic whisper.

The ticket collector came along and I bought Megan a return ticket. She sat in her corner looking at me in a kind of awed respect.

"I say," she said when the man had gone. "You are sudden, aren't you?"

"Very," I said. "It runs in our family."

How explain to Megan the impulse that had come over me? She had looked like a wistful dog being left behind. She now had on her face the incredulous pleasure of the dog who has been taken on the walk after all.

"I suppose you don't know London very well?" I said to Megan.

"Yes, I do," said Megan. "I always went through it to school. And I've been to the dentist there and to a pantomime."

"This," I said darkly, "will be a different London."

We arrived with half an hour to spare before my appointment in Harley Street.

I took a taxi and we drove straight to Mirotin, Joanna's dressmaker. Mirotin is, in the flesh, an unconventional and breezy woman of forty-five, Mary Grey. She is a clever woman and very good company. I have always liked her.

I said to Megan, "You're my cousin."

"Why?"

"Don't argue," I said.

Mary Grey was being firm with a stout Jewess who was enamoured of a skin-tight powder-blue evening dress. I detached her and took her aside.

"Listen," I said. "I've brought a little cousin of mine along. Joanna was coming up but was prevented. But she said I could leave it all to you. You see what the girl looks like now?"

"My God, I do," said Mary Grey with feeling.

"Well, I want her turned out right in every particular from head to foot. *Carte blanche.* Stockings, shoes, undies, everything! By the way, the man who does Joanna's hair is close round here, isn't he?"

"Antoine? Round the corner. I'll see to that too."

"You're a woman in a thousand."

"Oh, I shall enjoy it—apart from the money—and that's not to be sneezed at in these days—half my damned brutes of women never pay their bills. But as I say, I shall enjoy it." She shot a quick professional glance at Megan standing a little way away. "She's got a lovely figure."

"You must have X-ray eyes," I said. "She looks completely shapeless to me."

Mary Grey laughed.

"It's these schools," she said. "They seem to take a pride in turning out girls who preen themselves on looking like nothing on earth. They call it being sweet and unsophisticated. Sometimes it takes a whole season before a girl can pull herself together and look human. Don't worry, leave it all to me."

"Right," I said. "I'll come back and fetch her about six."

II

Marcus Kent was pleased with me. He told me that I surpassed his wildest expectations.

"You must have the constitution of an elephant," he said, "to make a come-back like this. Oh well, wonderful what country air and no late hours or excitements will do for a man if he can only stick it."

"I grant you your first two," I said. "But don't think that the country is free from excitements. We've had a good deal in my part."

"What sort of excitement?"

"Murder," I said.

Marcus Kent pursed up his mouth and whistled.

"Some bucolic love tragedy? Farm lad kills his lass?"

"Not at all. A crafty, determined lunatic killer."

"I haven't read anything about it. When did they lay him by the heels?"

"They haven't, and it's a she!"

"Whew! I'm not sure that Lymstock's quite the right place for you, old boy."

I said firmly:

"Yes, it is. And you're not going to get me out of it."

Marcus Kent has a low mind. He said at once:

"So that's it! Found a blonde?"

"Not at all," I said, with a guilty thought of Elsie Holland. "It's merely that the psychology of crime interests me a good deal."

"Oh, all right. It certainly hasn't done you any harm so far, but just make sure that your lunatic killer doesn't obliterate *you*."

"No fear of that," I said.

"What about dining with me this evening? You can tell me all about your revolting murder."

"Sorry. I'm booked."

"Date with a lady—eh? Yes, you're definitely on the mend."

"I suppose you could call it that," I said, rather tickled at the idea of Megan in the role.

I was at Mirotin's at six o'clock when the establishment was officially closing. Mary Grey came to meet me at the top of the stairs outside the showroom. She had a finger to her lips.

"You're going to have a shock! If I say it myself, I've put in a good bit of work."

I went into the big showroom. Megan was standing looking at herself in a long mirror. I give you my word I hardly recognised her! For a minute it took my breath away. Tall and slim as a willow with delicate ankles and feet shown off by sheer silk stockings and well-cut shoes. Yes, lovely feet and hands, small bones—quality and distinction in every line of her. Her hair had been trimmed and shaped to her head and it was glowing like a glossy chestnut. They'd had the sense to leave her face alone. She was not made up, or if she was it was so light and delicate that it did not show. Her mouth needed no lipstick.

Moreover there was about her something that I had never seen before, a new innocent pride in the arch of her neck. She looked at me gravely with a small shy smile.

"I do look—rather nice, don't I?" said Megan.

"Nice?" I said. "Nice isn't the word! Come on out to dinner and if every second man doesn't turn round to look at you I'll be surprised. You'll knock all the other girls into a cocked hat."

Megan was not beautiful, but she was unusual and striking looking. She had personality. She walked into the restaurant ahead of me and, as the head waiter hurried towards us, I felt the thrill of idiotic pride that a man feels when he has got something out of the ordinary with him.

We had cocktails first and lingered over them. Then we dined. And later we danced. Megan was keen to dance and I didn't want to disappoint her, but for some reason or other I hadn't thought she would dance well. But she did. She was light as a feather in my arms, and her body and feet followed the rhythm perfectly.

"Gosh!" I said. "You can dance!"

She seemed a little surprised. "Well, of course I can. We had dancing class every week at school."

"It takes more than dancing class to make a dancer," I said.

We went back to our table.

"Isn't this food lovely?" said Megan. "And everything!"

She heaved a delighted sigh.

"Exactly my sentiments," I said.

It was a delirious evening. I was still mad. Megan brought me down to earth when she said doubtfully:

"Oughtn't we to be going home?"

My jaw dropped. Yes, definitely I was mad. I had forgotten everything! I was in a world divorced from reality, existing in it with the creature I had created.

"Good Lord!" I said.

I realised that the last train had gone.

"Stay there," I said. "I'm going to telephone."

I rang up the Llewellyn Hire people and ordered their biggest and fastest car to come round as soon as possible.

I came back to Megan. "The last train has gone," I said. "So we're going home by car."

"Are we? What fun!"

What a nice child she was, I thought. So pleased with everything, so unquestioning, accepting all my suggestions without fuss or bother.

The car came, and it was large and fast, but all the same it was very late when we came into Lymstock.

Suddenly conscious-stricken, I said, "They'll have been sending out search parties for you!"

But Megan seemed in an equable mood. She said vaguely:

"Oh, I don't think so. I often go out and don't come home for lunch."

"Yes, my dear child, but you've been out for tea and dinner too."

However, Megan's lucky star was in the ascendant. The house was dark and silent. On Megan's advice, we went round to the back and threw stones at Rose's window.

In due course Rose looked out and with many suppressed exclamations and palpitations came down to let us in.

"Well now, and I saying you were asleep in your bed. The master and Miss Holland"—(slight sniff after Miss Holland's name)—"had early supper and went for a drive. I said I'd keep an eye to the boys. I thought I heard you come in when I was up in the nursery trying to quiet Colin, who was playing up, but you weren't about when I came down so I thought you'd gone up to bed. And that's what I said when the master came in and asked for you."

I cut short the conversation by remarking that that was where Megan had better go now.

"Good night," said Megan, "and thank you *awfully*. It's been the loveliest day I've ever had."

I drove home slightly light-headed still, and tipped the chauffeur handsomely, offering him a bed if he liked. But he preferred to drive back through the night.

The hall door had opened during our colloquy and as he drove away it was flung wide and Joanna said:

"So it's you at last, is it?"

"Were you worried about me?" I asked, coming in and shutting the door.

Joanna went into the drawing-room and I followed her. There was a coffee pot on the trivet and Joanna made herself coffee whilst I helped myself to a whisky and soda.

"Worried about you? No, of course not. I thought you'd decided to stay in town and have a binge."

"I've had a binge—of a kind."

I grinned and then began to laugh.

Joanna asked what I was laughing at and I told her.

"But Jerry, you must have been mad—quite mad!"

"I suppose I was."

"But, my dear boy, you can't do things like that—not in a place like this. It will be all round Lymstock to-morrow."

"I suppose it will. But, after all, Megan's only a child."

"She isn't. She's twenty. You can't take a girl of twenty to London and buy her clothes without a most frightful scandal. Good gracious, Jerry, you'll probably have to marry the girl."

Joanna was half-serious, half-laughing.

It was at that moment that I made a very important discovery. "Damn it all," I said. "I don't mind if I do. In fact—I should like it."

A very funny expression came over Joanna's face. She got up and said dryly, as she went towards the door:

"Yes, I've known that for some time. . . ."

She left me standing, glass in hand, aghast at my new discovery.

Chapter Twelve

I DON'T KNOW what the usual reactions are of a man who goes to propose marriage.

In fiction his throat is dry and his collar feels too tight and he is in a pitiable state of nervousness.

I didn't feel at all like that. Having thought of a good idea I just wanted to get it all settled as soon as possible. I didn't see any particular need for embarrassment.

I went along to the Symmingtons' house about eleven o'clock. I rang the bell and when Rose came, I asked for Miss Megan. It was the knowing look that Rose gave me that first made me feel slightly shy.

She put me in the little morning-room and whilst waiting there I hoped uneasily that they hadn't been upsetting Megan.

When the door opened and I wheeled round, I was instantly relieved. Megan was not looking shy or upset at all. Her head was still like a glossy chestnut, and she wore that air of pride and self-respect that she had acquired yesterday. She was in her old clothes again but she had managed to make them look different. It's wonderful what knowledge of her own attractiveness will do for a girl. Megan, I realised suddenly, had grown up.

I suppose I must really have been rather nervous, otherwise I should not have opened the conversation by saying affectionately, "Hallo, catfish!" It was hardly, in the circumstances, a lover-like greeting.

It seemed to suit Megan. She grinned and said, "Hallo!"

"Look here," I said. "You didn't get into a row about yesterday, I hope?"

Megan said with assurance, "Oh *no*," and then blinked, and said vaguely, "Yes, I believe I did. I mean, they said a lot of things and seemed to think it had been very odd—but then you know what people are and what fusses they make all about nothing."

I was relieved to find that shocked disapproval had slipped off Megan like water off a duck's back.

"I came round this morning," I said, "because I've a suggestion to make. You see I like you a lot, and I think you like me——"

"Frightfully," said Megan with rather disquieting enthusiasm.

"And we get on awfully well together, so I think it would be a good idea if we got married."

"Oh," said Megan.

She looked surprised. Just that. Not startled. Not shocked. Just mildly surprised.

"You mean you really want to marry me?" she asked with the air of one getting a thing perfectly clear.

"More than anything in the world," I said—and I meant it.

"You mean, you're in love with me?"

"I'm in love with you."

Her eyes were steady and grave. She said:

"I think you're the nicest person in the world—but I'm not in love with you."

"I'll make you love me."

"That wouldn't do. I don't want to be *made*."

She paused and then said gravely: "I'm not the sort of wife for you. I'm better at hating than at loving."

She said it with a queer intensity.

I said, "Hate doesn't last. Love does."

"Is that true?"

"It's what I believe."

Again there was a silence. Then I said:

"So it's 'No,' is it?"

"Yes, it's no."

"And you don't encourage me to hope?"

"What would be the good of that?"

"None whatever," I agreed. "Quite redundant, in fact—because I'm going to hope whether you tell me to or not."

II

Well, that was that. I walked away from the house feeling slightly dazed but irritatingly conscious of Rose's passionately interested gaze following me.

Rose had had a good deal to say before I could escape.

That she'd never felt the same since that awful day! That she wouldn't have stayed except for the children and being sorry for poor Mr. Symmington. That she wasn't going to stay unless they got another maid quick —and they wouldn't be likely to do that when there had been a murder in the house! That it was all very well for that Miss Holland to say she'd do the housework in the meantime. Very sweet and obliging she was—Oh yes, but it was mistress of the house that she was fancying herself going to be one fine day! Mr. Symmington, poor man, never saw anything—but one knew what a widower was, a poor helpless creature made to be the prey of a designing woman. And that it wouldn't be for want of trying if Miss Holland didn't step into the dead mistress's shoes!

I assented mechanically to everything, yearning to get away and unable to do so because Rose was holding firmly on to my hat whilst she indulged in her flood of spite.

I wondered if there was any truth in what she said. Had Elsie Holland envisaged the possibility of becoming the second Mrs. Symmington? Or was she just a decent kind-hearted girl doing her best to look after a bereaved household?

The result would quite likely be the same in either case. And why not? Symmington's young children needed a mother—Elsie was a decent soul— beside being quite indecently beautiful—a point which a man might appreciate—even such a stuffed fish as Symmington!

I thought all this, I know, because I was trying to put off thinking about Megan.

You may say that I had gone to ask Megan to marry me in an absurdly complacent frame of mind and that I deserved what I got—but it was not really like that. It was because I felt so assured, so certain, that Megan belonged to me—that she was my business, that to look after her and make her happy and keep her from harm was the only natural right way of life for me, that I had expected her to feel, too, that she and I belonged to each other.

But I was not giving up. Oh no! Megan was my woman and I was going to have her.

After a moment's thought, I went to Symmington's office. Megan might pay no attention to strictures on her conduct, but I would like to get things straight.

Mr. Symmington was disengaged, I was told, and I was shown into his room. By a pinching of the lips, and an additional stiffness of manner, I gathered that I was not exactly popular at the moment.

"Good morning," I said. "I'm afraid this isn't a professional call, but a personal one. I'll put it plainly. I dare say you'll have realised that I'm in love with Megan. I've asked her to marry me and she has refused. But I'm not taking that as final."

I saw Symmington's expression change, and I read his mind with ludicrous ease. Megan was a disharmonious element in his house. He was, I felt sure, a just and kindly man, and he would never have dreamed of not providing a home for his dead wife's daughter. But her marriage to me would certainly be a relief. The frozen halibut thawed. He gave me a pale cautious smile.

"Frankly, you know, Burton, I had no idea of such a thing. I know you've taken a lot of notice of her, but we've always regarded her as such a child."

"She's not a child," I said shortly.

"No, no, not in years."

"She can be her age any time she's allowed to be," I said, still slightly angry. "She's not twenty-one, I know, but she will be in a month or two. I'll let you have all the information about myself you want. I'm well off and have led quite a decent life. I'll look after her and do all I can to make her happy."

"Quite—quite. Still, it's up to Megan herself."

"She'll come round in time," I said. "But I just thought I'd like to get straight with you about it."

He said he appreciated that, and we parted amicably.

III

I ran into Miss Emily Barton outside. She had a shopping basket on her arm.

"Good morning, Mr. Burton, I hear you went to London yesterday."

Yes, she had heard all right. Her eyes were, I thought, kindly, but full of curiosity, too.

"I went to see my doctor," I said.

Miss Emily smiled.

That smile made little of Marcus Kent. She murmured:

"I hear Megan nearly missed the train. She jumped in when it was going."

"Helped by me," I said. "I hauled her in."

"How lucky you were there. Otherwise there might have been an accident."

It is extraordinary how much of a fool one gentle inquisitive old maiden lady can make a man feel!

I was saved further suffering by the onslaught of Mrs. Dane Calthrop. She had her own tame elderly maiden lady in tow, but she herself was full of direct speech.

"Good morning," she said. "I hear you've made Megan buy herself some decent clothes? Very sensible of you. It takes a man to think of something really practical like that. I've been so worried about that girl for a long time. Girls with brains are so liable to turn into morons, aren't they?"

With which remarkable statement, she shot into the fish shop.

Miss Marple, left standing by me, twinkled a little and said:

"Mrs. Dane Calthrop is a very remarkable woman, you know. She's nearly always right."

"It makes her rather alarming," I said.

"Sincerity has that effect," said Miss Marple.

Mrs. Dane Calthrop shot out of the fish shop again and rejoined us. She was holding a large red lobster.

"Have you ever seen anything so unlike Mr. Pye?" she said—"very virile and handsome, isn't it?"

IV

I was a little nervous of meeting Joanna but I found when I got home that I needn't have worried. She was out and she did not return for lunch. This aggrieved Partridge a good deal, who said sourly as she proffered two loin chops in an entrée dish: "Miss Burton said specially as she was going to be *in.*"

I ate both chops in an attempt to atone for Joanna's lapse. All the same, I wondered where my sister was. She had taken to be very mysterious about her doings of late.

It was half-past three when Joanna burst into the drawing-room. I had heard a car stop outside and I half expected to see Griffith, but the car drove on and Joanna came in alone.

Her face was very red and she seemed upset. I perceived that something had happened.

"What's the matter?" I asked.

Joanna opened her mouth, closed it again, sighed, plumped herself down in a chair and stared in front of her.

She said:

"I've had the most awful day."

"What's happened?"

"I've done the most incredible things. It was awful——"

"But what——"

"I just started out for a walk, an ordinary walk—I went up over the hill and on to the moor. I walked miles—I felt like it. Then I dropped down into a hollow. There's a farm there—a God-forsaken lonely sort of spot. I was thirsty and I wondered if they'd got any milk or something. So I wandered into the farmyard and then the door opened and Owen came out."

"Yes?"

"He thought it might be the district nurse. There was a woman in there having a baby. He was expecting the nurse and he'd sent word to her to get hold of another doctor. It—things were going wrong."

"Yes?"

"So he said—to *me,* 'Come on, you'll do—better than nobody.' I said I couldn't, and he said what did I mean? I said I'd never done anything like that, that I didn't know anything——

"He said what the hell did that matter? And then he was *awful*. He turned on me. He said, 'You're a woman, aren't you? I suppose you can do your durnedest to help another woman?' And he went on at me—said I'd talked as though I was interested in doctoring and had said I wished I was a nurse. 'All pretty talk, I suppose! You didn't mean anything real by it, but this *is* real and you're going to behave like a decent human being and not like a useless ornamental nit-wit!'

"I've done the most incredible things, Jerry. Held instruments and boiled them and handed things. I'm so tired I can hardly stand up. It was dreadful. But he saved her—and the baby. It was born alive. He didn't think at one time he could save it. Oh dear!"

Joanna covered her face with her hands.

I contemplated her with a certain amount of pleasure and mentally took my hat off to Owen Griffith. He'd brought Joanna slap up against reality for once.

I said, "There's a letter for you in the hall. From Paul, I think."

"Eh?" She paused for a minute and then said, "I'd no idea, Jerry, what doctors had to *do*. The nerve they've got to have!"

I went out into the hall and brought Joanna her letter. She opened it, glanced vaguely at its contents, and let it drop.

"He was really rather wonderful. The way he fought—the way he wouldn't be beaten! He was rude and horrible to *me*—but he *was* wonderful."

I observed Paul's disregarded letter with some pleasure. Plainly, Joanna was cured of Paul.

Chapter Thirteen

THINGS NEVER COME when they are expected.

I was full of Joanna's and my personal affairs and was quite taken aback the next morning when Nash's voice said over the telephone: "*We've got her*, Mr. Burton!"

I was so startled I nearly dropped the receiver.

"You mean the——"

He interrupted.

"Can you be overheard where you are?"

"No, I don't think so—well, perhaps——"

It seemed to me that the baize door to the kitchen had swung open a trifle.

"Perhaps you'd care to come down to the station?"

"I will. Right away."

I was at the police station in next to no time. In an inner room Nash and Sergeant Parkins were together. Nash was wreathed in smiles.

"It's been a long chase," he said. "But we're there at last."

He flicked a letter across the table. This time it was all typewritten. It was, of its kind, fairly mild.

"It's no use thinking you're going to step into a dead woman's shoes. The whole town is laughing at you. Get out now. Soon it will be too late. This is a warning. Remember what happened to that other girl. Get out and stay out."

It finished with some mildly obscene language.

"That reached Miss Holland this morning," said Nash.

"Thought it was funny she hadn't had one before," said Sergeant Parkins.

"Who wrote it?" I asked.

Some of the exultation faded out of Nash's face.

He looked tired and concerned. He said soberly:

"I'm sorry about it, because it will hit a decent man hard, but there it is. Perhaps he's had his suspicions already."

"Who wrote it?" I reiterated.

"Miss Aimée Griffith."

II

Nash and Parkins went to the Griffiths' house that afternoon with a warrant.

By Nash's invitation I went with them.

"The doctor," he said, "is very fond of you. He hasn't many friends in this place. I think if it is not too painful to you, Mr. Burton, that you might help him to bear up under the shock."

I said I would come. I didn't relish the job, but I thought I might be some good.

We rang the bell and asked for Miss Griffith and we were shown into the drawing-room. Elsie Holland, Megan and Symmington were there having tea.

Nash behaved very circumspectly.

He asked Aimée if he might have a few words with her privately.

She got up and came towards us. I thought I saw just a faint hunted look in her eye. If so, it went again. She was perfectly normal and hearty.

"Want me? Not in trouble over my car lights again, I hope?"

She led the way out of the drawing-room and across the hall into a small study.

As I closed the drawing-room door, I saw Symmington's head jerk up sharply. I supposed his legal training had brought him in contact with police cases, and he had recognized something in Nash's manner. He half rose.

That is all I saw before I shut the door and followed the others.

Nash was saying his piece. He was very quiet and correct. He cautioned her and then told her that he must ask her to accompany him. He had a warrant for her arrest and he read out the charge——

I forget now the exact legal term. It was the letters, not murder yet.

Aimée Griffith flung up her head and bayed with laughter. She boomed out: "What ridiculous nonsense! As though I'd write a packet of indecent stuff like that. You must be mad. I've never written a word of the kind."

Nash had produced the letter to Elsie Holland. He said:

"Do you deny having written this, Miss Griffith?"

If she hesitated it was only for a split second.

"Of course I do. I've never seen it before."

Nash said quietly: "I must tell you, Miss Griffith, that you were observed to type that letter on the machine at the Women's Institute between eleven and eleven-thirty p.m. on the night before last. Yesterday you entered the post office with a bunch of letters in your hand——"

"I never posted this."

"No, you did not. Whilst waiting for stamps, you dropped it inconspicuously on the floor, so that somebody should come along unsuspectingly and pick it up and post it."

"I never——"

The door opened and Symmington came in. He said sharply: "What's going on? Aimée, if there is anything wrong, you ought to be legally represented. If you wish me——"

She broke then. Covered her face with her hands and staggered to a chair. She said:

"Go away, Dick, go away. Not you! Not *you!*"

"You need a solicitor, my dear girl."

"Not you. I—I—couldn't bear it. I don't want you to know—all this."

He understood then, perhaps. He said quietly:

"I'll get hold of Mildmay, of Exhampton. Will that do?"

She nodded. She was sobbing now.

Symmington went out of the room. In the doorway he collided with Owen Griffith.

"What's this?" said Owen violently. "My sister——"

"I'm sorry, Dr. Griffith. Very sorry. But we have no alternative."

"You think she—was responsible for those letters?"

"I'm afraid there is no doubt of it, sir," said Nash—he turned to Aimée, "You must come with us now, please, Miss Griffith—you shall have every facility for seeing a solicitor, you know."

Owen cried: "Aimée?"

She brushed past him without looking at him.

She said: "Don't talk to me. Don't say anything. And for God's sake don't *look* at me!"

They went out. Owen stood like a man in a trance.

I waited a bit, then I came up to him.

"If there's anything I can do, Griffith, tell me."

He said like a man in a dream:

"Aimée? I don't believe it."

"It may be a mistake," I suggested feebly.

He said slowly: "She wouldn't take it like that if it were. But I would never have believed it. I *can't* believe it."

He sank down on a chair. I made myself useful by finding a stiff drink and bringing it to him. He swallowed it down and it seemed to do him good.

He said: "I couldn't take it in at first. I'm all right now. Thanks, Burton, but there's nothing you can do. Nothing *anyone* can do."

The door opened and Joanna came in. She was very white.

She came over to Owen and looked at me.

She said: "Get out, Jerry. This is my business."

As I went out of the door, I saw her kneel down by his chair.

III

I can't tell you coherently the events of the next twenty-four hours. Various incidents stand out, unrelated to other incidents.

I remember Joanna coming home, very white and drawn, and of how I tried to cheer her up, saying:

"Now who's being a ministering angel?"

And of how she smiled in a pitiful twisted way and said:

"He says he won't have me, Jerry. He's very, *very* proud and stiff!"

We sat there for a while, Joanna saying at last:

"The Burton family isn't exactly in demand at the moment!"

I said, "Never mind, my sweet, we still have each other," and Joanna said, "Somehow or other, Jerry, that doesn't comfort me much just now . . ."

IV

Owen came the next day and rhapsodised in the most fulsome way about Joanna. She was wonderful, marvellous! The way she'd come to him, the way she was willing to marry him—at once if he liked. But he wasn't going to let her do that. No, she was too good, too fine to be associated with the kind of muck that would start as soon as the papers got hold of the news.

I was fond of Joanna, and knew she was the kind who's all right when standing by in trouble, but I got rather bored with all this high-falutin' stuff. I told Owen rather irritably not to be so damned noble.

I went down to the High Street and found everybody's tongues wagging nineteen to the dozen. Emily Barton was saying that she had never really trusted Aimée Griffith. The grocer's wife was saying with gusto that she'd always thought Miss Griffith had a queer look in her eye——

They had completed the case against Aimée, so I learnt from Nash. A search of the house had brought to light the cut pages of Emily Barton's book—in the cupboard under the stairs, of all places, wrapped up in an old roll of wallpaper.

"And a jolly good place too," said Nash appreciatively. "You never know when a prying servant won't tamper with a desk or a locked drawer —but those junk cupboards full of last year's tennis balls and old wallpaper are never opened except to shove something more in."

"The lady would seem to have had a *penchant* for that particular hiding-place," I said.

"Yes. The criminal mind seldom has much variety. By the way, talking of the dead girl, we've got one fact to go upon. There's a large heavy pestle missing from the doctor's dispensary. I'll bet anything you like that's what she was stunned with."

"Rather an awkward thing to carry about," I objected.

"Not for Miss Griffith. She was going to the Guides that afternoon, but she was going to leave flowers and vegetables at the Red Cross stall on the way, so she'd got a whopping great basket with her."

"You haven't found the skewer?"

"No, and I shan't. The poor devil may be mad, but she wasn't mad enough to keep a blood-stained skewer just to make it easy for us, when all she'd got to do was to wash it and return it to a kitchen drawer."

"I suppose," I conceded, "that you can't have everything."

The vicarage had been one of the last places to hear the news. Old Miss Marple was very much distressed by it. She spoke to me very earnestly on the subject.

"It isn't *true*, Mr. Burton. I'm sure it isn't true."

"It's true enough, I'm afraid. They were lying in wait, you know. They actually *saw* her type that letter."

"Yes, yes—perhaps they did. Yes, I can understand *that*."

"And the printed pages from which the letters were cut were found where she'd hidden them in her house."

Miss Marple stared at me. Then she said, in a very low voice: "But that is horrible—really *wicked*."

Mrs. Dane Calthrop came up with a rush and joined us and said: "What's the matter, Jane?"

Miss Marple was murmuring helplessly:

"Oh dear, oh dear, what can one *do*?"

"What's upset you, Jane?"

Miss Marple said: "There must be *something*. But I am so old and ignorant, and I am afraid, so foolish."

I felt rather embarrassed and was glad when Mrs. Dane Calthrop took her friend away.

I was to see Miss Marple again that afternoon, however. Much later when I was on my way home.

She was standing near the little bridge at the end of the village, near Mrs. Cleat's cottage, and talking to Megan of all people.

I wanted to see Megan. I had been wanting to see her all day. I quickened my pace. But as I came up to them, Megan turned on her heel and went off in the other direction.

It made me angry and I would have followed her, but Miss Marple blocked my way.

She said: "I wanted to speak to you. No, don't go after Megan now. It wouldn't be wise."

I was just going to make a sharp rejoinder when she disarmed me by saying:

"That girl has great courage—a very high order of courage."

I still wanted to go after Megan, but Miss Marple said:

"Don't try and see her now. I do know what I am talking about. She must keep her courage intact."

There was something about the old lady's assertion that chilled me. It was as though she knew something that I didn't.

I was afraid and didn't know why I was afraid.

I didn't go home. I went back into the High Street and walked up and down aimlessly. I don't know what I was waiting for, nor what I was thinking about. . . .

I got caught by that awful old bore Colonel Appleton. He asked after my pretty sister as usual and then went on:

"What's all this about Griffith's sister being mad as a hatter? They say she's been at the bottom of this anonymous letter business that's been such a confounded nuisance to everybody? Couldn't believe it at first, but they say it's quite true."

I said it was true enough.

"Well, well—I must say our police force is pretty good on the whole. Give 'em time, that's all, give 'em time. Funny business this anonymous letter stunt—these desiccated old maids are always the ones who go in for it—though the Griffith woman wasn't bad-looking even if she was a bit long in the tooth. But there aren't any decent-looking girls in this part of the world. Except that governess girl of the Symmingtons. She's worth looking at. Pleasant girl, too. Grateful if one does any little thing for her.

Came across her having a picnic or something with those kids not long ago. They were romping about in the heather and she was knitting—ever so vexed she'd run out of wool. 'Well,' I said, 'like me to run you into Lymstock? I've got to call for a rod of mine there. I shan't be more than ten minutes getting it, then I'll run you back again.' She was a bit doubtful about leaving the boys. 'They'll be all right,' I said. 'Who's to harm them?' Wasn't going to have the boys along, no fear! So I ran her in, dropped her at the wool shop, picked her up again later and that was that. Thanked me very prettily. Grateful and all that. Nice girl."

I managed to get away from him.

It was after that, that I caught sight of Miss Marple for the third time. She was coming out of the police-station.

V

Where do one's fears come from? Where do they shape themselves? Where do they hide before coming out into the open?

Just one short phrase. Heard and noted and never quite put aside: "Take me away—it's so awful being here—feeling so wicked . . ."

Why had Megan said that? What had she to feel wicked about?

There could be nothing in Mrs. Symmington's death to make Megan feel wicked.

Why had the child felt wicked? Why? Why?

Could it be because she felt responsible in any way?

Megan? Impossible! *Megan* couldn't have had anything to do with those letters—those foul obscene letters.

Owen Griffith had known a case up North—a schoolgirl . . .

What had Inspector Graves said?

Something about an *adolescent mind . . .*

Innocent middle-aged ladies on operating tables babbling words they hardly knew. Little boys chalking up things on walls.

No, no, not *Megan.*

Heredity? Bad blood? An unconscious inheritance of something abnormal? Her misfortune, not her fault, a curse laid upon her by a past generation?

"I'm not the wife for you. I'm better at hating than loving."

Oh, my Megan, my little child. Not *that!* Anything but that. And that old Tabby is after you, she suspects. She says you have courage. Courage to do *what?*

It was only a brainstorm. It passed. But I wanted to see Megan—I wanted to see her badly.

At half-past nine that night I left the house and went down to the town and along to the Symmingtons'.

It was then that an entirely new idea came into my mind. The idea of a woman whom nobody had considered for a moment.

(Or had Nash considered her?)

Wildly unlikely, wildly improbable, and I would have said up to to-day impossible, too. But that was not so. No, not *impossible.*

I passed through the Symmingtons' gate and up to the house. It was a dark overcast night. A little rain was beginning to fall. The visibility was bad.

I saw a line of light from one of the windows. The little morning-room?

I hesitated a moment or two, then instead of going up to the front door, I swerved and crept very quietly up to the window, skirting a big bush and keeping low.

The light came from a chink in the curtains which were not quite drawn. It was easy to look through and see.

It was a strangely peaceful and domestic scene. Symmington in a big arm-chair, and Elsie Holland, her head bent, busily patching a boy's torn shirt.

I could hear as well as see for the window was open at the top.

Elsie Holland was speaking.

"But I do think, really, Mr. Symmington, that the boys are quite old enough to go to boarding school. Not that I shan't hate leaving them because I shall. I'm ever so fond of them both."

Symmington said: "I think perhaps you're right about Brian, Miss Holland. I've decided that he shall start next term at Winhays—my old prep school. But Colin is a little young yet. I'd prefer him to wait another year."

"Well of course I see what you mean. And Colin is perhaps a little young for his age——"

Quiet domestic talk—quiet domestic scene—and a golden head bent over needlework.

Then the door opened and Megan came in.

She stood very straight in the doorway, and I was aware at once of something tense and strung up about her. The skin of her face was tight and drawn and her eyes bright and resolute. There was no diffidence about her to-night and no childishness.

She said, addressing Symmington, but giving him no title (and I suddenly reflected that I never had heard her call him anything. Did she address him as father or as Dick or what?):

"I would like to speak to you, please. Alone."

Symmington looked surprised and, I fancied, not best pleased. He frowned, but Megan carried her point with a determination unusual in her.

She turned to Elsie Holland and said:

"Do you mind, Elsie?"

"Oh, of course not." Elsie Holland jumped up. She looked startled and a little flurried.

She went to the door and Megan came farther in so that Elsie passed her.

Just for a moment Elsie stood motionless in the doorway looking over her shoulder.

Her lips were closed, she stood quite still, one hand stretched out, the other clasping her needlework to her.

I caught my breath, overwhelmed suddenly by her beauty.

When I think of her now, I always think of her like that—in arrested motion, with that matchless deathless perfection that belonged to ancient Greece.

Then she went out shutting the door.

Symmington said rather fretfully:

"Well, Megan, what is it? What do you want?"

Megan had come right up to the table. She stood there looking down at Symmington. I was struck anew by the resolute determination of her face and by something else—a hardness new to me.

Then she opened her lips and said something that startled me to the core.

"I want some money," she said.

The request didn't improve Symmington's temper. He said sharply:

"Couldn't you have waited until to-morrow morning? What's the matter, do you think your allowance is inadequate?"

A fair man, I thought even then, open to reason, though not to emotional appeal.

Megan said: "I want a good deal of money."

Symmington sat up straight in his chair. He said coldly:

"You will come of age in a few months' time. Then the money left you by your grandmother will be turned over to you by the public trustee."

Megan said:

"You don't understand. I want money from *you*." She went on, speaking faster. "Nobody's ever talked much to me about my father. They've not wanted me to know about him. But I do know that he went to prison and I know why. It was for blackmail!"

She paused.

"Well, I'm his daughter. And perhaps I take after him. Anyway, I'm asking you to give me money because—if you don't"—she stopped and then went on very slowly and evenly—"if you don't—*I shall say what I saw you doing to the cachet that day in my mother's room.*"

There was a pause. Then Symmington said in a completely emotionless voice:

"I don't know what you mean."

Megan said: "I think you do."

And she smiled. It was not a nice smile.

Symmington got up. He went over to the writing-desk. He took a cheque-book from his pocket and wrote out a cheque. He blotted it carefully and then came back. He held it out to Megan.

"You're grown up now," he said. "I can understand that you may feel you want to buy something rather special in the way of clothes and all that. I don't know what you're talking about. I didn't pay attention. But here's a cheque."

Megan looked at it, then she said:

"Thank you. That will do to go on with."

She turned and went out of the room. Symmington stared after her and at the closed door, then he turned round and as I saw his face I made a quick uncontrolled movement forward.

It was checked in the most extraordinary fashion. The big bush that I had noticed by the wall stopped being a bush. Superintendent Nash's arms went round me and Superintendent Nash's voice just breathed in my ear:

"Quiet, Burton. For God's sake."

Then, with infinite caution he beat a retreat, his arm impelling me to accompany him.

Round the side of the house he straightened himself and wiped his forehead.

"Of course," he said. "You *would* have to butt in!"

"That girl isn't safe," I said urgently. "You saw his face? We've got to get her out of here."

Nash took a firm grip of my arm.

"Now, look here, Mr. Burton, you've got to *listen*."

VI

Well, I listened.

I didn't like it—but I gave in.

But I insisted on being on the spot and I swore to obey orders implicitly.

So that is how I came with Nash and Parkins into the house by the back door which was already unlocked.

And I waited with Nash on the upstairs landing behind the velvet curtain masking the window alcove until the clocks in the house struck two, and Symmington's door opened and he went across the landing and into Megan's room.

I did not stir or make a move for I knew that Sergeant Parkins was inside masked by the opening door, and I knew that Parkins was a good man and knew his job, and I knew that I couldn't have trusted myself to keep quiet and not break out.

And waiting there, with my heart thudding, I saw Symmington come out with Megan in his arms and carry her downstairs, with Nash and myself a discreet distance behind him.

He carried her through to the kitchen and he had just arranged her comfortably with her head in the gas-oven and had turned on the gas when Nash and I came through the kitchen door and switched on the light.

And that was the end of Richard Symmington. He collapsed. Even while I was hauling Megan out and turning off the gas I saw the collapse. He didn't even try to fight. He knew he'd played and lost.

VII

Upstairs I sat by Megan's bed waiting for her to come round and occasionally cursing Nash.

"How do you know she's all right? It was too big a risk."

Nash was very soothing.

"Just a soporific in the milk she always had by her bed. Nothing more. It stands to reason, he couldn't risk her being poisoned. As far as he's concerned the whole business is closed with Miss Griffith's arrest. He can't afford to have any mysterious death. No violence, no poison. But if a rather unhappy type of girl broods over her mother's suicide, and finally goes and puts her head in the gas-oven—well, people just say that she was never quite normal and the shock of her mother's death finished her."

I said, watching Megan:

"She's a long time coming round."

"You heard what Dr. Griffith said? Heart and pulse quite all right— she'll just sleep and wake naturally. Stuff he gives a lot of his patients, he says."

Megan stirred. She murmured something.

Superintendent Nash unobtrusively left the room.

Presently Megan opened her eyes. "Jerry."

"Hallo, sweet."

"Did I do it well?"

"You might have been blackmailing ever since your cradle!"

Megan closed her eyes again. Then she murmured:

"Last night—I was writing to you—in case anything went—went wrong. But I was too sleepy to finish. It's over there."

I went across to the writing-table. In a shabby little blotter I found Megan's unfinished letter.

"My dear Jerry," it began primly:

"I was reading my school Shakespeare and the sonnet that begins:

'So are you to my thoughts as food to life
Or as sweet-season'd showers are to the ground.'

and I see that I am in love with you after all, because that is what I feel. . . ."

Chapter Fourteen

"So you see," said Mrs. Dane Calthrop, "I was quite right to call in an expert."

I stared at her. We were all at the vicarage. The rain was pouring down outside and there was a pleasant log fire, and Mrs. Dane Calthrop had just wandered round, beat up a sofa cushion and put it for some reason of her own on the top of the grand piano.

"But did you?" I said, surprised. "Who was it? What did he do?"

"It wasn't a he," said Mrs. Dane Calthrop.

With a sweeping gesture she indicated Miss Marple. Miss Marple had finished the fleecy knitting and was now engaged with a crochet hook and a ball of cotton.

"That's my expert," said Mrs. Dane Calthrop. "Jane Marple. Look at her well. I tell you, that woman knows more about the different kinds of human wickedness than anyone I've ever known."

"I don't think you should put it quite like that, dear," murmured Miss Marple.

"But you do."

"One sees a good deal of human nature living in a village all the year round," said Miss Marple placidly. Then, seeming to feel it was expected of her, she laid down her crochet, and delivered a gentle old-maidish dissertation on murder.

"The great thing is in these cases to keep an absolutely open mind. Most crimes, you see, are so absurdly simple. This one was. Quite sane and straightforward—and quite understandable—in an unpleasant way, of course."

"Very unpleasant!"

"The truth was really so very obvious. *You* saw it, you know, Mr. Burton."

"Indeed, I did not."

"But you did. You indicated the whole thing to me. You saw perfectly the relationship of one thing to the other, but you just hadn't enough self-confidence to see what those feelings of yours meant. To begin with, that tiresome phrase 'No smoke without fire.' It irritated you, but you proceeded quite correctly to label it for what it was—a smoke screen. Misdirection, you see—everybody looking at the wrong thing—the anonymous letters, but the whole point was that there *weren't* any anonymous letters!"

"But my dear Miss Marple, I can assure you that there *were*. I had one."

"Oh yes, but they weren't real at all. Dear Maud here tumbled to that. Even in peaceful Lymstock there are plenty of scandals, and I can assure you any *woman* living in the place would have known about them and used them. But a man, you see, isn't interested in gossip in the same way—especially a detached logical man like Mr. Symmington. A genuine woman writer of those letters would have made her letters much more to the point.

"So you see that if you disregard the smoke and come to the fire you know where you are. You just come down to the actual facts of what happened—Mrs. Symmington died.

"So then, naturally, one thinks of who might have wanted Mrs. Symmington to die, and of course the very first person one thinks of in such a case is, I am afraid, the *husband*. And one asks oneself is there any *reason?*—any *motive?*—for instance, *any other woman?*

"And the very first thing I hear is that there is a very attractive young governess in the house. So clear, isn't it? Mr. Symmington, a rather dry repressed unemotional man, tied to a querulous and neurotic wife and then suddenly this radiant young creature comes along.

"I'm afraid, you know, that gentlemen, when they fall in love at a certain age, get the disease very badly. It's quite a madness. And Mr. Symmington, as far as I can make out, was never actually a *good* man—he wasn't very kind or very affectionate or very sympathetic—his qualities were all negative—so he hadn't really the strength to fight his madness. And in a place like this, only his wife's death would solve his problem. He wanted to marry the girl, you see. She's very respectable and so is he. And besides, he's devoted to his children and didn't want to give them up. He wanted everything, his home, his children, his respectability and Elsie. And the price he would have to pay for that was murder.

"He chose, I do think, a very clever way. He knew so well from his experience of criminal cases how soon suspicion falls on the husband if a wife dies unexpectedly—and the possibility of exhumation in the case of poison. So he created a death which seemed only incidental to something else. He created a non-existent anonymous letter-writer. And the clever thing was that the police were certain to suspect a *woman*—and they were quite right in a way. All the letters *were* a woman's letters; he cribbed them very cleverly from the letters in the case last year and from a case Dr. Griffith told him about. I don't mean that he was so crude as to reproduce any letter verbatim, but he took phrases and expressions from them and mixed them up, and the net result was that the letters definitely represented a woman's mind—a half-crazy repressed personality.

"He knew all the tricks that the police use, handwriting, typewriting tests, etc. He's been preparing his crime for some time. He typed all the envelopes before he gave away the typewriter to the Woman's Institute, and he cut the pages from the book at Little Furze probably quite a long time ago when he was waiting in the drawing-room one day. People don't open books of sermons much!

"And finally, having got his false Poison Pen well established, he staged the real thing. A fine afternoon when the governess and the boys and his stepdaughter would be out, and the servants having their regular day out. He couldn't foresee that the little maid Agnes would quarrel with her boy and come back to the house."

Joanna asked:

"But what did she *see*? Do you know that?"

"I don't *know*. I can only guess. My guess would be that she didn't see anything."

"That it was all a mare's nest?"

"No, no, my dear, I mean that she stood at the pantry window all the afternoon waiting for the young man to come and make it up and that— quite literally—she saw *nothing*. That is, *no one* came to the house at all, not the postman, nor anybody else.

"It would take her some time, being slow, to realise that that was very odd—because apparently Mrs. Symmington *had* received an anonymous letter that afternoon."

"Didn't she receive one?" I asked, puzzled.

"But of course not! As I say, this crime is so simple. Her husband just put the cyanide in the top cachet of the ones she took in the afternoon when her sciatica came on after lunch. All Symmington had to do was to get home before, or at the same time as Elsie Holland, call his wife, get no answer, go up to her room, drop a spot of cyanide in the plain glass of water she had used to swallow the cachet, toss the crumpled-up anonymous letter into the grate, and put by her hand the scrap of paper with '*I can't go on*' written on it."

Miss Marple turned to me.

"You were quite right about that, too, Mr. Burton. A 'scrap of paper' was all wrong. People don't leave suicide notes on small torn scraps of paper. They use a *sheet* of paper—and very often an envelope too. Yes, the scrap of paper was wrong and you knew it."

"You are rating me too high," I said. "I knew nothing."

"But you did, you really *did*, Mr. Burton. Otherwise why were you immediately impressed by the message your sister left scribbled on the telephone pad?"

I repeated slowly, " 'Say that I *can't go on* Friday'—I see! *I can't go on?*"

Miss Marple beamed on me.

"Exactly. Mr. Symmington came across such a message and saw its possibilities. He tore off the words he wanted for when the time came—a message genuinely in his wife's handwriting."

"Was there any further brilliance on my part?" I asked.

Miss Marple twinkled at me.

"You put me on the track, you know. You assembled those facts together for me—in sequence—and on top of it you told me the most important thing of all—that Elsie Holland had never received any anonymous letters."

"Do you know," I said, "last night I thought that *she* was the letter writer and that that was why there had been no letters written to her?"

"Oh dear me, no. . . . The person who writes anonymous letters practically always sends them to herself as well. That's part of the—well, the excitement, I suppose. No, no, the fact interested me for *quite* another reason. It was really, you see, Mr. Symmington's one weakness. He couldn't bring himself to write a foul letter to the girl he loved. It's a very interesting sidelight on human nature—and a credit to him, in a way—but it's where he gave himself away."

Joanna said:

"And he killed Agnes? But surely that was quite unnecessary?"

"Perhaps it was, but what you don't realise, my dear (not having killed anyone), is that your judgment is distorted afterwards and everything seems exaggerated. No doubt he heard the girl telephoning to Partridge, saying she'd been worried ever since Mrs. Symmington's death, that there was something she didn't understand. He can't take any chances—this stupid, foolish girl has seen *something*, knows something."

"Yet apparently he was at his office all that afternoon?"

"I should imagine he killed her before he went. Miss Holland was in the dining-room and kitchen. He just went out into the hall, opened and shut the front door as though he had gone out, then slipped into the little cloakroom. When only Agnes was left in the house, he probably rang the front-door bell, slipped back into the cloakroom, came out behind her and hit her on the head as she was opening the front door, and then after thrusting the body into the cupboard, he hurried along to his office, arriving just a little late if anyone had happened to notice it, but they probably didn't. You see, no one was suspecting a *man*."

"Abominable brute," said Mrs. Dane Calthrop.

"You're not sorry for him, Mrs. Dane Calthrop?" I inquired.

"Not in the least. Why?"

"I'm glad to hear it, that's all."

Joanna said:

"But why Aimée Griffith? I know that the police have found the pestle taken from Owen's dispensary—and the skewer too. I suppose it's not so easy for a man to return things to kitchen drawers. And guess where they were? Superintendent Nash only told me just now when I met him on my way here. In one of those musty old deedboxes in his office. Estate of Sir Jasper Harrington-West, deceased."

"Poor Jasper," said Mrs. Dane Calthrop. "He was a cousin of mine. Such a correct old boy. He would have had a fit!"

"Wasn't it madness to keep them?" I asked.

"Probably madder to throw them away," said Mrs. Dane Calthrop. "No one had any suspicions about Symmington."

"He didn't strike her with the pestle," said Joanna. "There was a clock weight there, too, with hair and blood on it. He pinched the pestle, they think, on the day Aimée was arrested, and hid the book pages in her house. And that brings me back to my original question. What about Aimée Griffith? The police actually *saw* her write that letter."

"Yes, of course," said Miss Marple. "She did write *that* letter."

"But why?"

"Oh, my dear, surely you have realised that Miss Griffith had been in love with Symmington all her life?"

"Poor thing!" said Mrs. Dane Calthrop mechanically.

"They'd always been good friends, and I dare say she thought, after Mrs. Symmington's death, that some day, perhaps—well——" Miss Marple coughed delicately. "And then the gossip began spreading about Elsie Holland and I expect that upset her badly. She thought of the girl as a designing minx worming her way into Symmington's affections and quite unworthy of him. And so, I think, she succumbed to temptation. Why not add one more anonymous letter, and frighten the girl out of the place? It must have seemed quite safe to her and she took, as she thought, every precaution."

"Well?" said Joanna. "Finish the story."

"I should imagine," said Miss Marple slowly, "that when Miss Holland showed that letter to Symmington he realised at once who had written it, and he saw a chance to finish the case once and for all, and make himself safe. Not very nice—no, not very nice, but he was frightened, you see. The police wouldn't be satisfied until they'd got the anonymous letter-writer. When he took the letter down to the police and he found they'd actually seen Aimée writing it, he felt he'd got a chance in a thousand of finishing the whole thing.

"He took the family to tea there that afternoon and as he came from the office with his attaché case, he could easily bring the torn-out book pages to hide under the stairs and clinch the case. Hiding them under the stairs was a neat touch. It recalled the disposal of Agnes's body, and, from the practical point of view, it was very easy for him. When he followed Aimée and the police, just a minute or two in the hall passing through would be enough."

"All the same," I said, "there's one thing I can't forgive you for, Miss Marple—roping in Megan."

Miss Marple put down her crochet which she had resumed. She looked at me over her spectacles and her eyes were stern.

"My dear young man, *something* had to be done. There was no evidence against this very clever and unscrupulous man. I needed someone to help me, someone of high courage and good brains. I found the person I needed."

"It was very dangerous for her."

"Yes, it was dangerous, but we are not put into this world, Mr. Burton, to avoid danger when an innocent fellow-creature's life is at stake. You understand me?"

I understood.

Chapter Fifteen

MORNING in the High Street.

Miss Emily Barton comes out of the grocer's with her shopping bag. Her cheeks are pink and her eyes are excited.

"Oh, dear, Mr. Burton, I really am in such a flutter. To think I really am going on a cruise at last!"

"I hope you'll enjoy it."

"Oh, I'm sure I shall. I should never have dared to go by myself. It does seem so *providential* the way everything has turned out. For a long time I've felt that I ought to part with Little Furze, that my means were really *too* straitened but I couldn't bear the idea of *strangers* there. But now that you have bought it and are going to live there with Megan—it is quite different. And then dear Aimée, after her terrible ordeal, not quite knowing what to do with herself, and her brother getting married (how nice to think you have *both* settled down with us!) and agreeing to come with me. We mean to be away quite a long time. We might even"—Miss Emily dropped her voice—"*go round the world!* And Aimée is so splendid and so practical. I really do think, don't you, that everything turns out for the *best?*"

Just for a fleeting moment I thought of Mrs. Symmington and Agnes Woddell in their graves in the churchyard and wondered if they would agree, and then I remembered that Agnes's boy hadn't been very fond of her and that Mrs. Symmington hadn't been very nice to Megan and, what the hell? we've all got to die some time! And I agreed with happy Miss Emily that everything was for the best in the best of possible worlds.

I went along the High Street and in at the Symmingtons' gate and Megan came out to meet me.

It was not a romantic meeting because an outsize Old English sheepdog came out with Megan and nearly knocked me over with his ill-timed exuberance.

"Isn't he *adorable?*" said Megan.

"A little overwhelming. Is he ours?"

"Yes, he's a wedding present from Joanna. We *have* had nice wedding presents, haven't we? That fluffy woolly thing that we don't know what it's for from Miss Marple, and the lovely Crown Derby tea-set from Mr. Pye, and Elsie has sent me a toast-rack——"

"How typical," I interjected.

"And she's got a post with a dentist and is very happy. And—where was I?"

"Enumerating wedding presents. Don't forget if you change your mind you'll have to send them all back."

"I shan't change my mind. What else have we got? Oh, yes, Mrs. Dane Calthrop has sent an Egyptian scarab."

"Original woman," I said.

"Oh! Oh! but you don't know the best. *Partridge* has actually sent me a present. It's the most hideous teacloth you've ever seen. But I think she *must* like me now because she says she embroidered it all with her own hands."

"In a design of sour grapes and thistles, I suppose?"

"No, true lovers' knots."

"Dear, dear," I said. "Partridge *is* coming on."

Megan had dragged me into the house.

She said:

"There's just one thing I can't make out. Besides the dog's own collar and lead, Joanna has sent an extra collar and lead. What do you think that's for?"

"That," I said, "is Joanna's little joke."